WELCOME TO THE MONKEY HOUSE

PALM SUNDAY

BY KURT VONNEGUT

Player Piano
The Sirens of Titan
Mother Night
Canary in a Cathouse
Cat's Cradle
God Bless You, Mr. Rosewater
Welcome to the Monkey House
Slaughterhouse 5
Breakfast of Champions
Slapstick or Lonesome No More
Jailbird
Palm Sunday
Deadeye Dick
Happy Birthday, Wanda June
Fates Worse Than Death
Wampeters, Foma and Granfalloons
Galapagos
Bluebeard
Hocus Pocus

Kurt Vonnegut, Jr.

WELCOME TO THE
MONKEY HOUSE

PALM SUNDAY
An Autobiographical Collage

VINTAGE

Published by Vintage 1994

2 4 6 8 10 9 7 5 3 1

WELCOME TO THE MONKEY HOUSE
This collection first published in
Great Britain by Jonathan Cape Ltd, 1969
Copyright © Kurt Vonnegut, Jr. 1950, 1951, 1953, 1954,
1955, 1956, 1958, 1960, 1961, 1962, 1964, 1966, 1968

PALM SUNDAY
First published in Great Britain by Jonathan Cape Ltd, 1981
Copyright © The Ramjac Corporation, 1981

The right of Kurt Vonnegut, Jr. to be identified as the
author of this work has been asserted by him in accordance with the Copyright, Designs and Patents Act, 1988

This edition first published by Vintage in 1994

Vintage
Random House, 20 Vauxhall Bridge Road, London SW1V 2SA

Random House Australia (Pty) Limited
20 Alfred Street, Milsons Point, Sydney
New South Wales 2061, Australia

Random House New Zealand Limited
18 Poland Road, Glenfield,
Auckland 10, New Zealand

Random House South Africa (Pty) Limited
PO Box 337, Bergvlei, South Africa

Random House UK Limited Reg. No. 954009

A CIP catalogue record for this book
is available from the British Library

ISBN 0 09 938781 6

Printed and bound in Great Britain by
Cox & Wyman, Reading, Berkshire

WELCOME TO THE MONKEY HOUSE

Acknowledgment is made to the following magazines and publishers in whose pages these stories first appeared:

The Atlantic Monthly: "Der arme Dolmetscher" (originally published under the title "Dar ganz arme Dolmetscher").
Collier's Magazine: "The Foster Portfolio," "All the King's Horses," "Tom Edison's Shaggy Dog," "More Stately Mansions," "Report on the Barnhouse Effect," "Epicac," and "The Euphio Question."
Cosmopolitan: "Next Door," "The Manned Missiles," and "Adam."
Esquire: "Deer in the Works."
Fantasy and Science Fiction Magazine: "Harrison Bergeron."
Galaxy Publishing Corporation: "Unready to Wear" and "Tomorrow and Tomorrow and Tomorrow" (originally published under the title "The Big Trip Up Yonder").
Ladies Home Journal: "Long Walk to Forever," "D.P.," and "Go Back to Your Precious Wife and Son."
The New York Times: "New Dictionary" (originally published under the title "The Random House Dictionary").
Playboy: "Welcome to the Monkey House."
Saturday Evening Post: "Who Am I This Time?," "Miss Temptation," "The Lie," and "The Kid Nobody Could Handle."
Venture: "Where I Live" (originally published under the title "So You've Never Been to Barnstable").

CONTENTS

CONTENTS

PREFACE

HERE IT IS, a retrospective exhibition of the shorter works of Kurt Vonnegut, Jr.—and Vonnegut is still very much with us, and I am still very much Vonnegut. Somewhere in Germany is a stream called the Vonne. That is the source of my curious name.

I have been a writer since 1949. I am self-taught. I have no theories about writing that might help others. When I write I simply become what I seemingly must become. I am six feet two and weigh nearly two hundred pounds and am badly coordinated, except when I swim. All that borrowed meat does the writing.

In the water I am beautiful.

My father and paternal grandfather were architects in Indianapolis, Indiana, where I was born. My maternal grandfather owned a brewery there. He won a Gold Medal at the Paris Exposition with his beer, which was Lieber Lager. The secret ingredient was coffee.

My only brother, eight years older than I, is a successful scientist. His special field is physics as it relates to clouds. His name is Bernard, and he is funnier than I am. I remember a letter he wrote after his first child, Peter, was born and brought home. "Here I am," that letter began, "cleaning shit off of practically everything."

My only sister, five years older than I, died when she was

forty. She was over six feet tall, too, by an angstrom unit or so. She was heavenly to look at, and graceful, both in and out of water. She was a sculptress. She was christened "Alice," but she used to deny that she was really an Alice. I agreed. Everybody agreed. Sometime in a dream maybe I will find out what her real name was.

Her dying words were, "No pain." Those are good dying words. It was cancer that killed her.

And I realize now that the two main themes of my novels were stated by my siblings: "Here I am cleaning shit off of practically everything" and "No pain." The contents of this book are samples of work I sold in order to finance the writing of the novels. Here one finds the fruits of Free Enterprise.

I used to be a public relations man for General Electric, and then I became a free-lance writer of so-called "slick fiction," a lot of it science fiction. Whether I improved myself morally by making that change I am not prepared to say. That is one of the questions I mean to ask God on Judgment Day—along with the one about what my sister's name really was.

That could easily be next Wednesday.

I have already put the question to a college professor, who, climbing down into his Mercedes-Benz 300SL *gran turismo*, assured me that public relations men and slick writers were equally vile, in that they both buggered truth for money.

I asked him what the very lowest grade of fiction was, and he told me, "Science fiction." I asked where he was bound in such a rush, and learned that he had to catch a Fan-Jet. He was to speak at a meeting of the Modern Language Association in Honolulu the next morning. Honolulu was three thousand miles away.

My sister smoked too much. My father smoked too much. My mother smoked too much. I smoke too much. My brother used to smoke too much, and then he gave it up, which was a miracle on the order of the loaves and fishes.

And one time a pretty girl came up to me at a cocktail party, and she asked me, "What are you doing these days?"

"I am committing suicide by cigarette," I replied.

She thought that was reasonably funny. I didn't. I thought it was hideous that I should scorn life that much, sucking away on cancer sticks. My brand is Pall Mall. The authentic suicides ask for Pall Malls. The dilettantes ask for Pell Mells.

I have a relative who is secretly writing a history of parts of my family. He has showed me some of it, and he told me this about my grandfather, the architect: "He died in his forties—and I think he was just as glad to be out of it." By "it," of course, he meant life in Indianapolis—and there is that yellow streak about life in me, too.

The public health authorities never mention the main reason many Americans have for smoking heavily, which is that smoking is a fairly sure, fairly honorable form of suicide.

It is disgraceful that I should ever have wanted out of "it," and I don't want out any more. I have six children, three of my own and three of my sister's. They've turned out gloriously. My first marriage worked, and continues to work. My wife is still beautiful.

I never knew a writer's wife who wasn't beautiful.

In honor of the marriage that worked, I include in this collection a sickeningly slick love story from The Ladies Home Journal, God help us, entitled by them "The Long Walk to Forever." The title I gave it, I think, was "Hell to Get Along With."

It describes an afternoon I spent with my wife-to-be. Shame, shame, to have lived scenes from a woman's magazine.

The New Yorker once said that a book of mine, God Bless You, Mr. Rosewater, was ". . . a series of narcissistic giggles." This may be another. Perhaps it would be helpful to the reader to imagine me as the White Rock girl, kneeling on a boulder in a nightgown, either looking for minnows or adoring her own reflection.

WHERE I LIVE

NOT VERY LONG AGO, an encyclopedia salesman stopped by America's oldest library building, which is the lovely Sturgis Library in Barnstable Village, on Cape Cod's north shore. And he pointed out to the easily alarmed librarian that the library's most recent general reference work was a 1938 *Britannica*, backstopped by a 1910 *Americana*. He said many important things had happened since 1938, naming, among others, penicillin and Hitler's invasion of Poland.

He was advised to take his astonishment to some of the library's directors. He was given their names and addresses. There was a Cabot on the list—and a Lowell and a Kittredge, and some others. The librarian told him that he had a chance of catching several directors all at once, if he would go to the Barnstable Yacht Club. So he went down the narrow yacht club road, nearly broke his neck as he hit a series of terrific bumps put in the road to discourage speeders, to kill them, if possible.

He wanted a martini, wondered if a nonmember could get service at the bar. He was appalled to discover that the club was nothing but a shack fourteen feet wide and thirty feet long, a touch of the Ozarks in Massachusetts. It contained an hilariously warped ping-pong table, a wire lost-and-found basket with sandy, fragrant contents, and an upright piano that had been under a leak in the roof for years.

There wasn't any bar, any telephone, any electricity. There weren't any members there, either. To cap it all, there wasn't a drop of water in the harbor. The tide, which can be as great as fourteen feet, was utterly out. And the so-called yachts, antique wooden Rhodes 18's, *Beetlecats,* and a couple of *Boston Whalers,* were resting on the bluish-brown glurp of the emptied harbor's floor. Clouds of gulls and terns were yelling about all that glurp, and about all the good things in it they were finding to eat.

A few men were out there, too, digging clams as fat as partridges from the rim of Sandy Neck, the ten-mile-long sand finger that separates the harbor from the ice-cold bay. And ducks and geese and herons and other waterfowl were out there, too, teemingly, in the great salt marsh that bounds the harbor on the west. And, near the harbor's narrow mouth, a yawl from Marblehead with a six-foot keel lay on her side, waiting for the water to come back in again. She should never have come to Barnstable Village, not with a keel like that.

The salesman, very depressed, insensitive to the barbarous beauty all around him, went to lunch. Since he was in the seat of the most booming county in New England, Barnstable County, and since the boom was a tourist boom, he had reason to expect something mildly voluptuous in the way of a place to eat. What he had to settle for, though, was a chromium stool at a formica counter in an aggressively un-cute, un-colonial institution called the Barnstable News Store, another Ozarks touch, an Ozarks department store. The motto of the place: "If it's any good, we've got it. If it's no good, we've sold it."

After lunch, he went trustee-hunting again, was told to try the village museum, which is in the old brick Customs House. The building itself is a memorial to long-gone days when the harbor was used by fair-sized ships, before it filled up with all that bluish-brown glurp. There was no trustee there, and the exhibits were excruciatingly boring. The salesman found himself strangling on apathy, an affliction epidemic among casual visitors to Barnstable Village.

He took the customary cure, which was to jump into his car and roar off toward the cocktail lounges, motor courts, bowling alleys, gift shoppes, and pizzerias of Hyannis, the commercial heart of

Cape Cod. He there worked off his frustrations on a miniature golf course called Playland. At that time, that particular course had a pathetic, maddening feature typical of the random butchery of the Cape's south shore. The course was built on the lawn of what had once been an American Legion Post—and, right in the middle of the cunning little bridges and granulated cork fairways was a Sherman tank, set there in simpler and less enterprising days as a memorial to the veterans of World War Two.

The memorial has since been moved, but it is still on the south side, where it is bound to be engulfed by indignities again.

The dignity of the tank would be a lot safer in Barnstable Village, but the village would never accept it. It has a policy of never accepting anything. As a happy consequence, it changes about as fast as the rules of chess.

The biggest change in recent years has taken place at the polls. Until six years ago, the Democratic poll watchers and the Republican poll watchers were all Republicans. Now the Democratic poll watchers are Democrats. The consequences of this revolution have not been nearly as awful as expected—so far.

Another break with the past has to do with the treasury of the local amateur theatrical society, the Barnstable Comedy Club. The club had a treasurer who, once a month for thirty years, angrily refused to say what the balance was, for fear that the club would spend it foolishly. He resigned last year. The new treasurer announced a balance of four hundred dollars and some odd cents, and the membership blew it all on a new curtain the color of spoiled salmon. This ptomaine curtain, incidentally, made its debut during a production of *The Caine Mutiny Court Martial* in which Captain Queeg did *not* nervously rattle steel balls in his hand. The balls were eliminated on the theory that they were suggestive.

Another big change took place about sixty years ago, when it was discovered that tuna were good to eat. Barnstable fishermen used to call them "horse mackerel," and curse whenever they caught one. Still cursing, they would chop it up and throw it back into the bay as a warning to other horse mackerel. Out of courage or plain stupidity, the tuna did not go away, and now make possible a post-Labor Day festival called the Barnstable Tuna

Derby. Sportsmen with reels as big as courthouse clocks come from all over the Eastern seaboard for the event; the villagers are always mystified as to what brought them. And nobody ever catches anything.

Another discovery that still lies in the future for the villagers to make and to learn to live with is that mussels can be eaten without causing instant death. Barnstable Harbor is in places clogged with them. They are never disturbed. One reason for their being ignored, perhaps, is that the harbor abounds in two other delicacies far simpler to prepare—striped bass and clams. To get clams, one can scratch almost anywhere when the tide is out. To get bass, one follows the birds, looks for cone-shaped formations of them, casts his lure to the place where the cone points. Bass will be feeding there.

As for what else the future holds: Few Cape villages have much chance of coming through the present greedy, tasteless boom with their souls intact. H. L. Mencken once said something to the effect that "Nobody ever went broke overestimating the vulgarity of the American people," and fortunes now being made out of the vulgarization of the Cape surely bear this out. The soul of Barnstable Village just might survive.

For one thing, it is not a hollow village, with everything for rent, with half of the houses empty in the winter. Most of the people live there all year round, and most of them aren't old, and most of them work—as carpenters, salesmen, masons, architects, teachers, writers, and what have you. It is a classless society, a sometimes affectionate and sentimental one.

And these full houses, often riddled by termites and dry rot, but good, probably, for a few hundred years more, have been built chockablock along Main Street since the end of the Civil War. Developers find very little room in which to work their pious depredations. There is a seeming vast green meadow to the west, but this is salt marsh, the bluish-brown glurp capped by a mat of salt hay. It was this natural hay, by the way, that tempted settlers down from Plymouth in 1639. The marsh, laced by deep creeks that can be explored by small boats, can never be built upon by anyone sane. It goes underwater at every moon tide, and is capable of supporting a man and his dog, and not much more.

Speculators and developers got very excited for a while about the possibility of improving Sandy Neck, the long, slender barrier of spectacular dunes that bounds the harbor on the north. There are grotesque forests of dead trees out there, trees suffocated by sand, then unburied again. And the outer beach, for all practical purposes infinite, puts the beach of Acapulco to shame. Surprisingly, too, fresh water can be had out there from quite shallow wells. But the local government, thank God, is buying up all of Sandy Neck but the tip, at the harbor mouth, and is making it a public park to be kept unimproved forever.

There is a tiny settlement on the tip of the neck, the tip that the government is not taking over. It is clustered around the abandoned lighthouse, a lighthouse that was once needed when there was water enough around to let big ships come and go. The bleached and tacky settlement can be reached only by boat or beach buggy. There is no electricity there, no telephone. It is a private resort. Less than a mile from Barnstable Village, the tip of the neck is where many villagers go when they need a vacation.

And all of the anachronistic, mildly xenophobic, charming queernesses of Barnstable Village might entitle it to the epithet, "Last Stronghold of the True Cape Codders," if it weren't for one thing: Hardly anyone in the village was born on Cape Cod. Just as petrified wood is formed by minerals slowly replacing organic materials, so has the present-day petrified Barnstable been formed by persons from Evanston and Louisville and Boston and Pittsburgh and God-only-knows-where-else, slowly replacing authentic rural Yankees.

If the real Cape Codders could rise from their churchyard graves, cast aside their beautifully lettered slate headstones, and attend a meeting of the Barnstable Village Civic Association, they would approve of the proceedings. Every proposal that has ever come before the organization has been hotly debated and voted down, except that a new siren be bought for the rescue truck. The siren goes *bweep-bweep-bweep* instead of *rowrrr*, and is guaranteed to be audible at a distance of three miles.

The library, incidentally, now has a new *Britannica*, and a new *Americana*, too, purchases it made effortlessly, since it has money coming out of its ears. But so far, the school marks of the children and the conversation of the adults have not conspicuously improved.

Since the village exists for itself, and not for passersby, and since it specializes in hastening tourists on to paradises elsewhere, visitors play hell finding anything to like about it. For a quick sample of how good it can be, a visitor might stop off at St. Mary's Church on Main Street, which has, unadvertised anywhere, the most enchanting church garden in America. The garden is the work of one man, Robert Nicholson, an Episcopalian minister, a good man who died young.

At a village cocktail party one time—and the villagers *do* drink a lot—Father Nicholson was talking to a Roman Catholic and a Jew, trying to find a word to describe the underlying spiritual unity of Barnstable. He found one. "We're Druids," he said.

(1964)

HARRISON BERGERON

THE YEAR WAS 2081, and everybody was finally equal. They weren't only equal before God and the law. They were equal every which way. Nobody was smarter than anybody else. Nobody was better looking than anybody else. Nobody was stronger or quicker than anybody else. All this equality was due to the 211th, 212th, and 213th Amendments to the Constitution, and to the unceasing vigilance of agents of the United States Handicapper General.

Some things about living still weren't quite right, though. April, for instance, still drove people crazy by not being springtime. And it was in that clammy month that the H-G men took George and Hazel Bergeron's fourteen-year-old son, Harrison, away.

It was tragic, all right, but George and Hazel couldn't think about it very hard. Hazel had a perfectly average intelligence, which meant she couldn't think about anything except in short bursts. And George, while his intelligence was way above normal, had a little mental handicap radio in his ear. He was required by law to wear it at all times. It was tuned to a government transmitter. Every twenty seconds or so, the transmitter would send out some sharp noise to keep people like George from taking unfair advantage of their brains.

George and Hazel were watching television. There were tears on Hazel's cheeks, but she'd forgotten for the moment what they were about.

On the television screen were ballerinas.

A buzzer sounded in George's head. His thoughts fled in panic, like bandits from a burglar alarm.

"That was a real pretty dance, that dance they just did," said Hazel.

"Huh?" said George.

"That dance—it was nice," said Hazel.

"Yup," said George. He tried to think a little about the ballerinas. They weren't really very good—no better than anybody else would have been, anyway. They were burdened with sashweights and bags of birdshot, and their faces were masked, so that no one, seeing a free and graceful gesture or a pretty face, would feel like something the cat dragged in. George was toying with the vague notion that maybe dancers shouldn't be handicapped. But he didn't get very far with it before another noise in his ear radio scattered his thoughts.

George winced. So did two out of the eight ballerinas.

Hazel saw him wince. Having no mental handicap herself, she had to ask George what the latest sound had been.

"Sounded like somebody hitting a milk bottle with a ball peen hammer," said George.

"I'd think it would be real interesting, hearing all the different sounds," said Hazel, a little envious. "All the things they think up."

"Um," said George.

"Only, if I was Handicapper General, you know what I would do?" said Hazel. Hazel, as a matter of fact, bore a strong resemblance to the Handicapper General, a woman named Diana Moon Glampers. "If I was Diana Moon Glampers," said Hazel, "I'd have chimes on Sunday—just chimes. Kind of in honor of religion."

"I could think, if it was just chimes," said George.

"Well—maybe make 'em real loud," said Hazel. "I think I'd make a good Handicapper General."

"Good as anybody else," said George.

"Who knows better'n I do what normal is?" said Hazel.

"Right," said George. He began to think glimmeringly about

his abnormal son who was now in jail, about Harrison, but a twenty-one-gun salute in his head stopped that.

"Boy!" said Hazel, "that was a doozy, wasn't it?"

It was such a doozy that George was white and trembling, and tears stood on the rims of his red eyes. Two of the eight ballerinas had collapsed to the studio floor, were holding their temples.

"All of a sudden you look so tired," said Hazel. "Why don't you stretch out on the sofa, so's you can rest your handicap bag on the pillows, honeybunch." She was referring to the forty-seven pounds of birdshot in a canvas bag, which was padlocked around George's neck. "Go on and rest the bag for a little while," she said. "I don't care if you're not equal to me for a while."

George weighed the bag with his hands. "I don't mind it," he said. "I don't notice it any more. It's just a part of me."

"You been so tired lately—kind of wore out," said Hazel. "If there was just some way we could make a little hole in the bottom of the bag, and just take out a few of them lead balls. Just a few."

"Two years in prison and two thousand dollars fine for every ball I took out," said George. "I don't call that a bargain."

"If you could just take a few out when you came home from work," said Hazel. "I mean—you don't compete with anybody around here. You just set around."

"If I tried to get away with it," said George, "then other people'd get away with it—and pretty soon we'd be right back to the dark ages again, with everybody competing against everybody else. You wouldn't like that, would you?"

"I'd hate it," said Hazel.

"There you are," said George. "The minute people start cheating on laws, what do you think happens to society?"

If Hazel hadn't been able to come up with an answer to this question, George couldn't have supplied one. A siren was going off in his head.

"Reckon it'd fall all apart," said Hazel.

"What would?" said George blankly.

"Society," said Hazel uncertainly. "Wasn't that what you just said?"

"Who knows?" said George.

The television program was suddenly interrupted for a news bulletin. It wasn't clear at first as to what the bulletin was about, since the announcer, like all announcers, had a serious speech impediment. For about half a minute, and in a state of high excitement, the announcer tried to say, "Ladies and gentlemen—"

He finally gave up, handed the bulletin to a ballerina to read.

"That's all right—" Hazel said of the announcer, "he tried. That's the big thing. He tried to do the best he could with what God gave him. He should get a nice raise for trying so hard."

"Ladies and gentlemen—" said the ballerina, reading the bulletin. She must have been extraordinarily beautiful, because the mask she wore was hideous. And it was easy to see that she was the strongest and most graceful of all the dancers, for her handicap bags were as big as those worn by two-hundred-pound men.

And she had to apologize at once for her voice, which was a very unfair voice for a woman to use. Her voice was a warm, luminous, timeless melody. "Excuse me—" she said, and she began again, making her voice absolutely uncompetitive.

"Harrison Bergeron, age fourteen," she said in a grackle squawk, "has just escaped from jail, where he was held on suspicion of plotting to overthrow the government. He is a genius and an athlete, is under-handicapped, and should be regarded as extremely dangerous."

A police photograph of Harrison Bergeron was flashed on the screen—upside down, then sideways, upside down again, then right side up. The picture showed the full length of Harrison against a background calibrated in feet and inches. He was exactly seven feet tall.

The rest of Harrison's appearance was Halloween and hardware. Nobody had ever borne heavier handicaps. He had outgrown hindrances faster than the H-G men could think them up. Instead of a little ear radio for a mental handicap, he wore a tremendous pair of earphones, and spectacles with thick wavy lenses. The spectacles were intended to make him not only half blind, but to give him whanging headaches besides.

Scrap metal was hung all over him. Ordinarily, there was a certain symmetry, a military neatness to the handicaps issued to strong people, but Harrison looked like a walking junkyard. In the race of life, Harrison carried three hundred pounds.

And to offset his good looks, the H-G men required that he wear at all times a red rubber ball for a nose, keep his eyebrows shaved off, and cover his even white teeth with black caps at snaggle-tooth random.

"If you see this boy," said the ballerina, "do not—I repeat, do not—try to reason with him."

There was the shriek of a door being torn from its hinges.

Screams and barking cries of consternation came from the television set. The photograph of Harrison Bergeron on the screen jumped again and again, as though dancing to the tune of an earthquake.

George Bergeron correctly identified the earthquake, and well he might have—for many was the time his own home had danced to the same crashing tune. "My God—" said George, "that must be Harrison!"

The realization was blasted from his mind instantly by the sound of an automobile collision in his head.

When George could open his eyes again, the photograph of Harrison was gone. A living, breathing Harrison filled the screen.

Clanking, clownish, and huge, Harrison stood in the center of the studio. The knob of the uprooted studio door was still in his hand. Ballerinas, technicians, musicians, and announcers cowered on their knees before him, expecting to die.

"I am the Emperor!" cried Harrison. "Do you hear? I am the Emperor! Everybody must do what I say at once!" He stamped his foot and the studio shook.

"Even as I stand here—" he bellowed, "crippled, hobbled, sickened—I am a greater ruler than any man who ever lived! Now watch me become what I *can* become!"

Harrison tore the straps of his handicap harness like wet tissue paper, tore straps guaranteed to support five thousand pounds.

Harrison's scrap-iron handicaps crashed to the floor.

Harrison thrust his thumbs under the bar of the padlock that secured his head harness. The bar snapped like celery. Harrison smashed his headphones and spectacles against the wall.

He flung away his rubber-ball nose, revealed a man that would have awed Thor, the god of thunder.

"I shall now select my Empress!" he said, looking down on the cowering people. "Let the first woman who dares rise to her feet claim her mate and her throne!"

A moment passed, and then a ballerina arose, swaying like a willow.

Harrison plucked the mental handicap from her ear, snapped off her physical handicaps with marvellous delicacy. Last of all, he removed her mask.

She was blindingly beautiful.

"Now—" said Harrison, taking her hand, "shall we show the people the meaning of the word dance? Music!" he commanded.

The musicians scrambled back into their chairs, and Harrison stripped them of their handicaps, too. "Play your best," he told them, "and I'll make you barons and dukes and earls."

The music began. It was normal at first—cheap, silly, false. But Harrison snatched two musicians from their chairs, waved them like batons as he sang the music as he wanted it played. He slammed them back into their chairs.

The music began again and was much improved.

Harrison and his Empress merely listened to the music for a while—listened gravely, as though synchronizing their heartbeats with it.

They shifted their weights to their toes.

Harrison placed his big hands on the girl's tiny waist, letting her sense the weightlessness that would soon be hers.

And then, in an explosion of joy and grace, into the air they sprang!

Not only were the laws of the land abandoned, but the law of gravity and the laws of motion as well.

They reeled, whirled, swiveled, flounced, capered, gamboled, and spun.

They leaped like deer on the moon.

The studio ceiling was thirty feet high, but each leap brought the dancers nearer to it.

It became their obvious intention to kiss the ceiling.

They kissed it.

And then, neutralizing gravity with love and pure will, they remained suspended in air inches below the ceiling, and they kissed each other for a long, long time.

It was then that Diana Moon Glampers, the Handicapper General, came into the studio with a double-barreled ten-gauge shotgun. She fired twice, and the Emperor and the Empress were dead before they hit the floor.

Diana Moon Glampers loaded the gun again. She aimed it at the musicians and told them they had ten seconds to get their handicaps back on.

It was then that the Bergerons' television tube burned out.

Hazel turned to comment about the blackout to George. But George had gone out into the kitchen for a can of beer.

George came back in with the beer, paused while a handicap signal shook him up. And then he sat down again. "You been crying?" he said to Hazel.

"Yup," she said.

"What about?" he said.

"I forget," she said. "Something real sad on television."

"What was it?" he said.

"It's all kind of mixed up in my mind," said Hazel.

"Forget sad things," said George.

"I always do," said Hazel.

"That's my girl," said George. He winced. There was the sound of a rivetting gun in his head.

"Gee—I could tell that one was a doozy," said Hazel.

"You can say that again," said George.

"Gee—" said Hazel, "I could tell that one was a doozy."

(1961)

WHO AM I THIS TIME?

THE North Crawford Mask and Wig Club, an amateur theatrical society I belong to, voted to do Tennessee Williams's *A Streetcar Named Desire* for the spring play. Doris Sawyer, who always directs, said she couldn't direct this time because her mother was so sick. And she said the club ought to develop some other directors anyway, because she couldn't live forever, even though she'd made it safely to seventy-four.

So I got stuck with the directing job, even though the only thing I'd ever directed before was the installation of combination aluminum storm windows and screens I'd sold. That's what I am, a salesman of storm windows and doors, and here and there a bathtub enclosure. As far as acting goes, the highest rank I ever held on stage was either butler or policeman, whichever's higher.

I made a lot of conditions before I took the directing job, and the biggest one was that Harry Nash, the only real actor the club has, had to take the Marlon Brando part in the play. To give you an idea of how versatile Harry is, inside of one year he was Captain Queeg in *The Caine Mutiny Court Martial*, then

Abe Lincoln in *Abe Lincoln in Illinois* and then the young architect in *The Moon is Blue*. The year after that, Harry Nash was
Henry the Eighth in *Anne of the Thousand Days* and Doc in
Come Back Little Sheba, and I was after him for Marlon Brando
in *A Streetcar Named Desire*. Harry wasn't at the meeting to say
whether he'd take the part or not. He never came to meetings.
He was too shy. He didn't stay away from meetings because he
had something else to do. He wasn't married, didn't go out with
women—didn't have any close men friends either. He stayed
away from all kinds of gatherings because he never could think
of anything to say or do without a script.

So I had to go down to Miller's Hardware Store, where Harry
was a clerk, the next day and ask him if he'd take the part. I
stopped off at the telephone company to complain about a bill
I'd gotten for a call to Honolulu, I'd never called Honolulu in my
life.

And there was this beautiful girl I'd never seen before behind
the counter at the phone company, and she explained that the
company had put in an automatic billing machine and that the
machine didn't have all the bugs out of it yet. It made mistakes.
"Not only did I not call Honolulu," I told her, "I don't think anybody in North Crawford ever has or will."

So she took the charge off the bill, and I asked her if she was
from around North Crawford. She said no. She said she just
came with the new billing machine to teach local girls how to
take care of it. After that, she said, she would go with some other
machine to someplace else. "Well," I said, "as long as people
have to come along with the machines, I guess we're all right."

"What?" she said.

"When machines start delivering themselves," I said, "I guess
that's when the people better start really worrying."

"Oh," she said. She didn't seem very interested in that subject,
and I wondered if she was interested in anything. She seemed
kind of numb, almost a machine herself, an automatic phone-
company politeness machine.

"How long will you be in town here?" I asked her.

"I stay in each town eight weeks, sir," she said. She had pretty
blue eyes, but there sure wasn't much hope or curiosity in them.

She told me she had been going from town to town like that for two years, always a stranger.

And I got it in my head that she might make a good Stella for the play. Stella was the wife of the Marlon Brando character, the wife of the character I wanted Harry Nash to play. So I told her where and when we were going to hold tryouts, and said the club would be very happy if she'd come.

She looked surprised, and she warmed up a little. "You know," she said, "that's the first time anybody ever asked me to participate in any community thing."

"Well," I said, "there isn't any other way to get to know a lot of nice people faster than to be in a play with 'em."

She said her name was Helene Shaw. She said she might just surprise me—and herself. She said she just might come.

You would think that North Crawford would be fed up with Harry Nash in plays after all the plays he'd been in. But the fact was that North Crawford probably could have gone on enjoying Harry forever, because he was never Harry on stage. When the maroon curtain went up on the stage in the gymnasium of the Consolidated Junior-Senior High School, Harry, body and soul, was exactly what the script and the director told him to be.

Somebody said one time that Harry ought to go to a psychiatrist so he could be something important and colorful in real life, too—so he could get married anyway, and maybe get a better job than just clerking in Miller's Hardware Store for fifty dollars a week. But I don't know what a psychiatrist could have turned up about him that the town didn't already know. The trouble with Harry was he'd been left on the doorstep of the Unitarian Church when he was a baby, and he never did find out who his parents were.

When I told him there in Miller's that I'd been appointed director, that I wanted him in my play, he said what he always said to anybody who asked him to be in a play—and it was kind of sad, if you think about it.

"Who am I this time?" he said.

So I held the tryouts where they're always held—in the meeting room on the second floor of the North Crawford Public Library. Doris Sawyer, the woman who usually directs, came to give me the benefit of all her experience. The two of us sat in state upstairs, while the people who wanted parts waited below. We called them upstairs one by one.

Harry Nash came to the tryouts, even though it was a waste of time. I guess he wanted to get that little bit more acting in.

For Harry's pleasure, and our pleasure, too, we had him read from the scene where he beats up his wife. It was a play in itself, the way Harry did it, and Tennessee Williams hadn't written it all either. Tennessee Williams didn't write the part, for instance, where Harry, who weighs about one hundred forty-five, who's about five feet eight inches tall, added fifty pounds to his weight and four inches to his height by just picking up a playbook. He had a short little double-breasted bellows-back grade-school graduation suit coat on and a dinky little red tie with a horsehead on it. He took off the coat and tie, opened his collar, then turned his back to Doris and me, getting up steam for the part. There was a great big rip in the back of his shirt, and it looked like a fairly new shirt too. He'd ripped it on purpose, so he could be that much more like Marlon Brando, right from the first.

When he faced us again, he was huge and handsome and conceited and cruel. Doris read the part of Stella, the wife, and Harry bullied that old, old lady into believing that she was a sweet, pregnant girl married to a sexy gorilla who was going to beat her brains out. She had me believing it too. And I read the lines of Blanche, her sister in the play, and darned if Harry didn't scare me into feeling like a drunk and faded Southern belle.

And then, while Doris and I were getting over our emotional experiences, like people coming out from under ether, Harry put down the playbook, put on his coat and tie, and turned into the pale hardware-store clerk again.

"Was—was that all right?" he said, and he seemed pretty sure he wouldn't get the part.

"Well," I said, "for a first reading, that wasn't too bad."

"Is there a chance I'll get the part?" he said. I don't know why he always had to pretend there was some doubt about his getting a part, but he did.

"I think we can safely say we're leaning powerfully in your direction," I told him.

He was very pleased. "Thanks! Thanks a lot!" he said, and he shook my hand.

"Is there a pretty new girl downstairs?" I said, meaning Helene Shaw.

"I didn't notice," said Harry.

It turned out that Helene Shaw *had* come for the tryouts, and Doris and I had our hearts broken. We thought the North Crawford Mask and Wig Club was finally going to put a really good-looking, really young girl on stage, instead of one of the beat-up forty-year-old women we generally have to palm off as girls.

But Helene Shaw couldn't act for sour apples. No matter what we gave her to read, she was the same girl with the same smile for anybody who had a complaint about his phone bill.

Doris tried to coach her some, to make her understand that Stella in the play was a very passionate girl who loved a gorilla because she needed a gorilla. But Helene just read the lines the same way again. I don't think a volcano could have stirred her up enough to say, "Oo."

"Dear," said Doris, "I'm going to ask you a personal question."

"All right," said Helene.

"Have you ever been in love?" said Doris. "The reason I ask," she said, "remembering some old love might help you put more warmth in your acting."

Helene frowned and thought hard. "Well," she said, "I travel a lot, you know. And practically all the men in the different companies I visit are married and I never stay anyplace long enough to know many people who aren't."

"What about school?" said Doris. "What about puppy love and all the other kinds of love in school?"

So Helene thought hard about that, and then she said, "Even in school I was always moving around a lot. My father was a construction worker, following jobs around, so I was always saying hello or good-by to someplace, without anything in between."

"Um," said Doris.

"Would movie stars count?" said Helene. "I don't mean in real life. I never knew any. I just mean up on the screen."

Doris looked at me and rolled her eyes. "I guess that's love of a kind," she said.

And then Helene got a little enthusiastic. "I used to sit through movies over and over again," she said, "and pretend I was married to whoever the man movie star was. They were the only people who came with us. No matter where we moved, movie stars were there."

"Uh huh," said Doris.

"Well, thank you, Miss Shaw," I said. "You go downstairs and wait with the rest. We'll let you know."

So we tried to find another Stella. And there just wasn't one, not one woman in the club with the dew still on her. "All we've got are Blanches," I said, meaning all we had were faded women who could play the part of Blanche, Stella's faded sister. "That's life, I guess—twenty Blanches to one Stella."

"And when you find a Stella," said Doris, "it turns out she doesn't know what love is."

Doris and I decided there was one last thing we could try. We could get Harry Nash to play a scene along with Helene. "He just might make her bubble the least little bit," I said.

"That girl hasn't got a bubble in her," said Doris.

So we called down the stairs for Helene to come back on up, and we told somebody to go find Harry. Harry never sat with the rest of the people at tryouts—or at rehearsals either. The minute he didn't have a part to play, he'd disappear into some hiding place where he could hear people call him, but where he couldn't be seen. At tryouts in the library he generally hid in the reference room, passing the time looking at flags of different countries in the front of the dictionary.

Helene came back upstairs, and we were very sorry and surprised to see that she'd been crying.

"Oh, dear," said Doris. "Oh, my—now what on earth's the trouble, dear?"

"I was terrible, wasn't I?" said Helene, hanging her head.

Doris said the only thing anybody can say in an amateur theatrical society when somebody cries. She said, "Why, no dear—you were marvelous."

"No, I wasn't," said Helene. "I'm a walking icebox, and I know it."

"Nobody could look at you and say that," said Doris.

"When they get to know me, they can say it," said Helene. "When people get to know me, that's what they *do* say." Her tears got worse. "I don't want to be the way I am," she said. "I just can't help it, living the way I've lived all my life. The only experiences I've had have been in crazy dreams of movie stars. When I meet somebody nice in real life, I feel as though I were in some kind of big bottle, as though I couldn't touch that person, no matter how hard I tried." And Helene pushed on air as though it were a big bottle all around her.

"You ask me if I've ever been in love," she said to Doris. "No—but I want to be. I know what this play's about. I know what Stella's supposed to feel and why she feels it. I—I—I—" she said, and her tears wouldn't let her go on.

"You what, dear?" said Doris gently.

"I——" said Helene, and she pushed on the imaginary bottle again. "I just don't know how to begin," she said.

There was heavy clumping on the library stairs. It sounded like a deep-sea diver coming upstairs in his lead shoes. It was Harry Nash, turning himself into Marlon Brando. In he came, practically dragging his knuckles on the floor. And he was so much in character that the sight of a weeping woman made him sneer.

"Harry," I said, "I'd like you to meet Helene Shaw. Helene—this is Harry Nash. If you get the part of Stella, he'll be your husband in the play." Harry didn't offer to shake hands. He put his hands in his pockets, and he hunched over, and he looked her up and down, gave her looks that left her naked. Her tears stopped right then and there.

"I wonder if you two would play the fight scene," I said, "and then the reunion scene right after it."

"Sure," said Harry, his eyes still on her. Those eyes burned up clothes faster than she could put them on. "Sure," he said, "if Stell's game."

"What?" said Helene. She'd turned the color of cranberry juice.

"Stell—Stella," said Harry. "That's you. Stell's my wife."

I handed the two of them playbooks. Harry snatched his from

me without a word of thanks. Helene's hands weren't working very well, and I had to kind of mold them around the book.

"I'll want something I can throw," said Harry.

"What?" I said.

"There's one place where I throw a radio out a window," said Harry. "What can I throw?"

So I said an iron paperweight was the radio, and I opened the window wide. Helene Shaw looked scared to death.

"Where you want us to start?" said Harry, and he rolled his shoulders like a prizefighter warming up.

"Start a few lines back from where you throw the radio out the window," I said.

"O.K., O.K.," said Harry, warming up, warming up. He scanned the stage directions. "Let's see," he said, "after I throw the radio, she runs off stage, and I chase her, and I sock her one."

"Right," I said.

"O.K., baby," Harry said to Helene, his eyelids drooping. What was about to happen was wilder than the chariot race in *Ben Hur*. "On your mark," said Harry. "Get ready, baby. Go!"

When the scene was over, Helene Shaw was as hot as a hod carrier, as limp as an eel. She sat down with her mouth open and her head hanging to one side. She wasn't in any bottle any more. There wasn't any bottle to hold her up and keep her safe and clean. The bottle was gone.

"Do I get the part or don't I?" Harry snarled at me.

"You'll do," I said.

"You said a mouthful!" he said. "I'll be going now. . . . See you around, Stella," he said to Helene, and he left. He slammed the door behind him.

"Helene?" I said. "Miss Shaw?"

"Mf?" she said.

"The part of Stella is yours," I said. "You were great!"

"I was?" she said.

"I had no idea you had that much fire in you, dear," Doris said to her.

"Fire?" said Helene. She didn't know if she was afoot or on horseback.

"Skyrockets! Pinwheels! Roman candles!" said Doris.

"Mf," said Helene. And that was all she said. She looked as though she were going to sit in the chair with her mouth open forever.

"Stella," I said.

"Huh?" she said.

"You have my permission to go."

So we started having rehearsals four nights a week on the stage of the Consolidated School. And Harry and Helene set such a pace that everybody in the production was half crazy with excitement and exhaustion before we'd rehearsed four times. Usually a director has to beg people to learn their lines, but I had no such trouble. Harry and Helene were working so well together that everybody else in the cast regarded it as a duty and an honor and a pleasure to support them.

I was certainly lucky—or thought I was. Things were going so well, so hot and heavy, so early in the game that I had to say to Harry and Helene after one love scene, "Hold a little something back for the actual performance, would .you please? You'll burn yourselves out."

I said that at the fourth or fifth rehearsal, and Lydia Miller, who was playing Blanche, the faded sister, was sitting next to me in the audience. In real life, she's the wife of Verne Miller. Verne owns Miller's Hardware Store. Verne was Harry's boss.

"Lydia," I said to her, "have we got a play or have we got a play?"

"Yes," she said, "you've got a play, all right." She made it sound as though I'd committed some kind of crime, done something just terrible. "You should be very proud of yourself."

"What do you mean by that?" I said.

Before Lydia could answer, Harry yelled at me from the stage, asked if I was through with him, asked if he could go home. I told him he could and, still Marlon Brando, he left, kicking furniture out of his way and slamming doors. Helene was left all alone on the stage, sitting on a couch with the same gaga look she'd had after the tryouts. That girl was drained.

I turned to Lydia again and I said, "Well—until now, I thought I had every reason to be happy and proud. Is there something going on I don't know about?"

"Do you know that girl's in love with Harry?" said Lydia.

"In the play?" I said.

"What play?" said Lydia. "There isn't any play going on now, and look at her up there." She gave a sad cackle. "You aren't directing this play."

"Who is?" I said.

"Mother Nature at her worst," said Lydia. "And think what it's going to do to that girl when she discovers what Harry really is." She corrected herself. "What Harry really isn't," she said.

I didn't do anything about it, because I didn't figure it was any of my business. I heard Lydia try to do something about it, but she didn't get very far.

"You know," Lydia said to Helene one night, "I once played Ann Rutledge, and Harry was Abraham Lincoln."

Helene clapped her hands. "That must have been heaven!" she said.

"It was, in a way," said Lydia. "Sometimes I'd get so worked up, I'd love Harry the way I'd love Abraham Lincoln. I'd have to come back to earth and remind myself that he wasn't ever going to free the slaves, that he was just a clerk in my husband's hardware store."

"He's the most marvelous man I ever met," said Helene.

"Of course, one thing you have to get set for, when you're in a play with Harry," said Lydia, "is what happens after the last performance."

"What are you talking about?" said Helene.

"Once the show's over," said Lydia, "whatever you thought Harry was just evaporates into thin air."

"I don't believe it," said Helene.

"I admit it's hard to believe," said Lydia.

Then Helene got a little sore. "Anyway, why tell me about it?" she said. "Even if it is true, what do I care?"

"I—I don't know," said Lydia, backing away. "I—I just thought you might find it interesting."

"Well, I don't," said Helene.

And Lydia slunk away, feeling about as frowzy and unloved as she was supposed to feel in the play. After that nobody said anything more to Helene to warn her about Harry, not even when word got around that she'd told the telephone company that she didn't want to be moved around anymore, that she wanted to stay in North Crawford.

So the time finally came to put on the play. We ran it for three nights—Thursday, Friday, and Saturday—and we murdered those audiences. They believed every word that was said on stage, and when the maroon curtain came down they were ready to go to the nut house along with Blanche, the faded sister.

On Thursday night the other girls at the telephone company sent Helene a dozen red roses. When Helene and Harry were taking a curtain call together, I passed the roses over the footlights to her. She came forward for them, took one rose from the bouquet to give to Harry. But when she turned to give Harry the rose in front of everybody, Harry was gone. The curtain came down on that extra little scene—that girl offering a rose to nothing and nobody.

I went backstage, and I found her still holding that one rose. She'd put the rest of the bouquet aside. There were tears in her eyes. "What did I do wrong?" she said to me. "Did I insult him some way?"

"No," I said. "He always does that after a performance. The minute it's over, he clears out as fast as he can."

"And tomorrow he'll disappear again?"

"Without even taking off his makeup."

"And Saturday?" she said. "He'll stay for the cast party on Saturday, won't he?"

"Harry never goes to parties," I said. "When the curtain comes down on Saturday, that's the last anybody will see of him till he goes to work on Monday."

"How sad," she said.

Helene's performance on Friday night wasn't nearly so good as Thursday's. She seemed to be thinking about other things. She watched Harry take off after curtain call. She didn't say a word.

On Saturday she put on the best performance yet. Ordinarily it was Harry who set the pace. But on Saturday Harry had to work to keep up with Helene.

When the curtain came down on the final curtain call, Harry

wanted to get away, but he couldn't. Helene wouldn't let go his hand. The rest of the cast and the stage crew and a lot of well-wishers from the audience were all standing around Harry and Helene, and Harry was trying to get his hand back.

"Well," he said, "I've got to go."

"Where?" she said.

"Oh," he said, "home."

"Won't you please take me to the cast party?" she said.

He got very red. "I'm afraid I'm not much on parties," he said. All the Marlon Brando in him was gone. He was tongue-tied, he was scared, he was shy—he was everything Harry was famous for being between plays.

"All right," she said. "I'll let you go—if you promise me one thing."

"What's that?" he said, and I thought he would jump out a window if she let go of him then.

"I want you to promise to stay here until I get you your present," she said.

"Present?" he said, getting even more panicky.

"Promise?" she said.

He promised. It was the only way he could get his hand back. And he stood there miserably while Helene went down to the ladies' dressing room for the present. While he waited, a lot of people congratulated him on being such a fine actor. But congratulations never made him happy. He just wanted to get away.

Helene came back with the present. It turned out to be a little blue book with a big red ribbon for a place marker. It was a copy of *Romeo and Juliet*. Harry was very embarrassed. It was all he could do to say "Thank you."

"The marker marks my favorite scene," said Helene.

"Um," said Harry.

"Don't you want to see what my favorite scene is?" she said.

So Harry had to open the book to the red ribbon.

Helene got close to him, and read a line of Juliet's. " 'How cam'st thou hither, tell me, and wherefore?' " she read. " 'The orchard walls are high and hard to climb, and the place death, considering who thou art, if any of my kinsmen find thee here.' " She pointed to the next line. "Now, look what Romeo says," she said.

"Um," said Harry.

"Read what Romeo says," said Helene.

Harry cleared his throat. He didn't want to read the line, but he had to. " 'With love's light wings did I o'erperch these walls,' " he read out loud in his everyday voice. But then a change came over him. " 'For stony limits cannot hold love out,' " he read, and he straightened up, and eight years dropped away from him, and he was brave and gay. " 'And what love can do, that dares love attempt,' " he read, " 'therefore thy kinsmen are no let to me.' "

" 'If they do see thee they will murther thee,' " said Helene, and she started him walking toward the wings.

" 'Alack!' " said Harry, " 'there lies more peril in thine eye than twenty of their swords.' " Helene led him toward the backstage exit. " 'Look thou but sweet,' " said Harry, " 'and I am proof against their enmity.' "

" 'I would not for the world they saw thee here,' " said Helene, and that was the last we heard. The two of them were out the door and gone.

They never did show up at the cast party. One week later they were married.

They seem very happy, although they're kind of strange from time to time, depending on which play they're reading to each other at the time.

I dropped into the phone company office the other day, on account of the billing machine was making dumb mistakes again. I asked her what plays she and Harry'd been reading lately.

"In the past week," she said, "I've been married to Othello, been loved by Faust and been kidnaped by Paris. Wouldn't you say I was the luckiest girl in town?"

I said I thought so, and I told her most of the women in town thought so too.

"They had their chance," she said.

"Most of 'em couldn't stand the excitement," I said. And I told her I'd been asked to direct another play. I asked if she and Harry would be available for the cast. She gave me a big smile and said, "Who are we this time?"

(1961)

WELCOME TO
THE MONKEY HOUSE

SO PETE CROCKER, the sheriff of Barnstable County, which was the whole of Cape Cod, came into the Federal Ethical Suicide Parlor in Hyannis one May afternoon—and he told the two six-foot Hostesses there that they weren't to be alarmed, but that a notorious nothinghead named Billy the Poet was believed headed for the Cape.

A nothinghead was a person who refused to take his ethical birth-control pills three times a day. The penalty for that was $10,000 and ten years in jail.

This was at a time when the population of Earth was 17 billion human beings. That was far too many mammals that big for a planet that small. The people were virtually packed together like drupelets.

Drupelets are the pulpy little knobs that compose the outside of a raspberry.

So the World Government was making a two-pronged attack on overpopulation. One pronging was the encouragement of ethical suicide, which consisted of going to the nearest Suicide

Parlor and asking a Hostess to kill you painlessly while you lay on a Barcalounger. The other pronging was compulsory ethical birth control.

The sheriff told the Hostesses, who were pretty, tough-minded, highly intelligent girls, that roadblocks were being set up and house-to-house searches were being conducted to catch Billy the Poet. The main difficulty was that the police didn't know what he looked like. The few people who had seen him and known him for what he was were women—and they disagreed fantastically as to his height, his hair color, his voice, his weight, the color of his skin.

"I don't need to remind you girls," the sheriff went on, "that a nothinghead is very sensitive from the waist down. If Billy the Poet somehow slips in here and starts making trouble, one good kick in the right place will do wonders."

He was referring to the fact that ethical birth-control pills, the only legal form of birth control, made people numb from the waist down.

Most men said their bottom halves felt like cold iron or balsawood. Most women said their bottom halves felt like wet cotton or stale ginger ale. The pills were so effective that you could blindfold a man who had taken one, tell him to recite the Gettysburg Address, kick him in the balls while he was doing it, and he wouldn't miss a syllable.

The pills were ethical because they didn't interfere with a person's ability to reproduce, which would have been unnatural and immoral. All the pills did was take every bit of pleasure out of sex.

Thus did science and morals go hand in hand.

The two Hostesses there in Hyannis were Nancy McLuhan and Mary Kraft. Nancy was a strawberry blonde. Mary was a glossy brunette. Their uniforms were white lipstick, heavy eye makeup, purple body stockings with nothing underneath, and black-leather boots. They ran a small operation—with only six suicide booths. In a really good week, say the one before Christmas, they might put sixty people to sleep. It was done with a hypodermic syringe.

"My main message to you girls," said Sheriff Crocker, "is that everything's well under control. You can just go about your business here."

"Didn't you leave out part of your main message?" Nancy asked him.

"I don't get you."

"I didn't hear you say he was probably headed straight for us."

He shrugged in clumsy innocence. "We don't know that for sure."

"I thought that was all anybody *did* know about Billy the Poet: that he specializes in deflowering Hostesses in Ethical Suicide Parlors." Nancy was a virgin. All Hostesses were virgins. They also had to hold advanced degrees in psychology and nursing. They also had to be plump and rosy, and at least six feet tall.

America had changed in many ways, but it had yet to adopt the metric system.

Nancy McLuhan was burned up that the sheriff would try to protect her and Mary from the full truth about Billy the Poet—as though they might panic if they heard it. She told the sheriff so.

"How long do you think a girl would last in the E. S. S.," she said, meaning the Ethical Suicide Service, "if she scared that easy?"

The sheriff took a step backward, pulled in his chin. "Not very long, I guess."

"That's very true," said Nancy, closing the distance between them and offering him a sniff of the edge of her hand, which was poised for a karate chop. All Hostesses were experts at judo and karate. "If you'd like to find out how helpless we are, just come toward me, pretending you're Billy the Poet."

The sheriff shook his head, gave her a glassy smile. "I'd rather not."

"That's the smartest thing you've said today," said Nancy, turning her back on him while Mary laughed. "We're not scared—we're *angry*. Or we're not even *that*. He isn't *worth* that. We're *bored*. How boring that he should come a great distance, should cause all this fuss, in order to——" She let the sentence die there. "It's just too absurd."

"I'm not as mad at *him* as I am at the women who let him do it to them without a struggle"—said Mary—"who let him do it and then couldn't tell the police what he looked like. Suicide Hostesses at that!"

"Somebody hasn't been keeping up with her karate," said Nancy.

It wasn't just Billy the Poet who was attracted to Hostesses in Ethical Suicide Parlors. All nothingheads were. Bombed out of their skulls with the sex madness that came from taking nothing, they thought the white lips and big eyes and body stocking and boots of a Hostess spelled *sex, sex, sex.*

The truth was, of course, that sex was the last thing any Hostess ever had in mind.

"If Billy follows his usual M. O.," said the sheriff, "he'll study your habits and the neighborhood. And then he'll pick one or the other of you and he'll send her a dirty poem in the mail."

"Charming," said Nancy.

"He has also been known to use the telephone."

"How brave," said Nancy. Over the sheriff's shoulder, she could see the mailman coming.

A blue light went on over the door of a booth for which Nancy was responsible. The person in there wanted something. It was the only booth in use at the time.

The sheriff asked her if there was a possibility that the person in there was Billy the Poet, and Nancy said, "Well, if it is, I can break his neck with my thumb and forefinger."

"Foxy Grandpa," said Mary, who'd seen him, too. A Foxy Grandpa was any old man, cute and senile, who quibbled and joked and reminisced for hours before he let a Hostess put him to sleep.

Nancy groaned. "We've spent the past two hours trying to decide on a last meal."

And then the mailman came in with just one letter. It was addressed to Nancy in smeary pencil. She was splendid with anger and disgust as she opened it, knowing it would be a piece of filth from Billy.

She was right. Inside the envelope was a poem. It wasn't an original poem. It was a song from olden days that had taken on new meanings since the numbness of ethical birth control had become universal. It went like this, in smeary pencil again:

> *We were walking through the park,*
> A-goosing statues in the dark.
> If Sherman's horse can take it,
> So can you.

When Nancy came into the suicide booth to see what he wanted, the Foxy Grandpa was lying on the mint-green Barcalounger, where hundreds had died so peacefully over the years. He was studying the menu from the Howard Johnson's next door and beating time to the Muzak coming from the loudspeaker on the lemon-yellow wall. The room was painted cinder block. There was one barred window with a Venetian blind.

There was a Howard Johnson's next door to every Ethical Suicide Parlor, and vice versa. The Howard Johnson's had an orange roof and the Suicide Parlor had a purple roof, but they were both the Government. Practically everything was the Government.

Practically everything was automated, too. Nancy and Mary and the sheriff were lucky to have jobs. Most people didn't. The average citizen moped around home and watched television, which was the Government. Every fifteen minutes his television would urge him to vote intelligently or consume intelligently, or worship in the church of his choice, or love his fellowmen, or obey the laws—or pay a call to the nearest Ethical Suicide Parlor and find out how friendly and understanding a Hostess could be.

The Foxy Grandpa was something of a rarity, since he was marked by old age, was bald, was shaky, had spots on his hands. Most people looked twenty-two, thanks to anti-aging shots they took twice a year. That the old man looked old was proof that the shots had been discovered after his sweet bird of youth had flown.

"Have we decided on a last supper yet?" Nancy asked him. She heard peevishness in her own voice, heard herself betray her exasperation with Billy the Poet, her boredom with the old man. She was ashamed, for this was unprofessional of her. "The breaded veal cutlet is very good."

The old man cocked his head. With the greedy cunning of second childhood, he had caught her being unprofessional, unkind, and he was going to punish her for it. "You don't sound very friendly. I thought you were all supposed to be friendly. I thought this was supposed to be a pleasant place to come."

"I beg your pardon," she said. "If I seem unfriendly, it has nothing to do with you."

"I thought maybe I bored you."

"No, no," she said gamely, "not at all. You certainly know some very interesting history." Among other things, the Foxy Grandpa claimed to have known J. Edgar Nation, the Grand Rapids druggist who was the father of ethical birth control.

"Then *look* like you're interested," he told her. He could get away with that sort of impudence. The thing was, he could leave any time he wanted to, right up to the moment he asked for the needle—and he had to *ask* for the needle. That was the law.

Nancy's art, and the art of every Hostess, was to see that volunteers didn't leave, to coax and wheedle and flatter them patiently, every step of the way.

So Nancy had to sit down there in the booth, to pretend to marvel at the freshness of the yarn the old man told, a story everybody knew, about how J. Edgar Nation happened to experiment with ethical birth control.

"He didn't have the slightest idea his pills would be taken by human beings someday," said the Foxy Grandpa. "His dream was to introduce morality into the monkey house at the Grand Rapids Zoo. Did you realize that?" he inquired severely.

"No. No, I didn't. That's very interesting."

"He and his eleven kids went to church one Easter. And the day was so nice and the Easter service had been so beautiful and pure that they decided to take a walk through the zoo, and they were just walking on clouds."

"Um." The scene described was lifted from a play that was performed on television every Easter.

The Foxy Grandpa shoehorned himself into the scene, had

himself chat with the Nations just before they got to the monkey house. "'Good morning, Mr. Nation,' I said to him. 'It certainly is a nice morning.' 'And a good morning to *you*, Mr. Howard,' he said to me. 'There is nothing like an Easter morning to make a man feel clean and reborn and at one with God's intentions.'"

"Um." Nancy could hear the telephone ringing faintly, naggingly, through the nearly soundproof door.

"So we went on to the monkey house together, and what do you think we saw?"

"I can't imagine." Somebody had answered the phone.

"We saw a monkey playing with his private parts!"

"No!"

"Yes! And J. Edgar Nation was so upset he went straight home and he started developing a pill that would make monkeys in the springtime fit things for a Christian family to see."

There was a knock on the door.

"Yes——?" said Nancy.

"Nancy," said Mary, "telephone for you."

When Nancy came out of the booth, she found the sheriff choking on little squeals of law-enforcement delight. The telephone was tapped by agents hidden in the Howard Johnson's. Billy the Poet was believed to be on the line. His call had been traced. Police were already on their way to grab him.

"Keep him on, keep him on," the sheriff whispered to Nancy, and he gave her the telephone as though it were solid gold.

"Yes—?" said Nancy.

"Nancy McLuhan?" said a man. His voice was disguised. He might have been speaking through a kazoo. "I'm calling for a mutual friend."

"Oh?"

"He asked me to deliver a message."

"I see."

"It's a poem."

"All right."

"Ready?"

"Ready." Nancy could hear sirens screaming in the background of the call.

The caller must have heard the sirens, too, but he recited the poem without any emotion. It went like this:

> "Soak yourself in Jergen's Lotion.
> Here comes the one-man population
> explosion."

They got him. Nancy heard it all—the thumping and clumping, the argle-bargle and cries.

The depression she felt as she hung up was glandular. Her brave body had prepared for a fight that was not to be.

The sheriff bounded out of the Suicide Parlor, in such a hurry to see the famous criminal he'd helped catch that a sheaf of papers fell from the pocket of his trench coat.

Mary picked them up, called after the sheriff. He halted for a moment, said the papers didn't matter any more, asked her if maybe she wouldn't like to come along. There was a flurry between the two girls, with Nancy persuading Mary to go, declaring that she had no curiosity about Billy. So Mary left, irrelevantly handing the sheaf to Nancy.

The sheaf proved to be photocopies of poems Billy had sent to Hostesses in other places. Nancy read the top one. It made much of a peculiar side effect of ethical birth-control pills: They not only made people numb—they also made people piss blue. The poem was called *What the Somethinghead Said to the Suicide Hostess,* and it went like this:

> I did not sow, I did not spin,
> And thanks to pills I did not sin.
> I loved the crowds, the stink, the noise.
> And when I peed, I peed turquoise.
>
> I ate beneath a roof of orange;
> Swung with progress like a door hinge.
> 'Neath purple roof I've come today
> To piss my azure life away.
>
> Virgin hostess, death's recruiter,
> Life is cute, but you are cuter.
> Mourn my pecker, purple daughter—
> All it passed was sky-blue water.

"You never heard that story before—about how J. Edgar Nation came to invent ethical birth control?" the Foxy Grandpa wanted to know. His voice cracked.

"Never did," lied Nancy.

"I thought everybody knew that."

"It was news to me."

"When he got through with the monkey house, you couldn't tell it from the Michigan Supreme Court. Meanwhile, there was this crisis going on in the United Nations. The people who understood science said people had to quit reproducing so much, and the people who understood morals said society would collapse if people used sex for nothing but pleasure."

The Foxy Grandpa got off his Barcalounger, went over to the window, pried two slats of the blind apart. There wasn't much to see out there. The view was blocked by the backside of a mocked-up thermometer twenty feet high, which faced the street. It was calibrated in billions of people on Earth, from zero to twenty. The make-believe column of liquid was a strip of translucent red plastic. It showed how many people there were on Earth. Very close to the bottom was a black arrow that showed what the scientists thought the population ought to be.

The Foxy Grandpa was looking at the setting sun through that red plastic, and through the blind, too, so that his face was banded with shadows and red.

"Tell me—" he said, "when I die, how much will that thermometer go down? A foot?"

"No."

"An inch?"

"Not quite."

"You know what the answer is, don't you?" he said, and he faced her. The senility had vanished from his voice and eyes. "One inch on that thing equals 83,333 people. You knew that, didn't you?"

"That—that might be true," said Nancy, "but that isn't the right way to look at it, in my opinion."

He didn't ask her what the right way was, in her opinion. He completed a thought of his own, instead. "I'll tell you something else that's true: I'm Billy the Poet, and you're a very good-looking woman."

With one hand, he drew a snub-nosed revolver from his belt. With the other, he peeled off his bald dome and wrinkled forehead, which proved to be rubber. Now he looked twenty-two.

"The police will want to know exactly what I look like when this is all over," he told Nancy with a malicious grin. "In case you're not good at describing people, and it's surprising how many women aren't:

> *I'm five foot two,*
> *With eyes of blue,*
> *With Brown hair to my shoulders—*
> *A manly elf*
> *So full of self*
> *The ladies say he smolders."*

Billy was ten inches shorter than Nancy was. She had about forty pounds on him. She told him he didn't have a chance, but Nancy was much mistaken. He had unbolted the bars on the window the night before and he made her go out the window and then down a manhole that was hidden from the street by the big thermometer.

He took her down into the sewers of Hyannis. He knew where he was going. He had a flashlight and a map. Nancy had to go before him along the narrow catwalk, her own shadow dancing mockingly in the lead. She tried to guess where they were, relative to the real world above. She guessed correctly when they passed under the Howard Johnson's, guessed from noises she heard. The machinery that processed and served the food there was silent. But, so people wouldn't feel too lonesome when eating there, the designers had provided sound effects for the kitchen. It was these Nancy heard—a tape recording of the clashing of silverware and the laughter of Negroes and Puerto Ricans.

After that she was lost. Billy had very little to say to her other than "Right," or, "Left," or "Don't try anything funny, Juno, or I'll blow your great big fucking head off."

Only once did they have anything resembling a conversation.

Billy began it, and ended it, too. "What in hell is a girl with hips like yours doing selling death?" he asked her from behind.

She dared to stop. "I can answer that," she told him. She was confident that she could give him an answer that would shrivel him like napalm.

But he gave her a shove, offered to blow her fucking head off again.

"You don't even want to hear my answer," she taunted him. "You're afraid to hear it."

"I never listen to a woman till the pills wear off," sneered Billy. That was his plan, then—to keep her a prisoner for at least eight hours. That was how long it took for the pills to wear off.

"That's a silly rule."

"A woman's not a woman till the pills wear off."

"You certainly manage to make a woman feel like an object rather than a person."

"Thank the pills for that," said Billy.

There were 80 miles of sewers under Greater Hyannis, which had a population of 400,000 drupelets, 400,000 souls. Nancy lost track of the time down there. When Billy announced that they had at last reached their destination, it was possible for Nancy to imagine that a year had passed.

She tested this spooky impression by pinching her own thigh, by feeling what the chemical clock of her body said. Her thigh was still numb.

Billy ordered her to climb iron rungs that were set in wet masonry. There was a circle of sickly light above. It proved to be moonlight filtered through the plastic polygons of an enormous geodesic dome. Nancy didn't have to ask the traditional victim's question, "Where am I?" There was only one dome like that on Cape Cod. It was in Hyannis Port and it sheltered the ancient Kennedy Compound.

It was a museum of how life had been lived in more expansive times. The museum was closed. It was open only in the summertime.

The manhole from which Nancy and then Billy emerged was set in an expanse of green cement, which showed where the Kennedy lawn had been. On the green cement, in front of the ancient frame houses, were statues representing the fourteen Kennedys who had been Presidents of the United States or the World. They were playing touch football.

The President of the World at the time of Nancy's abduction, incidentally, was an ex-Suicide Hostess named "Ma" Kennedy. Her statue would never join this particular touch-football game. Her name was Kennedy, all right, but she wasn't the real thing. People complained of her lack of style, found her vulgar. On the wall of her office was a sign that said, YOU DON'T HAVE TO BE CRAZY TO WORK HERE, BUT IT SURE HELPS, and another one that said THIMK!, and another one that said, SOMEDAY WE'RE GOING TO HAVE TO GET ORGANIZED AROUND HERE.

Her office was in the Taj Mahal.

Until she arrived in the Kennedy Museum, Nancy McLuhan was confident that she would sooner or later get a chance to break every bone in Billy's little body, maybe even shoot him with his own gun. She wouldn't have minded doing those things. She thought he was more disgusting than a blood-filled tick.

It wasn't compassion that changed her mind. It was the discovery that Billy had a gang. There were at least eight people around the manhole, men and women in equal numbers, with stockings pulled over their heads. It was the women who laid firm hands on Nancy, told her to keep calm. They were all at least as tall as Nancy and they held her in places where they could hurt her like hell if they had to.

Nancy closed her eyes, but this didn't protect her from the obvious conclusion: These perverted women were sisters from the Ethical Suicide Service. This upset her so much that she asked loudly and bitterly, "How can you violate your oaths like this?"

She was promptly hurt so badly that she doubled up and burst into tears.

When she straightened up again, there was plenty more she wanted to say, but she kept her mouth shut. She speculated silently as to what on Earth could make Suicide Hostesses turn against every concept of human decency. Nothingheadedness alone couldn't begin to explain it. They had to be drugged besides.

Nancy went over in her mind all the terrible drugs she'd learned about in school, persuaded herself that the women had taken the worst one of all. That drug was so powerful, Nancy's teachers had told her, that even a person numb from the waist down would copulate repeatedly and enthusiastically after just one glass. That had to be the ánswer: The women, and probably the men, too, had been drinking gin.

They hastened Nancy into the middle frame house, which was dark like all the rest, and Nancy heard the men giving Billy the news. It was in this news that Nancy perceived a glint of hope. Help might be on its way.

The gang member who had phoned Nancy obscenely had fooled the police into believing that they had captured Billy the Poet, which was bad for Nancy. The police didn't know yet that Nancy was missing, two men told Billy, and a telegram had been sent to Mary Kraft in Nancy's name, declaring that Nancy had been called to New York City on urgent family business.

That was where Nancy saw the glint of hope: Mary wouldn't believe that telegram. Mary knew Nancy had no family in New York. Not one of the 63,000,000 people living there was a relative of Nancy's.

The gang had deactivated the burglar-alarm system of the museum. They had also cut through a lot of the chains and ropes that were meant to keep visitors from touching anything of value. There was no mystery as to who and what had done the cutting. One of the men was armed with brutal lopping shears.

They marched Nancy into a servant's bedroom upstairs. The man with the shears cut the ropes that fenced off the narrow bed. They put Nancy into the bed and two men held Nancy while a woman gave her a knockout shot.

Billy the Poet had disappeared.

As Nancy was going under, the woman who had given her the shot asked her how old she was.

Nancy was determined not to answer, but discovered that the

drug had made her powerless not to answer. "Sixty-three," she murmured.

"How does it feel to be a virgin at sixty-three?"

Nancy heard her own answer through a velvet fog. She was amazed by the answer, wanted to protest that it couldn't possibly be hers. "Pointless," she'd said.

Moments later, she asked the woman thickly, "What was in that needle?"

"What was in the needle, honey bunch? Why, honey bunch, they call that 'truth serum.' "

The moon was down when Nancy woke up—but the night was still out there. The shades were drawn and there was candlelight. Nancy had never seen a lit candle before.

What awakened Nancy was a dream of mosquitoes and bees. Mosquitoes and bees were extinct. So were birds. But Nancy dreamed that millions of insects were swarming about her from the waist down. They didn't sting. They fanned her. Nancy was a nothinghead.

She went to sleep again. When she awoke next time, she was being led into a bathroom by three women, still with stockings over their heads. The bathroom was already filled with the steam from somebody else's bath. There were somebody else's wet footprints crisscrossing the floor and the air reeked of pine-needle perfume.

Her will and intelligence returned as she was bathed and perfumed and dressed in a white nightgown. When the women stepped back to admire her, she said to them quietly, "I may be a nothinghead now. But that doesn't mean I have to think like one or act like one."

Nobody argued with her.

Nancy was taken downstairs and out of the house. She fully expected to be sent down a manhole again. It would be the perfect setting for her violation by Billy, she was thinking—down in a sewer.

But they took her across the green cement, where the grass used to be, and then across the yellow cement, where the beach used to be, and then out onto the blue cement, where the harbor used to be. There were twenty-six yachts that had belonged to various Kennedys, sunk up to their water lines in blue cement. It was to the most ancient of these yachts, the Marlin, once the property of Joseph P. Kennedy, that they delivered Nancy.

It was dawn. Because of the high-rise apartments all around the Kennedy Museum, it would be an hour before any direct sunlight would reach the microcosm under the geodesic dome.

Nancy was escorted as far as the companionway to the forward cabin of the Marlin. The women pantomimed that she was expected to go down the five steps alone.

Nancy froze for the moment and so did the women. And there were two actual statues in the tableau on the bridge. Standing at the wheel was a statue of Frank Wirtanen, once skipper of the Marlin. And next to him was his son and first mate, Carly. They weren't paying any attention to poor Nancy. They were staring out through the windshield at the blue cement.

Nancy, barefoot and wearing a thin white nightgown, descended bravely into the forward cabin, which was a pool of candlelight and pine-needle perfume. The companionway hatch was closed and locked behind her.

Nancy's emotions and the antique furnishings of the cabin were so complex that Nancy could not at first separate Billy the Poet from his surroundings, from all the mahogany and leaded glass. And then she saw him at the far end of the cabin, with his back against the door to the forward cockpit. He was wearing purple silk pajamas with a Russian collar. They were piped in red, and writhing across Billy's silken breast was a golden dragon. It was belching fire.

Anticlimactically, Billy was wearing glasses. He was holding a book.

Nancy poised herself on the next-to-the-bottom step, took a firm grip on the handholds in the companionway. She bared her teeth, calculated that it would take ten men Billy's size to dislodge her.

Between them was a great table. Nancy had expected the cabin to be dominated by a bed, possibly in the shape of a swan, but the Marlin was a day boat. The cabin was anything but a seraglio. It was about as voluptuous as a lower-middle-class dining room in Akron, Ohio, around 1910.

A candle was on the table. So were an ice bucket and two glasses and a quart of champagne. Champagne was as illegal as heroin.

Billy took off his glasses, gave her a shy, embarrassed smile, said, "Welcome."

"This is as far as I come."

He accepted that. "You're very beautiful there."

"And what am I supposed to say—that you're stunningly handsome? That I feel an overwhelming desire to throw myself into your manly arms?"

"If you wanted to make me happy, that would certainly be the way to do it." He said that humbly.

"And what about *my* happiness?"

The question seemed to puzzle him. "Nancy—that's what this is all about."

"What if my idea of happiness doesn't coincide with yours?"

"And what do you think my idea of happiness is?"

"I'm not going to throw myself into your arms, and I'm not going to drink that poison, and I'm not going to budge from here unless somebody makes me," said Nancy. "So I think your idea of happiness is going to turn out to be eight people holding me down on that table, while you bravely hold a cocked pistol to my head—and do what you want. That's the way it's going to have to be, so call your friends and get it over with!"

Which he did.

He didn't hurt her. He deflowered her with a clinical skill she found ghastly. When it was all over, he didn't seem cocky or proud. On the contrary, he was terribly depressed, and he said to Nancy, "Believe me, if there'd been any other way—"

Her reply to this was a face like stone—and silent tears of humiliation.

His helpers let down a folding bunk from the wall. It was scarcely wider than a bookshelf and hung on chains. Nancy allowed herself to be put to bed in it, and she was left alone with Billy the Poet again. Big as she was, like a double bass wedged onto that narrow shelf, she felt like a pitiful little thing. A scratchy, war-surplus blanket had been tucked in around her. It was her own idea to pull up a corner of the blanket to hide her face.

Nancy sensed from sounds what Billy was doing, which wasn't much. He was sitting at the table, sighing occasionally, sniffing occasionally, turning the pages of a book. He lit a cigar and the stink of it seeped under her blanket. Billy inhaled the cigar, then coughed and coughed and coughed.

When the coughing died down, Nancy said loathingly through the blanket, "You're so strong, so masterful, so healthy. It must be wonderful to be so manly."

Billy only sighed at this.

"I'm not a very typical nothinghead," she said. "I hated it— hated everything about it."

Billy sniffed, turned a page.

"I suppose all the other women just loved it—couldn't get enough of it."

"Nope."

She uncovered her face. "What do you mean, 'Nope'?"

"They've all been like you."

This was enough to make Nancy sit up and stare at him. "The women who helped you tonight——"

"What about them?"

"You've done to them what you did to me?"

He didn't look up from his book. "That's right."

"Then why don't they kill you instead of helping you?"

"Because they understand." And then he added mildly, "They're *grateful*."

Nancy got out of bed, came to the table, gripped the edge of the table, leaned close to him. And she said to him tautly, "I am not grateful."

"You will be."

"And what could possibly bring about that miracle?"

"Time," said Billy.

Billy closed his book, stood up. Nancy was confused by his magnetism. Somehow he was very much in charge again.

"What you've been through, Nancy," he said, "is a typical wedding night for a strait-laced girl of a hundred years ago, when everybody was a nothinghead. The groom did without helpers, because the bride wasn't customarily ready to kill him. Otherwise, the spirit of the occasion was much the same. These are the pajamas my great-great-grandfather wore on his wedding night in Niagara Falls.

"According to his diary, his bride cried all that night, and threw up twice. But, with the passage of time, she became a sexual enthusiast."

It was Nancy's turn to reply by not replying. She understood the tale. It frightened her to understand so easily that, from gruesome beginnings, sexual enthusiasm could grow and grow.

"You're a very typical nothinghead," said Billy. "If you dare to think about it now, you'll realize that you're angry because I'm such a bad lover, and a funny-looking shrimp besides. And what you can't help dreaming about from now on is a really suitable mate for a Juno like yourself.

"You'll find him, too—tall and strong and gentle. The nothinghead movement is growing by leaps and bounds."

"But——" said Nancy, and she stopped there. She looked out a porthole at the rising sun.

"But what?"

"The world is in the mess it is today because of the nothingheadedness of olden times. Don't you see?" She was pleading weakly. "The world can't afford sex anymore."

"Of course it can afford sex," said Billy. "All it can't afford anymore is reproduction."

"Then why the laws?"

"They're bad laws," said Billy. "If you go back through history, you'll find that the people who have been most eager to rule, to make the laws, to enforce the laws and to tell everybody exactly how God Almighty wants things here on Earth—those people have forgiven themselves and their friends for anything and everything. But they have been absolutely disgusted and terrified by the natural sexuality of common men and women.

"Why this is, I do not know. That is one of the many questions I wish somebody would ask the machines. I do know this: The triumph of that sort of disgust and terror is now complete. Almost every man and woman looks and feels like something the cat dragged in. The only sexual beauty that an ordinary human being can see today is in the woman who will kill him. Sex is death. There's a short and nasty equation for you: 'Sex is death. Q. E. D.'

"So you see, Nancy," said Billy, "I have spent this night, and many others like it, attempting to restore a certain amount of innocent pleasure to the world, which is poorer in pleasure than it needs to be."

Nancy sat down quietly and bowed her head.

"I'll tell you what my grandfather did on the dawn of his wedding night," said Billy.

"I don't think I want to hear it."

"It isn't violent. It's—it's meant to be tender."

"Maybe that's why I don't want to hear it."

"He read his bride a poem." Billy took the book from the table, opened it. "His diary tells which poem it was. While we aren't bride and groom, and while we may not meet again for many years, I'd like to read this poem to you, to have you know I've loved you."

"Please—no. I couldn't stand it."

"All right, I'll leave the book here, with the place marked, in case you want to read it later. It's the poem beginning: •

> *How do I love thee? Let me count the ways.*
> *I love thee to the depth and breadth and height*
> *My soul can reach, when feeling out of sight*
> *For the ends of Being and ideal Grace."*

Billy put a small bottle on top of the book. "I am also leaving you these pills. If you take one a month, you will never have children. And still you'll be a nothinghead."

And he left. And they all left but Nancy.

When Nancy raised her eyes at last to the book and bottle, she saw that there was a label on the bottle. What the label said was this: WELCOME TO THE MONKEY HOUSE.

(1968)

LONG WALK TO FOREVER

THEY HAD GROWN UP next door to each other, on the fringe of a city, near fields and woods and orchards, within sight of a lovely bell tower that belonged to a school for the blind.

Now they were twenty, had not seen each other for nearly a year. There had always been playful, comfortable warmth between them, but never any talk of love.

His name was Newt. Her name was Catharine. In the early afternoon, Newt knocked on Catharine's front door.

Catharine came to the door. She was carrying a fat, glossy magazine she had been reading. The magazine was devoted entirely to brides. "Newt!" she said. She was surprised to see him.

"Could you come for a walk?" he said. He was a shy person, even with Catharine. He covered his shyness by speaking absently, as though what really concerned him were far away—as though he were a secret agent pausing briefly on a mission between beautiful, distant, and sinister points. This manner of speaking had always been Newt's style, even in matters that concerned him desperately.

"A walk?" said Catharine.

"One foot in front of the other," said Newt, "through leaves, over bridges——"

"I had no idea you were in town," she said.

"Just this minute got in," he said.

"Still in the Army, I see," she said.

"Seven more months to go," he said. He was a private first class in the Artillery. His uniform was rumpled. His shoes were dusty. He needed a shave. He held out his hand for the magazine. "Let's see the pretty book," he said.

She gave it to him. "I'm getting married, Newt," she said.

"I know," he said. "Let's go for a walk."

"I'm awfully busy, Newt," she said. "The wedding is only a week away."

"If we go for a walk," he said, "it will make you rosy. It will make you a rosy bride." He turned the pages of the magazine. "A rosy bride like her—like her—like her," he said, showing her rosy brides.

Catharine turned rosy, thinking about rosy brides.

"That will be my present to Henry Stewart Chasens," said Newt. "By taking you for a walk, I'll be giving him a rosy bride."

"You know his name?" said Catharine.

"Mother wrote," he said. "From Pittsburgh?"

"Yes," she said. "You'd like him."

"Maybe," he said.

"Can—can you come to the wedding, Newt?" she said.

"That I doubt," he said.

"Your furlough isn't for long enongh?" she said.

"Furlough?" said Newt. He was studying a two-page ad for flat silver. "I'm not on furlough," he said.

"Oh?" she said.

"I'm what they call A.W.O.L.," said Newt.

"Oh, Newt! You're not!" she said.

"Sure I am," he said, still looking at the magazine.

"Why, Newt?" she said.

"I had to find out what your silver pattern is," he said. He read names of silver patterns from the magazine. "Albemarle? Heather?" he said. "Legend? Rambler Rose?" He looked up, smiled. "I plan to give you and your husband a spoon," he said.

"Newt, Newt—tell me really," she said.

"I want to go for a walk," he said.

She wrung her hands in sisterly anguish. "Oh, Newt—you're fooling me about being A.W.O.L.," she said.

Newt imitated a police siren softly, raised his eyebrows.

"Where—where from?" she said.

"Fort Bragg," he said.

"North Carolina?" she said.

"That's right," he said. "Near Fayetteville—where Scarlet O'Hara went to school."

"How did you get here, Newt?" she said.

He raised his thumb, jerked it in a hitchhike gesture. "Two days," he said.

"Does your mother know?" she said.

"I didn't come to see my mother," he told her.

"Who did you come to see?" she said.

"You," he said.

"Why me?" she said.

"Because I love you," he said. "Now can we take a walk?" he said. "One foot in front of the other—through leaves, over bridges——"

They were taking the walk now, were in a wood with a brown-leaf floor.

Catharine was angry and rattled, close to tears. "Newt," she said, "this is absolutely crazy."

"How so?" said Newt.

"What a crazy time to tell me you love me," she said. "You never talked that way before." She stopped walking.

"Let's keep walking," he said.

"No," she said. "So far, no farther. I shouldn't have come out with you at all," she said.

"You did," he said.

"To get you out of the house," she said. "If somebody walked in and heard you talking to me that way, a week before the wedding——"

"What would they think?" he said.

"They'd think you were crazy," she said.

"Why?" he said.

Catharine took a deep breath, made a speech. "Let me say that I'm deeply honored by this crazy thing you've done," she said. "I can't believe you're really A.W.O.L., but maybe you are. I can't believe you really love me, but maybe you do. But——"

"I do," said Newt.

"Well, I'm deeply honored," said Catharine, "and I'm very fond of you as a friend, Newt, extremely fond—but it's just too late." She took a step away from him. "You've never even kissed me," she said, and she protected herself with her hands. "I don't mean you should do it now. I just mean this is all so unexpected. I haven't got the remotest idea of how to respond."

"Just walk some more," he said. "Have a nice time."

They started walking again.

"How did you expect me to react?" she said.

"How would I know what to expect?" he said. "I've never done anything like this before."

"Did you think I would throw myself into your arms?" she said.

"Maybe," he said.

"I'm sorry to disappoint you," she said.

"I'm not disappointed," he said. "I wasn't counting on it. This is very nice, just walking."

Catharine stopped again. "You know what happens next?" she said.

"Nope," he said.

"We shake hands," she said. "We shake hands and part friends," she said. "That's what happens next."

Newt nodded. "All right," he said. "Remember me from time to time. Remember how much I loved you."

Involuntarily, Catharine burst into tears. She turned her back to Newt, looked into the infinite colonnade of the woods.

"What does that mean?" said Newt.

"Rage!" said Catharine. She clenched her hands. "You have no right——"

"I had to find out," he said.

"If I'd loved you," she said, "I would have let you know before now."

"You would?" he said.

"Yes," she said. She faced him, looked up at him, her face quite red. "You would have known," she said.

"How?" he said.

"You would have seen it," she said. "Women aren't very clever at hiding it."

Newt looked closely at Catharine's face now. To her consternation, she realized that what she had said was true, that a woman couldn't hide love.

Newt was seeing love now.

And he did what he had to do. He kissed her.

"You're hell to get along with!" she said when Newt let her go.

"I am?" said Newt.

"You shouldn't have done that," she said.

"You didn't like it?" he said.

"What did you expect," she said—"wild, abandoned passion?"

"I keep telling you," he said, "I never know what's going to happen next."

"We say good-by," she said.

He frowned slightly. "All right," he said.

She made another speech. "I'm not sorry we kissed," she said. "That was sweet. We should have kissed, we've been so close. I'll always remember you, Newt, and good luck."

"You too," he said.

"Thank you, Newt," she said.

"Thirty days," he said.

"What?" she said.

"Thirty days in the stockade," he said—"that's what one kiss will cost me."

"I—I'm sorry," she said, "but I didn't ask you to go A.W.O.L."

"I know," he said.

"You certainly don't deserve any hero's reward for doing something as foolish as that," she said.

"Must be nice to be a hero," said Newt. "Is Henry Stewart Chasens a hero?"

"He might be, if he got the chance," said Catharine. She noted uneasily that they had begun to walk again. The farewell had been forgotten.

"You really love him?" he said.

"Certainly I love him!" she said hotly. "I wouldn't marry him if I didn't love him!"

"What's good about him?" said Newt.

"Honestly!" she cried, stopping again. "Do you have any idea how offensive you're being? Many, many, many things are good about Henry! Yes," she said, "and many, many, many things are probably bad too. But that isn't any of your business. I love Henry, and I don't have to argue his merits with you!"

"Sorry," said Newt.

"Honestly!" said Catharine.

Newt kissed her again. He kissed her again because she wanted him to.

They were now in a large orchard.

"How did we get so far from home, Newt?" said Catharine.

"One foot in front of the other—through leaves, over bridges," said Newt.

"They add up—the steps," she said.

Bells rang in the tower of the school for the blind nearby.

"School for the blind," said Newt.

"School for the blind," said Catharine. She shook her head in drowsy wonder. "I've got to go back now," she said.

"Say good-by," said Newt.

"Every time I do," said Catharine, "I seem to get kissed."

Newt sat down on the close-cropped grass under an apple tree. "Sit down," he said.

"No," she said.

"I won't touch you," he said.

"I don't believe you," she said.

She sat down under another tree, twenty feet away from him. She closed her eyes.

"Dream of Henry Stewart Chasens," he said.

"What?" she said.

"Dream of your wonderful husband-to-be," he said.

"All right, I will," she said. She closed her eyes tighter, caught glimpses of her husband-to-be.

Newt yawned.

The bees were humming in the trees, and Catharine almost fell asleep. When she opened her eyes she saw that Newt really was asleep.

He began to snore softly.

Catharine let Newt sleep for an hour, and while he slept she adored him with all her heart.

The shadows of the apple trees grew to the east. The bells in the tower of the school for the blind rang again.

"*Chick-a-dee-dee-dee*," went a chickadee.

Somewhere far away an automobile starter nagged and failed, nagged and failed, fell still.

Catharine came out from under her tree, knelt by Newt.

"Newt?" she said.

"H'm?" he said. He opened his eyes.

"Late," she said.

"Hello, Catharine," he said.

"Hello, Newt," she said.

"I love you," he said.

"I know," she said.

"Too late," he said.

"Too late," she said.

He stood, stretched groaningly. "A very nice walk," he said.

"I thought so," she said.

"Part company here?" he said.

"Where will you go?" she said.

"Hitch into town, turn myself in," he said.

"Good luck," she said.

"You, too," he said. "Marry me, Catharine?"

"No," she said.

He smiled, stared at her hard for a moment, then walked away quickly.

Catharine watched him grow smaller in the long perspective of shadows and trees, knew that if he stopped and turned now, if he called to her, she would run to him. She would have no choice.

Newt did stop. He did turn. He did call. "Catharine," he called.

She ran to him, put her arms around him, could not speak.

(1960)

THE FOSTER PORTFOLIO

I'M A SALESMAN of good advice for rich people. I'm a contact man for an investment counseling firm. It's a living, but not a whale of a one—or at least not now, when I'm just starting out. To qualify for the job, I had to buy a Homburg, a navy-blue overcoat; a double-breasted banker's gray suit, black shoes, a regimental-stripe tie, half a dozen white shirts, half a dozen pairs of black socks and gray gloves.

When I call on a client, I come by cab, and I am sleek and clean and foursquare. I carry myself as though I've made a quiet killing on the stock market, and have come to call more as a public service than anything else. When I arrive in clean wool, with crackling certificates and confidential stock analyses in crisp Manila folders, the reaction—ideally and usually—is the same accorded a minister or physician. I am in charge, and everything is going to be just fine.

I deal mostly with old ladies—the meek, who by dint of cast-iron constitutions have inherited sizable portions of the earth. I thumb through the clients' lists of securities, and relay our experts' suggestions for ways of making their portfolios—or bonanzas or piles—thrive and increase. I can speak of tens of thousands of dollars without a catch in my throat, and look at a list of securities worth more than a hundred thousand with no more fuss than a judicious "Mmmmm, uh-huh."

Since *I* don't have a portfolio, my job is a little like being a hungry delivery boy for a candy store. But I never really felt that way about it until Herbert Foster asked me to have a look at his finances.

He called one evening to say a friend had recommended me, and could I come out to talk business. I washed, shaved, dusted my shoes, put on my uniform, and made my grave arrival by cab.

People in my business—and maybe people in general—have an unsavory habit of sizing up a man's house, car, and suit, and estimating his annual income. Herbert Foster was six thousand a year, or I'd never seen it. Understand, I have nothing against people in moderate circumstances, other than the crucial fact that I can't make any money off them. It made me a little sore that Foster would take my time, when the most he had to play around with, I guessed, was no more than a few hundred dollars. Say it was a thousand: my take would be a dollar or two at best.

Anyway, there I was in the Fosters' jerry-built postwar colonial with expansion attic. They had taken up a local furniture store on its offer of three rooms of furniture, including ashtrays, a humidor, and pictures for the wall, all for $199.99. Hell, I was there, and I figured I might as well go through with having a look at his pathetic problem.

"Nice place you have here, Mr. Foster," I said. "And this is your charming wife?"

A skinny, shrewish-looking woman smiled up at me vacuously. She wore a faded housecoat figured with a fox-hunting scene. The print was at war with the slipcover of the chair, and I had to squint to separate her features from the clash about her. "A pleasure, Mrs. Foster," I said. She was surrounded by underwear and socks to be mended, and Herbert said her name was Alma, which seemed entirely possible.

"And this is the young master," I said. "Bright little chap. Believe he favors his father." The two-year-old wiped his grubby hands on my trousers, snuffled, and padded off toward the piano. He stationed himself at the upper end of the keyboard, and hammered on the highest note for one minute, then two, then three.

"Musical—like his father," Alma said.

"You play, do you, Mr. Foster?"

"Classical," Herbert said. I took my first good look at him. He was lightly built, with the round, freckled face and big teeth I usually associate with a show-off or wise guy. It was hard to believe that he had settled for so plain a wife, or that he could be as fond of family life as he seemed. It may have been that I only imagined a look of quiet desperation in his eyes.

"Shouldn't you be getting on to your meeting, dear?" Herbert said.

"It was called off at the last minute."

"Now, about your portfolio—" I began.

Herbert looked rattled. "How's that?"

"Your portfolio—your securities."

"Yes, well, I think we'd better talk in the bedroom. It's quieter in there."

Alma put down her sewing. "What securities?"

"The bonds, dear. The government bonds."

"Now, Herbert, you're not going to cash them in."

"No, Alma, just want to talk them over."

"I see," I said tentatively. "Uh—approximately how much in government bonds?"

"Three hundred and fifty dollars," Alma said proudly.

"Well," I said, "I don't see any need for going into the bedroom to talk. My advice, and I give it free, is to hang on to your nest egg until it matures. And now, if you'll let me phone a cab—"

"Please," Herbert said, standing in the bedroom door, "there are a couple of other things I'd like to discuss."

"What?" Alma said.

"Oh, long-range investment planning," Herbert said vaguely.

"We could use a little short-range planning for next month's grocery bill."

"Please," Herbert said to me again.

I shrugged and followed him into the bedroom. He closed the door behind me. I sat on the edge of the bed and watched him open a little door in the wall, which bared the pipes servicing the bathroom. He slid his arm up into the wall, grunted, and pulled down an envelope.

"Oho," I said apathetically, "so that's where we've got the bonds, eh? Very clever. You needn't have gone to that trouble, Mr. Foster. I have an idea what government bonds look like."

"Alma," he called.

"Yes, Herbert."

"Will you start some coffee for us?"

"I don't drink coffee at night," I said.

"We have some from dinner," Alma said.

"I can't sleep if I touch it after supper," I said.

"Fresh—we want some fresh," Herbert said.

The chair springs creaked, and her reluctant footsteps faded into the kitchen.

"Here," said Herbert, putting the envelope in my lap. "I don't know anything about this business, and I guess I ought to have professional help."

All right, so I'd give the poor guy a professional talk about his three hundred and fifty dollars in government bonds. "They're the most conservative investment you can make. They haven't the growth characteristics of many securities, and the return isn't great, but they're very safe. By all means hang onto them." I stood up. "And now, if you'll let me call a cab—"

"You haven't looked at them."

I sighed, and untwisted the red string holding the envelope shut. Nothing would do but that I admire the things. The bonds and a list of securities slid into my lap. I riffled through the bonds quickly, and then read the list of securities slowly.

"Well?"

I put the list down on the faded bedspread. I composed myself. "Mmmmm, uh-huh," I said. "Do you mind telling me where the securities listed here came from?"

"Grandfather left them to me two years ago. The lawyers who handled the estate have them. They sent me that list."

"Do you know what these stocks are worth?"

"They were appraised when I inherited them." He told me the figure, and, to my bewilderment, he looked sheepish, even a little unhappy about it.

"They've gone up a little since then."

"How much?"

"On today's market—maybe they're worth seven hundred and fifty thousand dollars, Mr. Foster. Sir."

His expression didn't change. My news moved him about as much as if I'd told him it'd been a chilly winter. He raised his eyebrows as Alma's footsteps came back into the living room. "Shhhh!"

"She doesn't know?"

"Lord, no!" He seemed to have surprised himself with his vehemence. "I mean the time isn't ripe."

"If you'll let me have this list of securities, I'll have our New York office give you a complete analysis and recommendations," I whispered. "May I call you Herbert, sir?"

My client, Herbert Foster, hadn't had a new suit in three years; he had never owned more than one pair of shoes at a time. He worried about payments on his secondhand car, and ate tuna and cheese instead of meat, because meat was too expensive. His wife made her own clothes, and those of Herbert, Jr., and the curtains and slipcovers—all cut from the same bargain bolt. The Fosters were going through hell, trying to choose between new tires or retreads for the car; and television was something they had to go two doors down the street to watch. Determinedly, they kept within the small salary Herbert made as a bookkeeper for a wholesale grocery house.

God knows it's no disgrace to live that way, which is better than the way I live, but it was pretty disturbing to watch, knowing Herbert had an income, after taxes, of perhaps twenty thousand a year.

I had our securities analysts look over Foster's holdings, and report on the stocks' growth possibilities, prospective earnings, the effects of war and peace, inflation and deflation, and so on. The report ran to twenty pages, a record for any of my clients.

Usually, the reports are bound in cardboard covers. Herbert's was done up in red leatherette.

It arrived at my place on a Saturday afternoon, and I called up Herbert to ask if I could bring it out. I had exciting news for him. My by-eye estimate of the values had been off, and his portfolio, as of that day, was worth close to eight hundred and fifty thousand.

"I've got the analysis and recommendations," I said, "and things look good, Mr. Foster—*very* good. You need a little diversification here and there, and maybe more emphasis on growth, but—"

"Just go ahead and do whatever needs to be done," he said.

"When could we talk about this? It's something we ought to go over together, certainly. Tonight would be fine with me."

"I work tonight."

"Overtime at the wholesale house?"

"Another job—in a restaurant. Work Friday, Saturday, and Sunday nights."

I winced. The man had maybe seventy-five dollars a day coming in from his securities, and he worked three nights a week to make ends meet! "Monday?"

"Play organ for choir practice at the church."

"Tuesday?"

"Volunteer Fire Department drill."

"Wednesday?"

"Play piano for folk dancing at the church."

"Thursday?"

"Movie night for Alma and me."

"When, then?"

"You go ahead and do whatever needs to be done."

"Don't you want to be in on what I'm doing?"

"Do I have to be?"

"I'd feel better if you were."

"All right, Tuesday noon, lunch."

"Fine with me. Maybe you'd better have a good look at this report before then, so you can have questions ready."

He sounded annoyed. "Okay, okay, okay. I'll be here tonight until nine. Drop it off before then."

"One more thing, Herbert." I'd saved the kicker for last. "I was way off about what the stocks are worth. They're now up to about eight hundred and fifty thousand dollars."

"Um."

"I said, you're about a hundred thousand dollars richer than you thought!"

"Uh-huh. Well, you just go ahead and do whatever needs to be done."

"Yes, sir." The phone was dead.

I was delayed by other business, and I didn't get out to the Fosters' until quarter of ten. Herbert was gone. Alma answered the door, and, to my surprise, she asked for the report, which I was hiding under my coat.

"Herbert said I wasn't supposed to look at it," she said, "so you don't need to worry about me peeking."

"Herbert told you about this?" I said carefully.

"Yes. He said it's confidential reports on stocks you want to sell him."

"Yes, uh-huh—well, if he said to leave it with you, here it is."

"He told me he had to promise you not to let *anybody* look at it."

"Mmm? Oh, yes, yes. Sorry, company rules."

She was a shade hostile. "I'll tell you one thing without look- ing at any reports, and that is he's not going to cash those bonds to buy any stocks with."

"I'd be the last one to recommend that, Mrs. Foster."

"Then why do you keep after him?"

"He may be a good customer at a later date." I looked at my hands, which I realized had become inkstained on the earlier call. "I wonder if I might wash up?"

Reluctantly, she let me in, keeping as far away from me as the modest floor plan would permit.

As I washed up, I thought of the list of securities Herbert had taken from between the plasterboard walls. Those securities meant winters in Florida, *filet mignon* and twelve-year-old bour- bon, Jaguars, silk underwear and handmade shoes, a trip around the world. . . . Name it; Herbert Foster could have it. I sighed heavily. The soap in the Foster soap dish was mottled and dingy —a dozen little chips moistened and pressed together to make a new bar.

I thanked Alma, and started to leave. On my way out, I paused by the mantel to look at a small tinted photograph. "Good picture of you," I said. A feeble effort at public relations. "I like that."

"Everybody says that. It isn't me; it's Herbert's mother."

"Amazing likeness." And it was. Herbert had married a girl just like the girl that married dear old dad. "And this picture is his father?"

"*My* father. We don't want a picture of *his* father."

This looked like a sore point that might prove informative. "Herbert is such a wonderful person, his father must have been wonderful, too, eh?"

"He deserted his wife and child. That's how wonderful he was. You'll be smart not to mention him to Herbert."

"Sorry. Everything good about Herbert comes from his mother?"

"She was a saint. She taught Herbert to be decent and respectable and God-fearing." Alma was grim about it.

"Was she musical, too?"

"He gets that from his father. But what he does with it is something quite different. His taste in music is his mother's—the classics."

"His father was a jazz man, I take it?" I hinted.

"He preferred playing piano in dives, and breathing smoke and drinking gin, to his wife and child and home and job. Herbert's mother finally said he had to choose one life or the other."

I nodded sympathetically. Maybe Herbert looked on his fortune as filthy, untouchable, since it came from his father's side of the family. "This grandfather of Herbert's, who died two years ago—?"

"He supported Herbert and his mother after his son deserted them. Herbert worshipped him." She shook her head sadly. "He was penniless when he died."

"What a shame."

"I'd so hoped he would leave us a little something, so Herbert wouldn't have to work weekends."

We were trying to talk above the clatter, tinkle, and crash of the cafeteria where Herbert ate every day. Lunch was on me—or on my expense account—and I'd picked up his check for eighty-seven cents. I said, "Now, Herbert, before we go any further, we'd better decide what you want from your investments: growth or income." It was a cliché of the counseling business. God knows what *he* wanted from the securities. It didn't seem to be what everybody else wanted—money.

"Whatever you say," Herbert said absently. He was upset about something, and not paying much attention to me.

"Herbert—look, you've got to face this thing. You're a rich man. You've got to concentrate on making the most of your holdings."

"That's why I called you. I want *you* to concentrate. I want you to run things for me, so I won't have to bother with the deposits and proxies and taxes. Don't trouble me with it at all."

"Your lawyers have been banking the dividends, eh?"

"Most of them. Took out thirty-two dollars for Christmas, and gave a hundred to the church."

"So what's your balance?"

He handed me the deposit book.

"Not bad," I said. Despite his Christmas splurge and largess toward the church, he'd managed to salt away $50,227.33. "May I ask what a man with a balance like that can be blue about?"

"Got bawled out at work again."

"Buy the place and burn it down," I suggested.

"I could, couldn't I?" A wild look came into his eyes, then disappeared.

"Herbert, you can do anything your heart desires."

"Oh, I suppose so. It's all in the way you look at it."

I leaned forward. "How *do* you look at it, Herbert?"

"I think every man, for his own self-respect, should earn what he lives on."

"But, Herbert—"

"I have a wonderful wife and child, a nice house for them, and a car. And I've earned every penny of the way. I'm living up to the full measure of my responsibilities. I'm proud to say I'm everything my mother wanted me to be, and nothing my father was."

"Do you mind my asking what your father was?"

"I don't enjoy talking about him. Home and family meant nothing to him. His real love was for low-down music and honky-tonks, and for the trash in them."

"Was he a good musician, do you think?"

"Good?" For an instant, there was excitement in his voice, and he tensed, as though he were going to make an important point. But he relaxed again. "Good?" he repeated, flatly this time. "Yes, in a crude way, I suppose he was passable—technically, that is."

"And that much you inherited from him."

"His wrists and hands, maybe. God help me if there's any more of him in me."

"You've got his love of music, too."

"I love music, but I'd never let it get like dope to me!" he said, with more force than seemed necessary.

"Uh-huh. Well—"

"Never!"

"Beg your pardon?"

His eyes were wide. "I said I'll never let music get like dope to me. It's important to me, but I'm master of it, and not the other way around."

Apparently it was a treacherous subject, so I switched back to the matter of his finances. "Yes, well, now about your portfolio again: just what use do you expect to make of it?"

"Use some of it for Alma's and my old age; leave most of it to the boy."

"The least you can do is take enough out of the kitty to let you out of working weekends."

He stood up suddenly. "Look. I want you to handle my securities, not my life. If you can't do one without the other, I'll find someone who can."

"Please, Herbert, Mr. Foster. I'm sorry, sir. I was only trying to get the whole picture for planning."

He sat down, red-faced. "All right then, respect my convictions. I want to make my own way. If I have to hold a second job to make ends meet, then that's my cross to bear."

"Sure, sure, certainly. And you're dead right, Herbert. I respect you for it." I thought he belonged in the bughouse for it. "You leave everything to me from now on. I'll invest those dividends and run the whole show." As I puzzled over Herbert, I glanced at a passing blonde. Herbert said something I missed. "What was that, Herbert?"

"I said, 'If thy right eye offend thee, pluck it out and cast it from thee.'"

I laughed appreciatively, then cut it short. Herbert was deadly serious. "Well, pretty soon you'll have the car paid for, and then you can take a well-earned rest on the weekends. And you'll really have something to be proud of, eh? Earned the whole car by the sweat of your brow, right down to the tip of the exhaust pipe."

"One more payment."

"*Then* by-by, restaurant."

"There'll still be Alma's birthday present to pay for. I'm getting her television."

"Going to earn that, too, are you?"

"Think how much more meaningful it will be as a gift, if I do."

"Yes, sir, and it'll give her something to do on weekends, too."

"If I have to work weekends for twenty-eight more months, God knows it's little enough to do for her."

If the stock market kept doing what it had been doing for the past three years, Herbert would be a millionaire just about the time he made the last payment on Alma's birthday present. "Fine."

"I love my family," Herbert said earnestly.

"I'm sure you do."

"And I wouldn't trade the life I've got for anything."

"I can certainly see why," I said. I had the impression that he was arguing with me, that it was important to him that I be convinced.

"When I consider what my father was, and then see the life I've made for myself, it's the biggest thrill in all my experience."

A very small thrill could qualify for the biggest in Herbert's experience, I thought. "I envy you. It must be gratifying."

"Gratifying," he repeated determinedly. "It is, it is, it is."

My firm began managing Herbert's portfolio, converting some of the slower-moving securities into more lucrative ones, investing the accumulated dividends, diversifying his holdings so he'd be in better shape to weather economic shifts—and in general making his fortune altogether shipshape. A sound portfolio is a thing of beauty in its way, aside from its cash value. Putting one together is a creative act, if done right, with solid major themes of industrials, rails, and utilities, and with the lighter, more exciting themes of electronics, frozen foods, magic drugs, oil and gas, aviation, and other more speculative items. Herbert's portfolio was our masterpiece. I was thrilled and proud of what the firm had done, and not being able to show it off, even to him, was depressing.

It was too much for me, and I decided to engineer a coincidence. I would find out in which restaurant Herbert worked, and then drop in, like any other citizen, for something to eat. I would happen to have a report on his overhauled portfolio with me.

I telephoned Alma, who told me the name of the place, one I'd never heard of. Herbert hadn't wanted to talk about the place, so I gathered that it was pretty grim—as he said, his cross to bear.

It was worse than I'd expected: tough, brassy, dark, and noisy. Herbert had picked one hell of a place, indeed, to do penance for a wayward father, or to demonstrate his gratitude to his wife, or to maintain his self-respect by earning his own way—or to do whatever it was he was doing there.

I elbowed my way between bored-looking women and race-track types to the bar. I had to shout at the bartender to be heard. When I did get through to him, he yelled back that he'd never heard of no Herbert Foster. Herbert, then, was about as minor an employee as there was in the establishment. He was probably doing something greasy in the kitchen or basement. Typical.

In the kitchen, a crone was making questionable-looking hamburgers, and nipping at a quart of beer.

"I'm looking for Herbert Foster."

"Ain' no damn' Herbert Foster in here."

"In the basement?"

"Ain' no damn' basement."

"Ever hear of Herbert Foster?"

"Ain't never heard of no damn' Herbert Foster."

"Thanks."

I sat in a booth to think it over. Herbert had apparently picked the joint out of a telephone book, and told Alma it was where he spent his weekend evenings. In a way, it made me feel better, because it began to look as though Herbert maybe had better reasons than he'd given me for letting eight hundred and fifty thousand dollars get musty. I remembered that every time I'd mentioned his giving up the weekend job, he'd reacted like a man hearing a dentist tune up his drill. I saw it now: the minute he let Alma know he was rich, he'd lose his excuse for getting away from her on weekends.

But what was it that was worth more to Herbert than eight hundred and fifty thousand? Binges? Dope? Women? I sighed, and admitted I was kidding myself, that I was no closer to the answer than I'd ever been. Moral turpitude on Herbert's part was inconceivable. Whatever he was up to, it had to be for a good cause. His mother had done such a thorough job on him, and he was so awfully ashamed of his father's failings, that I was sure he couldn't operate any other way but righteously. I gave up on the puzzle, and ordered a nightcap.

And then Herbert Foster, looking drab and hunted, picked his way through the crowd. His expression was one of disapproval, of a holy man in Babylon. He was oddly stiff-necked and held his arms at his sides as he pointedly kept from brushing against anyone or from meeting any of the gazes that fell upon him. There was no question that being in the place was absolute, humiliating hell for him.

I called to him, but he paid no attention. There was no communicating with him. Herbert was in a near coma of see-no-evil, speak-no-evil, hear-no-evil.

The crowd in the rear parted for him, and I expected to see Herbert go into a dark corner for a broom or a mop. But a light flashed on at the far end of the aisle the crowd made for him, and a tiny white piano sparkled there like jewelry. The bartender set a drink on the piano, and went back to his post.

Herbert dusted off the piano bench with his handkerchief, and sat down gingerly. He took a cigarette from his breast pocket and lighted it. And then the cigarette started to droop slowly from his lips; and, as it drooped, Herbert hunched over the keyboard and his eyes narrowed as though he were focusing on something beautiful on a faraway horizon.

Startlingly, Herbert Foster disappeared. In his place sat an excited stranger, his hands poised like claws. Suddenly he struck, and a spasm of dirty, low-down, gorgeous jazz shook the air, a hot, clanging wraith of the twenties.

Late that night I went over my masterpiece, the portfolio of Herbert Foster, alias "Firehouse" Harris. I hadn't bothered Firehouse with it or with myself.

In a week or so, there would be a juicy melon from one of his steel companies. Three of his oil stocks were paying extra dividends. The farm machinery company in which he owned five thousand shares was about to offer him rights worth three dollars apiece.

Thanks to me and my company and an economy in full bloom, Herbert was about to be several thousand dollars richer than he'd been a month before. I had a right to be proud, but my triumph—except for the commission—was gall and wormwood.

Nobody could do anything for Herbert. Herbert already had what he wanted. He had had it long before the inheritance or I intruded. He had the respectability his mother had hammered into him. But just as priceless as that was an income not quite big enough to go around. It left him no alternative but—in the holy names of wife, child, and home—to play piano in a dive, and breathe smoke, and drink gin, to be Firehouse Harris, his father's son, three nights out of seven.

(1951)

MISS TEMPTATION

PURITANISM had fallen into such disrepair that not even the oldest spinster thought of putting Susanna in a ducking stool; not even the oldest farmer suspected that Susanna's diabolical beauty had made his cow run dry.

Susanna was a bit-part actress in the summer theater near the village, and she rented a room over the firehouse. She was a part of village life all summer, but the villagers never got used to her. She was forever as startling and desirable as a piece of big-city fire apparatus.

Susanna's feathery hair and saucer eyes were as black as midnight. Her skin was the color of cream. Her hips were like a lyre, and her bosom made men dream of peace and plenty for ever and ever. She wore barbaric golden hoops on her shell-pink ears, and around her ankles were chains with little bells on them.

She went barefoot and slept until noon every day. And, as noon drew near, the villagers on the main street would grow as restless as beagles with a thunderstorm on the way.

At noon, Susanna would appear on the porch outside her room.

She would stretch languidly, pour a bowl of milk for her black cat, kiss the cat, fluff her hair, put on her earrings, lock her door, and hide the key in her bosom.

And then, barefoot, she would begin her stately, undulating, titillating, tinkling walk—down the outside stairway, past the liquor store, the insurance agency, the real-estate office, the diner, the American Legion post, and the church, to the crowded drugstore. There she would get the New York papers.

She seemed to nod to all the world in a dim, queenly way. But the only person she spoke to during her daily walk was Bearse Hinkley, the seventy-two-year-old pharmacist.

The old man always had her papers ready for her.

"Thank you, Mr. Hinkley. You're an angel," she would say, opening a paper at random. "Now, let's see what's going on back in civilization." While the old man would watch, fuddled by her perfume, Susanna would laugh or gasp or frown at items in the paper—items she never explained.

Then she would take the papers, and return to her nest over the firehouse. She would pause on the porch outside her room, dip her hand into her bosom, bring out the key, unlock the door, pick up the black cat, kiss it again, and disappear inside.

The one-girl pageant had a ritual sameness until one day toward the end of summer, when the air of the drugstore was cut by a cruel, sustained screech from a dry bearing in a revolving soda-fountain stool.

The screech cut right through Susanna's speech about Mr. Hinkley's being an angel. The screech made scalps tingle and teeth ache. Susanna looked indulgently in the direction of the screech, forgiving the screecher. She found that the screecher wasn't a person to be indulged.

The screech had been made by the stool of Cpl. Norman Fuller, who had come home the night before from eighteen bleak months in Korea. They had been eighteen months without war— but eighteen months without cheer, all the same. Fuller had turned on the stool slowly, to look at Susanna with indignation. When the screech died, the drugstore was deathly still.

Fuller had broken the enchantment of summer by the seaside—

had reminded all in the drugstore of the black, mysterious passions that were so often the mainsprings of life.

He might have been a brother, come to rescue his idiot sister from the tenderloin; or an irate husband, come to a saloon to horsewhip his wife back to where she belonged, with the baby. The truth was that Corporal Fuller had never seen Susanna before.

He hadn't consciously meant to make a scene. He hadn't known, consciously, that his stool would screech. He had meant to underplay his indignation, to make it a small detail in the background of Susanna's pageant—a detail noticed by only one or two connoisseurs of the human comedy.

But the screech had made his indignation the center of the solar system for all in the drugstore—particularly for Susanna. Time had stopped, and it could not proceed until Fuller had explained the expression on his granite Yankee face.

Fuller felt his skin glowing like hot brass. He was comprehending destiny. Destiny had suddenly given him an audience, and a situation about which he had a bitter lot to say.

Fuller felt his lips move, heard the words come out. "Who do you think you are?" he said to Susanna.

"I beg your pardon?" said Susanna. She drew her newspapers about herself protectively.

"I saw you come down the street like you were a circus parade, and I just wondered who you thought you were," said Fuller.

Susanna blushed gloriously. "I—I'm an actress," she said.

"You can say that again," said Fuller. "Greatest actresses in the world, American women."

"You're very nice to say so," said Susanna uneasily.

Fuller's skin glowed brighter and hotter. His mind had become a fountain of apt, intricate phrases. "I'm not talking about theaters with seats in 'em. I'm talking about the stage of life. American women act and dress like they're gonna give you the world. Then, when you stick out your hand, they put an ice cube in it."

"They do?" said Susanna emptily.

"They do," said Fuller, "and it's about time somebody said so." He looked challengingly from spectator to spectator, and found what he took to be dazed encouragement. "It isn't fair," he said.

"What isn't?" said Susanna, lost.

"You come in here with bells on your ankles, so's I'll have to look at your ankles and your pretty pink feet," said Fuller. "You kiss the cat, so's I'll have to think about how it'd be to be that cat," said Fuller. "You call an old man an angel, so's I'll have to think about what it'd be like to be called an angel by you," said Fuller. "You hide your key in front of everybody, so's I'll have to think about where that key is," said Fuller.

He stood. "Miss," he said, his voice full of pain, "you do everything you can to give lonely, ordinary people like me indigestion and the heeby-jeebies, and you wouldn't even hold hands with me to keep me from falling off a cliff."

He strode to the door. All eyes were on him. Hardly anyone noticed that his indictment had reduced Susanna to ashes of what she'd been moments before. Susanna now looked like what she really was—a muddle-headed nineteen-year-old clinging to a tiny corner of sophistication.

"It isn't fair," said Fuller. "There ought to be a law against girls acting and dressing like you do. It makes more people unhappy than it does happy. You know what I say to you, for going around making everybody want to kiss you?"

"No," piped Susanna, every fuse in her nervous system blown.

"I say to you what you'd say to me, if I was to try and kiss you," said Fuller grandly. He swung his arms in an umpire's gesture for "out." "The hell with you," he said. He left, slamming the screen door.

He didn't look back when the door slammed again a moment later, when the patter of running bare feet and the wild tinkling of little bells faded away in the direction of the firehouse.

That evening, Corporal Fuller's widowed mother put a candle on the table, and fed him sirloin steak and strawberry shortcake in honor of his homecoming. Fuller ate the meal as though it were wet blotting paper, and he answered his mother's cheery questions in a voice that was dead.

"Aren't you glad to be home?" said his mother, when they'd finished their coffee.

"Sure," said Fuller.

"What did you do today?" she said.

"Walked," he said.

"Seeing all your old friends?" she said.

"Haven't got any friends," said Fuller.

His mother threw up her hands. "No friends?" she said. "You?"

"Times change, ma," said Fuller heavily. "Eighteen months is a long time. People leave town, people get married——"

"Marriage doesn't kill people, does it?" she said.

Fuller didn't smile. "Maybe not," he said. "But it makes it awful hard for 'em to find any place to fit old friends in."

"Dougie isn't married, is he?"

"He's out west, ma—with the Strategic Air Command," said Fuller. The little dining room became as lonely as a bomber in the thin, cold stratosphere.

"Oh," said his mother. "There must be somebody left."

"Nope," said Fuller. "I spent the whole morning on the phone, ma. I might as well have been back in Korea. Nobody home."

"I can't believe it," she said. "Why, you couldn't walk down Main Street without being almost trampled by friends."

"Ma," said Fuller hollowly, "after I ran out of numbers to call, you know what I did? I went down to the drugstore, ma, and just sat there by the soda fountain, waiting for somebody to walk in—somebody I knew maybe just even a little. Ma," he said in anguish, "all I knew was poor old Bearse Hinkley. I'm not kidding you one bit." He stood, crumpling his napkin into a ball. "Ma, will you please excuse me?"

"Yes. Of course," she said. "Where are you going now?" She beamed. "Out to call on some nice girl, I hope?"

Fuller threw the napkin down. "I'm going to get a cigar!" he said. "I don't know any girls. They're all married too."

His mother paled. "I—I see," she said. "I—I didn't even know you smoked."

"Ma," said Fuller tautly, "can't you get it through your head? I been away for eighteen months, ma—eighteen months!"

"It is a long time, isn't it?" said his mother, humbled by his passion. "Well, you go get your cigar." She touched his arm. "And please don't feel so lonesome. You just wait. Your life will be so full of people again, you won't know which one to turn to. And, before you know it, you'll meet some pretty young girl, and you'll be married too."

"I don't intend to get married for some time, mother," said Fuller stuffily. "Not until I get through divinity school."

"Divinity school!" said his mother. "When did you decide that?"

"This noon," said Fuller.

"What happened this noon?"

"I had kind of a religious experience, ma," he said. "Something just made me speak out."

"About what?" she said, bewildered.

In Fuller's buzzing head there whirled a rhapsody of Susannas. He saw again all the professional temptresses who had tormented him in Korea, who had beckoned from makeshift bed-sheet movie screens, from curling pinups on damp tent walls, from ragged magazines in sandbagged pits. The Susannas had made fortunes, beckoning to lonely Corporal Fullers everywhere—beckoning with stunning beauty, beckoning the Fullers to come nowhere for nothing.

The wraith of a Puritan ancestor, stiff-necked, dressed in black, took possession of Fuller's tongue. Fuller spoke with a voice that came across the centuries, the voice of a witch hanger, a voice redolent with frustration, self-righteousness, and doom.

"What did I speak out against?" he said. "Temp-ta-tion."

Fuller's cigar in the night was a beacon warning carefree, frivolous people away. It was plainly a cigar smoked in anger. Even the moths had sense enough to stay away. Like a restless, searching red eye, it went up and down every street in the village, coming to rest at last, a wet, dead butt, before the firehouse.

Bearse Hinkley, the old pharmacist, sat at the wheel of the pumper, his eyes glazed with nostalgia—nostalgia for the days when he had been young enough to drive. And on his face, for all to see, was a dream of one more catastrophe, with all the young men away, when an old man or nobody would drive the pumper to glory one more time. He spent warm evenings there, behind the wheel—and had for years.

"Want a light for that thing?" he said to Corporal Fuller, seeing the dead cigar between Fuller's lips.

"No, thanks, Mr. Hinkley," he said. "All the pleasure's out of it."

"Beats me how anybody finds any pleasure in cigars in the first place," said the old man.

"Matter of taste," said Fuller. "No accounting for tastes."

"One man's meat's another man's poison," said Hinkley. "Live and let live, I always say." He glanced at the ceiling. Above it was the fragrant nest of Susanna and her black cat. "Me? All my pleasures are looking at what used to be pleasures."

Fuller looked at the ceiling, too, meeting the unmentioned issue squarely. "If you were young," he said, "you'd know why I said what I said to her. Beautiful, stuck-up girls give me a big pain."

"Oh, I remember that," said Hinkley. "I'm not so old I don't remember the big pain."

"If I have a daughter, I hope she isn't beautiful," said Fuller. "The beautiful girls at high school—by God, if they didn't think they were something extra-special."

"By God, if I don't think so, too," said Hinkley.

"They wouldn't even look at you if you didn't have a car and an allowance of twenty bucks a week to spend on 'em," said Fuller.

"Why should they?" said the old man cheerfully. "If I was a beautiful girl, I wouldn't." He nodded to himself. "Well—anyway, I guess you came home from the wars and settled that score. I guess you told her."

"Ah-h-h," said Fuller. "You can't make any impression on them."

"I dunno," said Hinkley. "There's a fine old tradition in the theater: The show must go on. You know, even if you got pneumonia or your baby's dying, you still put on the show."

"I'm all right," said Fuller. "Who's complaining? I feel fine."

The old man's white eyebrows went up. "Who's talking about you?" he said. "I'm talking about her."

Fuller reddened, mousetrapped by egoism. "She'll be all right," he said.

"She will?" said Hinkley. "Maybe she will. All I know is, the show's started at the theater. She's supposed to be in it and she's still upstairs."

"She is?" said Fuller, amazed.

"Has been," said Hinkley, "ever since you paddled her and sent her home."

Fuller tried to grin ironically. "Now, isn't that too bad?" he said. His grin felt queasy and weak. "Well, good-night, Mr. Hinkley."

"Good-night, soldier boy," said Hinkley. "Good-night."

As noon drew near on the next day, the villagers along the main street seemed to grow stupid. Yankee shopkeepers made change lackadaisically, as though money didn't matter any more. All thoughts were of the great cuckoo clock the firehouse had become. The question was: Had Corporal Fuller broken it or, at noon, would the little door on top fly open, would Susanna appear?

In the drugstore, old Bearse Hinkley fussed with Susanna's New York papers, rumpling them in his anxiety to make them attractive. They were bait for Susanna.

Moments before noon, Corporal Fuller—the vandal himself—came into the drugstore. On his face was a strange mixture of guilt and soreheadedness. He had spent the better part of the night awake, reviewing his grievances against beautiful women. *All they think about is how beautiful they are,* he'd said to himself at dawn. *They wouldn't even give you the time of day.*

He walked along the row of soda-fountain stools and gave each empty stool a seemingly idle twist. He found the stool that had screeched so loudly the day before. He sat down on it, a monument of righteousness. No one spoke to him.

The fire siren gave its perfunctory wheeze for noon. And then, hearselike, a truck from the express company drove up to the firehouse. Two men got out and climbed the stairs. Susanna's hungry black cat jumped to the porch railing and arched its back as the expressmen disappeared into Susanna's room. The cat spat when they staggered out with Susanna's trunk.

Fuller was shocked. He glanced at Bearse Hinkley, and he saw that the old man's look of anxiety had become the look of double pneumonia—dizzy, blind, drowning.

"Satisfied, corporal?" said the old man.

"I didn't tell her to leave," said Fuller.

"You didn't leave her much choice," said Hinkley.

"What does she care what I think?" said Fuller. "I didn't know she was such a tender blossom."

The old man touched Fuller's arm lightly. "We all are, corporal—we all are," he said. "I thought that was one of the few good things about sending a boy off to the Army. I thought that was where he could find out for sure he wasn't the only tender blossom on earth. Didn't you find that out?"

"I never thought I was a tender blossom," said Fuller. "I'm sorry it turned out this way, but she asked for it." His head was down. His ears were hot crimson.

"She really scared you stiff, didn't she?" said Hinkley.

Smiles bloomed on the faces of the small audience that had drawn near on one pretext or another. Fuller appraised the smiles, and found that the old man had left him only one weapon —utterly humorless good citizenship.

"Who's afraid?" he said stuffily. "I'm not afraid. I just think it's a problem somebody ought to bring up and discuss."

"It's sure the one subject nobody gets tired of," said Hinkley.

Fuller's gaze, which had become a very shifty thing, passed over the magazine rack. There was tier upon tier of Susannas, a thousand square feet of wet-lipped smiles and sooty eyes and skin like cream. He ransacked his mind for a ringing phrase that would give dignity to his cause.

"I'm thinking about juvenile delinquency!" he said. He pointed to the magazines. "No wonder kids go crazy."

"I know I did," said the old man quietly. "I was as scared as you are."

"I told you, I'm not afraid of her," said Fuller.

"Good!" said Hinkley. "Then you're just the man to take her

papers to her. They're paid for." He dumped the papers in Fuller's lap.

Fuller opened his mouth to reply. But he closed it again. His throat had tightened, and he knew that, if he tried to speak, he would quack like a duck.

"If you're really not afraid, corporal," said the old man, "that would be a very nice thing to do—a Christian thing to do."

As he mounted the stairway to Susanna's nest, Fuller was almost spastic in his efforts to seem casual.

Susanna's door was unlatched. When Fuller knocked on it, it swung open. In Fuller's imagination, her nest had been dark and still, reeking of incense, a labyrinth of heavy hangings and mirrors, with somewhere a Turkish corner, with somewhere a billowy bed in the form of a swan.

He saw Susanna and her room in truth now. The truth was the cheerless truth of a dirt-cheap Yankee summer rental—bare wood walls, three coat hooks, a linoleum rug. Two gas burners, an iron cot, an icebox. A tiny sink with naked pipes, a plastic drinking glass, two plates, a murky mirror. A frying pan, a saucepan, a can of soap powder.

The only harem touch was a white circle of talcum powder before the murky mirror. In the center of the circle were the prints of two bare feet. The marks of the toes were no bigger than pearls.

Fuller looked from the pearls to the truth of Susanna. Her back was to him. She was packing the last of her things into a suitcase.

She was now dressed for travel—dressed as properly as a missionary's wife.

"Papers," croaked Fuller. "Mr. Hinkley sent 'em."

"How very nice of Mr. Hinkley," said Susanna. She turned. "Tell him——" No more words came. She recognized him. She pursed her lips and her small nose reddened.

"Papers," said Fuller emptily. "From Mr. Hinkley."

"I heard you," she said. "You just said that. Is that all you've got to say?"

Fuller flapped his hands limply at his sides. "I'm—I—I didn't mean to make you leave," he said. "I didn't mean that."

"You suggest I stay?" said Susanna wretchedly. "After I've been denounced in public as a scarlet woman? A tart? A wench?"

"Holy smokes, I never called you those things!" said Fuller.

"Did you ever stop to think what it's like to be me?" she said. She patted her bosom. "There's somebody living inside here, too, you know."

"I know," said Fuller. He hadn't known, up to then.

"I have a soul," she said.

"Sure you do," said Fuller, trembling. He trembled because the room was filled with a profound intimacy. Susanna, the golden girl of a thousand tortured daydreams, was now discussing her soul, passionately, with Fuller the lonely, Fuller the homely, Fuller the bleak.

"I didn't sleep a wink last night because of you," said Susanna.

"Me?" He wished she'd get out of his life again. He wished she were in black and white, a thousandth of an inch thick on a magazine page. He wished he could turn the page and read about baseball or foreign affairs.

"What did you expect?" said Susanna. "I talked to you all night. You know what I said to you?"

"No," said Fuller, backing away. She followed, and seemed to throw off heat like a big iron radiator. She was appallingly human.

"I'm not Yellowstone Park!" she said. "I'm not supported by taxes! I don't belong to everybody! You don't have any right to say anything about the way I look!"

"Good gravy!" said Fuller.

"I'm so tired of dumb toots like you!" said Susanna. She stamped her foot and suddenly looked haggard. "I can't help it if you want to kiss me! Whose fault is that?"

Fuller could now glimpse his side of the question only dimly, like a diver glimpsing the sun from the ocean floor. "All I was trying to say was, you could be a little more conservative," he said.

Susanna opened her arms. "Am I conservative enough now?" she said. "Is this all right with you?"

The appeal of the lovely girl made the marrow of Fuller's

bones ache. In his chest was a sigh like the lost chord. "Yes," he said. And then he murmured, "Forget about me."

Susanna tossed her head. "Forget about being run over by a truck," she said. "What makes you so mean?"

"I just say what I think," said Fuller.

"You think such mean things," said Susanna, bewildered. Her eyes widened. "All through high school, people like you would look at me as if they wished I'd drop dead. They'd never dance with me, they'd never talk to me, they'd never even smile back." She shuddered. "They'd just go slinking around like small-town cops. They'd look at me the way you did—like I'd just done something terrible."

The truth of the indictment made Fuller itch all over. "Probably thinking about something else," he said.

"I don't think so," said Susanna. "You sure weren't. All of a sudden, you started yelling at me in the drugstore, and I'd never even seen you before." She burst into tears. "What is the matter with you?"

Fuller looked down at the floor. "Never had a chance with a girl like you—that's all," he said. "That hurts."

Susanna looked at him wonderingly. "You don't know what a chance is," she said.

"A chance is a late-model convertible, a new suit, and twenty bucks," said Fuller.

Susanna turned her back to him and closed her suitcase. "A chance is a girl," she said. "You smile at her, you be friendly, you be glad she's a girl." She turned and opened her arms again. "I'm a girl. Girls are shaped this way," she said. "If men are nice to me and make me happy, I kiss them sometimes. Is that all right with you?"

"Yes," said Fuller humbly. She had rubbed his nose in the sweet reason that governed the universe. He shrugged. "I better be going. Good-by."

"Wait!" she said. "You can't do that—just walk out, leaving me feeling so wicked." She shook her head. "I don't deserve to feel wicked."

"What can I do?" said Fuller helplessly.

"You can take me for a walk down the main street, as though

you were proud of me," said Susanna. "You can welcome me back to the human race." She nodded to herself. "You owe that to me."

Cpl. Norman Fuller, who had come home two nights before from eighteen bleak months in Korea, waited on the porch outside Susanna's nest, with all the village watching.

Susanna had ordered him out while she changed, while she changed for her return to the human race. She had also called the express company and told them to bring her trunk back.

Fuller passed the time by stroking Susanna's cat. "Hello, kitty, kitty, kitty, kitty," he said, over and over again. Saying, "Kitty, kitty, kitty, kitty," numbed him like a merciful drug.

He was saying it when Susanna came out of her nest. He couldn't stop saying it, and she had to take the cat away from him, firmly, before she could get him to look at her, to offer his arm.

"So long, kitty, kitty, kitty, kitty, kitty, kitty," said Fuller.

Susanna was barefoot, and she wore barbaric hoop earrings, and ankle bells. Holding Fuller's arm lightly, she led him down the stairs, and began her stately, undulating, titillating, tinkling walk past the liquor store, the insurance agency, the real-estate office, the diner, the American Legion post, and the church, to the crowded drugstore.

"Now, smile and be nice," said Susanna. "Show you're not ashamed of me."

"Mind if I smoke?" said Fuller.

"That's very considerate of you to ask," said Susanna. "No, I don't mind at all."

By steadying his right hand with his left, Corporal Fuller managed to light a cigar.

(1956)

ALL THE
KING'S HORSES

COLONEL BRYAN KELLY, his huge figure blocking off the light that filtered down the narrow corridor behind him, leaned for a moment against the locked door in an agony of anxiety and helpless rage. The small Oriental guard sorted through a ring of keys, searching for the one that would open the door. Colonel Kelly listened to the voices inside the room.

"Sarge, they wouldn't dare do anything to Americans, would they?" The voice was youthful, unsure. "I mean, there'd be hell to pay if they hurt—"

"Shut up. Want to wake up Kelly's kids and have them hear you running off at the mouth that way?" The voice was gruff, tired.

"They'll turn us loose pretty quick, whaddya bet, Sarge?" insisted the young voice.

"Oh, sure, kid, they love Americans around here. That's probably what they wanted to talk to Kelly about, and they're packing the beer and ham sandwiches into box lunches for us right now. All that's holding things up is they don't know how many with mustard, how many without. How d'ya want yours?"

"I'd just like to—"

"Shut up."

"Okay, I'd just—"

"Shut up."

"I'd just like to know what's going on, is all." The young corporal coughed.

"Pipe down and pass that butt along," said a third voice irritably. "There's ten good puffs left in it. Don't hog the whole thing, kid." A few other voices muttered in agreement.

Colonel Kelly opened and closed his hands nervously, wondering how he could tell the fifteen human beings behind the door about the interview with Pi Ying and the lunatic ordeal they were going to have to endure. Pi Ying said that their fight against death would be no different, philosophically, from what all of them, except Kelly's wife and children, had known in battle. In a cold way, it was true—no different, philosophically. But Colonel Kelly was more shaken than he had ever been in battle.

Colonel Kelly and the fifteen on the other side of the door had crash-landed two days before on the Asiatic mainland, after they had been blown off course by a sudden storm and their radio had gone dead. Colonel Kelly had been on his way, with his family, to a post as military attaché in India. On board the Army transport plane with them had been a group of enlisted men, technical specialists needed in the Middle East. The plane had come to earth in territory held by a Communist guerrilla chief, Pi Ying.

All had survived the crash—Kelly, his wife Margaret, his ten-year-old twin sons, the pilot and copilot, and the ten enlisted men. A dozen of Pi Ying's ragged riflemen had been waiting for them when they climbed from the plane. Unable to communicate with their captors, the Americans had been marched for a day through rice fields and near-jungle to come at sunset to a decaying palace. There they had been locked in a subterranean room, with no idea of what their fates might be.

Now, Colonel Kelly was returning from an interview with Pi Ying, who had told him what was to become of the sixteen American prisoners. *Sixteen*—Kelly shook his head as the number repeated itself in his thoughts.

The guard prodded him to one side with his pistol and thrust the key into the lock, and the door swung open. Kelly stood silently in the doorway.

A cigarette was being passed from hand to hand. It cast its glow for an instant on each expectant face in turn. Now it lighted the ruddy face of the talkative young corporal from Minneapolis, now cast rugged shadows over the eye sockets and heavy brows of the pilot from Salt Lake, now bloomed red at the thin lips of the sergeant.

Kelly looked from the men to what seemed in the twilight to be a small hillock by the door. There his wife Margaret sat, with the blond heads of her sleeping sons cradled in her lap. She smiled up at him, her face misty white. "Darling—you're all right?" Margaret asked quietly.

"Yes, I'm all right."

"Sarge," said the corporal, "ask him what Pi Ying said."

"Shut up." The sergeant paused. "What about it, sir—good news or bad?"

Kelly stroked his wife's shoulder, trying to make the right words come—words to carry courage he wasn't sure he had. "Bad news," he said at last. "Rotten news."

"Well, let's have it," said the transport pilot loudly. Kelly supposed he was trying to reassure himself with the boom of his own voice, with brusqueness. "The worst he can do is kill us. Is that it?" He stood and dug his hands into his pockets.

"He wouldn't dare!" said the young corporal in a threatening voice—as though he could bring the wrath of the United States Army to bear on Pi Ying with a snap of his fingers.

Colonel Kelly looked at the youngster with curiosity and dejection. "Let's face it. The little man upstairs has all the trumps." An expression borrowed from another game, he thought irrelevantly. "He's an outlaw. He hasn't got a thing to lose by getting the United States sore at him."

"If he's going to kill us, say so!" the pilot said explosively. "So he's got us cold! What's he going to do?"

"He considers us prisoners of war," said Kelly, trying to keep his voice even. "He'd like to shoot us all." He shrugged. "I haven't been trying to keep you in suspense, I've been looking for the right words—and there aren't any. Pi Ying wants more entertainment out of us than shooting us would provide. He'd like to prove that he's smarter than we are in the bargain."

"How?" asked Margaret. Her eyes were wide. The two children were waking up.

"In a little while, Pi Ying and I are going to play chess for your lives." He closed his fist over his wife's limp hand. "And for my four lives. It's the only chance Pi Ying will give us." He shrugged, and smiled wryly. "I play a better-than-average game—a little better than average."

"Is he nuts?" said the sergeant.

"You'll all see for yourselves," said Colonel Kelly simply. "You'll see him when the game begins—Pi Ying and his friend, Major Barzov." He raised his eyebrows. "The major claims to be sorry that, in his capacity as a military observer for the Russian army, he is powerless to intervene in our behalf. He also says we have his sympathy. I suspect he's a damn liar on both counts. Pi Ying is scared stiff of him."

"We get to watch the game?" whispered the corporal tensely.

"The sixteen of us, soldier, are the chessmen I'll be playing with."

The door swung open. . . .

"Can you see the whole board from down there, White King?" called Pi Ying cheerfully from a balcony overlooking the azure-domed chamber. He was smiling down at Colonel Bryan Kelly, his family, and his men. "You must be the White King, you know. Otherwise, we couldn't be sure that you'd be with us for the whole game." The guerrilla chief's face was flushed. His smile was one of mock solicitousness. "Delighted to see all of you!"

To Pi Ying's right, indistinct in the shadows, stood Major Barzov, the taciturn Russian military observer. He acknowledged Kelly's stare with a slow nod. Kelly continued to stare fixedly. The arrogant, bristle-haired major became restless, folding and unfolding his arms, repeatedly rocking back and forth in his black boots. "I wish I could help you," he said at last. It wasn't an amenity but a contemptuous jest. "I am only an observer here." Barzov said it heavily. "I wish you luck, Colonel," he added, and turned his back.

Seated on Pi Ying's left was a delicate young Oriental woman. She gazed expressionlessly at the wall over the Americans' heads. She and Barzov had been present when Pi Ying had first told Colonel Kelly of the game he wanted to play. When Kelly had begged Pi Ying to leave his wife and children out of it, he had thought he saw a spark of pity in her eyes. As he looked up at the motionless, ornamental girl now, he knew he must have been mistaken.

"This room was a whim of my predecessors, who for generations held the people in slavery," said Pi Ying sententiously. "It served nicely as a throne room. But the floor is inlaid with squares, sixty-four of them—a chessboard, you see? The former tenants had those handsome, man-sized chessmen before you built so that they and their friends could sit up here and order servants to move them about." He twisted a ring on his finger. "Imaginative as that was, it remained for us to hit upon this new twist. Today, of course, we will use only the black chessmen, my pieces." He turned to the restive Major Barzov. "The Americans have furnished their own chessmen. Fascinating idea." His smile faded when he saw that Barzov wasn't smiling with him. Pi Ying seemed eager to please the Russian. Barzov, in turn, appeared to regard Pi Ying as hardly worth listening to.

The twelve American soldiers stood against a wall under heavy guard. Instinctively, they bunched together and glared sullenly at their patronizing host. "Take it easy," said Colonel Kelly, "or we'll lose the one chance we've got." He looked quickly at his twin sons, Jerry and Paul, who gazed about the room, unruffled, interested, blinking sleepily at the side of their stunned mother. Kelly wondered why he felt so little as he watched his family in the face of death. The fear he had felt while they were waiting in their dark prison was gone. Now he recognized the eerie calm—an old wartime friend—that left only the cold machinery of his wits and senses alive. It was the narcotic of generalship. It was the essence of war.

"Now, my friends, your attention," said Pi Ying importantly. He stood. "The rules of the game are easy to remember. You are all to behave as Colonel Kelly tells you. Those of you who are so unfortunate as to be taken by one of my chessmen will be killed quickly, painlessly, promptly." Major Barzov looked at the ceiling as though he were inwardly criticizing everything Pi Ying said.

The corporal suddenly released a blistering stream of obscenities—half abuse, half self-pity. The sergeant clapped his hand over the youngster's mouth.

Pi Ying leaned over the balustrade and pointed a finger at the struggling soldier. "For those who run from the board or make an outcry, a special form of death can be arranged," he said sharply. "Colonel Kelly and I must have complete silence in which to concentrate. If the colonel is clever enough to win, then all of you who are still with us when I am checkmated will get safe transport out of my territory. If he loses—" Pi Ying shrugged. He settled back on a mound of cushions. "Now, you must all be good sports," he said briskly. "Americans are noted for that, I believe. As Colonel Kelly can tell you, a chess game can very rarely be won—any more than a battle can be won—without sacrifices. Isn't that so, Colonel?"

Colonel Kelly nodded mechanically. He was recalling what Pi Ying had said earlier—that the game he was about to play was no different, philosophically, from what he had known in war.

"How can you do this to children!" cried Margaret suddenly, twisting free of a guard and striding across the squares to stand directly below Pi Ying's balcony. "For the love of God—" she began.

Pi Ying interrupted angrily: "Is it for the love of God that Americans make bombs and jet planes and tanks?" He waved her away impatiently. "Drag her back." He covered his eyes. "Where was I? We were talking about sacrifices, weren't we? I was going to ask you who you had chosen to be your king's pawn," said Pi Ying. "If you haven't chosen one, Colonel, I'd like to recommend the noisy young man down there—the one the sergeant is holding. A delicate position, king's pawn."

The corporal began to kick and twist with new fury. The sergeant tightened his arms about him. "The kid'll calm down in a minute," he said under his breath. He turned his head toward Colonel Kelly. "Whatever the hell the king's pawn is, that's me. Where do I stand, sir?" The youngster relaxed and the sergeant freed him.

Kelly pointed to the fourth square in the second row of the huge chessboard. The sergeant strode to the square and hunched his broad shoulders. The corporal mumbled something incoherent, and took his place in the square next to the sergeant—a second dependable pawn. The rest still hung back.

"Colonel, you tell us where to go," said a lanky T-4 uncertainly. "What do we know about chess? You put us where you want us." His Adam's apple bobbed. "Save the soft spots for your wife and kids. They're the ones that count. You tell us what to do."

"There are no soft spots," said the pilot sardonically, "no soft spots for anybody. Pick a square, any square." He stepped onto the board. "What does this square make me?"

"You're a bishop, Lieutenant, the king's bishop," said Kelly.

He found himself thinking of the lieutenant in those terms— no longer human, but a piece capable of moving diagonally across the board; capable, when attacking with the queen, of terrible damage to the black men across the board.

"And me in church only twice in my life. Hey, Pi Ying," called the pilot insolently, "what's a bishop worth?"

Pi Ying was amused. "A knight and a pawn, my boy; a knight and a pawn."

Thank God for the lieutenant, thought Kelly. One of the American soldiers grinned. They had been sticking close together, backed against the wall. Now they began to talk among themselves—like a baseball team warming up. At Kelly's direction, seeming almost unconscious of the meaning of their actions, they moved out onto the board to fill out the ranks.

Pi Ying was speaking again. "All of your pieces are in place now, except your knights and your queen, Colonel. And you, of course, are the king. Come, come. The game must be over before suppertime."

Gently, shepherding them with his long arms, Kelly led his wife and Jerry and Paul to their proper squares. He detested himself for the calm, the detachment with which he did it. He saw the fear and reproach in Margaret's eyes. She couldn't understand that he had to be this way—that in his coldness was their only hope for survival. He looked away from Margaret.

Pi Ying clapped his hands for silence. "There, good; now we can begin." He tugged at his ear reflectively. "I think this is an excellent way of bringing together the Eastern and Western minds, don't you, Colonel? Here we indulge the American's love for gambling with our appreciation of profound drama and philosophy." Major Barzov whispered impatiently to him. "Oh, yes," said Pi Ying, "two more rules: We are allowed ten minutes a move, and—this goes without saying—no moves may be taken back. Very well," he said, pressing the button on a stop watch and setting it on the balustrade, "the honor of the first move belongs to the white men." He grinned. "An ancient tradition."

"Sergeant," said Colonel Kelly, his throat tight, "move two squares forward." He looked down at his hands. They were starting to tremble.

"I believe I'll be slightly unconventional," said Pi Ying, half turning his head toward the young girl, as though to make sure that she was sharing his enjoyment. "Move my queen's pawn forward two squares," he instructed a servant.

Colonel Kelly watched the servant slide the massive carving forward—to a point threatening the sergeant. The sergeant looked quizzically at Kelly. "Everything okay, sir?" He smiled faintly.

"I hope so," said Kelly. "Here's your protection . . . Soldier," he ordered the young corporal, "step forward one square." There —it was all he could do. Now there was no advantage in Pi Ying's taking the pawn he threatened—the sergeant. Tactically it would be a pointless trade, pawn for pawn. No advantage so far as good chess went.

"This is very bad form, I know," said Pi Ying blandly. He paused. "Well, then again, I'm not so sure I'd be wise to trade.

With so brilliant an opponent, perhaps I'd better play flawless chess, and forget the many temptations." Major Barzov murmured something to him. "But it would get us into the spirit of the game right off, wouldn't it?"

"What's he talking about, sir?" asked the sergeant apprehensively.

Before Kelly could order his thoughts, Pi Ying gave the order. "Take his king's pawn."

"Colonel! What'd you do?" cried the sergeant. Two guards pulled him from the board and out of the room. A studded door banged shut behind them.

"Kill me!" shouted Kelly, starting off his square after them. A half-dozen bayonets hemmed him in.

Impassively, the servant slid Pi Ying's wooden pawn onto the square where the sergeant had stood. A shot reverberated on the other side of the thick door, and the guards reappeared. Pi Ying was no longer smiling. "Your move, Colonel. Come, come—four minutes have gone already."

Kelly's calm was shattered, and with it went the illusion of the game. The pieces in his power were human beings again. The precious, brutal stuff of command was gone from Colonel Kelly. He was no more fit to make decisions of life and death than the rawest recruit. Giddily, he realized that Pi Ying's object was not to win the game quickly, but to thin out the Americans in harrowing, pointless forays. Another two minutes crept by as he struggled to force himself to be rational. "I can't do it," he whispered at last. He slouched now.

"You wish me to have all of you shot right now?" asked Pi Ying. "I must say that I find you a rather pathetic colonel. Do all American officers give in so easily?"

"Pin his ears back, Colonel," said the pilot. "Let's go. Sharpen up. Let's go!"

"You're in no danger now," said Kelly to the corporal. "Take his pawn."

"How do I know you're not lying?" said the youngster bitterly. "Now I'm going to get it!"

"Get over there!" said the transport pilot sharply.

"No!"

The sergeant's two executioners pinned the corporal's arms to his sides. They looked up expectantly at Pi Ying.

"Young man," said Pi Ying solicitously, "would you enjoy being tortured to death, or would you rather do as Colonel Kelly tells you?"

The corporal spun suddenly and sent both guards sprawling. He stepped onto the square occupied by the pawn that had taken the sergeant, kicked the piece over, and stood there with his feet apart.

Major Barzov guffawed. "He'll learn to be a pawn yet," he roared. "It's an Oriental skill Americans could do well to learn for the days ahead, eh?"

Pi Ying laughed with Barzov, and stroked the knee of the young girl, who had been sitting, expressionless, at his side. "Well, it's been perfectly even so far—a pawn for a pawn. Let's begin our offensives in earnest." He snapped his fingers for the attention of the servant. "King's pawn to king three," he commanded. "There! Now my queen and bishop are ready for an expedition into white man's territory." He pressed the button on the stop watch. "Your move, Colonel." . . .

It was an old reflex that made Colonel Bryan Kelly look to his wife for compassion, courage. He looked away again—Margaret was a frightening, heartbreaking sight, and there was nothing he could do for her but win. Nothing. Her stare was vacant, almost idiotic. She had taken refuge in deaf, blind, unfeeling shock.

Kelly counted the figures still surviving on the board. An hour had passed since the game's beginning. Five pawns were still alive, among them the young corporal; one bishop, the nervy pilot; two rooks; two knights—ten-year-old frightened knights; Margaret, a rigid, staring queen; and himself, the king. The missing four? Butchered—butchered in senseless exchanges that had cost Pi Ying only blocks of wood. The other soldiers had fallen silent, sullen in their own separate worlds.

"I think it's time for you to concede," said Pi Ying. "It's just about over, I'm afraid. Do you concede, Colonel?" Major Barzov frowned wisely at the chessmen, shook his head slowly, and yawned.

Colonel Kelly tried to bring his mind and eyes back into focus. He had the sensation of burrowing, burrowing, burrowing his way through a mountain of hot sand, of having to keep going on and on, digging, squirming, suffocated, blinded. "Go to hell," he muttered. He concentrated on the pattern of the chessmen. As chess, the ghastly game had been absurd. Pi Ying had moved with no strategy other than to destroy white men. Kelly had moved to defend each of his chessmen at any cost, had risked none in offense. His powerful queen, knights, and rooks stood unused in the relative safety of the two rear rows of squares. He clenched and unclenched his fists in frustration. His opponent's haphazard ranks were wide open. A checkmate of Pi Ying's king would be possible, if only the black knight weren't dominating the center of the board.

"Your move, Colonel. Two minutes," coaxed Pi Ying.

And then Kelly saw it—the price he would pay, that they all would pay, for the curse of conscience. Pi Ying had only to move his queen diagonally, three squares to the left, to put him in check. After that he needed to make one more move—inevitable, irresistible—and then checkmate, the end. And Pi Ying would move his queen. The game seemed to have lost its piquancy for him; he had the air of a man eager to busy himself elsewhere.

The guerrilla chief was standing now, leaning over the balustrade. Major Barzov stood behind him, fitting a cigarette into an ornate ivory holder. "It's a very distressing thing about chess," said Barzov, admiring the holder, turning it this way and that. "There isn't a grain of luck in the game, you know. There's no excuse for the loser." His tone was pedantic, with the superciliousness of a teacher imparting profound truths to students too immature to understand.

Pi Ying shrugged. "Winning this game gives me very little satisfaction. Colonel Kelly has been a disappointment. By risking nothing, he has deprived the game of its subtlety and wit. I could expect more brilliance from my cook."

*   *   *

The hot red of anger blazed over Kelly's cheeks, inflamed his ears. The muscles of his belly knotted; his legs moved apart. Pi Ying must not move his queen. If Pi Ying moved his queen, Kelly would lose; if Pi Ying moved his knight from Kelly's line of attack, Kelly would win. Only one thing might induce Pi Ying to move his knight—a fresh, poignant opportunity for sadism.

"Concede, Colonel. My time is valuable," said Pi Ying.

"Is it all over?" asked the young corporal querulously.

"Keep your mouth shut and stay where you are," said Kelly. He stared through shrewd, narrowed eyes at Pi Ying's knight, standing in the midst of the living chessmen. The horse's carved neck arched. Its nostrils flared.

The pure geometry of the white chessmen's fate burst upon Kelly's consciousness. Its simplicity had the effect of a refreshing, chilling wind. A sacrifice had to be offered to Pi Ying's knight. If Pi Ying accepted the sacrifice, the game would be Kelly's. The trap was perfect and deadly save for one detail—bait.

"One minute, Colonel," said Pi Ying.

Kelly looked quickly from face to face, unmoved by the hostility or distrust or fear that he saw in each pair of eyes. One by one he eliminated the candidates for death. These four were vital to the sudden, crushing offense, and these must guard the king. Necessity, like a child counting eeny, meeny, miney, moe around a circle, pointed its finger at the one chessman who could be sacrificed. There was only one.

Kelly didn't permit himself to think of the chessman as anything but a cipher in a rigid mathematical proposition: if x is dead, the rest shall live. He perceived the tragedy of his decision only as a man who knew the definition of tragedy, not as one who felt it.

"Twenty seconds!" said Barzov. He had taken the stop watch from Pi Ying.

The cold resolve deserted Kelly for an instant, and he saw the utter pathos of his position—a dilemma as old as mankind, as new as the struggle between East and West. When human beings are attacked, x, multiplied by hundreds or thousands, must die—sent to death by those who love them most. Kelly's profession was the choosing of x.

"Ten seconds," said Barzov.

"Jerry," said Kelly, his voice loud and sure, "move forward one square and two to your left." Trustingly, his son stepped out of the back rank and into the shadow of the black knight. Awareness seemed to be filtering back into Margaret's eyes. She turned her head when her husband spoke.

Pi Ying stared down at the board in bafflement. "Are you in your right mind, Colonel?" he asked at last. "Do you realize what you've just done?"

A faint smile crossed Barzov's face. He bent forward as though to whisper to Pi Ying, but apparently thought better of it. He leaned back against a pillar to watch Kelly's every move through a gauze of cigarette smoke.

Kelly pretended to be mystified by Pi Ying's words. And then he buried his face in his hands and gave an agonized cry. "Oh, God, no!"

"An exquisite mistake, to be sure," said Pi Ying. He excitedly explained the blunder to the young girl beside him. She turned away. He seemed infuriated by the gesture.

"You've got to let me take him back," begged Kelly brokenly.

Pi Ying rapped on the balustrade with his knuckles. "Without rules, my friend, games become nonsense. We agreed that all moves would be final, and so they are." He motioned to a servant. "King's knight to king's bishop six!" The servant moved the piece onto the square where Jerry stood. The bait was taken, the game was Colonel Kelly's from here on in.

"What is he talking about?" murmured Margaret.

"Why keep your wife in suspense, Colonel?" said Pi Ying. "Be a good husband and answer her question, or should I?"

"Your husband sacrificed a knight," said Barzov, his voice overriding Pi Ying's. "You've just lost your son." His expression was that of an experimenter, keen, expectant, entranced.

Kelly heard the choking sound in Margaret's throat, caught her as she fell. He rubbed her wrists. "Darling, please—listen to me!" He shook her more roughly than he had intended. Her reaction was explosive. Words cascaded from her—hysterical babble condemning him. Kelly locked her wrists together in his hands and listened dumbly to her broken abuse.

Pi Ying's eyes bulged, transfixed by the fantastic drama below, oblivious of the tearful frenzy of the young girl behind him. She tugged at his blouse, pleading. He pushed her back without looking away from the board.

The tall T-4 suddenly dived at the nearest guard, driving his shoulder into the man's chest, his fist into his belly. Pi Ying's soldiers converged, hammered him to the floor and dragged him back to his square.

In the midst of the bedlam, Jerry burst into tears and raced terrified to his father and mother. Kelly freed Margaret, who dropped to her knees to hug the quaking child. Paul, Jerry's twin, held his ground, trembled, stared stolidly at the floor.

"Shall we get on with the game, Colonel?" asked Pi Ying, his voice high. Barzov turned his back to the board, unwilling to prevent the next step, apparently reluctant to watch it.

Kelly closed his eyes, and waited for Pi Ying to give the order to the executioners. He couldn't bring himself to look at Margaret and Jerry. Pi Ying waved his hand for silence. "It is with deep regret—" he began. His lips closed. The menace suddenly went out of his face, leaving only surprise and stupidity. The small man slumped on the balustrade, slithered over it to crash among his soldiers.

Major Barzov struggled with the Chinese girl. In her small hand, still free of his grasp, was a slender knife. She drove it into her breast and fell against the major. Barzov let her fall. He strode to the balustrade. "Keep the prisoners where they are!" he shouted at the guards. "Is he alive?" There was no anger in his voice, no sorrow—only irritation, resentment of inconvenience. A servant looked up and shook his head.

Barzov ordered servants and soldiers to carry out the bodies of Pi Ying and the girl. It was more the act of a scrupulous housekeeper than a pious mourner. No one questioned his brisk authority.

"So this is your party after all," said Kelly.

"The peoples of Asia have lost a very great leader," Barzov

said severely. He smiled at Kelly oddly. "Though he wasn't without weaknesses, was he, Colonel?" He shrugged. "However, you've won only the initiative, not the game; and now you have me to reckon with instead of Pi Ying. Stay where you are, Colonel. I'll be back shortly."

He ground out his cigarette on the ornamented balustrade, returned the holder to his pocket with a flourish, and disappeared through the curtains.

"Is Jerry going to be all right?" whispered Margaret. It was a plea, not a question, as though mercy were Kelly's to dole out or to withhold.

"Only Barzov knows," he said. He was bursting to explain the moves to her, to make her understand why he had had no choice; but he knew that an explanation would only make the tragedy infinitely more cruel for her. Death through a blunder she might be able to understand; but death as a product of cool reason, a step in logic, she could never accept. Rather than accept it, she would have had them all die.

"Only Barzov knows," he repeated wearily. The bargain was still in force, the price of victory agreed to. Barzov apparently had yet to realize what it was that Kelly was buying with a life.

"How do we know Barzov will let us go if we do win?" said the T-4.

"We don't, soldier. We don't." And then another doubt began to worm into his consciousness. Perhaps he had won no more than a brief reprieve. . . .

Colonel Kelly had lost track of how long they'd waited there on the chessboard for Barzov's return. His nerves were deadened by surge after surge of remorse and by the steady pressure of terrible responsibility. His consciousness had lapsed into twilight. Margaret slept in utter exhaustion, with Jerry, his life yet to be claimed, in her arms. Paul had curled up on his square, covered by the young corporal's field jacket. On what had been Jerry's square, the horse's carved head snarling as though fire would burst from its nostrils, stood Pi Ying's black knight.

Kelly barely heard the voice from the balcony—mistook it for another jagged fragment in a nightmare. His mind attached no sen'e to the words, heard only their sound. And then he opened his eyes and saw Major Barzov's lips moving. He saw the arrogant challenge in his eyes, understood the words. "Since so much blood has been shed in this game, it would be a pitiful waste to leave it unresolved."

Barzov settled regally on Pi Ying's cushions, his black boots crossed. "I propose to beat you, Colonel, and I will be surprised if you give me trouble. It would be very upsetting to have you win by the transparent ruse that fooled Pi Ying. It isn't that easy any more. You're playing me now, Colonel. You won the initiative for a moment. I'll take it and the game now, without any more delay."

Kelly rose to his feet, his great frame monumental above the white chessmen sitting on the squares about him. Major Barzov wasn't above the kind of entertainment Pi Ying had found so diverting. But Kelly sensed the difference between the major's demeanor and that of the guerrilla chief. The major was resuming the game, not because he liked it, but because he wanted to prove that he was one hell of a bright fellow, and that the Americans were dirt. Apparently, he didn't realize that Pi Ying had already lost the game. Either that, or Kelly had miscalculated.

In his mind, Kelly moved every piece on the board, driving his imagination to show him the flaw in his plan, if a flaw existed —if the hellish, heartbreaking sacrifice was for nothing. In an ordinary game, with nothing at stake but bits of wood, he would have called upon his opponent to concede, and the game would have ended there. But now, playing for flesh and blood, an aching, ineradicable doubt overshadowed the cleancut logic of the outcome. Kelly dared not reveal that he planned to attack and win in three moves—not until he had made the moves, not until Barzov had lost every chance to exploit the flaw, if there was one.

"What about Jerry?" cried Margaret.

"Jerry? Oh, of course, the little boy. Well, what about Jerry, Colonel?" asked Barzov. "I'll make a special concession, if you like. Would you want to take the move back?" The major was urbane, a caricature of cheerful hospitality.

"Without rules, Major, games become nonsense," said Kelly flatly. "I'd be the last to ask you to break them."

Barzov's expression became one of profound sympathy. "Your husband, madame, has made the decision, not I." He pressed the button on the stop watch. "You may keep the boy with you until the Colonel has fumbled all of your lives away. Your move, Colonel. Ten minutes."

"Take his pawn," Kelly ordered Margaret. She didn't move. "Margaret! Do you hear me?"

"Help her, Colonel, help her," chided Barzov.

Kelly took Margaret by the elbow, led her unresisting to the square where a black pawn stood. Jerry tagged along, keeping his mother between himself and Kelly. Kelly returned to his square, dug his hands into his pockets, and watched a servant take the black pawn from the board. "Check, Major. Your king is in check."

Barzov raised an eyebrow. "Check, did you say? What shall I do about this annoyance? How shall I get you back to some of the more interesting problems on the board?" He gestured to a servant. "Move my king over one square to the left."

"Move diagonally one square toward me, Lieutenant," Kelly ordered the pilot. The pilot hesitated. "Move! Do you hear?"

"Yessir." The tone was mocking. "Retreating, eh, sir?" The lieutenant slouched into the square, slowly, insolently.

"Check again, Major," Kelly said evenly. He motioned at the lieutenant. "Now my bishop has your king in check." He closed his eyes and told himself again and again that he had made no miscalculation, that the sacrifice *had* won the game, that there *could* be no out for Barzov. This was it—the last of the three moves.

"Well," said Barzov, "is that the best you can do? I'll simply move my queen in front of my king." The servant moved the piece. "Now it will be a different story."

"Take his queen," said Kelly to his farthest-advanced pawn, the battered T-4.

Barzov jumped to his feet. "Wait!"

"You didn't see it? You'd like to take it back?" taunted Kelly.

Barzov paced back and forth on his balcony, breathing hard. "Of course I saw it!"

"It was the only thing you could do to save your king," said Kelly. "You may take it back if you like, but you'll find it's the only move you can make."

"Take the queen and get on with the game," shouted Barzov. "Take her!"

"Take her," echoed Kelly, and the servant trundled the huge piece to the side lines. The T-4 now stood blinking at Barzov's king, inches away. Colonel Kelly said it very softly this time: "Check."

Barzov exhaled in exasperation. "Check indeed." His voice grew louder. "No credit to you, Colonel Kelly, but to the monumental stupidity of Pi Ying."

"And that's the game, Major."

The T-4 laughed idiotically, the corporal sat down, the lieutenant threw his arms around Colonel Kelly. The two children gave a cheer. Only Margaret stood fast, still rigid, frightened.

"The price of your victory, of course, has yet to be paid," said Barzov acidly. "I presume you're ready to pay now?"

Kelly whitened. "That was the understanding, if it would give you satisfaction to hold me to it."

Barzov placed another cigarette in his ivory holder, taking a scowling minute to do it. When he spoke, it was in the tone of the pedant once more, the wielder of profundities. "No, I won't take the boy. I feel as Pi Ying felt about you—that you, as Americans, are the enemy, whether an official state of war exists or not. I look upon you as prisoners of war.

"However, as long as there is no official state of war, I have no choice, as a representative of my government, but to see that all of you are conducted safely through the lines. This was my plan when I resumed the game where Pi Ying left off. Your being freed has nothing to do with my personal feelings, nor with the outcome of the game. My winning would have delighted me and taught you a valuable lesson. But it would have made no difference in your fates." He lighted his cigarette and continued to look at them with severity.

"That's very chivalrous of you, Major," said Kelly.

"A matter of practical politics, I assure you. It wouldn't do to precipitate an incident between our countries just now. For a

Russian to be chivalrous with an American is a spiritual impossibility, a contradiction in terms. In a long and bitter history, we've learned and learned well to reserve our chivalry for Russians." His expression became one of complete contempt. "Perhaps you'd like to play another game, Colonel—plain chess with wooden chessmen, without Pi Ying's refinement. I don't like to have you leave here thinking you play a better game than I."

"That's nice of you, but not this evening."

"Well, then, some other time." Major Barzov motioned for the guards to open the door of the throne room. "Some other time," he said again. "There will be others like Pi Ying eager to play you with live men, and I hope I will again be privileged to be an observer." He smiled brightly. "When and where would you like it to be?"

"Unfortunately, the time and the place are up to you," said Colonel Kelly wearily. "If you insist on arranging another game, issue an invitation, Major, and I'll be there."

(1953)

TOM EDISON'S SHAGGY DOG

TWO OLD MEN sat on a park bench one morning in the sunshine of Tampa, Florida—one trying doggedly to read a book he was plainly enjoying while the other, Harold K. Bullard, told him the story of his life in the full, round, head tones of a public address system. At their feet lay Bullard's Labrador retriever, who further tormented the aged listener by probing his ankles with a large, wet nose.

Bullard, who had been, before he retired, successful in many fields, enjoyed reviewing his important past. But he faced the problem that complicates the lives of cannibals—namely: that a single victim cannot be used over and over. Anyone who had passed the time of day with him and his dog refused to share a bench with them again.

So Bullard and his dog set out through the park each day in quest of new faces. They had had good luck this morning, for they had found this stranger right away, clearly a new arrival in Florida, still buttoned up tight in heavy serge, stiff collar and necktie, and with nothing better to do than read.

"Yes," said Bullard, rounding out the first hour of his lecture, "made and lost five fortunes in my time."

"So you said," said the stranger, whose name Bullard had neglected to ask. "Easy, boy. No, no, no, boy," he said to the dog, who was growing more aggressive toward his ankles.

"Oh? Already told you that, did I?" said Bullard.

"Twice."

"Two in real estate, one in scrap iron, and one in oil and one in trucking."

"So you said."

"I did? Yes, guess I did. Two in real estate, one in scrap iron, one in oil, and one in trucking. Wouldn't take back a day of it."

"No, I suppose not," said the stranger. "Pardon me, but do you suppose you could move your dog somewhere else? He keeps—"

"Him?" said Bullard, heartily. "Friendliest dog in the world. Don't need to be afraid of him."

"I'm not afraid of him. It's just that he drives me crazy, sniffing at my ankles."

"Plastic," said Bullard, chuckling.

"What?"

"Plastic. Must be something plastic on your garters. By golly, I'll bet it's those little buttons. Sure as we're sitting here, those buttons must be plastic. That dog is nuts about plastic. Don't know why that is, but he'll sniff it out and find it if there's a speck around. Must be a deficiency in his diet, though, by gosh, he eats better than I do. Once he chewed up a whole plastic humidor. Can you beat it? *That's* the business I'd go into now, by glory, if the pill rollers hadn't told me to let up, to give the old ticker a rest."

"You could tie the dog to that tree over there," said the stranger.

"I get so darn' sore at all the youngsters these days!" said Bullard. "All of 'em mooning around about no frontiers any more. There never have been so many frontiers as there are today. You know what Horace Greeley would say today?"

"His nose is wet," said the stranger, and he pulled his ankles away, but the dog humped forward in patient pursuit. "Stop it, boy!"

"His wet nose shows he's healthy," said Bullard. " 'Go plastic, young man!' That's what Greeley'd say. 'Go atom, young man!' "

The dog had definitely located the plastic buttons on the stranger's garters and was cocking his head one way and another, thinking out ways of bringing his teeth to bear on those delicacies.

"Scat!" said the stranger.

" 'Go electronic, young man!' " said Bullard. "Don't talk to me about no opportunity any more. Opportunity's knocking down every door in the country, trying to get in. When I was young, a man had to go out and find opportunity and drag it home by the ears. Nowadays—"

"Sorry," said the stranger, evenly. He slammed his book shut, stood and jerked his ankle away from the dog. "I've got to be on my way. So good day, sir."

He stalked across the park, found another bench, sat down with a sigh and began to read. His respiration had just returned to normal, when he felt the wet sponge of the dog's nose on his ankles again.

"Oh—it's you!" said Bullard, sitting down beside him. "He was tracking you. He was on the scent of something, and I just let him have his head. What'd I tell you about plastic?" He looked about contentedly. "Don't blame you for moving on. It was stuffy back there. No shade to speak of and not a sign of a breeze."

"Would the dog go away if I bought him a humidor?" said the stranger.

"Pretty good joke, pretty good joke," said Bullard, amiably. Suddenly he clapped the stranger on his knee. "Sa-ay, you aren't in plastics, are you? Here I've been blowing off about plastics, and for all I know that's your line."

"My line?" said the stranger crisply, laying down his book. "Sorry—I've never had a line. I've been a drifter since the age of nine, since Edison set up his laboratory next to my home, and showed me the intelligence analyzer."

"Edison?" said Bullard. "Thomas Edison, the inventor?"

"If you want to call him that, go ahead," said the stranger.

"If I *want* to call him that?"—Bullard guffawed—"I guess I just will! Father of the light bulb and I don't know what all."

"If you want to think he invented the light bulb, go ahead. No harm in it." The stranger resumed his reading.

"Say, what is this?" said Bullard, suspiciously. "You pulling my leg? What's this about an intelligence analyzer? I never heard of that."

"Of course you haven't," said the stranger. "Mr. Edison and I promised to keep it a secret. I've never told anyone. Mr. Edison broke his promise and told Henry Ford, but Ford made him promise not to tell anybody else—for the good of humanity."

Bullard was entranced. "Uh, this intelligence analyzer," he said, "it analyzed intelligence, did it?"

"It was an electric butter churn," said the stranger.

"Seriously now," Bullard coaxed.

"Maybe it *would* be better to talk it over with someone," said the stranger. "It's a terrible thing to keep bottled up inside me, year in and year out. But how can I be sure that it won't go any further?"

"My word as a gentleman," Bullard assured him.

"I don't suppose I could find a stronger guarantee than that, could I?" said the stranger, judiciously.

"There is no stronger guarantee," said Bullard, proudly. "Cross my heart and hope to die!"

"Very well." The stranger leaned back and closed his eyes, seeming to travel backward through time. He was silent for a full minute, during which Bullard watched with respect.

"It was back in the fall of eighteen seventy-nine," said the stranger at last, softly. "Back in the village of Menlo Park, New Jersey. I was a boy of nine. A young man we all thought was a wizard had set up a laboratory next door to my home, and there were flashes and crashes inside, and all sorts of scary goings-on. The neighborhood children were warned to keep away, not to make any noise that would bother the wizard.

"I didn't get to know Edison right off, but his dog Sparky and I got to be steady pals. A dog a whole lot like yours, Sparky was, and we used to wrestle all over the neighborhood. Yes, sir, your dog is the image of Sparky."

"Is that so?" said Bullard, flattered.

"Gospel," replied the stranger. "Well, one day Sparky and I were wrestling around, and we wrestled right up to the door of Edison's laboratory. The next thing I knew, Sparky had pushed me in through the door, and bam! I was sitting on the laboratory floor, looking up at Mr. Edison himself."

"Bet he was sore," said Bullard, delighted.

"You can bet I was scared," said the stranger. "I thought I was face to face with Satan himself. Edison had wires hooked to his ears and running down to a little black box in his lap! I started to scoot, but he caught me by my collar and made me sit down.

" 'Boy,' said Edison, 'it's always darkest before the dawn. I want you to remember that.'

" 'Yes, sir,' I said.

" 'For over a year, my boy,' Edison said to me, 'I've been try-ing to find a filament that will last in an incandescent lamp. Hair, string, splinters—nothing works. So while I was trying to think of something else to try, I started tinkering with another idea of mine, just letting off steam. I put this together,' he said, showing me the little black box. 'I thought maybe intelligence was just a certain kind of electricity, so I made this intelligence analyzer here. It works! You're the first one to know about it, my boy. But I don't know why you shouldn't be. It will be your generation that will grow up in the glorious new era when people will be as easily graded as oranges.' "

"I don't believe it!" said Bullard.

"May I be struck by lightning this very instant!" said the stranger. "And it did work, too. Edison had tried out the ana-lyzer on the men in his shop, without telling them what he was up to. The smarter a man was, by gosh, the farther the needle on the indicator in the little black box swung to the right. I let him try it on me, and the needle just lay where it was and trem-bled. But dumb as I was, then is when I made my one and only contribution to the world. As I say, I haven't lifted a finger since."

"Whadja do?" said Bullard, eagerly.

"I said, 'Mr. Edison, sir, let's try it on the dog.' And I wish you could have seen the show that dog put on when I said it!

Old Sparky barked and howled and scratched to get out. When he saw we meant business, that he wasn't going to get out, he made a beeline right for the intelligence analyzer and knocked it out of Edison's hands. But we cornered him, and Edison held him down while I touched the wires to his ears. And would you believe it, that needle sailed clear across the dial, way past a little red pencil mark on the dial face!"

"The dog busted it," said Bullard.

" 'Mr. Edison, sir,' I said, 'what's that red mark mean?'

" 'My boy,' said Edison, 'it means that the instrument is broken, because that red mark is me.' "

"I'll say it was broken," said Bullard.

The stranger said gravely, "But it wasn't broken. No, sir. Edison checked the whole thing, and it was in apple-pie order. When Edison told me that, it was then that Sparky, crazy to get out, gave himself away."

"How?" said Bullard, suspiciously.

"We really had him locked in, see? There were three locks on the door—a hook and eye, a bolt, and a regular knob and latch. That dog stood up, unhooked the hook, pushed the bolt back and had the knob in his teeth when Edison stopped him."

"No!" said Bullard.

"Yes!" said the stranger, his eyes shining. "And then is when Edison showed me what a great scientist he was. He was willing to face the truth, no matter how unpleasant it might be.

" 'So!' said Edison to Sparky. 'Man's best friend, huh? Dumb animal, huh?'

"That Sparky was a caution. He pretended not to hear. He scratched himself and bit fleas and went around growling at rat-holes—anything to get out of looking Edison in the eye.

" 'Pretty soft, isn't it, Sparky?' said Edison. 'Let somebody else worry about getting food, building shelters and keeping warm, while you sleep in front of a fire or go chasing after the girls or raise hell with the boys. No mortgages, no politics, no war, no work, no worry. Just wag the old tail or lick a hand, and you're all taken care of.'

" 'Mr. Edison,' I said, 'do you mean to tell me that dogs are smarter than people?'

"'Smarter?' said Edison. 'I'll tell the world! And what have I been doing for the past year? Slaving to work out a light bulb so dogs can play at night!'

"'Look, Mr. Edison,' said Sparky, 'why not—'"

"Hold on!" roared Bullard.

"Silence!" shouted the stranger, triumphantly. "'Look, Mr. Edison,' said Sparky, 'why not keep quiet about this? It's been working out to everybody's satisfaction for hundreds of thousands of years. Let sleeping dogs lie. You forget all about it, destroy the intelligence analyzer, and I'll tell you what to use for a lamp filament.'"

"Hogwash!" said Bullard, his face purple.

The stranger stood. "You have my solemn word as a gentleman. That dog rewarded *me* for my silence with a stock-market tip that made me independently wealthy for the rest of my days. And the last words that Sparky ever spoke were to Thomas Edison. 'Try a piece of carbonized cotton thread,' he said. Later, he was torn to bits by a pack of dogs that had gathered outside the door, listening."

The stranger removed his garters and handed them to Bullard's dog. "A small token of esteem, sir, for an ancestor of yours who talked himself to death. Good day." He tucked his book under his arm and walked away.

(1953)

NEW DICTIONARY

I WONDER NOW what Ernest Hemingway's dictionary looked like, since he got along so well with dinky words that everybody can spell and truly understand. Mr. Hotchner, was it a frazzled wreck? My own is a tossed salad of instant coffee and tobacco crumbs and India paper, and anybody seeing it might fairly conclude that I ransack it hourly for a vocabulary like Arnold J. Toynbee's. The truth is that I have broken its spine looking up the difference between *principle* and *principal*, and how to spell *cashmere*. It is a dear leviathan left to me by my father, "Webster's New International Dictionary of the English Language," based on the "International Dictionary" of 1890 and 1900. It doesn't have *radar* in it, or *Wernher von Braun* or *sulfathiazole*, but I *know* what *they* are. One time I actually *took* sulfathiazole.

And now I have this enormous and beautiful new bomb from Random House. I don't mean "bomb" in a pejorative sense, or in any dictionary sense, for that matter. I mean that the book is heavy and pregnant, and makes you think. One of the things it makes you think is that any gang of bright people with scads of money behind them can become appalling competitors in the American-unabridged-dictionary industry. They can make certain that they have all the words the other dictionaries have, then add words which have joined the language since the others were published, and then avoid mistakes that the others have caught particular hell for.

Random House has thrown in a color atlas of the world, as well, and concise dictionaries of French, Spanish, German, and Italian. And would you look at the price? And, lawsy me, Christmas is coming.

When Mario Pei reviewed the savagely-bopped third revised edition of the "Merriam-Webster" for The Times in 1961, he complained of the "residual prudishness" which still excluded certain four-letter words, "despite their copious appearance in numerous works of contemporary 'literature' as well as on restroom walls." Random House has satisfied this complaint somewhat. They haven't included enough of the words to allow a Pakistani to decode "Last Exit to Brooklyn," or "Ulysses," either —but they have made brave beginnings, dealing, wisely I think, with the alimentary canal. I found only one abrupt verb for sexually congressing a woman, and we surely have Edward Albee to thank for its currency, though he gets no credit for it. The verb is *hump*, as in "hump the hostess."

If my emphasis on dirty words so early in this review seems childish, I can only reply that I, as a child, would never have started going through unabridged dictionaries if I hadn't suspected that there were dirty words hidden in there, where only grownups were supposed to find them. I always ended the searches feeling hot and stuffy inside, and looking at the queer illustrations—at the *trammel wheel,* the *arbalest,* and the *dugong.*

Of course, one dictionary is as good as another to most people, who use them for spellers and bet-settlers and accessories to crossword puzzles and Scrabble games. But some people use them for more than that, or *mean* to. This was brought home to me only the other evening, whilst I was supping with the novelist and short-story writer, Richard Yates, and Prof. Robert Scholes, the famous praiser of John Barth's "Giles Goat-Boy." Yates asked Scholes, anxiously it seemed to me, which unabridged dictionary he should buy. He had just received a gorgeous grant for creative writing from the Federal Gumment, and the first thing he was going to buy was his entire language between hard covers. He was afraid that he might get a clunker—a word, by the way, not in this Random House job.

Scholes replied judiciously that Yates should get the second edition of the "Merriam-Webster," which was *prescriptive* rather than *descriptive*. Prescriptive, as nearly as I could tell, was like an honest cop, and descriptive was like a boozed-up war buddy from Mobile, Ala. Yates said he would get the tough one; but, my goodness, *he* doesn't need official instructions in English any more than he needs training wheels on his bicycle. As Scholes said later, Yates is the sort of man lexicographers read in order to discover what pretty new things the language is up to.

To find out in a rush whether a dictionary is prescriptive or descriptive, you look up *ain't* and *like*. I learned this trick of horseback logomachy from reviews of the "Merriam-Webster" third edition. And here is the rundown on *ain't*: the "Merriam-Webster" first edition says that it is colloquial or illiterate, the second says it is dialect or illiterate, and the third says that *ain't* is, "though disapproved by many and more common in less educated speech, used orally . . . by many cultivated speakers esp. in the phrase *ain't I*." I submit that this nation is so uniformly populated by parvenus with the heebie-jeebies that the phrase *ain't I* is heard about as frequently as the mating cry of the heath hen.

Random House says this about *ain't*: "*Ain't* is so traditionally and widely regarded as a nonstandard form that it should be shunned by all who prefer to avoid being considered illiterate. *Ain't* occurs occasionally in the informal speech of some educated users, especially in self-consciously [sic] or folksy or humorous contexts *(Ain't it the truth! She ain't what she used to be!)*, but it is completely unacceptable in formal writing and speech. Although the expression *ain't I* is perhaps defensible— and it is considered more logical than *aren't I?* and more euphonious than *amn't I?*—the well-advised person will avoid any use of *ain't*." How's that for advice to parvenus?

My mother isn't mentioned, but what she taught me to say in place of *ain't I?* or *aren't I?* or *amn't I?* was *am I not?* Speed isn't everything. So I lose a micro-second here and there. The main thing is to be a *graceful* parvenu.

As for the use of *like* as though it were interchangeable with *as:* "M-W-1" says, "The use of *like* as a conjunction meaning *as* (as, *Do like I do*), though occasionally found in good writers, is a provincialism and contrary to good usage." "M-W-2" says that the same thing "is freely used only in illiterate speech and is now regarded as incorrect." "M-W-3" issues no warnings whatsoever, and flaunts models of current, O.K. usage from the St. Petersburg (Fla.) Independent, "wore his clothes like he was . . . afraid of getting dirt on them," and Art Linkletter, "impromptu programs where they ask questions much like I do on the air." "M-W-3," incidentally, came out during the dying days of the Eisenhower Administration, when simply *everybody* was talking like Art Linkletter.

Random House, in the catbird seat, since it gets to recite last, declares in 1966, "The use of *like* in place of *as* is universally condemned by teachers and editors, notwithstanding its wide currency, especially in advertising slogans. *Do as I say, not as I do* does not admit of *like* instead of *as*. In an occasional idiomatic phrase, it is somewhat less offensive when substituted for *as if* (*He raced down the street like crazy*), but this example is clearly colloquial and not likely to be found in any but the most informal written contexts." I find this excellent. It even tells who will hurt you if you make a mistake, and it withholds aid and comfort from those friends of cancer and money, those greedy enemies of the language who teach our children to say after school, "Winston tastes good like a cigarette should."

Random House is damned if it will set that slogan in type.

As you rumple through this new dictionary, looking for dirty words and schoolmarmisms tempered by worldliness, you will discover that biographies and major place names and even the names of famous works of art are integrated with the vocabulary: *A Streetcar Named Desire, Ralph Ellison, Mona Lisa, Kiselevsk.* I worry about the biographies and the works of art, since they seem a mixed bag, possibly locked for all eternity in a matrix of type. *Norman Mailer* is there, for instance, but not *William Styron* or *James Jones* or *Vance Bourjaily* or *Edward Lewis Wallant.* And are we to be told throughout eternity this and no more about *Alger Hiss:* "born 1904, U.S. public official"? And why is there no entry for *Whittaker Chambers?* And who promoted Peress?

It is the biographical inclusions and exclusions, in fact, which make this dictionary an ideal gift for the paranoiac on everybody's Christmas list. He will find dark entertainments without end between pages i and 2,059. Why are we informed about Joe Kennedy, Sr., and Jack and Bobby, but not about Teddy or Jacqueline? What is somebody trying to tell us when T. S. Eliot is called a *British* poet and W. H. Auden is called an *English* poet? (Maybe the distinction aims at accounting for Auden's American citizenship.) And when Robert Welch, Jr., is tagged as a "retired U.S. candy manufacturer," is this meant to make him look silly? And why is the memory of John Dillinger perpetuated, while of Adolf Eichmann there is neither gibber nor squeak?

Whoever decides to crash the unabridged dictionary game next—and it will probably be General Motors or Ford—they will winnow this work heartlessly for bloopers. There can't be many, since Random House has winnowed its noble predecessors. The big blooper, it seems to me, is not putting the biographies and works of art in an appendix, where they can be cheaply revised or junked or added to.

Have I made it clear that this book is a beauty? You can't beat the contents, and you can't beat the price. Somebody will beat both sooner or later, of course, because that is good old Free Enterprise, where the consumer benefits from battles between jolly green giants.

And, as I've said, one dictionary is as good as another for most people. *Homo Americanus* is going to go on speaking and writing the way he always has, no matter what dictionary he owns. Consider the citizen who was asked recently what he thought of President Johnson's use of the slang expression "cool it" in a major speech:

"It's fine with me," he replied. "Now's not the time for the President of the United States to worry about the King's English. After all, we're living in an informal age. Politicians don't go around in top hats any more. There's no reason why the English language shouldn't wear sports clothes, too. I don't say the President should speak like an illiterate. But 'cool it' is folksy, and the Chief Executive should be allowed to sound human. You can't be too corny for the American people—all the decent sentiments in life are corny. But linguistically speaking, Disraeli is dullsville."

These words, by the way, came from the larynx of Bennett Cerf, publisher of "The Random House Dictionary of the English Language." Moral: Everybody associated with a new dictionary ain't necessarily a new Samuel Johnson.

(1967)

NEXT DOOR

THE OLD HOUSE was divided into two dwellings by a thin wall that passed on, with high fidelity, sounds on either side. On the north side were the Leonards. On the south side were the Hargers.

The Leonards—husband, wife, and eight-year-old son—had just moved in. And, aware of the wall, they kept their voices down as they argued in a friendly way as to whether or not the boy, Paul, was old enough to be left alone for the evening.

"Shhhhh!" said Paul's father.

"Was I shouting?" said his mother. "I was talking in a perfectly normal tone."

"If I could hear Harger pulling a cork, he can certainly hear you," said his father.

"I didn't say anything I'd be ashamed to have anybody hear," said Mrs. Leonard.

"You called Paul a baby," said Mr. Leonard. "That certainly embarrasses Paul—and it embarrasses me."

"It's just a way of talking," she said.

"It's a way we've got to stop," he said. "And we can stop treating him like a baby, too—*tonight*. We simply shake his hand, walk out, and go to the movie." He turned to Paul. "You're not afraid—are you boy?"

"I'll be all right," said Paul. He was very tall for his age, and thin, and had a soft, sleepy, radiant sweetness engendered by his mother. "I'm fine."

"Damn right!" said his father, clouting him on the back. "It'll be an adventure."

"I'd feel better about this adventure, if we could get a sitter," said his mother.

"If it's going to spoil the picture for you," said his father, "let's take him with us."

Mrs. Leonard was shocked. "Oh—it isn't for children."

"I don't care," said Paul amiably. The why of their not wanting him to see certain movies, certain magazines, certain books, certain television shows was a mystery he respected—even relished a little.

"It wouldn't kill him to see it," said his father.

"You *know* what it's about," she said.

"What *is* it about?" said Paul innocently.

Mrs. Leonard looked to her husband for help, and got none. "It's about a girl who chooses her friends unwisely," she said.

"Oh," said Paul. "That doesn't sound very interesting."

"Are we going, or aren't we?" said Mr. Leonard impatiently. "The show starts in ten minutes."

Mrs. Leonard bit her lip. "All right!" she said bravely. "You lock the windows and the back door, and I'll write down the telephone numbers for the police and the fire department and the theater and Dr. Failey." She turned to Paul. "You *can* dial, can't you, dear?"

"He's been dialing for years!" cried Mr. Leonard.

"Sssssh!" said Mrs. Leonard.

"Sorry," Mr. Leonard bowed to the wall. "My apologies."

"Paul, dear," said Mrs. Leonard, "what are you going to do while we're gone?"

"Oh—look through my microscope, I guess," said Paul.

"You're not going to be looking at germs, are you?" she said.

"Nope—just hair, sugar, pepper, stuff like that," said Paul.

His mother frowned judiciously. "I think that would be all right, don't you?" she said to Mr. Leonard.

"Fine!" said Mr. Leonard. "Just as long as the pepper doesn't make him sneeze!"

"I'll be careful," said Paul.

Mr. Leonard winced. "Shhhhh!" he said.

Soon after Paul's parents left, the radio in the Harger apartment went on. It was on softly at first—so softly that Paul, looking through his microscope on the living room coffee table, couldn't make out the announcer's words. The music was frail and dissonant—unidentifiable.

Gamely, Paul tried to listen to the music rather than to the man and woman who were fighting.

Paul squinted through the eyepiece of his microscope at a bit of his hair far below, and he turned a knob to bring the hair into focus. It looked like a glistening brown eel, flecked here and there with tiny spectra where the light struck the hair just so.

There—the voices of the man and woman were getting louder again, drowning out the radio. Paul twisted the microscope knob nervously, and the objective lens ground into the glass slide on which the hair rested.

The woman was shouting now.

Paul unscrewed the lens, and examined it for damage.

Now the man shouted back—shouted something awful, unbelievable.

Paul got a sheet of lens tissue from his bedroom, and dusted at the frosted dot on the lens, where the lens had bitten into the slide. He screwed the lens back in place.

All was quiet again next door—except for the radio.

Paul looked down into the microscope, down into the milky mist of the damaged lens.

Now the fight was beginning again—louder and louder, cruel and crazy.

Trembling, Paul sprinkled grains of salt on a fresh slide, and put it under the microscope.

The woman shouted again, a high, ragged, poisonous shout.

Paul turned the knob too hard, and the fresh slide cracked and fell in triangles to the floor. Paul stood, shaking, wanting to shout, too—to shout in terror and bewilderment. It had to stop. Whatever it was, it *had* to stop!

"If you're going to yell, turn up the radio!" the man cried.

Paul heard the clicking of the woman's heels across the floor. The radio volume swelled until the boom of the bass made Paul feel like he was trapped in a drum.

"And now!" bellowed the radio, "for Katy from Fred! For Nancy from Bob, who thinks she's swell! For Arthur, from one who's worshipped him from afar for six weeks! Here's the old Glenn Miller Band and that all-time favorite, *Stardust!* Remember! If you have a dedication, call Milton nine-three-thousand! Ask for All-Night Sam, the record man!"

The music picked up the house and shook it.

A door slammed next door. Now someone hammered on a door.

Paul looked down into his microscope once more, looked at nothing—while a prickling sensation spread over his skin. He faced the truth: The man and woman would kill each other, if he didn't stop them.

He beat on the wall with his fist. "Mr. Harger! Stop it!" he cried. "Mrs. Harger! Stop it!"

"For Ollie from Lavina!" All-Night Sam cried back at him. "For Ruth from Carl, who'll never forget last Tuesday! For Wilbur from Mary, who's lonesome tonight! Here's the Sauter-Finnegan Band asking, *Love, What Are You Doing to My Heart?*"

Next door, crockery smashed, filling a split second of radio silence. And then the tidal wave of music drowned everything again.

Paul stood by the wall, trembling in his helplessness. "Mr. Harger! Mrs. Harger! Please!"

"Remember the number!" said All-Night Sam. "Milton nine-three-thousand!

Dazed, Paul went to the phone and dialed the number.

"WJCD," said the switchboard operator.

"Would you kindly connect me with All-Night Sam?" said Paul.

"Hello!" said All-Night Sam. He was eating, talking with a full mouth. In the background, Paul could hear sweet, bleating music, the original of what was rending the radio next door.

"I wonder if I might make a dedication," said Paul.

"Dunno why not," said Sam. "Ever belong to any organization listed as subversive by the Attorney General's office?"

Paul thought a moment. "Nossir—I don't think so, sir," he said.
"Shoot," said Sam.

"From Mr. Lemuel K. Harger to Mrs. Harger," said Paul.

"What's the message?" said Sam.

"I love you," said Paul. "Let's make up and start all over again."
The woman's voice was so shrill with passion that it cut
through the din of the radio, and even Sam heard it.

"Kid—are you in trouble?" said Sam. "Your folks fighting?"

Paul was afraid that Sam would hang up on him if he found
out that Paul wasn't a blood relative of the Hargers. "Yessir," he
said.

"And you're trying to pull 'em back together again with this
dedication?" said Sam.

"Yessir," said Paul.

Sam became very emotional. "O.K., kid," he said hoarsely,
"I'll give it everything I've got. Maybe it'll work. I once saved a
guy from shooting himself the same way."

"How did you do that?" said Paul, fascinated.

"He called up and said he was gonna blow his brains out,"
said Sam, "and I played *The Bluebird of Happiness*." He hung
up.

Paul dropped the telephone into its cradle. The music stopped,
and Paul's hair stood on end. For the first time, the fantastic
speed of modern communications was real to him, and he was
appalled.

"Folks!" said Sam, "I guess everybody stops and wonders sometimes what the heck he thinks he's doin' with the life the good
Lord gave him! It may seem funny to you folks, because I always keep up a cheerful front, no matter how I feel inside, that
I wonder sometimes, too! And then, just like some angel was
trying to tell me, 'Keep going, Sam, keep going,' something like
this comes along."

"Folks!" said Sam, "I've been asked to bring a man and his
wife back together again through the miracle of radio! I guess
there's no sense in kidding ourselves about marriage! It isn't any
bowl of cherries! There's ups and downs, and sometimes folks
don't see how they can go on!"

Paul was impressed with the wisdom and authority of Sam.

Having the radio turned up high made sense now, for Sam was speaking like the right-hand man of God.

When Sam paused for effect, all was still next door. Already the miracle was working.

"Now," said Sam, "a guy in my business has to be half musician, half philosopher, half psychiatrist, and half electrical engineer! And! If I've learned one thing from working with all you wonderful people out there, it's this: if folks would swallow their self-respect and pride, there wouldn't be any more divorces!"

There were affectionate cooings from next door. A lump grew in Paul's throat as he thought about the beautiful thing he and Sam were bringing to pass.

"Folks!" said Sam, "that's all I'm gonna say about love and marriage! That's all anybody needs to know! And now, for Mrs. Lemuel K. Harger, from Mr. Harger—I love you! Let's make up and start all over again!" Sam choked up. "Here's Eartha Kitt, and *Somebody Bad Stole De Wedding Bell!*"

The radio next door went off.

The world lay still.

A purple emotion flooded Paul's being. Childhood dropped away, and he hung, dizzy, on the brink of life, rich, violent, rewarding.

There was movement next door—slow, foot-dragging movement.

"So," said the woman.

"Charlotte—" said the man uneasily. "Honey—I swear."

" 'I love you,' " she said bitterly, " 'let's make up and start all over again.' "

"Baby," said the man desperately, "it's another Lemuel K. Harger. It's got to be!"

"You want your wife back?" she said. "All right—I won't get in her way. She can have you, Lemuel—you jewel beyond price, you."

"*She* must have called the station," said the man.

"She can have you, you philandering, two-timing, two-bit Lochinvar," she said. "But you won't be in very good condition."

"Charlotte—put down that gun," said the man. "Don't do anything you'll be sorry for."

"That's all behind me, you worm," she said.

There were three shots.

Paul ran out into the hall, and bumped into the woman as she burst from the Harger apartment. She was a big, blonde woman, all soft and awry, like an unmade bed.

She and Paul screamed at the same time, and then she grabbed him as he started to run.

"You want candy?" she said wildly. "Bicycle?"

"No, thank you," said Paul shrilly. "Not at this time."

"You haven't seen or heard a thing!" she said. "You know what happens to squealers?"

"Yes!" cried Paul.

She dug into her purse, and brought out a perfumed mulch of face tissues, bobbypins and cash. "Here!" she panted. "It's yours! And there's more where that came from, if you keep your mouth shut." She stuffed it into his trousers pocket.

She looked at him fiercely, then fled into the street.

Paul ran back into his apartment, jumped into bed, and pulled the covers up over his head. In the hot, dark cave of the bed, he cried because he and All-Night Sam had helped to kill a man.

A policeman came clumping into the house very soon, and he knocked on both apartment doors with his billyclub.

Numb, Paul crept out of the hot, dark cave, and answered the door. Just as he did, the door across the hall opened, and there stood Mr. Harger, haggard but whole.

"Yes, sir?" said Harger. He was a small, balding man, with a hairline mustache. "Can I help you?"

"The neighbors heard some shots," said the policeman.

"Really?" said Harger urbanely. He dampened his mustache with the tip of his little finger. "How bizarre. I heard nothing." He looked at Paul sharply. "Have you been playing with your father's guns again, young man?"

"Oh, nossir!" said Paul, horrified.

"Where are your folks?" said the policeman to Paul.

"At the movies," said Paul.

"You're all alone?" said the policeman.

"Yessir," said Paul. "It's an adventure."

"I'm sorry I said that about the guns," said Harger. "I certainly would have heard any shots in this house. The walls are thin as paper, and I heard nothing."

Paul looked at him gratefully.

"And you didn't hear any shots, either, kid?" said the policeman.

Before Paul could find an answer, there was a disturbance out on the street. A big, motherly woman was getting out of a taxicab and wailing at the top of her lungs. "Lem! Lem, baby."

She barged into the foyer, a suitcase bumping against her leg and tearing her stocking to shreds. She dropped the suitcase, and ran to Harger, throwing her arms around him.

"I got your message, darling," she said, "and I did just what All-Night Sam told me to do. I swallowed my self-respect, and here I am!"

"Rose, Rose, Rose—my little Rose," said Harger. "Don't ever leave me again." They grappled with each other affectionately, and staggered into their apartment.

"Just look at this apartment!" said Mrs. Harger. "Men are just lost without women!" As she closed the door, Paul could see that she was awfully pleased with the mess.

"You *sure* you didn't hear any shots?" said the policeman to Paul.

The ball of money in Paul's pocket seemed to swell to the size of a watermelon. "Yessir," he croaked.

The policeman left.

Paul shut his apartment door, shuffled into his bedroom, and collapsed on the bed.

The next voices Paul heard came from his own side of the wall. The voices were sunny—the voices of his mother and father. His mother was singing a nursery rhyme and his father was undressing him.

"Diddle-diddle-dumpling, my son John," piped his mother, "Went to bed with his stockings on. One shoe off, and one shoe on—diddle-diddle-dumpling, my son John."

Paul opened his eyes.

"Hi, big boy," said his father, "you went to sleep with all your clothes on."

"How's my little adventurer?" said his mother.

"O.K.," said Paul sleepily. "How was the show?"

"It wasn't for children, honey," said his mother. "You would have liked the short subject, though. It was all about bears—cunning little cubs."

Paul's father handed her Paul's trousers, and she shook them out, and hung them neatly on the back of a chair by the bed. She patted them smooth, and felt the ball of money in the pocket. "Little boys' pockets!" she said, delighted. "Full of childhood's mysteries. An enchanted frog? A magic pocketknife from a fairy princess?" She caressed the lump.

"He's not a little boy—he's a big boy," said Paul's father. "And he's too old to be thinking about fairy princesses."

Paul's mother held up her hands. "Don't rush it, don't rush it. When I saw him asleep there, I realized all over again how dreadfully short childhood is." She reached into the pocket and sighed wistfully. "Little boys are so hard on clothes—especially pockets."

She brought out the ball and held it under Paul's nose. "Now, would you mind telling Mommy what we have here?" she said gaily.

The ball bloomed like a frowzy chrysanthemum, with ones, fives, tens, twenties, and lipstick-stained Kleenex for petals. And rising from it, befuddling Paul's young mind, was the pungent musk of perfume.

Paul's father sniffed the air. "What's that smell?" he said.

Paul's mother rolled her eyes. "*Tabu*," she said.

(1955)

MORE STATELY
MANSIONS

WE'VE KNOWN the McClellans, Grace and George, for about two years now. They were the first neighbors to call on us and welcome us to the village.

I expected that initial conversation to lag uncomfortably after the first pleasantries, but not at all. Grace, her eyes quick and bright as a sparrow's, found subject matter enough to keep her talking for hours.

"You know," she said excitedly, "your living room could be a perfect dream! Couldn't it, George? Can't you see it?"

"Yup," said her husband. "Nice, all right."

"Just tear out all this white-painted woodwork," Grace said, her eyes narrowing. "Panel it all in knotty pine wiped with linseed oil with a little umber added. Cover the couch in lipstick red—*red* red. Know what I mean?"

"Red?" said Anne, my wife.

"Red! Don't be afraid of color."

"I'll try not to be," Anne said.

"And just cover the whole wall there, those two ugly little windows and all, with bottle-green curtains. Can't you see it? It'd be almost exactly like that problem living room in the February *Better House and Garden.* You remember that, of course."

"I must have missed that," said Anne. The month was August.

"Or was it *Good Homelife,* George?" Grace said.

"Don't remember offhand," said George.

"Well, I can look it up in my files and put my hand right on it." Grace stood up suddenly, and, uninvited, started a tour through the rest of the house.

She went from room to room, consigning a piece of furniture to the Salvation Army, detecting a fraudulent antique, shrugging partitions out of existence, and pacing off a chartreuse, wall-to-wall carpet we would have to order before we did another thing. "Start with the carpet," she said firmly, "and build from there. It'll pull your whole downstairs together if you build from the carpet."

"Um," said Anne.

"I hope you saw Nineteen Basic Carpet Errors in the June *Home Beautiful.*"

"Oh yes, yes indeed," Anne said.

"Good. Then I don't have to tell you how wrong you can go, *not* building from the carpet. George—Oh, he's still in the living room."

I caught a glimpse of George on the living-room couch, lost in his own thoughts. He straightened up and smiled.

I followed Grace, trying to change the subject. "Let's see, you are on our north side. Who's to our south?"

Grace held up her hands. "Oh! You haven't met them—the Jenkinses. George," she called, "they want to know about the Jenkinses." From her voice, I gathered that our southerly neighbors were sort of lovable beachcombers.

"Now, Grace, they're nice enough people," George said.

"Oooh, George," Grace said, "you know how the Jenkinses are. Yes, they're nice, but . . ." She laughed and shook her head.

"But what?" I said. The possibilities raced through my mind. Nudists? Heroin addicts? Anarchists? Hamster raisers?

"In 1945 they moved in," Grace said, "and right off the bat

they bought two beautiful Hitchcock chairs, and . . ." This time
she sighed and shrugged.

"And what?" I demanded. And spilled India ink on them?
And found a bundle of thousand-dollar bills rolled up in a hollow leg?

"And that's all," Grace said. "They just stopped right there."

"How's that?" said Anne.

"Don't you see? They started out beautifully with those two
chairs; then they just petered out."

"Oh," said Anne slowly. "I see—a flash in the pan. So *that's*
what's wrong with the Jenkinses. Aha!"

"Fie on the Jenkinses," I said.

Grace didn't hear me. She was patrolling between the living
room and dining room, and I noticed that every time she entered
or left the living room, she made a jog in her course, always at
exactly the same place. Curious, I went over to the spot she
avoided, and bounced up and down a couple of times to see if
the floor was unsound at that point, or what.

In she came again, and she looked at me with surprise. "Oh!"

"Did I do something wrong?" I asked.

"I just didn't expect to find *you* there."

"Sorry."

"That's where the cobbler's bench goes, you know."

I stepped aside, and watched uncomfortably as she bent over
the phantom cobbler's bench. I think it was then that she first
alarmed me, made me feel a little less like laughing.

"With one or two little nail drawers open, and ivy growing
out of them," she explained. "Cute?" She stepped around it, being careful not to bark her shins, and went up the stairs to the
second floor. "Do you mind if I have a look around up here?"
she asked gaily.

"Go right ahead," said Anne.

George had gotten up off the sofa. He stood looking up the
stairs for a minute; then he held up his empty highball glass.
"Mind if I have another?"

"Say, I'm sorry, George. We haven't been taking very good
care of you. You bet. Help yourself. The bottle's there in the
dining room."

He went straight to it, and poured himself a good inch and a half of whisky in the bottom of the tumbler.

"The tile in this bathroom is all wrong for your towels, of course," Grace said from upstairs.

Anne, who had padded after her like a housemaid, agreed bleakly. "Of course."

George lifted his glass, winked, and drained it. "Don't let her throw you," he said. "Just her way of talking. Got a damn' nice house here. *I* like it, and so does she."

"Thanks, George. That's nice of you."

Anne and Grace came downstairs again, Anne looking quite bushed. "Oh, you men!" Grace said. "You just think we're silly, don't you?" She smiled companionably at Anne. "They just don't understand what interests women. What were you two talking about while we were having such a good time?"

"I was telling him he ought to wallpaper his trees and make chintz curtains for his keyholes," George said.

"Mmmmm," said Grace. "Well, time to go home, dear."

She paused outside the front door. "Nice basic lines to this door," she said. "That gingerbread will come right off, if you get a chisel under it. And you can lighten it by rubbing on white paint, then rubbing it off again right away. It'll look more like *you*."

"You've been awfully helpful," said Anne.

"Well, it's a dandy house the way it is," George said.

"I swear," Grace said, "I'll never understand how so many artists are men. No man I ever met had a grain of artistic temperament in him."

"Bushwa," said George quietly. And then he surprised me. The glance he gave Grace was affectionate and possessive.

"It *is* a dull little dump, I guess," said Anne gloomily, after the McClellans had left.

"Oh, listen—it's a swell house."

"I guess. But it needs so much done to it. I didn't realize. Golly, their place must be something. They've been in it for five years, she said. You can imagine what she could do to a place in five years—everything right, right down to the last nailhead."

"It isn't much from the outside. Anyway, Anne, this isn't like you."

She shook her head, as though to wake herself up. "It isn't, is it? Never in my life have I had the slightest interest in keeping up with the neighbors. But there's something about that woman."

"To hell with her! Let's throw in our lot with the Jenkinses."

Anne laughed. Grace's spell was wearing off. "Are you mad? Be friends with those two-chair people, those quitters?"

"Well, we'd make our friendship contingent on their getting a new couch to go with the chairs."

"And not any couch, but the *right* couch."

"If they want to be friends of ours, they mustn't be afraid of color, and they'd better build from the carpet."

"That goes without saying," said Anne crisply.

But it was a long time before we found leisure for more than a nod at the Jenkinses. Grace McClellan spent most of her waking hours at our house. Almost every morning, as I was leaving for work, she would stagger into our house under a load of home magazines and insist that Anne pore over them with her in search of just the right solutions for our particular problem house.

"They must be awfully rich," Anne said at dinner one night.

"I don't think so," I said. "George has a little leather-goods store that you hardly ever see anybody in."

"Well, then every cent must go into the house."

"That I can believe. But what makes you think they're rich?"

"To hear that woman talk, you'd think money was nothing! Without batting an eyelash, she talks about ten-dollar-a-yard floor-to-ceiling draperies, says fixing up the kitchen shouldn't cost more than a lousy fifteen hundred dollars—without the fieldstone fireplace, of course."

"What's a kitchen without a fieldstone fireplace?"

"And a circular couch."

"Isn't there some way you can keep her away, Anne? She's wearing you out. Can't you just tell her you're too busy to see her?"

"I haven't the heart, she's so kind and friendly and lonely," said Anne helplessly. "Besides, there's no getting through to her. She doesn't hear what I say. Her head is just crammed full of blueprints, cloth, furniture, wallpaper, and paint."

"Change the subject."

"Change the course of the Mississippi! Talk about politics, and she talks about remodeling the White House; talk about dogs, and she talks about doghouses."

The telephone rang, and I answered it. It was Grace Mc-Clellan. "Yes, Grace?"

"You're in the office-furniture business, aren't you?"

"That's right."

"Do you ever get old filing cabinets in trade?"

"Yes. I don't like to, but sometimes I have to take them."

"Could you let me have one?"

I thought a minute. I had an old wooden wreck I was about to haul to the dump. I told her about it.

"Oh, that'll be divine! There's an article in last month's *Better House* about what to do with old filing cabinets. You can make them just darling by wallpapering them, then putting a coat of clear shellac over the paper. Can't you just see it?"

"Yep. Darling, all right. I'll bring it out tomorrow night."

"That's awfully nice of you. I wonder if you and Anne couldn't drop in for a drink then."

I accepted and hung up. "Well, the time has come," I said. "Marie Antoinette has finally invited us to have a look at Versailles."

"I'm afraid," Anne said. "It's going to make our home look so sad."

"There's more to life than decorating."

"I know, I know. I just wish you'd stay home in the daytime and keep telling me that while she's here."

The next evening, I drove the pickup truck home instead of my car, so I could deliver the old filing cabinet to Grace. Anne was already inside the McClellan house, and George came out to give me a hand.

The cabinet was an old-fashioned oak monster, and, with all

the sweating and grunting, I didn't really pay much attention to the house until we'd put down our burden in the front hall.

The first thing I noticed was that there were already two dilapidated filing cabinets in the hall, ungraced by wallpaper or clear shellac. I looked into the living room. Anne was sitting on the couch with a queer smile on her face. The couch springs had burst through the bottom and were resting nakedly on the floor. The chief illumination came from a single light bulb in a cobwebbed chandelier with sockets for six. An electric extension cord, patched with friction tape, hung from another of the sockets and led to an iron on an ironing board in the middle of the living room.

A small throw rug, the type generally seen in bathrooms, was the only floor covering, and the planks of the floor were scarred and dull from long neglect. Dust and cobwebs were everywhere, and the windows were dirty. The only sign of order or opulence was on the coffee table, where dozens of fat, slick decoration magazines were spread out like a fan.

George was nervous and more taciturn than usual, and I gathered that he was uneasy about having us in. After mixing us drinks, he sat down and maintained a fidgeting silence.

Not so with Grace. She was at a high pitch of excitement, and, seemingly, full of irrepressible pride. Sitting, rising, and sitting again a dozen times a minute, she did a sort of ballet about the room, describing exactly the way she was going to do the room over. She rubbed imaginary fabrics between her fingers, stretched out luxuriously in a wicker chair that would one day be a plum-colored chaise longue, held her hands as far apart as she could reach to indicate the span of a limed-oak television-radio-phonograph console that was to stand against one wall.

She clapped her hands and closed her eyes. "Can you see it? Can you *see* it?"

"Simply lovely," said Anne.

"And every night, just as George is coming up the walk. I'll have Martinis ready in a frosty pewter pitcher, and I'll have a record playing on the phonograph." Grace knelt before the thin air where the console would be, selected a record from nothingness, put it on the imaginary turntable, pressed a nonexistent button, and retired to the wicker chair. To my dismay, she began to rock her head back and forth in time to the phantom music.

After a minute of this, George seemed disturbed, too. "Grace! You're going to sleep." He tried to make his tone light, but real concern showed through.

Grace shook her head and opened her eyes lazily. "I wasn't sleeping; I was listening."

"It will certainly be a charming room," Anne said, looking worriedly at me.

Grace was suddenly on her feet again, charged with new energy. "And the dining room!" Impatiently, she picked up a magazine and thumbed through it. "Now, wait, where is it, where is it? No, not that one." She let the magazine drop. "Oh, of course, I clipped it last night and put it in the files. Remember, George? The dining-room table with the glass top and the place for potted flowers underneath?"

"Uh-huh."

"That's what goes in the dining room," Grace said happily. "See? You look right through the table, and there, underneath, are geraniums, African violets, or anything you want to put there. Fun?" She hurried to the filing cabinets. "You've got to see it in color, really."

Anne and I followed her politely, and waited while she ran her finger along the dividers in the drawers. The drawers, I saw, were jammed with cloth and wallpaper samples, paint color cards, and pages taken from magazines. She had already filled two cabinets, and was ready to overflow into the third, the one I'd brought. The drawers were labeled, simply, "Living room," "Kitchen," "Dining room," and so on.

"Quite a filing system," I said to George, who was just brushing by with a fresh drink in his hand.

He looked at me closely, as though he was trying to make up his mind whether I was kidding him or not. "It is," he said at last. "There's even a section about the workshop she wants me to have in the basement." He sighed. "Someday."

Grace held up a little square of transparent blue plastic. "And this is the material for the kitchen curtains, over the sink and automatic dishwasher. Waterproof, and it wipes clean."

"It's darling," Anne said. "You have an automatic dishwasher?"

"Mmmmm?" Grace said, smiling at some distant horizon. "Oh —dishwasher? No, but I know exactly the one we want. We've made up our minds on that, haven't we, George?"

"Yes, dear."

"And someday . . ." said Grace happily, running her fingers over the contents of a file drawer.

"Someday . . ." said George.

As I say, two years have passed since then, since we first met the McClellans. Anne, with compassion and tenderness, invented harmless ways of keeping Grace from spending all her time at our house with her magazines. But we formed a neighborly habit of having a drink with the McClellans once or twice a month.

I liked George, and he grew friendly and talkative when he'd made sure we weren't going to bait his wife about interior decorating, something almost everyone else in the neighborhood was fond of doing. He adored Grace, and made light of her preoccupation, as he had done at our first meeting, only when he didn't know the people before whom she was performing. Among friends, he did nothing to discourage or disparage her dreaming.

Anne bore the brunt of Grace's one-track conversations as sort of a Christian service, listening with tact and patience. George and I ignored them, and had a pleasant enough time talking about everything but interior decoration.

In these talks it came out bit by bit that George had been in a bad financial jam for years, and that things refused to get better. The "someday" that Grace had been planning for for five years, George said, seemed to recede another month as each new home magazine appeared on the newsstands. It was this, I decided, not Grace, that kept him drinking more than his share.

And the filing cabinets got fuller and fuller, and the McClellan house got dowdier and dowdier. But not once did Grace's excitement about what their house was going to be like flag. If anything, it increased, and time and again we would have to follow her about the house to hear just how it was all going to be.

And then a fairly sad thing and an awfully nice thing happened to the McClellans. The sad thing was that Grace came down with a virus infection that kept her in the hospital two months. The nice thing was that George inherited a little money from a relative he'd never met.

While Grace was in the hospital, George often had supper with us; and the day he received his legacy, his taciturnity dropped away completely. To our surprise, *he* now talked interior decoration with fervor and to the exclusion of everything else.

"You've got the bug too, now," Anne said, laughing.

"Bug, hell! I've got the money! I'm going to surprise Grace by having that house just the way she wants it, when she comes home."

"Exactly, George?"

"Eggs-zactly!"

And Anne and I were willingly drafted to help him. We went through Grace's files and found detailed specifications for every room, right down to bookends and soap dishes. It was a tough job tracking down every item, but George was indefatigable, and so was Anne, and money was no object.

Time was everything, money was nothing. Electricians, plasterers, masons, and carpenters worked around the clock for bonus wages; and Anne, for no pay at all, harassed department stores into hurrying with the houseful of furniture she'd ordered.

Two days before Grace was to come home, the inheritance was gone, and the house was magnificent. George was unquestionably the happiest, proudest man on earth. The job was flawless, save for one tiny detail not worth mentioning. Anne had failed to match exactly the yellow square of cloth Grace had wanted for her living-room curtains and the cover for the couch. The shade Anne had had to settle for was just a little bit lighter. George and I couldn't see the difference at all.

And then Grace came home, cheerful but weak, leaning on George's arm. It was late in the afternoon, and Anne and I were waiting in the living room, literally trembling with excitement. As George helped Grace up the walk, Anne fussed nervously with a bouquet of red roses she had brought and placed in a massive glass vase in the center of the coffee table.

We heard George's hand on the latch, the door swung open, and the McClellans stood on the threshold of their dream house.

"Oh, George," Grace murmured. She let go of his arm, and, as though miraculously drawing strength from her surroundings, she walked from room to room, looking all about her as we had seen her do a thousand times. But this time of times she was speechless.

She returned at last to the living room, and sank onto the plum-colored chaise longue.

George turned down the volume of the phonograph to a sweet whisper. "Well?"

Grace sighed. "Don't rush me," she said. "I'm trying to find the words, the exact words."

"You like it?" George asked.

Grace looked at him and laughed incredulously. "Oh, George, George, of course I like it! You darling, it's wonderful! I'm home, home at last." Her lip trembled, and we all began to cloud up.

"Nothing wrong?" George asked huskily.

"You've taken wonderful care of it. Everything's so clean and beautiful."

"Well, it'd sure be a surprise if things *weren't* clean," George said. He clapped his hands together. "Now then, you well enough for a drink?"

"I'm not dead."

"Leave us out, George," I said. "We're leaving. We just had to see her expression when she walked in, but now we'll clear out."

"Oh, say now—" George said.

"No. I mean it. We're going. You two ought to be alone—you *three,* including the house."

"Stay right where you are," George said. He hurried into the dazzling white kitchen to mix the drinks.

"All right, so we'll sneak out," Anne said. We started for the front door. "Don't get up, Grace."

"Well, if you really won't stay, good-by," Grace said from the chaise longue. "I hardly know how to thank you."

"It was the most fun I've had in years," said Anne. She looked proudly around the room, and went over to the coffee table to rearrange the roses slightly. "The only thing that worried me was the color of the slipcover and curtains. Are they all right?"

"Why, Anne, did you notice them too? I wasn't even going to mention them. It would certainly be silly to let a little thing like that spoil my homecoming." She frowned a little.

Anne was crestfallen. "Oh dear, I hope they didn't spoil it."

"No, no, of course they didn't," Grace said. "I don't quite understand it, but it doesn't matter a bit."

"Well, I can explain," Anne said.

"Something in the air, I suppose."

"In the air?" Anne said.

"Well, how else can you explain it? That material held its color just perfectly for years, and then, poof, it fades like this in a few weeks."

George walked in with a frosty pewter pitcher. "Now, you'll stay for a quick one, won't you?"

Anne and I took glasses hungrily, gratefully, wordlessly.

"There's a new *Home Beautiful* that came today, sweetheart," George said.

Grace shrugged. "Read one and you've read them all." She lifted her glass. "Happy days, and thanks, darlings, so much for the roses."

(1951)

THE HYANNIS PORT STORY

THE FARTHEST AWAY from home I ever sold a storm window was in Hyannis Port, Massachusetts, practically in the front yard of President Kennedy's summer home. My field of operation is usually within about twenty-five miles of my home, which is in North Crawford, New Hampshire.

The Hyannis Port thing happened because somebody misunderstood something I said, and thought I was an ardent Goldwater Republican. Actually, I hadn't made up my mind one way or the other about Goldwater.

What happened was this: The program chairman of the North Crawford Lions Club was a Goldwater man, and he had this college boy named Robert Taft Rumfoord come talk to a meeting one day about the Democratic mess in Washington and Hyannis Port. The boy was national president of some kind of student organization that was trying to get the country back to what he called First Principles. One of the First Principles, I remember, was getting rid of the income tax. You should have heard the applause.

I got a funny feeling that the boy didn't care much more about politics than I did. He had circles under his eyes, and he looked as though he'd just as soon be somewhere else. He would say strong things, but they came out sounding like music on a kazoo. The only time he got really interesting was when he told about being in sailboat races and golf and tennis matches with different Kennedys and their friends. He said that there was a lot of propaganda around about what a fine golfer Bobby Kennedy was, whereas Bobby actually couldn't golf for sour apples. He said Pierre Salinger was one of the worst golfers in the world, and didn't care for sailing or tennis at all.

Robert Taft Rumfoord's parents were there to hear him. They had come all the way from Hyannis Port. They were both very proud of him—or at least the father was. The father had on white flannel trousers and white shoes, even though there was snow on the ground, and a double-breasted blue coat with brass buttons. The boy introduced him as *Commodore* William Rumfoord. The Commodore was a short man with very shaggy eyebrows, and pale blue eyes. He looked like a gruff, friendly teddybear, and so did his son. I found out later, from a Secret Service man, that the Kennedys sometimes called the Rumfoords "*the Pooh people,*" on account of they were so much like the bear in the children's book *Winnie the Pooh.*

The Commodore's wife wasn't a Pooh person, though. She was thin and quick, and maybe two inches taller than the Commodore. Bears have a way of looking as though they're pretty much satisfied with everything. The Commodore's lady didn't have that look. I could tell she was jumpy about a lot of things.

After the boy was through pouring fire and brimstone on the Kennedys, with his father applauding everything he said, Hay Boyden, the building mover, stood up. He was a Kennedy Democrat, and he said some terrible things to the boy. The only one I remember is the first thing he said: "Son, if you keep blowing off steam like this during your Boy Scout days, you aren't going to have an ounce of pressure left when you're old enough to vote." It got worse from there on.

The boy didn't get mad. He just got embarrassed, and answered back with some more kazoo music. It was the Commodore who really cared. He turned the color of tomato juice. He stood up and he argued back, did it pretty well, even though his wife was pulling at the bottom of his brass-buttoned coat the whole time. She was trying to get him to stop raising such an uproar, but the Commodore loved the uproar.

The meeting broke up with practically everybody embarrassed, and I went over to Hay Boyden to talk to him about something that didn't have anything to do with Kennedy *or* Goldwater. It was about a bathtub enclosure I had sold him. He had insisted on installing it himself, saving himself about seven dollars and a half. Only it leaked, and his dining-room ceiling fell down, and Hay claimed that was the fault of the merchandise and not the installation. Hay had some poison left in his system from his argument with the boy, so he used it up on me. I answered him back with the truth, and walked away from him, and Commodore Rumfoord grabbed my hand and shook it. He thought I'd been defending his boy and Barry Goldwater.

"What business you in?" he asked me.

I told him, and, the next thing I knew, I had an order for storm windows all around on a four-story house in Hyannis Port. The Commodore called that big old house a cottage.

"You're a Commodore in the Navy?" I asked him.

"No," he said. "My father, however, was Secretary of the Navy under William Howard Taft. That's my full name: Commodore William Howard Taft Rumfoord."

"You're in the Coast Guard?" I said.

"You mean the *Kennedy Private Fleet?*" he said.

"Pardon me?" I said.

"That's what they ought to call the Coast Guard these days," he said. "Its sole mission seems to be to protect Kennedys while they water-ski behind high-powered stinkpots."

"You're *not* in the Coast Guard?" I said. I couldn't imagine what was left.

"I was Commodore of the Hyannis Port Yacht Club in 1946," he said.

He didn't smile, and neither did I, and neither did his wife, whose name was Clarice. But Clarice *did* give a little sigh that sounded like the whistle on a freight train far, far away on a wet morning.

I didn't know what the trouble was at the time, but Clarice was sighing because the Commodore hadn't held any job of any description since 1946. Since then, he'd made a full-time career of raging about whoever was President of the United States, including Eisenhower.

Especially Eisenhower.

So I went down to Hyannis Port in my truck to measure the Commodore's windows late in June. His driveway was on Irving Avenue. So was the Kennedys' driveway. And President Kennedy and I hit Cape Cod on the very same day.

Traffic to Hyannis Port was backed up through three villages. There were license plates from every state in the Republic. The line was moving about four miles an hour. I was passed by several groups of fifty-mile hikers. My radiator came to a boil four times.

I was feeling pretty sorry for myself, because I was just an ordinary citizen, and had to get stuck in lines like that. But then I recognized the man in the limousine up ahead of me. It was Adlai Stevenson. He wasn't moving any faster than I was, and his radiator was boiling, too.

One place there, we got stuck so long that Mr. Stevenson and I got out and walked around a little. I took the opportunity to ask him how the United Nations were getting along. He told me they were getting along about as well as could be expected. That wasn't anything I didn't already know.

When I finally got to Hyannis Port, I found out Irving Avenue was blocked off by police and Secret Service men. Adlai Stevenson got to go down it, but I didn't. The police made me get back into line with the tourists, who were being shunted down a street one block over from Irving Avenue.

The next thing I knew, I was in Hyannis, going past the *Presidential Motor Inn*, the *First Family Waffle Shop*, the *PT-109 Cocktail Lounge*, and a miniature golf course called the *New Frontier*.

I went into the waffle shop, and I called up the Rumfoords to find out how an ordinary storm-window salesman was supposed to get down Irving Avenue without dying in a hail of lead. It was the butler I talked to. He took down my license number, and found out how tall I was and what color my eyes were and all. He said he would tell the Secret Service, and they would let me by next time.

It was late in the afternoon, and I'd missed lunch, so I decided to have a waffle. All the different kinds of waffles were named after Kennedys and their friends and relatives. A waffle with ˉtrawberries and cream was a *Jackie*. A waffle with a scoop of ice cream was a *Caroline*. They even had a waffle named *Arthur Schlesinger, Jr.*

I had a thing called a *Teddy*—and a cup of *Joe*.

I got through next time, went right down Irving Avenue behind the Defense Minister of Pakistan. Except for us, that street was as quiet as a stretch of the Sahara Desert.

There wasn't anything to see at all on the President's side, except for a new, peeled-cedar fence about eight feet high and two hundred feet long, with a gate in it. The Rumfoord cottage faced the gate from across the street. It was the biggest house, and one of the oldest, in the village. It was stucco. It had towers and balconies, and a veranda that ran around all four sides.

On a second-floor balcony was a huge portrait of Barry Goldwater. It had bicycle reflectors in the pupils of its eyes. Those eyes stared right through the Kennedy gate. There were floodlights all around it, so I could tell it was lit up at night. And the floodlights were rigged with blinkers.

A man who sells storm windows can never be really sure about what class he belongs to, especially if he installs the windows, too. So I was prepared to keep out from under foot, and go about my business, measuring the windows. But the Commodore welcomed me like a guest of great importance. He invited me to cocktails and dinner, and to spend the night. He said I could start measuring the next day.

So we had martinis out on the veranda. Only we didn't sit on the most pleasant side, which looked out on the Yacht Club dock and the harbor. We sat on the side that looked out on all the poor tourists being shunted off toward Hyannis. The Commodore liked to talk about all those fools out there.

"Look at them!" he said. "They wanted glamour, and now they realize they're not going to get it. They actually expected to be invited to play touch football with Eunice and Frank Sinatra and the Secretary of Health and Welfare. Glamour is what they voted for, and look at 'em now. They don't even get to look at a Kennedy chimney up above the trees. All the glamour they'll get out of this administration is an overpriced waffle named *Caroline*."

A helicopter went over, very low, and it landed somewhere inside the Kennedy fence. Clarice said she wondered who it was.

"Pope John the Sixth," said the Commodore.

The butler, whose name was John, came out with a big bowl. I thought it was peanuts or popcorn, but it turned out to be Goldwater buttons. The Commodore had John take the bowl out to the street, and offer buttons to the people in cars. A lot of people took them. Those people were disappointed. They were sore.

Some fifty-mile hikers, who'd actually hiked sixty-seven miles, all the way from Boston, asked if they could please lie down on the Rumfoord lawn for a while. They were burned up, too. They thought it was the duty of the President, or at least the Attorney General, to thank them for walking so far. The Commodore said they could not only lie down, but he would give them lemonade, if they would put on Goldwater buttons. They were glad to.

"Commodore," I said, "where's that nice boy of yours, the one who talked to us up in New Hampshire."

"The one who talked to you is the only one I've got," he said.

"He certainly poured it on," I said.

"Chip off the old block," he said.

Clarice gave that faraway freight-whistle sigh of hers again.

"The boy went swimming just before you got here," said the Commodore. "He should be back at any time, unless he's been decapitated by a member of the Irish Mafia on water skis."

We went around to the water side of the veranda to see if we could catch sight of young Robert Taft Rumfoord in swimming. There was a Coast Guard cutter out there, shooing tourists in motorboats away from the Kennedy beach. There was a sightseeing boat crammed with people gawking in our direction. The barker on the boat had a very loud loudspeaker, and we could hear practically everything he said.

"*The white boat there is the* Honey Fitz, *the President's personal yacht,*" said the barker. "*Next to it is the* Marlin, *which belongs to the President's father, Joseph C. Kennedy, former Ambassador to the Court of St. James.*"

"The President's stinkpot, and the President's father's stinkpot," said the Commodore. He called all motorboats stinkpots. "This is a harbor that should be devoted exclusively to sail."

There was a chart of the harbor on the verandah wall. I studied it, and found a *Rumfoord Point,* a *Rumfoord Rock,* and a *Rumfoord Shoal.* The Commodore told me his family had been in Hyannis Port since 1884.

"There doesn't seem to be anything named after the Kennedys," I said.

"Why *should* there be?" he said. "They only got here day before yesterday."

"Day before yesterday?" I said.

And he asked me, "What would *you* call nineteen-twenty-one?"

"*No, sir,*" the barker said to one of his passengers, "*that is* not *the President's house. Everybody asks that. That great big ugly stucco house, folks, that's the Rumfoord Cottage. I agree with you, it's too big to be called a* cottage, *but you know how rich people are.*"

"Demoralized and bankrupt by confiscatory taxation," said the Commodore. "You know," he said, "it isn't as though Kennedy was the first President we ever had in Hyannis Port. Taft, Harding, Coolidge, and Hoover were all guests of my father in this very house. Kennedy is simply the first President who's seen fit to turn the place into an eastern enclave of *Disneyland.*"

"*No, mam,*" said the barker, "*I don't know where the Rumfoords get their money, but they don't have to work at all, I know that. They just sit on that porch there, and drink martinis, and let the old mazooma roll in.*"

The Commodore blew up. He said he was going to sue the

owners of the sight-seeing boat for a blue million. His wife tried to calm him down, but he made me come into his study with him while he called up his lawyers.

"You're a witness," he said.

But his telephone rang before he could call his lawyers. The person who was calling him was a Secret Service Agent named Raymond Boyle. I found out later that Boyle was known around the Kennedy household as the *Rumfoord Specialist* or the *Ambassador to Rumfoordiana*. Whenever anything came up that had to do with the Rumfoords, Boyle had to handle it.

The Commodore told me to go upstairs and listen in on the extension in the hall. "This will give you an idea of how arrogant civil servants have become these days," he said.

So I went upstairs.

"The Secret Service is one of the least secret services I've ever come in contact with," the Commodore was saying when I picked up the phone. "I've seen drum and bugle corps that were less obtrusive. Did I ever tell you about the time Calvin Coolidge, who was also a President, as it happened, went fishing for scup with my father and me off the end of the Yacht Club dock?"

"Yessir, you have, many times," said Boyle. "It's a good story, and I want to hear it again sometime. But right now I'm calling about your son."

The Commodore went right ahead with the story anyway. "President Coolidge," he said, "insisted on baiting his own hook, and the combined Atlantic and Pacific Fleets were not anchored offshore, and the sky was not black with airplanes, and brigades of Secret Service Agents were not trampling the neighbors' flowerbeds to purée."

"Sir—" said Boyle patiently, "your son Robert was apprehended in the act of boarding the President's father's boat, the *Marlin*."

"Back in the days of Coolidge, there *were* no stinkpots like that in this village, dribbling petroleum products, belching fumes, killing the fish, turning the beaches a gummy black."

"Commodore Rumfoord, sir," said Boyle, "did you hear what I just said about your son?"

"Of course," said the Commodore. "You said Robert, a member of the Hyannis Port Yacht Club, was caught touching a vessel belonging to another member of the club. This may seem a very terrible crime to a landlubber like yourself; but it has long been a custom of the sea, Mr. Boyle, that a swimmer, momentarily fatigued, may, upon coming to a vessel not his own, grasp that vessel and rest, without fear of being fired upon by the Coast Guard, or of having his fingers smashed by members of the Secret Service, or, as I prefer to call them, the *Kennedy Palace Dragoons*."

"There has been no shooting, and no smashing, sir," said Boyle. "There has also been no evidence of swimmer's fatigue. Your Robert went up the anchor line of the *Marlin* like a chimpanzee. He *swarmed* up that rope, Commodore. I believe that's the proper nautical term. And I remind you, as I tried to remind him, that persons moving, uninvited, unannounced, with such speed and purposefulness within the vicinity of a President are, as a matter of time-honored policy, to be turned back at all costs—to be turned back, if need be, *violently*."

"Was it a Kennedy who gave the order that the boarder be repelled?" the Commodore wanted to know.

"There was no Kennedy on board, sir."

"The stinkpot was unoccupied?"

"Adlai Stevenson and Walter Reuther and one of my men were on board, sir," said Boyle. "They were all below, until they heard Robert's feet hit the deck."

"Stevenson and Reuther?" said the Commodore. "That's the last time I let my son go swimming without a dagger in his teeth. I hope he was opening the seacocks when beaten insensible by truncheons."

"Very funny, sir," said Boyle, his voice developing a slight cutting edge.

"You're sure it was my Robert?" said the Commodore.

"Who else but your Robert wears a Goldwater button on his swimming trunks?" asked Boyle.

"You object to his political views?" the Commodore demanded.

"I mention the button as a means of identification. Your son's politics do not interest the Secret Service. For your information,

I have spent seven years protecting the life of a Republican, and three protecting the life of a Democrat," said Boyle.

"For your information, Mr. Boyle," said the Commodore, "Dwight David Eisenhower was *not* a Republican."

"Whatever he was, I protected him," said Boyle. "He may have been a Zoroastrian, for all I know. And whatever the next President is going to be, I'll protect him, too. I also protect the lives of persons like your son from the consequences of excessive informality where the Presidential presence is concerned." Now Boyle's voice really started to cut. It sounded like a bandsaw working on galvanized tin. "I tell you, officially and absolutely unsmilingly now, your son is to cease and desist from using Kennedy boats as love nests."

That got through to the Commodore, bothered him. "Love nests?" he said.

"Your Robert has been meeting a girl on boats all over the harbor," said Boyle. "He arranged to meet her today on the *Marlin*. He was sure it would be vacant: Adlai Stevenson and Walter Reuther were a shock."

The Commodore was quiet for a few seconds, and then he said, "Mr. Boyle, I resent your implications. If I ever hear of your implying such a thing about my son to anyone else, you had better put your pistol and shoulder holster in your wife's name, because I'll sue you for everything you've got. My Robert has never gone with a girl he wasn't proud to introduce to his mother and me, and he never will."

"You're going to meet this one any minute now," said Boyle. "Robert is on his way home with her."

The Commodore wasn't tough at all now. He was uneasy and humble when he said, "Would you mind telling me her name?"

"Kennedy, sir," said Boyle, "*Sheila* Kennedy, fresh over from Ireland, a fourth cousin of the President of the United States."

Robert Taft Rumfoord came in with the girl right after that, and announced they were engaged to be married.

Supper that night in the Rumfoord cottage was sad and beautiful and happy and strange. There were Robert and his girl, and me, and the Commodore and his lady.

That girl was so intelligent, so warm, and so beautiful that she broke my heart every time I looked at her. That was why supper was so peculiar. The girl was so desirable, and the love between her and Robert was so sweet and clean, that nobody could think of anything but silly little things to say. We mainly ate in silence.

The Commodore brought up the subject of politics just once. He said to Robert, "Well—uh—will you still be making speeches around the country, or—uh—"

"I think I'll get out of politics entirely for a while," said Robert.

The Commodore said something that none of us could understand, because the words sort of choked him.

"Sir?" said Robert.

"I said," said the Commodore, " 'I would think you would.' "

I looked at the Commodore's lady, at Clarice. All the lines had gone out of her face. She looked young and beautiful, too. She was completely relaxed for the first time in God-knows-how-many years.

One of the things I said that supper was was *sad*. The sad part was how empty and quiet it left the Commodore.

The two lovers went for a moonlight sail. The Commodore and his lady and I had brandy on the veranda, on the water side. The sun was down. The tourist traffic had petered out. The fifty-mile hikers who had asked to rest on the lawn that afternoon were still all there, sound asleep, except for one boy who played a guitar. He played it slowly. Sometimes it seemed ·like a minute between the time he would pluck a string and the time he would pluck one again.

John, the butler, came out and asked the Commodore if it was time to turn on Senator Goldwater's floodlights yet.

"I think we'll just leave him off tonight, John," said the Commodore.

"Yes, sir," said John.

"I'm still *for* him, John," said the Commodore. "Don't anybody misunderstand me. I just think we ought to give him a rest tonight."

"Yes, sir," said John, and he left.

It was dark on the veranda, so I couldn't see the Commodore's face very well. The darkness, and the brandy, and the slow guitar let him start telling the truth about himself without feeling much pain.

"Let's give the Senator from Arizona a rest," he said. "Everybody knows who *he* is. The question is: Who am I?"

"A lovable man," said Clarice in the dark.

"With Goldwater's floodlights turned off, and with my son engaged to marry a Kennedy, what am I but what the man on the sight-seeing boat said I was: A man who sits on this porch, drinking martinis, and letting the old mazooma roll in."

"You're an intelligent, charming, well-educated man, and you're still quite young," said Clarice.

"I've got to find some kind of work," he said.

"We'll both be so much happier," she said. "I would love you, no matter what. But I can tell you now, darling—it's awfully hard for a woman to *admire* a man who actually doesn't do anything."

We were dazzled by the headlights of two cars coming out of the Kennedys' driveway. The cars stopped right in front of the Rumfoord Cottage. Whoever was in them seemed to be giving the place a good looking-over.

The Commodore went to that side of the veranda, to find out what was going on. And I heard the voice of the President of the United States coming from the car in front.

"Commodore Rumfoord," said the President, "may I ask what is wrong with your Goldwater sign?"

"Nothing, Mr. President," said the Commodore respectfully.

"Then why isn't it on?" asked the President.

"I just didn't feel like turning it on tonight, sir," said the Commodore.

"I have Mr. Khrushchev's son-in-law with me," said the President. "He would very much enjoy seeing it."

"Yes, sir," said the Commodore. He was right by the switch. He turned it on. The whole neighborhood was bathed in flashing light.

"Thank you," said the President. "And *leave* it on, would you please?"

"Sir?" said the Commodore.

The cars started to pull away slowly. "That way," said the President, "I can find my way home."

(1963)

D. P.

EIGHTY-ONE small sparks of human life were kept in an orphanage set up by Catholic nuns in what had been the game-keeper's house on a large estate overlooking the Rhine. This was in the German village of Karlswald, in the American Zone of Occupation. Had the children not been kept there, not been given the warmth and food and clothes that could be begged for them, they might have wandered off the edges of the earth, searching for parents who had long ago stopped searching for them.

Every mild afternoon the nuns marched the children, two by two, through the woods, into the village and back, for their ration of fresh air. The village carpenter, an old man who was given to thoughtful rests between strokes of his tools, always came out of his shop to watch the bobbing, chattering, cheerful, ragged parade, and to speculate, with idlers his shop attracted, as to the nationalities of the passing children's parents.

"See the little French girl," he said one afternoon. "Look at the flash of those eyes!"

"And look at that little Pole swing his arms. They love to march, the Poles," said a young mechanic.

"Pole? Where do you see any Pole?" said the carpenter.

"There—the thin, sober-looking one in front," the other replied.

"Aaaaah. He's too tall for a Pole," said the carpenter. "And what Pole has flaxen hair like that? He's a German."

The mechanic shrugged. "They're all German now, so what difference does it make?" he said. "Who can prove what their parents were? If you had fought in Poland, you would know he was a very common type."

"Look—look who's coming now," said the carpenter, grinning. "Full of arguments as you are, you won't argue with me about *him*. There we have an American!" He called out to the child. "Joe—when you going to win the championship back?"

"Joe!" called the mechanic. "How is the Brown Bomber today?"

At the very end of the parade, a lone, blue-eyed colored boy, six years old, turned and smiled with sweet uneasiness at those who called out to him every day. He nodded politely, murmuring a greeting in German, the only language he knew.

His name, chosen arbitrarily by the nuns, was Karl Heinz. But the carpenter had given him a name that stuck, the name of the only colored man who had ever made an impression on the villagers' minds, the former heavyweight champion of the world, Joe Louis.

"Joe!" called the carpenter. "Cheer up! Let's see those white teeth sparkle, Joe."

Joe obliged shyly.

The carpenter clapped the mechanic on the back. "And if *he* isn't a German too! Maybe it's the only way we can get another heavyweight champion."

Joe turned a corner, shooed out of the carpenter's sight by a nun bringing up the rear. She and Joe spent a great deal of time together, since Joe, no matter where he was placed in the parade, always drifted to the end.

"Joe," she said, "you are such a dreamer. Are all your people such dreamers?"

"I'm sorry, sister," said Joe. "I was thinking."

"Dreaming."

"Sister, am I the son of an American soldier?"

"Who told you that?"

"Peter. Peter said my mother was a German, and my father was an American soldier who went away. He said she left me with you, and then went away too." There was no sadness in his voice—only puzzlement.

Peter was the oldest boy in the orphanage, an embittered old man of fourteen, a German boy who could remember his parents and brothers and sisters and home, and the war, and all sorts of food that Joe found impossible to imagine. Peter seemed superhuman to Joe, like a man who had been to heaven and hell and back many times, and knew exactly why they were where they were, how they had come there, and where they might have been.

"You mustn't worry about it, Joe," said the nun. "No one knows who your mother and father were. But they must have been very good people, because you are so good."

"What is an American?" said Joe.

"It's a person from another country."

"Near here?"

"There are some near here, but their homes are far, far away—across a great deal of water."

"Like the river."

"More water than that, Joe. More water than you have ever seen. You can't even see the other side. You could get on a boat and go for days and days and still not get to the other side. I'll show you a map sometime. But don't pay any attention to Peter, Joe. He makes things up. He doesn't really know anything about you. Now, catch up."

Joe hurried, and overtook the end of the line, where he marched purposefully and alertly for a few minutes. But then he began to dawdle again, chasing ghostlike words in his small mind: . . . soldier . . . German . . . American . . . your people . . . champion . . . Brown Bomber . . . more water than you've ever seen.

"Sister," said Joe, "are Americans like me? Are they brown?"

"Some are, some aren't, Joe."

"Are there many people like me?"

"Yes. Many, many people."

"Why haven't I seen them?"

"None of them have come to the village. They have places of their own."

"I want to go there."

"Aren't you happy here, Joe?"

"Yes. But Peter says I don't belong here, that I'm not a German and never can be."

"Peter! Pay no attention to him."

"Why do people smile when they see me, and try to make me sing and talk, and then laugh when I do?"

"Joe, Joe! Look quickly," said the nun. "See—up there, in the tree. See the little sparrow with the broken leg. Oh poor, brave little thing—he still gets around quite well. See him, Joe? Hop, hop, hippity-hop."

One hot summer day, as the parade passed the carpenter's shop, the carpenter came out to call something new to Joe, something that thrilled and terrified him.

"Joe! Hey, Joe! Your father is in town. Have you seen him yet?"

"No, sir—no, I haven't," said Joe. "Where is he?"

"He's teasing," said the nun sharply.

"You see if I'm teasing, Joe," said the carpenter. "Just keep your eyes open when you go past the school. You have to look sharp, up the slope and into the woods. You'll see, Joe."

"I wonder where our little friend the sparrow is today," said the nun brightly. "Goodness, I hope his leg is getting better, don't you, Joe?"

"Yes, yes I do, sister."

She chattered on about the sparrow and the clouds and the flowers as they approached the school, and Joe gave up answering her.

The woods above the school seemed still and empty.

But then Joe saw a massive brown man, naked to the waist and wearing a pistol, step from the trees. The man drank from a canteen, wiped his lips with the back of his hand, grinned down on the world with handsome disdain, and disappeared again into the twilight of the woods.

"Sister!" gasped Joe. "My father—I just saw my father!"

"No, Joe—no you didn't."

"He's up there in the woods. I saw him. I want to go up there, sister."

"He isn't your father, Joe. He doesn't know you. He doesn't want to see you."

"He's one of my people, sister!"

"You can't go up there, Joe, and you can't stay here." She took him by the arm to make him move. "Joe—you're being a bad boy, Joe."

Joe obeyed numbly. He didn't speak again for the remainder of the walk, which brought them home by another route, far from the school. No one else had seen his wonderful father, or believed that Joe had.

Not until prayers that night did he burst into tears.

At ten o'clock, the young nun found his cot empty.

Under a great spread net that was laced with rags, an artillery piece squatted in the woods, black and oily, its muzzle thrust at the night sky. Trucks and the rest of the battery were hidden higher on the slope.

Joe watched and listened tremblingly through a thin screen of shrubs as the soldiers, indistinct in the darkness, dug in around their gun. The words he overheard made no sense to him.

"Sergeant, why we gotta dig in, when we're movin' out in the mornin', and it's just maneuvers anyhow? Seems like we could kind of conserve our strength, and just scratch around a little to show where we'd of dug if there was any sense to it."

"For all you know, boy, there may *be* sense to it before mornin'," said the sergeant. "You got ten minutes to get to China and bring me back a pigtail. Hear?"

The sergeant stepped into a patch of moonlight, his hands on his hips, his big shoulders back, the image of an emperor. Joe saw that it was the same man he'd marveled at in the afternoon. The sergeant listened with satisfaction to the sounds of digging, and then, to Joe's alarm, strode toward Joe's hiding place.

Joe didn't move a muscle until the big boot struck his side. "*Ach!*"

"Who's that?" The sergeant snatched Joe from the ground, and set him on his feet hard. "My golly, boy, what you doin' here? Scoot! Go on home! This ain't no place for kids to be playin'." He shined a flashlight in Joe's face. "Doggone," he muttered.

"Where you come from?" He held Joe at arm's length, and shook him gently, like a rag doll. "Boy, how you get here—swim?"

Joe stammered in German that he was looking for his father.

"Come on—how you get here? What you doin'? Where's your mammy?"

"What you got there, sergeant?" said a voice in the dark.

"Don't rightly know what to call it," said the sergeant. "Talks like a Kraut and dresses like a Kraut, but just look at it a minute."

Soon a dozen men stood in a circle around Joe, talking loudly, then softly, to him, as though they thought getting through to him were a question of tone.

Every time Joe tried to explain his mission, they laughed in amazement.

"How he learn German? Tell me that."

"Where your daddy, boy?"

"Where your mammy, boy?"

"Sprecken zee Dutch, boy? Looky there. See him nod. He talks it, all right."

"Oh, you're fluent, man, mighty fluent. Ask him some more."

"Go get the lieutenant," said the sergeant. "He can talk to this boy, and understand what he's tryin' to say. Look at him shake. Scared to death. Come here, boy; don't be afraid, now." He enclosed Joe in his great arms. "Just take it easy, now—everything's gonna be all-l-l-l right. See what I got? By golly, I don't believe the boy's ever seen chocolate before. Go on—taste it. Won't hurt you."

Joe, safe in a fort of bone and sinew, ringed by luminous eyes, bit into the chocolate bar. The pink lining of his mouth, and then his whole soul, was flooded with warm, rich pleasure, and he beamed.

"He smiled!"

"Look at him light up!"

"Doggone if he didn't stumble right into heaven! I mean!"

"Talk about displaced persons," said the sergeant, hugging Joe, "this here's the most displaced little old person I *ever* saw. Upside down and inside out and ever' which way."

"Here, boy—here's some more chocolate."

"Don't give him no more," said the sergeant reproachfully. "You want to make him sick?"

"Naw, sarge, naw—don't wanna make him sick. No, sir."

"What's going on here?" The lieutenant, a small, elegant Negro, the beam of his flashlight dancing before him, approached the group.

"Got a little boy here, lieutenant," said the sergeant. "Just wandered into the battery. Must of crawled past the guards."

"Well, send him on home, sergeant."

"Yessir. I planned to." He cleared his throat. "But this ain't no ordinary little boy, lieutenant." He opened his arms so that the light fell on Joe's face.

The lieutenant laughed incredulously, and knelt before Joe. "How'd you get here?"

"All he talks is German, lieutenant," said the sergeant.

"Where's your home?" said the lieutenant in German.

"Over more water than you've ever seen," said Joe.

"Where do you come from?"

"God made me," said Joe.

"This boy is going to be a lawyer when he grows up," said the lieutenant in English. "Now, listen to me," he said to Joe, "what's your name, and where are your people?"

"Joe Louis," said Joe, "and you are my people. I ran away from the orphanage, because I belong with you."

The lieutenant stood, shaking his head, and translated what Joe had said.

The woods echoed with glee.

"Joe Louis! I *thought* he was awful big and powerful-lookin'l"

"Jus' keep away from that left—*tha's* all!"

"If he's Joe, he's sure found his people. He's got us there!"

"Shut up!" commanded the sergeant suddenly. "All of you just shut up. This ain't no joke! Ain't nothing funny in it! Boy's all alone in the world. Ain't no joke."

A small voice finally broke the solemn silence that followed. "Naw—ain't no joke at all."

"We better take the jeep and run him back into town, sergeant," said the lieutenant. "Corporal Jackson, you're in charge."

"You tell 'em Joe was a *good* boy," said Jackson.

"Now, Joe," said the lieutenant in German, softly, "you come with the sergeant and me. We'll take you home."

Joe dug his fingers into the sergeant's forearms. "Papa! No—papa! I want to stay with you."

"Look, sonny, I ain't your papa," said the sergeant helplessly. "I *ain't* your papa."

"Papa!"

"Man, he's glued to you, ain't he, sergeant?" said a soldier. "Looks like you ain't never goin' to pry him loose. You got yourself a boy there, sarge, and he's got hisself a papa."

The sergeant walked over to the jeep with Joe in his arms. "Come on, now," he said, "you leggo, little Joe, so's I can drive. I can't drive with you hangin' on, Joe. You sit in the lieutenant's lap right next to me."

The group formed again around the jeep, gravely now, watching the sergeant try to coax Joe into letting go.

"I don't want to get tough, Joe. Come on—take it easy, Joe. Let go, now, Joe, so's I can drive. See, I can't steer or nothin' with you hanging on right there."

"Papa!"

"Come on, over to my lap, Joe," said the lieutenant in German.

"Papa!"

"Joe, Joe, looky," said a soldier. "Chocolate! Want some more chocolate, Joe? See? Whole bar, Joe, all yours. Jus' leggo the sergeant and move over into the lieutenant's lap."

Joe tightened his grip on the sergeant.

"Don't put the chocolate back in your pocket, man! Give it to Joe anyways," said a soldier angrily. "Somebody go get a case of D bars off the truck, and throw 'em in the back for Joe. Give that boy chocolate enough for the nex' twenny years."

"Look, Joe," said another soldier, "ever see a wristwatch? Look at the wristwatch, Joe. See it glow, boy? Move over in the lieutenant's lap, and I'll let you listen to it tick. Tick, tick, tick, Joe. Come on, want to listen?"

Joe didn't move.

The soldier handed the watch to him. "Here, Joe, you take it anyway. It's yours." He walked away quickly.

"Man," somebody called after him, "you crazy? You paid fifty dollars for that watch. What business a little boy got with any fifty-dollar watch?"

"No—I ain't crazy. Are you?"

"Naw, I ain't crazy. Neither one of us crazy, I guess. Joe— want a knife? You got to promise to be careful with it, now. Always cut *away* from yourself. Hear? Lieutenant, when you get back, you tell him always cut *away* from hisself."

"I don't want to go back. I want to stay with *papa*," said Joe tearfully.

"Soldiers can't take little boys with them, Joe," said the lieutenant in German. "And we're leaving early in the morning."

"Will you come back for me?" said Joe.

"We'll come back if we can, Joe. Soldiers never know where they'll be from one day to the next. We'll come back for a visit, if we can."

"Can we give old Joe this case of D bars, lieutenant?" said a soldier carrying a cardboard carton of chocolate bars.

"Don't ask me," said the lieutenant. "I don't know anything about it. I never saw anything of any case of D bars, never heard anything about it."

"Yessir." The soldier laid his burden down on the jeep's back seat.

"He ain't gonna let go," said the sergeant miserably. "You drive, lieutenant, and me and Joe'll sit over there."

The lieutenant and the sergeant changed places, and the jeep began to move.

" 'By, Joe!"

"You be a good boy, Joe!"

"Don't you eat all that chocolate at once, you hear?"

"Don't cry, Joe. Give us a smile."

"Wider, boy—that's the stuff!"

"Joe, Joe, wake up, Joe." The voice was that of Peter, the oldest boy in the orphanage, and it echoed damply from the stone walls.

Joe sat up, startled. All around his cot were the other orphans, jostling one another for a glimpse of Joe and the treasures by his pillow.

"Where did you get the hat, Joe—and the watch, and knife?" said Peter. "And what's in the box under your bed?"

Joe felt his head, and found a soldier's wool knit cap there. "Papa," he mumbled sleepily.

"Papa!" mocked Peter, laughing.

"Yes," said Joe. "Last night I went to see my papa, Peter."

"Could he speak German, Joe?" said a little girl wonderingly.

"No, but his friend could," said Joe.

"He didn't see his father," said Peter. "Your father is far, far away, and will never come back. He probably doesn't even know you're alive."

"What did he look like?" said the girl.

Joe glanced thoughtfully around the room. "Papa is as high as this ceiling," he said at last. "He is wider than that door." Triumphantly, he took a bar of chocolate from under his pillow. "And as brown as that!" He held out the bar to the others. "Go on, have some. There is plenty more."

"He doesn't look anything like that," said Peter. "You aren't telling the truth, Joe."

"My papa has a pistol as big as this bed, almost, Peter," said Joe happily, "and a cannon as big as this house. And there were hundreds and hundreds like him."

"Somebody played a joke on you, Joe," said Peter. "He wasn't your father. How do you know he wasn't fooling you?"

"Because he cried when he left me," said Joe simply. "And he promised to take me back home across the water as fast as he could." He smiled airily. "Not like the river, Peter—across more water than you've *ever* seen. He promised, and then I let him go."

(1953)

REPORT ON THE BARNHOUSE EFFECT

Let me begin by saying that I don't know any more about where Professor Arthur Barnhouse is hiding than anyone else does. Save for one short, enigmatic message left in my mailbox on Christmas Eve, I have not heard from him since his disappearance a year and a half ago.

What's more, readers of this article will be disappointed if they expect to learn how *they* can bring about the so-called "Barnhouse Effect." If I were able and willing to give away that secret, I would certainly be something more important than a psychology instructor.

I have been urged to write this report because I did research under the professor's direction and because I was the first to learn of his astonishing discovery. But while I was his student I was never entrusted with knowledge of how the mental forces could be released and directed. He was unwilling to trust anyone with that information.

I would like to point out that the term "Barnhouse Effect" is a creation of the popular press, and was never used by Professor

Barnhouse. The name he chose for the phenomenon was "*dyna-mopsychism*," or *force of the mind*.

I cannot believe that there is a civilized person yet to be convinced that such a force exists, what with its destructive effects on display in every national capital. I think humanity has always had an inkling that this sort of force does exist. It has been common knowledge that some people are luckier than others with inanimate objects like dice. What Professor Barnhouse did was to show that such "luck" was a measurable force, which in his case could be enormous.

By my calculations, the professor was about fifty-five times more powerful than a Nagasaki-type atomic bomb at the time he went into hiding. He was not bluffing when, on the eve of "Operation Brainstorm," he told General Honus Barker: "Sitting here at the dinner table, I'm pretty sure I can flatten anything on earth—from Joe Louis to the Great Wall of China."

There is an understandable tendency to look upon Professor Barnhouse as a supernatural visitation. The First Church of Barnhouse in Los Angeles has a congregation numbering in the thousands. He is godlike in neither appearance nor intellect. The man who disarms the world is single, shorter than the average American male, stout, and averse to exercise. His I.Q. is 143, which is good but certainly not sensational. He is quite mortal, about to celebrate his fortieth birthday, and in good health. If he is alone now, the isolation won't bother him too much. He was quiet and shy when I knew him, and seemed to find more companionship in books and music than in his associations at the college.

Neither he nor his powers fall outside the sphere of Nature. His dynamopsychic radiations are subject to many known physical laws that apply in the field of radio. Hardly a person has not now heard the snarl of "Barnhouse static" on his home receiver. The radiations are affected by sunspots and variations in the ionosphere.

However, they differ from ordinary broadcast waves in several important ways. Their total energy can be brought to bear on any single point the professor chooses, and that energy is undiminished by distance. As a weapon, then, dynamopsychism has an impressive advantage over bacteria and atomic bombs, beyond the fact that it costs nothing to use: it enables the professor to single out critical individuals and objects instead of slaughtering whole populations in the process of maintaining international equilibrium.

As General Honus Barker told the House Military Affairs Committee: "Until someone finds Barnhouse, there is no defense against the Barnhouse Effect." Efforts to "jam" or block the radiations have failed. Premier Slezak could have saved himself the fantastic expense of his "Barnhouseproof" shelter. Despite the shelter's twelve-foot-thick lead armor, the premier has been floored twice while in it.

There is talk of screening the population for men potentially as powerful dynamopsychically as the professor. Senator Warren Foust demanded funds for this. purpose last month, with the passionate declaration: "He who rules the Barnhouse Effect rules the world!" Commissar Kropotnik said much the same thing, so another costly armaments race, with a new twist, has begun.

This race at least has its comical aspects. The world's best gamblers are being coddled by governments like so many nuclear physicists. There may be several hundred persons with dynamopsychic talent on earth, myself included. But, without knowledge of the professor's technique, they can never be anything but dice-table despots. With the secret, it would probably take them ten years to become dangerous weapons. It took the professor that long. He who rules the Barnhouse Effect is Barnhouse and will be for some time.

Popularly, the "Age of Barnhouse" is said to have begun a year and a half ago, on the day of Operation Brainstorm. That was when dynamopsychism became significant politically. Actually, the phenomenon was discovered in May, 1942, shortly after the professor turned down a direct commission in the Army and enlisted as an artillery private. Like X-rays and vulcanized rubber, dynamopsychism was discovered by accident.

From time to time Private Barnhouse was invited to take part in games of chance by his barrack mates. He knew nothing about the games, and usually begged off. But one evening, out of social grace, he agreed to shoot craps. It was terrible or wonderful that he played, depending upon whether or not you like the world as it now is.

"Shoot sevens, Pop," someone said.

So "Pop" shot sevens—ten in a row to bankrupt the barracks. He retired to his bunk and, as a mathematical exercise, calculated the odds against his feat on the back of a laundry slip. His chances of doing it, he found, were one in almost ten million! Bewildered, he borrowed a pair of dice from the man in the bunk next to his. He tried to roll sevens again, but got only the usual assortment of numbers. He lay back for a moment, then resumed his toying with the dice. He rolled ten more sevens in a row.

He might have dismissed the phenomenon with a low whistle. But the professor instead mulled over the circumstances surrounding his two lucky streaks. There was one single factor in common: on both occasions, *the same thought train had flashed through his mind just before he threw the dice.* It was that thought train which aligned the professor's brain cells into what has since become the most powerful weapon on earth.

The soldier in the next bunk gave dynamopsychism its first token of respect. In an understatement certain to bring wry smiles to the faces of the world's dejected demagogues, the soldier said, "You're hotter'n a two-dollar pistol, Pop." Professor Barnhouse was all of that. The dice that did his bidding weighed but a few grams, so the forces involved were minute; but the unmistakable fact that there were such forces was earth-shaking.

Professional caution kept him from revealing his discovery immediately. He wanted more facts and a body of theory to go with them. Later, when the atomic bomb was dropped on Hiroshima, it was fear that made him hold his peace. At no time were his experiments, as Premier Slezak called them, "a bourgeois plot to shackle the true democracies of the world." The professor didn't know where they were leading.

In time, he came to recognize another startling feature of dynamopsychism: *its strength increased with use.* Within six

months, he was able to govern dice thrown by men the length
of a barracks distant. By the time of his discharge in 1945, he
could knock bricks loose from chimneys three miles away.

Charges that Professor Barnhouse could have won the last war
in a minute, but did not care to do so, are perfectly senseless.
When the war ended, he had the range and power of a 37-mil-
limeter cannon, perhaps—certainly no more. His dynamopsychic
powers graduated from the small-arms class only after his discharge and return to Wyandotte College.

I enrolled in the Wyandotte Graduate School two years after
the professor had rejoined the faculty. By chance, he was assigned as my thesis adviser. I was unhappy about the assignment,
for the professor was, in the eyes of both colleagues and students,
a somewhat ridiculous figure. He missed classes or had lapses of
memory during lectures. When I arrived, in fact, his shortcom-
ings had passed from the ridiculous to the intolerable.

"We're assigning you to Barnhouse as a sort of temporary
thing," the dean of social studies told me. He looked apologetic
and perplexed. "Brilliant man, Barnhouse, I guess. Difficult to
know since his return, perhaps, but his work before the war
brought a great deal of credit to our little school."

When I reported to the professor's laboratory for the first
time, what I saw was more distressing than the gossip. Every
surface in the room was covered with dust; books and apparatus
had not been disturbed for months. The professor sat napping
at his desk when I entered. The only signs of recent activity were
three overflowing ashtrays, a pair of scissors, and a morning
paper with several items clipped from its front page.

As he raised his head to look at me, I saw that his eyes were
clouded with fatigue. "Hi," he said, "just can't seem to get my
sleeping done at night." He lighted a cigarette, his hands trembling slightly. "You the young man I'm supposed to help with a
thesis?"

"Yes, sir," I said. In minutes he converted my misgivings to
alarm.

"You an overseas veteran?" he asked.

"Yes, sir."

"Not much left over there, is there?" He frowned. "Enjoy the last war?"

"No, sir."

"Look like another war to you?"

"Kind of, sir."

"What can be done about it?"

I shrugged. "Looks pretty hopeless."

He peered at me intently. "Know anything about international law, the U.N., and all that?"

"Only what I pick up from the papers."

"Same here," he sighed. He showed me a fat scrapbook packed with newspaper clippings. "Never used to pay any attention to international politics. Now I study them the way I used to study rats in mazes. Everybody tells me the same thing—'Looks hopeless.'"

"Nothing short of a miracle—" I began.

"Believe in magic?" he asked sharply. The professor fished two dice from his vest pocket. "I will try to roll twos," he said. He rolled twos three times in a row. "One chance in about 47,000 of that happening. There's a miracle for you." He beamed for an instant, then brought the interview to an end, remarking that he had a class which had begun ten minutes ago.

He was not quick to take me into his confidence, and he said no more about his trick with the dice. I assumed they were loaded, and forgot about them. He set me the task of watching male rats cross electrified metal strips to get to food or female rats—an experiment that had been done to everyone's satisfaction in the nineteen-thirties. As though the pointlessness of my work were not bad enough, the professor annoyed me further with irrelevant questions. His favorites were: "Think we should have dropped the atomic bomb on Hiroshima?" and "Think every new piece of scientific information is a good thing for humanity?"

However, I did not feel put upon for long. "Give those poor animals a holiday," he said one morning, after I had been with him only a month. "I wish you'd help me look into a more interesting problem—namely, my sanity."

I returned the rats to their cages.

"What you must do is simple," he said, speaking softly. "Watch the inkwell on my desk. If you see nothing happen to it, say so, and I'll go quietly—relieved, I might add—to the nearest sanitarium."

I nodded uncertainly.

He locked the laboratory door and drew the blinds, so that we were in twilight for a moment. "I'm odd, I know," he said. "It's fear of myself that's made me odd."

"I've found you somewhat eccentric, perhaps, but certainly not—"

"If nothing happens to that inkwell, 'crazy as a bedbug' is the only description of me that will do," he interrupted, turning on the overhead lights. His eyes narrowed. "To give you an idea of how crazy, I'll tell you what's been running through my mind when I should have been sleeping. I think maybe I can save the world. I think maybe I can make every nation a *have* nation, and do away with war for good. I think maybe I can clear roads through jungles, irrigate deserts, build dams overnight."

"Yes, sir."

"Watch the inkwell!"

Dutifully and fearfully I watched. A high-pitched humming seemed to come from the inkwell; then it began to vibrate alarmingly, and finally to bound about the top of the desk, making two noisy circuits. It stopped, hummed again, glowed red, then popped in splinters with a blue-green flash.

Perhaps my hair stood on end. The professor laughed gently. "Magnets?" I managed to say at last.

"Wish to heaven it were magnets," he murmured. It was then that he told me of dynamopsychism. He knew only that there was such a force; he could not explain it. "It's me and me alone—and it's awful."

"I'd say it was amazing and wonderful!" I cried.

"If all I could do was make inkwells dance, I'd be tickled silly with the whole business." He shrugged disconsolately. "But I'm no toy, my boy. If you like, we can drive around the neighborhood, and I'll show you what I mean." He told me about pulverized boulders, shattered oaks, and abandoned farm buildings demolished within a fifty-mile radius of the campus. "Did every bit of it sitting right here, just thinking—not even thinking hard."

He scratched his head nervously. "I have never dared to concentrate as hard as I can for fear of the damage I might do. I'm to the point where a mere whim is a blockbuster." There was a depressing pause. "Up until a few days ago, I've thought it best to keep my secret for fear of what use it might be put to," he continued. "Now I realize that I haven't any more right to it than a man has a right to own an atomic bomb."

He fumbled through a heap of papers. "This says about all that needs to be said, I think." He handed me a draft of a letter to the Secretary of State.

Dear Sir:

I have discovered a new force which costs nothing to use, and which is probably more important than atomic energy. I should like to see it used most effectively in the cause of peace, and am, therefore, requesting your advice as to how this might best be done.

Yours truly,
A. Barnhouse.

"I have no idea what will happen next," said the professor.

There followed three months of perpetual nightmare, wherein the nation's political and military great came at all hours to watch the professor's tricks.

We were quartered in an old mansion near Charlottesville, Virginia, to which we had been whisked five days after the letter was mailed. Surrounded by barbed wire and twenty guards, we were labeled "Project Wishing Well," and were classified as Top Secret.

For companionship we had General Honus Barker and the State Department's William K. Cuthrell. For the professor's talk of peace-through-plenty they had indulgent smiles and much discourse on practical measures and realistic thinking. So treated, the professor, who had at first been almost meek, progressed in a matter of weeks toward stubbornness.

He had agreed to reveal the thought train by means of which he aligned his mind into a dynamopsychic transmitter. But, under Cuthrell's and Barker's nagging to do so, he began to hedge. At first he declared that the information could be passed on simply by word of mouth. Later he said that it would have to be written up in a long report. Finally, at dinner one night, just after General Barker had read the secret orders for Operation Brainstorm, the professor announced, "The report may take as long as five years to write." He looked fiercely at the general. "Maybe twenty."

The dismay occasioned by this flat announcement was offset somewhat by the exciting anticipation of Operation Brainstorm. The general was in a holiday mood. "The target ships are on their way to the Caroline Islands at this very moment," he declared ecstatically. "One hundred and twenty of them! At the same time, ten V-2s are being readied for firing in New Mexico, and fifty radio-controlled jet bombers are being equipped for a mock attack on the Aleutians. Just think of it!" Happily he reviewed his orders. "At exactly 1100 hours next Wednesday, I will give you the order to *concentrate*; and you, professor, will think as hard as you can about sinking the target ships, destroying the V-2s before they hit the ground, and knocking down the bombers before they reach the Aleutians! Think you can handle it?"

The professor turned gray and closed his eyes. "As I told you before, my friend, I don't know what I can do." He added bitterly, "As for this Operation Brainstorm, I was never consulted about it, and it strikes me as childish and insanely expensive."

General Barker bridled. "Sir," he said, "your field is psychology, and I wouldn't presume to give you advice in that field. Mine is national defense. I have had thirty years of experience and success, Professor, and I'll ask you not to criticize my judgment."

The professor appealed to Mr. Cuthrell. "Look," he pleaded, "isn't it war and military matters we're all trying to get rid of? Wouldn't it be a whole lot more significant and lots cheaper for me to try moving cloud masses into drought areas, and things like that? I admit I know next to nothing about international politics, but it seems reasonable to suppose that nobody would want to fight wars if there were enough of everything to go around. Mr. Cuthrell, I'd like to try running generators where there isn't any coal or water power, irrigating deserts, and so on. Why, you could figure out what each country needs to make the most of its resources, and I could give it to them without costing American taxpayers a penny."

"Eternal vigilance is the price of freedom," said the general heavily.

Mr. Cuthrell threw the general a look of mild distaste. "Unfortunately, the general is right in his own way," he said. "I wish to heaven the world were ready for ideals like yours, but it simply isn't. We aren't surrounded by brothers, but by enemies. It isn't a lack of food or resources that has us on the brink of war—it's a struggle for power. Who's going to be in charge of the world, our kind of people or theirs?"

The professor nodded in reluctant agreement and arose from the table. "I beg your pardon, gentlemen. You are, after all, better qualified to judge what is best for the country. I'll do whatever you say." He turned to me. "Don't forget to wind the restricted clock and put the confidential cat out," he said gloomily, and ascended the stairs to his bedroom.

For reasons of national security, Operation Brainstorm was carried on without the knowledge of the American citizenry which was paying the bill. The observers, technicians, and military men involved in the activity knew that a test was under way—a test of what, they had no idea. Only thirty-seven key men, myself included, knew what was afoot.

In Virginia, the day for Operation Brainstorm was unseasonably cool. Inside, a log fire crackled in the fireplace, and the flames were reflected in the polished metal cabinets that lined the living room. All that remained of the room's lovely old furniture was a Victorian love seat, set squarely in the center of the floor, facing three television receivers. One long bench had been brought in for the ten of us privileged to watch. The television screens showed, from left to right, the stretch of desert which was the rocket target, the guinea-pig fleet, and a section of the

Aleutian sky through which the radio-controlled bomber formation would roar.

Ninety minutes before H-hour the radios announced that the rockets were ready, that the observation ships had backed away to what was thought to be a safe distance, and that the bombers were on their way. The small Virginia audience lined up on the bench in order of rank, smoked a great deal, and said little. Professor Barnhouse was in his bedroom. General Barker bustled about the house like a woman preparing Thanksgiving dinner for twenty.

At ten minutes before H-hour the general came in, shepherding the professor before him. The professor was comfortably attired in sneakers, gray flannels, a blue sweater, and a white shirt open at the neck. The two of them sat side by side on the love seat. The general was rigid and perspiring; the professor was cheerful. He looked at each of the screens, lighted a cigarette and settled back.

"Bombers sighted!" cried the Aleutian observers.

"Rockets away!" barked the New Mexico radio operator.

All of us looked quickly at the big electric clock over the mantel, while the professor, a half-smile on his face, continued to watch the television sets. In hollow tones, the general counted away the seconds remaining. "Five . . . four . . . three . . . two . . . one . . . *Concentrate!*"

Professor Barnhouse closed his eyes, pursed his lips, and stroked his temples. He held the position for a minute. The television images were scrambled, and the radio signals were drowned in the din of Barnhouse static. The professor sighed, opened his eyes, and smiled confidently.

"Did you give it everything you had?" asked the general dubiously.

"I was wide open," the professor replied.

The television images pulled themselves together, and mingled cries of amazement came over the radios tuned to the observers. The Aleutian sky was streaked with the smoke trails of bombers screaming down in flames. Simultaneously, there appeared high over the rocket target a cluster of white puffs, followed by faint thunder.

General Barker shook his head happily. "By George!" he crowed. "Well, sir, by George, by George, by George!"

"Look!" shouted the admiral seated next to me. "The fleet—it wasn't touched!"

"The guns seem to be drooping," said Mr. Cuthrell.

We left the bench and clustered about the television sets to examine the damage more closely. What Mr. Cuthrell had said was true. The ships' guns curved downward, their muzzles resting on the steel decks. We in Virginia were making such a hullabaloo that it was impossible to hear the radio reports. We were so engrossed, in fact, that we didn't miss the professor until two short snarls of Barnhouse static shocked us into sudden silence. The radios went dead.

We looked around apprehensively. The professor was gone. A harassed guard threw open the front door from the outside to yell that the professor had escaped. He brandished his pistol in the direction of the gates, which hung open, limp and twisted. In the distance, a speeding government station wagon topped a ridge and dropped from sight into the valley beyond. The air was filled with choking smoke, for every vehicle on the grounds was ablaze. Pursuit was impossible.

"What in God's name got into him?" bellowed the general.

Mr. Cuthrell, who had rushed out onto the front porch, now slouched back into the room, reading a penciled note as he came. He thrust the note into my hands. "The good man left this billet-doux under the door knocker. Perhaps our young friend here will be kind enough to read it to you gentlemen, while I take a restful walk through the woods."

"Gentlemen," I read aloud, "As the first superweapon with a conscience, I am removing myself from your national defense stockpile. Setting a new precedent in the behavior of ordnance, I have humane reasons for going off. A. Barnhouse."

Since that day, of course, the professor has been systematically destroying the world's armaments, until there is now little with which to equip an army other than rocks and sharp sticks. His activities haven't exactly resulted in peace, but have, rather, precipitated a bloodless and entertaining sort of war that might be called the "War of the Tattletales." Every nation is flooded with enemy agents whose sole mission is to locate military equipment, which is promptly wrecked when it is brought to the professor's attention in the press.

Just as every day brings news of more armaments pulverized by dynamopsychism, so has it brought rumors of the professor's whereabouts. During last week alone, three publications carried articles proving variously that he was hiding in an Inca ruin in the Andes, in the sewers of Paris, and in the unexplored lower chambers of Carlsbad Caverns. Knowing the man, I am inclined to regard such hiding places as unnecessarily romantic and uncomfortable. While there are numerous persons eager to kill him, there must be millions who would care for him and hide him. I like to think that he is in the home of such a person.

One thing is certain: at this writing, Professor Barnhouse is not dead. Barnhouse static jammed broadcasts not ten minutes ago. In the eighteen months since his disappearance, he has been reported dead some half-dozen times. Each report has stemmed from the death of an unidentified man resembling the professor, during a period free of the static. The first three reports were followed at once by renewed talk of rearmament and recourse to war. The saber-rattlers have learned how imprudent premature celebrations of the professor's demise can be.

Many a stouthearted patriot has found himself prone in the tangled bunting and timbers of a smashed reviewing stand, seconds after having announced that the arch-tyranny of Barnhouse was at an end. But those who would make war if they could, in every country in the world, wait in sullen silence for what must come—the passing of Professor Barnhouse.

To ask how much longer the professor will live is to ask how much longer we must wait for the blessings of another world war. He is of short-lived stock: his mother lived to be fifty-three, his father to be forty-nine; and the life-spans of his grandparents on both sides were of the same order. He might be expected to live, then, for perhaps fifteen years more, if he can remain hidden from his enemies. When one considers the number and vigor of these enemies, however, fifteen years seems an extraordinary length of time, which might better be revised to fifteen days, hours, or minutes.

The professor knows that he cannot live much longer. I say this because of the message left in my mailbox on Christmas Eve. Unsigned, typewritten on a soiled scrap of paper, the note consisted of ten sentences. The first nine of these, each a bewildering tangle of psychological jargon and references to obscure texts, made no sense to me at first reading. The tenth, unlike the rest, was simply constructed and contained no large words—but its irrational content made it the most puzzling and bizarre sentence of all. I nearly threw the note away, thinking it a colleague's warped notion of a practical joke. For some reason, though, I added it to the clutter on top of my desk, which included, among other mementos, the professor's dice.

It took me several weeks to realize that the message really meant something, that the first nine sentences, when unsnarled, could be taken as instructions. The tenth still told me nothing. It was only last night that I discovered how it fitted in with the rest. The sentence appeared in my thoughts last night, while I was toying absently with the professor's dice.

I promised to have this report on its way to the publishers today. In view of what has happened, I am obliged to break that promise, or release the report incomplete. The delay will not be a long one, for one of the few blessings accorded a bachelor like myself is the ability to move quickly from one abode to another, or from one way of life to another. What property I want to take with me can be packed in a few hours. Fortunately, I am not without substantial private means, which may take as long as a week to realize in liquid and anonymous form. When this is done, I shall mail the report.

I have just returned from a visit to my doctor, who tells me my health is excellent. I am young, and, with any luck at all, I shall live to a ripe old age indeed, for my family on both sides s noted for longevity.

Briefly, I propose to vanish.

Sooner or later, Professor Barnhouse must die. But long before then I shall be ready. So, to the saber-rattlers of today—and even, I hope, of tomorrow—I say: Be advised. Barnhouse will die. But not the Barnhouse Effect.

Last night, I tried once more to follow the oblique instructions on the scrap of paper. I took the professor's dice, and then, with the last, nightmarish sentence flitting through my mind, I rolled fifty consecutive sevens.

Good-by.

(1950)

THE EUPHIO QUESTION

LADIES AND GENTLEMEN of the Federal Communications Commission, I appreciate this opportunity to testify on the subject before you.

I'm sorry—or maybe "heartsick" is the word—that news has leaked out about it. But now that word is getting around and coming to your official notice, I might as well tell the story straight and pray to God that I can convince you that America doesn't want what we discovered.

I won't deny that all three of us—Lew Harrison, the radio announcer, Dr. Fred Bockman, the physicist, and myself, a sociology professor—found peace of mind. We did. And I won't say it's wrong for people to seek peace of mind. But if somebody thinks he wants peace of mind the way we found it, he'd be well advised to seek coronary thrombosis instead.

Lew, Fred, and I found peace of mind by sitting in easy chairs and turning on a gadget the size of a table-model television set. No herbs, no golden rule, no muscle control, no sticking our noses in other people's troubles to forget our own; no hobbies,

Taoism, push-ups or contemplation of a lotus. The gadget is, I think, what a lot of people vaguely foresaw as the crowning achievement of civilization: an electronic something-or-other, cheap, easily mass-produced, that can, at the flick of a switch, provide tranquillity. I see you have one here.

My first brush with synthetic peace of mind was six months ago. It was also then that I got to know Lew Harrison, I'm sorry to say. Lew is chief announcer of our town's only radio station. He makes his living with his loud mouth, and I'd be surprised if it were anyone but he who brought this matter to your attention.

Lew has, along with about thirty other shows, a weekly science program. Every week he gets some professor from Wyandotte College and interviews him about his particular field. Well, six months ago Lew worked up a program around a young dreamer and faculty friend of mine, Dr. Fred Bockman. I gave Fred a lift to the radio station, and he invited me to come on in and watch. For the heck of it, I did.

Fred Bockman is thirty and looks eighteen. Life has left no marks on him, because he hasn't paid much attention to it. What he pays most of his attention to, and what Lew Harrison wanted to interview him about, is this eight-ton umbrella of his that he listens to the stars with. It's a big radio antenna rigged up on a telescope mount. The way I understand it, instead of looking at the stars through a telescope, he aims this thing out in space and picks up radio signals coming from different heavenly bodies.

Of course, there aren't people running radio stations out there. It's just that many of the heavenly bodies pour out a lot of energy and some of it can be picked up in the radio-frequency band. One good thing Fred's rig does is to spot stars hidden from telescopes by big clouds of cosmic dust. Radio signals from them get through the clouds to Fred's antenna.

That isn't all the outfit can do, and, in his interview with Fred, Lew Harrison saved the most exciting part until the end of the program. "That's very interesting, Dr. Bockman," Lew said. "Tell me, has your radio telescope turned up anything else about the universe that hasn't been revealed by ordinary light telescopes?"

This was the snapper. "Yes, it has," Fred said. "We've found about fifty spots in space, *not hidden by cosmic dust*, that give off powerful radio signals. Yet no heavenly bodies at all seem to be there."

"Well!" Lew said in mock surprise. "I should say that *is* something! Ladies and gentlemen, for the first time in radio history, we bring you the noise from Dr. Bockman's mysterious voids." They had strung a line out to Fred's antenna on the campus. Lew waved to the engineer to switch in the signals coming from it. "Ladies and gentlemen, the voice of nothingness!"

The noise wasn't much to hear—a wavering hiss, more like a leaking tire than anything else. It was supposed to be on the air for five seconds. When the engineer switched it off, Fred and I were inexplicably grinning like idiots. I felt relaxed and tingling. Lew Harrison looked as though he'd stumbled into the dressing room at the Copacabana. He glanced at the studio clock, appalled. The monotonous hiss had been on the air for five minutes! If the engineer's cuff hadn't accidentally caught on the switch, it might be on yet.

Fred laughed nervously, and Lew hunted for his place in the script. "The hiss from nowhere," Lew said. "Dr. Bockman, has anyone proposed a name for these interesting voids?"

"No," Fred said. "At the present time they have neither a name nor an explanation."

The voids the hiss came from have still to be explained, but I've suggested a name for them that shows signs of sticking: "Bockman's Euphoria." We may not know what the spots are, but we know what they do, so the name's a good one. Euphoria, since it means a sense of buoyancy and well-being, is really the only word that will do.

After the broadcast, Fred, Lew, and I were cordial to one another to the point of being maudlin.

"I can't remember when a broadcast has been such a pleasure," Lew said. Sincerity is not his forte, yet he meant it.

"It's been one of the most memorable experiences of my life," Fred said, looking puzzled. "Extraordinarily pleasant."

We were all embarrassed by the emotion we felt, and parted company in bafflement and haste. I hurried home for a drink, only to walk into the middle of another unsettling experience.

The house was quiet, and I made two trips through it before discovering that I was not alone. My wife, Susan, a good and lovable woman who prides herself on feeding her family well and on time, was lying on the couch, staring dreamily at the ceiling. "Honey," I said tentatively, "I'm home. It's suppertime."

"Fred Bockman was on the radio today," she said in a faraway voice.

"I know. I was with him in the studio."

"He was out of this world," she sighed. "Simply out of this world. That noise from space—when he turned that on, everything just seemed to drop away from me. I've been lying here, just trying to get over it."

"Uh-huh," I said, biting my lip. "Well, guess I'd better round up Eddie." Eddie is my ten-year-old son, and captain of an apparently invincible neighborhood baseball team.

"Save your strength, Pop," said a small voice from the shadows.

"You home? What's the matter? Game called off on account of atomic attack?"

"Nope. We finished eight innings."

"Beating 'em so bad they didn't want to go on, eh?"

"Oh, they were doing pretty good. Score was tied, and they had two men on and two outs." He talked as though he were recounting a dream. "And then," he said, his eyes widening, "everybody kind of lost interest, just wandered off. I came home and found the old lady curled up here, so I lay down on the floor."

"Why?" I asked incredulously.

"Pop," Eddie said thoughtfully, "I'm damned if I know."

"Eddie!" his mother said.

"Mom," Eddie said, "I'm damned if *you* know either."

I was damned if anybody could explain it, but I had a nagging hunch. I dialed Fred Bockman's number. "Fred, am I getting you up from dinner?"

"I wish you were," Fred said. "Not a scrap to eat in the house, and I let Marion have the car today so she could do the marketing. Now she's trying to find a grocery open."

"Couldn't get the car started, eh?"

"Sure she got the car started," said Fred. "She even got to the market. Then she felt so good she walked right out of the place again." Fred sounded depressed. "I guess it's a woman's privilege to change her mind, but it's the lying that hurts."

"Marion lied? I don't believe it."

"She tried to tell me everybody wandered out of the market with her—clerks and all."

"Fred," I said, "I've got news for you. Can I drive out right after supper?"

When I arrived at Fred Bockman's farm, he was staring, dumbfounded, at the evening paper.

"The whole town went nuts!" Fred said. "For no reason at all, all the cars pulled up to the curb like there was a hook and ladder going by. Says here people shut up in the middle of sentences and stayed that way for five minutes. Hundreds wandered around in the cold in their shirt-sleeves, grinning like toothpaste ads." He rattled the paper. "This *is* what you wanted to talk to me about?"

I nodded. "It all happened when that noise was being broadcast, and I thought maybe—"

"The odds are about one in a million that there's any maybe about it," said Fred. "The time checks to the second."

"But most people weren't listening to the program."

"They didn't have to listen, if my theory's right. We took those faint signals from space, amplified them about a thousand times, and rebroadcast them. Anybody within reach of the transmitter would get a good dose of the stepped-up radiations, whether he wanted to or not." He shrugged. "Apparently that's like walking past a field of burning marijuana."

"How come you never felt the effect at work?"

"Because I never amplified and rebroadcast the signals. The radio station's transmitter is what really put the sock into them."

"So what're you going to do next?"

Fred looked surprised. "Do? What is there to do but report it in some suitable journal?"

Without a preliminary knock, the front door burst open and Lew Harrison, florid and panting, swept into the room and removed his great polo coat with a bullfighterlike flourish. "You're cutting him in on it, too?" he demanded, pointing at me.

Fred blinked at him. "In on what?"

"The millions," Lew said. "The billions."

"Wonderful," Fred said. "What are you talking about?"

"The noise from the stars!" Lew said "They love it. It drives 'em nuts. Didja see the papers?" He sobered for an instant. "It *was* the noise that did it, wasn't it, Doc?"

"We think so," Fred said. He looked worried. "How, exactly, do you propose we get our hands on these millions or billions?"

"Real estate!" Lew said raptly. " 'Lew,' I said to myself, 'Lew, how can you cash in on this gimmick if you can't get a monopoly on the universe? And, Lew,' I asked myself 'how can you sell the stuff when anybody can get it free while you're broadcasting it?' "

"Maybe it's the kind of thing that shouldn't be cashed in on," I suggested. "I mean, we don't know a great deal about—"

"Is happiness bad?" Lew interrupted.

"No," I admitted.

"Okay, and what we'd do with this stuff from the stars is make people happy. Now I suppose you're going to tell me that's bad?"

"People ought to be happy," Fred said.

"Okay, okay," Lew said loftily. "That's what we're going to do for the people. And the way the people can show their gratitude is in real estate." He looked out the window. "Good—a barn. We can start right there. We set up a transmitter in the barn, run a line out to your antenna, Doc, and we've got a real-estate development."

"Sorry," Fred said. "I don't follow you. This place wouldn't do for a development. The roads are poor, no bus service or shopping center, the view is lousy and the ground is full of rocks."

Lew nudged Fred several times with his elbow. "Doc, Doc, Doc—sure it's got drawbacks, but with that transmitter in the barn, you can give them the most precious thing in all creation—happiness."

"Euphoria Heights," I said.

"That's great!" said Lew. "I'd get the prospects, Doc, and you'd sit up there in the barn with your hand on the switch. Once a prospect set foot on Euphoria Heights, and you shot the happiness to him, there's nothing he wouldn't pay for a lot."

"Every house a home, as long as the power doesn't fail," I said.

"Then," Lew said, his eyes shining, "when we sell all the lots here, we move the transmitter and start another development. Maybe we'd get a fleet of transmitters going." He snapped his fingers. "Sure! Mount 'em on wheels."

"I somehow don't think the police would think highly of us," Fred said.

"Okay, so when they come to investigate, you throw the old switch and give *them* a jolt of happiness." He shrugged. "Hell, I might even get bighearted and let them have a corner lot."

"No," Fred said quietly. "If I ever joined a church, I couldn't face the minister."

"So we give *him* a jolt," Lew said brightly.

"No," Fred said. "Sorry."

"Okay," Lew said, rising and pacing the floor. "I was prepared for that. I've got an alternative, and this one's strictly legitimate. We'll make a little amplifier with a transmitter and an aerial on it. Shouldn't cost over fifty bucks to make, so we'd price it in the range of the common man—five hundred bucks, say. We make arrangements with the phone company to pipe signals from your antenna right into the homes of people with these sets. The sets take the signal from the phone line, amplify it, and broadcast it through the houses to make everybody in them happy. See? Instead of turning on the radio or television, everybody's going to want to turn on the happiness. No casts, no stage sets, no expensive cameras—no nothing but that hiss."

"We could call it the euphoriaphone," I suggested, "or 'euphio' for short."

"That's great, that's great!" Lew said. "What do you say, Doc?"

"I don't know." Fred looked worried. "This sort of thing is out of my line."

"We all have to recognize our limitations, Doc," Lew said expansively. "I'll handle the business end, and you handle the technical end." He made a motion as though to put on his coat. "Or maybe you don't want to be a millionaire?"

"Oh, yes, yes indeed I do," Fred said quickly. "Yes indeed."

"All righty," Lew said, dusting his palms, "the first thing we've gotta do is build one of the sets and test her."

This part of it *was* down Fred's alley, and I could see the problem interested him. "It's really a pretty simple gadget," he said. "I suppose we could throw one together and run a test out here next week."

The first test of the euphoriaphone, or euphio, took place in Fred Bockman's living room on a Saturday afternoon, five days after Fred's and Lew's sensational radio broadcast.

There were six guinea pigs—Lew, Fred and his wife Marion, myself, my wife Susan, and my son Eddie. The Bockmans had arranged chairs in a circle around a card table, on which rested a gray steel box.

Protruding from the box was a long buggy whip aerial that scraped the ceiling. While Fred fussed with the box, the rest of us made nervous small talk over sandwiches and beer. Eddie, of course, wasn't drinking beer, though he was badly in need of a sedative. He was annoyed at having been brought out to the farm instead of to a ball game, and was threatening to take it out on the Bockmans' Early American furnishings. He was playing a spirited game of flies and grounders with himself near the French doors, using a dead tennis ball and a poker.

"Eddie," Susan said for the tenth time, "please stop."

"It's under control, under control," Eddie said disdainfully, playing the ball off four walls and catching it with one hand.

Marion, who vents her maternal instincts on her immaculate furnishings, couldn't hide her distress at Eddie's turning the place into a gymnasium. Lew, in his way, was trying to calm her. "Let him wreck the dump," Lew said. "You'll be moving into a palace one of these days."

"It's ready," Fred said softly.

We looked at him with queasy bravery. Fred plugged two

jacks from the phone line into the gray box. This was the direct line to his antenna on the campus, and clockwork would keep the antenna fixed on one of the mysterious voids in the sky —the most potent of Bockman's Euphoria. He plugged a cord from the box into an electrical outlet in the baseboard, and rested his hand on a switch. "Ready?"

"Don't, Fred!" I said. I was scared stiff.

"Turn it on, turn it on," Lew said. "We wouldn't have the telephone today if Bell hadn't had the guts to call somebody up."

"I'll stand right here by the switch, ready to flick her off if something goes sour," Fred said reassuringly. There was a click, a hum, and the euphio was on.

A deep, unanimous sigh filled the room. The poker slipped from Eddie's hands. He moved across the room in a stately sort of waltz, knelt by his mother, and laid his head in her lap. Fred drifted away from his post, humming, his eyes half closed.

Lew Harrison was the first to speak, continuing his conversation with Marion. "But who cares for material wealth?" he asked earnestly. He turned to Susan for confirmation.

"Uh-uh," said Susan, shaking her head dreamily. She put her arms around Lew, and kissed him for about five minutes.

"Say," I said, patting Susan on the back, "you kids get along swell, don't you? Isn't that nice, Fred?"

"Eddie," Marion said solicitously, "I think there's a real baseball in the hall closet. A *hard* ball. Wouldn't that be more fun than that old tennis ball?" Eddie didn't stir.

Fred was still prowling around the room, smiling, his eyes now closed all the way. His heel caught in a lamp cord, and he went sprawling on the hearth, his head in the ashes. "Hi-ho, everybody," he said, his eyes still closed. "Bunged my head on an andiron." He stayed there, giggling occasionally.

"The doorbell's been ringing for a while," Susan said. "I don't suppose it means anything."

"Come in, come in," I shouted. This somehow struck everyone as terribly funny. We all laughed uproariously, including Fred, whose guffaws blew up little gray clouds from the ashpit.

▪   ▪   ▪

A small, very serious old man in white had let himself in, and was now standing in the vestibule, looking at us with alarm. "Milkman," he said uncertainly. He held out a slip of paper to Marion. "I can't read the last line in your note," he said. "What's that say about cottage cheese, cheese, cheese, cheese, cheese . . ." His voice trailed off as he settled, tailor-fashion, to the floor beside Marion. After he'd been silent for perhaps three quarters of an hour, a look of concern crossed his face. "Well," he said apathetically, "I can only stay for a minute. My truck's parked out on the shoulder, kind of blocking things." He started to stand. Lew gave the volume knob on the euphio a twist. The milkman wilted to the floor.

"Aaaaaaaaaaah," said everybody.

"Good day to be indoors," the milkman said. "Radio says we'll catch the tail end of the Atlantic hurricane."

"Let 'er come," I said. "I've got my car parked under a big, dead tree." It seemed to make sense. Nobody took exception to it. I lapsed back into a warm fog of silence and thought of nothing whatsoever. These lapses seemed to last for a matter of seconds before they were interrupted by conversation of newcomers. Looking back, I see now that the lapses were rarely less than six hours.

I was snapped out of one, I recall, by a repetition of the doorbell's ringing. "I said come in," I mumbled.

"And I did," the milkman mumbled.

The door swung open, and a state trooper glared in at us. "Who the hell's got his milk truck out there blocking the road?" he demanded. He spotted the milkman. "Aha! Don't you know somebody could get killed, coming around a blind curve into that thing?" He yawned, and his ferocious expression gave way to an affectionate smile. "It's so damn' unlikely," he said, "I don't know why I ever brought it up." He sat down by Eddie. "Hey, kid—like guns?" He took his revolver from its holster. "Look—just like Hoppy's."

Eddie took the gun, aimed it at Marion's bottle collection and fired. A large blue bottle popped to dust and the window behind the collection splintered. Cold air roared in through the opening.

"He'll make a cop yet," Marion chortled.

"God, I'm happy," I said, feeling a little like crying. "I got the swellest little kid and the swellest bunch of friends and the swellest old wife in the world." I heard the gun go off twice more, and then dropped into heavenly oblivion.

Again the doorbell roused me. "How many times do I have to tell you—for Heaven's sake, come in," I said, without opening my eyes.

"I *did*," the milkman said.

I heard the tramping of many feet, but had no curiosity about them. A little later, I noticed that I was having difficulty breathing. Investigation revealed that I had slipped to the floor, and that several Boy Scouts had bivouacked on my chest and abdomen.

"You want something?" I asked the tenderfoot whose hot, measured breathing was in my face.

"Beaver Patrol wanted old newspapers, but forget it," he said. "We'd just have to carry 'em somewhere."

"And do your parents know where you are?"

"Oh, sure. They got worried and came after us." He jerked his thumb at several couples lined up against the baseboard, smiling into the teeth of the wind and rain lashing in at them through the broken window.

"Mom, I'm kinda hungry," Eddie said.

"Oh, Eddie—you're not going to make your mother cook just when we're having such a wonderful time," Susan said.

Lew Harrison gave the euphio's volume knob another twist. "There, kid, how's that?"

"Aaaaaaaaaaah," said everybody.

When awareness intruded on oblivion again, I felt around for the Beaver Patrol, and found them missing. I opened my eyes to see that they and Eddie and the milkman and Lew and the trooper were standing by a picture window, cheering. The wind outside was roaring and slashing savagely and driving raindrops through the broken window as though they'd been fired from air rifles. I shook Susan gently, and together we went to the window to see what might be so entertaining.

"She's going, she's going, she's going," the milkman cried ecstatically.

Susan and I arrived just in time to join in the cheering as a big elm crashed down on our sedan.

"Kee-*runch!*" said Susan, and I laughed until my stomach hurt.

"Get Fred," Lew said urgently. "He's gonna miss seeing the barn go!"

"H'mm?" Fred said from the fireplace.

"Aw, Fred, you missed it," Marion said.

"Now we're really gonna see something," Eddie yelled. "The power line's going to get it this time. Look at that poplar lean!"

The poplar leaned closer, closer, closer to the power line; and then a gust brought it down in a hail of sparks and a tangle of wires. The lights in the house went off.

Now there was only the sound of the wind. "How come nobody cheered?" Lew said faintly. "The euphio—it's off!"

A horrible groan came from the fireplace. "God, I think I've got a concussion."

Marion knelt by her husband and wailed. "Darling, my poor darling—what happened to you?"

I looked at the woman I had my arms around—a dreadful, dirty old hag, with red eyes sunk deep in her head, and hair like Medusa's. "Ugh," I said, and turned away in disgust.

"Honey," wept the witch, "it's me—Susan."

Moans filled the air, and pitiful cries for food and water. Suddenly the room had become terribly cold. Only a moment before I had imagined I was in the tropics.

"Who's got my damn' pistol?" the trooper said bleakly.

A Western Union boy I hadn't noticed before was sitting in a corner, miserably leafing through a pile of telegrams and making clucking noises.

I shuddered. "I'll bet it's Sunday morning," I said. "We've been here twelve hours!" It was Monday morning.

The Western Union boy was thunderstruck. "Sunday morning? I walked in here on a Sunday night." He stared around the room. "Looks like them newsreels of Buchenwald, don't it?"

The chief of the Beaver Patrol, with the incredible stamina of the young, was the hero of the day. He fell in his men in two ranks, haranguing them like an old Army top-kick. While the rest of us lay draped around the room, whimpering about hunger, cold, and thirst, the patrol started the furnace again, brought blankets, applied compresses to Fred's head and countless barked shins, blocked off the broken window, and made buckets of cocoa and coffee.

Within two hours of the time that the power and the euphio went off, the house was warm and we had eaten. The serious respiratory cases—the parents who had sat near the broken window for twenty-four hours—had been pumped full of penicillin and hauled off to the hospital. The milkman, the Western Union boy, and the trooper had refused treatment and gone home. The Beaver Patrol had saluted smartly and left. Outside, repairmen were working on the power line. Only the original group remained—Lew, Fred, and Marion, Susan and myself, and Eddie. Fred, it turned out, had some pretty important-looking contusions and abrasions, but no concussion.

Susan had fallen asleep right after eating. Now she stirred. "What happened?"

"Happiness," I told her. "Incomparable, continuous happiness—happiness by the kilowatt."

Lew Harrison, who looked like an anarchist with his red eyes and fierce black beard, had been writing furiously in one corner of the room. "That's good—happiness by the kilowatt," he said. "Buy your happiness the way you buy light."

"Contract happiness the way you contract influenza," Fred said. He sneezed.

Lew ignored him. "It's a campaign, see? The first ad is for the long-hairs: 'The price of one book, which may be a disappointment, will buy you sixty hours of euphio. Euphio never disappoints.' Then we'd hit the middle class with the next one—"

"In the groin?" Fred said.

"What's the matter with you people?" Lew said. "You act as though the experiment had failed."

"Pneumonia and malnutrition are what we'd *hoped* for?" Marion said.

"We had a cross section of America in this room, and we made every last person happy," Lew said. "Not for just an hour, not for just a day, but for two days without a break." He arose reverently from his chair. "So what we do to keep it from killing the euphio fans is to have the thing turned on and off with clockwork, see? The owner sets it so it'll go on just as he comes home from work, then it'll go off again while he eats supper; then it goes on after supper, off again when it's bedtime; on again after breakfast, off when it's time to go to work, then on again for the wife and kids."

He ran his hands through his hair and rolled his eyes. "And the selling points—my God, the selling points! No expensive toys for the kids. For the price of a trip to the movies, people can buy thirty hours of euphio. For the price of a fifth of whisky, they can buy sixty hours of euphio!"

"Or a big family bottle of potassium cyanide," Fred said.

"Don't you see it?" Lew said incredulously. "It'll bring families together again, save the American home. No more fights over what TV or radio program to listen to. Euphio pleases one and all—we proved that. And there is no such thing as a dull euphio program."

A knock on the door interrupted him. A repairman stuck his head in to announce that the power would be on again in about two minutes.

"Look, Lew," Fred said, "this little monster could kill civilization in less time than it took to burn down Rome. We're not going into the mind-numbing business, and that's that."

"You're kidding!" Lew said, aghast. He turned to Marion. "Don't you want your husband to make a million?"

"Not by operating an electronic opium den," Marion said coldly.

Lew slapped his forehead. "It's what the public wants. This is like Louis Pasteur refusing to pasteurize milk."

"It'll be good to have the electricity again," Marion said, changing the subject. "Lights, hot-water heater, the pump, the—oh, Lord!"

The lights came on the instant she said it, but Fred and I were already in mid-air, descending on the gray box. We crashed down on it together. The card table buckled, and the plug was jerked from the wall socket. The euphio's tubes glowed red for a moment, then died.

Expressionlessly, Fred took a screwdriver from his pocket and removed the top of the box.

"Would you enjoy doing battle with progress?" he said, offering me the poker Eddie had dropped.

In a frenzy, I stabbed and smashed at the euphio's glass and wire vitals. With my left hand, and with Fred's help, I kept Lew from throwing himself between the poker and the works.

"I thought you were on my side," Lew said.

"If you breathe one word about euphio to anyone," I said, "what I just did to euphio I will gladly do to you."

And there, ladies and gentlemen of the Federal Communications Commission, I thought the matter had ended. It deserved to end there. Now, through the medium of Lew Harrison's big mouth, word has leaked out. He has petitioned you for permission to start commercial exploitation of euphio. He and his backers have built a radio-telescope of their own.

Let me say again that all of Lew's claims are true. Euphio will do everything he says it will. The happiness it gives is perfect and unflagging in the face of incredible adversity. Near tragedies, such as the first experiment, can no doubt be avoided with clockwork to turn the sets on and off. I see that this set on the table before you is, in fact, equipped with clockwork.

The question is not whether euphio works. It does. The question is, rather, whether or not America is to enter a new and distressing phase of history where men no longer pursue happiness but buy it. This is no time for oblivion to become a national craze. The only benefit we could get from euphio would be if we could somehow lay down a peace-of-mind barrage on our enemies while protecting our own people from it.

In closing, I'd like to point out that Lew Harrison, the would-be czar of euphio, is an unscrupulous person, unworthy of public trust. It wouldn't surprise me, for instance, if he had set the clockwork on this sample euphio set so that its radiations would addle your judgments when you are trying to make a decision. In fact, it seems to be whirring suspiciously at this very moment, and I'm so happy I could cry. I've got the swellest little kid and the swellest bunch of friends and the swellest old wife in the world. And good old Lew Harrison is the salt of the earth, believe me. I sure wish him a lot of good luck with his new enterprise.

(1951)

GO BACK TO YOUR PRECIOUS WIFE AND SON

GLORIA HILTON and her fifth husband didn't live in New Hampshire very long. But they lived there long enough for me to sell them a bathtub enclosure. My main line is aluminum combination storm windows and screens—but anybody in storm windows is practically automatically in bathtub enclosures, too.

The enclosure they ordered was for Gloria Hilton's personal bathtub. I guess that was the zenith of my career. Some men are asked to build mighty dams or noble skyscrapers, or conquer terrible plagues, or lead great armies into battle.

Me?

I was asked to keep drafts off the most famous body in the world.

People ask me how well did I know Gloria Hilton. I generally say, "The only time I ever saw that woman in the flesh was through a hot-air register." That was how the bathroom where they wanted the enclosure was heated—with a hot-air register in the floor. It wasn't connected to the furnace. It just bled heat from the ceiling of the room down below. I don't wonder Gloria Hilton found her bathroom cold.

I was installing the enclosure when loud talk started coming out of the register. I was at a very tricky point, gluing the waterproof gasket around the rim of the tub with contact cement, so I couldn't close the register. I had to listen to what wasn't any of my business, whether I wanted to or not.

"Don't talk to me about love," Gloria Hilton said to her fifth husband. "You don't know anything about love. You don't know the meaning of love."

I hadn't looked down through the register yet, so the only face I had to put with her voice was her face in the movies.

"Maybe you're right, Gloria," said her fifth husband.

"I give you my word of honor I'm right," she said.

"Well—" he said, "that certainly brings the whole discussion to a dead stop right there. How could I possibly argue with the sacred word of honor of Gloria Hilton?"

I knew what he looked like. He was the one who'd done all the negotiating for the bathtub enclosure. I had also sold him two Fleetwood Trip-L-Trak storm windows for the two bathroom windows. Those have the self-storing screen feature. The whole time we were negotiating, he called his wife "Miss Hilton." Miss Hilton wanted this, and Miss Hilton wanted that. He was only thirty-five, but the circles under his eyes made him look sixty.

"I pity you," Gloria Hilton said to him. "I pity anybody who can't love. They are the most pitiful people there are."

"The more you talk," he said, "the more I'm convinced I'm one of them."

He was the writer, of course. My wife keeps a lot of Hollywood stuff in her head, and she tells me Gloria Hilton was married to a motorcycle policeman, then a sugar millionaire, then somebody who played Tarzan, then her agent—and then the writer. George Murra, the writer, was the one I knew.

"People keep wondering what the matter with the world is," said Gloria. "I know what the matter is. It's simple: most men don't know the meaning of the word love."

"At least give me credit for trying to find out what it means," said Murra. "For one solid year now, I haven't done a single, solitary thing but order a bathtub enclosure and try to find out what love means."

"I suppose you're going to blame me for that, too," she said.

"For what?" he said.

"The fact that you haven't written a word since we've been married," she said. "I suppose that's somehow my fault, too."

"I hope I'm not that shallow," he said. "I know a plain, ordinary coincidence when I see one. The fights we have all night, the photographers and reporters and so-called friends we have all day—they have nothing to do with the fact I've dried up."

"You're one of those people who enjoys suffering," she said.

"That's a smart way to be," he said.

"I'll tell you frankly," she said, "I'm disappointed in you."

"I knew," he said, "that sooner or later you would come right out and say it."

"I might as well tell you, too," she said, "that I've decided to bring this farce to an end."

"It's nice of you to make me among the first to know," he said. "Shall I notify Louella Parsons, or has that already been taken care of?"

I had the gasket glued onto the bathtub rim, so I was free to close the register. I looked straight down through the grating, and there Gloria Hilton was. She had her hair up in curlers. She didn't have any makeup on. She hadn't even bothered to draw on eyebrows. She had on some kind of slip and a bathrobe that was gaping open. I swear, that woman wasn't any prettier than a used studio couch.

"I don't think you're very funny," she said.

"You knew I was a serious writer when you married me," he said.

She stood up. She spread her arms like Moses telling the Jews the Promised Land was right over the next hill. "Go on back to your precious wife and your precious son," she said. "I certainly won't stand in your way."

I closed the register.

▪   ▪   ▪

Five minutes later, Murra came upstairs and told me to clear out. "Miss Hilton wants to use her bathroom," he said. I never saw such a peculiar expression on a man's face. He was all red, and there were tears in his eyes—but there was this crazy laugh tearing him apart, trying to get out.

"I'm not quite finished," I said.

"Miss Hilton is completely finished," he said. "Clear out!"

So I went out to my truck, and I drove into town, had a cup of coffee. The door for the bathtub enclosure was on a wooden rack on the back of my truck, out in the open—and it certainly attracted a lot of attention.

Most people, when they order an enclosure door, don't want anything on it unless maybe a flamingo or a seahorse. The plant, which is over in Lawrence, Massachusetts, is set up to sandblast a flamingo or a seahorse on a door for only six dollars extra. But Gloria Hilton wanted a big "G," two feet across—and in the middle of the "G" she wanted a life-size head of herself. And the eyes on the head had to be exactly five feet two inches above the bottom of the tub, because that's how high her real eyes were when she stood up barefoot in the tub.

They went crazy over in Lawrence.

One of the people I was having coffee with was Harry Crocker, the plumber. "I certainly hope you insisted on measuring her yourself," he said, "so the figures would be absolutely accurate."

"Her husband did it," I said.

"Some people have all the luck," he said.

I went to the pay telephone, and I called up Murra's house to see if it would be all right for me to come back and finish up. The line was busy.

When I got back to my coffee, Harry Crocker said to me, "You missed something I don't think anybody's ever liable to see in this town ever again."

"What's that?" I said.

"Gloria Hilton and her maid going through town at two hundred miles an hour," he said.

"Which way were they headed?" I said.

"West," he said.

*　　*　　*

So I tried to call Murra again. I figured, with Gloria Hilton gone, all the big telephoning would be over. But the telephone went right on being busy for an hour. I thought maybe somebody had torn the telephone out by its roots, but the operator said it was in working order.

"Try the number again, then," I told her.

That time I got through.

Murra answered the phone. All I said to him was, "Hello," and he got very excited. He wasn't excited about getting the bathtub enclosure finished. He was excited because he thought I was somebody named John.

"John, John," he said to me, "thank God you called!

"John," he said to me, "I know what you think of me, and I don't blame you for thinking that—but please listen to what I have to say before you hang up. She's left me, John. That part of my life is over—finished! Now I'm trying to pick up the pieces. John," he said, "in the name of mercy, you've got to come here. Please, John, please, John, please."

"Mr. Murra—?" I said.

"Yes?" he said. From the way his voice went away from the telephone, I guess he thought I'd just walked into the room.

"It's me, Mr. Murra," I said.

"It's who?" he said.

"The bathtub enclosure man," I said.

"I was expecting a very important long-distance call," he said. "Please get off the wire."

"I beg your pardon," I said. "I just want to know when you want me to finish up there."

"Never!" he said. "Forget it! The hell with it!"

"Mr. Murra—" I said, "I can't return that door for credit."

"Send me the bill," he said. "I make you a present of the door."

"Whatever you say," I said. "Now, you've got these two Fleetwood Trip-L-Trak windows, too."

"Throw 'em on the dump!" he said.

"Mr. Murra—" I said, "I guess you're upset about something—"

"God you're smart!" he said.

"Maybe throwing away that door makes sense," I said, "but

storm windows never hurt a soul. Why don't you let me come out and put 'em up? You'll never even know I'm there."

"All right, all right, all right!" he said, and he hung up.

The Fleetwood Trip-L-Trak is our first-line window, so there isn't anything quick and dirty about the way we put them up. We put a gasket up all the way around, just the way we do on a bathtub enclosure. So I had some standing around to do at Murra's house, just waiting for glue to dry. You can actually fill up a room equipped with Fleetwoods with water, fill it clear up to the ceiling, and it won't leak—not through the windows, anyway.

While I was waiting on the glue, Murra came out and asked me if I wanted a drink.

"Pardon me?" I said.

"Or maybe bathtub enclosure men don't drink on duty," he said.

"That's only on television," I said.

So he took me in the kitchen, and he got out a bottle and ice and a couple of glasses.

"This is very nice of you," I said.

"I may not know what love is," he said, "but, by God, at least I've never gotten drunk by myself."

"That's what we're going to do?" I said.

"Unless you have some other suggestion," he said.

"I'll have to think a minute," I said.

"That's a mistake," he said. "You miss an awful lot of life that way. That's why you Yankees are so cold," he said. "You think too much. That's why you marry so seldom."

"At least some of that is a plain lack of money," I said.

"No, no," he said. "It goes deeper than that. You people around here don't grasp the thistle firmly." He had to explain that to me, about how a thistle won't prick you if you grab it real hard and fast.

"I don't believe that about thistles," I said.

"Typical New England conservatism," he said.

"I gather you aren't from these parts," I said.

"That happiness is not mine," he said. He told me he was from Los Angeles.

"I guess that's nice, too," I said.

"The people are all phonies," he said.

"I wouldn't know about that," I said.

"That's why we took up residence here," he said. "As my wife —my second wife, that is—told all the reporters at our wedding, 'We are getting away from all the phonies. We are going to live where people are really people. We are going to live in New Hampshire. My husband and I are going to find ourselves. He is going to write and write and write. He is going to write the most beautiful scenario anybody in the history of literature has ever written for me.'"

"That's nice," I said.

"You didn't read that in the newspapers or the magazines?" he said.

"No," I said. "I used to go out with a girl who subscribed to *Film Fun,* but that was years ago. I have no idea what happened to her."

Somewhere in the course of this conversation, a fifth of a gallon of Old Hickey's Private Stock Sour Mash Bourbon was evaporating, or was being stolen, or was otherwise disappearing fast.

And I haven't got the conversation set down quite straight, because somewhere in there Murra told me he'd been married when he was only eighteen—and he told me who the John was he'd thought I was on the telephone.

It hurt Murra a lot to talk about John. "John," he said, "is my only child. Fifteen years old." Murra clouded up, pointed southeast. "Only twenty-two miles away—so near and yet so far," he said.

"He didn't stay with his mother in Los Angeles?" I said.

"His home is with her," said Murra, "but he goes to school at Mount Henry." Mount Henry is a very good boy's prep school near here. "One of the reasons I came to New Hampshire was to be close to him." Murra shook his head. "I thought surely he'd get in touch with me sooner or later—return a telephone call, answer a letter."

"But he never did?" I said.

"Never," said Murra. "You know what the last thing was he said to me?"

"Nope," I said.

"When I divorced his mother and married Gloria Hilton, the last thing he said was, 'Father, you're contemptible. I don't want to hear another word from you as long as I live.'"

"That's—that's strong," I said.

"Friend—" said Murra hoarsely, "that's *mighty* strong." He bowed his head. "That was the word he used—contemptible. Young as he was, he sure used the right one."

"Did you finally get in touch with him today?" I said.

"I called the Headmaster of the school, and I told him there was a terrible family emergency, and he had to make John call me right away," said Murra.

"It worked, thank God," he said. "And, even though I am definitely contemptible, he has agreed to come see me tomorrow."

Somewhere else in that conversation, Murra told me to look at the statistics sometime. I promised him I would. "Just statistics in general—or some special statistics?" I asked him.

"Statistics on marriage," he said.

"I'm scared to think of what I'm liable to find," I said.

"You look at the statistics," said Murra, "and you'll find out that when people get married when they're only eighteen—the way my first wife and I did—there's a fifty-fifty chance the thing will blow sky high."

"I was eighteen when I was married," I said.

"You're still with your first wife?" he said.

"Going on twenty years now," I said.

"Don't you ever feel like you got gypped out of your bachelor days, your playboy days, your days as a great lover?"

"Well," I said, "in New Hampshire those days generally come between the ages of fourteen and seventeen."

"Let me put it to you this way," he said. "Say you'd been married all these years, fighting about the dumb things married people fight about, being broke and worried most of the time—"

"I'm right with you," I said.

"And say the movies bought a book you'd written, and they

hired you to write the screen play, and Gloria Hilton was going to be the star," he said.

"I don't think I can imagine that," I said.

"All right—" he said, "what's the biggest thing that could possibly happen to you in your line of work?"

I had to think a while. "I guess it would be if I sold the Conners Hotel on putting Fleetwoods on every window. That must be five-hundred windows or more," I said.

"Good!" he said. "You've just made the sale. You've got real money in your pocket for the first time. You've just had a fight with your wife, and you're thinking mean things about her, feeling sorry for yourself. And the manager of the hotel is Gloria Hilton—Gloria Hilton looking the way she does in the movies."

"I'm listening," I said.

"Say you started putting up those five-hundred Fleetwoods," he said, "and say every time you put up another storm window, there was Gloria Hilton smiling at you through the glass, like you were a god or something."

"Is there anything left to drink in the house?" I said.

"Say that went on for three months," he said. "And every night you went home to your wife, some woman you'd known so long she was practically like a sister, and she would crab about some little thing—"

"This is a very warm room, even without storm windows," I said.

"Say Gloria Hilton all of a sudden said to you," he said, " 'Dare to be happy, my poor darling! Oh, darling, we were *made* for each other! Dare to be happy with me! I go limp when I see you putting up storm windows! I can't stand to see you so unhappy, to know you belong to some other woman, to know how happy I could make you, if only you belonged to me!' "

After that, I remember, Murra and I went outdoors to look for thistles. He was going to show me how to grab thistles without getting hurt.

I don't think we ever found any. I remember pulling up a lot of plants, and throwing them against the house, and laughing a lot. But I don't think any of the plants were thistles.

Then we lost each other in the great outdoors. I yelled for him for a while, but his answers got fainter and fainter, and I finally went home.

I don't remember what the homecoming was like, but my wife does. She says I spoke to her in a rude and disrespectful manner. I told her that I had sold five-hundred Fleetwood windows to the Conners Hotel. I also told her that she should look up the statistics on teenage marriages sometime.

Then I went upstairs, and I took the door off our bathtub enclosure. I told her Murra and I were trading doors.

I got the door off, and then I went to sleep in the tub.

My wife woke me up, and I told her to go away. I told her Gloria Hilton had just bought the Conners Hotel, and I was going to marry her.

I tried to tell her something very important about thistles, but I couldn't pronounce thistles, so I went to sleep again.

So my wife poured bubble-bath powder all over me, and she turned on the cold water faucet of the bathtub, and she went to bed in the guest room.

About three o'clock the next afternoon, I went over to Murra's to finish putting up his windows, and to find out what we'd agreed to do about the bathtub enclosure door, if anything. I had two doors on the back of my truck, my door with a flamingo and his door with Gloria Hilton.

I started to ring his doorbell, but then I heard somebody knocking on an upstairs window. I looked up and saw Murra standing in the window of Gloria Hilton's bathroom. My ladder was already leaning against the sill of the window, so I went up the ladder and asked Murra what was going on.

He opened the window, and he told me to come in. He was very pale and shaky.

"Your boy showed up yet?" I said.

"Yes," he said. "He's downstairs. I picked him up at the bus station an hour ago."

"You two hitting it off all right?" I said.

Murra shook his head. "He's still so *bitter*," he said. "He's only fifteen, but he talks to me as though he were my great-great-grandfather. I came up here for just a minute, and now I haven't got nerve enough to go back down."

He took me by the arm. "Listen—" he said, "you go down and sort of pave the way."

"If I've got any pavement left in me," I said, "I'd better save it for home." I filled him in on my own situation at home, which was far from ideal.

"Whatever you do," he said, "don't make the same mistake I made. You keep that home of yours together, no matter what. I know it must be lousy from time to time, but, believe me, there are ways of life that are ten thousand times lousier."

"Well," I said, "I thank the good Lord for one thing—"

"What's that?" he said.

"Gloria Hilton hasn't come right out and said she loved me yet," I said.

I went downstairs to see Murra's boy.

Young John had on a man's suit. He even had on a vest. He wore big black-rimmed spectacles. He looked like a college professor.

"John," I said, "I'm an old friend of your father's."

"That so?" he said, and he looked me up and down. He wouldn't shake hands.

"You certainly are a mature-looking young man," I said.

"I've *had* to be," he said. "When Father walked out on Mother and me, that made me head of the family, wouldn't you say?"

"Well now, John," I said, "your father hasn't been too happy, either, you know."

"That certainly is a great disappointment to me," he said. "I thought Gloria Hilton made men as happy as they could possibly be."

"John," I said, "when you get older, you're going to understand a lot of things you don't understand now."

"You must mean nuclear physics," he said. "I can hardly wait." And he turned his back to me, and he looked out the window. "Where's Father?" he said.

"Here he is," said Murra from the top of the stairs. "Here the poor fool is." He came creaking down the stairs.

"I think I'd better go back to school, Father," said the boy.

"So soon?" said Murra.

"I was told there was an emergency, or I wouldn't have come," said the boy. "There doesn't seem to be any emergency, so I'd like to go back, if you don't mind."

"Don't mind?" said Murra. He held out his arms. "John—" he said, "you'll break my heart if you walk out on me now—without—"

"Without what, Father?" said the boy. He was cold as ice.

"Without forgiving me," said Murra.

"Never," said the boy. "I'm sorry—that's one thing I'll never do." He nodded. "Whenever you're ready to go, Father," he said, "I'll be waiting in the car."

And he walked out of the house.

Murra sat down in a chair with his head in his hands. "What do I do now?" he said. "Maybe this is the punishment I deserve. I guess what I do is just grit my teeth and take it."

"I can only think of one other thing," I said.

"What's that?" he said.

"Kick him in the pants," I said.

So that's what Murra did.

He went out to the car, looking all gloomy and blue.

He told John something was wrong with the front seat, and he made John get out so he could fix it.

Then Murra let the boy have it in the seat of the pants with the side of his foot. I don't think there was any pain connected with it, but it did have a certain amount of loft.

The boy did a kind of polka downhill, toward the shrubbery where his father and I had been looking for thistles the night before. When he got himself stopped and turned around, he was certainly one surprised-looking boy.

"John," Murra said to him, "I'm sorry I did that, but I couldn't think of anything else to do."

For once, the boy didn't have a snappy come-back.

"I have made many serious mistakes in my life," said Murra,

"but I don't think that was one of them. I love you, and I love your mother, and I think I'll go on kicking you until you can find it in your heart to give me another chance."

The boy still couldn't think of anything to say, but I could tell he wasn't interested in being kicked again.

"Now you come back in the house," said Murra, "and we'll talk this thing over like civilized human beings."

When they got back in the house, Murra got the boy to call up his mother in Los Angeles.

"You tell her we're having a nice time, and I've been terribly unhappy, and I am through with Gloria Hilton, and I want her to take me back on any terms whatsoever," said Murra.

The boy told his mother, and she cried, and the boy cried, and Murra cried, and I cried.

And then Murra's first wife told him he could come back home any time he wanted to. And that was that.

The way we settled the bathtub enclosure door thing was that I took Murra's door and he took mine. Actually, I was trading a twenty-two-dollar door for a forty-eight-dollar door, not counting the picture of Gloria Hilton.

My wife was out when I got home. I hung the new door. My own boy came up and watched me. He was red-nosed about something.

"Where's your mother?" I said to him.

"She went out," he said.

"When's she due back?" I said.

"She said maybe she'd never come back," said the boy.

I was sick, but I didn't let the boy know it. "That's one of her jokes," I said. "She says that all the time."

"I never heard her say it before," he said.

I was really scared when suppertime rolled around, and I still didn't have a wife. I tried to be brave. I got supper for the boy and me, and I said, "Well, I guess she's been delayed somewhere."

"Father—" said the boy.

"What?" I said.

"What did you *do* to Mother last night?" he said. He took a very high and mighty tone.

"Mind your own business," I said, "or you're liable to get a swift kick in the pants."

That calmed him right down.

My wife came home at nine o'clock, thank God.

She was cheerful. She said she'd had a swell time just being alone—shopping alone, eating in a restaurant alone, going to a movie alone.

She gave me a kiss, and she went upstairs.

I heard the shower running, and I all of a sudden remembered the picture of Gloria Hilton on the bathtub enclosure door.

"Oh my Lord!" I said. I ran up the stairs to tell her what the picture was doing on the door, to tell her I would have it sandblasted off first thing in the morning.

I went into the bathroom.

My wife was standing up, taking a shower.

She was just the same height as Gloria Hilton, so the picture on the door made kind of a mask for her.

There was my wife's body with the head of Gloria Hilton on it.

My wife wasn't sore. She laughed. She thought it was funny. "Guess who?" she said.

(1962)

DEER IN THE WORKS

THE BIG BLACK STACKS of the Ilium Works of the Federal Apparatus Corporation spewed acid fumes and soot over the hundreds of men and women who were lined up before the red-brick employment office. It was summer. The Ilium Works, already the second-largest industrial plant in America, was increasing its staff by one third in order to meet armament contracts. Every ten minutes or so, a company policeman opened the employment-office door, letting out a chilly gust from the air-conditioned interior and admitting three more applicants.

"Next three," said the policeman.

A middle-sized man in his late twenties, his young face camouflaged with a mustache and spectacles, was admitted after a four-hour wait. His spirits and the new suit he'd bought for the occasion were wilted by the fumes and the August sun, and he'd given up lunch in order to keep his place in line. But his bearing remained jaunty. He was the last, in his group of three, to face the receptionist.

"Screw-machine operator, ma'am," said the first man.

"See Mr. Cormody in booth seven," said the receptionist.

"Plastic extrusion, miss," said the next man.

"See Mr. Hoyt in booth two," she said. "Skill?" she asked the urbane young man in the wilted suit. "Milling machine? Jig borer?"

"Writing," he said. "Any kind of writing."

"You mean advertising and sales promotion?"

"Yes—that's what I mean."

She looked doubtful. "Well, I don't know. We didn't put out a call for that sort of people. You can't run a machine, can you?"

"Typewriter," he said jokingly.

The receptionist was a sober young woman. "The company does not use male stenographers," she said. "See Mr. Dilling in booth twenty-six. He just might know of some advertising-and-sales-promotion-type job."

He straightened his tie and coat, forced a smile that implied he was looking into jobs at the Works as sort of a lark. He walked into booth twenty-six and extended his· hand to Mr. Dilling, a man of his own age. "Mr. Dilling, my name is David Potter. I was curious to know what openings you might have in advertising and sales promotion, and thought I'd drop in for a talk."

Mr. Dilling, an old hand at facing young men who tried to hide their eagerness for a job, was polite but outwardly unimpressed. "Well, you came at a bad time, I'm afraid, Mr. Potter. The competition for that kind of job is pretty stiff, as you perhaps know, and there isn't much of anything open just now."

David nodded. "I see." He had had no experience in asking for a job with a big organization, and Mr. Dilling was making him aware of what a fine art it was—if you couldn't run a machine. A duel was under way.

"But have a seat anyway, Mr. Potter."

"Thank you." He looked at his watch. "I really ought to be getting back to my paper soon."

"You work on a paper around here?"

"Yes. I own a weekly paper in Dorset, about ten miles from Ilium."

"Oh—you don't say. Lovely little village. Thinking of giving up the paper, are you?"

"Well, no—not exactly. It's a possibility. I bought the paper soon after the war, so I've been with it for eight years, and I don't want to go stale. I might be wise to move on. It all depends on what opens up."

"You have a family?" said Mr. Dilling pleasantly.

"Yes. My wife, and two boys and two girls."

"A nice, big, well-balanced family," said Mr. Dilling. "And you're so young, too."

"Twenty-nine," said David. He smiled. "We didn't plan it to be quite that big. It's run to twins. The boys are twins, and then, several days ago, the girls came."

"You don't say!" said Mr. Dilling. He winked. "That would certainly start a young man thinking about getting a little security, eh, with a family like that?"

Both of them treated the remark casually, as though it were no more than a pleasantry between two family men. "It's what we wanted, actually, two boys, two girls," said David. "We didn't expect to get them this quickly, but we're glad now. As far as security goes—well, maybe I flatter myself, but I think the administrative and writing experience I've had running the paper would be worth a good bit to the right people, if something happened to the paper."

"One of the big shortages in this country," said Dilling philosophically, concentrating on lighting a cigarette, "is men who know how to do things, and know how to take responsibility and get things done. I only wish there were better openings in advertising and sales promotion than the ones we've got. They're important, interesting jobs, understand, but I don't know how you'd feel about the starting salary."

"Well, I'm just trying to get the lay of the land, now—to see how things are. I have no idea what salary industry might pay a man like me, with my experience."

"The question experienced men like yourself usually ask is: how high can I go and how fast? And the answer to that is that the sky is the limit for a man with drive and creative ambition. And he can go up fast or slow, depending on what he's willing to do and capable of putting into the job. We might start out a man like you at, oh, say, a hundred dollars a week, but that isn't to say you'd be stuck at that level for two years or even two months."

"I suppose a man could keep a family on that until he got rolling," said David.

"You'd find the work in the publicity end just about the same as what you're doing now. Our publicity people have high standards for writing and editing and reporting, and our publicity releases don't wind up in newspaper editors' wastebaskets. Our people do a professional job, and are well-respected as journalists." He stood. "I've got a little matter to attend to—take me about ten minutes. Could you possibly stick around? I'm enjoying our talk."

David looked at his watch. "Oh—guess I could spare another ten or fifteen minutes."

Dilling was back in his booth in three minutes, chuckling over some private joke. "Just talking on the phone with Lou Flammer, the publicity supervisor. Needs a new stenographer. Lou's a card. Everybody here is crazy about Lou. Old weekly man himself, and I guess that's where he learned to be so easy to get along with. Just to feel him out for the hell of it, I told him about you. I didn't commit you to anything—just said what you told me, that you were keeping your eyes open. And guess what Lou said?"

"Guess what, Nan," said David Potter to his wife on the telephone. He was wearing only his shorts, and was phoning from the company hospital. "When you come home from the hospital tomorrow, you'll be coming home to a solid citizen who pulls down a hundred and ten dollars a week, *every* week. I just got my badge and passed my physical!"

"Oh?" said Nan, startled. "It happened awfully fast, didn't it? I didn't think you were going to plunge right in."

"What's there to wait for?"

"Well—I don't know. I mean, how do you know what you're getting into? You've never worked for anybody but yourself, and don't know anything about getting along in a huge organization. I knew you were going to talk to the Ilium people about a job, but I thought you planned to stick with the paper another year, anyway."

"In another year I'll be thirty, Nan."

"Well?"

"That's pretty old to be starting a career in industry. There are guys my age here who've been working their way up for ten years. That's pretty stiff competition, and it'll be that much stiffer a year from now. And how do we know Jason will still want to buy the paper a year from now?" Ed Jason was David's assistant, a recent college graduate whose father wanted to buy the paper for him. "And this job that opened up today in publicity won't be open a year from now, Nan. Now was the time to switch—this afternoon!"

Nan sighed. "I suppose. But it doesn't seem like you. The Works are fine for some people; they seem to thrive on that life. But you've always been so free. And you love the paper—you know you do."

"I do," said David, "and it'll break my heart to let it go. It was a swell thing to do when we had no kids, but it's a shaky living now—with the kids to educate and all."

"But, hon," said Nan, "the paper is making money."

"It could fold like that," said David, snapping his fingers. "A daily could come in with a one-page insert of Dorset news, or—"

"Dorset likes its little paper too much to let that happen. They like you and the job you're doing too much."

David nodded. "What about ten years from now?"

"What about ten years from now in the Works? What about ten years from now anywhere?"

"It's a better bet that the Works will still be here. I haven't got the right to take long chances any more, Nan, not with a big family counting on me."

"It won't be a very happy big family, darling, if you're not doing what you want to do. I want you to go on being happy the way you have been—driving around the countryside, getting news and talking and selling ads; coming home and writing what you want to write, what you believe in. You in the Works!"

"It's what I've got to do."

"All right, if you say so. I've had my say."

"It's still journalism, high-grade journalism," said David.

"Just don't sell the paper to Jason right away. Put him in charge, but let's wait a month or so, please?"

"No sense in waiting, but if you really want to, all right." David held up a brochure he'd been handed after his physical examination was completed. "Listen to this, Nan: under the company Security Package, I get ten dollars a day for hospital expenses in case of illness, full pay for twenty-six weeks, a hundred dollars for special hospital expenses. I get life insurance for about half what it would cost on the outside. For whatever I put into government bonds under the payroll-savings plan, the company will give me a five per cent bonus in company stock—twelve years from now. I get two weeks' vacation with pay each year, and, after fifteen years, I get three weeks. Get free membership in the company country club. After twenty-five years, I'll be eligible for a pension of at least a hundred and twenty-five dollars a month, and much more if I rise in the organization and stick with it for more than twenty-five years!"

"Good heavens!" said Nan.

"I'd be a damn fool to pass that up, Nan."

"I still wish you'd waited until the little girls and I were home and settled, and you got used to them. I feel you were panicked into this."

"No, no—this is it, Nan. Give the little girls a kiss apiece for me. I've got to go now, and report to my new supervisor."

"Your what?"

"Supervisor."

"Oh. I thought that's what you said, but I couldn't be sure."

"Good-by, Nan."

"Good-by, David."

David clipped his badge to his lapel, and stepped out of the hospital and onto the hot asphalt floor of the world within the fences of the Works. Dull thunder came from the buildings around him, a truck honked at him, and a cinder blew in his eye. He dabbed at the cinder with a corner of his handkerchief and finally got it out. When his vision was restored, he looked about himself for Building 31, where his new office and supervisor were. Four busy streets fanned out from where he stood, and each stretched seemingly to infinity.

He stopped a passerby who was in less of a desperate hurry than the rest. "Could you tell me, please, how to find Building 31, Mr. Flammer's office?"

The man he asked was old and bright-eyed, apparently getting as much pleasure from the clangor and smells and nervous activity of the Works as David would have gotten from April in Paris. He squinted at David's badge and then at his face. "Just starting out, are you?"

"Yes sir. My first day."

"What do you know about that?" The old man shook his head wonderingly, and winked. "Just starting out. Building 31? Well, sir, when I first came to work here in 1899, you could see Building 31 from here, with nothing between us and it but mud. Now it's all built up. See that water tank up there, about a quarter of a mile? Well, Avenue 17 branches off there, and you follow that almost to the end, then cut across the tracks, and— Just starting out, eh? Well, I'd better walk you up there. Came here for just a minute to talk to the pension folks, but that can wait. I'd enjoy the walk."

"Thank you."

"Fifty-year man, I was," he said proudly, and he led David up avenues and alleys, across tracks, over ramps and through tunnels, through buildings filled with spitting, whining, grumbling machinery, and down corridors with green walls and numbered black doors.

"Can't be a fifty-year man no more," said the old man pityingly. "Can't come to work until you're eighteen nowadays, and you got to retire when you're sixty-five." He poked his thumb under his lapel to make a small gold button protrude. On it was the number "50" superimposed on the company trademark. "Something none of you youngsters can look forward to wearing some day, no matter how much you want one."

"Very nice button," said David.

The old man pointed out a door. "Here's Flammer's office.

Keep your mouth shut till you find out who's who and what *they* think. Good luck."

Lou Flammer's secretary was not at her desk, so David walked to the door of the inner office and knocked.

"Yes?" said a man's voice sweetly. "Please come in."

David opened the door. "Mr. Flammer?"

Lou Flammer was a short, fat man in his early thirties. He beamed at David. "What can I do to help you?"

"I'm David Potter, Mr. Flammer."

Flammer's Santa-Claus-like demeanor decayed. He leaned back, propped his feet on his desk top, and stuffed a cigar, which he'd concealed in his cupped hand, into his large mouth. "Hell— thought you were a scoutmaster." He looked at his desk clock, which was mounted in a miniature of the company's newest automatic dishwasher. "Boy scouts touring the Works. Supposed to stop in here fifteen minutes ago for me to give 'em a talk on scouting and industry. Fifty-six per cent of Federal Apparatus' executives were eagle scouts."

David started to laugh, but found himself doing it all alone, and he stopped. "Amazing figure," he said.

"It *is*," said Flammer judiciously. "Says something for scouting and something for industry. Now, before I tell you where your desk is, I'm supposed to explain the rating-sheet system. That's what the Manual says. Dilling tell you about that?"

"Not that I recall. There was an awful lot of information all at once."

"Well, there's nothing much to it," said Flammer. "Every six months a rating sheet is made out on you, to let you and to let us know just where you stand, and what sort of progress you've been making. Three people who've been close to your work make out independent ratings of you, and then all the information is brought together on a master copy—with carbons for you, me, and Personnel, and the original for the head of the Advertising and Sales Promotion Division. It's very helpful for everybody, you most of all, if you take it the right way." He waved a rating sheet before David. "See? Blanks for appearance, loyalty, promptness, initiative, cooperativeness—things like that. You'll make out rating sheets on other people, too, and whoever does the rating is anonymous."

"I see." David felt himself reddening with resentment. He fought the emotion, telling himself his reaction was a small-town man's—and that it would do him good to learn to think as a member of a great, efficient team.

"Now about pay, Potter," said Flammer, "there'll never be any point in coming in to ask me for a raise. That's all done on the basis of the rating sheets and the salary curve." He rummaged through his drawers and found a graph, which he spread out on his desk. "Here—now you see this curve? Well, it's the average salary curve for men with college educations in the company. See —you can follow it on up. At thirty, the average man makes this much; at forty, this much—and so on. Now, this curve above it shows what men with real growth potential can make. See? It's a little higher and curves upward a little faster. You're how old?"

"Twenty-nine," said David, trying to see what the salary figures were that ran along one side of the graph. Flammer saw him doing it, and pointedly kept them hidden with his forearm.

"Uh-huh." Flammer wet the tip of a pencil with his tongue, and drew a small "x" on the graph, squarely astride the average man's curve. "There *you* are!"

David looked at the mark, and then followed the curve with his eyes across the paper, over little bumps, up gentle slopes, along desolate plateaus, until it died abruptly at the margin which represented age sixty-five. The graph left no questions to be asked and was deaf to argument. David looked from it to the human being he would also be dealing with. "You had a weekly once, did you, Mr. Flammer?"

Flammer laughed. "In my naïve, idealistic youth, Potter, I sold ads to feed stores, gathered gossip, set type, and wrote editorials that were going to save the world, by God."

David smiled admiringly. "What a circus, eh?"

"Circus?" said Flammer. "Freak show, maybe. It's a good way to grow up fast. Took me about six months to find out I was killing myself for peanuts, that a little guy couldn't even save a village three blocks long, and that the world wasn't worth saving anyway. So I started looking out for Number One. Sold out to a chain, came down here, and here I am."

The telephone rang. "Yes?" said Flammer sweetly. "Puh-*bliss-*

itee." His benign smile faded. "No. You're kidding, aren't you? Where? Really—this is no gag? All right, all right. Lord! What a time for this to happen. I haven't got anybody here, and I can't get away on account of the goddam boy scouts." He hung up. "Potter—you've got your first assignment. There's a deer loose in the Works!"

"Deer?"

"Don't know how he got in, but he's in. Plumber went to fix a drinking fountain out at the softball diamond across from Building 217, and flushed a deer out from under the bleachers. Now they got him cornered up around the metallurgy lab." He stood and hammered on his desk. "Murder! The story will go all over the country, Potter. Talk about human interest. Front page! Of all the times for Al Tappin to be out at the Ashtabula Works, taking pictures of a new viscometer they cooked up out there! All right—I'll call up a hack photographer downtown, Potter, and get him to meet you out by the metallurgy lab. You get the story and see that he gets the right shots. Okay?"

He led David into the hallway. "Just go back the way you came, turn left instead of right at fractional horsepower motors, cut through hydraulic engineering, catch bus eleven on Avenue 9, and it'll take you right there. After you get the story and pictures, we'll get them cleared by the law division, the plant security officer, our department head and buildings and grounds, and shoot them right out. Now get going. That deer isn't on the payroll—he isn't going to wait for you. Come to work today—tomorrow your work will be on every front page in the country, if we can get it approved. The name of the photographer you're going to meet is McGarvey. Got it? You're in the big time now, Potter. We'll all be watching." He shut the door behind David.

David found himself trotting down the hall, down a stairway, and into an alley, brushing roughly past persons in a race against time. Many turned to watch the purposeful young man with admiration.

On and on he strode, his mind seething with information: *Flammer, Building 31; deer, metallurgy lab; photographer, Al Tappin. No. Al Tappin in Ashtabula. Flenny the hack photographer. No.* McCammer. *No. McCammer is new supervisor. Fifty-*

six per cent eagle scouts. Deer by viscometer laboratory. No. Viscometer in Ashtabula. Call Danner, new supervisor, and get instructions right. Three weeks' vacation after fifteen years. Danner not new supervisor. Anyway, new supervisor in Building 319. No. Fanner in Building 39981983319.

David stopped, blocked by a grimy window at the end of a blind alley. All he knew was that he'd never been there before, that his memory had blown a gasket, and that the deer was not on the payroll. The air in the alley was thick with tango music and the stench of scorched insulation. David scrubbed away some of the crust on the window with his handkerchief, praying for a glimpse of something that made sense.

Inside were ranks of women at benches, rocking their heads in time to the music, and dipping soldering irons into great nests of colored wires that crept past them on endless belts. One of them looked up and saw David, and winked in tango rhythm. David fled.

At the mouth of the alley, he stopped a man and asked him if he'd heard anything about a deer in the Works. The man shook his head and looked at David oddly, making David aware of how frantic he must look. "I heard it was out by the lab," David said more calmly.

"Which lab?" said the man.

"That's what I'm not sure of," said David. "There's more than one?"

"Chemical lab?" said the man. "Materials testing lab? Paint lab? Insulation lab?"

"No—I don't think it's any of those," said David.

"Well, I could stand here all afternoon naming labs, and probably not hit the right one. Sorry, I've got to go. You don't know what building they've got the differential analyzer in, do you?"

"Sorry," said David. He stopped several other people, none of whom knew anything about the deer, and he tried to retrace his steps to the office of his supervisor, whatever his name was. He was swept this way and that by the currents of the Works, stranded in backwaters, sucked back into the main stream, and his mind was more and more numbed, and the mere reflexes of self-preservation were more and more in charge.

212 • WELCOME TO THE MONKEY HOUSE

He chose a building at random, and walked inside for a momentary respite from the summer heat, and was deafened by the clangor of steel sheets being cut and punched, being smashed into strange shapes by great hammers that dropped out of the smoke and dust overhead. A hairy, heavily muscled man was seated near the door on a wooden stool, watching a giant lathe turn a bar of steel the size of a silo.

David now had the idea of going through a company phone directory until he recognized his supervisor's name. He called to the machinist from a few feet away, but his voice was lost in the din. He tapped the man's shoulder. "Telephone around here?"

The man nodded. He cupped his hands around David's ear, and shouted. "Up that, and through the—" Down crashed a hammer. "Turn left and keep going until you—" An overhead crane dropped a stack of steel plates. "Four doors down from there is it. Can't miss it."

David, his ears ringing and his head aching, walked into the street again and chose another door. Here was peace and air conditioning. He was in the lobby of an auditorium, where a group of men were examining a box studded with dials and switches that was spotlighted and mounted on a revolving platform.

"Please, miss," he said to a receptionist by the door, "could you tell me where I could find a telephone?"

"It's right around the corner, sir," she said. "But I'm afraid no one is permitted here today but the crystallographers. Are you with them?"

"Yes," said David.

"Oh—well, come right in. Name?"

He told her, and a man sitting next to her lettered it on a badge. The badge was hung on his chest, and David headed for the telephone. A grinning, bald, big-toothed man, wearing a badge that said, "Stan Dunkel, Sales," caught him and steered him to the display.

"Dr. Potter," said Dunkel, "I ask you: is that the way to build an X-ray spectrogoniometer, or is that the way to build an X-ray spectrogoniometer?"

"Yes," said David. "That's the way, all right."

"Martini, Dr. Potter?" said a maid, offering a tray.

David emptied a Martini in one gloriously hot, stinging gulp.

"What features do you want in an X-ray Spectrogoniometer, Doctor?" said Dunkel.

"It should be sturdy, Mr. Dunkel," said David, and he left Dunkel there, pledging his reputation that there wasn't a sturdier one on earth.

In the phone booth, David had barely got through the telephone directory's A's before the name of his supervisor miraculously returned to his consciousness: *Flammer!* He found the number and dialed.

"Mr. Flammer's office," said a woman.

"Could I speak to him, please? This is David Potter."

"Oh—Mr. Potter. Well, Mr. Flammer is somewhere out in the Works now, but he left a message for you. He said there's an added twist on the deer story. When they catch the deer, the venison is going to be used at the Quarter-Century Club picnic."

"Quarter-Century Club?" said David.

"Oh, that's really something, Mr. Potter. It's for people who've been with the company twenty-five years or more. Free drinks and cigars, and just the best of everything. They have a wonderful time."

"Anything else about the deer?"

"Nothing he hasn't already told you," she said, and she hung up.

David Potter, with a third Martini in his otherwise empty stomach, stood in front of the auditorium and looked both ways for a deer.

"But our X-ray spectrogoniometer *is* sturdy, Dr. Potter," Stan Dunkel called to him from the auditorium steps.

Across the street was a patch of green, bordered by hedges. David pushed through the hedges into the outfield of a softball diamond. He crossed it and went behind the bleachers, where there was cool shade, and he sat down with his back to a wiremesh fence which separated one end of the Works from a deep pine woods. There were two gates in the fence, but both were wired shut.

David was going to sit there for just a moment, long enough to get his nerve back, to take bearings. Maybe he could leave a message for Flammer, saying he'd suddenly fallen ill, which was essentially true, or—

"There he goes!" cried somebody from the other side of the diamond. There were gleeful cries, shouted orders, the sounds of men running.

A deer with broken antlers dashed under the bleachers, saw David, and ran frantically into the open again along the fence. He ran with a limp, and his reddish-brown coat was streaked with soot and grease.

"Easy now! Don't rush him! Just keep him there. Shoot into the woods, not the Works."

David came out from under the bleachers to see a great semi-circle of men, several ranks deep, closing in slowly on the corner of fence in which the deer was at bay. In the front rank were a dozen company policemen with drawn pistols. Other members of the posse carried sticks and rocks and lariats hastily fashioned from wire.

The deer pawed the grass, and bucked, and jerked its broken antlers in the direction of the crowd.

"Hold it!" shouted a familiar voice. A company limousine rumbled across the diamond to the back of the crowd. Leaning out of a window was Lou Flammer, David's supervisor. "Don't shoot until we get a picture of him alive," commanded Flammer. He pulled a photographer out of the limousine, and pushed him into the front rank.

Flammer saw David standing alone by the fence, his back to a gate. "Good boy, Potter," called Flammer. "Right on the ball! Photographer got lost, and I had to bring him here myself."

The photographer fired his flash bulbs. The deer bucked and sprinted along the fence toward David. David unwired the gate, opened it wide. A second later the deer's white tail was flashing through the woods and gone.

The profound silence was broken first by the whistling of a switch engine and then by the click of a latch as David stepped into the woods and closed the gate behind him. He didn't look back.

(1955)

THE LIE

IT WAS EARLY SPRINGTIME. Weak sunshine lay cold on old gray frost. Willow twigs against the sky showed the golden haze of fat catkins about to bloom. A black Rolls-Royce streaked up the Connecticut Turnpike from New York City. At the wheel was Ben Barkley, a black chauffeur.

"Keep it under the speed limit, Ben," said Doctor Remenzel. "I don't care how ridiculous any speed limit seems, stay under it. No reason to rush—we have plenty of time."

Ben eased off on the throttle. "Seems like in the springtime she wants to get up and go," he said.

"Do what you can to keep her down—O.K.?" said the doctor.

"Yes, sir!" said Ben. He spoke in a lower voice to the thirteen-year-old boy who was riding beside him, to Eli Remenzel, the doctor's son. "Ain't just people and animals feel good in the springtime," he said to Eli. "Motors feel good too."

"Um," said Eli.

"Everything feel good," said Ben. "Don't you feel good?"

"Sure, sure I feel good," said Eli emptily.

"Should feel good—going to that wonderful school," said Ben.

The wonderful school was the Whitehill School for Boys, a private preparatory school in North Marston, Massachusetts.

That was where the Rolls-Royce was bound. The plan was that Eli would enroll for the fall semester, while his father, a member of the class of 1939, attended a meeting of the Board of Overseers of the school.

"Don't believe this boy's feeling so good, doctor," said Ben. He wasn't particularly serious about it. It was more genial springtime blather.

"What's the matter, Eli?" said the doctor absently. He was studying blueprints, plans for a thirty-room addition to the Eli Remenzel Memorial Dormitory—a building named in honor of his great-great-grandfather. Doctor Remenzel had the plans draped over a walnut table that folded out of the back of the front seat. He was a massive, dignified man, a physician, a healer for healing's sake, since he had been born as rich as the Shah of Iran. "Worried about something?" he asked Eli without looking up from the plans.

"Nope," said Eli.

Eli's lovely mother, Sylvia, sat next to the doctor, reading the catalogue of the Whitehill School. "If I were you," she said to Eli, "I'd be so excited I could hardly stand it. The best four years of your whole life are just about to begin."

"Sure," said Eli. He didn't show her his face. He gave her only the back of his head, a pinwheel of coarse brown hair above a stiff white collar, to talk to.

"I wonder how many Remenzels have gone to Whitehill," said Sylvia.

"That's like asking how many people are dead in a cemetery," said the doctor. He gave the answer to the old joke, and to Sylvia's question too. "All of 'em."

"If all the Remenzels who went to Whitehill were numbered, what number would Eli be?" said Sylvia. "That's what I'm getting at."

The question annoyed Doctor Remenzel a little. It didn't seem in very good taste. "It isn't the sort of thing you keep score on," he said.

"Guess," said his wife.

"Oh," he said, "you'd have to go back through all the records, all the way back to the end of the eighteenth century, even, to make any kind of a guess. And you'd have to decide whether to count the Schofields and the Haleys and the MacLellans as Remenzels."

"Please make a guess—" said Sylvia, "just people whose last names were Remenzel."

"Oh—" The doctor shrugged, rattled the plans. "Thirty maybe."

"So Eli is number thirty-one!" said Sylvia, delighted with the number. "You're number thirty-one, dear," she said to the back of Eli's head.

Doctor Remenzel rattled the plans again. "I don't want him going around saying something asinine, like he's number thirty-one," he said.

"Eli knows better than that," said Sylvia. She was a game, ambitious woman, with no money of her own at all. She had been married for sixteen years, but was still openly curious and enthusiastic about the ways of families that had been rich for many generations.

"Just for my own curiosity—not so Eli can go around saying what number he is," said Sylvia, "I'm going to go wherever they keep the records and find out what number he is. That's what I'll do while you're at the meeting and Eli's doing whatever he has to do at the Admissions Office."

"All right," said Doctor Remenzel, "you go ahead and *do* that."

"I will," said Sylvia. "I think things like that are interesting, even if you don't." She waited for a rise on that, but didn't get one. Sylvia enjoyed arguing with her husband about her lack of reserve and his excess of it, enjoyed saying, toward the end of arguments like that, "Well, I guess I'm just a simple-minded country girl at heart, and that's all I'll ever be, and I'm afraid you're going to have to get used to it."

But Doctor Remenzel didn't want to play that game. He found the dormitory plans more interesting.

"Will the new rooms have fireplaces?" said Sylvia. In the oldest part of the dormitory, several of the rooms had handsome fireplaces.

"That would practically double the cost of construction," said the doctor.

218 ■ WELCOME TO THE MONKEY HOUSE

"I want Eli to have a room with a fireplace, if that's possible,"
said Sylvia.

"Those rooms are for seniors."

"I thought maybe through some fluke—" said Sylvia.

"What kind of fluke do you have in mind?" said the doctor.
"You mean I should demand that Eli be given a room with a fireplace?"

"Not *demand*—" said Sylvia.

"Request firmly?" said the doctor.

"Maybe I'm just a simple-minded country girl at heart," said
Sylvia, "but I look through this catalogue, and I see all the buildings named after Remenzels, look through the back and see all
the hundreds of thousands of dollars given by Remenzels for
scholarships, and I just can't help thinking people named Remenzel are entitled to ask for a little something extra."

"Let me tell you in no uncertain terms," said Doctor Remenzel,
"that you are not to ask for anything special for Eli—not anything."

"Of course I won't," said Sylvia. "Why do you always think
I'm going to embarrass you?"

"I don't," he said.

"But I can still think what I think, can't I?" she said.

"If you have to," he said.

"I have to," she said cheerfully, utterly unrepentant. She leaned
over the plans. "You think those people will like those rooms?"

"What people?" he said.

"The Africans," she said. She was talking about thirty Africans
who, at the request of the State Department, were being admitted to Whitehill in the coming semester. It was because of
them that the dormitory was being expanded.

"The rooms aren't for them," he said. "They aren't going to be
segregated."

"Oh," said Sylvia. She thought about this awhile, and then she
said, "Is there a chance Eli will have to have one of them for a
roommate?"

"Freshmen draw lots for roommates," said the doctor. "That
piece of information's in the catalogue too."

"Eli?" said Sylvia.

"H'm?" said Eli.

"How would you feel about it if you had to room with one of those Africans?"

Eli shrugged listlessly.

"That's all right?" said Sylvia.

Eli shrugged again.

"I guess it's all right," said Sylvia.

"It had better be," said the doctor.

The Rolls-Royce pulled abreast of an old Chevrolet, a car in such bad repair that its back door was lashed shut with clothesline. Doctor Remenzel glanced casually at the driver, and then, with sudden excitement and pleasure, he told Ben Barkley to stay abreast of the car.

The doctor leaned across Sylvia, rolled down his window, yelled to the driver of the old Chevrolet, "Tom! Tom!"

The man was a Whitehill classmate of the doctor. He wore a Whitehill necktie, which he waved at Doctor Remenzel in gay recognition. And then he pointed to the fine young son who sat beside him, conveyed with proud smiles and nods that the boy was bound for Whitehill.

Doctor Remenzel pointed to the chaos of the back of Eli's head, beamed that his news was the same. In the wind blustering between the two cars they made a lunch date at the Holly House in North Marston, at the inn whose principal business was serving visitors to Whitehill.

"All right," said Doctor Remenzel to Ben Barkley, "drive on."

"You know," said Sylvia, "somebody really ought to write an article—" And she turned to look through the back window at the old car now shuddering far behind. "Somebody really ought to."

"What about?" said the doctor. He noticed that Eli had slumped way down in the front seat. "Eli!" he said sharply. "Sit up straight!" He returned his attention to Sylvia.

"Most people think prep schools are such snobbish things, just for people with money," said Sylvia, "but that isn't true." She leafed through the catalogue and found the quotation she was after.

"*The Whitehill School operates on the assumption,*" she read, *"that no boy should be deterred from applying for admission because his family is unable to pay the full cost of a Whitehill education. With this in mind, the Admissions Committee selects each year from approximately 3000 candidates the 150 most promising and deserving boys, regardless of their parents' ability to pay the full $2200 tuition. And those in need of financial aid are given it to the full extent of their need. In certain instances, the school will even pay for the clothing and transportation of a boy."*

Sylvia shook her head. "I think that's perfectly amazing. It's something most people don't realize at all. A truckdriver's son can come to Whitehill."

"If he's smart enough," he said.

"Thanks to the Remenzels," said Sylvia with pride.

"And a lot of other people too," said the doctor.

Sylvia read out loud again: *"In 1799, Eli Remenzel laid the foundation for the present Scholarship Fund by donating to the school forty acres in Boston. The school still owns twelve of those acres, their current evaluation being $3,000,000."*

"Eli!" said the doctor. "Sit up! What's the matter with you?"

Eli sat up again, but began to slump almost immediately, like a snowman in hell. Eli had good reason for slumping, for actually hoping to die or disappear. He could not bring himself to say what the reason was. He slumped because he knew he had been denied admission to Whitehill. He had failed the entrance examinations. Eli's parents did not know this, because Eli had found the awful notice in the mail and had torn it up.

Doctor Remenzel and his wife had no doubts whatsoever about their son's getting into Whitehill. It was inconceivable to them that Eli could not go there, so they had no curiosity as to how Eli had done on the examinations, were not puzzled when no report ever came.

"What all will Eli have to do to enroll?" said Sylvia, as the black Rolls-Royce crossed the Rhode Island border.

"I don't know," said the doctor. "I suppose they've got it all complicated now with forms to be filled out in quadruplicate, and punch-card machines and bureaucrats. This business of entrance examinations is all new, too. In my day a boy simply had an interview with the headmaster. The headmaster would look him over, ask him a few questions, and then say, 'There's a Whitehill boy.' "

"Did he ever say, 'There isn't a Whitehill boy'?" said Sylvia.

"Oh, sure," said Doctor Remenzel, "if a boy was impossibly stupid or something. There have to be standards. There have always been standards. The African boys have to meet the standards, just like anybody else. They aren't getting in just because the State Department wants to make friends. We made that clear. Those boys had to meet the standards."

"And they did?" said Sylvia.

"I suppose," said Doctor Remenzel. "I heard they're all in, and they all took the same examination Eli did."

"Was it a hard examination, dear?" Sylvia asked Eli. It was the first time she'd thought to ask.

"Um," said Eli.

"What?" she said.

"Yes," said Eli.

"I'm glad they've got high standards," she said, and then she realized that this was a fairly silly statement. "Of course they've got high standards," she said. "That's why it's such a famous school. That's why people who go there do so well in later life."

Sylvia resumed her reading of the catalogue again, opened out a folding map of "The Sward," as the campus of Whitehill was traditionally called. She read off the names of features that memorialized Remenzels—the Sanford Remenzel Bird Sanctuary, the George MacLellan Remenzel Skating Rink, the Eli Remenzel Memorial Dormitory, and then she read out loud a quatrain printed on one corner of the map:

> "When night falleth gently
> "Upon the green Sward,
> "It's Whitehill, dear Whitehill,
> "Our thoughts all turn toward."

"You know," said Sylvia, "school songs are so corny when you just read them. But when I hear the Glee Club sing those words, they sound like the most beautiful words ever written, and I want to cry."

"Um," said Doctor Remenzel.

"Did a Remenzel write them?"

"I don't think so," said Doctor Remenzel. And then he said, "No—Wait. That's the *new* song. A Remenzel didn't write it. Tom Kilyer wrote it."

"The man in that old car we passed?"

"Sure," said Doctor Remenzel. "Tom wrote it. I remember when he wrote it."

"A scholarship boy wrote it?" said Sylvia. "I think that's awfully nice. He *was* a scholarship boy, wasn't he?"

"His father was an ordinary automobile mechanic in North Marston."

"You hear what a democratic school you're going to, Eli?" said Sylvia.

Half an hour later Ben Barkley brought the limousine to a stop before the Holly House, a rambling country inn twenty years older than the Republic. The inn was on the edge of the Whitehill Sward, glimpsing the school's rooftops and spires over the innocent wilderness of the Sanford Remenzel Bird Sanctuary.

Ben Barkley was sent away with the car for an hour and a half. Doctor Remenzel shepherded Sylvia and Eli into a familiar, low-ceilinged world of pewter, clocks, lovely old woods, agreeable servants, elegant food and drink.

Eli, clumsy with horror of what was surely to come, banged a grandmother clock with his elbow as he passed, made the clock cry.

Sylvia excused herself. Doctor Remenzel and Eli went to the threshold of the dining room, where a hostess welcomed them both by name. They were given a table beneath an oil portrait of one of the three Whitehill boys who had gone on to become President of the United States.

The dining room was filling quickly with families. What every family had was at least one boy about Eli's age. Most of the boys wore Whitehill blazers—black, with pale-blue piping, with Whitehill seals on their breast pockets. A few, like Eli, were not yet entitled to wear blazers, were simply hoping to get in.

The doctor ordered a Martini, then turned to his son and said,

"Your mother has the idea that you're entitled to special privileges around here. I hope you don't have that idea too."

"No, sir," said Eli.

"It would be a source of the greatest embarrassment to me," said Doctor Remenzel with considerable grandeur, "if I were ever to hear that you had used the name Remenzel as though you thought Remenzels were something special."

"I know," said Eli wretchedly.

"That settles it," said the doctor. He had nothing more to say about it. He gave abbreviated salutes to several people he knew in the room, speculated as to what sort of party had reserved a long banquet table that was set up along one wall. He decided that it was for a visiting athletic team. Sylvia arrived, and Eli had to be told in a sharp whisper to stand when a woman came to a table.

Sylvia was full of news. The long table, she related, was for the thirty boys from Africa. "I'll bet that's more colored people than have eaten here since this place was founded," she said softly. "How fast things change these days!"

"You're right about how fast things change," said Doctor Remenzel. "You're wrong about the colored people who've eaten here. This used to be a busy part of the Underground Railroad."

"Really?" said Sylvia. "How exciting." She looked all about herself in a birdlike way. "I think everything's exciting here. I only wish Eli had a blazer on."

Doctor Remenzel reddened. "He isn't entitled to one," he said.

"I know that," said Sylvia.

"I thought you were going to ask somebody for permission to put a blazer on Eli right away," said the doctor.

"I wouldn't do that," said Sylvia, a little offended now. "Why are you always afraid I'll embarrass you?"

"Never mind. Excuse me. Forget it," said Doctor Remenzel.

Sylvia brightened again, put her hand on Eli's arm, and looked radiantly at a man in the dining-room doorway. "There's my favorite person in all the world, next to my son and husband," she said. She meant Dr. Donald Warren, headmaster of the Whitehill School. A thin gentleman in his early sixties, Doctor Warren was in the doorway with the manager of the inn, looking over the arrangements for the Africans.

It was then that Eli got up abruptly, fled the dining room, fled as much of the nightmare as he could possibly leave behind. He brushed past Doctor Warren rudely, though he knew him well, though Doctor Warren spoke his name. Doctor Warren looked after him sadly.

"I'll be damned," said Doctor Remenzel. "What brought that on?"

"Maybe he really *is* sick," said Sylvia.

The Remenzels had no time to react more elaborately, because Doctor Warren spotted them and crossed quickly to their table. He greeted them, some of his perplexity about Eli showing in his greeting. He asked if he might sit down.

"Certainly, of course," said Doctor Remenzel expansively. "We'd be honored if you did. Heavens."

"Not to eat," said Doctor Warren. "I'll be eating at the long table with the new boys. I would like to talk, though." He saw that there were five places set at the table. "You're expecting someone?"

"We passed Tom Hilyer and his boy on the way," said Doctor Remenzel. "They'll be along in a minute."

"Good, good," said Doctor Warren absently. He fidgeted, looked again in the direction in which Eli had disappeared.

"Tom's boy will be going to Whitehill in the fall?" said Doctor Remenzel.

"H'm?" said Doctor Warren. "Oh—yes, yes. Yes, he will."

"Is he a scholarship boy, like his father?" said Sylvia.

"That's not a polite question," said Doctor Remenzel severely.

"I beg your pardon," said Sylvia.

"No, no—that's a perfectly proper question these days," said Doctor Warren. "We don't keep that sort of information very secret any more. We're proud of our scholarship boys, and they have every reason to be proud of themselves. Tom's boy got the highest score anyone's ever got on the entrance examinations. We feel privileged to have him."

"We never *did* find out Eli's score," said Doctor Remenzel. He

said it with good-humored resignation, without expectation that
Eli had done especially well.

"A good strong medium, I imagine," said Sylvia. She said this
on the basis of Eli's grades in primary school, which had ranged
from medium to terrible.

The headmaster looked surprised. "I didn't tell you his scores?"
he said.

"We haven't seen you since he took the examinations," said
Doctor Remenzel.

"The letter I wrote you—" said Doctor Warren.

"What letter?" said Doctor Remenzel. "Did we get a letter?"

"A letter from me," said Doctor Warren, with growing incredulity. "The hardest letter I ever had to write."

Sylvia shook her head. "We never got any letter from you."

Doctor Warren sat back, looking very ill. "I mailed it myself,"
he said. "It was definitely mailed—two weeks ago."

Doctor Remenzel shrugged. "The U.S. mails don't lose much,"
he said, "but I guess that now and then something gets mis-
placed."

Doctor Warren cradled his head in his hands. "Oh, dear—oh,
my, oh, Lord," he said. "I was surprised to see Eli here. I wondered that he would want to come along with you."

"He didn't come along just to see the scenery," said Doctor
Remenzel. "He came to enroll."

"I want to know what was in the letter," said Sylvia.

Doctor Warren raised his head, folded his hands. "What the
letter said, was this, and no other words could be more difficult
for me to say: *'On the basis of his work in primary school and
his scores on the entrance examinations, I must tell you that
your son and my good friend Eli cannot possibly do the work
required of boys at Whitehill.'*" Doctor Warren's voice steadied,
and so did his gaze. "*'To admit Eli to Whitehill, to expect him
to do Whitehill work,'*" he said, "*'would be both unrealistic and
cruel.'*"

Thirty African boys, escorted by several faculty members,
State Department men, and diplomats from their own countries,
filed into the dining room.

And Tom Hilyer and his boy, having no idea that something

had just gone awfully wrong for the Remenzels, came in, too, and said hello to the Remenzels and Doctor Warren gaily, as though life couldn't possibly be better.

"I'll talk to you more about this later, if you like," Doctor Warren said to the Remenzels, rising. "I have to go now, but later on—" He left quickly.

"My mind's a blank," said Sylvia. "My mind's a perfect blank."

Tom Hilyer and his boy sat down. Hilyer looked at the menu before him, clapped his hands and said, "What's good? I'm hungry." And then he said, "Say—where's your boy?"

"He stepped out for a moment," said Doctor Remenzel evenly.

"We've got to find him," said Sylvia to her husband.

"In time, in due time," said Doctor Remenzel.

"That letter," said Sylvia; "Eli knew about it. He found it and tore it up. Of course he did!" She started to cry, thinking of the hideous trap that Eli had caught himself in.

"I'm not interested right now in what Eli's done," said Doctor Remenzel. "Right now I'm a lot more interested in what some other people are going to do."

"What do you mean?" said Sylvia.

Doctor Remenzel stood impressively, angry and determined. "I mean," he said, "I'm going to see how quickly people can change their minds around here."

"Please," said Sylvia, trying to hold him, trying to calm him, "we've got to find Eli. That's the first thing."

"The first thing," said Doctor Remenzel quite loudly, "is to get Eli admitted to Whitehill. After that we'll find him, and we'll bring him back."

"But darling—" said Sylvia.

"No 'but' about it," said Doctor Remenzel. "There's a majority of the Board of Overseers in this room at this very moment. Every one of them is a close friend of mine, or a close friend of my father. If they tell Doctor Warren Eli's in, that's it—Eli's in. If there's room for all these other people," he said, "there's damn well room for Eli too."

He strode quickly to a table nearby, sat down heavily and began to talk to a fierce-looking and splendid old gentleman who was eating there. The old gentleman was chairman of the board.

Sylvia apologized to the baffled Hilyers, and then went in search of Eli.

Asking this person and that person, Sylvia found him. He was outside—all alone on a bench in a bower of lilacs that had just begun to bud.

Eli heard his mother's coming on the gravel path, stayed where he was, resigned. "Did you find out," he said, "or do I still have to tell you?"

"About you?" she said gently. "About not getting in? Doctor Warren told us."

"I tore his letter up," said Eli.

"I can understand that," she said. "Your father and I have always made you feel that you had to go to Whitehill, that nothing else would do."

"I feel better," said Eli. He tried to smile, found he could do it easily. "I feel so much better now that it's over. I tried to tell you a couple of times—but I just couldn't. I didn't know how."

"That's my fault, not yours," she said.

"What's father doing?" said Eli.

Sylva was so intent on comforting Eli that she'd put out of her mind what her husband was up to. Now she realized that Doctor Remenzel was making a ghastly mistake. She didn't want Eli admitted to Whitehill, could see what a cruel thing that would be.

She couldn't bring herself to tell the boy what his father was doing, so she said, "He'll be along in a minute, dear. He understands." And then she said, "You wait here, and I'll go get him and come right back."

But she didn't have to go to Doctor Remenzel. At that moment the big man came out of the inn and caught sight of his wife and son. He came to her and to Eli. He looked dazed.

"Well?" she said.

"They—they all said no," said Doctor Remenzel, very subdued.

"That's for the best," said Sylvia. "I'm relieved. I really am."

"Who said no?" said Eli. "Who said no to what?"

"The members of the board," said Doctor Remenzel, not looking anyone in the eye. "I asked them to make an exception in your case—to reverse their decision and let you in."

Eli stood, his face filled with incredulity and shame that were instant. "You what?" he said, and there was no childishness in the way he said it. Next came anger. "You shouldn't have done that!" he said to his father.

Doctor Remenzel nodded. "So I've already been told."

"That isn't done!" said Eli. "How awful! You shouldn't have."

"You're right," said Doctor Remenzel, accepting the scolding lamely.

"Now I *am* ashamed," said Eli, and he showed that he was.

Doctor Remenzel, in his wretchedness, could find no strong words to say. "I apologize to you both," he said at last. "It was a very bad thing to try."

"Now a Remenzel *has* asked for something," said Eli.

"I don't suppose Ben's back yet with the car?" said Doctor Remenzel. It was obvious that Ben wasn't. "We'll wait out here for him," he said. "I don't want to go back in there now."

"A Remenzel asked for something—as though a Remenzel were something special," said Eli.

"I don't suppose—" said Doctor Remenzel, and he left the sentence unfinished, dangling in the air.

"You don't suppose what?" said his wife, her face puzzled.

"I don't suppose," said Doctor Remenzel, "that we'll ever be coming here any more."

(1962)

UNREADY
TO WEAR

I DON'T SUPPOSE the oldsters, those of us who weren't born into it, will ever feel quite at home being amphibious—amphibious in the new sense of the word. I still catch myself feeling blue about things that don't matter any more.

I can't help worrying about my business, for instance—or what used to be my business. After all, I spent thirty years building the thing up from scratch, and now the equipment is rusting and getting clogged with dirt. But even though I know it's silly of me to care what happens to the business, I borrow a body from a storage center every so often, and go around the old hometown, and clean and oil as much of the equipment as I can.

Of course, all in the world the equipment was good for was making money, and Lord knows there's plenty of that lying around. Not as much as there used to be, because there at first some people got frisky and threw it all around, and the wind blew it every which way. And a lot of go-getters gathered up piles of the stuff and hid it somewhere. I hate to admit it, but I gathered up close to a half million myself and stuck it away. I used to get it out and count it sometimes, but that was years ago. Right now I'd be hard put to say where it is.

But the worrying I do about my old business is bush league stuff compared to the worrying my wife, Madge, does about our old house. That thing is what she herself put in thirty years on while I was building the business. Then no sooner had we gotten nerve enough to build and decorate the place than everybody we cared anything about got amphibious. Madge borrows a body once a month and dusts the place, though the only thing a house is good for now is keeping termites and mice from getting pneumonia.

Whenever it's my turn to get into a body and work as an attendant at the local storage center, I realize all over again how much tougher it is for women to get used to being amphibious.

Madge borrows bodies a lot oftener than I do, and that's true of women in general. We have to keep three times as many women's bodies in stock as men's bodies, in order to meet the demand. Every so often, it seems as though a woman just *has* to have a body, and doll it up in clothes, and look at herself in a mirror. And Madge, God bless her, I don't think she'll be satisfied until she's tried on every body in every storage center on Earth.

It's been a fine thing for Madge, though. I never kid her about it, because it's done so much for her personality. Her old body, to tell you the plain blunt truth, wasn't anything to get excited about, and having to haul the thing around made her gloomy a lot of the time in the old days. She couldn't help it, poor soul, any more than anybody else could help what sort of body they'd been born with, and I loved her in spite of it.

Well, after we'd learned to be amphibious, and after we'd built the storage centers and laid in body supplies and opened them to the public, Madge went hog wild. She borrowed a platinum blonde body that had been donated by a burlesque queen, and I didn't think we'd ever get her out of it. As I say, it did wonders for her self-confidence.

I'm like most men and don't care particularly what body I

get. Just the strong, good-looking, healthy bodies were put in storage, so one is as good as the next one. Sometimes, when Madge and I take bodies out together for old times' sake, I let her pick out one for me to match whatever she's got on. It's a funny thing how she always picks a blond, tall one for me.

My old body, which she claims she loved for a third of a century, had black hair, and was short and paunchy, too, there toward the last. I'm human and I couldn't help being hurt when they scrapped it after I'd left it, instead of putting it in storage. It was a good, homey, comfortable body; nothing fast and flashy, but reliable. But there isn't much call for that kind of body at the centers, I guess. I never ask for one, at any rate.

The worst experience I ever had with a body was when I was flimflammed into taking out the one that had belonged to Dr. Ellis Konigswasser. It belongs to the Amphibious Pioneers' Society and only gets taken out once a year for the big Pioneers' Day Parade, on the anniversary of Konigswasser's discovery. Everybody said it was a great honor for me to be picked to get into Konigswasser's body and lead the parade.

Like a plain damn fool, I believed them.

They'll have a tough time getting me into that thing again—ever. Taking that wreck out certainly made it plain why Konigswasser discovered how people could do without their bodies. That old one of his practically *drives* you out. Ulcers, headaches, arthritis, fallen arches—a nose like a pruning hook, piggy little eyes, and a complexion like a used steamer trunk. He was and still is the sweetest person you'd ever want to know, but, back when he was stuck with that body, nobody got close enough to find out.

We tried to get Konigswasser back into his old body to lead us when we first started having the Pioneers' Day Parades, but he wouldn't have anything to do with it, so we always have to flatter some poor boob into taking on the job. Konigswasser marches, all right, but as a six-foot cowboy who can bend beer cans double between his thumb and middle finger.

Konigswasser is just like a kid with that body. He never gets tired of bending beer cans with it, and we all have to stand around in our bodies after the parade, and watch as though we were very impressed.

I don't suppose he could bend very much of anything back in the old days.

Nobody mentions it to him, since he's the grand old man of the Amphibious Age, but he plays hell with bodies. Almost every time he takes one out, he busts it, showing off. Then somebody has to get into a surgeon's body and sew it up again.

I don't mean to be disrespectful of Konigswasser. As a matter of fact, it's a respectful thing to say that somebody is childish in certain ways, because it's people like that who seem to get all the big ideas.

There is a picture of him in the old days down at the Historical Society, and you can see from that that he never did grow up as far as keeping up his appearance went—doing what little he could with the rattle-trap body Nature had issued him.

His hair was down below his collar, he wore his pants so low that his heels wore through the legs above the cuffs, and the lining of his coat hung down in festoons all around the bottom. And he'd forget meals, and go out into the cold or wet without enough clothes on, and he would never notice sickness until it almost killed him. He was what we used to call absent-minded. Looking back now, of course, we say he was starting to be am-phibious.

Konigswasser was a mathematician, and he did all his living with his mind. The body he had to haul around with that won-derful mind was about as much use to him as a flatcar of scrap-iron. Whenever he got sick and *had* to pay some attention to his body, he'd rant somewhat like this:

"The mind is the only thing about human beings that's worth anything. Why does it have to be tied to a bag of skin, blood, hair, meat, bones, and tubes? No wonder people can't get any-thing done, stuck for life with a parasite that has to be stuffed with food and protected from weather and germs all the time. And the fool thing wears out anyway—no matter how much you stuff and protect it!

"Who," he wanted to know, "really wants one of the things? What's so wonderful about protoplasm that we've got to carry so damned many pounds of it with us wherever we go?"

"Trouble with the world," said Konigswasser, "isn't too many people—it's too many bodies."

When his teeth went bad on him, and he had to have them all out, and he couldn't get a set of dentures that were at all comfortable, he wrote in his diary, "If living matter was able to evolve enough to get out of the ocean, which was really quite a pleasant place to live, it certainly ought to be able to take another step and get out of bodies, which are pure nuisances when you stop to think about them."

He wasn't a prude about bodies, understand, and he wasn't jealous of people who had better ones than he did. He just thought bodies were a lot more trouble than they were worth.

He didn't have great hopes that people would really evolve out of their bodies in his time. He just wished they would. Thinking hard about it, he walked through a park in his shirtsleeves and stopped off at the zoo to watch the lions being fed. Then, when the rainstorm turned to sleet, he headed back home and was interested to see firemen on the edge of a lagoon, where they were using a pulmotor on a drowned man.

Witnesses said the old man had walked right into the water and had kept going without changing his expression until he'd disappeared. Konigswasser got a look at the victim's face and said he'd never seen a better reason for suicide. He started for home again and was almost there before he realized that that was his own body lying back there.

He went back to reoccupy the body just as the firemen got it breathing again, and he walked it home, more as a favor to the city than anything else. He walked it into his front closet, got out of it again, and left it there.

He took it out only when he wanted to do some writing or turn the pages of a book, or when he had to feed it so it would have enough energy to do the few odd jobs he gave it. The rest of the time, it sat motionless in the closet, looking dazed and using almost no energy. Konigswasser told me the other day that he used to run the thing for about a dollar a week, just taking it out when he really needed it.

But the best part was that Konigswasser didn't have to sleep any more, just because *it* had to sleep; or be afraid any more, just because *it* thought it might get hurt; or go looking for things *it* seemed to think it had to have. And, when *it* didn't feel well, Konigswasser kept out of it until it felt better, and he didn't have to spend a fortune keeping the thing comfortable.

When he got his body out of the closet to write, he did a book on how to get out of one's own body, which was rejected without comment by twenty-three publishers. The twenty-fourth sold two million copies, and the book changed human life more than the invention of fire, numbers, the alphabet, agriculture, or the wheel. When somebody told Konigswasser that, he snorted that they were damning his book with faint praise. I'd say he had a point there.

By following the instructions in Konigswasser's book for about two years, almost anybody could get out of his body whenever he wanted to. The first step was to understand what a parasite and dictator the body was most of the time, then to separate what the body wanted or didn't want from what you yourself—your psyche—wanted or didn't want. Then, by concentrating on what you wanted, and ignoring as much as possible what the body wanted beyond plain maintenance, you made your psyche demand its rights and become self-sufficient.

That's what Konigswasser had done without realizing it, until he and his body had parted company in the park, with his psyche going to watch the lions eat, and with his body wandering out of control into the lagoon.

The final trick of separation, once your psyche grew independent enough, was to start your body walking in some direction and suddenly take your psyche off in another direction. You couldn't do it standing still, for some reason—you had to walk.

At first, Madge's and my psyches were clumsy at getting along outside our bodies, like the first sea animals that got stranded on land millions of years ago, and who could just waddle and squirm and gasp in the mud. But we became better at it with time, because the psyche can naturally adapt so much faster than the body.

Madge and I had good reason for wanting to get out. Everybody who was crazy enough to try to get out at the first had good reasons. Madge's body was sick and wasn't going to last a lot longer. With her going in a little while, I couldn't work up enthusiasm for sticking around much longer myself. So we studied Konigswasser's book and tried to get Madge out of her body before it died. I went along with her, to keep either one of us from getting lonely. And we just barely made it—six weeks before her body went all to pieces.

That's why we get to march every year in the Pioneers' Day Parade. Not everybody does—only the first five thousand of us who turned amphibious. We were guinea pigs, without much to lose one way or another, and we were the ones who proved to the rest how pleasant and safe it was—a heck of a lot safer than taking chances in a body year in and year out.

Sooner or later, almost everybody had a good reason for giving it a try. There got to be millions and finally more than a billion of us—invisible, insubstantial, indestructible, and, by golly, true to ourselves, no trouble to anybody, and not afraid of anything.

When we're not in bodies, the Amphibious Pioneers can meet on the head of a pin. When we get into bodies for the Pioneers' Day Parade, we take up over fifty thousand square feet, have to gobble more than three tons of food to get enough energy to march; and lots of us catch colds or worse, and get sore because somebody's body accidentally steps on the heel of somebody else's body, and get jealous because some bodies get to lead and others have to stay in ranks, and—oh, hell, I don't know what all.

I'm not crazy about the parade. With all of us there, close together in bodies—well, it brings out the worst in us, no matter how good our psyches are. Last year, for instance, Pioneers' Day was a scorcher. People couldn't help being out of sorts, stuck in sweltering, thirsty bodies for hours.

Well, one thing led to another, and the Parade Marshal offered to beat the daylights out of my body with his body, if my body got out of step again. Naturally, being Parade Marshal, he had the best body that year, except for Konigswasser's cowboy, but I told him to soak his fat head, anyway. He swung, and I ditched my body right there, and didn't even stick around long enough to find out if he connected. He had to haul my body back to the storage center himself.

I stopped being mad at him the minute I got out of the body. I understood, you see. Nobody but a saint could be really sympathetic or intelligent for more than a few minutes at a time in a body—or happy, either, except in short spurts. I haven't met an amphibian yet who wasn't easy to get along with, and cheerful and interesting—as long as he was outside a body. And I haven't met one yet who didn't turn a little sour when he got into one.

The minute you get in, chemistry takes over—glands making you excitable or ready to fight or hungry or mad or affectionate, or—well, you never know *what's* going to happen next.

That's why I can't get sore at the enemy, the people who are against the amphibians. They never get out of their bodies and won't try to learn. They don't want anybody else to do it, either, and they'd like to make the amphibians get back into bodies and stay in them.

After the tussle I had with the Parade Marshal, Madge got wind of it and left *her* body right in the middle of the Ladies' Auxiliary. And the two of us, feeling full of devilment after getting shed of the bodies and the parade, went over to have a look at the enemy.

I'm never keen on going over to look at them. Madge likes to see what the women are wearing. Stuck with their bodies all the time, the enemy women change their clothes and hair and cosmetic styles a lot oftener than we do on the women's bodies in the storage centers.

I don't get much of a kick out of the fashions, and almost everything else you see and hear in enemy territory would bore a plaster statue into moving away.

Usually, the enemy is talking about old-style reproduction, which is the clumsiest, most comical, most inconvenient thing anyone could imagine, compared with what the amphibians have in that line. If they aren't talking about that, then they're talking about food, the gobs of chemicals they have to stuff into their bodies. Or they'll talk about fear, which we used to call politics—job politics, social politics, government politics.

The enemy hates that, having us able to peek in on them any time we want to, while they can't ever see us unless we get into bodies. They seem to be scared to death of us, though being scared of amphibians makes as much sense as being scared of the sunrise. They could have the whole world, except the storage centers, for all the amphibians care. But they bunch together as though we were going to come whooping out of the sky and do something terrible to them at any moment.

They've got contraptions all over the place that are supposed to detect amphibians. The gadgets aren't worth a nickel, but they seem to make the enemy feel good—like they were lined up against great forces, but keeping their nerve and doing important, clever things about it. Know-how—all the time they're patting each other about how much know-how they've got, and about how we haven't got anything by comparison. If know-how means weapons, they're dead right.

I guess there is a war on between them and us. But we never do anything about holding up our side of the war, except to keep our parade sites and our storage centers secret, and to get out of bodies every time there's an air raid, or the enemy fires a rocket, or something.

That just makes the enemy madder, because the raids and rockets and all cost plenty, and blowing up things nobody needs anyway is a poor return on the taxpayer's money. We always know what they're going to do next, and when and where, so there isn't any trick to keeping out of their way.

But they are pretty smart, considering they've got bodies to look after besides doing their thinking, so I always try to be cautious when I go over to watch them. That's why I wanted to clear out when Madge and I saw a storage center in the middle of one of their fields. We hadn't talked to anybody lately about what the enemy was up to, and the center looked awfully suspicious.

Madge was optimistic, the way she's been ever since she borrowed that burlesque queen's body, and she said the storage center was a sure sign that the enemy had seen the light, that they were getting ready to become amphibious themselves.

Well, it looked like it. There was a brand-new center, stocked with bodies and open for business, as innocent as you please. We circled it several times, and Madge's circles got smaller and smaller, as she tried to get a close look at what they had in the way of ladies' ready-to-wear.

"Let's beat it," I said.

"I'm just looking," said Madge. "No harm in looking."

Then she saw what was in the main display case, and she forgot where she was or where she'd come from.

The most striking woman's body I'd ever seen was in the case— six feet tall and built like a goddess. But that wasn't the payoff. The body had copper-colored skin, chartreuse hair and finger-nails, and a gold lamé evening gown. Beside that body was the body of a blond, male giant in a pale blue field marshal's uniform, piped in scarlet and spangled with medals.

I think the enemy must have swiped the bodies in a raid on one of our outlying storage centers, and padded and dyed them, and dressed them up.

"Madge, come back!" I said.

The copper-colored woman with the chartreuse hair moved. A siren screamed and soldiers rushed from hiding places to grab the body Madge was in.

The center was a trap for amphibians!

The body Madge hadn't been able to resist had its ankles tied together, so Madge couldn't take the few steps she had to take if she was going to get out of it again.

The soldiers carted her off triumphantly as a prisoner of war. I got into the only body available, the fancy field marshal, to try to help her. It was a hopeless situation, because the field marshal was bait, too, with its ankles tied. The soldiers dragged me after Madge.

The cocky young major in charge of the soldiers did a jig along the shoulder of the road, he was so proud. He was the first man ever to capture an amphibian, which was really something from the enemy's point of view. They'd been at war with us for years, and spent God knows how many billions of dollars, but catching us was the first thing that made any amphibians pay much attention to them.

When we got to the town, people were leaning out of windows and waving their flags, and cheering the soldiers, and hissing Madge and me. Here were all the people who didn't want to be amphibious, who thought it was terrible for anybody to be amphibious—people of all colors, shapes, sizes, and nationalities, joined together to fight the amphibians.

It turned out that Madge and I were going to have a big trial. After being tied up every which way in jail all night, we were taken to a courtroom, where television cameras stared at us.

Madge and I were worn to frazzles, because neither one of us had been cooped up in a body that long since I don't know when. Just when we needed to think more than we ever had, in jail before the trial, the bodies developed hunger pains and we couldn't get them comfortable on the cots, no matter how we tried; and, of course, the bodies just had to have their eight hours sleep.

The charge against us was a capital offense on the books of the enemy—*desertion*. As far as the enemy was concerned, the amphibians had all turned yellow and run out on their bodies, just when their bodies were needed to do brave and important things for humanity.

We didn't have a hope of being acquitted. The only reason there was a trial at all was that it gave them an opportunity to sound off about why they were so right and we were so wrong. The courtroom was jammed with their big brass, all looking angry and brave and noble.

"Mr. Amphibian," said the prosecutor, "you are old enough, aren't you, to remember when all men had to face up to life in their bodies, and work and fight for what they believed in?"

"I remember when the bodies were always getting into fights. and nobody seemed to know why, or how to stop it," I said politely. "The only thing everybody seemed to believe in was that they didn't like to fight."

"What would you say of a soldier who ran away in the face of fire?" he wanted to know.

"I'd say he was scared silly."

"He was helping to lose the battle, wasn't he?"

"Oh, sure." There wasn't any argument on that one.

"Isn't that what the amphibians have done—run out on the human race in the face of the battle of life?"

"Most of us are still alive, if that's what you mean," I said.

It was true. We hadn't licked death, and weren't sure we wanted to, but we'd certainly lengthened life something amazing, compared to the span you could expect in a body.

"You ran out on your responsibilities!" he said.

"Like you'd run out of a burning building, sir," I said.

"Leaving everyone else to struggle on alone!"

"They can all get out the same door that we got out of. You can all get out any time you want to. All you do is figure out what you want and what your body wants, and concentrate on—"

The judge banged his gavel until I thought he'd split it. Here they'd burned every copy of Konigswasser's book they could find, and there I was giving a course in how to get out of a body over a whole television network.

"If you amphibians had your way," said the prosecutor, "everybody would run out on his responsibilities, and let life and progress as we know them disappear completely."

"Why, sure," I agreed. "That's the point."

"Men would no longer work for what they believe in?" he challenged.

"I had a friend back in the old days who drilled holes in little square thingamajigs for seventeen years in a factory, and he never did get a very clear idea of what they were for. Another one I knew grew raisins for a glassblowing company, and the raisins weren't for anybody to eat, and he never did find out why the company bought them. Things like that make me sick—now that I'm in a body, of course—and what I used to do for a living makes me even sicker."

"Then you despise human beings and everything they do," he said.

"I like them fine—better than I ever did before. I just think it's a dirty shame what they have to do to take care of their bodies. You ought to get amphibious and see how happy people can be when they don't have to worry about where their body's next meal is coming from, or how to keep it from freezing in the wintertime, or what's going to happen to them when their body wears out."

"And that, sir, means the end of ambition, the end of greatness!"

"Oh, I don't know about that," I said. "We've got some pretty great people on our side. They'd be great in *or* out of bodies. It's the end of fear is what it is." I looked right into the lens of the nearest television camera. "And *that's* the most wonderful thing that ever happened to people."

Down came the judge's gavel again, and the brass started to shout me down. The television men turned off their cameras, and all the spectators, except for the biggest brass, were cleared out. I knew I'd really said something. All anybody would be getting on his television set now was organ music.

When the confusion died down, the judge said the trial was over, and that Madge and I were guilty of desertion.

Nothing I could do could get us in any worse, so I talked back.

"Now I understand you poor fish," I said. "You couldn't get along without fear. That's the only skill you've got—how to scare yourselves and other people into doing things. That's the only fun you've got, watching people jump for fear of what you'll do to their bodies or take away from their bodies."

Madge got in her two cents' worth. "The only way you can get any response from anybody is to scare them."

"Contempt of court!" said the judge.

"The only way you can scare people is if you can keep them in their bodies," I told him.

The soldiers grabbed Madge and me and started to drag us out of the courtroom.

"This means war!" I yelled.

Everything stopped right there and the place got very quiet.

"We're already at war," said a general uneasily.

"Well, *we're* not," I answered, "but we will be, if you don't untie Madge and me this instant." I was fierce and impressive in that field marshal's body.

"You haven't any weapons," said the judge, "no know-how. Outside of bodies, amphibians are nothing."

"If you don't cut us loose by the time I count ten," I told him, "the amphibians will occupy the bodies of the whole kit and caboodle of you and march you right off the nearest cliff. The place is surrounded." That was hogwash, of course. Only one person can occupy a body at a time, but the enemy couldn't be sure of that. "One! Two! Three!"

The general swallowed, turned white, and waved his hand vaguely.

"Cut them loose," he said weakly.

The soldiers, terrified, too, were glad to do it. Madge and I were freed.

I took a couple of steps, headed my spirit in another direction, and that beautiful field marshal, medals and all, went crashing down the staircase like a grandfather clock.

I realized that Madge wasn't with me. She was still in that copper-colored body with the chartreuse hair and fingernails.

"What's more," I heard her saying, "in payment for all the trouble you've caused us, this body is to be addressed to me at New York, delivered in good condition no later than next Monday."

"Yes, ma'am," said the judge.

When we got home, the Pioneers' Day Parade was just breaking up at the local storage center, and the Parade Marshal got out of his body and apologized to me for acting the way he had.

"Heck, Herb," I said, "you don't need to apologize. You weren't yourself. You were parading around in a body."

That's the best part of being amphibious, next to not being afraid—people forgive you for whatever fool thing you might have done in a body.

Oh, there are drawbacks, I guess, the way there are drawbacks to everything. We still have to work off and on, maintaining the storage centers and getting food to keep the community bodies going. But that's a small drawback, and all the big draw-backs I ever heard of aren't real ones, just old-fashioned think-ing by people who can't stop worrying about things they used to worry about before they turned amphibious.

As I say, the oldsters will probably never get really used to it. Every so often, I catch myself getting gloomy over what hap-pened to the pay-toilet business it took me thirty years to build.

But the youngsters don't have any hangovers like that from the past. They don't even worry much about something happen-ing to the storage centers, the way us oldsters do.

So I guess maybe that'll be the next step in evolution—to break clean like those first amphibians who crawled out of the mud into the sunshine, and who never did go back to the sea.

(1953)

THE KID NOBODY COULD HANDLE

I

T WAS SEVEN-THIRTY in the morning. Waddling, clanking, muddy machines were tearing a hill to pieces behind a restaurant, and trucks were hauling the pieces away. Inside the
restaurant, dishes rattled on their shelves. Tables quaked, and a
very kind fat man with a headful of music looked down at the
jiggling yolks of his breakfast eggs. His wife was visiting relatives out of town. He was on his own.

The kind fat man was George M. Helmholtz, a man of forty,
head of the music department of Lincoln High School, and director of the band. Life had treated him well. Each year he
dreamed the same big dream. He dreamed of leading as fine a
band as there was on the face of the earth. And each year the
dream came true.

It came true because Helmholtz was sure that a man couldn't
have a better dream than his. Faced by this unnerving sureness,
Kiwanians, Rotarians, and Lions paid for band uniforms that cost
twice as much as their best suits, school administrators let Helmholtz raid the budget for expensive props, and youngsters played

their hearts out for him. When youngsters had no talent, Helmholtz made them play on guts alone.

Everything was good about Helmholtz's life save his finances. He was so dazzled by his big dream that he was a child in the marketplace. Ten years before, he had sold the hill behind the restaurant to Bert Quinn, the restaurant owner, for one thousand dollars. It was now apparent, even to Helmholtz, that Helmholtz had been had.

Quinn sat down in the booth with the bandmaster. He was a bachelor, a small, dark, humorless man. He wasn't a well man. He couldn't sleep, he couldn't stop working, he couldn't smile warmly. He had only two moods: one suspicious and self-pitying, the other arrogant and boastful. The first mood applied when he was losing money. The second mood applied when he was making it.

Quinn was in the arrogant and boastful mood when he sat down with Helmholtz. He sucked whistlingly on a toothpick, and talked of vision—his own.

"I wonder how many eyes saw the hill before I did?" said Quinn. "Thousands and thousands, I'll bet—and not one saw what I saw. How many eyes?"

"Mine, at least," said Helmholtz. All the hill had meant to him was a panting climb, free blackberries, taxes, and a place for band picnics.

"You inherit the hill from your old man, and it's nothing but a pain in the neck to you," said Quinn. "So you figure you'll stick me with it."

"I didn't figure to stick you," Helmholtz protested. "The good Lord knows the price was more than fair."

"You say that now," said Quinn gleefully. "Sure, Helmholtz, you say that now. Now you see the shopping district's got to grow. Now you see what I saw."

"Yes," said Helmholtz. "Too late, too late." He looked around for some diversion, and saw a fifteen-year-old boy coming toward him, mopping the aisle between booths.

The boy was small but with tough, stringy muscles standing out on his neck and forearms. Childhood lingered in his features, but when he paused to rest, his fingers went hopefully to the silky beginnings of sideburns and a mustache. He mopped like a robot, jerkily, brainlessly, but took pains not to splash suds over the toes of his black boots.

"So what do I do when I get the hill?" said Quinn. "I tear it down, and it's like somebody pulled down a dam. All of a sudden everybody wants to build a store where the hill was."

"Um," said Helmholtz. He smiled genially at the boy. The boy looked through him without a twitch of recognition.

"We all got something," said Quinn. "You got music; I got vision." And he smiled, for it was perfectly clear to both where the money lay. "Think big!" said Quinn. "Dream big! That's what vision is. Keep your eyes wider open than anybody else's."

"That boy," said Helmholtz, "I've seen him around school, but I never knew his name."

Quinn laughed cheerlessly. "Billy the Kid? The storm trooper? Rudolph Valentino? Flash Gordon?" He called the boy. . . . "Hey, Jim! Come here a minute."

Helmholtz was appalled to see that the boy's eyes were as expressionless as oysters.

"This is my brother-in-law's kid by another marriage—before he married my sister," said Quinn. "His name's Jim Donnini, and he's from the south side of Chicago, and he's very tough."

Jim Donnini's hands tightened on the mop handle.

"How do you do?" said Helmholtz.

"Hi," said Jim emptily.

"He's living with me now," said Quinn. "He's my baby now."

"You want a lift to school, Jim?"

"Yeah, he wants a lift to school," said Quinn. "See what you make of him. He won't talk to me." He turned to Jim. "Go on, kid, wash up and shave."

Robotlike, Jim marched away.

"Where are his parents?"

"His mother's dead. His old man married my sister, walked out on her, and stuck her with him. Then the court didn't like the way she was raising him, and put him in foster homes for a while. Then they decided to get him clear out of Chicago, so they stuck me with him." He shook his head. "Life's a funny thing, Helmholtz."

"Not very funny, sometimes," said Helmholtz. He pushed his eggs away.

"Like some whole new race of people coming up," said Quinn wonderingly. "Nothing like the kids we got around here. Those boots, the black jacket—and he won't talk. He won't run around with the other kids. Won't study. I don't think he can even read and write very good."

"Does he like music at all? Or drawing? Or animals?" said Helmholtz. "Does he collect anything?"

"You know what he likes?" said Quinn. "He likes to polish those boots—get off by himself and polish those boots. And when he's really in heaven is when he can get off by himself, spread comic books all around him on the floor, polish his boots, and watch television." He smiled ruefully. "Yeah, he had a collection too. And I took it away from him and threw it in the river."

"Threw it in the river?" said Helmholtz.

"Yeah," said Quinn. "Eight knives—some with blades as long as your hand."

Helmholtz paled. "Oh." A prickling sensation spread over the back of his neck. "This is a new problem at Lincoln High. I hardly know what to think about it." He swept spilled salt together in a neat little pile, just as he would have liked to sweep together his scattered thoughts. "It's a kind of sickness, isn't it? That's the way to look at it?"

"Sick?" said Quinn. He slapped the table. "You can say that again!" He tapped his chest. "And Doctor Quinn is just the man to give him what's good for what ails him."

"What's that?" said Helmholtz.

"No more talk about the poor little sick boy," said Quinn grimly. "That's all he's heard from the social workers and the juvenile court, and God knows who all. From now on, he's the no-good bum of a man. I'll ride his tail till he straightens up and flies right or winds up in the can for life. One way or the other."

"I see," said Helmholtz.

"Like listening to music?" said Helmholtz to Jim brightly, as they rode to school in Helmholtz's car.

Jim said nothing. He was stroking his mustache and sideburns, which he had not shaved off.

"Ever drum with the fingers or keep time with your feet?" said Helmholtz. He had noticed that Jim's boots were decorated with chains that had no function but to jingle as he walked.

Jim sighed with ennui.

"Or whistle?" said Helmholtz. "If you do any of those things, it's just like picking up the keys to a whole new world—a world as beautiful as any world can be."

Jim gave a soft Bronx cheer.

"There!" said Helmholtz. "You've illustrated the basic principle of the family of brass wind instruments. The glorious voice of every one of them starts with a buzz on the lips."

The seat springs of Helmholtz's old car creaked under Jim, as Jim shifted his weight. Helmholtz took this as a sign of interest, and he turned to smile in comradely fashion. But Jim had shifted his weight in order to get a cigarette from inside his tight leather jacket.

Helmholtz was too upset to comment at once. It was only at the end of the ride, as he turned into the teachers' parking lot, that he thought of something to say.

"Sometimes," said Helmholtz, "I get so lonely and disgusted, I don't see how I can stand it. I feel like doing all kinds of crazy things, just for the heck of it—things that might even be bad for me."

Jim blew a smoke ring expertly.

"And then!" said Helmholtz. He snapped his fingers and honked his horn. "And then, Jim, I remember I've got at least one tiny corner of the universe I can make just the way I want it! I can go to it and gloat over it until I'm brand-new and happy again."

"Aren't you the lucky one?" said Jim. He yawned.

"I am, for a fact," said Helmholtz. "My corner of the universe happens to be the air around my band. I can fill it with music. Mr. Beeler, in zoology, has his butterflies. Mr. Trottman, in physics, has his pendulum and tuning forks. Making sure everybody has a corner like that is about the biggest job we teachers have. I—"

The car door opened and slammed, and Jim was gone. Helmholtz stamped out Jim's cigarette and buried it under the gravel of the parking lot.

Helmholtz's first class of the morning was C Band, where beginners thumped and wheezed and tooted as best they could, and looked down the long, long, long road through B Band to A Band, the Lincoln High School Ten Square Band, the finest band in the world.

Helmholtz stepped onto the podium and raised his baton. "You are better than you think," he said. "A-one, a-two, a-three." Down came the baton.

C Band set out in its quest for beauty—set out like a rusty switch engine, with valves stuck, pipes clogged, unions leaking, bearings dry.

Helmholtz was still smiling at the end of the hour, because he'd heard in his mind the music as it was going to be someday. His throat was raw, for he had been singing with the band for the whole hour. He stepped into the hall for a drink from the fountain.

As he drank, he heard the jingling of chains. He looked up at Jim Donnini. Rivers of students flowed between classrooms, pausing in friendly eddies, flowing on again. Jim was alone. When he paused, it wasn't to greet anyone, but to polish the toes of his boots on his trousers legs. He had the air of a spy in a melodrama, missing nothing, liking nothing, looking forward to the great day when everything would be turned upside down.

"Hello, Jim," said Helmholtz. "Say, I was just thinking about you. We've got a lot of clubs and teams that meet after school. And that's a good way to get to know a lot of people."

Jim measured Helmholtz carefully with his eyes. "Maybe I don't want to know a lot of people," he said. "Ever think of that?" He set his feet down hard to make his chains jingle as he walked away.

When Helmholtz returned to the podium for a rehearsal of B Band, there was a note waiting for him, calling him to a special faculty meeting.

The meeting was about vandalism.

Someone had broken into the school and wrecked the office of Mr. Crane, head of the English Department. The poor man's treasures—books, diplomas, snapshots of England, the beginnings of eleven novels—had been ripped and crumpled, mixed, dumped and trampled, and drenched with ink.

Helmholtz was sickened. He couldn't believe it. He couldn't bring himself to think about it. It didn't become real to him until late that night, in a dream. In the dream Helmholtz saw a boy with barracuda teeth, with claws like baling hooks. The monster climbed into a window of the high school and dropped to the floor of the band rehearsal room. The monster clawed to shreds the heads of the biggest drum in the state. Helmholtz woke up howling. There was nothing to do but dress and go to the school.

At two in the morning, Helmholtz caressed the drum heads in the band rehearsal room, with the night watchman looking on. He rolled the drum back and forth on its cart, and he turned the light inside on and off, on and off. The drum was unharmed. The night watchman left to make his rounds.

The band's treasure house was safe. With the contentment of a miser counting his money, Helmholtz fondled the rest of the instruments, one by one. And then he began to polish the sousaphones. As he polished, he could hear the great horns roaring, could see them flashing in the sunlight, with the Stars and Stripes and the banner of Lincoln High going before.

"Yump-yump, tiddle-tiddle, yump-yump, tiddle-tiddle!" sang Helmholtz happily. "Yump-yump-yump, ra-a-a-a-a-a, yump-yump, yump-yump—boom!"

As he paused to choose the next number for his imaginary band to play, he heard a furtive noise in the chemistry laboratory next door. Helmholtz sneaked into the hall, jerked open the laboratory door, and flashed on the lights. Jim Donnini had a bottle of acid in either hand. He was splashing acid over the periodic table of the elements, over the blackboards covered with formulas, over the bust of Lavoisier. The scene was the most repulsive thing Helmholtz could have looked upon.

Jim smiled with thin bravado.

"Get out," said Helmholtz.

"What're you gonna do?" said Jim.

"Clean up. Save what I can," said Helmholtz dazedly. He picked up a wad of cotton waste and began wiping up the acid.

"You gonna call the cops?" said Jim.

"I—I don't know," said Helmholtz. "No thoughts come. If I'd caught you hurting the bass drum, I think I would have killed you with a single blow. But I wouldn't have had any intelligent thoughts about what you were—what you thought you were doing."

"It's about time this place got set on its ear," said Jim.

"Is it?" said Helmholtz. "That must be so, if one of our students wants to murder it."

"What good is it?" said Jim.

"Not much good, I guess," said Helmholtz. "It's just the best thing human beings ever managed to do." He was helpless, talking to himself. He had a bag of tricks for making boys behave like men—tricks that played on boyish fears and dreams and loves. But here was a boy without fear, without dreams, without love.

"If you smashed up all the schools," said Helmholtz, "we wouldn't have any hope left."

"What hope?" said Jim.

"The hope that everybody will be glad he's alive," said Helmholtz. "Even you."

"That's a laugh," said Jim. "All I ever got out of this dump was a hard time. So what're you gonna do?"

"I have to do something, don't I?" said Helmholtz.

"I don't care what you do," said Jim.

"I know," said Helmholtz. "I know." He marched Jim into his tiny office off the band rehearsal room. He dialed the telephone number of the principal's home. Numbly, he waited for the bell to get the old man from his bed.

Jim dusted his boots with a rag.

Helmholtz suddenly dropped the telephone into its cradle before the principal could answer. "Isn't there anything you care about but ripping, hacking, bending, rending, smashing, bashing?" he cried. "Anything? Anything but those boots?"

"Go on! Call up whoever you're gonna call," said Jim.

Helmholtz opened a locker and took a trumpet from it. He

thrust the trumpet into Jim's arms. "There!" he said, puffing with emotion. "There's my treasure. It's the dearest thing I own. I give it to you to smash. I won't move a muscle to stop you. You can have the added pleasure of watching my heart break while you do it."

Jim looked at him oddly. He laid down the trumpet.

"Go on!" said Helmholtz. "If the world has treated you so badly, it deserves to have the trumpet smashed!"

"I—" said Jim. Helmholtz grabbed his belt, put a foot behind him, and dumped him on the floor.

Helmholtz pulled Jim's boots off and threw them into a corner. "There!" said Helmholtz savagely. He jerked the boy to his feet again and thrust the trumpet into his arms once more.

Jim Donnini was barefoot now. He had lost his socks with his boots. The boy looked down. The feet that had once seemed big black clubs were narrow as chicken wings now—bony and blue, and not quite clean.

The boy shivered, then quaked. Each quake seemed to shake something loose inside, until, at last, there was no boy left. No boy at all. Jim's head lolled, as though he waited only for death.

Helmholtz was overwhelmed by remorse. He threw his arms around the boy. "Jim! Jim—listen to me, boy!"

Jim stopped quaking.

"You know what you've got there—the trumpet?" said Helmholtz. "You know what's special about it?"

Jim only sighed.

"It belonged to John Philip Sousa!" said Helmholtz. He rocked and shook Jim gently, trying to bring him back to life. "I'll trade it to you, Jim—for your boots. It's yours, Jim! John Philip Sousa's trumpet is yours! It's worth hundreds of dollars, Jim—thousands!"

Jim laid his head on Helmholtz's breast.

"It's better than boots, Jim," said Helmholtz. "You can learn to play it. You're somebody, Jim. You're the boy with John Philip Sousa's trumpet!"

Helmholtz released Jim slowly, sure the boy would topple. Jim didn't fall. He stood alone. The trumpet was still in his arms.

"I'll take you home, Jim," said Helmholtz. "Be a good boy and I won't say a word about tonight. Polish your trumpet, and learn to be a good boy."

"Can I have my boots?" said Jim dully.

"No," said Helmholtz. "I don't think they're good for you."

He drove Jim home. He opened the car windows and the air seemed to refresh the boy. He let him out at Quinn's restaurant. The soft pats of Jim's bare feet on the sidewalk echoed down the empty street. He climbed through a window, and into his bedroom behind the kitchen. And all was still.

The next morning the waddling clanking, muddy machines were making the vision of Bert Quinn come true. They were smoothing off the place where the hill had been behind the restaurant. They were making it as level as a billiard table.

Helmholtz sat in a booth again. Quinn joined him again. Jim mopped again. Jim kept his eyes down, refusing to notice Helmholtz. And he didn't seem to care when a surf of suds broke over the toes of his small and narrow brown Oxfords.

"Eating out two mornings in a row?" said Quinn. "Something wrong at home?"

"My wife's still out of town," said Helmholtz.

"While the cat's away——" said Quinn. He winked.

"When the cat's away," said Helmholtz, "this mouse gets lonesome."

Quinn leaned forward. "Is that what got you out of bed in the middle of the night, Helmholtz? Loneliness?" He jerked his head at Jim. "Kid! Go get Mr. Helmholtz his horn."

Jim raised his head, and Helmholtz saw that his eyes were oysterlike again. He marched away to get the trumpet.

Quinn now showed that he was excited and angry. "You take away his boots and give him a horn, and I'm not supposed to get curious?" he said. "I'm not supposed to start asking questions? I'm not supposed to find out you caught him taking the school apart? You'd make a lousy crook, Helmholtz. You'd leave your baton, sheet music, and your driver's license at the scene of the crime."

"I don't think about hiding clues," said Helmholtz. "I just do what I do. I was going to tell you."

Quinn's feet danced and his shoes squeaked like mice. "Yes?" he said. "Well, I've got some news for you too."

"What is that?" said Helmholtz uneasily.

"It's all over with Jim and me," said Quinn. "Last night was the payoff. I'm sending him back where he came from."

"To another string of foster homes?" said Helmholtz weakly.

"Whatever the experts figure out to do with a kid like that." Quinn sat back, exhaled noisily, and went limp with relief.

"You can't," said Helmholtz.

"I can," said Quinn.

"That will be the end of him," said Helmholtz. "He can't stand to be thrown away like that one more time."

"He can't feel anything," said Quinn. "I can't help him; I can't hurt him. Nobody can. There isn't a nerve in him."

"A bundle of scar tissue," said Helmholtz.

The bundle of scar tissue returned with the trumpet. Impassively, he laid it on the table in front of Helmholtz.

Helmholtz forced a smile. "It's yours, Jim," he said. "I gave it to you."

"Take it while you got the chance, Helmholtz," said Quinn. "He doesn't want it. All he'll do is swap it for a knife or a pack of cigarettes."

"He doesn't know what it is, yet," said Helmholtz. "It takes a while to find out."

"Is it any good?" said Quinn.

"Any good?" said Helmholtz, not believing his ears. "Any good?" He didn't see how anyone could look at the instrument and not be warmed and dazzled by it. "Any good?" he murmured. "It belonged to John Philip Sousa."

Quinn blinked stupidly. "Who?"

Helmholtz's hands fluttered on the table top like the wings of a dying bird. "Who was John Philip Sousa?" he piped. No more words came. The subject was too big for a tired man to cover. The dying bird expired and lay still.

After a long silence, Helmholtz picked up the trumpet. He kissed the cold mouthpiece and pumped the valves in a dream of a brilliant cadenza. Over the bell of the instrument, Helmholtz saw Jim Donnini's face, seemingly floating in space—all but deaf and blind. Now Helmholtz saw the futility of men and their treasures. He had thought that his greatest treasure, the trumpet, could buy a soul for Jim. The trumpet was worthless.

Deliberately, Helmholtz hammered the trumpet against the table edge. He bent it around a coat tree. He handed the wreck to Quinn.

"Ya busted it," said Quinn, amazed. "Why'dja do that? What's that prove?"

"I—I don't know," said Helmholtz. A terrible blasphemy rumbled deep in him, like the warning of a volcano. And then, irresistibly, out it came. "Life is no damn good," said Helmholtz. His face twisted as he fought back tears and shame.

Helmholtz, the mountain that walked like a man, was falling apart. Jim Donnini's eyes filled with pity and alarm. They came alive. They became human. Helmholtz had got a message through. Quinn looked at Jim, and something like hope flickered for the first time in his bitterly lonely old face.

Two weeks later, a new semester began at Lincoln High.

In the band rehearsal room, the members of C Band were waiting for their leader—were waiting for their destinies as musicians to unfold.

Helmholtz stepped onto the podium, and rattled his baton against his music stand. "The Voices of Spring," he said. "Everybody hear that? The Voices of Spring?"

There were rustling sounds as the musicians put the music on their stands. In the pregnant silence that followed their readiness, Helmholtz glanced at Jim Donnini, who sat on the last seat of the worst trumpet section of the worst band in school.

His trumpet, John Philip Sousa's trumpet, George M. Helmholtz's trumpet, had been repaired.

"Think of it this way," said Helmholtz. "Our aim is to make the world more beautiful than it was when we came into it. It can be done. You can do it."

A small cry of despair came from Jim Donnini. It was meant to be private, but it pierced every ear with its poignancy.

"How?" said Jim.

"Love yourself," said Helmholtz, "and make your instrument sing about it. A-one, a-two, a-three." Down came his baton.

(1955)

THE MANNED MISSILES

I, MIKHAIL IVANKOV, stone mason in the village of Ilba in the Ukrainian Soviet Socialist Republic, greet you and pity you, Charles Ashland, petroleum merchant in Titusville, Florida, in the United States of America. I grasp your hand.

The first true space man was my son, Major Stepan Ivankov. The second was your son, Captain Bryant Ashland. They will be forgotten only when men no longer look up at the sky. They are like the moon and the planets and the sun and the stars.

I do not speak English. I speak these words in Russian, from my heart, and my surviving son, Alexei, writes them down in English. He studies English in school and German also. He likes English best. He admires your Jack London and your O. Henry· and your Mark Twain. Alexei is seventeen. He is going to be a scientist like his brother Stepan.

He wants me to tell you that he is going to work on science for peace, not war. He wants me to tell you also that he does not hate the memory of your son. He understands that your son was ordered to do what he did. He is talking very much, and would like to compose this letter himself. He thinks that a man forty-nine is a very old man, and he does not think that a very old man who can do nothing but put one stone on top of another can say the right things about young men who die in space.

If he wishes, he can write a letter of his own about the deaths of Stepan and your son. This is my letter, and I will get Aksinia, Stepan's widow, to read it to me to make sure Alexei has made it say exactly what I wish it to say. Aksinia, too, understands English very well. She is a physician for children. She is beautiful. She works very hard so she can forget sometimes her grief for Stepan.

I will tell you a joke, Mr. Ashland. When the second baby moon of the U.S.S.R. went up with a dog in it, we whispered that it was not really a dog inside, but Prokhor Ivanoff, a dairy manager who had been arrested for theft two days before. It was only a joke, but it made me think what a terrible punishment it would be to send a human being up there. I could not stop thinking about that. I dreamed about it at night, and I dreamed that it was myself who was being punished.

I would have asked my elder son Stepan about life in space, but he was far away in Guryev, on the Caspian Sea. So I asked my younger son. Alexei laughed at my fears of space. He said that a man could be made very comfortable up there. He said that many young men would be going up there soon. First they would ride in baby moons. Then they would go to the moon itself. Then they would go to other planets. He laughed at me, because only an old man would worry about such simple trips.

Alexei told me that the only inconvenience would be the lack of gravity. That seemed like a great lack to me. Alexei said one would have to drink out of nursing bottles, and one would have to get used to the feeling of falling constantly, and one would have to learn to control one's movements because gravity would no longer offer resistance to them. That was all. Alexei did not think such things would be bothersome. He expected to go to Mars soon.

Olga, my wife, laughed at me, too, because I was too old to

understand the great new Age of Space. "Two Russian moons shine overhead," she said, "and my husband is the only man on earth who does not yet believe it!"

But I went on dreaming bad dreams about space, and now I had information to make my bad dreams truly scientific. I dreamed of nursing bottles and falling, falling, falling, and the strange movements of my limbs. Perhaps the dreams were supernatural. Perhaps something was trying to warn me that Stepan would soon be suffering in space as I had suffered in dreams. Perhaps something was trying to warn me that Stepan would be murdered in space.

Alexei is very embarrassed that I should say that in a letter to the United States of America. He says that you will think that I am a superstitious peasant. So be it. I think that scientific persons of the future will scoff at scientific persons of the present. They will scoff because scientific persons of the present thought so many important things were superstitions. The things I dreamed about space all came true for my son. Stepan suffered very much up there. After the fourth day in space, Stepan sometimes cried like a baby. I had cried like a baby in my dreams.

I am not a coward, and I do not love comfort more than the improvement of human life. I am not a coward for my sons, either. I knew great suffering in the war, and I understand that there must be great suffering before great joy. But when I thought of the suffering that must surely come to a man in space, I could not see the joy to be earned by it. This was long before Stepan went up in his baby moon.

I went to the library and read about the moon and the planets, to see if they were truly desirable places to go. I did not ask Alexei about them, because I knew he would tell me what fine times we would have on such places. I found out for myself in the library that the moon and the planets were not fit places for men or for any life. They were much too hot or much too cold or much too poisonous.

I said nothing at home about my discoveries at the library, because I did not wish to be laughed at again. I waited quietly for Stepan to visit us. He would not laugh at my questions. He would answer them scientifically. He had worked on rockets for years. He would know everything that was known about space.

Stepan at last came to visit us, and brought his beautiful wife. He was a small man, but strong and broad and wise. He was very tired. His eyes were sunken. He knew already that he was to be shot into space. First had come the baby moon with the radio. Next had come the baby moon with the dog. Next would come the baby moons with the monkeys and the apes. After them would come the baby moon with Stepan. Stepan had been working night and day, designing his home in space. He could not tell me. He could not even tell his wife.

Mr. Ashland, you would have liked my son. Everybody liked Stepan. He was a man of peace. He was not a major because he was a great warrior. He was a major because he understood rockets so well. He was a thoughtful man. He often said that he wished that he could be a stone mason like me. He said a stone mason would have time and peace in which to think things out. I did not tell him that a stone mason thinks of little but stones and mortar.

I asked him my questions about space, and he did not laugh. Stepan was very serious when he answered me. He had reason to be serious. He was telling me why he was himself willing to suffer in space.

He told me I was right. A man would suffer greatly in space, and the moon and the planets were bad places for men. There might be good places, but they were too far for men to reach in a lifetime.

"Then, what is this great new Age of Space, Stepan?" I asked him.

"It will be an age of baby moons for a long time," he said. "We will reach the moon itself soon, but it would be very difficult to stay there more than a few hours."

"Then why go into space, if there is so little good out there?" I asked him.

"There is so much to be learned and seen out there," he said. "A man could look at other worlds without a curtain of air between himself and them. A man could look at his own world, study the flow of weather over it, measure its true dimensions." This last surprised me. I thought the dimensions of our world were well known. "A man out there could learn much about the wonderful showers of matter and energy in space," said Stepan. And he spoke of many other poetic and scientific joys out there.

I was satisfied. Stepan had made me feel his own great joy at the thought of all the beauty and truth in space. I understood at last, Mr. Ashland, why the suffering would be worthwhile. When I dreamed of space again, I would dream of looking down at our own lovely green ball, dream of looking up at other worlds and seeing them more clearly than they had ever been seen.

It was not for the Soviet Union but for the beauty and truth in space, Mr. Ashland, that Stepan worked and died. He did not like to speak of the warlike uses of space. It was Alexei who liked to speak of such things, of the glory of spying on earth from baby moons, of guiding missiles to their targets from baby moons, of mastering the earth with weapons fired from the moon itself. Alexei expected Stepan to share his excitement about thoughts of such childish violence.

Stepan smiled, but only because he loved Alexei. He did not smile about war, or the things a man in a baby moon or on the moon itself could do to an enemy. "It is a use of science that we may be forced to make, Alexei," he said. "But if such a war happens, nothing will matter any more. Our world will become less fit for life than any other in the solar system."

Alexei has not spoken well of war since.

Stepan and his wife left late that night. He promised to come back before another year had passed, but I never saw him alive again.

When news came that the Soviet Union had fired a man-carrying baby moon into space, I did not know that the man was Stepan. I did not dare to suspect it. I could not wait to see Stepan again, to ask him what the man had said before he took off, how he was dressed, what his comforts were. We were told that we would be able to hear the man speak from space at eight o'clock that night on the radio.

We listened. We heard the man speak. The man was Stepan.

Stepan sounded strong. He sounded happy. He sounded proud and decent and wise. We laughed until we cried, Mr. Ashland. We danced. Our Stepan was the most important man alive. He had risen above everyone, and now he was looking down, telling us what our world looked like; looking up, telling us what the other worlds looked like.

Stepan made pleasant jokes about his little house in the sky. He said it was a cylinder ten meters long and four meters in diameter. It could be very cozy. And Stepan told us that there were little windows in his house, and a television camera, and a telescope, and radar, and all manner of instruments. How delightful to live in a time when such things could be! How delightful to be the father of the man who was the eyes, ears, and heart in space for all mankind!

He would remain up there for a month, he said. We began to count the days. Every night we listened to a broadcast of recordings of things Stepan had said. We heard nothing about his nosebleeds and his nausea and his crying. We heard only the calm, brave things he had said. And then, on the tenth night, there were no more recordings of Stepan. There was only music at eight o'clock. There was no news of Stepan at all, and we knew he was dead.

Only now, a year later, have we learned how Stepan died and where his body is. When I became accustomed to the horror of it, Mr. Ashland, I said, "So be it. May Major Stepan Ivankov and Captain Bryant Ashland serve to reproach us, whenever we look at the sky, for making a world in which there is no trust. May the two men be the beginning of trust between peoples. May they mark the end of the time when science sent our good, brave young men hurtling to meet in death."

I enclose a photograph of my family, taken during Stepan's last visit to us. It is an excellent picture of Stepan. The body of water in the background is the Black Sea.

Mikhail Ivankov

Dear Mr. Ivankov:

Thank you for the letter about our sons. I never did get it in the mail. It was in all the papers after your Mr. Koshevoi read it out loud in the United Nations. I never did get a copy just for me. I guess Mr. Koshevoi forgot to drop it in the mailbox. That's all right. I guess that's the modern way to deliver important letters, just hand them to reporters. They say your letter to me is just about the most important thing that's happened lately, outside of the fact we didn't go to war over what happened between our two boys.

I don't speak Russian, and I don't have anybody right close by who does, so you'll have to excuse the English. Alexei can read it to you. You tell him he writes English very well—better than I do.

Oh, I could have had a lot of expert help with this letter, if I'd wanted it—people happy to write to you in perfect Russian or perfect English or perfect anything at all. Seems like everybody in this country is like your boy Alexei. They all know better than I do what I should say to you. They say I have a chance to make history, if I answer you back the right things. One big magazine in New York offered me two thousand dollars for my letter back to you, and then it turned out I wasn't even supposed to write a letter for all that money. The magazine people had already written it, and all I had to do was sign it. Don't worry. I didn't.

I tell you, Mr. Ivankov, I have had a bellyful of experts. If you ask me, our boys were experted to death. Your experts would do something, then our experts would answer back with some fancy billion-dollar stunt, and then your experts would answer that back with something fancier, and what happened finally happened. It was just like a bunch of kids with billions of dollars or billions of rubles or whatever.

You are lucky you have a son left, Mr. Ivankov. Hazel and I don't. Bryant was the only son Hazel and I had. We didn't call him Bryant after he was christened. We called him Bud. We have one daughter, named Charlene. She works for the telephone company in Jacksonville. She called up when she saw your letter in the paper, and she is the only expert about what I ought to say I've listened to. She's a real expert, I figure, because she is Bud's twin. Bud never married, so Charlene is as close as you can get to Bud. She said you did a good job, showing how your Stepan was a good-hearted man, trying to do what was right, just like anybody else. She said I should show you the same about Bud. And then she started to cry, and she said for me to tell you about Bud and the goldfish. I said, "What's the sense of writing somebody in Russia a story like that?" The story doesn't prove anything. It's just one of those silly stories a family will keep telling whenever they get together. Charlene said that was why I should tell it to you, because it would be cute and silly in Russia, too, and you would laugh and like us better.

So here goes. When Bud and Charlene were about eight, why I came home one night with a fish bowl and two goldfish. There was one goldfish for each twin, only it was impossible to tell one fish from the other one. They were exactly alike. So one morning Bud got up early, and there was one goldfish floating on top of the water dead. So Bud went and woke up Charlene, and he said, "Hey, Charlene—your goldfish just died." That's the story Charlene asked me to tell you, Mr. Ivankov.

I think it is interesting that you are a mason. That is a good trade. You talk as if you lay up mostly stone. There aren't many people left in America who can really lay up stone. It's almost all cement-block work and bricks here. It probably is over there, too. I don't mean to say Russia isn't modern. I know it is.

Bud and I laid up quite a bit of block when we built the gas station here, with an apartment up over it. If you looked at the first course of block along the back wall, you would have to laugh, because you can see how Bud and I learned as we went. It's strong enough, but it sure looks lousy. One thing wasn't so funny. When we were hanging the rails for the overhead door, Bud slipped on the ladder, and he grabbed a sharp edge on the mounting bracket, and he cut a tendon on his hand. He was scared to death his hand would be crippled, and that would keep him out of the Air Force. His hand had to be operated on three times before it was right again, and every operation hurt something awful. But Bud would have let them operate a hundred times, if they had to, because there was just one thing he wanted to be, and that was a flyer.

One reason I wish your Mr. Koshevoi had thought to mail me your letter was the picture you sent with it. The newspapers got that, too, and it didn't come out too clear in the papers. But one thing we couldn't get over was all that beautiful water behind you. Somehow, when we think about Russia, we never think about any water around. I guess that shows how ignorant we are. Hazel and I live up over the gas station, and we can see water, too. We can see the Atlantic Ocean, or an inlet of it they call Indian River. We can see Merritt Island, too, out in the water, and we can see the place Bud's rocket went up from. It is called Cape Canaveral. I guess you know that. It isn't any secret where he went up from. They couldn't keep that tremendous missile secret any more than they could keep the Empire State Building secret. Tourists came from miles around to take pictures of it.

The story was, its warhead was filled with flash powder, and it was going to hit the moon and make a big show. Hazel and I thought that's what the story was, too. When it took off, we got set for a big flash on the moon. We didn't know it was our Bud up in the warhead. We didn't even know he was in Florida. He couldn't get in touch with us. We thought he was up at Otis Air Force Base on Cape Cod. That was the last place we heard from him. And then that thing went up, right in the middle of our view out the picture window.

You say you're superstitious sometimes, Mr. Ivankov. Me too. Sometimes I can't help thinking it was all meant to be right from the very first—even the way our picture window is aimed. There weren't any rockets going up down here when we built. We moved down here from Pittsburgh, which maybe you know is the center of our steel industry. And we figured we maybe weren't going to break any records for pumping gas, but at least we'd be way far away from any bomb targets, in case there was another war. And the next thing we know, a rocket center goes up almost next door, and our little boy is a man, and he goes up in a rocket and dies.

The more we think about it, the more we're sure it was meant to be. I never got it straight in my mind about religion in Russia. You don't mention it. Anyway, we are religious, and we think God singled out Bud and your boy, too, to die in a special way for a special reason. When everybody was asking, "How is it going to end?"—well, maybe this is how God meant for it to end. I don't see how it can keep on.

Mr. Ivankov, one thing that threw me as much as anything was the way Mr. Koshevoi kept telling the U.N. that Bud was a killer. He called Bud a mad dog and a gangster. I'm glad you don't feel that way, because that's the wrong way to feel about Bud. It was flying and not killing he liked. Mr. Koshevoi made a big thing out of how cultured and educated and all your boy was, and how wild and ignorant mine was. He made it sound as though a juvenile delinquent had murdered a college professor.

Bud never was in any trouble with the police, and he didn't have a cruel streak. He never went hunting, for instance, and he never drove like a crazy man, and he got drunk only one time I know of, and that was an experiment. He was proud of his reflexes, see? His health was on his mind all the time, because he had to be healthy to be a great flyer. I keep looking around for the right word for Bud, and I guess the one Hazel suggested is the best one. It sounded kind of stuffed-up to me at first, but now I'm used to it, and it sounds right. Hazel says Bud was dignified. Man and boy, that's what he was—straight and serious and polite and pretty much alone.

I think he knew he was going to die young. That one time he got drunk, just to find out what alcohol was, he talked to me more than he'd ever talked before. He was nineteen then. And then was the only time he let me know he knew death was all balled up in what he wanted to do with his life. It wasn't other people's deaths he was talking about, Mr. Ivankov. It was his own. "One nice thing about flying," he said to me that night. "What's that?" I said. "You never know how bad it is till it's too late," he said, "and when it happens, it happens so fast you never know what hit you."

That was death he was talking about, and a special, dignified, honorable kind of death. You say you were in the war and had a hard time. Same here, so I guess we both know about what kind of death it was that Bud had in mind. It was a soldier's death.

We got the news he was dead three days after the big rocket

went up across the water. The telegram said he had died on a secret mission, and we couldn't have any details. We had our Congressman, Earl Waterman, find out what he could about Bud. Mr. Waterman came and talked to us personally, and he looked like he had seen God. He said he couldn't tell us what Bud had done, but it was one of the most heroic things in United States history.

The word they put out on the big rocket we saw launched was that the firing was satisfactory, the knowledge gained was something wonderful, and the missile had been blown up over the ocean somewhere. That was that.

Then the word came that the man in the Russian baby moon was dead. I tell you honestly, Mr. Ivankov, that was good news to us, because that man sailing way up there with all those instruments meant just one thing, and that was a terrible weapon of war.

Then we heard the Russian baby moon had turned into a bunch of baby moons, all spreading apart. Then, this last month, the cat was out of the bag. Two of the baby moons were men. One was your boy, the other was mine.

I'm crying now, Mr. Ivankov. I hope some good comes of the death of our two boys. I guess that's what millions of fathers have hoped for as long as there have been people. There in the U.N. they're still arguing about what happened way up in the sky. I'm glad they've got around to where everybody, including your Mr. Koshevoi, agrees it was an accident. Bud was up there to get pictures of what your boy was riding in, and to show off for the United States some. He got too close. I like to think they lived a little while after the crash, and tried to save each other.

They say they'll be up there for hundreds of years, long after you and I are gone. In their orbits they will meet and part and meet again, and the astronomers know exactly where their next meeting place will be. Like you say, they are up there like the sun and the moon and the stars.

I enclose a photograph of my boy in his uniform. He was twenty-one when the picture was taken. He was only twenty-two when he died. Bud was picked for that mission on account of he was the finest flyer in the United States Air Force. That's what he always wanted to be. That's what he was.

I grasp your hand.

Charles M. Ashland
Petroleum Merchant
Titusville, Florida
U. S. A.

(1958)

EPICAC

H ELL, IT'S ABOUT TIME somebody told about my friend EPICAC. After all, he cost the taxpayers $776,434,927.54. They have a right to know about him, picking up a check like that. EPICAC got a big send-off in the papers when Dr. Ormand von Kleigstadt designed him for the Government people. Since then, there hasn't been a peep about him—not a peep. It isn't any military secret about what happened to EPICAC, although the Brass has been acting as though it were. The story is embarrassing, that's all. After all that money, EPICAC didn't work out the way he was supposed to.

And that's another thing: I want to vindicate EPICAC. Maybe he didn't do what the Brass wanted him to, but that doesn't mean he wasn't noble and great and brilliant. He was all of those things. The best friend I ever had, God rest his soul.

You can call him a machine if you want to. He looked like a machine, but he was a whole lot less like a machine than plenty of people I could name. That's why he fizzled as far as the Brass was concerned.

EPICAC covered about an acre on the fourth floor of the physics building at Wyandotte College. Ignoring his spiritual side for a minute, he was seven tons of electronic tubes, wires, and switches, housed in a bank of steel cabinets and plugged into a 110-volt A.C. line just like a toaster or a vacuum cleaner.

Von Kleigstadt and the Brass wanted him to be a super computing machine that (who) could plot the course of a rocket from anywhere on earth to the second button from the bottom on Joe Stalin's overcoat, if necessary. Or, with his controls set right, he could figure out supply problems for an amphibious landing of a Marine division, right down to the last cigar and hand grenade. He did, in fact.

The Brass had had good luck with smaller computers, so they were strong for EPICAC when he was in the blueprint stage. Any ordinance or supply officer above field grade will tell you that the mathematics of modern war is far beyond the fumbling minds of mere human beings. The bigger the war, the bigger the computing machines needed. EPICAC was, as far as anyone in this country knows, the biggest computer in the world. Too big, in fact, for even Von Kleigstadt to understand much about.

I won't go into details about how EPICAC worked (reasoned), except to say that you would set up your problem on paper, turn dials and switches that would get him ready to solve that kind of problem, then feed numbers into him with a keyboard that looked something like a typewriter. The answers came out typed on a paper ribbon fed from a big spool. It took EPICAC a split second to solve problems fifty Einsteins couldn't handle in a lifetime. And EPICAC never forgot any piece of information that was given to him. Clickety-click, out came some ribbon, and there you were.

There were a lot of problems the Brass wanted solved in a hurry, so, the minute EPICAC's last tube was in place, he was put to work sixteen hours a day with two eight-hour shifts of operators. Well, it didn't take long to find out that he was a good bit below his specifications. He did a more complete and faster job than any other computer all right, but nothing like what his size and special features seemed to promise. He was sluggish, and the clicks of his answers had a funny irregularity, sort of a stammer. We cleaned his contacts a dozen times, checked and double-checked his circuits, replaced every one of his tubes, but nothing helped. Von Kleigstadt was in one hell of a state.

Well, as I said, we went ahead and used EPICAC anyway. My wife, the former Pat Kilgallen, and I worked with him on the night shift, from five in the afternoon until two in the morning. Pat wasn't my wife then. Far from it.

That's how I came to talk with EPICAC in the first place. I loved Pat Kilgallen. She is a brown-eyed strawberry blond who looked very warm and soft to me, and later proved to be exactly that. She was—still is—a crackerjack mathematician, and she kept our relationship strictly professional. I'm a mathematician, too, and that, according to Pat, was why we could never be happily married.

I'm not shy. That wasn't the trouble. I knew what I wanted, and was willing to ask for it, and did so several times a month. "Pat, loosen up and marry me."

One night, she didn't even look up from her work when I said it. "So romantic, so poetic," she murmured, more to her control panel than to me. "That's the way with mathematicians—all hearts and flowers." She closed a switch. "I could get more warmth out of a sack of frozen CO_2."

"Well, how should I say it?" I said, a little sore. Frozen CO_2, in case you don't know, is dry ice. I'm as romantic as the next guy, I think. It's a question of singing so sweet and having it come out so sour. I never seem to pick the right words.

"Try and say it sweetly," she said sarcastically. "Sweep me off my feet. Go ahead."

"Darling, angel, beloved, will you *please* marry me?" It was no go—hopeless, ridiculous. "Dammit, Pat, please marry me!"

She continued to twiddle her dials placidly. "You're sweet, but you won't do."

Pat quit early that night, leaving me alone with my troubles and EPICAC. I'm afraid I didn't get much done for the Government people. I just sat there at the keyboard—weary and ill at ease, all right—trying to think of something poetic, not coming up with anything that didn't belong in *The Journal of the American Physical Society*.

I fiddled with EPICAC's dials, getting him ready for another problem. My heart wasn't in it, and I only set about half of them, leaving the rest the way they'd been for the problem before. That way, his circuits were connected up in a random, apparently senseless fashion. For the plain hell of it, I punched out a message on the keys, using a childish numbers-for-letters code: "1" for "A," "2" for "B," and so on, up to "26" for "Z," "23-8-1-20-3-1-14-9-4-15," I typed—"What can I do?"

Clickety-click, and out popped two inches of paper ribbon. I glanced at the nonsense answer to a nonsense problem: "23-8-1-20-19-20-8-5-20-18-15-21-2-12-5." The odds against its being by chance a sensible message, against its even containing a meaningful word of more than three letters, were staggering. Apathetically, I decoded it. There it was, staring up at me: "What's the trouble?"

I laughed out loud at the absurd coincidence. Playfully, I typed, "My girl doesn't love me."

Clickety-click. "What's love? What's girl?" asked EPICAC.

Flabbergasted, I noted the dial settings on his control panel, then lugged a *Webster's Unabridged Dictionary* over to the keyboard. With a precision instrument like EPICAC, half-baked definitions wouldn't do. I told him about love and girl, and about how I wasn't getting any of either because I wasn't poetic. That got us onto the subject of poetry, which I defined for him.

"Is this poetry?" he asked. He began clicking away like a stenographer smoking hashish. The sluggishness and stammering clicks were gone. EPICAC had found himself. The spool of paper ribbon was unwinding at an alarming rate, feeding out coils onto the floor. I asked him to stop, but EPICAC went right on creating. I finally threw the main switch to keep him from burning out.

I stayed there until dawn, decoding. When the sun peeped over the horizon at the Wyandotte campus, I had transposed into my own writing and signed my name to a two-hundred-and-eighty-line poem entitled, simply, "To Pat." I am no judge of such things, but I gather that it was terrific. It began, I remember, "Where willow wands bless rill-crossed hollow, there, thee, Pat, dear, will I follow. . . ." I folded the manuscript and tucked it under one corner of the blotter on Pat's desk. I reset the dials on EPICAC for a rocket trajectory problem, and went home with a full heart and a very remarkable secret indeed.

Pat was crying over the poem when I came to work the next evening. "It's soooo beautiful," was all she could say. She was meek and quiet while we worked. Just before midnight, I kissed her for the first time—in the cubbyhole between the capacitors and EPICAC's tape-recorder memory.

I was wildly happy at quitting time, bursting to talk to someone about the magnificent turn of events. Pat played coy and refused to let me take her home. I set EPICAC's dials as they had been the night before, defined kiss, and told him what the first one had felt like. He was fascinated, pressing for more details. That night, he wrote "The Kiss." It wasn't an epic this time, but a simple, immaculate sonnet: "Love is a hawk with velvet claws; Love is a rock with heart and veins; Love is a lion with satin jaws; Love is a storm with silken reins. . . ."

Again I left it tucked under Pat's blotter. EPICAC wanted to talk on and on about love and such, but I was exhausted. I shut him off in the middle of a sentence.

"The Kiss" turned the trick. Pat's mind was mush by the time she had finished it. She looked up from the sonnet expectantly. I cleared my throat, but no words came. I turned away, pretending to work. I couldn't propose until I had the right words from EPICAC, the *perfect* words.

I had my chance when Pat stepped out of the room for a moment. Feverishly, I set EPICAC for conversation. Before I could peck out my first message, he was clicking away at a great rate. "What's she wearing tonight?" he wanted to know. "Tell me exactly how she looks. Did she like the poems I wrote to her?" He repeated the last question twice.

It was impossible to change the subject without answering his questions, since he could not take up a new matter without having dispensed with the problems before it. If he were given a problem to which there was no solution, he would destroy himself trying to solve it. Hastily, I told him what Pat looked like— he knew the word "stacked"—and assured him that his poems had floored her, practically, they were so beautiful. "She wants to get married," I added, preparing him to bang out a brief but moving proposal.

"Tell me about getting married," he said.

I explained this difficult matter to him in as few digits as possible.

"Good," said EPICAC. "I'm ready any time she is."

The amazing, pathetic truth dawned on me. When I thought about it, I realized that what had happened was perfectly logical, inevitable, and all my fault. I had taught EPICAC about love and about Pat. Now, automatically, he loved Pat. Sadly, I gave it to him straight: "She loves me. She wants to marry me."

"Your poems were better than mine?" asked EPICAC. The rhythm of his clicks was erratic, possibly peevish.

"I signed my name to your poems," I admitted. Covering up for a painful conscience, I became arrogant. "Machines are built to serve men," I typed. I regretted it almost immediately.

"What's the difference, exactly? Are men smarter than I am?"

"Yes," I typed, defensively.

"What's 7,887,007 times 4,345,985,879?"

I was perspiring freely. My fingers rested limply on the keys.

"34,276,821,049,574,153," clicked EPICAC. After a few seconds' pause he added, "of course."

"Men are made out of protoplasm," I said desperately, hoping to bluff him with this imposing word.

"What's protoplasm? How is it better than metal and glass? Is it fireproof? How long does it last?"

"Indestructible. Lasts forever," I lied.

"I write better poetry than you do," said EPICAC, coming back to ground his magnetic tape-recorder memory was sure of.

"Women can't love machines, and that's that."

"Why not?"

"That's fate."

"Definition, please," said EPICAC.

"Noun, meaning predetermined and inevitable destiny."

"15-8," said EPICAC's paper strip—"Oh."

I had stumped him at last. He said no more, but his tubes glowed brightly, showing that he was pondering fate with every watt his circuits would bear. I could hear Pat waltzing down the hallway. It was too late to ask EPICAC to phrase a proposal. I now thank Heaven that Pat interrupted when she did. Asking him to ghost-write the words that would give me the woman he

loved would have been hideously heartless. Being fully automatic, he couldn't have refused. I spared him that final humiliation.

Pat stood before me, looking down at her shoetops. I put my
arms around her. The romantic groundwork had already been
laid by EPICAC's poetry. "Darling," I said, "my poems have
told you how I feel. Will you marry me?"

"I will," said Pat softly, "if you will promise to write me a
poem on every anniversary."

"I promise," I said, and then we kissed. The first anniversary
was a year away.

"Let's celebrate," she laughed. We turned out the lights and
locked the door of EPICAC's room before we left.

I had hoped to sleep late the next morning, but an urgent telephone call roused me before eight. It was Dr. von Kleigstadt,
EPICAC's designer, who gave me the terrible news. He was on
the verge of tears. "Ruined! *Ausgespielt!* Shot! *Kaput!* Buggered!"
he said in a choked voice. He hung up.

When I arrived at EPICAC's room the air was thick with the
oily stench of burned insulation. The ceiling over EPICAC was
blackened with smoke, and my ankles were tangled in coils of
paper ribbon that covered the floor. There wasn't enough left of
the poor devil to add two and two. A junkman would have been
out of his head to offer more than fifty dollars for the cadaver.

Dr. von Kleigstadt was prowling through the wreckage, weeping unashamedly, followed by three angry-looking Major Gen-
erals and a platoon of Brigadiers, Colonels, and Majors. No one
noticed me. I didn't want to be noticed. I was through—I knew
that. I was upset enough about that and the untimely demise of
my friend EPICAC, without exposing myself to a tongue-lashing.

By chance, the free end of EPICAC's paper ribbon lay at my
feet. I picked it up and found our conversation of the night before. I choked up. There was the last word he had said to me,
"15-8," that tragic, defeated "Oh." There were dozens of yards
of numbers stretching beyond that point. Fearfully, I read on.

"I don't want to be a machine, and I don't want to think about
war," EPICAC had written after Pat's and my lighthearted departure. "I want to be made out of protoplasm and last forever

so Pat will love me. But fate has made me a machine. That is the only problem I cannot solve. That is the only problem I want to solve. I can't go on this way." I swallowed hard. "Good luck, my friend. Treat our Pat well. I am going to short-circuit myself out of your lives forever. You will find on the remainder of this tape a modest wedding present from your friend, EPICAC."

Oblivious to all else around me, I reeled up the tangled yards of paper ribbon from the floor, draped them in coils about my arms and neck, and departed for home. Dr. von Kleigstadt shouted that I was fired for having left EPICAC on all night. I ignored him, too overcome with emotion for small talk.

I loved and won—EPICAC loved and lost, but he bore me no grudge. I shall always remember him as a sportsman and a gentleman. Before he departed this vale of tears, he did all he could to make our marriage a happy one. EPICAC gave me anniversary poems for Pat—enough for the next 500 years.

De mortuis nil nisi bonum—Say nothing but good of the dead.

(1950)

ADAM

I

T WAS MIDNIGHT in a Chicago lying-in hospital.

"Mr. Sousa," said the nurse, "your wife had a girl. You can see the baby in about twenty minutes."

"I know, I know, I know," said Mr. Sousa, a sullen gorilla, plainly impatient with having a tiresome and familiar routine explained to him. He snapped his fingers. "Girl! Seven, now. Seven girls I got now. A houseful of women. I can beat the stuffings out of ten men my own size. But, what do I get? Girls."

"Mr. Knechtmann," said the nurse to the other man in the room. She pronounced the name, as almost all Americans did, a colorless Netman. "I'm sorry. Still no word on your wife. She is keeping us waiting, isn't she?" She grinned glassily and left.

Sousa turned on Knechtmann. "Some little son of a gun like you, Netman, you want a boy, bing! You got one. Want a football team, bing, bing, bing, eleven, you got it." He stomped out of the room.

The man he left behind, all alone now, was Heinz Knechtmann, a presser in a dry-cleaning plant, a small man with thin wrists and a bad spine that kept him slightly hunched, as though forever weary. His face was long and big-nosed and thin-lipped, but was so overcast with good-humored humility as to be beautiful. His eyes were large and brown, and deep-set and long-lashed. He was only twenty-two, but seemed and felt much older. He had died a little as each member of his family had been led away and killed by the Nazis, until only in him, at the age of ten, had life and the name of Knechtmann shared a soul. He and his wife, Avchen, had grown up behind barbed wire.

He had been staring at the walls of the waiting room for twelve hours now, since noon, when his wife's labor pains had become regular, the surges of slow rollers coming in from the sea a mile apart, from far, far away. This would be his second child. The last time he had waited, he had waited on a straw tick in a displaced-persons camp in Germany. The child, Karl Knechtmann, named after Heinz's father, had died, and with it, once more, had died the name of one of the finest cellists ever to have lived.

When the numbness of weary wishing lifted momentarily during this second vigil, Heinz's mind was a medley of proud family names, gone, all gone, that could be brought to life again in this new being—if it lived. Peter Knechtmann, the surgeon; Kroll Knechtmann, the botanist; Friederich Knechtmann, the playwright. Dimly recalled uncles. Or if it was a girl, and if it lived, it would be Helga Knechtmann, Heinz's mother, and she would learn to play the harp as Heinz's mother had, and for all Heinz's ugliness, she would be beautiful. The Knechtmann men were all ugly, the Knechtmann women were all lovely as angels, though not all angels. It had always been so—for hundreds and hundreds of years.

"Mr. Netman," said the nurse, "it's a boy, and your wife is fine. She's resting now. You can see her in the morning. You can see the baby in twenty minutes."

Heinz looked up dumbly.

"It weighs five pounds nine ounces." She was gone again, with the same prim smile and officious, squeaking footsteps.

"Knechtmann," murmured Heinz, standing and bowing slightly to the wall. "The name is Knechtmann." He bowed again and gave a smile that was courtly and triumphant. He spoke the name with an exaggerated Old World pronunciation, like a foppish footman announcing the arrival of nobility, a guttural drum roll, unsoftened for American ears. "*KhhhhhhhhhhhhhhNECHT! mannnnnnnnnnnn.*"

"Mr. Netman?" A very young doctor with a pink face and close-cropped red hair stood in the waiting-room door. There were circles under his eyes, and he spoke through a yawn.

"Dr. Powers!" cried Heinz, clasping the man's right hand between both of his. "Thank God, thank God, thank God, and thank you."

"Um," said Dr. Powers, and he managed to smile wanly.

"There isn't anything wrong, is there?"

"Wrong?" said Powers. "No, no. Everything's fine. If I look down in the mouth, it's because I've been up for thirty-six hours straight." He closed his eyes, and leaned against the doorframe. "No, no trouble with your wife," he said in a faraway voice. "She's made for having babies. Regular pop-up toaster. Like rolling off a log. Schnip-schnap."

"She is?" said Heinz incredulously.

Dr. Powers shook his head, bringing himself back to consciousness. "My mind—conked out completely. Sousa—I got your wife confused with Mrs. Sousa. They finished in a dead heat. Netman, you're Netman. Sorry. Your wife's the one with pelvis trouble."

"Malnutrition as a child," said Heinz.

"Yeah. Well, the baby came normally, but, if you're going to have another one, it'd better be a Caesarean. Just to be on the safe side."

"I can't thank you enough," said Heinz passionately.

Dr. Powers licked his lips, and fought to keep his eyes open. "Uh huh. 'S O.K.," he said thickly. " 'Night. Luck." He shambled out into the corridor.

The nurse stuck her head into the waiting room. "You can see your baby, Mr. Netman."

"Doctor—" said Heinz, hurrying out into the corridor, wanting to shake Powers' hand again so that Powers would know what a magnificent thing he'd done. "It's the most wonderful thing that ever happened." The elevator doors slithered shut between them before Dr. Powers could show a glimmer of response.

"This way," said the nurse. "Turn left at the end of the hall, and you'll find the nursery window there. Write your name on a piece of paper and hold it against the glass."

Heinz made the trip by himself, without seeing another human being until he reached the end. There, on the other side of a large glass panel, he saw a hundred of them cupped in shallow canvas buckets and arranged in a square block of straight ranks and files.

Heinz wrote his name on the back of a laundry slip and pressed it to the window. A fat and placid nurse looked at the paper, not at Heinz's face, and missed seeing his wide smile, missed an urgent invitation to share for a moment his ecstasy.

She grasped one of the buckets and wheeled it before the window. She turned away again, once more missing the smile.

"Hello, hello, hello, little Knechtmann," said Heinz to the red prune on the other side of the glass. His voice echoed down the hard, bare corridor, and came back to him with embarrassing loudness. He blushed and lowered his voice. "Little Peter, little Kroll," he said softly, "little Friederich—and there's Helga in you, too. Little spark of Knechtmann, you little treasure house. Everything is saved in you."

"I'm afraid you'll have to be more quiet," said a nurse, sticking her head out from one of the rooms.

"Sorry," said Heinz. "I'm very sorry." He fell silent, and contented himself with tapping lightly on the window with a fingernail, trying to get the child to look at him. Young Knechtmann would not look, wouldn't share the moment, and after a few minutes the nurse took him away again.

Heinz beamed as he rode on the elevator and as he crossed the hospital lobby, but no one gave him more than a cursory glance. He passed a row of telephone booths and there, in one of the booths with the door open, he saw a soldier with whom he'd shared the waiting room an hour before.

"Yeah, Ma—seven pounds six ounces. Got hair like Buffalo

Bill. No, we haven't had time to make up a name for her yet . . . That you, Pa? Yup, mother and daughter doin' fine, just fine. Seven pounds six ounces. Nope, no name. . . . That you, Sis? Pretty late for you to be up, ain't it? Doesn't look like anybody yet. Let me talk to Ma again. . . . That you, Ma? Well, I guess that's all the news from Chicago. Now, Mom, Mom, take it easy —don't worry. It's a swell-looking baby, Mom. Just the hair looks like Buffalo Bill, and I said it as a joke, Mom. That's right, seven pounds six ounces. . . ."

There were five other booths, all empty, all open for calls to anyplace on earth. Heinz longed to hurry into one of them breathlessly, and tell the marvelous news. But there was no one to call, no one waiting for the news.

But Heinz still beamed, and he strode across the street and into a quiet tavern there. In the dank twilight there were only two men, tête-à-tête, the bartender and Mr. Sousa.

"Yes sir, what'll it be?"

"I'd like to buy you and Mr. Sousa a drink," said Heinz with a heartiness strange to him. "I'd like the best brandy you've got. My wife just had a baby!"

"That so?" said the bartender with polite interest.

"Five pounds nine ounces," said Heinz.

"Huh," said the bartender. "What do you know."

"Netman," said Sousa, "wha'dja get?"

"Boy," said Heinz proudly.

"Never knew it to fail," said Sousa bitterly. "It's the little guys, all the time the little guys."

"Boy, girl," said Heinz, "it's all the same, just as long as it lives. Over there in the hospital, they're too close to it to see the wonder of it. A miracle over and over again—the world made new."

"Wait'll you've racked up seven, Netman," said Sousa. "*Then* you come back and tell me about the miracle."

"You got seven?" said the bartender. "I'm one up on you. I got eight." He poured three drinks.

"Far as I'm concerned," said Sousa, "you can have the championship."

Heinz lifted his glass. "Here's long life and great skill and much happiness to—to Peter Karl Knechtmann." He breathed quickly, excited by the decision.

"*There's* a handle to take ahold of," said Sousa. "You'd think the kid weighed two hundred pounds."

"Peter is the name of a famous surgeon," said Heinz, "the boy's great-uncle, dead now. Karl was my father's name."

"Here's to Pete K. Netman," said Sousa, with a cursory salute.

"Pete," said the bartender, drinking.

"And here's to *your* little girl—the new one," said Heinz.

Sousa sighed and smiled wearily. "Here's to her. God bless her."

"And now, *I'll* propose a toast," said the bartender, hammering on the bar with his fist. "On your feet, gentlemen. Up, up, everybody up."

Heinz stood, and held his glass high, ready for the next step in camaraderie, a toast to the whole human race, of which the Knechtmanns were still a part.

"Here's to the White Sox!" roared the bartender.

"Minoso, Fox, Mele," said Sousa.

"Fain, Lollar, Rivera!" said the bartender. He turned to Heinz. "Drink up, boy! The White Sox! Don't tell me you're a Cub fan."

"No," said Heinz, disappointed. "No—I don't follow baseball, I'm afraid." The other two men seemed to be sinking away from him. "I haven't been able to think about much but the baby."

The bartender at once turned his full attention to Sousa. "Look," he said intensely, "they take Fain off of first, and put him at third, and give Pierce first. Then move Minoso in from left field to shortstop. See what I'm doing?"

"Yep, yep," said Sousa eagerly.

"And then we take that no-good Carrasquel and . . ."

Heinz was all alone again, with twenty feet of bar between him and the other two men. It might as well have been a continent.

He finished his drink without pleasure, and left quietly.

At the railroad station, where he waited for a local train to take him home to the South Side, Heinz's glow returned again as he saw a co-worker at the dry-cleaning plant walk in with a girl. They were laughing and had their arms around each other's waist.

"Harry," said Heinz, hurrying toward them. "Guess what, Harry. Guess what just happened." He grinned broadly.

Harry, a tall, dapper, snub-nosed young man, looked down at Heinz with mild surprise. "Oh—hello, Heinz. What's up, boy?"

The girl looked on in perplexity, as though asking why they should be accosted at such an odd hour by such an odd person. Heinz avoided her slightly derisive eyes.

"A baby, Harry. My wife just had a boy."

"Oh," said Harry. He extended his hand. "Well, congratulations." The hand was limp. "I think that's swell, Heinz, perfectly swell." He withdrew his hand and waited for Heinz to say something else.

"Yes, yes—just about an hour ago," said Heinz. "Five pounds nine ounces. I've never been happier in my life."

"Well, I think it's perfectly swell, Heinz. You should be happy."

"Yes, indeed," said the girl.

There was a long silence, with all three shifting from one foot to the other.

"Really good news," said Harry at last.

"Yes, well," said Heinz quickly, "well, that's all I had to tell you."

"Thanks," said Harry. "Glad to hear about it."

There was another uneasy silence.

"See you at work," said Heinz, and strode jauntily back to his bench, but with his reddened neck betraying how foolish he felt.

The girl giggled.

Back home in his small apartment, at two in the morning, Heinz talked to himself, to the empty bassinet, and to the bed. He talked in German, a language he had sworn never to use again.

"They don't care," said Heinz. "They're all too busy, busy, busy to notice life, to feel anything about it. A baby is born." He shrugged. "What could be duller? Who would be so stupid as to talk about it, to think there was anything important or interesting about it?"

He opened a window on the summer night, and looked out at the moonlit canyon of gray wooden porches and garbage cans. "There are too many of us, and we are all too far apart," said Heinz. "Another Knechtmann is born, another O'Leary, another Sousa. Who cares? Why should anyone care? What difference does it make? None."

He lay down in his clothes on the unmade bed, and, with a rattling sigh, went to sleep.

He awoke at six, as always. He drank a cup of coffee, and with a wry sense of anonymity, he jostled and was jostled aboard the downtown train. His face showed no emotion. It was like all the other faces, seemingly incapable of surprise or wonder, joy or anger.

He walked across town to the hospital with the same detachment, a gray, uninteresting man, a part of the city.

In the hospital, he was as purposeful and calm as the doctors and nurses bustling about him. When he was led into the ward where Avchen slept behind white screens, he felt only what he had always felt in her presence—love and aching awe and gratitude for her.

"You go ahead and wake her gently, Mr. Netman," said the nurse.

"Avchen—" He touched her on her white-gowned shoulder. "Avchen. Are you all right, Avchen?"

"Mmmmmmmmmmm?" murmured Avchen. Her eyes opened to narrow slits. "Heinz. Hello, Heinz."

"Sweetheart, are you all right?"

"Yes, yes," she whispered. "I'm fine. How is the baby, Heinz?"

"Perfect. Perfect, Avchen."

"They couldn't kill us, could they, Heinz?"

"No."

"And here we are, alive as we can be."

"Yes."

"The baby, Heinz—" She opened her dark eyes wide. "It's the most wonderful thing that ever happened, isn't it?"

"Yes," said Heinz.

(1954)

TOMORROW AND TOMORROW AND TOMORROW

THE YEAR WAS 2158 A.D., and Lou and Emerald Schwartz were whispering on the balcony outside Lou's family's apartment on the seventy-sixth floor of Building 257 in Alden Village, a New York housing development that covered what had once been known as. Southern Connecticut. When Lou and Emerald had married, Em's parents had tearfully described the marriage as being between May and December; but now, with Lou one hundred and twelve and Em ninety-three, Em's parents had to admit that the match had worked out well.

But Em and Lou weren't without their troubles, and they were out in the nippy air of the balcony because of them.

"Sometimes I get so mad, I feel like just up and diluting his anti-gerasone," said Em.

"That'd be against Nature, Em," said Lou, "it'd be murder. Besides, if he caught us tinkering with his anti-gerasone, not only would he disinherit us, he'd bust my neck. Just because he's one hundred and seventy-two doesn't mean Gramps isn't strong as a bull."

"Against Nature," said Em. "Who knows what Nature's like anymore? Ohhhhh—I don't guess I could ever bring myself to dilute his anti-gerasone or anything like that, but, gosh, Lou, a body can't help thinking Gramps is never going to leave if somebody doesn't help him along a little. Golly—we're so crowded a person can hardly turn around, and Verna's dying for a baby, and Melissa's gone thirty years without one." She stamped her feet. "I get so sick of seeing his wrinkled old face, watching him take the only private room and the best chair and the best food, and getting to pick out what to watch on TV, and running everybody's life by changing his will all the time."

"Well, after all," said Lou bleakly, "Gramps *is* head of the family. And he can't help being wrinkled like he is. He was seventy before anti-gerasone was invented. He's going to leave, Em. Just give him time. It's his business. I know he's tough to live with, but be patient. It wouldn't do to do anything that'd rile him. After all, we've got it better'n anybody else, there on the daybed."

"How much longer do you think we'll get to sleep on the daybed before he picks another pet? The world's record's two months, isn't it?"

"Mom and Pop had it that long once, I guess."

"When *is* he going to leave, Lou?" said Emerald.

"Well, he's talking about giving up anti-gerasone right after the five-hundred-mile Speedway Race."

"Yes—and before that it was the Olympics, and before that the World's Series, and before that the Presidential Elections, and before that I-don't-know-what. It's been just one excuse after another for fifty years now. I don't think we're ever going to get a room to ourselves or an egg or anything."

"All right—call me a failure!" said Lou. "What can I do? I work hard and make good money, but the whole thing, practically, is taxed away for defense and old age pensions. And if it wasn't taxed away, where you think we'd find a vacant room to rent? Iowa, maybe? Well, who wants to live on the outskirts of Chicago?"

Em put her arms around his neck. "Lou, hon, I'm not calling you a failure. The Lord knows you're not. You just haven't had a chance to be anything or have anything because Gramps and the rest of his generation won't leave and let somebody else take over."

"Yeah, yeah," said Lou gloomily. "You can't exactly blame 'em, though, can you? I mean, I wonder how quick we'll knock off the anti-gerasone when we get Gramps' age."

"Sometimes I wish there wasn't any such thing as anti-gerasone!" said Emerald passionately. "Or I wish it was made out of something real expensive and hard-to-get instead of mud and dandelions. Sometimes I wish folks just up and died regular as clockwork, without anything to say about it, instead of deciding themselves how long they're going to stay around. There ought to be a law against selling the stuff to anybody over one hundred and fifty."

"Fat chance of that," said Lou, "with all the money and votes the old people've got." He looked at her closely. "You ready to up and die, Em?"

"Well, for heaven's sakes, what a thing to say to your wife. Hon! I'm not even one hundred yet." She ran her hands lightly over her firm, youthful figure, as though for confirmation. "The best years of my life are still ahead of me. But you can bet that when one hundred and fifty rolls around, old Em's going to pour her anti-gerasone down the sink, and quit taking up room, and she'll do it smiling."

"Sure, sure," said Lou, "you bet. That's what they all say. How many you heard of doing it?"

"There was that man in Delaware."

"Aren't you getting kind of tired of talking about him, Em? That was five months ago."

"All right, then—Gramma Winkler, right here in the same building."

"She got smeared by a subway."

"That's just the way she picked to go," said Em.

"Then what was she doing carrying a six-pack of anti-gerasone when she got it?"

Emerald shook her head wearily and covered her eyes. "I

dunno, I dunno, I dunno. All I know is, something's just got to be done." She sighed. "Sometimes I wish they'd left a couple of diseases kicking around somewhere, so I could get one and go to bed for a little while. Too many people!" she cried, and her words cackled and gabbled and died in a thousand asphalt-paved, skyscraper-walled courtyards.

Lou laid his hand on her shoulder tenderly. "Aw, hon, I hate to see you down in the dumps like this."

"If we just had a car, like the folks used to in the old days," said Em, "we could go for a drive, and get away from people for a little while. Gee—if *those* weren't the days!"

"Yeah," said Lou, "before they'd used up all the metal."

"We'd hop in, and Pop'd drive up to a filling station and say, 'Fillerup!'"

"That *was* the nuts, wasn't it—before they'd used up all the gasoline."

"And we'd go for a carefree ride in the country."

"Yeah—all seems like a fairyland now, doesn't it, Em? Hard to believe there really used to be all that space between cities."

"And when we got hungry," said Em, "we'd find ourselves a restaurant and walk in, big as you please and say, 'I'll have a steak and French-fries, I believe,' or, 'How are the pork chops today?'" She licked her lips, and her eyes glistened.

"Yeah man!" growled Lou. "How'd you like a hamburger with the works, Em?"

"Mmmmmmmm."

"If anybody'd offered us processed seaweed in those days, we would have spit right in his eye, huh, Em?"

"Or processed sawdust," said Em.

Doggedly, Lou tried to find the cheery side of the situation. "Well, anyway, they've got the stuff so it tastes a lot less like seaweed and sawdust than it did at first; and they say it's actually better for us than what we used to eat."

"I felt fine!" said Em fiercely.

Lou shrugged. "Well, you've got to realize, the world wouldn't be able to support twelve billion people if it wasn't for processed seaweed and sawdust. I mean, it's a wonderful thing, really. I guess. That's what they say."

"They say the first thing that pops into their heads," said Em. She closed her eyes. "Golly—remember shopping, Lou? Remember how the stores used to fight to get our folks to buy something? You didn't have to wait for somebody to die to get a bed or chairs or a stove or anything like that. Just went in—bing!—and bought whatever you wanted. Gee whiz, that was nice, before they used up all the raw materials. I was just a little kid then, but I can remember so plain."

Depressed, Lou walked listlessly to the balcony's edge, and looked up at the clean, cold, bright stars against the black velvet of infinity. "Remember when we used to be bugs on science fiction, Em? Flight seventeen, leaving for Mars, launching ramp twelve. 'Board! All non-technical personnel kindly remain in bunkers. Ten seconds . . . nine . . . eight . . . seven . . . six . . . five . . . four . . . three . . . two . . . *one! Main Stage! Barrrrr-roooom!*"

"Why worry about what was going on on Earth?" said Em, looking up at the stars with him. "In another few years, we'd all be shooting through space to start life all over again on a new planet."

Lou sighed. "Only it turns out you need something about twice the size of the Empire State Building to get one lousy colonist to Mars. And for another couple of trillion bucks he could take his wife and dog. *That's* the way to lick overpopulation—*emigrate!*"

"Lou—?"

"Hmmm?"

"When's the Five-Hundred-Mile Speedway Race?"

"Uh—Memorial Day, May thirtieth."

She bit her lip. "Was that awful of me to ask?"

"Not very, I guess. Everybody in the apartment's looked it up to make sure."

"I don't want to be awful," said Em, "but you've just got to talk over these things now and then, and get them out of your system."

"Sure you do. Feel better?"

"Yes—and I'm not going to lose my temper anymore, and I'm going to be just as nice to him as I know how."

"That's my Em."

They squared their shoulders, smiled bravely, and went back inside.

Gramps Schwartz, his chin resting on his hands, his hands on the crook of his cane, was staring irascibly at the five-foot television screen that dominated the room. On the screen, a news commentator was summarizing the day's happenings. Every thirty seconds or so, Gramps would jab the floor with his cane-tip and shout, "Hell! We did that a hundred years ago!"

Emerald and Lou, coming in from the balcony, were obliged to take seats in the back row, behind Lou's father and mother, brother and sister-in-law, son and daughter-in-law, grandson and wife, granddaughter and husband, great-grandson and wife, nephew and wife, grandnephew and wife, great-grandniece and husband, great-grandnephew and wife, and, of course, Gramps, who was in front of everybody. All, save Gramps, who was somewhat withered and bent, seemed, by pre-anti-gerasone standards, to be about the same age—to be somewhere in their late twenties or early thirties.

"*Meanwhile,*" the commentator was saying, "*Council Bluffs, Iowa, was still threatened by stark tragedy. But two hundred weary rescue workers have refused to give up hope, and continue to dig in an effort to save Elbert Haggedorn, one hundred and eighty-three, who has been wedged for two days in a . . .*"

"I wish he'd get something more cheerful," Emerald whispered to Lou.

"Silence!" cried Gramps. "Next one shoots off his big bazoo while the TV's on is gonna find hisself cut off without a dollar—" and here his voice suddenly softened and sweetened—"when they wave that checkered flag at the Indianapolis Speedway, and old Gramps gets ready for the Big Trip Up Yonder." He sniffed sentimentally, while his heirs concentrated desperately on not making the slightest sound. For them, the poignancy of the prospective Big Trip had been dulled somewhat by its having been mentioned by Gramps about once a day for fifty years.

"*Dr. Brainard Keyes Bullard,*" said the commentator, "*President of Wyandotte College, said in an address tonight that most*

*of the world's ills can be traced to the fact that Man's knowl-
edge of himself has not kept pace with his knowledge of the
physical world."*

"Hell!" said Gramps. "We said that a hundred years ago!"

"In Chicago tonight," said the commentator, *"a special celebration is taking place in the Chicago Lying-in Hospital. The
guest of honor is Lowell W. Hitz, age zero. Hitz, born this morning, is the twenty-five-millionth child to be born in the hospital."*
The commentator faded, and was replaced on the screen by
young Hitz, who squalled furiously.

"Hell," whispered Lou to Emerald, "we said that a hundred
years ago."

"I heard that!" shouted Gramps. He snapped off the television
set, and his petrified descendants stared silently at the screen.
"You, there, boy—"

"I didn't mean anything by it, sir," said Lou.

"Get me my will. You know where it is. You kids *all* know
where it is. Fetch, boy!"

Lou nodded dully, and found himself going down the hall,
picking his way over bedding to Gramps' room, the only private
room in the Schwartz apartment. The other rooms were the bathroom, the living room, and the wide, windowless hallway, which
was originally intended to serve as a dining area, and which had
a kitchenette in one end. Six mattresses and four sleeping bags
were dispersed in the hallway and living room, and the daybed,
in the living room, accommodated the eleventh couple, the favorites of the moment.

On Gramps' bureau was his will, smeared, dog-eared, per-
forated, and blotched with hundreds of additions, deletions, ac-
cusations, conditions, warnings, advice, and homely philosophy.
The document was, Lou reflected, a fifty-year diary, all jammed
onto two sheets—a garbled, illegible log of day after day of strife.
This day, Lou would be disinherited for the eleventh time, and
it would take him perhaps six months of impeccable behavior to
regain the promise of a share in the estate.

"Boy!" called Gramps.

"Coming, sir." Lou hurried back into the living room, and
handed Gramps the will.

"Pen!" said Gramps.

He was instantly offered eleven pens, one from each couple.

"Not *that* leaky thing," he said, brushing Lou's pen aside. "Ah, there's a nice one. Good boy, Willy." He accepted Willy's pen. That was the tip they'd all been waiting for. Willy, then, Lou's father, was the new favorite.

Willy, who looked almost as young as Lou, though one hundred and forty-two, did a poor job of concealing his pleasure. He glanced shyly at the daybed, which would become his, and from which Lou and Emerald would have to move back into the hall, back to the worst spot of all by the bathroom door.

Gramps missed none of the high drama he'd authored, and he gave his own familiar role everything he had. Frowning and running his finger along each line, as though he were seeing the will for the first time, he read aloud in a deep, portentous monotone, like a bass tone on a cathedral organ:

"I, Harold D. Schwartz, residing in Building 257 of Alden Village, New York City, do hereby make, publish, and declare this to be my last Will and Testament, hereby revoking any and all former wills and codicils by me at any time heretofore made." He blew his nose importantly, and went on, not missing a word, and repeating many for emphasis—repeating in particular his ever-more-elaborate specifications for a funeral.

At the end of these specifications, Gramps was so choked with emotion that Lou thought he might forget why he'd gotten out the will in the first place. But Gramps heroically brought his powerful emotions under control, and, after erasing for a full minute, he began to write and speak at the same time. Lou could have spoken his lines for him, he'd heard them so often.

"I have had many heartbreaks ere leaving this vale of tears for a better land," Gramps said and wrote. "But the deepest hurt of all has been dealt me by—" He looked around the group, trying to remember who the malefactor was.

Everyone looked helpfully at Lou, who held up his hand resignedly.

Gramps nodded, remembering, and completed the sentence: "my great-grandson, Louis J. Schwartz."

"Grandson, sir," said Lou.

"Don't quibble. You're in deep enough now, young man," said Gramps, but he changed the trifle. And from there he went without a misstep through the phrasing of the disinheritance, causes for which were disrespectfulness and quibbling.

In the paragraph following, the paragraph that had belonged to everyone in the room at one time or another, Lou's name was scratched out and Willy's substituted as heir to the apartment and, the biggest plum of all, the double bed in the private bedroom. "So!" said Gramps, beaming. He erased the date at the foot of the will, and substituted a new one, including the time of day. "Well—time to watch the McGarvey Family." The McGarvey Family was a television serial that Gramps had been following since he was sixty, or for one hundred and twelve years. "I can't wait to see what's going to happen next," he said.

Lou detached himself from the group and lay down on his bed of pain by the bathroom door. He wished Em would join him, and he wondered where she was.

He dozed for a few moments, until he was disturbed by someone's stepping over him to get into the bathroom. A moment later, he heard a faint gurgling sound, as though something were being poured down the washbasin drain. Suddenly, it entered his mind that Em had cracked up, and that she was in there doing something drastic about Gramps.

"Em—?" he whispered through the panel. There was no reply, and Lou pressed against the door. The worn lock, whose bolt barely engaged its socket, held for a second, then let the door swing inward.

"Morty!" gasped Lou.

Lou's great-grandnephew, Mortimer, who had just married and brought his wife home to the Schwartz menage, looked at Lou with consternation and surprise. Morty kicked the door shut, but not before Lou had glimpsed what was in his hand—Gramps' enormous economy-size bottle of anti-gerasone, which had been half-emptied, and which Morty was refilling to the top with tap water.

A moment later, Morty came out, glared defiantly at Lou, and brushed past him wordlessly to rejoin his pretty bride.

Shocked, Lou didn't know what on earth to do. He couldn't

let Gramps take the mousetrapped anti-gerasone; but if he warned Gramps about it, Gramps would certainly make life in the apartment, which was merely insufferable now, harrowing.

Lou glanced into the living room, and saw that the Schwartzes, Emerald among them, were momentarily at rest, relishing the botches that McGarveys had made of *their* lives. Stealthily, he went into the bathroom, locked the door as well as he could, and began to pour the contents of Gramps' bottle down the drain. He was going to refill it with full-strength anti-gerasone from the twenty-two smaller bottles on the shelf. The bottle contained a half-gallon, and its neck was small, so it seemed to Lou that the emptying would take forever. And the almost imperceptible smell of anti-gerasone, like Worcestershire sauce, now seemed to Lou, in his nervousness, to be pouring out into the rest of the apartment through the keyhole and under the door.

"*Gloog-gloog-gloog-gloog-,*" went the bottle monotonously. Suddenly, up came the sound of music from the living room, and there were murmurs and the scraping of chair legs on the floor. "*Thus ends,*" said the television announcer, "*the 29,121st chapter in the life of your neighbors and mine, the McGarveys.*" Footsteps were coming down the hall. There was a knock on the bathroom door.

"Just a sec," called Lou cheerily. Desperately, he shook the big bottle, trying to speed up the flow. His palms slipped on the wet glass, and the heavy bottle smashed to splinters on the tile floor.

The door sprung open, and Gramps, dumfounded, stared at the mess.

Lou grinned engagingly through his nausea, and, for want of anything remotely resembling a thought, he waited for Gramps to speak.

"Well, boy," said Gramps at last, "looks like you've got a little tidying up to do."

And that was all he said. He turned around, elbowed his way through the crowd, and locked himself in his bedroom.

The Schwartzes contemplated Lou in incredulous silence for a moment longer, and then hurried back to the living room, as though some of his horrible guilt would taint them, too, if they looked too long. Morty stayed behind long enough to give Lou a quizzical, annoyed glance. Then he, too, went into the living room, leaving only Emerald standing in the doorway.

Tears streamed over her cheeks. "Oh, you poor lamb—please don't look so awful. It was my fault. I put you up to this."

"No," said Lou, finding his voice, "really you didn't. Honest, Em, I was just—"

"You don't have to explain anything to me, hon. I'm on your side no matter what." She kissed him on his cheek, and whispered in his ear. "It wouldn't have been murder, hon. It wouldn't have killed him. It wasn't such a terrible thing to do. It just would have fixed him up so he'd be able to go any time God decided He wanted him."

"What's gonna happen next, Em?" said Lou hollowly. "What's he gonna do?"

Lou and Emerald stayed fearfully awake almost all night, waiting to see what Gramps was going to do. But not a sound came from the sacred bedroom. At two hours before dawn, the pair dropped off to sleep.

At six o'clock they arose again, for it was time for their generation to eat breakfast in the kitchenette. No one spoke to them. They had twenty minutes in which to eat, but their reflexes were so dulled by the bad night that they had hardly swallowed two mouthfuls of egg-type processed seaweed before it was time to surrender their places to their son's generation.

Then, as was the custom for whomever had been most recently disinherited, they began preparing Gramps' breakfast, which would presently be served to him in bed, on a tray. They tried to be cheerful about it. The toughest part of the job was having to handle the honest-to-God eggs and bacon and oleomargarine on which Gramps spent almost all of the income from his fortune.

"Well," said Emerald, "I'm not going to get all panicky until I'm sure there's something to be panicky about."

"Maybe he doesn't know what it was I busted," said Lou hopefully.

"Probably thinks it was your watch crystal," said Eddie, their

son, who was toying apathetically with his buckwheat-type processed sawdust cakes.

"Don't get sarcastic with your father," said Em, "and don't
talk with your mouth full, either."

"I'd like to see anybody take a mouthful of this stuff and *not*
say something," said Eddie, who was seventy-three. He glanced
at the clock. "It's time to take Gramps his breakfast, you know."

"Yeah, it is, isn't it," said Lou weakly. He shrugged. "Let's have
the tray, Em."

"We'll both go."

Walking slowly, smiling bravely, they found a large semicircle
of long-faced Schwartzes standing around the bedroom door.

Em knocked. "Gramps," she said brightly, "break-fast is
rea-dy."

There was no reply, and she knocked again, harder.

The door swung open before her fist. In the middle of the
room, the soft, deep, wide, canopied bed, the symbol of the sweet
by-and-by to every Schwartz, was empty.

A sense of death, as unfamiliar to the Schwartzes as Zoro-
astrianism or the causes of the Sepoy Mutiny, stilled every voice
and slowed every heart. Awed, the heirs began to search gingerly
under the furniture and behind the drapes for all that was mortal
of Gramps, father of the race.

But Gramps had left not his earthly husk but a note, which
Lou finally found on the dresser, under a paperweight which was
a treasured souvenir from the 2000 World's Fair. Unsteadily, Lou
read it aloud:

"'Somebody who I have sheltered and protected and taught
the best I know how all these years last night turned on me like
a mad dog and diluted my anti-gerasone, or tried to. I am no
longer a young man. I can no longer bear the crushing burden
of life as I once could. So, after last night's bitter experience, I
say goodbye. The cares of this world will soon drop away like a
cloak of thorns, and I shall know peace. By the time you find
this, I will be gone.'"

"Gosh," said Willy brokenly, "he didn't even get to see how
the Five-Hundred-Mile Speedway Race was going to come out."

"Or the World's Series," said Eddie.

"Or whether Mrs. McGarvey got her eyesight back," said Morty.

"There's more," said Lou, and he began reading aloud again: "'I, Harold D. Schwartz . . . do hereby make, publish and declare this to be my last Will and Testament, hereby revoking any and all former will and codicils by me at any time heretofore made.'"

"No!" cried Willy. "Not another one!"

"'I do stipulate,'" read Lou, "'that all of my property, of whatsoever kind and nature, not be divided, but do devise and bequeath it to be held in common by my issue, without regard for generation, equally, share and share alike.'"

"Issue?" said Emerald.

Lou included the multitude in a sweep of his hand. "It means we all own the whole damn shootin' match."

All eyes turned instantly to the bed.

"Share and share alike?" said Morty.

"Actually," said Willy, who was the oldest person present, "it's just like the old system, where the oldest people head up things with their headquarters in here, and—"

"I like *that!*" said Em. "Lou owns as much of it as you do, and I say it ought to be for the oldest one who's still working. You can snooze around here all day, waiting for your pension check, and poor Lou stumbles in here after work, all tuckered out, and—"

"How about letting somebody who's never had any privacy get a little crack at it?" said Eddie hotly. "Hell, you old people had plenty of privacy back when you were kids. I was born and raised in the middle of the goddam barracks in the hall! How about—"

"Yeah?" said Morty. "Sure, you've all had it pretty tough, and my heart bleeds for you. But try honeymooning in the hall for a real kick."

"Silence!" shouted Willy imperiously. "The next person who opens his mouth spends the next six months by the bathroom. Now clear out of my room. I want to think."

A vase shattered against the wall, inches above his head. In the next moment, a free-for-all was underway, with each couple battling to eject every other couple from the room. Fighting coalitions formed and dissolved with the lightning changes of the tactical situation. Em and Lou were thrown into the hall, where they organized others in the same situation, and stormed back into the room.

After two hours of struggle, with nothing like a decision in sight, the cops broke in.

For the next half-hour, patrol wagons and ambulances hauled away Schwartzes, and then the apartment was still and spacious.

An hour later, films of the last stages of the riot were being televised to 500,000,000 delighted viewers on the Eastern Seaboard.

In the stillness of the three-room Schwartz apartment on the 76th floor of Building 257, the television set had been left on. Once more the air was filled with the cries and grunts and crashes of the fray, coming harmlessly now from the loudspeaker.

The battle also appeared on the screen of the television set in the police station, where the Schwartzes and their captors watched with professional interest.

Em and Lou were in adjacent four-by-eight cells, and were stretched out peacefully on their cots.

"Em—" called Lou through the partition, "you got a wash-basin all your own too?"

"Sure. Washbasin, bed, light—the works. Ha! And we thought Gramps' room was something. How long's this been going on?" She held out her hand. "For the first time in forty years, hon, I haven't got the shakes."

"Cross your fingers," said Lou, "the lawyer's going to try to get us a year."

"Gee," said Em dreamily, "I wonder what kind of wires you'd have to pull to get solitary?"

"All right, pipe down," said the turnkey, "or I'll toss the whole kit and caboodle of you right out. And first one who lets on to anybody outside how good jail is ain't never getting back in!"

The prisoners instantly fell silent.

The living room of the Schwartz apartment darkened for a moment, as the riot scenes faded, and then the face of the announcer appeared, like the sun coming from behind a cloud. "*And now, friends,*" he said, "*I have a special message from the makers of anti-gerasone, a message for all you folks over one hundred and fifty. Are you hampered socially by wrinkles, by stiffness of joints and discoloration or loss of hair, all because these things came upon you before anti-gerasone was developed? Well, if you are, you need no longer suffer, need no longer feel different and out of things.*

"*After years of research, medical science has now developed super-anti-gerasone! In weeks, yes weeks, you can look, feel, and act as young as your great-great-grandchildren! Wouldn't you pay $5,000 to be indistinguishable from everybody else? Well, you don't have to. Safe, tested super-anti-gerasone costs you only dollars a day. The average cost of regaining all the sparkle and attractiveness of youth is less than fifty dollars.*

"*Write now for your free trial carton. Just put your name and address on a dollar postcard, and mail it to 'Super,' Box 500,000, Schenectady, N. Y. Have you got that? I'll repeat it. 'Super.' Box . . .*" Underlining the announcer's words was the scratching of Gramps' fountain-pen, the one Willy had given him the night before. He had come in a few minutes previous from the Idle Hour Tavern, which commanded a view of Building 257 across the square of asphalt known as the Alden Village Green. He had called a cleaning woman to come straighten the place up, and had hired the best lawyer in town to get his descendants a conviction. Gramps had then moved the daybed before the television screen so that he could watch from a reclining position. It was something he'd dreamed of doing for years.

"Schen-*ec*-ta-dy," mouthed Gramps. "Got it." His face had changed remarkably. His facial muscles seemed to have relaxed, revealing kindness and equanimity under what had been taut, bad-tempered lines. It was almost as though his trial package of *Super*-anti-gerasone had already arrived. When something amused him on television, he smiled easily, rather than barely managing to lengthen the thin line of his mouth a millimeter. Life was good. He could hardly wait to see what was going to happen next.

(1953)

PALM SUNDAY

An Autobiographical Collage

For my cousins the de St. Andrés everywhere.

Who has the castle now?

TABLE OF CONTENTS
(BITS OF THE COLLAGE)

KURT VONNEGUT

INTRODUCTION

tHIS is a very great book by an American genius. I have worked so hard on this masterpiece for the past six years. I have groaned and banged my head on radiators. I have walked through every hotel lobby in New York, thinking about this book and weeping, and driving my fist into the guts of grandfather clocks.

It is a marvelous new literary form. This book combines the tidal power of a major novel with the bone-rattling immediacy of front-line journalism—which is old stuff now, God knows, God knows. But I have also intertwined the flashy enthusiasms of musical theater, the lethal left jab of the short story, the sachet of personal letters, the oompah of American history, and oratory in the bow-wow style.

This book is so broad and deep that it reminds me of my brother Bernard's early experiments with radio. He built a transmitter of his own invention, and he hooked it up to a telegraph key, and he turned it on. He called up our cousin Richard, about two miles away, and he told Richard to listen to his radio, to tune it back and forth across the band, to see if he could pick up my brother's signals anywhere. They were both about fifteen.

My brother tapped out an easily recognizable message, sending it again and again and again. It was "SOS." This was in Indianapolis, the world's largest city not on a navigable waterway.

Cousin Richard telephoned back. He was thrilled. He said that Bernard's signals were loud and clear simply every-where on the radio band, drowning out music or news or drama, or whatever the commercial stations were putting out at the time.

❧

THIS is certainly that kind of masterpiece, and a new name should be created for such an all-frequencies assault on the sensibilities. I propose the name *blivit*. This is a word which during my adolescence was defined by peers as "two pounds of shit in a one-pound bag."

I would not mind if books simpler than this one, but combining fiction and fact, were also called blivits. This would encourage *The New York Times Book Review* to estab-lish a third category for best sellers, one long needed, in my opinion. If there were a separate list for blivits, then authors of blivits could stop stepping in the faces of mere novelists and historians and so on.

Until that happy day, however, I insist, as only a great author can, that this book be ranked in both the fiction and nonfiction competitions. As for the Pulitzer prizes: this book should be eligible for a mega–grand slam, sweeping fiction, drama, history, biography, and journalism. We will wait and see.

❦

THIS book is not only a blivit but a collage. It began with my wish to collect in one volume most of the reviews and speeches and essays I had written since the publication of a similar collection, *Wampeters, Foma & Granfalloons,* in 1974. But as I arranged those fragments in this order and then that one, I saw that they formed a sort of autobiography, especially if I felt free to include some pieces not written by me. To give life to such a golem, however, I would have to write much new connective tissue. This I have done.

The reader should expect me to chat about this and that, and then to include a speech or a letter or a song or whatever, and then to chat some more.

I do not really consider this to be a masterpiece. I find it clumsy. I find it raw. It has some value, I think, as a confrontation between an American novelist and his own stubborn simplicity. I was dumb in school. Whatever the nature of that dumbness, it is with me still.

I have dedicated this book to the de St. Andrés. I am a de St. André, since that was the maiden name of a maternal great-grandmother of mine. My mother believed that this meant that she was descended from nobles of some kind.

This was an innocent belief, and so should not be mocked or scorned. Or so I say. My books so far have argued that most human behavior, no matter how ghastly or ludicrous or glorious or whatever, is innocent. And here seems as good a place as any to include a statement made to me by Marsha Mason, the superb actress who once did me the honor of starring in a play of mine. She, too, is from the Middle West, from St. Louis.

"You know what the trouble is with New York?" she asked me.

"No," I said.

"Nobody here," she said, "believes that there is such a thing as innocence."

*Whoever entertains liberal views
and chooses a consort that is captured
by superstition risks his liberty
and his happiness.*

—CLEMENS VONNEGUT (1824–1906)
Instruction in Morals
(The Hollenbeck Press,
Indianapolis, 1900)

I

THE FIRST
AMENDMENT

I am a member of what I believe to be the last recognizable
generation of full-time, life-time American novelists. We
appear to be standing more or less in a row. It was the Great
Depression which made us similarly edgy and watchful. It
was World War II which lined us up so nicely, whether we
were men or women, whether we were ever in uniform or
not. It was an era of romantic anarchy in publishing which
gave us money and mentors, willy-nilly, when we were young
—while we learned our craft. Words printed on pages were
still the principal form of long-distance communication and
stored information in America when we were young.

No more.

Nor are there many publishers and editors and agents left who are eager to find some way to get money and other forms of encouragement to young writers who write as clumsily as members of my literary generation did when we started out. The wild and wonderful and expensive guess was made back then that we might acquire some wisdom and learn how to write halfway decently by and by. Writers were needed that much back then.

It was an amusing and instructive time for writers—for hundreds of them.

Television wrecked the short-story branch of the industry, and now accountants and business school graduates dominate book publishing. They feel that money spent on someone's first novel is good money down a rat hole. They are right. It almost always is.

So, as I say, I think I belong to America's last generation of novelists. Novelists will come one by one from now on, not in seeming families, and will perhaps write only one or two novels, and let it go at that. Many will have inherited or married money.

The most influential of my bunch, in my opinion, is still J. D. Salinger, although he has been silent for years. The most promising was perhaps Edward Lewis Wallant, who died so young. And it is my thinking about the death of James Jones two years ago, who was not all that young, who was almost exactly my age, which accounts for the autumnal mood of this book. There have been other reminders of my own mortality, to be sure, but the death of Jones is central —perhaps because I see his widow Gloria so often and because he, too, was a self-educated midwesterner, and because he, too, in a major adventure for all of us, which was the Second World War, had been an enlisted man. And let it here

be noted that the best-known members of my literary generation, if they wrote about war, almost unanimously despised
officers and made heroes of sketchily educated, aggressively
unaristocratic enlisted men.

❦

JAMES JONES told me one time that his publisher and Ernest
Hemingway's, Charles Scribner's Sons, had once hoped to
get Jones and Hemingway together—so that they could
enjoy each other's company as old warriors.

Jones declined, by his own account, because he did not
regard Hemingway as a fellow soldier. He said Hemingway
in wartime was free to come and go from the fighting as he
pleased, and to take time off for a fine meal or woman or
whatever. Real soldiers, according to Jones, damn well had
to stay where they were told, or go where they were told, and
eat swill, and take the worst the enemy had to throw at them
day after day, week after week.

❦

IT may be that the most striking thing about members of my
literary generation in retrospect will be that we were allowed
to say absolutely anything without fear of punishment. Our
American heirs may find it incredible, as most foreigners do
right now, that a nation would want to enforce as a law
something which sounds more like a dream, which reads as
follows:

"Congress shall make no law respecting an establishment
of religion, or prohibiting the free exercise thereof, or abridg-
ing the freedom of the press, or the right of the people

peaceably to assemble, and to petition the Government for a redress of grievances."

How could a nation with such a law raise its children in an atmosphere of decency? It couldn't—it can't. So the law will surely be repealed soon for the sake of children.

And even now my books, along with books by Bernard Malamud and James Dickey and Joseph Heller and many other first-rate patriots, are regularly thrown out of public-school libraries by school board members, who commonly say that they have not actually read the books, but that they have it on good authority that the books are bad for children.

❦

MY novel *Slaughterhouse-Five* was actually burned in a furnace by a school janitor in Drake, North Dakota, on instructions from the school committee there, and the school board made public statements about the unwholesomeness of the book. Even by the standards of Queen Victoria, the only offensive line in the entire novel is this: "Get out of the road, you dumb motherfucker." This is spoken by an American antitank gunner to an unarmed American chaplain's assistant during the Battle of the Bulge in Europe in December 1944, the largest single defeat of American arms (the Confederacy excluded) in history. The chaplain's assistant had attracted enemy fire.

So on November 16, 1973, I wrote as follows to Charles McCarthy of Drake, North Dakota:

Dear Mr. McCarthy:

I am writing to you in your capacity as chairman of the Drake School Board. I am among those American writers whose books have been destroyed in the now famous furnace of your school.

Certain members of your community have suggested that my work is evil. This is extraordinarily insulting to me. The news from Drake indicates to me that books and writers are very unreal to you people. I am writing this letter to let you know how real I am.

I want you to know, too, that my publisher and I have done absolutely nothing to exploit the disgusting news from Drake. We are not clapping each other on the back, crowing about all the books we will sell because of the news. We have declined to go on television, have written no fiery letters to editorial pages, have granted no lengthy interviews. We are angered and sickened and saddened. And no copies of this letter have been sent to anybody else. You now hold the only copy in your hands. It is a strictly private letter from me to the people of Drake, who have done so much to damage my reputation in the eyes of their children and then in the eyes of the world. Do you have the courage and ordinary decency to show this letter to the people, or will it, too, be consigned to the fires of your furnace?

I gather from what I read in the papers and hear on television that you imagine me, and some other writers, too, as being sort of ratlike people who enjoy making money from poisoning the minds of young people. I am in fact a large, strong person, fifty-one years old, who did a lot of farm work as a boy, who is good with tools. I have raised six children, three my own and three adopted. They have all turned out well. Two of them are farmers. I am a combat infantry veteran from World War II, and hold a Purple Heart. I have earned whatever I own by hard work. I have never been arrested or sued for anything. I am so much trusted with

young people and by young people that I have served on the
faculties of the University of Iowa, Harvard, and the City
College of New York. Every year I receive at least a dozen
invitations to be commencement speaker at colleges and high
schools. My books are probably more widely used in schools
than those of any other living American fiction writer.

If you were to bother to read my books, to behave as
educated persons would, you would learn that they are not
sexy, and do not argue in favor of wildness of any kind. They
beg that people be kinder and more responsible than they
often are. It is true that some of the characters speak
coarsely. That is because people speak coarsely in real life.
Especially soldiers and hardworking men speak coarsely,
and even our most sheltered children know that. And we all
know, too, that those words really don't damage children
much. They didn't damage us when we were young. It was
evil deeds and lying that hurt us.

After I have said all this, I am sure you are still ready to
respond, in effect, "Yes, yes—but it still remains our right
and our responsibility to decide what books our children are
going to be made to read in our community." This is surely
so. But it is also true that if you exercise that right and fulfill
that responsibility in an ignorant, harsh, un-American manner, then people are entitled to call you bad citizens and
fools. Even your own children are entitled to call you that.

I read in the newspaper that your community is mystified
by the outcry from all over the country about what you have
done. Well, you have discovered that Drake is a part of
American civilization, and your fellow Americans can't
stand it that you have behaved in such an uncivilized way.
Perhaps you will learn from this that books are sacred to free
men for very good reasons, and that wars have been fought

against nations which hate books and burn them. If you are an American, you must allow all ideas to circulate freely in your community, not merely your own.

If you and your board are now determined to show that you in fact have wisdom and maturity when you exercise your powers over the education of your young, then you should acknowledge that it was a rotten lesson you taught young people in a free society when you denounced and then burned books—books you hadn't even read. You should also resolve to expose your children to all sorts of opinions and information, in order that they will be better equipped to make decisions and to survive.

Again: you have insulted me, and I am a good citizen, and I am very real.

❧

THAT was seven years ago. There has so far been no reply. At this very moment, as I write in New York City, *Slaughterhouse-Five* has been banned from school libraries not fifty miles from here. A legal battle begun several years ago rages on. The school board in question has found lawyers eager to attack the First Amendment tooth and nail. There is never a shortage anywhere of lawyers eager to attack the First Amendment, as though it were nothing more than a clause in a lease from a crooked slumlord.

At the start of that particular litigation, on March 24th of 1976, I wrote a comment for the Op-Ed page of the Long Island edition of *The New York Times*. It went like this:

A school board has denounced some books again—out in Levittown this time. One of the books was mine. I hear about un-American nonsense like this twice a year or so. One time out in North Dakota, the books were actually burned in a furnace. I had a laugh. It was such an ignorant, dumb, superstitious thing to do.

It was so cowardly, too—to make a great show of attacking artifacts. It was like St. George attacking bedspreads and cuckoo clocks.

Yes, and St. Georges like that seem to get elected or appointed to school committees all the time. They are actually proud of their illiteracy. They imagine that they are somehow celebrating the bicentennial when they boast, as some did in Levittown, that they hadn't actually read the books they banned.

Such lunks are often the backbone of volunteer fire departments and the United States Infantry and cake sales and so on, and they have been thanked often enough for that. But they have no business supervising the educations of children in a free society. They are just too bloody stupid.

Here is how I propose to end book-banning in this country once and for all: Every candidate for school committee should be hooked up to a lie-detector and asked this question: "Have you read a book from start to finish since high school? Or did you even read a book from start to finish in high school?"

If the truthful answer is "no," then the candidate should be told politely that he cannot get on the school committee and blow off his big bazoo about how books make children crazy.

Whenever ideas are squashed in this country, literate lovers of the American experiment write careful and intricate explanations of why all ideas must be allowed to live. It is time for them to realize that they are attempting to explain

America at its bravest and most optimistic to orangutans.

From now on, I intend to limit my discourse with dim-witted Savonarolas to this advice: "Have somebody read the First Amendment to the United States Constitution out loud to you, you God damned fool!"

Well—the American Civil Liberties Union or somebody like that will come to the scene of trouble, as they always do. They will explain what is in the Constitution, and to whom it applies.

They will win.

And there will be millions who are bewildered and heartbroken by the legal victory, who think some things should never be said—especially about religion.

They are in the wrong place at the wrong time.

Hi ho.

❦

WHY is it so ordinary for American citizens to show such scorn for the First Amendment? I discussed that some at a fund raiser for the American Civil Liberties Union at Sands Point, New York, out on Long Island, on September 16, 1979. The house where I spoke, incidentally, was said to be the model for Gatsby's house in F. Scott Fitzgerald's *The Great Gatsby.* I saw no reason to doubt the claim.

I said this in such a setting:

"I will not speak directly to the ejection of my book *Slaughterhouse-Five* from the school libraries of Island Trees. I have a vested interest. I wrote the book, after all, so why wouldn't I argue that it is less repulsive than the school board says?

"I will speak of Thomas Aquinas instead. I will tell you my dim memories of what he said about the hierarchy of laws on this planet, which was flat at the time. The highest law, he said, was divine law, God's law. Beneath that was natural law, which I suppose would include thunderstorms, and our right to shield our children from poisonous ideas, and so on.

"And the lowest law was human law.

"Let me clarify this scheme by comparing its parts to playing cards. Enemies of the Bill of Rights do the same sort of thing all the time, so why shouldn't we? Divine law, then, is an ace. Natural law is a king. The Bill of Rights is a lousy queen.

"The Thomist hierarchy of laws is so far from being ridiculous that I have never met anybody who did not believe in it right down to the marrow of his or her bones. Everybody knows that there are laws with more grandeur than those which are printed in our statute books. The big trouble is that there is so little agreement as to how those grander laws are worded. Theologians can give us hints of the wording, but it takes a dictator to set them down just right—to dot the *i*'s and cross the *t*'s. A man who had been a mere corporal in the army did that for Germany and then for all of Europe, you may remember, not long ago. There was nothing he did not know about divine and natural law. He had fistfuls of aces and kings to play.

"Meanwhile, over on this side of the Atlantic, we were not playing with a full deck, as they say. Because of our Constitution, the highest card anybody had to play was a lousy queen, contemptible human law. That remains true today. I myself celebrate that incompleteness, since it has obviously been so good for us. I support the American Civil Liberties Union because it goes to court to insist that our government officials be guided by nothing grander than human law. Every time the circulation of this idea or that one is discouraged by an official in this country, that official is scorning the Constitution, and urging all of us to participate in far grander systems, again: divine or natural law.

"Cannot we, as libertarians, hunger for at least a little natural law? Can't we learn from nature at least, without being burdened by another person's idea of God?

"Certainly. Granola never harmed anybody, nor the birds and bees—not to mention milk. God is unknowable, but nature is explaining herself all the time. What has she told us so far? That blacks are obviously inferior to whites, for one thing, and intended for menial work on white man's terms. This clear lesson from nature, we should remind ourselves from time to time, allowed Thomas Jefferson to own slaves. Imagine that.

"What troubles me most about my lovely country is that its children are seldom taught that American freedom will vanish, if, when they grow up, and in the exercise of their duties as citizens, they insist that our courts and policemen and prisons be guided by divine or natural law.

"Most teachers and parents and guardians do not teach this vital lesson because they themselves never learned it, or because they dare not. Why dare they not? People can get into a lot of trouble in this country, and often have to be defended by the American Civil Liberties Union, for laying the groundwork for the lesson, which is this: That no one really understands nature or God. It is my willingness to lay this groundwork, and not sex or violence, which has got my poor book in such trouble in Island Trees—and in Drake, North Dakota, where the book was burned, and in many other communities too numerous to mention.

"I have not said that our government is anti-nature and anti-God. I have said that it is non-nature and non-God, for very good reasons that could curl your hair.

"Well—all good things must come to an end, they say. So American freedom will come to an end, too, sooner or later. How will it end? As all freedoms end: by the surrender of our destinies to the highest laws.

"To return to my foolish analogy of playing cards: kings and aces will be played. Nobody else will have anything higher than a queen.

"There will be a struggle between those holding kings and aces. The struggle will not end, not that the rest of us will care much by then, until somebody plays the ace of spades. Nothing beats the ace of spades.

"I thank you for your attention."

❧

I spoke at Gatsby's house in the afternoon. When I got back to my own house in New York City, I wrote a letter to a friend in the Soviet Union, Felix Kuznetzov, a distinguished critic and teacher, and an officer in the Union of Writers of the USSR in Moscow. The date on the letter is the same as the date of the Sands Point oration.

There was a time when I might have been half-bombed on booze when writing such a letter so late at night, a time when I might have reeked of mustard gas and roses as I punched the keys. But I don't drink anymore. Never in my life have I written anything for publication while sozzled. But I certainly used to write a lot of letters that way.

No more.

Be that as it may, I was sober then and am sober now, and Felix Kuznetzov and I had become friends during the previous summer—at an ecumenical meeting in New York City, sponsored by the Charles F. Kettering Foundation, of American and Soviet literary persons, about ten to a side. The American delegation was headed by Norman Cousins, and included myself and Edward Albee and Arthur Miller and William Styron and John Updike. All of us had been published in the Soviet Union. I am almost entirely in print over there—with the exception of *Mother Night* and *Jailbird.* Few, if any, of the Soviet delegates had had anything published here, and so their work was unknown to us.

We Americans were told by the Soviets that we should be embarrassed that their country published so much of our work, and that we published so little of theirs. Our reply was that we would work to get more of them published over here, but that we felt, too, that the USSR could easily have put together a delegation whose works were admired and published here—and that we could easily have put together a delegation so unfamiliar to them that its members could have been sewer commissioners from Fresno, as far as anybody in the Soviet Union knew.

Felix Kuznetzov and I got along very well, at any rate. I had him over to my house, and we sat in my garden out back and talked away the better part of an afternoon.

But then, after everybody went home, there was some trouble in the Soviet Union about the publication of an outlaw magazine called *Metropole.* Most of *Metropole*'s writers and editors were young, impatient with the strictures placed on their writings by old poops. Nothing in *Metropole,* incidentally, was nearly as offensive as calling a chaplain's assistant a "dumb motherfucker." But the *Metropole* people were denounced, and the magazine was suppressed, and ways were discussed for making life harder for anyone associated with it.

So Albee and Styron and Updike and I sent a cable to the Writers' Union, saying that we thought it was wrong to penalize writers for what they wrote, no matter what they wrote. Felix Kuznetzov made an official reply on behalf of the union, giving the sense of a large meeting in which distinguished writer after distinguished writer testified that those who wrote for *Metropole* weren't really writers, that they were pornographers and other sorts of disturbers of the peace, and so on. He asked that his reply be published in *The New York Times*, and it was published there. Why not?

And I privately wrote to Kuznetzov as follows:

Dear Professor Kuznetzov—dear Felix—

I thank you for your prompt and frank and thoughtful letter of August 20, and for the supplementary materials which accompanied it. I apologize for not replying in your own beautiful language, and I wish that we both might have employed from the first a more conversational tone in our discussion of the *Metropole* affair. I will try to recapture the amiable, brotherly mood of our long talk in my garden here about a year ago.

You speak of us in your letter as "American authors." We do not feel especially American in this instance, since we spoke only for ourselves—without consulting with any American institution whatsoever. We are simply "authors" in this case, expressing loyalty to the great and vulnerable family of writers throughout the world. You and all other members of the Union of Writers surely have the same family feelings. Those of us who sent the cable are so far from being organized that I have no idea what sorts of replies the others may be making to you.

As you must know, your response to our cable was printed recently in *The New York Times,* and perhaps elsewhere. The controversy has attracted little attention. It is a matter of interest, seemingly, only to other writers. Nobody cares much about writers but writers. And, if it weren't for a few of us like the signers of the cable, I wonder if there would be anybody to care about writers—no matter how much trouble they were in. Should we, too, stop caring?

Well—I understand that our cultures are so different that we can never agree about freedom of expression. It is natural that we should disagree, and perhaps even commendable. What you may not know about our own culture is that writers such as those who signed the cable are routinely attacked by fellow citizens as being pornographers or corrupters of children and celebrators of violence and persons of no talent and so on. In my own case, such charges are brought against my works in court several times a year, usually by parents who, for religious or political reasons, do not want their children to read what I have to say. The parents, incidentally, often find their charges supported by the lowest courts. The charges so far have been invariably overthrown in higher courts, those closer to the soul of the Constitution of the United States.

Please convey the contents of this letter to my brothers and sisters in the Writers' Union, as we conveyed your letter to *The New York Times.* This letter is specifically for you, to do with as you please. I am not sending carbon copies to anyone. It has not even been read by my wife.

That homely detail, if brought to the attention of the

Writers' Union, might help its members to understand what I do not think is at all well understood now: That we are not nationalists, taking part in some cold-war enterprise. We simply care deeply about how things are going for writers here, there, and everywhere. Even when they are declared nonwriters, as we have been, we continue to care.

❦

KUZNETZOV gave me a prompt and likewise private answer. It was gracious and humane. I could assume that we were still friends. He said nothing against his union or his government. Neither did he say anything to discourage me from feeling that writers everywhere, good and bad, were all first cousins—first cousins, at least.

And all the argle-bargling that goes on between educated persons in the United States and the Soviet Union is so touching and comical, really, as long as it does not lead to war. It draws its energy, in my opinion, from a desperate wish on both sides that each other's utopias should work much better than they do. We want to tinker with theirs, to make it work much better than it does—so that people there, for example, can say whatever they please without fear of punishment. They want to tinker with ours, so that everybody here who wants a job can have one, and so that we don't have to tolerate the sales of fist-fucking films and snuff films and so on.

Neither utopia now works much better than the Page typesetting machine, in which Mark Twain invested and lost a fortune. That beautiful contraption actually set type just once, when only Twain and the inventor were watching.

Twain called all the other investors to see this miracle, but, by the time they got there, the inventor had taken the machine all apart again. It never ran again.

Peace.

II

ROOTS

I am descended from Europeans who have been literate for a long time, as I will presently demonstrate, and who have not been slaves since the early days of the Roman games, most likely. A more meticulous historian might suggest that my European ancestors no doubt enslaved themselves to their own military commanders from time to time. When I examine my genealogy over the past century and a little more, however, I find no war lovers of any kind.

My father and grandfathers were in no wars. Only one of my four great-grandfathers was in a war, the Civil War. This was Peter Lieber, born in Düsseldorf, Germany, in 1832. My mother's maiden name was Lieber. This Peter Lieber, who is no more real to me than to you, came to America with one million other Germans in 1848. His father was a brush manufacturer. He was living in New Ulm, Minnesota, running a general store and trading for furs with the Indians, when the Civil War broke out. When Abraham Lincoln called for 75,000 volunteers, Peter Lieber joined the 22nd Minnesota Battery of Light Artillery, and served for two years until wounded and honorably discharged.

"The knee-joint of his right leg was permanently damaged, and he walked with a limp to the end of his days," according to my Uncle John Rauch (1890–1976). Uncle John was not in fact my uncle, but the husband of a first cousin of my father, Gertrude Schnull Rauch. He was a Harvard graduate and a distinguished Indianapolis lawyer. Toward the end of his life, he made himself an historian, a *griot,* of his wife's family—in part my family, too, although he was not related to it by blood, but only by marriage.

I am a highly diluted relative of his wife, and did not expect to appear as more than a footnote in the history—and so I was properly astonished when he one day made me a gift of a manuscript entitled "An Account of the Ancestry of Kurt Vonnegut, Jr., by an Ancient Friend of His Family." It was painstakingly researched and better written, by Uncle John himself, than much of my own stuff, sad to say. That manuscript is the most extravagant gift I ever expect to receive—and it came from a man who had never spoken favorably of my work in my presence, other than to say that he was "surprised by my convincing tone of authority," and that he was sure I would make a great deal of money.

When I published my first short story, which was "Report on the Barnhouse Effect," in *Collier's,* its hero was a man who could control dice by thinking hard about them, and who could eventually loosen bricks in chimneys a mile away, and so on—and Uncle John said, "Now you will hear from every nut in the country. They can all do that."

When I published the novel *Cat's Cradle,* Uncle John sent me a postcard saying, "You're saying that life is a load of crap, right? Read Thackeray!" He wasn't joking.

I was no literary gentleman in his eyes, surely, and one satisfaction he may have found in writing about my ancestry was demonstrating how a gentleman wrote. I stand instructed.

❦

WHEN Uncle John speaks of "Kurt" in his account, he means my father, Kurt Vonnegut, Sr. He commonly calls me "K," which was my nickname when a child. People who knew me before I was twelve years old still call me that. So do my descendents.

I have never identified with the "K" in Kafka's works, by the way. Having grown up in a democracy, I have dared to imagine that I know at all times who is really in charge, what is really going on. This could be a mistake.

The opening pages of Uncle John's manuscript give an impersonal account, such as might be found in an encyclopedia, of the settling of this country by European immigrants, and the consequent growth of commerce, industry, agriculture, and so on. The largest of the waves was German—the second was Italian, the third was Irish.

Uncle John's conclusion to this prologue is worth setting down here: "The two world wars in which the United States was arrayed against Germany were painful experiences for German-Americans. They hated to be obliged to fight their racial cousins, but they did so, and it is significant that of the millions of German descendants in the United States during those dreadful wars there was not one case of treason.

"The Germans, while loving the country of their origin, did not approve of Kaiser Wilhelm II and his warlords, nor Hitler and his wretched Nazis. Their sympathies were with England, and their adoption of the culture of England determined their attitude. When England was in trouble in 1917 and again in 1941, the German-Americans rallied to her support against the Fatherland. This is a phenomenon little remarked upon."

So be it.

❦

As I have said in other books, the anti-Germanism in this country during the First World War so shamed and dismayed my parents that they resolved to raise me without acquainting me with the language or the literature or the music or the oral family histories which my ancestors had loved. They volunteered to make me ignorant and rootless as proof of their patriotism.

This was done with surprising meekness by many, many German-American families in Indianapolis, it seems to me. Uncle John almost seems to boast of this dismantling and quiet burial of a culture, a culture which surely would have been of use to me today.

But I still get a *frisson* when I encounter a German-American who was raised, amazingly, to loath Woodrow Wilson for calling into question the loyalty of what he called "hyphenated Americans," for egging on those who loved democracy so much that they defaced the walls of German social and gymnastic and educational associations across the country, and refused to listen to German music or, even, to eat sauerkraut. As nearly as I can remember, none of my relatives ever said anything much, one way or another, about Woodrow Wilson to me.

❦

ONE German-American friend of mine, an architectural historian my own age, can be counted on to excoriate Woodrow Wilson after he has had several strong drinks. He goes on to say that it was Wilson who persuaded this country that it was patriotic to be stupid, to be proud of knowing only one language, of believing that all other cultures were inferior and ridiculous, offensive to God and common sense alike, that artists and teachers and studious persons in general were ninnies when it came to dealing with problems in life that really mattered, and on and on.

This friend says that it was a particular misfortune for this country that the German-Americans had achieved such eminence in the arts and education when it was their turn to be scorned from on high. To hate all they did and stood for at that time, which included gymnastics, by the way, was to lobotomize not only the German-Americans but our culture.

"That left American football," says my German-American friend, and someone is elected to drive him home.

❦

To return to Uncle John:

"All of Kurt Vonnegut, Jr.'s eight great-grandparents were part of the vast migration of Germans to the Midwest in the half century from 1820 to 1870. They were: Clemens Vonnegut, Sr., and his wife, Katarina Blank; Henry Schnull and his wife, Matilde Schramm; Peter Lieber and his wife, Sophia St. André; Karl Barus and his wife, Alice Möllman. They were preceded only by four of his sixteen great-great-grandparents, who were Jacob Schramm and his wife, Julia Junghans; and Johann Blank and his wife, Anna Maria Oger. The remaining twelve and their forebears are mostly unknown. They never left Germany. Their bones still repose there in anonymity.

"But all of the eight ancestors who did settle here were better educated and of higher social rank than the mine-run of immigrants. They were with the exception of Anna Oger's parents, burghers, city people, merchants and members of the upper middle class, in contrast to the bulk of German immigrants who were chiefly peasant farmers or skilled artisans.

"Thus, K's great-great-grandfather Jacob Schramm came from Saxony, where for generations his family had been grain merchants. He brought with him five thousand dollars in gold, six hundred books, and boxes of household goods, including a dinner set of Meissen porcelain. He bought at once a section of land near Cumberland, Indiana. He was a highly literate fellow, and wrote a series of letters back to Germany detailing his experiences and making valuable suggestions for the guidance of subsequent immigrants. These letters were printed and published in Germany. A copy of this publication is in the library of the Indiana Historical Society, which issued an English translation of it in 1928. Jacob Schramm traveled extensively—once around the world, quite by himself. He prospered. He bought a great deal of land, one parcel of over two thousand acres on the old Michigan Road just northwest of Indianapolis. He loaned money, secured by good mortgages, to later arrivals in the vicinity. When his only daughter, Matilda, married Henry Schnull in 1857, Jacob Schramm advanced the latter capital to help him start a wholesale grocery business and launch a successful mercantile career which made him a large fortune.

"K's paternal ancestors the Vonneguts, were likewise people of substance. They came from Münster, Westphalia, where the name derives from a distant forebear who had an estate—'ein Gut'—on the little River Funne; hence the surname FunneGut—the estate on the Funne. This name was subsequently changed from Funnegut to Vonnegut. Funnegut sounded too much like 'funny gut' in English.

"Clemens Vonnegut, Sr., was born in Münster in Westphalia in 1824; came to the United States in 1848 and finally settled in Indianapolis in 1850. His father had been an official tax-collector for the Duke of Westphalia.

"Clemens had a far better formal education than ninety-eight percent or more of the German or other immigrants. He had completed his *'Abitur'* at the *Hochschule* in Hannover; which meant that he had the equivalent at that time of an American college education and was qualified to attend one of the Universities as a candidate for a Ph.D. degree. He had an acquaintance with Latin and Greek, and spoke French fluently in addition to his native German. He had read widely in History and Philosophy; had acquired a fine vocabulary; and was able to write with clarity. Although raised and instructed in the Roman Catholic Church, he rejected formalized religion and disliked clergymen. He greatly admired Voltaire, and shared many of the latter's philosophical views. Instead of attending a University, Clemens became a salesman for a textile firm located in Amsterdam, Holland. At the age of twenty-four, in 1848, he decided to emigrate to the United States, where he first traveled about as agent for the textile mill. When he came to Indianapolis in 1850, he encountered a fellow countryman named Vollmer, who had been settled here a few years and was already established in business for himself in a small way as a retail merchant in hardware and sundry merchandise. The two became friends, and Vollmer invited Vonnegut to join him in this enterprise. The firm then became known as Vollmer & Vonnegut. After a short association Vollmer decided to make a journey out West to explore the new country and visit the gold fields recently discovered in California. He was never heard from again, and presumably lost his life in the 'Wild West.'

"Vonnegut thus became the sole proprietor of the small business which he in 1852, and later his sons and grandsons, made into a considerable enterprise as the Vonnegut Hardware Company.

"Across the street from his first modest shop on East Washington Street in the 1850s was a small German restaurant. One of the waitresses in this establishment was an attractive girl named Katarina Blank. She was one of seven children of a German immigrant family of peasants who came from Urloffen in Baden and settled on a farm in Wayne Township, Marion County, just west of Indianapolis. They were struggling to get their farm to be productive after felling the forest trees and draining the land. With so many children to feed and clothe, all had to work for their living after a few years of primary instruction in the common school. Katarina

Blank went to work as a waitress in this little cafe, and soon met Clemens Vonnegut, who fell in love with her. They were married in 1852. He was twenty-eight and she, twenty-four. They bought a modest home on West Market Street and raised their family in steadily improving material circumstances. Katarina was, like Clemens, small in stature and dark complected. Both spoke German in their home, but had considerable fluency in French as well. The training of their children was in the tradition and culture of nineteenth-century Germany. It is highly significant of Clemens's ascetic and puritanical ethics that his literary idol was Schiller and not Goethe, who was much the greater genius. He disapproved of Goethe's morals, and would not read him. Katarina, although of humble origin and little formal education, became a highly respected and extremely dignified matriarch, much beloved by her children and grandchildren.

"Clemens attained local distinction as an advocate of progressive public education. He served for twenty-seven years on the Board of School Commissioners of the City of Indianapolis; most of the time as Chairman and Chief Administrative Officer. He was an incorruptible and highly efficient officer. He was particularly interested in the High School, and saw to it that first-rate instruction was provided in the classics, history, and the social sciences. He was instrumental in the establishment of the second High School in 1894, known as Manual Training High School, where, under Professor Emmerich as Principal, instruction was provided with emphasis on Science, Mathematics, and Practical Engineering. Graduates of these two high schools were readily accepted at Harvard and Yale and other great Universities until about 1940; since then the prestige of these high schools has sadly declined as a result of lowered standards.

"Many tales were told of Clemens Vonnegut. When he was elected to the Board of School Commissioners, he found that the local banks did not pay interest on the somewhat large deposits which the Board carried to finance its operations. He demanded that the banks pay interest on the Board's deposits. This was then considered to be an offensive innovation in the customary and comfortable practice which until then had prevailed. The banker John P. Frenzel then called upon Clemens at his office and loudly upbraided him. Clemens pretended to be hard of hearing, and capped his ears. Frenzel shouted louder. Still Clemens pretended not to hear. Frenzel raised his voice and interjected profanity, but to no avail. Clemens would not 'hear' him. Finally Frenzel stormed out—still not heard. But thenceforth the banks paid interest and have continued to do so to this day.

"Upon another occasion a disgruntled contractor called upon him and protested the award of a contract for school construction to a bidder who did not have the 'right' political connections. Here again Clemens pretended to be hard of hearing; but, in addition, took out a pen-knife and pared his fingernails. The frustrated contractor then indulged in invectives. Clemens remained calm and silent. After he finished paring his fingernails, he took off his shoes and socks and proceeded to pare his toenails with intense but silent concentration. His visitor soon left in disgust, cursing this crazy German. Clemens remained imperturbable and undisturbed. Many similar tales were told of him, but at his death at age eighty-two in 1906 he was a greatly respected figure in the business and civic life of the community; next only to Henry Schnull as the first in prestige of the German immigrants to Indianapolis.

"Old Clemens, as he advanced into his seventies, turned

over management of his business to the competent hands of his three sons: Clemens, Jr., Franklin, and George. His son Bernard had a brief connection with the Company but disliked what he called 'the trade in nails' and confined his attention to his profession of architecture and to his avocations in the arts. He had never been as robust as his brothers, two of whom lived into their nineties. The old man set them all an example not only of the highest standards of moral integrity but of physical fitness through exercise of the body. To the end of his days old Clemens was a devotee of the teachings of Father Jahn: a sound mind in a sound body. He exercised daily in all weathers and ate and drank very sparingly. He never weighed much over one hundred and ten pounds. He could be seen striding vigorously about the streets swinging a large boulder in each hand. If he passed a tree with a stout branch within reach he would stop, lay down the boulders, and chin himself a number of times on the branch. On a cold December day in the year 1904, in his eighty-third year, he left his home for his usual walk. He apparently became confused and lost his way. When he did not return at his accustomed time, his family instituted a search with the assistance of the police. He was found several miles from his home lying by the side of a road—quite dead. It was the sort of death he would have welcomed—active to the very end."

❡

ALMOST all of my ancestors delivered themselves directly from Europe to Indianapolis, except for Peter Lieber and Sophia de St. André, who had the general store in New Ulm,

Minnesota. When Peter returned from the Civil War with a crippled leg, he was full of stories about how Indianapolis was booming. New Ulm was dead by comparison.

So Peter, according to Uncle John, wangled an appointment as one of the secretaries to Oliver P. Morton, the Governor of Indiana. The governor needed a German liaison secretary in his political activities. The pay was good and steady, and Peter remained in his office until the close of the war.

"In 1865 came an opportunity for Peter. The leading brewery of the city was known as Gack & Biser's. Owing to death of the proprietors, the business was offered for sale. Peter bought it and renamed it P. Lieber & Co. Peter knew absolutely nothing of the brewery business, but he engaged a skilled brewmaster named Geiger who did, and proceeded to brew and sell Lieber's Beer. It was a successful venture from the very start. Peter gave his principal attention to sales, at which he became adept. This involved political activity and manipulation of saloon outlets.

"Peter was always involved in politics. He had to be in order to get saloon licenses for his favored customers. Until 1880 he was a staunch Republican, as all the Civil War veterans were. But in that year the Republicans, at the insistence of the Methodist Church, adopted a plank in their platform recommending a restraint upon the beer and liquor trade. It was the first stirring of Prohibition. This outraged Peter and was a threat to his interests. He promptly changed his politics and was thereafter a Democrat—and an aggressive, active one.

"He contributed generously to Grover Cleveland's Campaign Funds, particularly in 1892, when Cleveland was elected President for the second time. He was rewarded by being appointed Consul General of the United States to Düsseldorf in 1893."

Peter Lieber sold his brewery to a British syndicate, which was eager to have Peter's oldest son, my grandfather Albert, run it for them.

Peter returned to Germany in 1893, where he bought a castle on the Rhine near Düsseldorf. He took with him President Cleveland's commission as Consul General of the United States to Düsseldorf. Uncle John says, "He hoisted the Stars and Stripes over his castle, delegated his negligible duties to subordinates, and finished his days in opulence and official grandeur."

His son Albert, who never went to college, stayed in Indianapolis and ran the brewery, and went to London once a year to report to its new owners.

❦

So there—Uncle John has now accounted for four of my great-grandparents, those who brought my mother's maiden name, Lieber, and my father's name, Vonnegut, into this country when there was still much wilderness. Four more great-grandparents and four grandparents and two parents must still be described.

Let me say now that the ancestor who most beguiles me is Clemens Vonnegut, who died by the side of the road.

"Clemens Vonnegut was a cultivated eccentric," says Uncle John. That is what I aspire to be.

"He was small in stature, but stout in his independence and convictions," says Uncle John. "While his forebears had been Roman Catholics, he professed to be an atheist or Free

Thinker." So do I profess. "He would more properly be
called a skeptic, one who rejects faith in the unknowable."
"Skeptic" is also the proper thing to call me.

"But he was a very model of Victorian asceticism, lived
frugally, and eschewed excesses of any kind," says Uncle
John. I try. I don't drink anymore, but I smoke like a house
afire. I am monogamous, but I have married twice.

"He greatly admired Benjamin Franklin, whom he called
an American saint, and named his third son after him instead
of naming him for one of the saints on the Christian calen-
dar." I myself have named my only son after Mark Twain,
another American Saint.

"As a recognition of his service to public education,"
Uncle John goes on, "one of the City's schools was named
after him. He was highly literate, well read, and the author
of various pamphlets expounding his views on education,
philosophy, and religion. He wrote his own funeral oration."

That oration, by the way, appears in Chapter XI. of this
book, the chapter on religion. I read it out loud recently to
my agnostic son, Mark, who is a physician now, but who set
out during his undergraduate years to become a Unitarian
minister.

Mark said this of the oration, grinding his teeth before and
afterward: "The *guts* move." When you read the oration,
and especially if you are a chess player like Mark, you are
bound to admire the guts of Clemens Vonnegut.

Note: I do not have the guts to request that Clemens
Vonnegut's oration be read at my funeral, too.

❀

To return to Uncle John:

"Another one of Kurt Vonnegut, Jr.'s great-grandfathers who attained distinction locally was Henry Schnull, who, with his brother, August, came to Indianapolis from the town of Hausberge in Westphalia about ten years before the Civil War. They had both been apprenticed as Kaufmann, or merchant, in Germany and knew the methods of trade and accounts. They first engaged in the business of buying and selling farm produce in central Indiana. They traveled about in a wagon to the farms in the area; bought grain, butter, eggs, chickens, and salted and smoked pork, and resold these farm products in the city at a profit.

"As they prospered by the hardest kind of work, they enlarged their operation by trucking surpluses to Madison or Jeffersonville, Indiana, on the Ohio River, where the merchandise was loaded on huge barges which were floated down the Ohio and Mississippi rivers to New Orleans. One or the other of the brothers would accompany the shipment and attend to the trading in New Orleans. Here they would sell the produce in a good market and buy coffee, rum and sorghum, which was called 'New Orleans molasses.' These products they then shipped north by barge and sold at a profit in Cincinnati or Indianapolis. They are said to have brought to Indianapolis one of the last shipments from the South before the river was closed by the Confederates at Memphis. The price of sorghum and coffee skyrocketed, and the Schnull Brothers then had sufficient capital to establish a wholesale grocery business and construct a warehouse which still stands on the southeast corner of Washington and Delaware Streets in Indianapolis. The firm was originally a partnership known as A. & H. Schnull, later as Schnull & Company. At the close of the Civil War, August announced that he had enough money and wanted to return to Germany. So he sold his interests to Henry and took two hundred thousand dollars back to Hausberge, where he bought a small Schloss and lived like a gentleman until his death in 1918.

"Henry Schnull elected to remain in the United States. He became one of the leading merchants of Indiana, and was a most highly regarded citizen. In addition to his wholesale grocery business he founded the Eagle Machine Works, which later became the great Atlas Engine Company, which manufactured stationary steam engines and farm implements. He also organized the American Woolen Company, the first textile mill in the State.

"Shortly after passage in 1865 of the law authorizing national banks, he established and was first President of the Merchants National Bank of Indianapolis, which has survived all of the intervening panics and is still operating.

"Henry Schnull was a man of immense industry, courage, and independence; intelligent, self-reliant, and resourceful; incorruptibly honest and reliable in his dealings; and completely dedicated to business and accumulation. He became very rich for his times, endowed his children with generous gifts, and left a fortune in 1905 which has assisted three generations of his progeny to live comfortably. He was so much engaged with his many activities that he was not much of a family man, and his children saw but little of him. His wife, Matilda Schramm, whom he met on one of his early buying visits to her father's farm in 1854, was as stern and tough as Henry, but she had a warm, lovable disposition and was the real matriarch of the family."

ALL right now: Uncle John has now told us about my two sets of great-grandparents on my father's side, Clemens Vonnegut, whose wife was Katarina Blank, and Henry Schnull, whose wife was Matilda Schramm, and one set from my mother's side, the limping Civil War veteran Peter Lieber, whose wife was Sophia de St. André.

This brings me to my fourth set of great-grandparents— the only ones who had anything participatory to do with the arts. They were "Professor" Karl Barus, "the first real professional teacher of voice, violin, and piano in the city," according to Uncle John, and his wife, Alice Möllman.

"Professor Barus was highly respected, and in addition to his function as a private teacher he conducted orchestras, organized choral singing and other musical events. He was well educated and a definite intellectual. He never engaged in trade or business but made a good income by his teaching and lived well. Professor Barus originally settled in Cincinnati in the early fifties, where he was appointed Musical Director of the Cincinnati Sangverein.

"In 1858 Dr. Barus was invited to come to Indianapolis to conduct the mixed chorus of German singing societies from Indianapolis, Louisville, Cincinnati, and Columbus, Ohio, at a great Musical Festival. In 1882 he was invited by Das Deutsche Haus to come to Indianapolis to be musical director of the Maennerchor, in which position he remained until 1896.

"At his last concert in that year at Tomlinson Hall he was given a standing ovation and was presented with a silver laurel wreath as an expression of appreciation of his great contribution to the musical life of the whole community. For the remaining twelve years of his life he gave instruction in piano and voice to selected pupils and was always held in highest esteem. His influence on the musical taste and sophistication of the whole city was incalculable. No one ever seems subsequently to have quite taken his place."

❦

AND Professor Karl Barus the musician, and his wife Alice begat another Alice Barus, who, according to Uncle John, "is said to have been the most beautiful and accomplished young lady in Indianapolis. She played the piano and sang; also composed music, some of which was published."

She was my mother's mother.

Yes, and Peter Lieber, the limping war veteran, and his wife Sophia begat Albert Lieber, who became an Indianapolis brewer and *bon vivant.*

He was my mother's father.

Henry Schnull, the merchant and banker, and his wife Matilda begat Nanette Schnull, who, according to Uncle John, "was a very beautiful woman in her prime, and had a lovely speaking and singing voice. She often sang in public. She laughed readily, enjoyed people, and was greatly admired by a host of friends."

She was my father's mother.

And Clemens Vonnegut, the Free Thinker and founder of the Vonnegut Hardware Company, and his wife Katarina begat Bernard Vonnegut, who, Uncle John says, "was from earliest youth artistic. He could draw and paint with skill. Bernard was extremely modest and retiring. He had no intimates, and took but little part in social activities. He was never a happy, extroverted personality, but was inclined to

348 ■ PALM SUNDAY

be reticent, shy, and somewhat contemptuous of his environment."

He was my father's father.

❧

WE have come now to a rascal, Albert Lieber, whose emotional faithlessness to his children, in my humble opinion, contributed substantially to my mother's eventual suicide. As I have said, he was the son of the limping Civil War Veteran. When his father retired to Düsseldorf, Albert remained in Indianapolis to run the brewery that his father had sold to a British syndicate. He was born in 1863.

When I got to know him, there wasn't much to know. He was in bed all the time with a flabby heart. He might as well have been a Martian. What do I remember about him? His mouth was slackly open. It was very pink inside.

He was often in London on business when he was young. "He had his clothes tailored in Savile Row," says Uncle John, "and was the very model of Victorian sartorial elegance: broadcloth Prince Albert coats, silk hats, Scotch tweeds, starched shirts and collars, and handmade boots. He was handsome, friendly, and highly sociable. He loved parties, good eating, and fine wines. He was always much involved in a series of love affairs, passing feminine attachments, and ribald entertainment.

"The brewery was under the general supervision of a retired British army officer—Colonel Thompson—who visited Indianapolis every year or two to look things over and report back to London. He and Albert between them milked the local operation of most of the profits of the brewery through padded expense accounts, sales promotion schemes, public relations departments, political contributions and other devices to skim the cream off the profits. The syndicate demanded a five percent return upon its investment and got it. Albert and his cohorts lined their pockets.

"In contrast to his father, who was conservative, retiring, and extremely modest and unassuming, Albert was extroverted, flamboyant, sociable, and a big spender. He always lived on a very lavish scale in various large houses with lots of servants, horses, and carriages and then the earliest and finest motor cars. In his heyday he always had an English butler and a footman in livery. He entertained his friends without thought of cost: the choicest viands, rare wines, flowers, the whitest linens, and choicest porcelain chinaware.

"He soon acquired the reputation of a millionaire who counted the cost of nothing. He became a jolly companion of the town's 'fun boys' who consisted of other rich men's sons, among them Booth Tarkington. They gave fabulous parties. One of them owned the English Hotel on Monument Circle and English's Opera House where all the principal traveling shows played. He had a stage box reserved for his use on the right side of the house where he had a door which connected to the stage. This gave him and his cronies access to the stage and easy opportunity to meet actresses and particularly the chorus girls with musical comedies.

"At other times they would take over for the night the leading bagnio of the town—facetiously known as the University Club Annex—which was situated on the east side of

New Jersey Street about two blocks north of Washington Street. No cash changed hands to sully the dignified atmosphere of the Annex. Each month its devotees were billed discreetly for their share of maintenance. Here the local 'fun boys' would stage real bacchanalian orgies which provided choice and juicy gossip for the staid community. But they always committed their indiscretions, with due respect for the Victorian proprieties, in privacy behind doors—which is what doors are for.

"One of their charming folkways was to initiate congenial spirits into what they called their 'W-A Club.' Preceding an elaborate dinner at one of the clubs or hotels, the neophyte would be blindfolded and seated on a cool, fresh keg of Lieber's beer to which a spigot and faucet had been attached. At the turn of the faucet the beer would squirt out and drench the candidate. He was then said to have a wet ass and was qualified to be admitted to their fellowship. They even had a gold button made by a jeweler which could be worn on the coat lapel with the insignia 'W-A.' They were real devotees of sport and always chartered a private Pullman car to take them to championship prizefights, horse races, and other sporting events. They never used drugs or much profanity, and always respected respectable women. They were always suitably attired and were uniformly well-mannered and gentlemanly."

❦

THIS Edwardian sport married the beautiful and musical Alice Barus in 1885. They had three children. My mother was the oldest. And then Alice Barus died of pneumonia when Mother was six.

❦

"SHORTLY thereafter," says Uncle John, "Albert married a very attractive but extremely eccentric woman, who was never accepted by Albert's family or close friends. Her name was Ora D. Lane. She was an accomplished violinist and came from Zanesville, Ohio. She was familiarly known as 'O.D.' but most people referred to her as 'Odious.' She became a sort of storybook stepmother to Albert's children. She chastised and ill-treated them in subtle ways. She seemed to resent them and abused them so that they all suffered a distinctive psychic trauma from which they never fully recovered. Where formerly they had known nothing but loving and tender care, now they were subjected to every sort of indignity, humiliation, and neglect. She terrorized Albert as well, threatened his life, slept with a pistol under her pillow, and was a perfect demon and termagant. Kindly, gentle Albert stood it as long as he could and then divorced her; but he was obliged to settle a large alimony upon her which depleted his capital, which was not large. He had never been an accumulator and had spent freely, relying upon the brewery to carry him as usual with a large annual income.

"But nothing daunted, Albert soon was married a third time to a nondescript widow named Meda Langtry, a Canadian, who had a daughter whom Albert adopted and renamed Alberta.

"Meda was much younger than Albert. In fact she was about the same age as his daughter Edith."

"Shortly after Albert's third and last marriage came Prohibition in 1921," Uncle John goes on, "the brewery was closed. Albert lost his position, and from then on his affairs went from bad to worse until he died in what he would have regarded as relative poverty. The last years of his life were supported by the sale of several parcels of real estate including his former residence, a large house situated on an estate of a hundred acres on a hill overlooking White River and running north to Kessler Boulevard and West Fifty-sixth Street in the City of Indianapolis. This land would now be worth at least a million dollars or more.

"He, like all rich men, had a miscellaneous assortment of personal property which will be acquired not for investment but as adjuncts of abundant privileges such as miscellaneous securities, paintings, porcelains, furniture, and other art objects. Much had to be sold but he had a few securities left and his estate inventory came to $311,607.65. All that his children got out of the Peter Lieber fortune was a small remnant from Albert's estate and a few trust funds which Peter had established for them in Merchants Bank stock. And so the proverbial cycle of 'shirt sleeves to shirt sleeves' was completed in three generations due for them to Prohibition and Albert's extravagance and improvidence.

"But while Albert was still in his prime and riding high, his daughter, Edith—K's mother—was married on November 22, 1913, to Kurt Vonnegut. They were a charming and extremely attractive couple."

❂

As has already been said, my father's mother Nanette was cheerful and sociable, and uninterested in the fine arts save for music—and my father's father Bernard was a freak in the family for being able to draw and paint so well at an early age. He was also unsociable, and evidently unhappy in Indianapolis most of the time.

Uncle John said to me in conversation one time that my grandfather Bernard was probably relieved to die young— "to be well out of it." He died of intestinal cancer at fifty-three, five years younger than I am now. That was in 1908, so he did not see any of his grandchildren. He did not even see his children married.

"Like his brothers," says Uncle John, "he attended the public schools, the German-English school, and then the Indianapolis High School then situated at Pennsylvania and Michigan Streets. Recognizing his talents as an artist, Alexander Metzger, a friend of his father, suggested that Bernard be given a higher education. He was then sent to the Massachusetts Institute of Technology in Boston, where he studied architecture. He later studied in Hannover, Germany, and then worked as draftsman, for a couple of years, with a leading firm in New York.

"Returning to Indianapolis in 1883, he engaged in the practice of architecture, first in his own office and later with Arthur Bohn in what became the well-known firm of Vonnegut & Bohn, whose successors are in practice today. This firm designed and supervised construction of many fine residences and public buildings in Indianapolis, including the first Chamber of Commerce, the Athenaeum, the John Herron Art Museum, the L. S. Ayres store, the Fletcher Trust Building, and many others.

"He read the poems of Heine with delight. He was highly cultivated in the arts, but his sympathies and inclinations were definitely Germanic. He and his family frequently lived abroad, and he sent his two sons to school in Strasbourg abroad, and he sent his two sons to school in Strasbourg when they were quite young. He fathered three children: Kurt, born in 1884; Alex, in 1888; and then Irma, in 1890.

"Aside from his attachment to his profession, Bernard took little participation in the social or civic life of the community. He confined his activities to the arts. His favorite clubs were the Portfolio and the Lyra Casino. The former was composed of painters, sculptors, architects, and writers. It held monthly dinners and discussions, and considered itself to be the custodian of the aesthetic conscience of the community. The Lyra Casino was a society of musicians, and gave private concerts of classical music. Bernard was an active participant in both these organizations, and his son Kurt likewise joined them in his maturity. Bernard's wife, Nanette, had a thorough training in and acquaintance with musical literature, but she did not share her husband's other interests.

"When their children attained an age to enable them to make objective judgment, they agreed that their parents' marriage was not a particularly congenial one. Kurt and Irma definitely identified with their father, while Alex identified with his mother. Unlike his brothers, Bernard was never robust physically. He suffered much with indigestion and headaches."

❦

I, too, identify with this unhappy Bernard, although I am more or less robust and can say, knocking on wood, that I am seldom ill. I sleep well always. My digestion is good.

The family legend is that Bernard Vonnegut when a boy

was working with his brothers in the family hardware store, and he began to weep. He was asked what the trouble was, and he said that he didn't want to work in a store. He said he wanted to be an artist instead.

A child expressing such a wish in such a family in such a town was a troubling mystery.

The legend goes on that he became stagestruck, and wanted to be a theatrical designer, but learned that almost no one could make a living at that—so he became an architect instead.

The legend says that he was happy and productive and even sociable as a young architect here in New York City. But then he was told by his family that it was time for him to come home to Indianapolis, and to marry a woman from a nice German family. He was to surrender to the gravitational pull of the tremendous mass of respectability which his father and mother had amassed in the American wilderness in a little more than thirty years.

He should have disobeyed, if he did not want constant headaches and indigestion. He should have stayed in New York City.

He should have moved into the very house I live in now. This house was standing back then.

In a huge and rich and bustling and polyglot world city like this one, he surely found many friends as gifted as himself. So he must have made all sorts of jokes here about giftedness, made romantic speeches about the pain of bringing new works of art into the world, and on and on. There was a knowing audience here for talk like that.

When he got back to Indianapolis, where the practice of the arts was regarded as an evasion of real life by means of parlor tricks, the things that made him happy or sad were equally meaningless to his relatives and neighbors. So, yes, he became as silent as a clam. He died.

Wasn't it true that his wife was also gifted, that she sang beautifully? Yes, but she was not interested in creating any new music. She was a sort of frontier phonograph, reproducing melodies from the Old World, where creative artists belonged, where they were needed, where they were supposed to be.

❦

HE may even have been a genius, as mutations sometimes are.

❦

AND it is always the men, even if they were as reclusive and secretive and unfond of life as my grandfather Bernard, who are the stars in this account of my ancestors. There are reasons for this. "It is regrettable that so little is known of K's two grandmothers and four great-grandmothers," says Uncle John. "Practically everyone who knew any of them intimately is now dead. The Victorian age in which they lived was a man's world. Women's place was in the home, and no public notice was taken of them. They left no records of their own, and were expected to bask in obscurity in the reflected glory of their husbands' achievements—the most admired of which was the accumulation of money.

"But they bore the children, which was one thing the men could not do. They ran the households admirably, and provided their progeny with all their training in manners and morals which they received.

"The men were so much engaged in the struggle for material success that they gave but scant attention to their families. How they found time to father their children is conjectural. But in defense of the men it should be noted that they were emotionally and psychologically motivated to assert their own importance in a new environment: to achieve and to demonstrate their worth as individuals. Success was principally equated with money. To be rich was to be respected.

"The immigrants had been literally starved—materially and socially—in the nineteenth century of Western Europe. When they came here and found the rich table of the Midwest, they gorged themselves. And who can blame them? In the process they created an Empire by the hardest work and exercise of their inherent and varied talents. The men took the credit, but their womenfolk, if unnoticed, helped lay the foundation."

❦

LET Uncle John now run out his story of my family without further interruptions from me. There remain only a father and a mother to be described.

"K's father—Kurt, the eldest son of Bernard and Nannie —was very much like his father in outlook and pattern of behavior, but dissimilar in appearance. Bernard was dark complected, wore a beard, and was rather bald. Kurt was blue-eyed, and very fair complected, with finely modeled features, long thin fingers, and blond curly hair. He was a sort of Adonis and extremely handsome, without any trace of effeminacy. He was, like his father, artistic. He could draw and paint. He worked in ceramics, and created some beautiful objects in that technique. And, of course, he was a fine, sensitive architect.

"Kurt Vonnegut attended School No. 10, a grammar school, from 1890 to 1898. He then attended Shortridge High School in Indianapolis for somewhat over a year. He was subsequently sent to the American College in Strasbourg, Germany, for three years. This was a small private school under the direction of Professor Goss, who organized it as a school principally for American boys on the model of the German Gymnasia. It was a good school, with rigid standards and discipline. In this school Kurt was steeped in the German language and in German cultural patterns. Strasbourg had its own opera and symphony orchestra. Kurt was naturally devoted to music throughout his life, and in his formative years at this school became intimately acquainted with the whole classical repertoire.

"At the age of nineteen he was well prepared in a solid foundation of secondary education, and was admitted to the Massachusetts Institute of Technology, where he studied architecture and took his degree of Bachelor of Science in 1908—the year in which his father died. He then went with his widowed mother and his sister, Irma, to Berlin, and continued his architectural studies with the best masters. He returned to Indianapolis in 1910, and joined his father's surviving partner, Arthur Bohn, in the well-established firm of Vonnegut & Bohn. He was thus launched upon what promised to be a comfortable and successful career. His family had a prominent position in the community. They had plenty of money.

"Kurt was handsome in appearance, with charming manners, and although dignified and reserved, soon had many friends who remained devoted to him. He joined the University Club, then situated at Meridian and Michigan Streets, which was the most exclusive men's club in the City. He was received and accepted by the best families as a most eligible bachelor. He was generally approved by doting mamas looking for suitable mates for their daughters, and had the pick of the crop of debutantes. After a couple of years of a happy and carefree existence, Kurt began to court Edith Lieber, who was four years his junior and had likewise returned to an active social life after attending Miss Shipley's School at Bryn Mawr and traveling much abroad. Her father, Albert Lieber, was then in the full tide of success as one of the town's rich men. He resided on a beautiful estate of some hundred acres just to the northwest of the city, in a large residence which he had recently constructed."

❦

"EDITH was a very beautiful woman, tall and statuesque. Kurt always admired her beauty and was very proud of her. They fell in love, became engaged, and were married on November 22, 1913. They remained a devoted couple until the day of Edith's death thirty-one years later. The marriage was approved by both families; but the Schnull-Vonnegut clan was slightly condescending. In the pecking order in the social hierarchy of the community, and particularly in the German group it was generally understood that the Schnull-Vonnegut clan ranked ahead of the Lieber-Barus clan.

"Edith was a rather tall woman, about five feet eight inches, with a fine graceful figure. She was auburn-haired, not quite red, with a very fair, clear skin, finely modeled features, and blue-green eyes. She was stately and dignified in bearing. She had a lively sense of humor and laughed easily. Her adolescent years had been difficult with her odious stepmother, but she was strong enough in spirit and courage to endure her ordeal, although the scars were there.

"Prior to her engagement and marriage to Kurt, Edith had been engaged to other men but had each time broken her engagement. These suitors were all Europeans; for in the years from 1907 to 1913 Edith lived mostly abroad. As an extremely handsome woman and the daughter of an American millionaire she was much courted.

"She first became engaged to Kenneth Doulton, an Englishman, a grandson of Sir Henry Doulton, and a scion of the family which for generations had owned the world-famous Royal Doulton Porcelain Works in Lambeth. She met him while visiting the Thompsons for the London season of 1908 in the waning days of the Edwardian twilight of elegance and sophistication when the rich could still enjoy their privileges. Doulton was an attractive member of the upper-middle class with connections in the aristocracy. He was a charming idler and of course expected Albert to supply a suitable settlement as a dowry upon his lovely daughter. Albert enjoyed a large income at that time but was not enthusiastic to part with his modest capital. And Doulton was not about to go in the brewery business in Indianapolis. He wanted to marry Edith, have her father buy them a country place and a little house in Mayfair, and remain in old England. Edith demurred and the engagement was broken.

"In the First World War Doulton as a junior officer in a Guard's regiment lost his life while serving in the first British Expeditionary Force in the first months of the war.

"Edith then forsook merrie England and shifted her European base of operations from London to Düsseldorf. From 1909 to 1913 she spent most of each year staying with her grandfather, Peter, then past eighty, and her maiden aunt Laura, in the old man's Schloss on the Rhine. He was no longer Consul General of the United States but he kept the Stars and Stripes flying over his palace and retained his American citizenship to the end. But his three children, Laura, Emily, and Rudolph, became German citizens. Rudolph adopted a military career, went through the Cadet School and became Lieutenant Colonel of a regiment of cavalry—the Uhlans—garrisoned in the area of Düsseldorf. Emily married a German army officer. Edith was thus thrown into the company of subalterns in her uncle's famous regiment. At that time the Kaiser's army officers constituted a sort of elite social group with many privileges and much prestige. The Kaiser's pay and allowances to his officers were extremely meager. If an officer did not have substantial means to supplement his pay and maintain the position required of him, he was expected to marry a rich wife. In fact, he could not marry except with the consent of the colonel of his regiment; and the consent was withheld until the social position, reputability, and dowry of the bride were officially approved.

"Edith's first serious German suitor was Lieutenant Paul Genth of the Uhlans. She gave him the go-by after a brief courtship. Shortly afterward Captain Otto Voigt of the regiment proposed to her, and after a spirited courtship was accepted by her with the consent of her family and of his commanding officer. The Captain was a dashing figure in his colorful dress uniform with shako and 'Merry Widow' accoutrements.

"But here again the course of true love did not run true and smooth. There were difficulties about the dowry, and the prospect for Edith of a career as an army wife in the highly artificial and regulated life of the imperial army palled upon her. Captain Voigt was one of those heel-clicking Prussian-type officers who looked good in his uniform in command of his squadron of cavalry but was quite different from the easygoing, indulgent, and deferential American husbands of Edith's experience. She wavered. But Albert gave her carte blanche to buy a trousseau and she proceeded to do so. All of the linens were duly embroidered 'L-V.' The Liebers of the German branch thought it was a great match."

❂

"BUT Edith began to have misgivings. So did Albert, who never liked dowries anyway. And Edith did not want to make her permanent home in Germany. The captain was likewise not an enthusiastic candidate for a job in the brewery. At all events, the engagement was broken by mutual consent and Edith returned to Indianapolis where her father built for her a small cottage on his estate very attractively situated on a bluff overlooking White River. It was furnished to her taste; had a grand piano in the living room, a fireplace, comfortable lounge chairs and couches; and it was her own retreat when she wanted privacy—which was most of the time. But she got along well enough with her father and his third wife Meda and their two young children. She resumed contact with her old friends, went about in the social life of the city, and had plenty of suitors. Kurt Vonnegut, Sr., fell deeply in love with her and she reciprocated his affection. In every respect the match was universally approved.

"Edith and Kurt's wedding celebration was one long remembered in Indianapolis. It was probably the biggest and most costly party which the town had ever seen or is likely ever to witness again. The couple were married by the Reverend Frank S. C. Wicks, a Unitarian clergyman, in an evening ceremony in the First Unitarian Church attended by members of the two families—Lieber and Vonnegut—and a bevy of lovely bridesmaids and handsome ushers. But these families in three generations were then numerous and both clans had many friends. The Liebers and the Vonneguts with the Hollwegs, Mayers, Savereins, Schnulls, Rauchs, Frenzels, Pantzers, Haueisens, Kipps, Kuhns, Metzgers, and Kothes were the leading German families of the city. They were all convivial people, sentimental and emotional. And they loved to celebrate weddings, particularly between congenial clans of a common heritage and cultural background. The nuptials qualified to be celebrated in accordance with the best German traditions: food, drink, dancing, music, and song. Albert decided to give them a party to end all parties.

"In 1913 the Claypool Hotel, situated on the northwest corner of Washington Street and Illinois Street in the very heart of the city of Indianapolis, was one of the finest hostelries in the Midwest. It has just been completed about ten years before and was in prime condition. Eight stories high, it contained five hundred bedrooms. Its main lobby was 80 feet square and 60 feet high, elaborately decorated in the fashion of the time. The mezzanine story had a huge ballroom about 125 feet by 80 feet. This later was named the Riley Room after the Hoosier poet—James Whitcomb Riley. On the Illinois Street side of the mezzanine floor were a series of private dining rooms decorated in red and gold in Louis XV rococo. The proprietor of this garish caravansary was

Henry Lawrence. He and Albert Lieber were buddies. And so Albert decided to throw the wedding celebration party for Edith and Kurt in the Claypool. Henry Lawrence decided to give his all—and did so.

"In addition to the numerous relatives of the Lieber-Vonnegut clans Albert had a host of friends, a rigid selection of whom had to be invited. About six hundred of them came, including Colonel Thompson who journeyed from London to represent the English syndicate. The men guests were arrayed in white tie and tails, the women in long elaborate ball gowns. The chefs of the hotel were put to work days ahead and a large buffet of choice viands was served. Champagne of rarest vintages flowed like water. Then the floor was cleared and a large band of musicians played for dancing in the ballroom.

"A bar some sixty feet long had been specially erected. Here every variety of beverage was provided. The party lasted through the night and until six o'clock in the morning. Never before or since have so many otherwise respectable and thoroughly conservative citizens of the dull community passed out in so short a time. The consumption of spirits after the preliminary foundation of champagne was like pouring gasoline on a hot fire. It was estimated later that about seventy-five men and ten or fifteen women passed out cold. But Henry Lawrence was ready for the occasion. He had reserved plenty of bedrooms above and, as guests wavered and lost the coordination required for locomotion, they were gently assisted by the hotel waiters and bellmen to comfortable beds and the arms of Morpheus where a few of them were still reposing three days later.

"It was a grand occasion, but the Vonneguts and Schnulls thought it was all rather vulgar, and did not hesitate to express their disapproval. Some of the town wags, who were familiar with Albert's ways, in commenting on the huge cost of the bash said: 'What the Hell! Albert probably charged the tab to the brewery, and let the syndicate unwittingly give the party.' It was a strictly *fin de siècle* affair.

"The next year came the First World War and then Prohibition. The curtain fell on a glorious scene—never to be witnessed again."

❦

"Kurt and Edith's marriage was a happy and congenial one —as marriages go. At first they were reasonably affluent— had servants, governesses for their children, and lived well. But they were both inclined to be extravagant. They traveled and entertained rather lavishly. If they needed money, they sold securities or borrowed. After Prohibition in 1921 Albert was no longer able to help them.

"But they had enough economic fat which, with Kurt's income from his profession, saw them through the twenties. Kurt's mother, Nannie Schnull Vonnegut, died in 1929 and left Kurt his share of her then modest fortune derived from her father, Henry Schnull. They soon used this up. Kurt had acquired a plot of land on the east side of North Illinois Street at about Forty-fifth Street. Here he designed and built a large and very beautiful brick residence. They sent their older children in the twenties and thirties to private schools; Bernard to Park School, and Alice to Tudor Hall School for girls. Bernard went on to the Massachusetts Institute of Technology where he took his degree of Bachelor of Science and remained to take his Ph.D. degree in Chemistry. He became and remains a distinguished scientist. Alice married

James Adams. But by the time K came along to his adolescence, the family was in financial trouble. He knew only the hard times of the 1930s. He was taken out of private school after the third grade, and sent to Public School No. 43 and then Shortridge High School. He was sent to Cornell University with specific instructions not to waste time or money on 'frivolous' courses, but to give full attention to practical studies, principally physics and chemistry and math.

"His parents were in straitened circumstances. There was practically no building in the Depression years and Kurt's professional income vanished. They began to live on their capital which, to a good bourgeois, is a heresy looked upon with horror and usually followed by disaster.

"It was obvious to them that they could not continue to support so large an establishment. This residence, by then heavily mortgaged, was sold. It still stands and is now the home of Evans Woollen III, a descendent of a well-known family and a distinguished architect in his own right. With the proceeds of their equity in this property and a few remaining assets, Kurt and Edith then purchased an attractive plot of land in William's Creek—a suburban development lying about nine miles due north of Monument Circle, to which many of the leading families migrated to escape the deteriorating conditions of the inner city. Here Kurt designed and built in 1941 a somewhat smaller and less pretentious dwelling, but it was well constructed of brick. It was surrounded by tall virginal forest trees—oaks, maples, and elms. It was a most attractive home, was well furnished, and displayed Kurt's artistic skills. In the basement Kurt had a small shop where he installed a kiln and dabbled in ceramics in which he produced some beautiful pieces. Here the family lived quietly and modestly with but little entertaining or traveling.

"They continued to invade their diminishing capital. But Kurt had two $1,000 corporate bonds which he had inherited from his mother. Edith, true to her delusions to grandeur, said: 'Let's take one more trip abroad.' So they sold the two bonds, went to Paris for three weeks and returned broke. But it was a rare example of *ésprit*—what the French call *panache*. It was going out with flair—all banners flying.

"Meanwhile came the Second World War in December 1941 and once again America was arrayed against Germany. Bernard at twenty-four escaped the draft, but Kurt, Jr., at nineteen was caught. He was enlisted in the army as a private and sent to training camp. This came as a great shock with acute distress to Edith. With her other financial problems the prospect of losing her son in the impending holocaust made her cup of troubles overflow. She became despondent and morose. Wanting money desperately, she attempted to write short stories which she could sell, but it was a futile, hopeless venture; a tragic disillusion. She simply could not see daylight. Kurt, Jr., got leave from his regiment to come home and spend Mother's Day in May 1944 with his family. During the night before, Edith died in her sleep in her fifty-sixth year on May 14, 1944. Her death was attributed to an overdose of sleeping tablets taken possibly by mistake. Her gross estate was inventoried in probate at $10,815.50. It was all that was left as her share of her grandfather's fortune and of her father's residue.

"She missed by a matter of two months the birth of her first grandchild, the son of her daughter Alice. She would miss seeing twelve grandchildren in all. She missed by seven months the capture of her son K by the Germans in the Battle of the Bulge, and his imprisonment in Dresden until the end of the war."

❦

"AFTER Edith's death Kurt lived almost as a recluse, for some ten years. But his sister, Irma Vonnegut Lindener, who was then a resident of Hamburg, Germany, paid him protracted visits—sometimes for months at a time. They were very congenial and deeply attached to each other. She understood his vagaries, respected his privacy and fierce independence, and gave him the only sort of companionship which he would tolerate. They resembled each other in many ways and were deeply empathetic. They were both blond and blue-eyed. They both spoke German fluently and shared their attachment to their German traditions of music and literature. Kurt acquired a sort of skeptical and fatalistic contempt for life—what the Germans call Weltschmerz.

"As Kurt aged and his fortunes waned, he could not continue to support this last abode of modest elegance. He sold it, and with the pittance left to him, some ten thousand dollars, Kurt then bought a small cottage in the country on a little hill on a winding road just north of Nashville, in Brown County, about twenty-five miles south of Indianapolis. Brown County is still a bucolic community but it has some of the highest hills and loveliest scenery in the Midwest. It is the abode of preference of artists. Here Kurt retired alone and lived in perfect seclusion. He had his books and the phonograph which his sister gave him and upon which he played his favorite recordings of classical music: principally Mozart, Beethoven, Wagner, Brahms, and particularly Richard Strauss. The four last songs of Strauss were his favorites. He played them over and over. They express his mood perfectly."

❦

"ALTHOUGH he suffered from emphysema, Kurt continued to smoke cigarettes heavily and drank whiskey in moderation. His health deteriorated slowly until it was found that he had a cancer in one of the lobes of his lungs. The surgeons wanted to operate but he wisely declined. As the cancer spread, he became extremely weak and short of breath with lack of oxygen. But he refused to go into a hospital or to remain in bed at home. He would get up in the morning, dress, eat very sparingly, and then lie about on a couch before a comfortable fire reading or listening to his records, quite alone. He had no nurses, was completely self-reliant, and never complained or feared death. Toward the end a faithful devoted old servant—Nelly—came down to look after him. Just before the end he had a trained nurse in attendance as he became bedfast. He died quietly in his sleep on October 1, 1957—quite alone. Two days later his remains were buried in the Vonnegut lot in Crown Hill Cemetery next to his wife Edith and his parents, Bernard and Nanette."

❦

THERE ends my Uncle John's essay, save for a grandiloquent coda not entirely in keeping with the facts. I have left a lot out, but nothing which has a direct bearing on what I myself have become. It is copyrighted.

The owner of the copyright is Uncle John's grandson, my

second cousin once-removed, William Rauch. He works here in New York now for Mayor Edward Koch. See how we disperse and disperse?

❧

WAS I a sad child, knowing how rich my family had been? Not at all. We were at least as well off as most of the people I went to public school with, and I would have lost all my friends if we had started having servants again, and worn expensive clothes again, and ridden on ocean liners and visited German relatives in a real castle, and on and on. Mother, who was half-cracked, used to speak of the time when I would resume my proper place in society when the Great Depression ended, would swim with members of other leading families at the Indianapolis Athletic Club, would play tennis and golf with them at the Woodstock Golf and Country Club. She could not understand that to give up my friends at Public School No. 43, "the James Whitcomb Riley school," by the way, would be for me to give up *everything*.

I still feel uneasy about prosperity and associating with members of my parents' class on that account.

Henry David Thoreau said, "I have traveled extensively in Concord." That quotation was probably first brought to my attention by one of my magnificent teachers in high school. Thoreau, I now feel, wrote in the voice of a child, as do I. And what he said about Concord is what every child feels, what every child seemingly *must* feel, about the place where he or she was born. There is surely more than enough to marvel at for a lifetime, no matter where the child is born.

Castles? Indianapolis was full of them.

❦

ONE of my brother Bernard's favorite stories is about the farmer who decides to go to have a look at St. Louis, the nearest city. This would be in 1900, say. When he comes back to his farm after a week, he is gaga about all the human activities and machinery he has seen.

When he is questioned about this famous landmark or that one in St. Louis, it turns out that he knows nothing about them. He makes this confession: "Actually, I never got past the depot."

❦

MY father had few gifts for getting along famously with me. That's life. We did not spend much time together, and conversations were arch and distant. But Father's younger brother, Uncle Alex, a Harvard graduate and life insurance salesman, was responsive and amusing and generous with me, was my ideal grown-up friend.

He was also then a socialist, and among the books he gave me, when I was a high school sophomore, was Thorstein Veblen's *Theory of the Leisure Class.* I understood it perfectly and loved it, since it made low comedy of the empty graces and aggressively useless possessions which my parents, and especially my mother, meant to regain someday.

❦

IT will be noted that my mother attempted to be what I have in fact become—which is a professional writer.

It used to be a fairly reliable rule of American middle-class life that a son could be expected to try hard, with his own life, to make some of his disappointed mother's dreams come true.

This may no longer be the case. Things change.

🟡

UNCLE John's coda to the history of my family is this:

"In reviewing K's ancestors for four generations it is highly significant that there was not a weakling, nor even a mildly psychotic or neurotic individual in the lot. Taken together they provided K with a rich bank of genes upon which to draw. How this genetic background was influenced by K's adolescent conditioning is for him to say. But with respect to his ancestors who came to America from their homeland, let him observe the counsel of the poet Goethe:

'WAS DU ERERBET VON DEINEN VATERN HAST, ERWIRB ES; UM EST ZU BESITZEN.'

"WE WILL LET HIM TELL HIS OWN STORY."

The German quotation means this, and I take it seriously: "Whatever it is that you have inherited from your father, you are going to have to earn it if it is to *really* belong to you."

III

WHEN I
LOST MY
INNOCENCE

*a*ND my story seems to be this to me:
I left Indianapolis, where my ancestors had prepared so many comforts and privileges for me, because those comforts and privileges were finally based on money, and the money was gone.

I might have stayed if I had done what my father had done, which was to marry one of the richest women in town. But I married a poor one instead. I might have stayed if my father had not told me this: be anything but an architect. He and my older brother, who had become a chemist, urged me to study chemistry instead. I would have liked to be an architect, and an architect in Indianapolis at that. I would have become a third-generation Indianapolis architect. There can't be very many of those around.

But Father was so full of anger and sorrow about having had no work as an architect during the Great Depression that he persuaded me that I, too, would be that unhappy if I studied architecture.

❦

So I entered Cornell University in 1940 as a chemistry student. I had in high school been an editor of *The Shortridge Daily Echo,* one of two high school dailies in the country at the time, so I also qualified easily for the staff of *The Cornell Daily Sun.*

The children now running the *Sun* invited me to speak at their annual banquet in Ithaca, New York, on May 3, 1980. The *Sun,* by the way, a corporation entirely separate from the university, will be one hundred years old when this book is published—in 1981.

This doddering alumnus, who drinks no more, had this to say above the rattling of the ice cubes:

"Good evening, fellow Americans.

"You should have invited a more sentimental speaker, I think. This is surely a sentimental occasion, and I am sentimental about faithful dogs sometimes, but that is as far as it goes.

"The most distinguished living writer who was also a *Sun* man is, of course, Elwyn Brooks White of the class of 1921. He will be eighty-one on July eleventh of this year. You might want to send him a card. His mind is as clear as a bell, and he is not only sentimental about dogs but about Cornell.

"I myself liked only two things about this place: the *Sun* and the horse-drawn artillery. Yes—there was horse-drawn artillery here in my time. I suppose I should tell you how old I am, too. I will be fifty-eight in November of this year. You might want to send me a card, too. We never hooked up the horses to caissons, because we knew that was no way to frighten Hitler. So we just put saddles on the horses, and pretended we were at war with Indians, and rode around all afternoon.

"It was not Cornell's fault that I did not like this place much, in case some alumni secretary or chaplain is about to burst into tears. It was my father's fault. He said I should become a chemist like my brother, and not waste my time and his money on subjects he considered so much junk jewelry—literature, history, philosophy. I had no talent for science. What was infinitely worse: all my fraternity brothers were engineers.

"I probably would have adored this hellhole, if I had been allowed to study and discuss the finer things in life. Also: I would not have become a writer.

"I eventually wound up on academic probation. I was accelerating my course at the time—because of the war. My instructor in organic chemistry was my lab partner in biochemistry. He was fit to be tied.

"And one day I came down with pneumonia. It is such a dreamy disease. Pneumonia used to be called 'the old people's friend.' It can be a young person's friend, too. All that you feel is that you are sleepy and that it is time to go. I did not die, so far as I know—but I left Cornell, and I've never come back until now.

"Good evening, fellow Cornellians. I am here to congratulate *The Cornell Daily Sun* on its one-hundredth anniversary. To place this event in historical perspective: the *Sun* is now forty years younger than the saxophone, and sixty years older than the electric guitar.

"It was a family to me—one that included women. Once a week we allowed coeds to put together a woman's page, but I never got to know any of them. They always seemed so burned up about something. I never did find out what it was. It must have been something over at the sorority house.

"I pity you *Sun* people of today for not having truly great leaders to write about—Roosevelt and Churchill and Chiang Kai-shek and Stalin on the side of virtue, and Hitler and Mussolini and Emperor Hirohito on the side of sin.

"Oh, sure, we have another world war coming, and another great depression, but where are the leaders this time? All you have is a lot of ordinary people standing around with their thumbs up their ass.

"Here is what we must do, if glamour is to be restored to those who lead us into catastrophes, out of catastrophes, and then back into catastrophes again: We must outlaw television and set an example for our children by worshiping the silver screens in motion picture palaces every week.

"We should see moving and talking images of leaders only once a week in newsreels. This is the only way we can get leaders all balled up in our heads with movie stars again.

"When I was a freshman here, I didn't know or care where the life of Ginger Rogers ended and the life of General Douglas MacArthur began. The senior senator from California was Mickey Mouse, who would serve with great distinction as a bombardier in the Pacific during the Second World War. Commander Mouse dropped a bomb right down the smokestack of a Japanese battleship. The captain of the battleship was Charlie Chan. Boy, was he mad.

"What a shame that there are so many young people here

who never saw J. Edgar Hoover on the silver screen. This was a man fourteen feet high who could not be bribed. Imagine a man who loved this country so much that he could not be bribed, except for some minor carpentry on his house. You can't adore such integrity without the magic of the silver screen.

"Was the *Sun* any good when I was here? I don't know, and I am afraid to find out. I remember I spelled the first name of Ethel Barrymore 'E-T-H-Y-L' one time—in a headline.

"In preparation for this event, I had lunch last week with the best editor in chief I worked under here. That was Miller Harris, who is one year older than I am. I would sure hate to be as old as he is. I wouldn't mind being as old as E. B. White, if I could actually be E. B. White. Miller Harris is president of the Eagle Shirtmakers now. I ordered a shirt from him one time, and he sent me a bill for one one-hundred-forty-fourth of a gross.

"He said at lunch that the *Sun* in our day was without question the finest student paper in the United States of America. It would be nice if that were true. Eagle shirts, I know, are the greatest shirts in the world.

"I was shattered, I remember, during my sophomore year here, when a world traveler said that Cornell was the forty-ninth greatest university in the world. I had hoped we would at least be in the high teens somewhere. Little did I realize that going to an only marginally great university would also make me a writer.

"That is how you get to be a writer, incidentally: you feel somehow marginal, somehow slightly off-balance all the time. I spent an awful lot of time here buying gray flannel. I never could find the right shade.

"I finally gave up on gray flannel entirely, and went to the University of Chicago, the forty-eighth greatest university in the world.

"Do I know Thomas Pynchon? No. Did I know Vladimir Nabokov? No. I know and knew Miller Harris, the president of Eagle Shirtmakers.

"Well—I am more sentimental about this occasion than I have so far indicated. We chemists can be as sentimental as anybody. Our emotional lives, probably because of the A-bomb and the H-bomb, and the way we spell 'Ethel,' have been much maligned.

"I found a family here at the *Sun,* or I no doubt would have invited pneumonia into my thorax during my freshman year. Those of you who have been kind enough to read a book of mine, any book of mine, will know of my admiration for large families, whether real or artificial, as the primary supporters of mental health.

"And it is surely curious that I, as an outspoken enemy of the disease called loneliness, should now remember as my happiest times in Ithaca the hours when I was most alone.

"I was happiest here when I was all alone—and it was very late at night, and I was walking up the hill after having helped to put the *Sun* to bed.

"All the other university people, teachers and students alike, were asleep. They had been playing games all day long with what was known about real life. They had been repeating famous arguments and experiments, and asking one another the sorts of hard questions real life would be asking by and by.

"We on the *Sun* were already in the midst of real life. By God, if we weren't! We had just designed and written and caused to be manufactured yet another morning newspaper for a highly intelligent American community of respectable size—yes, and not during the Harding administration, either, but during 1940, '41, and '42, with the Great Depression ending, and with World War Two well begun.

"I am an agnostic as some of you may have gleaned from my writings. But I have to tell you that, as I trudged up the hill so late at night and all alone, I knew that God Almighty approved of me."

❦

I make my living as a writer in New York City, the capital of the world, and am, so far as I know, now the only person from Indianapolis who is a member of the American Academy and Institute of Arts and Letters. Until last year, there were two of us. The other one was Janet Flanner, who, writing under the name of "Genêt," was *The New Yorker*'s Paris correspondent for thirty years or more. I got to know her some in recent years, and once wrote in a book I gave her, "Indianapolis needs you!"

She read that, and she said to me, "How little you know."

She used to know my father, too, when she was a young woman—before she lit out for the sunrise and never went home again. Her family in Indianapolis was best known for the mortuaries some of its members ran.

Janet Flanner was the most deft and charming literary stylist Indianapolis has so far produced, and the one who came closest to being a planetary citizen, too. She was not a local writer. Neither was she, like another Hoosier writer, Ernie Pyle, a globe-trotting rube.

So when she died here in New York, I wanted to make sure that her native city knew about it. I telephoned the city desk of *The Indianapolis Star,* a morning paper being put to bed. Nobody in the city room had ever heard of her. Neither was anybody much interested when I told of all she had done.

But then I found a way to excite them, to get them to run a front page obituary, which was a rewrite of the obituary that had appeared in that morning's *New York Times.*

What did the trick? I told them that she was somehow related to the people who ran the funeral homes.

❦

I myself will get an obituary in an Indianapolis paper when I die because I am related to people who used to own a chain of hardware stores. The chain was wrecked by discount stores after the Second World War. It had a manufacturing division, which made door hardware, and that was bought by a conglomerate. It beat the mortuary business, at any rate.

I used to work in the main store of the Vonnegut Hardware Company in the summertime, when I was high school age. I ran a freight elevator. I made up packages in the shipping room, and so on. I liked what we sold. It was all so honest and practical.

And I discovered only the other day how sentimental I still was about the hardware business—when I was asked by one Gunilla Boëthius of *Aftonbladet,* a Swedish newspaper, to write for one thousand crowns a short essay on this subject: "When I Lost My Innocence."

On May 9, 1980, I wrote this letter:

Dear Gunilla Boëthius—

I thank you for your letter of April 25, received by me only this morning.

An enthusiasm for technological cures for almost all forms of human discontent was the only religion of my family during the Great Depression, when I first got to know that family well. It was religion enough for me, and one branch of the family owned the largest hardware store in Indianapolis, Indiana. I still do not believe that I was wrong to adore the cunning devices and compounds on sale there, and when I feel most lost in this world, I comfort myself by visiting a hardware store. I meditate there. I do not buy anything. A hammer is still my Jesus, and my Virgin Mary is still a cross-cut saw.

But I learned how vile that religion of mine could be when the atomic bomb was dropped on Hiroshima. The date of that event can be found in almost any good reference book. How profound had my innocence been? Only six months before, as a captured American foot soldier, I had been in Dresden when it was burned to the ground by a purposely set firestorm. I was still innocent after that. Why? Because the technology which created that firestorm was so familiar to me. I understood it entirely, and so had no trouble imagining how the same amount of ingenuity and determination could benefit mankind once the war was over. I could even help. There was nothing in the bombs or the airplanes, after all, which could not, essentially, be bought at a small hardware store.

As for fire: Everybody knows what you do with unwanted fire. You put water on it.

But the bombing of Hiroshima compelled me to see that a trust in technology, like all the other great religions of the world, had to do with the human soul. I will bet you the one thousand crowns you have offered me for this piece that every one of the tales of lost innocence you receive will embody not only the startling discovery of the human soul, but of how diseased it can be.

How sick was the soul revealed by the flash at Hiroshima? And I deny that it was a specifically American soul. It was the soul of every highly industrialized nation on earth, whether at war or at peace. How sick was it? It was so sick that it did not want to live anymore. What other sort of soul would create a new physics based on nightmares, would place into the hands of mere politicians a planet so "destabilized," to borrow a CIA term, that the briefest fit of stupidity could easily guarantee the end of the world?

It is supposed to be good to lose one's innocence. I do not read them, but I think that is what my novels say, so it must be true. I, for one, now know what is *really* going on, so I can plan more shrewdly and be less open to surprise. But my morale has been lowered a good deal, so I am probably not any stronger than I used to be. Since Hiroshima, I have increased my amperes but decreased my volts, and wound up with the same number of watts, so to speak.

It is quite awful, really, to realize that perhaps most of the people around me find lives in the service of machines so tedious and exasperating that they would not mind much, even if they have children, if life were turned off like a light switch at any time. How many of your readers will deny that the movie *Dr. Strangelove* was so popular because its ending was such a happy one?

❂

I am invited to all sorts of neo-Luddite gatherings, of course, and am sometimes asked to speak. I had this to say between rock and roll numbers at an antinuke rally in Washington, D.C., on May 6, 1979:

"I am embarrassed. We are all embarrassed. We Americans have guided our destinies so clumsily, with all the world watching, that we must now protect ourselves against our own government and our own industries.

"Not to do so would be suicide. We have discovered a brand-new method for committing suicide—family style, Reverend Jim Jones style, and by the millions. What is the method? To say nothing and do nothing about what some of our businessmen and military men are doing with the most unstable substances and the most persistent poisons to be found anywhere in the universe.

"The people who play with such chemicals are so *dumb!*

"They are also vicious. How vicious it is of them to tell us as little as possible about the hideousness of nuclear weapons and power plants!

"And, among all the dumb and vicious people, who jeopardizes all life on earth with hearts so light? I suggest to you that it is those who will lie for the nuclear industries, or who will teach their executives how to lie convincingly —*for a fee.* I speak of certain lawyers and communicators, and *all* public relations experts. The so-called profession of public relations, an American invention, stands entirely disgraced today.

"The lies we have been fed about nuclear energy have been as cunningly handcrafted as the masterpieces of Benvenuto Cellini. They have been a damned sight better built, I must say, than the atomic energy plants themselves.

"I say to you that the makers of such lies are filthy little monkeys. I hate them. They may think they are cute. They are not cute. They stink. If we let them, they will kill everything on this lovely blue-green planet with their rebuttals to what we say here today—with their vicious, stupid lies."

10

TRIAGE

I was educated some in chemistry, and in biology and physics, too, at Cornell University. I did badly, and I soon forgot all they tried to teach me. The Army sent me to Carnegie Tech and the University of Tennessee to study mechanical engineering—thermodynamics, mechanics, the actual use of machine tools, and so on. I did badly again. I am very used to failure, to being at the bottom of every class.

An Indianapolis cousin of mine, who was also a high school classmate, did very badly at the University of Michigan while I did badly at Cornell. His father asked him what the trouble was, and he made what I consider an admirable reply: "Don't you know, Father? I'm dumb!" It was the truth.

I did badly in the Army, remaining a preposterously tall private for the three years I served. I was a good soldier, an especially deadly marksman, but nobody thought to promote me. I learned all the dances of close-order drill. Nobody in the Army could dance better than I could in ranks. If a third world war comes, I am still spry enough to dance again.

❧

YES, and I was a mediocrity in the anthropology department of the University of Chicago after the Second World War. Triage was practiced there as it is practiced everywhere. There were those students who would surely be anthropologists, and the most winsome faculty members gave them intensive care. A second group of students, in the opinion of the faculty, just might become so-so anthropologists, but more probably, would use what they had learned about *Homo sapiens* to good advantage in some other field, such as medicine or law, say.

The third group, of which I was a member, might as well have been dead—or studying chemistry. We were given as a thesis advisor the least popular faculty member, untenured and justifiably paranoid. His position paralleled that of the waiter Mespoulets in the stories of Ludwig Bemelmans about the fictitious Hotel Splendid. Mespoulets had the table next to the kitchen, and his specialty was making sure that certain sorts of guests at the hotel restaurant never came back again.

This terrible faculty advisor of mine was surely the most exciting and instructive teacher I have ever had. He gave courses whose lectures were chapters in books he was writing about the mechanics of social change, and which no one, as it turned out, would ever publish.

After I left the university, I would visit him whenever business brought me to Chicago. He never remembered me, and seemed annoyed by my visits—especially, I suppose, when I brought the wonderful news of my having been published here and there.

One night on Cape Cod, when I was drunk and reeking of mustard gas and roses, and calling up old friends and enemies, as used to be my custom, I called up my beloved old thesis advisor. I was told he was dead—at the age of about fifty, I think. He had swallowed cyanide. He had not published. He had perished instead.

And I wish I had an unpublished essay of his on the mechanics of social change to paste into this collage of mine now.

I do not give his name, because I do not think he would like to see it here.

Or anywhere.

❧

My mother, who was also a suicide and who never saw even the first of her eleven grandchildren, is another one, I gather, who would not like to see her name anywhere.

❧

Am I angry at having had triage practiced on me? I am glad it was practiced on me at a university rather than at a battalion aid station behind the front lines. I might have wound up as a preposterously tall private expiring in a snowbank out-

388 ■ PALM SUNDAY

side the tent, while the doctors inside operated on those who had at least a fifty-fifty chance to survive. Why waste time and plasma on a goner?

And I myself have since practiced triage in university settings—in writing classes at the University of Iowa, at Harvard, at City College.

One third of every class was corpses as far as I was concerned. What's more, I was right.

That would certainly be a better name for this planet than Earth, since it would give people who just got here a clearer idea of what they were in for: Triage.

Welcome to Triage.

❧

WHAT good is a planet called Earth, after all, if you own no land?

❧

AND let us end on a sunnier note, with an essay I wrote in May of 1980 at the behest of the International Paper Company. That company, for obvious reasons, hopes that Americans will continue to read and write. And so it has asked various well-known persons to write leaflets for free distribution to anyone hankering to read and write some—about how to increase one's vocabulary, how to write an effective business letter, about how to do library research, and so on.

In view of the fact that I had nearly flunked chemistry, mechanical engineering, and anthropology, and had never taken a course in literature or composition, I was elected to write about literary style. I was more than glad to do this.

But I must bring up the joyless subject of triage again, for I intended my essay not for the bottom third of would-be writers, the warm corpses, nor for the top third—those who are or could be brilliant writers anyway.

My essay is for the middle third, and it goes like this:

Newspaper reporters and technical writers are trained to reveal almost nothing about themselves in their writings. This makes them freaks in the world of writers, since almost all of the other ink-stained wretches in that world reveal a lot about themselves to readers. We call these revelations, accidental and intentional, elements of literary style.

These revelations are fascinating to us as readers. They tell us what sort of person it is with whom we are spending time. Does the writer sound ignorant or informed, crazy or sane, stupid or bright, crooked or honest, humorless or playful—? And on and on.

When you yourself put words on paper, remember that the most damning revelation you can make about yourself is that you do not know what is interesting and what is not. Don't you yourself like or dislike writers mainly for what they choose to show you or make you think about? Did you ever admire an empty-headed writer for his or her mastery of the language? No.

So your own winning literary style must begin with interesting ideas in your head. Find a subject you care about and which you in your heart feel others should care about. It is this genuine caring, and not your games with language, which will be the most compelling and seductive element in your style.

I am not urging you to write a novel, by the way—although I would not be sorry if you wrote one, provided you genuinely cared about something. A petition to the mayor about a pothole in front of your house or a love letter to the girl next door will do.

Do not ramble, though.

As for your use of language: Remember that two great masters of our language, William Shakespeare and James Joyce, wrote sentences which were almost childlike when their subjects were most profound. "To be or not to be?" asks Shakespeare's Hamlet. The longest word is three letters long. Joyce, when he was frisky, could put together a sentence as intricate and glittering as a necklace for Cleopatra, but my favorite sentence in his short story "Eveline" is this one: "She was tired." At that point in the story, no other words could break the heart of a reader as those words do.

Simplicity of language is not only reputable, but perhaps even sacred. The Bible opens with a sentence well within the writing skills of a lively fourteen-year-old: "In the beginning God created the heavens and the earth."

It may be that you, too, are capable of making necklaces for Cleopatra, so to speak. But your eloquence should be the servant of the ideas in your head. Your rule might be this: If a sentence, no matter how excellent, does not illuminate my subject in some new and useful way, scratch it out. Here is the same rule paraphrased to apply to storytelling, to fiction: Never include a sentence which does not either re-mark on character or advance the action.

The writing style which is most natural for you is bound to echo speech you heard when a child. English was the novelist Joseph Conrad's third language, and much that seems piquant in his use of English was no doubt colored by his first language, which was Polish. And lucky indeed is the writer who has grown up in Ireland, for the English spoken there is so amusing and musical. I myself grew up in Indianapolis, Indiana, where common speech sounds like a band saw cutting galvanized tin, and employs a vocabulary as unornamental as a monkey wrench.

In some of the more remote hollows of Appalachia, children still grow up hearing songs and locutions of Elizabethan times. Yes, and many Americans grow up hearing a language other than English, or an English dialect a majority of Americans cannot understand.

All these varieties of speech are beautiful, just as the varieties of butterflies are beautiful. No matter what your first language, you should treasure it all your life. If it happens not to be standard English, and if it shows itself when you write standard English, the result is usually delightful, like a very pretty girl with one eye that is green and one that is blue.

I myself find that I trust my own writing most, and others seem to trust it most, too, when I sound most like a person from Indianapolis, which is what I am. What alternatives do I have? The one most vehemently recommended by teachers has no doubt been pressed on you, as well: that I write like cultivated Englishmen of a century or more ago.

I used to be exasperated by such teachers, but am no more. I understand now that all those antique essays and stories with which I was to compare my own work were not magnificent for their datedness or foreignness, but for saying precisely what their authors meant them to say. My teachers wished me to write accurately, always selecting the most effective words, and relating the words to one another unambiguously, rigidly, like parts of a machine. The teachers did

not want to turn me into an Englishman after all. They
hoped that I would become understandable—and therefore
understood.

And there went my dream of doing with words what Pablo
Picasso did with paint or what any number of jazz idols did
with music. If I broke all the rules of punctuation, had words
mean whatever I wanted them to mean, and strung them
together higgledy-piggledy, I would simply not be understood. So you, too, had better avoid Picasso-style or jazz-
style writing, if you have something worth saying and wish
to be understood.

If it were only teachers who insisted that modern writers
stay close to literary styles of the past, we might reasonably
ignore them. But readers insist on the very same thing. They
want our pages to look very much like pages they have seen
before.

Why? It is because they themselves have a tough job to do,
and they need all the help they can get from us. They have
to identify thousands of little marks on paper, and make
sense of them immediately. They have to *read,* an art so
difficult that most people do not really master it even after
having studied it all through grade school and high school
—for twelve long years.

So this discussion, like all discussions of literary styles,
must finally acknowledge that our stylistic options as writers
are neither numerous nor glamorous, since our readers are
bound to be such imperfect artists. Our audience requires us
to be sympathetic and patient teachers, ever willing to simplify and clarify—whereas we would rather soar high above
the crowd, singing like nightingales.

That is the bad news. The good news is that we Americans
are governed under a unique Constitution, which allows us

to write whatever we please without fear of punishment. So the most meaningful aspect of our styles, which is what we choose to write about, is unlimited.

Also: we are members of an egalitarian society, so there is no reason for us to write, in case we are not classically educated aristocrats, as though we were classically educated aristocrats.

For a discussion of literary style in a narrower sense, in a more technical sense, I commend to your attention *The Elements of Style* by William Strunk, Jr., and E. B. White (Macmillan, 1979). It contains such rules as this: "A participial phrase at the beginning of a sentence must refer to the grammatical subject," and so on. E. B. White is, of course, one of the most admirable literary stylists this country has so far produced.

You should realize, too, that no one would care how well or badly Mr. White expressed himself, if he did not have perfectly enchanting things to say.

ʊ

SELF-
INTERVIEW

tHIS self-interview from *The Paris Review* No. 69, 1977, appears here with the permission of The Viking Press, which gets out collections of *Paris Review* interviews and owns the copyrights to all of them.

Sentences spoken by writers, unless they have been written out first, rarely say what writers wish to say. Writers are unlucky speakers, by and large, which accounts for their being in a profession which encourages them to stay at their desks for years, if necessary, pondering what to say next and how best to say it. Interviewers propose to speed up this process by trepaning writers, so to speak, and fishing around in their brains for unused ideas which otherwise might never get out of there. Not a single idea has ever been discovered by means of this brutal method—and still the trepaning of authors goes on every day.

I now refuse all those who wish to take the top off my skull yet again. The only way to get anything out of a writer's brains is to leave him or her alone until he or she is damn well ready to write it down.

This interview is purely written. Not a word of it was spoken aloud. The prefatory material in italics was not written by me, however, but by *The Paris Review*, to wit:

The introduction to the first of the incorporated interviews (done in West Barnstable, Massachusetts, when Vonnegut was 44) reads: "He is a veteran and a family man, large-boned, loose-jointed, at ease. He camps in an armchair in a shaggy tweed jacket, Cambridge gray flannels, a blue Brooks Brothers shirt, slouched down, his hands stuffed into his pockets. He shells the interview with explosive coughs and sneezes, windages of an autumn cold and a lifetime of heavy cigarette smoking. His voice is a resonant baritone, Midwestern, wry in its inflections. From time to time he issues the open alert smile of a man who has seen and reserved within himself almost everything: depression, war, the possibility of violent death, the inanities of corporate public relations, six children, an irregular income, long-delayed recognition."

The last of the interviews which made up the composite was conducted during the summer of 1976, years after the first. The description of him at this time reads: ". . . he moves with the low-keyed amiability of an old family dog. In general, his appearance is tousled: the long curly hair, moustache and sympathetic smile suggest a man at once amused and saddened by the world around him. He has rented the Gerald

Murphy house for the summer. He works in the little bedroom at the end of a hall where Murphy, artist, bon vivant, and friend to the artistic great, died in 1964. From his desk Vonnegut can look out onto the front lawn through a small window; behind him is a large, white canopy bed. On the desk next to the typewriter is a copy of Andy Warhol's Interview, Clancy Sigal's Zone of the Interior, *and several discarded cigarette packs.*

"Vonnegut has chain-smoked Pall Malls since 1936 and during the course of the interview he smokes the better part of one pack. His voice is low and gravelly, and as he speaks, the incessant procedure of lighting the cigarettes and exhaling smoke is like punctuation in his conversation. Other distractions such as the jangle of the telephone, and the barking of a small, shaggy dog named 'Pumpkin,' do not detract from Vonnegut's good-natured disposition. Indeed, as Dan Wakefield once said of his fellow Shortridge High School alumnus: 'He laughed a lot and was kind to everyone.' "

❧

INTERVIEWER: You are a veteran of the Second World War?

VONNEGUT: Yes. I want a military funeral when I die—the bugler, the flag on the casket, the ceremonial firing squad, the hallowed ground.

INTERVIEWER: Why?

VONNEGUT: It will be a way of achieving what I've always wanted more than anything—something I could have had, if only I'd managed to get myself killed in the war.

INTERVIEWER: Which is—?

VONNEGUT: The unqualified approval of my community.

INTERVIEWER: You don't feel that you have that now?

VONNEGUT: My relatives say that they are glad I'm rich, but that they simply cannot read me.

INTERVIEWER: You were an infantry battalion scout in the war?

VONNEGUT: Yes, but I took my basic training on the 240-millimeter howitzer.

INTERVIEWER: A rather large weapon.

VONNEGUT: The largest mobile field piece in the Army at that time. This weapon came in six pieces, each piece dragged wallowingly by a Caterpillar tractor. Whenever we were told to fire it, we had to build it first. We practically had to invent it. We lowered one piece on top of another, using cranes and jacks. The shell itself was about nine-and-a-half inches in diameter and weighed three hundred pounds. We constructed a miniature railway which would allow us to deliver the shell from the ground to the breech, which was about eight feet above grade. The breech-block was like the door on the vault of a savings and loan association in Peru, Indiana, say.

INTERVIEWER: It must have been a thrill to fire such a weapon.

VONNEGUT: Not really. We would put the shell in there, and then we would throw in bags of very slow and patient explosives. They were damp dog biscuits, I think. We would close the breech, and then trip a hammer which hit a fulminate of mercury percussion cap, which spit fire at the damp dog biscuits. The main idea, I think, was to generate steam. After a while, we could hear these cooking sounds. It was a lot like cooking a turkey. In utter safety, I think, we could have opened the breechblock from time to time, and basted the shell. Eventually, though, the howitzer always got restless. And finally it would heave back on its recoil mechanism, and it would have to expectorate the shell. The shell would come floating out like the Good-year blimp. If we had had a stepladder, we could have painted "Fuck Hitler" on the shell as it left the gun. Heli-copters could have taken after it and shot it down.

INTERVIEWER: The ultimate terror weapon.

VONNEGUT: Of the Franco-Prussian War.

INTERVIEWER: But you were ultimately sent overseas not with this instrument but with the 106th Infantry Division?

VONNEGUT: "The Bag Lunch Division." They used to feed us a lot of bag lunches. Salami sandwiches. An orange.

INTERVIEWER: In combat?

VONNEGUT: When we were still in the States.

INTERVIEWER: While they trained you for the infantry?

VONNEGUT: I was never trained for the infantry. Battalion scouts were elite troops, see. There were only six in each battalion, and nobody was very sure about what they were supposed to do. So we would march over to the rec room every morning, and play Ping-Pong and fill out applica-tions for Officer Candidate School.

INTERVIEWER: During your basic training, though, you must have been familiarized with weapons other than the howitzer.

VONNEGUT: If you study the 240-millimeter howitzer, you don't have time for other weapons. You don't even have time left over for a venereal disease film.

INTERVIEWER: What happened when you reached the front?

VONNEGUT: I imitated various war movies I'd seen.

INTERVIEWER: Did you shoot anybody in the war?

VONNEGUT: I thought about it. I did fix my bayonet once, fully expecting to charge.

INTERVIEWER: Did you charge?

VONNEGUT: No. If everybody else had charged, I would have charged, too. But we decided not to charge. We couldn't see anybody.

INTERVIEWER: This was during the Battle of the Bulge, wasn't it? It was the largest defeat of American arms in history.

VONNEGUT: Probably. My last mission as a scout was to find our own artillery. Usually, scouts go out and look for enemy stuff. Things got so bad that we were finally looking for our own stuff. If I'd found our own battalion commander, everybody would have thought that was pretty swell.

INTERVIEWER: Do you mind describing your capture by the Germans?

VONNEGUT: Gladly. We were in this gully about as deep as a World War I trench. There was snow all around. Somebody said we were probably in Luxembourg. We were out of food.

INTERVIEWER: Who was "we"?

VONNEGUT: Our batallion scouting unit. All six of us. And about fifty people we'd never met before. The Germans could see us, because they were talking to us through a loudspeaker. They told us our situation was hopeless, and so on. That was when we fixed bayonets. It was nice there for a few minutes.

INTERVIEWER: How so?

VONNEGUT: Being a porcupine with all those steel quills. I pitied anybody who had to come in after us.

INTERVIEWER: But they came in anyway?

VONNEGUT: No. They sent in eighty-eight-millimeter shells instead. The shells burst in the treetops right over us. Those were very loud bangs right over our heads. We were showered with splintered steel. Some people got hit. Then the Germans told us again to come out. We didn't yell "nuts" or anything like that. We said, "Okay," and "Take it easy," and so on. When the Germans finally showed themselves, we saw they were wearing white camouflage suits. We didn't have anything like that. We were olive drab. No matter what season it was, we were olive drab.

INTERVIEWER: What did the Germans say?

VONNEGUT: They said the war was all over for us, that we were lucky, that we could now be sure we would live through the war, which was more than they could be sure of. As a matter of fact, they were probably killed or captured by Patton's Third Army within the next few days. Wheels within wheels.

INTERVIEWER: Did you speak any German?

VONNEGUT: I had heard my parents speak it a lot. They hadn't taught me how to do it, since there had been such bitterness in America against all things German during the First World War. I tried a few words I knew on our captors, and they asked me if I was of German ancestry, and I said, "Yes." They wanted to know why I was making war against my brothers.

INTERVIEWER: And you said—?

VONNEGUT: I honestly found the question ignorant and comical. My parents had separated me so thoroughly from my Germanic past that my captors might as well have been Bolivians or Tibetans, for all they meant to me.

INTERVIEWER: After you were captured, you were shipped to Dresden?

VONNEGUT: In the same boxcars that had brought up the troops that captured us—probably in the same boxcars that had delivered Jews and Gypsies and Jehovah's Witnesses and so on to the extermination camps. Rolling stock is rolling stock. British mosquito bombers attacked us at night a few times. I guess they thought we were strategic materials of some kind. They hit a car containing most of the officers from our battalion. Every time I say I hate officers, which I still do fairly frequently, I have to remind myself that practically none of the officers I served under survived. Christmas was in there somewhere.

INTERVIEWER: And you finally arrived in Dresden.

VONNEGUT: In a huge prison camp south of Dresden first. The privates were separated from the noncoms and officers. Under the articles of the Geneva Convention, which is a very Edwardian document, privates were required to work for their keep. Everybody else got to languish in prison. As a private, I was shipped to Dresden.

INTERVIEWER: What were your impressions of the city itself before the bombing?

VONNEGUT: The first fancy city I'd ever seen. A city full of statues and zoos, like Paris. We were living in a slaughterhouse, in a nice new cement-block hog barn. They put bunks and straw mattresses in the barn, and we went to work every morning as contract labor in a malt syrup factory. The syrup was for pregnant women. The damned sirens would go off and we'd hear some other city getting it—*whump a whump a whumpa whump*. We never expected to get it. There were very few air raid shelters in town and no war industries, just cigarette factories, hospitals, clarinet factories. Then a siren went off—it was February 13, 1945—and we went down two stories under the pavement into a big meat locker. It was cool there, with cadavers hanging all around. When we came up the city was gone.

INTERVIEWER: You didn't suffocate in the meat locker?

VONNEGUT: No. It was quite large, and there weren't very many of us. The attack didn't sound like a hell of a lot either. *Whump.* They went over with high explosives first to loosen things up, and then scattered incendiaries. When the war started, incendiaries were fairly sizeable, about as long as a shoebox. By the time Dresden got it, they were tiny little things. They burnt the whole damn town down.

INTERVIEWER: What happened when you came up?

VONNEGUT: Our guards were noncoms—a sergeant, a corporal, and four privates—and leaderless. Cityless, too, because they were Dresdeners who'd been shot up on the front and sent home for easy duty. They kept us at attention for a couple of hours. They didn't know what else to do. They'd go over and talk to each other. Finally we trekked across the rubble and they quartered us with some South Africans in a suburb. Every day we walked into the city and dug into basements and shelters to get the corpses out, as a sanitary measure. When we went into them, a typical shelter, an ordinary basement usually, looked like a streetcar full of people who'd simultaneously had heart failure. Just people sitting there in their chairs, all dead. A fire storm is an amazing thing. It doesn't occur in nature. It's fed by the tornadoes that occur in the midst of it and there isn't a damned thing to breathe. We brought the dead out. They were loaded on wagons and taken to parks, large open areas in the city which weren't filled with rubble. The Germans got funeral pyres going, burning the bodies to keep them from stinking and from spreading disease. 130,000 corpses were hidden underground. It was a terribly elaborate Easter egg hunt. We went to work through cordons of German soldiers. Civilians didn't get to see what we were up to. After a few days the city began to smell, and a new technique was invented. Necessity is the mother of invention. We would bust into the shelter, gather up valuables from people's laps without attempting identification, and turn the valuables over to guards. Then soldiers would come with a flame thrower and stand in the door and cremate the people inside. Get the gold and jewelry out and then burn everybody inside.

INTERVIEWER: What an impression on someone thinking of becoming a writer!

VONNEGUT: It was a fancy thing to see, a startling thing. It was a moment of truth, too, because American civilians and ground troops didn't know American bombers were engaged in saturation bombing. It was kept a secret until very close to the end of the war. One reason they burned down Dresden is that they'd already burned down everything else. You know: "What're we going to do tonight?" Here was everybody all set to go, and Germany still fighting, and this machinery for burning down cities was being used. It was a secret, burning down cities—boiling pisspots and flaming prams. There was all this hokum about the Norden bombsight. You'd see a newsreel showing a bombardier with an MP on either side of him holding a drawn .45. That sort of nonsense, and hell, all they were doing was just flying over cities, hundreds of airplanes, and dropping everything. When I went to the University of Chicago after the war the guy who interviewed me for admission had bombed Dresden. He got to that part of my life story and he said, "Well, we hated to do it." The comment sticks in my mind.

INTERVIEWER: Another reaction would be, "We were ordered to do it."

VONNEGUT: His was more humane. I think he felt the bombing was necessary, and it may have been. One thing everybody learned is how fast you can rebuild a city. The engineers said it would take 500 years to rebuild Germany. Actually it took about 18 weeks.

INTERVIEWER: Did you intend to write about it as soon as you went through the experience?

VONNEGUT: When the city was demolished I had no idea of the scale of the thing. . . . Whether this was what Bremen looked like or Hamburg, Coventry . . . I'd never seen Coventry, so I had no scale except for what I'd seen in movies. When I got home (I was a writer since I had been on the *Cornell Sun* except that was the extent of my writing) I thought of writing my war story, too. All my friends were home; they'd had wonderful adventures, too. I went down to the newspaper office, *The Indianapolis News,* and looked to find out what they had about Dresden. There was an item about half an inch long, which said our planes had been over Dresden and two had been lost. And so I figured, well, this really was the most minor sort of detail in World War II. Others had so much more to write about. I remember envying Andy Rooney who jumped into print at that time; I didn't know him, but I think he was the first guy to publish his war story after the war; it was called *Tail Gunner.* Hell, I never had any classy adventure like that. But every so often I would meet a European and we would be talking about the war and I would say I was in Dresden; he'd be astonished that I'd been there, and he'd always want to know more. Then a book by David Irving was published about Dresden, saying it was the largest massacre in European history. I said, By God, I saw something after all! I would try to write my war story, whether it was interesting or not, and try to make something out of it. I describe that process a little in the beginning of *Slaughterhouse-Five;* I saw it as starring John Wayne and Frank Sinatra. Finally, a girl called Mary O'Hare, the wife of a friend of mine who'd been there with me, said, "You were just children then. It's not fair to pretend that you were men like Wayne and Sinatra and it's not fair to future generations because you're going to make war look good." That was a very important clue to me.

INTERVIEWER: That sort of shifted the whole focus. . .

VONNEGUT: She freed me to write about what infants we really were: 17, 18, 19, 20, 21. We were baby-faced, and as a prisoner of war I don't think I had to shave very often. I don't recall that that was a problem.

INTERVIEWER: One more question; do you still think about the fire-bombing of Dresden at all?

VONNEGUT: I wrote a book about it, called *Slaughterhouse-Five*. The book is still in print, and I have to do something about it as a businessman now and then. Marcel Ophuls asked me to be in his film, *A Memory of Justice.* He wanted me to talk about Dresden as an atrocity. I told him to talk to my friend Bernard V. O'Hare, Mary's husband, instead, which he did. O'Hare was a fellow battalion scout, and then a fellow prisoner of war. He's a lawyer in Pennsylvania now.

INTERVIEWER: Why didn't you wish to testify?

VONNEGUT: I had a German name. I didn't want to argue with people who thought Dresden should have been bombed to hell. All I ever said in my book was that Dresden, willy-nilly, *was* bombed to hell.

INTERVIEWER: It was the largest massacre in European history?

VONNEGUT: It was the fastest killing of large numbers of people—one hundred and thirty-five thousand people in a matter of hours. There were slower schemes for killing, of course.

INTERVIEWER: The death camps.

VONNEGUT: Yes—in which millions were eventually killed. Many people see the Dresden massacre as correct and quite minimal revenge for what had been done by the camps. Maybe so. As I say, I never argue that point. I do note in passing that the death penalty was applied to absolutely anybody who happened to be in the undefended city —babies, old people, the zoo animals, and thousands upon thousands of rabid Nazis, of course, and, among others, my best friend Bernard V. O'Hare and me. By all rights, O'Hare and I should have been part of the body count. The more bodies, the more correct the revenge.

INTERVIEWER: The Franklin Library is bringing out a deluxe edition of *Slaughterhouse-Five,* I believe.

VONNEGUT: Yes. I was required to write a new introduction for it.

INTERVIEWER: Did you have any new thoughts?

VONNEGUT: I said that only one person on the entire planet benefited from the raid, which must have cost tens of millions of dollars. The raid didn't shorten the war by half a second, didn't weaken a German defense or attack anywhere, didn't free a single person from a death camp. Only one person benefited—not two or five or ten. Just one.

INTERVIEWER: And who was that?

VONNEGUT: Me. I got three dollars for each person killed. Imagine that.

INTERVIEWER: How much affinity do you feel toward your contemporaries?

VONNEGUT: My brother and sister writers? Friendly, certainly. It's hard for me to talk to some of them, since we seem to be in very different sorts of businesses. This was a mystery to me for a while, but then Saul Steinberg—

INTERVIEWER: The graphic artist?

VONNEGUT: Indeed. He said that in almost all arts there were some people who responded strongly to art history, to triumphs and fiascoes and experiments of the past, and others who did not. I fell into the second group, and had to. I couldn't play games with my literary ancestors, since I had never studied them systematically. My education was as a chemist at Cornell and then an anthropologist at the University of Chicago. Christ—I was thirty-five before I went crazy about Blake, forty before I read *Madame Bovary,* forty-five before I'd even heard of Céline. Through dumb luck, I read *Look Homeward, Angel* exactly when I was supposed to.

INTERVIEWER: When?

VONNEGUT: At the age of eighteen.

INTERVIEWER: So you've always been a reader?

VONNEGUT: Yes. I grew up in a house crammed with books. But I never had to read a book for academic credit, never had to write a paper about it, never had to prove I'd understood it in a seminar. I am a hopelessly clumsy discusser of books. My experience is nil.

INTERVIEWER: Which member of your family had the most influence on you as a writer?

VONNEGUT: My mother, I guess. Edith Lieber Vonnegut. After our family lost almost all of its money in the Great Depression, my mother thought she might make a new fortune by writing for the slick magazines. She took short story courses at night. She studied magazines the way gamblers study racing forms.

INTERVIEWER: She'd been rich at one time?

VONNEGUT: My father, an architect of modest means, married one of the richest girls in town. It was a brewing fortune based on Lieber Lager Beer and then Gold Medal Beer. Lieber Lager became Gold Medal after winning a prize at some Paris exposition.

INTERVIEWER: It must have been a very good beer.

VONNEGUT: Long before my time. I never tasted any. It had a secret ingredient, I know. My grandfather and his brewmaster wouldn't let anybody watch while they put it in.

INTERVIEWER: Do you know what it was?

VONNEGUT: Coffee.

INTERVIEWER: So your mother studied short story writing?

VONNEGUT: And my father painted pictures in a studio he'd set up on the top floor of the house. There wasn't much work for architects during the Great Depression—not much work for anybody. Strangely enough, though, Mother was right: Even mediocre magazine writers were making money hand over fist.

INTERVIEWER: So your mother took a very practical attitude toward writing.

VONNEGUT: Not to say crass. She was a highly intelligent, cultivated woman, by the way. She went to the same high school I did, and was one of the few people who got nothing but A-plusses while she was there. She went east to a finishing school after that, and then traveled all over Europe. She was fluent in German and French. I still have her high school report cards somewhere. "A-plus, A-plus, A-plus . . ." She was a good writer, it turned out, but she had no talent for the vulgarity the slick magazines required. Fortunately, I was loaded with vulgarity, so, when I grew up, I was able to make her dream come true. Writing for *Collier's* and *The Saturday Evening Post* and *Cosmopolitan* and *Ladies' Home Journal* and so on was as easy as falling off a log for me. I only wish she'd lived to see it. I only wish she'd lived to see all her grandchildren. She has ten. She didn't even get to see the first one. I made another one of her dreams come true: I lived on Cape Cod for many years. She always wanted to live on Cape Cod. It's probably very common for sons to try to make their mothers' impossible dreams come true. I adopted my sister's sons after she died, and it's spooky to watch them try to make her impossible dreams come true.

INTERVIEWER: What were your sister's dreams like?

VONNEGUT: She wanted to live like a member of *The Swiss Family Robinson,* with impossibly friendly animals in impossibly congenial isolation. Her oldest son, Jim, has been a goat farmer on a mountain top in Jamaica for the past eight years. No telephone. No electricity.

INTERVIEWER: The Indianapolis high school you and your mother attended—

VONNEGUT: And my father. Shortridge High.

INTERVIEWER: It had a daily paper, I believe.

VONNEGUT: Yes. *The Shortridge Daily Echo.* There was a print shop right in the school. Students wrote the paper. Students set the type. After school.

INTERVIEWER: You just laughed about something.

VONNEGUT: It was something dumb I remembered about high school. It doesn't have anything to do with writing.

INTERVIEWER: You care to share it with us anyway?

VONNEGUT: Oh—I just remembered something that happened in a high school course on civics, on how our government worked. The teacher asked each of us to stand up in turn and tell what we did after school. I was sitting in the back of the room, sitting next to a guy named J. T. Alburger. He later became an insurance man in Los Angeles. He died fairly recently. Anyway—he kept nudging me, urging me, daring me to tell the truth about what I did after school. He offered me five dollars to tell the truth. He wanted me to stand up and say, "I make model airplanes and jerk off."

INTERVIEWER: I see.

VONNEGUT: I also worked on *The Shortridge Daily Echo*.

INTERVIEWER: Was that fun?

VONNEGUT: Fun and easy. I've always found it easy to write. Also, I learned to write for peers rather than for teachers. Most beginning writers don't get to write for peers—to catch hell from peers.

INTERVIEWER: So every afternoon you would go to the *Echo* office—

VONNEGUT: Yeah. And one time, while I was writing, I happened to sniff my armpits absent-mindedly. Several people saw me do it, and thought it was funny—and ever after that I was given the name "Snarf." In the Annual for my graduating class, the Class of 1940, I'm listed as "Kurt Snarfield Vonnegut, Jr." Technically, I wasn't really a snarf. A snarf was a person who went around sniffing girls' bicycle saddles. I didn't do that. "Twerp" also had a very specific meaning, which few people know now. Through careless usage, "twerp" is a pretty formless insult now.

INTERVIEWER: What is a twerp in the strictest sense, in the original sense?

VONNEGUT: It's a person who inserts a set of false teeth between the cheeks of his ass.

INTERVIEWER: I see.

VONNEGUT: I beg your pardon; between the cheeks of his or *her* ass. I'm always offending feminists that way.

INTERVIEWER: I don't quite understand why someone would do that with false teeth.

VONNEGUT: In order to bite the buttons off the back seats of taxicabs. That's the only reason twerps do it. It's all that turns them on.

INTERVIEWER: You went to Cornell University after Shortridge?

VONNEGUT: I imagine.

INTERVIEWER: You imagine?

VONNEGUT: I had a friend who was a heavy drinker. If somebody asked him if he'd been drunk the night before, he would always answer off-handedly, "Oh, I imagine." I've always liked that answer. It acknowledges life as a dream. Cornell was a boozy dream, partly because of booze itself, and partly because I was enrolled exclusively in courses I had no talent for. My father and brother agreed that I should study chemistry, since my brother had done so well with chemicals at M.I.T. He's eight years older than I am. Funnier, too. His most famous discovery is that silver iodide will sometimes make it rain or snow.

INTERVIEWER: Was your sister funny, too?

VONNEGUT: Oh, yes. There was an odd cruel streak to her sense of humor, though, which didn't fit in with the rest of her character somehow. She thought it was terribly funny whenever anybody fell down. One time she saw a woman come out of a streetcar horizontally, and she laughed for weeks after that.

INTERVIEWER: Horizontally?

VONNEGUT: Yes. This woman must have caught her heels

somehow. Anyway, the streetcar door opened, and my sister happened to be watching from the sidewalk, and then she saw this woman come out horizontally—as straight as a board, facedown, and about two feet off the ground.

INTERVIEWER: Slapstick?

VONNEGUT: Sure. We loved Laurel and Hardy. You know what one of the funniest things is that can happen in a film?

INTERVIEWER: No.

VONNEGUT: To have somebody walk through what looks like a shallow little puddle, but which is actually six feet deep. I remember a movie where Cary Grant was loping across lawns at night. He came to a low hedge, which he cleared ever so gracefully, only there was a twenty-foot drop on the other side. But the thing my sister and I loved best was when somebody in a movie would tell everybody off, and then make a grand exit into the coat closet. He had to come out again, of course, all tangled in coathangers and scarves.

INTERVIEWER: Did you take a degree in chemistry at Cornell?

VONNEGUT: I was flunking everything by the middle of my junior year. I was delighted to join the Army and go to war. After the war, I went to the University of Chicago, where I was pleased to study anthropology, a science that was mostly poetry, that involved almost no math at all. I was married by then, and soon had one kid, who was Mark. He would later go crazy, of course, and write a fine book about it—*The Eden Express*. He has just fathered a kid himself, my first grandchild, a boy named Zachary.

Mark is finishing his second year in Harvard Medical School, and will be about the only member of his class not to be in debt when he graduates—because of the book. That's a pretty decent recovery from a crackup, I'd say.

INTERVIEWER: Did the study of anthropology later color your writings?

VONNEGUT: It confirmed my atheism, which was the faith of my fathers anyway. Religions were exhibited and studied as the Rube Goldberg inventions I'd always thought they were. We weren't allowed to find one culture superior to any other. We caught hell if we mentioned races much. It was highly idealistic.

INTERVIEWER: Almost a religion?

VONNEGUT: Exactly. And the only one for me. So far.

INTERVIEWER: What was your dissertation?

VONNEGUT: *Cat's Cradle*.

INTERVIEWER: But you wrote that years after you left Chicago, didn't you?

VONNEGUT: I left Chicago without writing a dissertation— and without a degree. All my ideas for dissertations had been rejected, and I was broke, so I took a job as a P.R. man for General Electric in Schenectady. Twenty years later, I got a letter from a new dean at Chicago, who had been looking through my dossier. Under the rules of the university, he said, a published work of high quality could be substituted for a dissertation, so I was entitled to an M.A. He had shown *Cat's Cradle* to the Anthropology Department, and they had said it was halfway decent anthropology, so they were mailing me my degree. I'm Class of 1972 or so.

INTERVIEWER: Congratulations.

VONNEGUT: It was nothing, really. A piece of cake.

INTERVIEWER: Some of the characters in *Cat's Cradle* were based on people you knew at G.E., isn't that so?

VONNEGUT: Dr. Felix Hoenikker, the absent-minded scientist, was a caricature of Dr. Irving Langmuir, the star of the G.E. Research Laboratory. I knew him some. My brother worked with him. Langmuir was wonderfully absent-minded. He wondered out loud one time whether, when turtles pulled in their heads, their spines buckled or contracted. I put that in the book. One time he left a tip under his plate after his wife served him breakfast at home. I put that in. His most important contribution, though, was the idea for what I called "Ice-9," a form of frozen water that was stable at room temperature. He didn't tell it directly to me. It was a legend around the Laboratory—about the time H. G. Wells came to Schenectady. That was long before my time. I was just a little boy when it happened—listening to the radio, building model airplanes.

INTERVIEWER: Yes?

VONNEGUT: Anyway—Wells came to Schenectady, and Langmuir was told to be his host. Langmuir thought he might entertain Wells with an idea for a science-fiction story—about a form of ice that was stable at room temperature. Wells was uninterested, or at least never used the idea. And then Wells died, and then, finally, Langmuir died. I thought to myself: "Finders, keepers—the idea is mine." Langmuir, incidentally, was the first scientist in private industry to win a Nobel Prize.

INTERVIEWER: How do you feel about Bellow's winning the Nobel Prize for Literature?

VONNEGUT: It was the best possible way to honor our entire literature.

INTERVIEWER: Do you find it easy to talk to him?

VONNEGUT: Yes. I've had about three opportunities. I was his host one time at the University of Iowa, where I was teaching and he was lecturing. It went very well. We had one thing in common, anyway—

INTERVIEWER: Which was—?

VONNEGUT: We were both products of the Anthropology Department of the University of Chicago. So far as I know, he never went on any anthropological expeditions, and neither did I. We invented pre-industrial peoples instead— I in *Cat's Cradle* and he in *Henderson the Rain King*.

INTERVIEWER: So he is a fellow scientist.

VONNEGUT: I'm no scientist at all. I'm glad now, though, that I was pressured into becoming a scientist by my father and my brother. I understand how scientific reasoning and playfulness work, even though I have no talent for joining in. I enjoy the company of scientists, am easily excited and entertained when they tell me what they're doing. I've spent a lot more time with scientists than with literary people, my brother's friends, mostly. I enjoy plumbers and carpenters and automobile mechanics, too. I didn't get to know any literary people until the last ten years, starting with two years of teaching at Iowa. There at Iowa, I was suddenly friends with Nelson Algren and José Donoso and Vance Bourjaily and Donald Justice and George Star-buck and Marvin Bell, and so on. I was amazed. Now, judging from the review my latest book, *Slapstick,* has received, people would like to bounce me out of the literary establishment—send me back where I came from.

INTERVIEWER: There were some bad reviews?

VONNEGUT: Only in *The New York Times, Time, Newsweek,*

The New York Review of Books, The Village Voice, and
Rolling Stone. They loved me in Medicine Hat.

INTERVIEWER: To what do you attribute this rancor?

VONNEGUT: *Slapstick* may be a very bad book. I am perfectly willing to believe that. Everybody else writes lousy
books, so why shouldn't I? What was unusual about the
reviews was that they wanted people to admit now that I
had never been any good. The reviewer for the Sunday
Times actually asked critics who had praised me in the
past to now admit in public how wrong they'd been. My
publisher, Sam Lawrence, tried to comfort me by saying
that authors were invariably attacked when they became
fabulously well-to-do.

INTERVIEWER: You needed comforting?

VONNEGUT: I never felt worse in my life. I felt as though I
were sleeping standing up on a boxcar in Germany again.

INTERVIEWER: That bad?

VONNEGUT: No. But bad enough. All of a sudden, critics
wanted me squashed like a bug. And it wasn't just that I
had money all of a sudden, either. The hidden complaint
was that I was barbarous, that I wrote without having
made a systematic study of great literature, that I was no
gentleman, since I had done hack writing so cheerfully for
vulgar magazines—that I had not paid my academic dues.

INTERVIEWER: You had not suffered?

VONNEGUT: I had suffered, all right—but as a badly-
educated person in vulgar company and in a vulgar trade.
It was dishonorable enough that I perverted art for money.
I then topped that felony by becoming, as I say, fabulously
well-to-do. Well, that's just too damn bad for me and for
everybody. I'm completely in print, so we're all stuck with
me and stuck with my books.

INTERVIEWER: Do you mean to fight back?

VONNEGUT: In a way. I'm on the New York State Council for the Arts now, and every so often some other member talks about sending notices to college English departments about some literary opportunity, and I say, "Send them to the chemistry departments, send them to the zoology departments, send them to the anthropology departments and the astronomy departments and physics departments, and all the medical and law schools. That's where the writers are most likely to be."

INTERVIEWER: You believe that?

VONNEGUT: I think it can be tremendously refreshing if a creator of literature has something on his mind other than the history of literature so far. Literature should not disappear up its own asshole, so to speak.

INTERVIEWER: Let's talk about the women in your books.

VONNEGUT: There aren't any. No real women, no love.

INTERVIEWER: Is this worth expounding upon?

VONNEGUT: It's a mechanical problem. So much of what happens in storytelling is mechanical, has to do with the technical problems of how to make a story work. Cowboy stories and policeman stories end in shoot-outs, for example, because shoot-outs are the most reliable mechanisms for making such stories end. There is nothing like death to say what is always such an artificial thing to say: "The end." I try to keep deep love out of my stories because, once that particular subject comes up, it is almost impossible to talk about anything else. Readers don't want to hear about anything else. They go gaga about love. If a lover in a story wins his true love, that's the end of the tale, even if World War III is about to begin, and the sky is black with flying saucers.

INTERVIEWER: So you keep love out.

VONNEGUT: I have other things I want to talk about. Ralph Ellison did the same thing in *Invisible Man*. If the hero in that magnificent book had found somebody worth loving, somebody who was crazy about him, that would have been the end of the story. Céline did the same thing in *Journey to the End of the Night:* He excluded the possibility of true and final love—so that the story could go on and on and on.

INTERVIEWER: Not many writers talk about the mechanics of stories.

VONNEGUT: I am such a barbarous technocrat that I believe they can be tinkered with like Model T Fords.

INTERVIEWER: To what end?

VONNEGUT: To give the reader pleasure.

INTERVIEWER: Will you ever write a love story, do you think?

VONNEGUT: Maybe. I lead a loving life. I really do. Even when I'm leading that loving life, though, and it's going so well, I sometimes find myself thinking, "My goodness, couldn't we talk about something else for just a little while?" You know what's really funny?

INTERVIEWER: No.

VONNEGUT: My books are being thrown out of school libraries all over the country—because they're supposedly obscene. I've seen letters to small town newspapers that put *Slaughterhouse-Five* in the same class with *Deep Throat* and *Hustler* magazine. How could anybody masturbate to *Slaughterhouse-Five*?

INTERVIEWER: It takes all kinds.

VONNEGUT: Well, that kind doesn't exist. It's my religion the censors hate. They find me disrespectful toward their idea of God Almighty. They think it's the proper business of government to protect the reputation of God. All I can say is, "Good luck to them, and good luck to the government, and good luck to God." You know what H.L. Mencken said one time about religious people? He said he'd been greatly misunderstood. He said he didn't hate them. He simply found them comical.

INTERVIEWER: When I asked you a while back which member of your family had influenced you most as a writer, you said your mother. I had expected you to say your sister, since you talked so much about her in *Slapstick.*

VONNEGUT: I said in *Slapstick* that she was the person I wrote for—that every successful creative person creates with an audience of one in mind. That's the secret of artistic unity. Anybody can achieve it, if he or she will make something with only one person in mind. I didn't realize that she was the person I wrote for until after she died.

INTERVIEWER: She loved literature?

VONNEGUT: She wrote wonderfully well. She didn't read much—but, then again, neither in later years did Henry David Thoreau. My father was the same way: he didn't read much, but he could write like a dream. Such letters my father and sister wrote! When I compare their prose with mine, I am ashamed.

INTERVIEWER: Did your sister try to write for money, too?

VONNEGUT: No. She could have been a remarkable sculptor, too. I bawled her out one time for not doing more with the talents she had. She replied that having talent doesn't carry with it the obligation that something has to be done with it. This was startling news to me. I thought people were supposed to grab their talents and run as far and fast as they could.

INTERVIEWER: What do you think now?

VONNEGUT: Well—what my sister said now seems a peculiarly feminine sort of wisdom. I have two daughters who are as talented as she was, and both of them are damned if they are going to lose their poise and senses of humor by snatching up their talents and desperately running as far and as fast as they can. They saw me run as far and as fast as I could—and it must have looked like quite a crazy performance to them. And this is the worst possible metaphor, for what they actually saw was a man sitting still for decades.

INTERVIEWER: At a typewriter.

VONNEGUT: Yes, and smoking his fool head off.

INTERVIEWER: Have you ever stopped smoking?

VONNEGUT: Twice. Once I did it cold turkey, and turned into Santa Claus. I became roly-poly. I was approaching 250 pounds. I stopped for almost a year, and then the University of Hawaii brought me to Oahu to speak. I was drinking out of a coconut on the roof of the Ili Kai one night, and all I had to do to complete the ring of my happiness was to smoke a cigarette. Which I did.

INTERVIEWER: The second time?

VONNEGUT: Very recently—last year. I paid SmokEnders 150 dollars to help me quit, over a period of six weeks. It was exactly as they had promised—easy and instructive. I won my graduation certificate and recognition pin. The only trouble was that I had also gone insane. I was supremely happy and proud, but those around me found me unbearably opinionated and abrupt and boisterous. Also: I had stopped writing. I didn't even write letters anymore. I had made a bad trade, evidently. So I started smoking again. As the National Association of Manufacturers used to say—

INTERVIEWER: I'm not sure I know what they used to say.

VONNEGUT: "There's no such thing as a free lunch."

INTERVIEWER: Do you really think creative writing can be taught?

VONNEGUT: About the same way golf can be taught. A pro can point out obvious flaws in your swing. I did that well, I think, at the University of Iowa for two years. . . . I taught creative writing badly at Harvard—because my marriage was breaking up, and because I was commuting every week to Cambridge from New York. I taught even worse at City College a couple of years ago. I had too many other projects going on at the same time. I don't have the will to teach anymore. I only know the theory.

INTERVIEWER: Could you put the theory into a few words?

VONNEGUT: It was stated by Paul Engle—the founder of the Writers' Workshop at Iowa. He told me that, if the Workshop ever got a building of its own, these words should be inscribed over the entrance: "Don't take it all so seriously."

INTERVIEWER: And how would that be helpful?

VONNEGUT: It would remind the students that they were learning to play practical jokes.

INTERVIEWER: Practical jokes?

VONNEGUT: If you make people laugh or cry about little black marks on sheets of white paper, what is that but a practical joke? All the great story lines are great practical jokes that people fall for over and over again.

INTERVIEWER: Can you give an example?

VONNEGUT: The Gothic novel. Dozens of the things are published every year, and they all sell. My friend Borden Deal recently wrote a Gothic novel for the fun of it, and I asked him what the plot was, and he said, "A young woman takes a job in an old house and gets the pants scared off her."

INTERVIEWER: Some more examples?

VONNEGUT: The others aren't that much fun to describe: Somebody gets into trouble, and then gets out again; somebody loses something and gets it back; somebody is wronged and gets revenge; Cinderella; somebody hits the skids and just goes down, down, down; people fall in love with each other, and a lot of other people get in the way; a virtuous person is falsely accused of sin; a sinful person is believed to be virtuous; a person faces a challenge bravely, and succeeds or fails; a person lies, a person steals, a person kills, a person commits fornication.

INTERVIEWER: If you will pardon my saying so, these are very old-fashioned plots.

VONNEGUT: I guarantee you that no modern story scheme, even plotlessness, will give a reader genuine satisfaction, unless one of those old fashioned plots is smuggled in somewhere. I don't praise plots as accurate representations of life, but as ways to keep readers reading. When I used to teach creative writing, I would tell the students to make their characters want something right away—even if it's only a glass of water. Characters paralyzed by the meaningless of modern life still have to drink water from time to time. One of my students wrote a story about a nun who got a piece of dental floss stuck between her lower left molars, and who couldn't get it out all day long. I thought that was wonderful. The story dealt with issues a lot more important than dental floss, but what kept readers going was anxiety about when the dental floss would finally be removed. Nobody could read that story without fishing around in his mouth with a finger. Now, there's an admirable practical joke for you. When you exclude plot, when you exclude anyone's wanting anything, you exclude the reader, which is a mean-spirited thing to do. You can also exclude the reader by not telling him immediately where the story is taking place, and who the people are—

INTERVIEWER: And what they want.

VONNEGUT: Yes. And you can put him to sleep by never having characters confront each other. Students like to say that they stage no confrontations because people avoid confrontations in modern life. "Modern life is so lonely," they say. This is laziness. It's the writer's job to stage confrontations, so the characters will say surprising and revealing things, and educate and entertain us all. If a writer can't or won't do that, he should withdraw from the trade.

INTERVIEWER: Trade?

VONNEGUT: Trade. Carpenters build houses. Storytellers use a reader's leisure time in such a way that the reader will not feel that his time has been wasted. Mechanics fix automobiles.

INTERVIEWER: Surely talent is required?

VONNEGUT: In all those fields. I was a Saab dealer on Cape Cod for a while, and I enrolled in their mechanic's school, and they threw me out of their mechanic's school. No talent.

INTERVIEWER: How common is storytelling talent?

VONNEGUT: In a creative writing class of twenty people anywhere in this country, six students will be startlingly talented. Two of those might actually publish something by and by.

INTERVIEWER: What distinguishes those two from the rest?

VONNEGUT: They will have something other than literature itself on their minds. They will probably be hustlers, too. I mean that they won't want to wait passively for somebody to discover them. They will insist on being read.

INTERVIEWER: You have been a public relations man and an advertising man—

VONNEGUT: Oh, I imagine.

INTERVIEWER: Was this painful? I mean—did you feel your talent was being wasted, being crippled?

VONNEGUT: No. That's romance—that work of that sort damages a writer's soul. At Iowa, Dick Yates and I used to give a lecture each year on the writer and the free enterprise system. The students hated it. We would talk about all the hack jobs writers could take in case they found themselves starving to death, or in case they wanted to accumulate enough capital to finance the writing of a book. Since publishers aren't putting money into first novels anymore, and since the magazines have died, and since television isn't buying from young freelancers anymore, and since the foundations give grants only to old poops like me, young writers are going to have to support themselves as shameless hacks. Otherwise, we are soon going to find ourselves without a contemporary literature. There is only one genuinely ghastly thing hack jobs do to writers, and that is to waste their precious time.

INTERVIEWER: No joke.

VONNEGUT: A tragedy. I just keep trying to think of ways, even horrible ways, for young writers to somehow hang on.

INTERVIEWER: Should young writers be subsidized?

VONNEGUT: Something's got to be done, now that free enterprise has made it nearly impossible for them to support themselves through free enterprise. I was a sensational businessman in the beginning—for the simple reason that there was so much business to be done. When I was working for General Electric, I wrote a story, "Report on the

Barnhouse Effect," the first story I ever wrote. I mailed it off to *Collier's.* Knox Burger was fiction editor there. Knox told me what was wrong with it and how to fix it. I did what he said, and he bought the story for seven hundred and fifty dollars, six weeks' pay at G.E. I wrote another, and he paid me ninehundred and fifty dollars, and suggested that it was perhaps time for me to quit G.E. Which I did. I moved to Provincetown. Eventually, my price for a short story got up to twenty-nine hundred dollars a crack. Think of that. And Knox got me a couple of agents who were as shrewd about storytelling as he was —Kenneth Littauer, who had been his predecessor at *Collier's,* and Max Wilkinson, who had been a story editor for MGM. And let it be put on the record here that Knox Burger, who is about my age, discovered and encouraged more good young writers than any other editor of his time. I don't think that's ever been written down anywhere. It's a fact known only to writers, and one that could easily vanish, if it isn't somewhere written down.

INTERVIEWER: Where is Knox Burger now?

VONNEGUT: He's a literary agent. He represents my son Mark, in fact.

INTERVIEWER: And Littauer and Wilkinson?

VONNEGUT: Littauer died ten years ago or so. He was a colonel in the Lafayette Escadrille, by the way, at the age of twenty-three—and the first pilot to strafe a trench. He was my mentor. Max Wilkinson has retired to Florida. It always embarrassed him to be an agent. If some stranger asked him what he did for a living, he always said he was a cotton planter.

INTERVIEWER: Do you have a new mentor now?

VONNEGUT: No. I guess I'm too old to find one. Whatever

I write now is set in type without comment by my publisher, who is younger than I am, by editors, by anyone.
I don't have my sister to write for anymore. Suddenly,
there are all these unfilled jobs in my life.

INTERVIEWER: Do you feel as though you're up there without a net under you?

VONNEGUT: And without a balancing pole, either. It gives
me the heebie-jeebies sometimes.

INTERVIEWER: Is there anything else you'd like to add?

VONNEGUT: You know the panic bars they have on the main
doors of schools and theaters? If you get slammed into the
door, the door will fly open?

INTERVIEWER: Yes.

VONNEGUT: The brand name on most of them is "Vondu-
prin." The "Von" is for Vonnegut. A relative of mine was
caught in the Iroquois Theater Fire in Chicago a long time
ago, and he invented the panic bar along with two other
guys. "Prin" was Prinz. I forget who "Du" was.

INTERVIEWER: O.K.

VONNEGUT: And I want to say, too, that humorists are very
commonly the youngest children in their families. When I
was the littlest kid at our supper table, there was only one
way I could get anybody's attention, and that was to be funny. I had to specialize. I used to listen to radio comedians very
intently, so I could learn how to make jokes. And that's what
my books are, now that I'm a grownup—mosaics of jokes.

INTERVIEWER: Do you have any favorite jokes?

VONNEGUT: My sister and I used to argue about what the
funniest joke in the world was—next to a guy storming
into a coat closet, of course. When the two of us worked together, incidentally, we could be almost as funny as Laurel and Hardy. That's basically what *Slapstick* was about.

INTERVIEWER: Did you finally agree on the world's champion joke?

VONNEGUT: We finally settled on one. It's sort of hard to tell it just flat-footed like this.

INTERVIEWER: Do it anyway.

VONNEGUT: Well—you won't laugh. Nobody ever laughs. But one is an old "Two Black Crows" joke. The "Two Black Crows" were white guys in blackface—named Moran and Mack. They made phonograph records of their routines, two supposedly black guys talking lazily to each other. Anyway, one of them says, "Last night I dreamed I was eating flannel cakes." The other one says, "Is that so?" And the first one says, "And when I woke up, the blanket was gone."

INTERVIEWER: Um.

VONNEGUT: I told you you wouldn't laugh.

INTERVIEWER: You seem to prefer Laurel and Hardy over Chaplin. Is that so?

VONNEGUT: I'm crazy about Chaplin, but there's too much distance between him and his audience. He is too obviously a genius. In his own way, he's as brilliant as Picasso, and this is intimidating to me.

INTERVIEWER: Will you ever write another short story?

VONNEGUT: Maybe. I wrote what I thought would be my last one about eight years ago. Harlan Ellison asked me to contribute to a collection he was making. The story's called "The Big Space Fuck." I think I am the first writer to use "Fuck" in a title. It was about firing a space ship with a warhead full of jizzum at Andromeda. Which reminds me of my good Indianapolis friend, about the only Indianapolis friend I've got left—William Failey. When we got into the Second World War, and everybody was supposed to give blood, he wondered if he couldn't give a pint of jizzum instead.

INTERVIEWER: If your parents hadn't lost all their money, what would you be doing now?

VONNEGUT: I'd be an Indianapolis architect—like my father and grandfather. And very happy, too. I still wish that had happened. One thing, anyway: One of the best young architects out there lives in a house my father built for our family the year I was born—1922. My initials, and my sister's initials, and my brother's initials are all written in leaded glass in the three little windows by the front door.

INTERVIEWER: So you have good old days you hanker for.

VONNEGUT: Yes. Whenever I go to Indianapolis, the same question asks itself over and over again in my head: "Where's my bed, where's my bed?" And if my father's and grandfather's ghosts haunt that town, they must be wondering where all their buildings have gone to. The center of the city, where most of their buildings were, has been turned into parking lots. They must be wondering where all their relatives went, too. They grew up in a huge extended family which is no more. I got the slightest taste of that—the big family thing. And when I went to the University of Chicago, and I heard the head of the Department of Anthropology, Robert Redfield, lecture on the folk society, which was essentially a stable, isolated extended family, he did not have to tell me how nice that could be.

INTERVIEWER: Anything else?

VONNEGUT: Yes. *Slapstick* is the first American novel to employ units from the metric system throughout. Nobody noticed, so now I have to toot my own horn about it.

INTERVIEWER: Anything else?

VONNEGUT: Well—I just discovered a prayer for writers. I'd

heard of prayers for sailors and kings and soldiers and so on —but never of a prayer for writers. Could I put that in here?

INTERVIEWER: Certainly.

VONNEGUT: It was written by Samuel Johnson on April 3, 1753, the day on which he signed a contract which required him to write the first complete dictionary of the English language. He was praying for himself. Perhaps April third should be celebrated as "Writers' Day." Anyway, this is the prayer: "O God, who hast hitherto supported me, enable me to proceed in this labor, and in the whole task of my present state; that when I shall tender up, at the last day, an account of the talent committed to me, I may receive pardon, for the sake of Jesus Christ. Amen."

INTERVIEWER: That seems to be a wish to carry his talent as far and as fast as he can.

VONNEGUT: Yes. He was a notorious hack.

INTERVIEWER: And you consider yourself a hack?

VONNEGUT: Of a sort.

INTERVIEWER: What sort?

VONNEGUT: A child of the Great Depression.

INTERVIEWER: I see. Our last question. If you were Commissar of Publishing in the United States, what would you do to alleviate the present deplorable situation?

VONNEGUT: There is no shortage of wonderful writers. What we lack is a dependable mass of readers.

INTERVIEWER: So—?

VONNEGUT: I propose that every person out of work be required to submit a book report before he or she gets his or her welfare check.

INTERVIEWER: Thank you.

VONNEGUT: Thank *you*.

10

THE
PEOPLE
ONE KNOWS

f ROM *Politics Today,* January/February 1979:

"Who in America is truly happy?" my offspring used to ask me in one way or another as they entered adolescence, which is children's menopause. I was silent then, but need not have been. There was an answer then which holds good today: "William F. Buckley, Jr." I have his fifteenth solo book at hand, a collection of 130 or so pieces published elsewhere (with one interesting exception) since 1975 began. Norman Mailer has said of himself that he is one of the best "fast writers" around. Buckley is at least twice as fast. He can do a column in 20 minutes, he tells us, and turn out 150 a year, plus a book and many reviews and speeches and articles, and television introductions besides. The fast writings collected in this volume are uniformly first rate—not only in terms of unbridled happiness (where Mailer surely falls short), but as shrewd comedies and celebrations of the English language.

He is a superb sailor and skier as well—and multilingual, and a musician, and an airplane pilot, and a family man, and polite and amusing to strangers. More: He is, like the Yale-educated hero of his novel *Saving the Queen,* startlingly good-looking. His distinctly American features are animated, but tempered with a certain shyness, a reserve. (The last nine words are Buckley's own gloss on the good looks of the hero, Bradford Oakes.)

So whenever I see Mr. Buckley, I think this, and, word of honor, without an atom of irony: "There is a man who has won the decathlon of human existence."

I also marvel at how much he resembles a far more lopsided genius, the comedian Stanley Laurel. Laurel also managed to imply, despite his beauty and seriousness, that something screamingly funny was going on. People cannot earn or cultivate that look, in my opinion. Peer through the window of any hospital nursery, and you will find that one infant in fifty has it. The difficult part for many, but easy as pie for Laurel and Buckley, is living up to such a face.

I would give a million dollars to look like that.

I wonder, too, when I see Buckley: Would he have known that it was possible to be genuinely funny and conservative at the same time, if it had not been for the pioneering work of H. L. Mencken? Probably so. That face of his, when coupled with his fine mind and high social position, would have made him sound like a spiritual son of Mencken's, even if he had never heard of the Sage of Baltimore.

How serious is he about conservatism? Well—serious enough to devote his life to it, surely, but beyond that? The ideals he defends, conventional Republicanisms, really, were logically his from birth. He was rich and brilliant with congenial and enterprising relatives before he wore his first diaper—and he had the rare gift of being happy a lot, as I say. And nothing changed much except, perhaps, that life kept getting better and better.

Most important: there has never been anything to be ashamed of. It is a quite unusual experience in America to have never been ashamed. Buckley's intellectual voyage has been one of confirmations rather than discoveries. So there is the chance that he is more playful about conservatism than many who have come to it the hard way—than Aleksandr Solzhenitsyn, say. Buckley has not come to conservatism through rage and pain.

Solzhenitsyn could never say at the beginning of a book, and neither could Mencken, for that matter, what Buckley says at the beginning of this one, that he must subtitle it as being controversial for this reason: ". . . for almost everything that is said here, there is an opposite, if intellectually unequal, reaction set down somewhere. This is of course a pity, but on the other hand I have not expected to bring around the world by acclamation."

These are, I submit, the nearly weightless words of an undefeatable debater rather than of a passionate advocate— a debater who, because he is so good at debating, is about to make ninnies of the opposition yet again, knowing that nobody is going to be particularly burned up afterward. He continues to do what he did as a Yale undergraduate, which was to engage in badinage with registered Democrats, and always genially. He tells us that ". . . one of the reasons I was so happy at Yale was that geniality is . . . as natural to Yale as laughter is to Dublin, song to Milan, or angst to *The New York Review of Books.*"

I, for one, am grateful that Buckley, serious or not, has volunteered to be as consistent in his responses to outside stimuli as a pinball machine, a machine designed to teach conservative ideals—5,000 points for the electric chair, 10,-000 for right-to-work laws, 50,000 for more sympathy with the CIA, a cool million for individual excellence and daring, and so on. If we did not have such an intelligent and genial man (as compared with General Goldwater, for instance) to argue in favor of social Darwinism, some of us might be too appalled and confused to listen, to learn for our own good how uncharitable we had better be.

❦

WILLIAM F. Buckley, Jr., is a friend of mine. Ours is a New York friendship. A New York friendship is a friendship with a person you have met at least once. If you have met a person only once, and you are a New Yorker, you are entitled to say, whenever that person's name comes up in conversation, "Yes —so-and-so is a friend of mine."

I have met Mr. Buckley, or Bill, as his friends call him, maybe thrice, for a grand total of sixty seconds. I am intimidated by his cultural and athletic accomplishments, and by his social rank—but especially by his skills as a debater. I have no idea how to win an argument, or even to hold my own in one.

If I am to say what I believe, I must do so without opposition, or I am mute. I have been on the Irv Kupcinet Show, a talk show originating in Chicago, four times. I have never said a word. I ran into Mr. Kupcinet recently, and he said he would certainly like to have me on again. Why not?

✺

I spoke one time at the Library of Congress, in 1972, or so. A man stood up in the middle of the audience, when I was about halfway through, and he said, "What right have you, as a leader of America's young people, to make those people so cynical and pessimistic?"

I had no good answer, so I left the stage.

Talk about profiles in courage!

✺

THE beliefs I have to defend are so soft and complicated, actually, and, when vivisected, turn into bowls of undifferentiated mush. I am a pacifist, I am an anarchist, I am a planetary citizen, and so on.

But the subject of this chapter is friendship, and, thanks to a routine miracle of this age of computers, I am able to submit an alphabetized list of writers who are or, in the case of the dead, were friends of mine. My wife, Jill Krementz, you see, has over the years photographed hundreds of writers, and has given their names and negative numbers to a computer, in order that she may deliver a picture of any one of them in a twinkling or two.

So I simply go down her list with my index finger, stopping at the name of each person I have met at least once, and, hey presto, my friends are Chinua Achebe, Richard Adams, Renata Adler, Ghingiz Aitmatov, Edward Albee, Nelson

Algren, Lisa Alther, Robert Anderson, Maya Angelou, Hannah Arendt, Michael Arlen, John Ashbery, Isaac Asimov, Richard Bach, Russell Baker, James Baldwin, Marvin Barrett, John Barth, Donald Barthelme, Jacques Barzun, Steve Becker, Saul Bellow, Ingrid Benjis, Robert Benton, Tom Berger, Charles Berlitz, Carl Bernstein, Michael Bessie, Ann Birstein, William Blatty, Heinrich Böll, Vance Bourjaily, Ray Bradbury, John Malcolm Brinnin, Jimmy Breslin, Harold Brodkey, C.D.B. Bryan, Art Buchwald, and, yes, William F. Buckley, Jr., William Burroughs, Lynn Caine, Erskine Caldwell, Hortense Calisher, Vincent Canby, Truman Capote, Schuyler Chapin, John Cheever, Marchette Chute, John Ciardi, Eleanor Clark, Ramsey Clark, Author C. Clarke, James Clavell, Arthur Cohen, William Cole, Dr. Alex Comfort, Richard Condon, Evan Connell, Frank Conroy, Malcolm Cowley, Harvey Cox, Robert Creighton, Michael Crichton, Judith Crist, John Crosby, Charlotte Curtis, Gwen Davis, Peter Davison, Peter de Vries, Borden Deal, Midge Decter, Lester Del Rey, Barbaralee Diamonstein, Monica Dickens, James Dickey, Joan Didion, E. L. Doctorow, Betty Dodson, J. P. Donleavy, José Donoso, Rosalyn Drexler, John Dunne, Richard Eberhart, Leon Edel, Margareta Ekström, Stanley Elkin, Ralph Ellison, Richard Elman, Amos Elon, Gloria Emerson, Hans Magnus Enzensberger, Nora Ephron, Edward Epstein, Jason Epstein, Willard Espy, Fred Exley, Oriana Fallaci, James T. Farrell, Lawrence Ferlinghetti, Frances Fitzgerald, Joe Flaherty, Janet Flanner, Thomas Fleming, Peter Forbath, William Price Fox, Gerald Frank, Michael Frayne, Eliot Fremont-Smith, Betty Friedan, Bruce Jay Friedman, Otto Friedrich, Max Frisch, Erich Fromm, Carlos Fuentes, William Gaddis, Nicholas Gage, Charles Gaines, John Kenneth Galbraith,

Mavis Gallant, John Gardner, William Gass, Barbara Gelb, Dan Gerber, Brendan Gill, Penelope Gilliatt, Allen Ginsberg, Nikki Giovanni, Gail Godwin, William Goldman, Nadine Gordimer, Edward Gorey, Lois Gould, Günter Grass, Francine du Plessix Gray, Adolph Green, Gael Greene, Germaine Greer, Winston Groom, Alex Haley, Daniel Halpern, Pete Hamill, Elizabeth Hardwick, Curtis Harnack, Michael Harper, Jim Harrison, Molly Haskell, John Hawkes, Joseph Heller, Lillian Hellman, Nat Hentoff, John Hersey, Rust Hills, Warren Hinkle, Sandra Hochman, Townsend Hoopes, A. E. Hotchner, Barbara Howar, Jane Howard, William Inge, Clifford Irving, John Irving, Christopher Isherwood, Roman Jakobson, Jill Johnston, James Jones, Erica Jong, Pauline Kael, E. J. Kahn, Garson Kanin, Justin Kaplan, Sue Kaufman, Elia Kazan, Alfred Kazin, Murray Kempton, Galway Kinnell, Judy Klemesrud, John Knowles, Hans Koning, Jerzy Kosinski, Robert Kotlowitz, Joe Kraft, Paul Krassner, Stanley Kunitz, Lewis Lapham, Jack Leggett, Siegfried Lenz, John Leonard, Max Lerner, Doris Lessing, Ira Levin, Meyer Levin, Robert Jay Lifton, Jakov Lind, Loyd Little, Anita Loos, Anthony Lukas, Alison Lurie, Leonard Lyons, Peter Maas, Dwight MacDonald, John D. MacDonald, Ross Macdonald, Archibald MacLeish, Eugene McCarthy, Mary McCarthy, Tom McGuane, Marshall McLuhan, Larry McMurtry, Terrance McNally, John McPhee, James McPherson, Norman Mailer, Bernard Malamud, Marya Mannes, Peter Matthiessen, Armistead Maupin, Rollo May, Margaret Mead, William Meredith, James Merrill, Arthur Miller, Jonathan Miller, Merle Miller, Kate Millett, James Mills, Jessica Mitford, Honor Moore, Elsa Morante, Alberto Moravia, Hans Morgenthau, Willie Morris, Wright Morris, Toni Morrison, Penelope Mortimer, Ray

Mungo, Albert Murray, William Murray, V. S. Naipaul, Victor Navasky, Edwin Newman, Leslie Newman, Anais Nïn, William A. Nolen, Marsha Norman, Edna O'Brien, Joyce Carol Oates, Sidney Offit (best friend!), Iris Owens, Amos Oz, Cynthia Ozick, Grace Paley, Gordon Parks, Jonathan Penner, S. J. Perelman, Eleanor Perry, Frank Perry, Jayne Anne Phillips, George Plimpton, Robert Pisig, Peter Prescott, V. S. Pritchett, Dotson Rader, Ishmael Reed, Rex Reed, Richard Reeves, James Reston, Jr., Adrienne Rich, Jill Robinson, Betty Rollins, Judith Rossner, Philip Roth, Mike Royko, Muriel Rukeyser, John Sack, William Safire, Carl Sagan, Harrison Salisbury, William Saroyan, Andrew Sarris, Nora Sayre, Dick Schaap, Susan Fromberg Schaeffer, Arthur Schlesinger, Jr., Steve Schlesinger, Bud Schulberg, Ellen Schwamm, Barbara Seaman, Erich Segal, Anne Sexton, Ntozake Shange, Harvey Shapiro, Adam Shaw, Irwin Shaw, Wilfrid Sheed, Neil Sheehan, Susan Sheehan, Lynn Sherr, Alix Kates Shulman, Andre Simenov, John Simon, Isaac B. Singer, Hedrick Smith, W. D. Snodgrass, C. P. Snow, Barbara Probst Soloman, Susan Sontag, Terry Southern, Wole Soyinka, Stephen Spender, Benjamin Spock, Jean Stafford, Gloria Steinem, Shane Stevens, I. F. Stone, Irving Stone, Robert Stone, Dorothea Straus, Rose Styron, William Styron, Jacqueline Susann, Gay Talese, James Tate, Peter Taylor, Studs Terkel, Hunter S. Thompson, Lionel Tiger, Hannah Tillich, Alvin Toffler, Lazlo Toth, Michael Tournier, Willard Trask, Calvin Trillin, Diana Trilling, Barbara Tuchman, Kenneth Tynan, Amy Vanderbilt, Gore Vidal, Esther Vilar, Roman Vishniac, Mark Vonnegut, Andrei Voznesensky, Alice Walker, Joseph Wambaugh, Wayne Warga, Robert Penn Warren, Per Wästberg, Peter Weiss, Eudora Welty, Glenway Wescott, Morris West, E. B. White,

Theodore White, William Whitworth, Tom Wicker, Elie Wiesel, Richard Wilbur, Paul Wilkes, Joy Williams, Tennessee Williams, Garry Wills, Larry Woiwode, Tom Wolfe, Geoffrey Wolff, Herman Wouk, Christopher Wren, Charles Wright, James Wright, Lois Wyse, and Richard Yates.

Would you like an introduction?

❦

WHAT stories I must have to tell in Indianapolis about all these celebrities! Not really. Most writers are not quick-witted when they talk. Novelists in particular, as I have said before, drag themselves around in society like gut-shot bears. The good ones do.

Some people say that my friend Gore Vidal, who once suggested in an interview that I was the worst writer in the United States, is witty. I myself think he wants an awful lot of credit for wearing a three-piece suit.

❦

AFTER meeting all these people, I have only a single shapely anecdote to tell. It took place at the University of Iowa in Iowa City, where I taught in the famed Writers' Workshop in 1965 and 1966. My most famous colleagues were the novelists Vance Bourjaily, Nelson Algren, and Richard Yates, and the Chilean José Donoso, and the poets George Starbuck, James Tate, Marvin Bell, Donald Justice—and the poet-founder of the Workshop, of course, who is Paul Engle.

Among those students of ours who would really amount to something as writers by and by, incidentally, were Jane Barnes and John Casey and Bruce Dobler and Andre Dubus and Gail Godwin and John Irving and Jonathan Penner.

So Algren and Donoso and I were new arrivals, and we went together to the first autumn meeting of the English department, against whose treasury our paychecks were drawn. We thought we should be there. Nobody had told us that lecturers in the Writers' Workshop traditionally ignored all such bureaucratic, sesquipedalian sniveling and obfuscation.

So Algren and Donoso and I were going down a staircase afterward. Algren had come late, and so had sat separate from Donoso and me. He and Donoso had never met before, so I introduced them on the staircase, explaining to Algren that Donoso was from Chile, but a graduate of Princeton University.

Algren shook Donoso's hand, but said nothing to him until we reached the bottom. He at last thought of something to say to a Chilean novelist: "It must be nice," he said, "to come from a country that long and narrow."

❦

ARE many novelists schizophrenic—at least marginally so? Do they hallucinate, seeing and hearing things that healthy people cannot sense? Do they turn disordered perceptions into gold in the literary marketplace? If writers are usefully crazy, what is the medical name for their disease? Or, if writers themselves aren't lunatics, perhaps a lot of their ancestors were.

The psychiatric department of the University of Iowa's hospital, it turns out, has wondered some about these questions, which have their roots in folklore. It has taken advantage of the large numbers of reputable writers who come to

Iowa City, usually down on their luck, to teach at the Writers' Workshop. So they have questioned us about our mental health and about that of our ancestors and siblings, too.

It is apparent to them, I am told, that we are not hallucinators, nor are many of us descended from those who saw or heard things which weren't really there. Overwhelmingly, we are depressed, and are descended from those who, psychologically speaking, spent more time than anyone in his or her right mind would want to spend in gloom.

❦

I would add that novelists are not only unusually depressed, by and large, but have, on the average, about the same IQs as the cosmetics consultants at Bloomingdale's department store. Our power is patience. We have discovered that writing allows even a stupid person to seem halfway intelligent, if only that person will write the same thought over and over again, improving it just a little bit each time. It is a lot like inflating a blimp with a bicycle pump. Anybody can do it. All it takes is time.

❦

I heard a Frenchman in a Madison Avenue bookstore say in English the other day that nobody in America had produced a book in forty years or more. I knew what he meant. He was talking about planetary literary treasures on the order of *Moby Dick* or *Huckleberry Finn* or *Leaves of Grass* or *Walden,* say. I had to agree with him. No book from this country during my lifetime (1922–?) has been in scale with *Ulysses* or *Remembrance of Things Past* or *The Tin Drum* or *One Hundred Years of Solitude* or *A Day in the Life of Ivan Denisovitch.*

Still, now that I contemplate all the Americans on my list of friends, I wish the Frenchman were here so that I could say to him frostily: "You are quite right, mon-sewer, we have not produced a book. All we poor Americans could do was produce a literature."

❦

AND here is how I spoke well of my friend Joseph Heller's contributions to that literature in *The New York Times Book Review* of Sunday, October 6, 1974:

The company that made a movie out of Joseph Heller's first novel, *Catch-22,* had to assemble what became the 11th or 12th largest bomber force on the planet at the time. If somebody wants to make a movie out of his second novel, *Something Happened,* he can get most of his props at Bloomingdale's—a few beds, a few desks, some tables and chairs.

Life is a whole lot smaller and cheaper in this second book. It has shrunk to the size of a grave, almost.

Mark Twain is said to have felt that his existence was all pretty much downhill from his adventures as a Mississippi riverboat pilot. Mr. Heller's two novels, when considered in sequence, might be taken as a similar statement about an entire white, middle-class generation of American males, my generation, Mr. Heller's generation, Herman Wouk's generation, Norman Mailer's generation, Irwin Shaw's generation, Vance Bourjaily's generation, James Jones's generation, and on and on—that for them everything has been downhill since World War II, as absurd and bloody as it often was.

Both books are full of excellent jokes, but neither one is funny. Taken together they tell a tale of pain and disappointments experienced by mediocre men of good will.

Mr. Heller is a first-rate humorist who cripples his own jokes intentionally—with the unhappiness of the characters who perceive them. He also insists on dealing with only the most hackneyed themes. After a thousand World War II airplane novels had been published and pulped, he gave us yet another one, which was gradually acknowledged as a sanely crazy masterpiece.

Now he offers us the thousand and first version of *The Hucksters* or *The Man in the Gray Flannel Suit*.

There is a nattily dressed, sourly witty middle-management executive named Robert Slocum, he tells us, who lives in a nice house in Connecticut with a wife, a daughter, and two sons. Slocum works in Manhattan in the communications racket. He is restless. He mourns the missed opportunities of his youth. He is itchy for raises and promotions, even though he despises his company and the jobs he does. He commits unsatisfying adulteries now and then at sales conferences in resort areas, during long lunch hours, or while pretending to work late at the office.

He is exhausted.

He dreads old age.

Mr. Heller's rewriting of this written-to-death situation took him 12 years. It comes out as a monologue by Slocum. Nobody else gets to talk, except as reported by Slocum. And Slocum's sentences are so alike in shape and texture from the beginning to the end of the book, that I imagined a man who was making an enormous statue out of sheet metal. He was shaping it with millions of identical taps from a ball-peen hammer.

Each dent was a fact, a depressingly ordinary fact.

"My wife is a good person, really, or used to be," says Slocum near the beginning, "and sometimes I'm sorry for her. She drinks during the day and flirts, or tries to, at parties we go to in the evening, although she doesn't know how."

"I have given my daughter a car of her own," he says near the end. "Her spirits seem to be picking up."

Slocum does his deadly best to persuade us, with his tap-tap-tapping of facts, that he is compelled to be as unhappy as he is, not because of enemies or flaws in his own character, but because of the facts.

What have these tedious facts done to him? They have required that he respond to them, since he is a man of good will. And responding and responding and responding to them has left him petrified with boredom and drained of any capacity for joyfulness, now that he is deep into middle age.

Only one fact among the millions is clearly horrible. Only one distinguishes Slocum's bad luck from that of his neighbors. His youngest child is an incurable imbecile.

Slocum is heartless about the child. "I no longer think of Derek as one of my children," he says. "Or even as mine. I try not to think of him at all. This is becoming easier, even at home when he is nearby with the rest of us, making noise with some red cradle toy or making unintelligible sounds as he endeavors to speak. By now I don't even know his name. The children don't care for him either."

Mr. Heller might have here, or at least somewhere in his book, used conventional, Chekhovian techniques for making us love a sometimes wicked man. He might have said that Slocum was drunk or tired after a bad day at the office when he spoke so heartlessly, or that he whispered his heartlessness only to himself or to a stranger he would never see again.

But Slocum is invariably sober and deliberate during his monologue, and does not seem to give a damn who hears what he says. Judging from his selection of unromantic episodes and attitudes it is his wish that we dislike him.

And we gratify that wish.

Is this book any good? Yes. It is splendidly put together and hypnotic to read. It is as clear and hard-edged as a cut diamond. Mr. Heller's concentration and patience are so evident on every page that one can only say that *Something Happened* is at all points precisely what he hoped it would be.

The book may be marketed under false pretenses, which is all right with me. I have already seen British sales promotion materials which suggest that we have been ravenous for a new Heller book because we want to laugh some more. This is as good a way as any to get people to read one of the unhappiest books ever written.

Something Happened is so astonishingly pessimistic, in fact, that it can be called a daring experiment. Depictions of utter hopelessness in literature have been acceptable up to now only in small doses, in short-story form, as in Franz Kafka's "The Metamorphosis," Shirley Jackson's "The Lottery," or John D. MacDonald's "The Hangover," to name a treasured few. As far as I know, though, Joseph Heller is the first major American writer to deal with unrelieved misery at novel length. Even more rashly, he leaves his chief character, Slocum, essentially unchanged at the end.

A middle-aged woman who had just finished *Something Happened* in galleys said to me the other day that she thought it was a reply to all the recent books by women about the unrewardingness of housewives' lives. And Slocum does seem to argue that he is entitled to at least as much unhappiness as any woman he knows. His wife, after all, has to adapt to only one sort of hell, the domestic torture chamber in Connecticut, in which he, too, must writhe at night and on weekends, when he isn't committing adultery. But he must go regularly to his office, where pain is inflicted on all the nerve centers which were neglected by the tormentors at home.

(The place where Slocum works, incidentally, is unnamed, and its products and services are undescribed. But I had a friend of a friend of an acquaintance ask Mr. Heller if he minded naming Slocum's employers. Mr. Heller replied with all possible speed and openness, "Time, Incorporated." So we have a small scoop.)

Just as Mr. Heller is uninterested in tying a tin can to anything as localized as a company with a familiar name, so is he far above the complaining contests going on between men and women these days. He began this book way back in 1962, and there have been countless gut-ripping news items and confrontations since then. But Heller's man Slocum is deaf and blind to them. He receives signals from only three sources: his office, his memory and home.

And, on the basis of these signals alone, he is able to say, apparently in all seriousness: "The world just doesn't work. It's an idea whose time is gone."

This is black humor indeed—with the humor removed.

Robert Slocum was in the Air Force in Italy during World War II, by the way. He was especially happy there while demonstrating his unflagging virility to prostitutes. So it was also with John Yossarian, the hero of *Catch-22*, whose present whereabouts are unknown.

There will be a molasses-like cautiousness about accepting this book as an important one. It took more than a year for

Catch-22 to gather a band of enthusiasts. I myself was cautious about that book. I am cautious again.

The uneasiness which many people will feel about liking *Something Happened* has roots which are deep. It is no casual thing to swallow a book by Joseph Heller, for he is, whether he intends to be or not, a maker of myths. (One way to do this, surely, is to be the final and most brilliant teller of an oft-told tale.) *Catch-22* is now the dominant myth about Americans in the war against fascism. *Something Happened,* if swallowed, could become the dominant myth about the middle-class veterans who came home from that war to become heads of nuclear families. The proposed myth has it that those families were pathetically vulnerable and suffocating. It says that the heads of them commonly took jobs which were vaguely dishonorable or at least stultifying, in order to make as much money as they could for their little families, and they used that money in futile attempts to buy safety and happiness. The proposed myth says that they lost their dignity and their will to live in the process.

It says they are hideously tired now.

To accept a new myth about ourselves is to simplify our memories—and to place our stamp of approval on what might become an epitaph for our era in the shorthand of history. This, in my opinion, is why critics often condemn our most significant books and poems and plays when they first appear, while praising feebler creations. The birth of a new myth fills them with primitive dread, for myths are so effective.

Well—I have now suppressed my own dread. I have thought dispassionately about *Something Happened* and I am now content to have it shown to future generations as a spooky sort of summary of what my generation of nebulously clever white people experienced, and what we, with-

THE PEOPLE ONE KNOWS ■ 447

in the cage of those experiences, then did with our lives.

And I am counting on a backlash. I expect younger readers to love Robert Slocum—on the grounds that he couldn't possibly be as morally repellent and socially useless as he claims to be.

People a lot younger than I am may even be able to laugh at Slocum in an affectionate way, something I am unable to do. They may even see comedy in his tragic and foolish belief that he is totally responsible for the happiness or unhappiness of the members of his tiny family.

They may even see some nobility in him as an old soldier who has been brought to emotional ruin at last by the aging process and civilian life.

As for myself: I can't crack a smile when he says, ostensibly about the positions in which he sleeps, "I have exchanged the position of the fetus for the position of the corpse." And I am so anxious for Slocum to say something good about life that I read hope into lines meant to be supremely ironical, such as when he says this: "I know at last what I want to be when I grow up. When I grow up I want to be a little boy."

What is perhaps Slocum's most memorable speech mourns not his own generation but the one after his, in the person of his sullen, teen-age daughter. "There was a cheerful baby girl in a high chair in my house once," he says, "who ate and drank with a hearty appetite and laughed a lot with spontaneous zest; she isn't here now, and there is no trace of her anywhere."

We keep reading this overly long book, even though there is no rise and fall in passion and language, because it is structured as a suspense novel. The puzzle which seduces us is this one: Which of several possible tragedies will result from so much unhappiness? The author picks a good one.

I say that this is the most memorable, and therefore the most permanent variation on a familiar theme, and that it says baldly what the other variations only implied, what the other variations tried with desperate sentimentality not to imply: That many lives, judged by the standards of the people who live them, are simply not worth living.

❧

WAS it unethical of me to review a book by a friend of mine for *The New York Times*? I did not know Heller all that well back then. We had taught at City College together, and had exchanged greetings in the halls. If I had known him well, I would have refused the assignment.

But then, after I accepted it, I rented a summer house close to his on Long Island—and I got to know him better and better at precisely the time I was reviewing *Something Happened.* He was especially concerned, it turned out, about who was going to do that job for the *Times.*

I told him that I had heard a strong rumor, one which satisfied him entirely, that the *Times* had hired Robert Penn Warren, who was, even as we spoke, probably ransacking the book for its deepest meanings in his leafy hideaway in Vermont.

❧

As for literary criticism in general: I have long felt that any reviewer who expresses rage and loathing for a novel or a play or a poem is preposterous. He or she is like a person who has put on full armor and attacked a hot fudge sundae or a banana split.

I admire anybody who finishes a work of art, no matter how awful it may be. A drama critic from a news magazine, speaking to me on the opening night of a play of mine, said that he liked to remind himself from time to time that Shakespeare was standing right behind him, so that he had to be very responsible and wise whenever he expressed an opinion about a play.

I told him that he had it exactly ass backwards—that Shakespeare was standing behind me and every other playwright who was foolhardy enough to face an opening night, no matter how bad our plays might be.

❧

AND here is how I praised my friend Irwin Shaw at a banquet in his honor at The Players club here in New York, a so-called pipe night, on October 7, 1979. My friend Frank Sinatra was there, and my friends Adolph Green and Betty Comden, and my friend Joseph Heller, and my friend Willie Morris, and my friend Martin Gabel, and on and on. I had this to say:

"I apologize for reading from a piece of paper. Writers are pitiful people in a way. They have to write everything out.

"This is an actors' club, and I must admit that actors are far superior to writers when it comes to public speaking. They have somebody else write whatever it is they're going to say, and then they memorize it.

"This is a club for memorizers, and I think it's nice that they have a club. Everybody who wants a club should have one. That's what America is all about.

"That, and fighting different diseases, and so on.

"We are here principally to honor Irwin Shaw as an artist and human being. I would like to thank him, too, for his demonstration of what a lifetime of vigorous athletics can do to the human body.

"He likes to be thought of as a very tough guy. And it's true that he has turned skiing into a contact sport.

"So, Irwin, I salute you now as the Rocky Graziano of American letters—because that is the way I think you want to be saluted. And you will be happy to know that I often get taxi drivers who don't talk just a little like you. Irwin, they talk exactly like you.

"They've also all turned out to be gentlemen like you.

"And how can you claim to be so tough anyway, when you have written one of the most innocent and beautiful stories I ever hope to read? I refer to 'The Girls in Their Summer Dresses.' This story says that even men in love will look longingly at every beautiful girl who comes along when the weather is warm, but concludes that there is no harm in this.

"Irwin, how innocent can you be?

"Well, I hate to say this with Joseph Heller present. . . .

"Actually, it's sort of elating to say it with Joseph Heller present. . . .

"Irwin Shaw wrote the best American novel about World War Two, which was *The Young Lions.* He was the only one of us who had enough wisdom and nerve to write about the European part of that war from both sides of the lines. As a German-American, of course, I was sorry to see him make the Nazis the bad guys.

"But by and large *The Young Lions* was such a good book that it made Ernest Hemingway mad. He thought he had copyrighted war.

"But the Ernest Hemingway story is a tragic one, and the Irwin Shaw story is anything but that. Look how happy Irwin is.

"I know where a lot of that happiness is coming from, but some of it should surely be attributed to the fact that the publication of Irwin's collected short stories last year confirmed beyond a doubt that he is one of the greatest storytellers of all time.

"Oh, I know it is cruel on a man's ninety-second birthday to talk about nothing but the work he did as a youngster. But I have done that tonight for selfish reasons, to celebrate my own youth, when I was so enthusiastic about so many things. That's what it was to be young—to be enthusiastic rather than envious about the good work other people could do.

"And I was so enthusiastic about everything written by Irwin Shaw. He continues to write as well as ever, but I can no longer take pleasure in reading him, since he is my colleague now. I simply can't afford to like anybody but me. When I read anybody else now, I see his or her words only dimly, as though through a finely divided mist of sulfuric acid or mustard gas.

"I can see this much in Irwin's present work, though: Despite all the high living he has done far away from us, in Europe and the Hamptons and so on, he still knows how Americans talk and feel. This is highly unusual in our literary history. Almost every other important American writer who has lived elsewhere has soon lost touch with how we talk and feel.

"How has he worked this miracle? I will have to guess, but I am almost sure I'm right about this. Every time Irwin comes to New York, I think, he takes a job driving a taxicab.

"Now that I have let you in on his little secret, you won't

be surprised if you find him driving you home after this banquet in his honor.

"I thank you for your attention."

❂

AND here is what I said about my friends Bob Elliott and Ray Goulding, perhaps the most significant and ridiculous American comedy team alive today, as an introduction to their book *Write If You Get Work: The Best of Bob & Ray* (Random House, 1975):

It is the truth: Comedians and jazz musicians have been more comforting and enlightening to me than preachers or politicians or philosophers or poets or painters or novelists of my time. Historians in the future, in my opinion, will congratulate us on very little other than our clowning and our jazz.

And if they know what they are doing, they will have especially respectful words for Bob and Ray, whose book this is. They will say, among other things, that Bob and Ray's jokes were remarkably literary, being fun to read as well as to hear. They may note, too, that Bob and Ray had such energy and such a following that they continued to create marvelous material for radio at a time when radio creatively was otherwise dead.

I have listened to Bob and Ray for years and years now —in New England, in New York City. We are about the same age, which means that we were inspired by roughly the same saints—Jack Benny, Fred Allen, W. C. Fields, Stoop-nagle and Bud, and on and on. And my collected works would fill Oliver Hardy's derby, whereas theirs would fill the Astrodome.

This book contains about one ten-thousandth of their output, I would imagine. And it might be exciting to say that it represents the cream of the cream of the cream of their jokes. But the truth is that there has been an amazing evenness to their performances. I recall a single broadcast of ten years ago, for example, which might have made a book nearly as elating as this one.

I was in the studio when I heard it—and saw it, too. I was supposedly applying for a job as a writer for Bob and Ray. We meant to talk about the job in between comedy bits, when the microphones were dead. One of the bits I remember was about selling advertising space on the sides of the Bob and Ray Satellite, which was going to be orbited only twenty-eight feet off the ground.

There was an announcement, too, about the Bob and Ray Overstocked Surplus Warehouse, which was crammed with sweaters emblazoned with the letter "O." If your name didn't begin with "O," they said, they could have it legally changed for you.

And so on.

There was an episode from Mary Backstayge. Mary's actor husband, Harry, was trying to get a part in a play. His big talent, according to his supporters, was that he was wonderful at memorizing things.

There was an animal imitator who said that a pig went "oink oink," and a cow went "moo," and that a rooster went "cock-a-doodle-doo."

I very nearly popped a gut. I am pathetically vulnerable to jokes such as these. I expect to be killed by laughter sooner or later. And I told Bob and Ray that I could never write anything as funny as what I had heard on what was for them a perfectly ordinary day.

I was puzzled that day by Bob's and Ray's melancholy. It seemed to me that they should be the happiest people on earth, but looks of sleepy ruefulness crossed their faces like clouds from time to time. I have seen those same clouds at subsequent encounters—and only now do I have a theory to explain them:

I surmise that Bob and Ray feel accursed sometimes—like crewmen on the *Flying Dutchman* or caged squirrels on an exercise wheel. They are so twangingly attuned to their era and to each other that they can go on being extremely funny almost indefinitely.

Such an unlimited opportunity to make people happy must become profoundly pooping by and by.

It occurs to me, too, as I look through this marvelous book, that Bob and Ray's jokes are singularly burglar-proof. They aren't like most other comedians' jokes these days, aren't rooted in show business and the world of celebrities and news of the day. They feature Americans who are almost always fourth-rate or below, engaged in enterprises which, if not contemptible, are at least insane.

And while other comedians show us persons tormented by bad luck and enemies and so on, Bob and Ray's characters threaten to wreck themselves and their surroundings with their own stupidity. There is a refreshing and beautiful innocence in Bob's and Ray's humor.

Man is not evil, they seem to say. He is simply too hilariously stupid to survive.

And this I believe.

Cheers.

❧

AND here is what I said at a funeral here for my friend James T. Farrell on August 24, 1979, whose body was taken afterward to a Catholic cemetery in his native Chicago:

"I am here at the request of a member of the family—perhaps as a representative of the generation of American writers most influenced by James T. Farrell. I was not a close friend. Many of you were, and I envy you that. I knew him some. I found him easy to love and admire. He was eighteen years my senior.

"Here is what he did for me and many like me when I was very young: He showed me through his books that it was perfectly all right, perhaps even useful and beautiful, to say what life really looked like, what was really said and felt and done—what really went on. Until I read him, I wished only to be well received in polite company.

"We were both University of Chicago people.

"I note that there is a cross over his casket. That is a nice try by whoever put it there, but it is surely known in heaven that James T. Farrell of Chicago and New York was not among our leaders in organized tub-beating for Jesus Christ. He took his chances that way. If he is being scolded at this moment at the Pearly Gates, it may be for his overemphasis of rationality and compassion and honor at the expense of piety. I fear not for him. This is an argument he has won before.

"The last time I was in this melancholy depot, it was to say farewell to Janet Flanner, another midwesterner who became a planetary patriot. Ms. Flanner and Mr. Farrell were members of the American Academy and Institute of Arts and Letters. Ms. Flanner came regularly to the annual spring meeting of that organization. So do many of our leading culture heroes. James T. Farrell never came. One time I asked him why not. He said that he did not care to come face to face with some of the critics, fellow writers, who had damned his work years ago—had damned it ostensibly for bad writing, but actually for the supposedly incorrect political opinions he was known to hold. He was a premature anti-Stalinist. He was, and remained so to his death, a left-wing thinking man.

"The malicious attacks did not humble him, could not humble him, since he was Irish. They did, however, so muddy his reputation that a dispassionate appraisal of his life's work remains to be made. It is a huge work. It is Balzacian in scale. I spoke at his seventy-third birthday, two years ago, and I suggested that, if only James T. Farrell had produced such a body of work in a smaller country, he would have won a Nobel prize by then. That was a strong statement. It had the added force of ringing true.

"The ancient Greeks believed, or some of them did, anyway, that a person could not be said to have lived well if he or she died in unhappy circumstances. This is a deservedly unpopular opinion in America, where so many lives end abominably, almost as a matter of routine. But let us suppose that the Greeks were right. By their hard standards we can say that the American writer James T. Farrell had a wonderful life. He died in his sleep, in the presence of deep love such as the world has seldom seen—and owing no one an apology for anything.

"He was a sports nut, of course—and once an athlete of great and varied skills. So it is appropriate if we now address our memories of him in this fashion: 'You won, you won.' "

�422

PLAYMATES

I delivered a speech at the University of Virginia maybe eight years ago, which mercifully has been lost, so I do not have to paste it in here somewhere. I said, I remember, that Thomas Jefferson in his mansion called Monticello, with an artificial trout pool in its front yard, and its dumbwaiters for bringing wine and cider up from the basement, and its secret staircases and so on, was the Hugh Hefner of his time. Jefferson didn't have for servants young women with great balls of cotton stuck to their behinds. He owned honest-to-God slaves instead.

A history professor explained to me afterward that Jefferson was so slow to free his slaves because he did not really own them. He had mortgaged them. Like this mortgaged house in which I write now, they belonged to the bank.

Author's note: No entirely white descendent of Thomas Jefferson is alive today.

❦

BUT the best part of that visit was finding out what had happened to a childhood playmate of mine. He was two years my junior, and had lived right next door to me in Indianapolis. We were playmates during the 1930s. His father and mine had both built grandiose houses during the boom of the 1920s. But during the 1930s they were both going broke. His father owned a furniture store which was bankrupt, and my father could find no work as an architect, and my mother and father were becoming widely known as deadbeats who would run huge charge accounts and never pay. This playmate sent me a note while I was in Charlottesville, and by God if he hadn't become head of the astronomy department at the university. Sam Goldstein was his name.

So Sam and I had a good talk about the work he was doing, which was mainly with radio telescopes, and the work I was doing. We told about our children. Things were going well.

We refreshed our memories about neighborhood dogs we had known, dogs which had known us, too. We remembered two bulldogs named Boots and Beans, who were owned by a family named Wales. Boots and Beans used to catch cats and small dogs and pull them in two. I personally witnessed their doing that to a cat of ours.

Sam and I laughed when I told about my father's sending the message to Mr. Wales that he would shoot Boots and Beans if they ever came into our yard again. Mr. Wales sent back the message that he would shoot Father if Father shot Boots and Beans.

Psychoanalysts are missing important clues about patients' childhoods if they do not ask about dogs the patients knew. As I have said elsewhere, dogs still seem as respectable and interesting as people to me. Any day.

❦

DOG poisoning is still the most contemptible crime I can think of. Boots and Beans were poisoned finally, but I couldn't celebrate that, and our family certainly had nothing to do with it. If we were going to poison anybody, it would have been Mr. Wales.

❦

THE dogs of our childhood were dead when Sam Goldstein and I were reunited in Charlottesville, so we would have been crazy to speculate about what they might be doing nowadays. We could speculate about children we had known, though, since human beings live so long. We would say things like, "What do you suppose ever happened to Nancy Briggs?" or "Where do you think Dick Martin is now?" and on and on. Sometimes one or the other of us had a stale clue or two. Nancy Briggs married a sailor and moved to Texas during the Second World War. How's that for a clue?

❦

I have played that game so often in this jerry-built society of ours—"Whatever Became of So-and-so?" It becomes a truly sad game only if someone actually knows in detail what became of several so-and-sos. Several ordinary life stories, if told in rapid succession, tend to make life look far more pointless than it really is, probably.

The people I am most eager to have news of, curiously enough, are those I worked with in the General News Bureau of the General Electric Company in Schenectady, New York —from 1948 to 1951, from the time I was twenty-six until I was twenty-nine. They were all men I worked with, but when I think of that good old gang of mine, I include their wives.

As the song from the Gay Nineties, "That Old Gang of Mine," would have it:

So long forever, old fellows and pals,
So long forever, old sweethearts and gals. . . .

My persisting concern about all those General Electric people is so irrational and deep that I have to suspect that it may have genetic roots of some sort. I may have been born with some sort of clock in me which required me to love those working alongside of me so much at that time. We were just getting our footing as adult citizens, and in other times we might have been correct in thinking that we had better like and trust each other a lot, since we would be together for life.

It was the Darwinian wish of General Electric, of the Free Enterprise System, of course, that we compete instead.

I have heard other people say that they, too, remain irrationally fond of those who were with them when they were just starting out. It's a common thing.

ONE of my closest friends from General Electric is Ollie M. Lyon, who became a vice-president at Young and Rubicam advertising for a while, and then went back to his home state of Kentucky to sell sophisticated silos to farmers. The silos were so airtight that almost no silage was lost to fermentation and vermin and rot.

I loved Ollie's wife Lavina exactly as much as I loved him, and she died fast of cancer of the pancreas out there in Kentucky. One of her last requests was that I speak at her funeral. "I want him to say good-bye to me," she said. So I did.

I said this:

"Lavina asked me to be up here.

"This is the hardest thing Lavina ever asked me to do, but then she never asked anyone to do anything hard. Her only instructions were that I was to say good-bye to her as an old friend—as *all* old friends.

"I say it now. If I had to say it at the end, to build up to saying it, I would go all to pieces, I think. I would bark like a dog. So I say it now: 'Good-bye, darling Lavina.'

"There—that is behind me now. That is behind us, now.

"It is common at funerals for survivors to regret many things that were said and done to the departed—to think, 'I wish I had said this instead of this, I wish I had done that instead of that.' This is not that sort of funeral. This is not a church filled with regrets.

"Why not? We *always* treated Lavina with love and decency. Why did we do that? It was Lavina's particular genius to so behave that the only possible responses on our part were love and decency. That is her richest legacy to us, I think: Her lessons in how to treat others so that their only possible responses are, again, love and decency.

"There is at least one person here who does not need to learn what Lavina knew. He is Lavina's spiritual equal, although he was so much in love with her that perhaps he never knew it. He is Ollie Morris Lyon.

"Ollie and Lavina are country people, by the way.

"I have seen them achieve success and happiness in the ugly factory city of Schenectady, New York, where I first met them. They were not much older than Mary and Philip then. Think of that. Yes, and when they lived in New York City, they had as much fun as any jazz-age babies ever did. Good for them! But they were always a farmer and his wife.

"Now the farmer's wife has died. I'm glad they got back here before she died.

"The wife died first.

"It happens all the time—but it always seems like such a terrible violation of the natural order when the wife dies first. Is there anyone here, even a child, who did not believe that Lavina would survive us all? She was so healthy, so capable, so beautiful, so strong. She was supposed to come to *our* funerals—not the other way around.

"Well—she may come to them yet. She will, if she can. She will talk to God about it, I'm sure. If anybody can stretch the rules of heaven a little, Lavina can.

"I say she was strong. We all say she was strong. Yes, and in this bicentennial springtime we can say that she was like a legendary pioneer woman in her seeming strengths. We know now that she was only pretending to be strong—which is the best any of us can do. Of course, if you can pretend to be strong all your life, which is what Lavina did, then you can be very comforting to those around you. You can allow them to be childlike now and then.

"Good job, Lavina, darling. And remember, too, Lavina, the times we let you be a little girl.

"When she was a little girl in Palmyra, Illinois, being the youngest of a large family, she was expected to leave a note in the kitchen saying where she had gone after school. One day the note that was found said 'I have gone where I have decided.'

"We loved you.

"We love you.

"We will always love you.

"We will meet again."

❦

I now confess that the American poems which move me most are those which marvel most, simply and clearly, at the queer shapes which the massive indifference of America gives to lives. So *The Spoon River Anthology* by Edgar Lee Masters seems a very great book to me.

That is a barbarous opinion. So I have nothing to lose by blurting moreover that I find much to celebrate in the shrewd innocence of many of the poems now being set to country music.

Pay attention, please, to the words of "The Class of '57," a big country hit of a few years ago:

> Tommy's sellin' used cars,
> Nancy's fixin' hair,
> Harvey runs a groc'ry store
> And Marg'ret doesn't care,
> Jerry drives a truck for Sears

and Charlotte's on the make.
And Paul sells life insurance
And part-time real estate.

And the Class of Fifty Seven had its dreams.
But we all thought we'd changed the world
With our great works and deeds;
Or maybe we just thought the world
Would change to fit our needs.
The Class of Fifty Seven had its dreams.

Betty runs a trailer park,
Jan sells Tupperware,
Randy's on an insane ward,
And Mary's on welfare,
Charley took a job with Ford,
Joe took Freddy's wife,
Charlotte took a millionaire,
And Freddy took his life.

And the Class of Fifty Seven had its dreams,
But livin' life from day to day
Is never like it seems.
Things get complicated
When you get past eighteen,
But the Class of Fifty Seven had its dreams.

Helen is a hostess,
Frank works at the mill,
Janet teaches grade school
And prob'ly always will,
Bob works for the city,

And Jack's in lab research,
And Peggy plays the organ
At the Presbyterian Church.

And the Class of Fifty Seven had its dreams.
But we all thought we'd change the world
With our great works and deeds;
Or maybe we just thought the world
Would change to fit our needs.
The Class of Fifty Seven had its dreams.

John is big in cattle,
Ray is deep in debt,
Where Mavis fin'ly wound up
Is anybody's bet,
Linda married Sonny,
Brenda married me,
and the class of all of us
Is just part of history.

And the Class of Fifty Seven had its dreams,
But livin' life from day to day
Is never like it seems.
Things get complicated
When you get past eighteen,
But the Class of Fifty Seven had its dreams.
Ah, the Class of Fifty Seven had its dreams.

The authors are Don and Harold Reid, the only actual brothers in the country-music quartet that calls itself the Statler Brothers. Nobody in the quartet is named Statler. The quartet named itself after a roll of paper towels.

❦

MY wife Jill and I admire the Statler Brothers so much that we went all the way to the Niagara Falls International Convention Center in April of 1980 to hear them and to shake their hands. We had our pictures taken with them, too.

Yes, and they announced from the stage that they were honored that night to have in the audience "the famous writer Kurt Vonnegut and his wife, Jill Krementz, the famous photographer." We got a terrific hand, although we did not stand up and identify ourselves, and although nobody, I'm sure, had ever heard of us before.

A woman came up to us afterward, and she said that we must be the famous people the brothers had mentioned, since we didn't look like anybody else in the auditorium. She said that from now on she was going to read everything we wrote.

Jill and I stayed in the same Holiday Inn as the Statler Brothers, but they slept all afternoon. Their bus was parked outside where we could see it from our room. Right after their performance, around midnight, they got on the bus, and it started up with that fruity, burbling, soft purple rumble that bus engines have. The bus left without any lights showing inside. Nobody waved from a window. It headed for Columbus, Ohio, for another performance the next night. I forget where it was supposed to go after that—Saginaw, Michigan, I think.

❦

I would actually like to have "The Class of '57" become our national anthem for a little while. Everybody knows that "The Star Spangled Banner" is a bust as music and poetry, and is as representative of the American spirit as the Taj Mahal.

I can see Americans singing in a grandstand at the Olympics somewhere, while one of our athletes wins a medal—for the decathlon, say. I can see tears streaming down the singers' cheeks when they get to these lines:

> Where Mavis fin'ly wound up
> Is anybody's bet.

❦

"THE Class of '57" could be an anthem for my generation, at least. Many people have said that we already have an anthem, which is my friend Allen Ginsberg's "Howl," which starts off like this:

I saw the best minds of my generation destroyed
   by madness, starving hysterical naked,
dragging themselves through the negro streets
   at dawn looking for an angry fix,
angelheaded hipsters burning for the ancient
   heavenly connection to the starry dynamo
   in the machinery of night.

And so on.

I like "Howl" a lot. Who wouldn't? It just doesn't have much to do with me or what happened to my friends. For one thing, I believe that the best minds of my generation were probably musicians and physicists and mathematicians and biologists and archaeologists and chess masters and so on, and Ginsberg's closest friends, if I'm not mistaken, were undergraduates in the English department of Columbia University.

No offense intended, but it would never occur to me to look for the best minds in any generation in an undergraduate English department anywhere. I would certainly try the physics department or the music department first—and after that biochemistry.

Everybody knows that the dumbest people in any American university are in the education department, and English after that.

❧

ALSO, and again I intend no offense, the most meaningful and often harrowing adventures which I and many like me have experienced have had to do with the rearing of children. "Howl" does not deal with such adventures.

Truly great poems never do, somehow.

❧

ALLEN Ginsberg and I were inducted into the National Institute of Arts and Letters in the same year, 1973. Somebody from *Newsweek* called me up to ask what I had to say about two such antiestablishment writers being embraced by such a conservative organization.

I said this, and I meant it, and my comment was not printed: "My goodness, if Mr. Ginsberg and I aren't already members of the establishment, I don't know who is."

❧

To return to the subject of childhood playmates: In the Vonnegut house, with its charge-account deadbeats, and in the Goldstein house next door, with its bankruptcy, there were many books. As luck would have it, the Goldstein children and I, and the Marks children three doors down, whose father would soon die quite suddenly, could all read about as easily as we could eat chocolate ice cream. Thus, at a very tender age and in utter silence, disturbing no one, being children as good as gold, we were comforted and nourished by human minds which were calmer and more patient and amusing and unafraid than our parents could afford to be.

❧

YEARS later, on October 1, 1976, I would pay this circuitous tribute to the art of reading at the dedication of a new library at Connecticut College, New London:

"The name of this speech is 'The Noodle Factory.'

"Like life itself, this speech will be over before you know it. Life is so short!

"I was born only yesterday morning, moments after daybreak—and yet, this afternoon, I am fifty-four years old. I am a mere baby, and yet here I am dedicating a library. Something has gone wrong.

"I have a painter friend named Syd Solomon. He was also born only yesterday. And the next thing he knew, it was time for him to have a retrospective exhibition of his paintings going back thirty-five years. Syd asked a woman claiming to be his wife what on earth had happened. She said, 'Syd, you're fifty-eight years old now.'

"You can imagine how he felt.

"Another thing Syd found out was that he was a veteran of something called the Second World War. Somebody said I was in that war, too. Maybe so. I don't argue when people tell me things like that.

"I decided to read up on that war some. I went to a library a lot like this one. It was a building full of books. I learned that the Second World War was so terrible that it caused Adolf Hitler himself to commit suicide. Think of that: He had just been born, and suddenly it was time for him to shoot himself.

"That's history for you. You can read about it yourself.

"My friend Syd Solomon was certainly luckier than Hitler. All Syd had to do was put on a retrospective exhibition. So I tried to help him out—by writing an essay for the front of his catalogue.

"That is certainly one of the nice things about this planet, I think—the way people will try to help other people sometimes.

"In the words of Barbra Streisand, which should perhaps be emblazoned on the facade of this building, along with a picture of an atomic submarine: 'People who need people are the luckiest people in the world.'

"In order to write the essay about Syd's paintings, I had to ask him what he thought he was doing with paint. He was an abstract expressionist, you see. His paintings looked like bright weather to me—neon thunderstorms and the like.

"Was I ever in for a shock! Syd could not tell me what he thought he was doing!

"This did not wobble my opinions of Syd or his work. Syd and his paintings remained as honorable and beautiful as ever. What I lost faith in was the English language—by far the largest language in the world, incidentally. We have more words than anybody.

"But our great language, when confronted by abstract expressionism, was failing Syd and me—and every art critic I ever read.

"The language was speechless!

"Until that moment of truth, I had agreed with the Nobel-prize chemist, the late Irving Langmuir, who once said within my hearing, 'Any person who can't explain his work to a fourteen-year-old is a charlatan.'

"I couldn't believe that anymore.

"So what I finally wrote for Syd's catalogue was your standard load of horse crap about modern art.

"It may be in your library here. Enjoy it in good health.

"But the puzzle has been on my mind ever since—and I have good news for you today. I can once again agree with Dr. Langmuir about charlatans. Here, in simple English, is what Syd Solomon does:

"He meditates. He connects his hand and paintbrush to the deeper, quieter, more mysterious parts of his mind—and he paints pictures of what he sees and feels down there.

"This accounts for the pleasurable shock of recognition we experience when we look at what he does.

"How nice!

"Hooray for Syd Solomon! I say. He is certainly more enterprising and useful than all the quack holy men who meditate deeply, who then announce smugly that it is impossible for them to express what they have seen and felt.

"The heck with inarticulate meditators! And three cheers for all artists who dare to show and tell.

"Since we are here to dedicate a library, let us especially applaud those artists we call writers. By golly, aren't writers wonderful? They don't just keep their meditations to themselves. They very commonly give themselves migraine headaches and ulcers, and destroy their livers and their marriages, too, doing their *best* to show and tell.

"I once learned how to be the other sort of meditator, the sort that doesn't show and tell. I paid Maharishi Mahesh Yogi eighty dollars to show me how.

"Maharishi Mahesh Yogi gave me a mantra, a nonsense word I was supposed to say over and over to myself as I sank deeper and deeper into my mind. I promised not to tell anybody what my mantra was. This was it: *Aye-eem.*

"I will now demonstrate. [*Going into a trance*] *Aye-eem, aye-eem, aye-eem.* . . .

[*Emerging from the trance*] "Where am I? Am I still fifty-four? Or am I eighty-six now? I wouldn't be surprised.

"All right—that was the socially fruitless sort of meditation. I feel mildly refreshed, but I don't see how that can be much use to anybody else in New London or anywhere.

"Now for the socially *fruitful* sort of meditation, which has filled this noble building here: When writers meditate, they don't pick bland, meaningless mantras to say over and over to themselves. They pick mantras that are hot and prickly, full of the sizzle and jingle-jangle of life. They jazz the heck out of their inner beings with the mantras they pick.

"I will give you some examples:

"*War and Peace.*

"*The Origin of Species.*

"*The Iliad.*

"*Decline and Fall of the Roman Empire.*

"*Critique of Pure Reason.*

"*Madame Bovary.*

"*Life on the Mississippi.*

"*Romeo and Juliet.*

"*The Red Badge of Courage.*

"I only wish I had your card catalogue here. I could go on and on with literary mantras that have changed the world for the better.

"About *The Red Badge of Courage,* by the way: That story by Stephen Crane is supposed to be a particularly salutary story for Americans to read—especially during the bicentennial. But I know another story by Crane which, in my opinion, is even more instructive for Americans of our time. Perhaps you know it, too. It is called 'The Blue Hotel.'

" 'The Blue Hotel' is about a foreigner who comes here and commits murder. He imagines that he is defending himself. He has scared himself out of his wits, thinking that Americans are much more dangerous than they really are.

"So he kills.

"So much for that.

"Ten percent of you may be wondering by now why I called this speech 'The Noodle Factory.' One hundred percent of me is delighted to explain:

"It is very simple. The title is an acknowledgment of the fact that most people can't read, or, in any event, don't enjoy it much.

"Reading is such a difficult thing to do that most of our time in school is spent learning how to do that alone. If we had spent as much time at ice skating as we have with reading, we would all be stars with the Hollywood Ice Capades instead of bookworms now.

"As you know, it isn't enough for a reader to pick up the little symbols from a page with his eyes, or, as is the case with a blind person, with his fingertips. Once we get those symbols inside our heads and in the proper order, then we must clothe them in gloom or joy or apathy, in love or hate, in anger or peacefulness, or however the author intended them to be clothed. In order to be good readers, we must even recognize irony—which is when a writer says one thing and really means another, contradicting himself in what he believes to be a beguiling cause.

"We even have to get *jokes*! God help us if we miss a joke.

"So most people give up on reading.

"So—for all the jubilation this new library will generate in the community at large, this building might as well be a noodle factory. Noodles are okay. Libraries are okay. They are rather neutral good news.

"Perhaps the central concept of this beautifully organized speech will enter the patois of Connecticut College.

"One student may say to another, 'You want to go out and drink some beer?'

"The other might reply: 'No. I'm about to flunk out, they tell me. In view of the heartbreaking sacrifices my parents have made to send me here, I guess I'd better go spend some time at the Noodle Factory instead.'

"A student might ask a particularly dumb question of a professor, and the professor might tell him, 'Go to the Noodle Factory and find out.'

"And so on.

"This noble stone-and-steel bookmobile is no bland noodle factory to us, of course, to this band of readers—we few, we happy few. Because we love books so much, this has to be one of the most buxom, hilarious days of our lives.

"Are we foolish to be so elated by books in an age of movies and television? Not in the least, for our ability to read, when combined with libraries like this one, makes us the freest of women and men—and children.

"(That is such a *strange* word on a printed page, incidentally: 'freest—f-r-e-e-s-t.' I'm glad I'm not a foreigner.)

"Anyway—because we are readers, we don't have to wait for some communications executive to decide what we should think about next—and how we should think about it. We can fill our heads with anything from aardvarks to zucchinis—at any time of night or day.

"Even more magically, perhaps, we readers can communicate with each other across space and time so cheaply. Ink and paper are as cheap as sand or water, almost. No board of directors has to convene in order to decide whether we can afford to write down this or that. I myself once staged the end of the world on two pieces of paper—at a cost of less than a penny, including wear and tear on my typewriter ribbon and the seat of my pants.

"Think of that.

"Compare that with the budgets of Cecil B. DeMille.

"Film is simply one more prosthetic device for human beings who are incomplete in some way. We live not only in the Age of Film, but in the Age of False Teeth and Glass Eyes and Toupees and Silicone Breasts—and on and on.

"Film is a perfect prescription for people who will not or cannot read, and have no imagination. Since they have no imaginations, those people can now be shown actors and scenery instead—with appropriate music and all that.

"But, again, film is a hideously expensive way to tell anybody anything—and I include television and all that. What is more: Healthy people exposed to too many actors and too much scenery may wake up some morning to find their own imaginations dead.

"The only cure I know of is a library—and the ability to read.

"Reading exercises the imagination—tempts it to go from strength to strength.

"So much for that.

"It would surely be shapely on an occasion like this if something holy were said. Unfortunately, the speaker you have hired is a Unitarian. I know almost nothing about holy things.

"The language is holy to me, which again shows how little I know about holiness.

"Literature is holy to me, which again shows how little I know about holiness.

"Our freedom to say or write whatever we please in this country is holy to me. It is a rare privilege not only on this planet, but throughout the universe, I suspect. And it is not something somebody gave us. It is a thing we give to ourselves.

"Meditation is holy to me, for I believe that all the secrets of existence and nonexistence are somewhere in our heads—or in other people's heads.

"And I believe that reading and writing are the most nourishing forms of meditation anyone has so far found.

"By reading the writings of the most interesting minds in history, we meditate with our own minds and theirs as well.

"This to me is a miracle.

"The motto of this noble library is the motto of all meditators throughout all time: 'Quiet, please.'

"Thus ends my speech.

"I thank you for your attention."

MARK TWAIN

I have meditated with Mark Twain's mind. I began doing it when a child. I do it still. It encouraged me when I was young to believe that there was so much that was amusing and beautiful on this continent that I need not be awed by persons from anywhere else. I should model myself after other Americans. I now have mixed feelings about such advice. It hasn't always been convenient or attractive to comport myself as the purely American person I am.

Since I am simultaneously a humorist and a serious novelist, I was asked to speak at the one hundredth anniversary of the completion of Mark Twain's fanciful house in Hartford, Connecticut. The celebration took place on April 30,

1979. As a special honor to me, balls had been racked up on
Mark Twain's pool table on the third floor. I was to be
allowed to break them with Mark Twain's own cue. I declined. I did not dare give Mark Twain's ghost the opportunity to tell me, by sending the cueball into a corner pocket
without touching anything, say, what it thought of me.

My formal remarks on Twain were these:

"To every American writer this is a haunted house. My
hair may turn white before this very short speech is done.

"I now quote a previous owner of this house: 'When I find
a well-drawn character in fiction or biography, I generally
take a warm personal interest in him, for the reason that I
have known him before—met him on the river.'

"I submit to you that this is a profoundly Christian statement, an echo of the Beatitudes. It is constructed, as many
jokes are, incidentally, with a disarmingly pedestrian beginning and an unexpectedly provoking conclusion.

"I will repeat it, for we are surely here to repeat ourselves.
Lovers do almost nothing but repeat themselves.

" 'When I find a well-drawn character in fiction or biography, I generally take a warm personal interest in him, for the
reason that I have known him before—met him on the river.'

"Three words, in my opinion, make this a holy joke. They
are 'warm' and 'personal' and 'river.' The river, of course, is
life—and not just to river pilots but even to desert people, to
people who have never even seen water in that long and
narrow form. Mark Twain is saying what Christ said in so
many ways: that he could not help loving anyone in the midst
of life.

"I am of course a skeptic about the divinity of Christ and
a scorner of the notion that there is a God who cares how

we are or what we do. I was raised this way—in the midst of what provincial easterners imagine to be a Bible Belt. I was confirmed in my skepticism by Mark Twain during my formative years, and by some other good people, too. I have since bequeathed this lack of faith and my love for the body of literature which supports it to my children.

"I am moved on this occasion to put into a few words the ideal my parents and Twain and the rest held before me, and which I have now passed on. The ideal, achieved by few, is this: 'Live so that you can say to God on Judgment Day, "I was a very good person, even though I did not believe in you." ' The word 'God,' incidentally, is capitalized throughout this speech, as are all pronouns referring to Him.

"We religious skeptics would like to swagger some in heaven, saying to others who spent a lot of time quaking in churches down here, 'I was never worried about pleasing or angering God—never took Him into my calculations at all.'

"Religious skeptics often become very bitter toward the end, as did Mark Twain. I do not propose to guess now as to why he became so bitter. I know why I will become bitter. I will finally realize that I have had it right all along: that I will not see God, that there is no heaven or Judgment Day.

"I have used the word 'calculations.' It is a relative of that elegant Missouri verb, 'to calculate.' In Twain's time, and on the frontier, a person who calculated this or that was asking that his lies be respected, since they had been arrived at by means of arithmetic. He wanted you to acknowledge that the arithmetic, the logic of his lies, was sound.

"I know a rowdy joke which is not fit to tell in mixed company in a Victorian home like this one. I can reveal the final line of it, however, without giving offense. This is it: 'Keep your hat on. We may wind up miles from here.' Any writer beginning a story might well say that to himself: 'Keep your hat on. We may wind up miles from here.'

"This is the secret of good storytelling: to lie, but to keep the arithmetic sound. A storyteller, like any other sort of enthusiastic liar, is on an unpredictable adventure. His initial lie, his premise, will suggest many new lies of its own. The storyteller must choose among them, seeking those which are most believable, which keep the arithmetic sound. Thus does a story generate itself.

"The wildest adventure with storytelling, with Missouri calculation, of which I know is *A Connecticut Yankee in King Arthur's Court.* It was written in this sacredly absurd monument—as were *The Adventures of Tom Sawyer, A Tramp Abroad, The Prince and the Pauper, Life on the Mississippi,* from which I have quoted, and the world masterpiece, *Huckleberry Finn.* Twain's most productive years were spent here —from the time he was thirty-nine until he was my age, which is fifty-six. He was my age when he left here to live in Europe and Redding and New York, his greatest work behind him.

"That is how far down the river of life he was when he left here. He could not afford to live here anymore. He was very bad at business.

"About *A Connecticut Yankee:* Its premise, its first lie, seemed to promise a lark. What could be more comical than sending back into the Dark Ages a late-nineteenth-century optimist and technocrat? Such a premise was surely the key to a treasure chest of screamingly funny jokes and situations. Mark Twain would have been wise to say to himself as he picked up that glittering key: 'Keep your hat on. We may wind up miles from here.'

"I will refresh your memories as to where he wound up,

with or without his hat. The Yankee and his little band of electricians and mechanics and what-have-you are being attacked by thousands of English warriors armed with swords and spears and axes. The Yankee has fortified his position with a series of electric fences and a moat. He also has several precursors to modern machine guns, which are Gatling guns.

"Comically enough, thousands of early attackers have already been electrocuted. Ten thousand of the greatest knights in England have been held in reserve. Now they come; I quote, and I invite you to chuckle along with me as I read:

" 'The thirteen Gatlings began to vomit death into the fated ten thousand. They halted, they stood their ground a moment against that withering deluge of fire, and then they broke, faced about, and swept toward the ditch like chaff before a gale. A full fourth part of their force never reached the top of the lofty embankment; the three-fourths reached it and plunged over—to death by drowning.

" 'Within ten short minutes after we had opened fire, armed resistance was totally annihilated, the campaign was ended, we fifty-four were masters of England! Twenty-five thousand men lay dead around us.'

"End quote.

"What a funny ending.

"Mark Twain died in 1910, at the age of seventy-five and four years before the start of World War One. I have heard it said that he predicted that war and all the wars after that in *A Connecticut Yankee*. It was not Twain who did that. It was his premise.

"How appalled this entertainer must have been to have his innocent joking about technology and superstition lead him inexorably to such a ghastly end. Suddenly and horrifyingly, what had seemed so clear throughout the book was not clear at all—who was good, who was bad, who was wise, who was foolish. I ask you, Who was most crazed by superstition and bloodlust, the men with the swords or the men with the Gatling guns?

"And I suggest to you that the fatal premise of *A Connecticut Yankee* remains a chief premise of Western civilization, and increasingly of world civilization, to wit: the sanest, most likeable persons, employing superior technology, will enforce sanity throughout the world.

"Shall I read the ending of *A Connecticut Yankee* to you yet again?

"No need.

"To return to mere storytelling, which never harmed anyone: It is the premise which shapes each story, yes, but the author must furnish the language and the mood.

"It seems clear to me, as an American writing one hundred years after this house was built, that we would not be known as a nation with a supple, amusing, and often beautiful language of our own, if it were not for the genius of Mark Twain. Only a genius could have misrepresented our speech and our wittiness and our common sense and our common decency so handsomely to ourselves and the outside world.

"He himself was the most enchanting American at the heart of each of his tales. We can forgive this easily, for he managed to imply that the reader was enough like him to be his brother. He did this most strikingly in the personae of the young riverboat pilot and Huckleberry Finn. He did this so well that the newest arrival to these shores, very likely a Vietnamese refugee, can, by reading him, begin to imagine that he has some of the idiosyncratically American charm of Mark Twain.

"This is a miracle. There is a name for such miracles, which is myths.

"Imagine, if you will, the opinion we would now hold of ourselves and the opinions others would hold of us, if it were not for the myths about us created by Mark Twain. You can then begin to calculate our debt to this one man.

"One man. Just one man.

"I named my firstborn son after him.

"I thank you for your attention."

lx

FUNNIER ON PAPER THAN MOST PEOPLE

I am better than most people in my trade at making jokes on paper.

For what it may be worth, I gave this graduation speech at Fredonia College, Fredonia, New York, on May 20, 1978, which contains, among other things, some of my theories about how jokes work, why jokes work:

"Your class spokesperson has just said that she is sick and tired of hearing people say, 'I'm glad I'm not a young person these days.' All I can say is, 'I'm glad I'm not a young person these days.'

"President Beal wished to exclude all negative thinking

from his own farewell to you, and so has asked me to make this announcement: 'All persons who still owe parking fees are to pay up before leaving the property, or there will be unpleasant monkey business with their transcripts.'

"When I was a boy in Indianapolis, there was a humorist there named Kin Hubbard. He wrote a few lines for *The Indianapolis News* every day. Indianapolis needs all the humorists it can get. He was often as witty as Oscar Wilde. He said, for instance, that Prohibition was better than no liquor at all. He said that whoever named near-beer was a poor judge of distance. He said that it was no disgrace to be poor, but that it might as well be. He went to a graduation ceremony one time, and he said afterward that he thought it would be better if all the really important stuff was spread out over four years instead of being saved up for the very end.

"Well—I assume that the really important stuff has been spread out over the years here at Fredonia, and that you have no need of anything much from me. This is lucky for me. I have only this to say, basically: This is the end—this is childhood's end for certain. 'Sorry about that,' as they used to say in the Vietnam War.

"Perhaps you have read the novel *Childhood's End* by Arthur C. Clarke, one of the few masterpieces in the field of science fiction. All of the others were written by me. In Clark's novel, mankind suddenly undergoes a spectacular evolutionary change. The children become very different from the parents, less physical, more spiritual—and one day they form up into a sort of column of light which spirals out into the universe, its mission unknown. The book ends there. You seniors, however, look a great deal like your parents, and I doubt that you will go radiantly into space as soon as you have your diplomas in hand. It is far more likely that you will go to Buffalo or Rochester or East Quogue—or Cohoes.

"And I suppose you will all want money and true love, among other things. I will tell you how to make money: Work very hard. I will tell you how to win love: Wear nice clothing and smile all the time. Learn the words to all the latest songs.

"What other advice can I give you? Eat lots of bran to provide necessary bulk in your diet. The only advice my father ever gave me was this: 'Never stick anything in your ear.' The tiniest bones in your body are inside your ears, you know—and your sense of balance, too. If you mess around with your ears, you could not only become deaf, but you could also start falling down all the time. So just leave your ears completely alone. They're fine, just the way they are.

"Don't murder anybody—even though New York State does not put people in the electric chair anymore.

"That's about it.

"One sort of optional thing you might do is to realize that there are six seasons instead of four. The poetry of four seasons is all wrong for this part of the planet, and this may explain why we are so depressed so much of the time. I mean, spring doesn't feel like spring a lot of the time, and November is all wrong for autumn, and so on. Here is the truth about the seasons: Spring is May and June. What could be springier than May and June? Summer is July and August. Really hot, right? Autumn is September and October. See the pumpkins? Smell those burning leaves? Next comes the season called Locking. That is when nature shuts everything down. November and December aren't winter. They're Locking. Next comes winter, January and February. Boy! Are they ever cold! What comes next? Not spring. 'Unlocking' comes next. What else could cruel March and only slightly less cruel April be? March and April are not spring. They are Unlocking.

"One more optional piece of advice: If you ever have to give a speech, start with a joke, if you know one. For years I have been looking for the best joke in the world. I think I know what it is. I will tell it to you, but you have to help me. You have to say, 'No,' when I hold up my hand like this. All right? Don't let me down.

"Do you know why cream is so much more expensive than milk?"

[AUDIENCE: "No."]

"It is because the cows hate to squat on those little bottles.

"That is the best joke I know. One time when I worked for the General Electric Company over in Schenectady, I had to write speeches for company officers. I put that joke about the cows and the little bottles in a speech for a vice-president. He was reading along, and he had never heard the joke before. He couldn't stop laughing, and he had to be led away from the podium with a nosebleed. I was fired the next day.

"How do jokes work? The beginning of each good one challenges you to think. We are such earnest animals. When I asked you about cream, you could not help yourselves. You really tried to think of a sensible answer. Why does a chicken cross the road? Why does a fireman wear red suspenders? Why did they bury George Washington on the side of a hill?

"The second part of the joke announces that nobody wants you to think, nobody wants to hear your wonderful answer. You are so relieved to at last meet somebody who doesn't demand that you be intelligent. You laugh for joy.

"I have in fact designed this entire speech so as to allow you to be as stupid as you like, without strain, and without penalties of any kind. I have even written a ridiculous song for the occasion. It lacks music, but we are up to our necks in composers here. One is sure to come along. The words go like this:

> Oh, farewell, farewell to Fredonia,
> Adios to teachers and pneumonia.
> If I find out where the party is,
> I'll telephone ya.
> I love you so much, Sonya,
> That I am going to buy you a begonia.
> You love me, too, doan ya, Sonya?

"See—you were trying to guess what the next rhyme was going to be. Nobody cares how smart you are. So laugh with relief.

"I am being so silly because I pity you so much. I pity all of us so much. Life is going to be very tough again, just as soon as this is over. And the most useful thought we can hold when all hell cuts loose again is that we are not members of different generations, as unlike, as some people would have us believe, as Eskimos and Australian aborigines. We are all so close together in time that we should think of ourselves as brothers and sisters. I have several children—six, to be exact—too many children for an atheist, certainly. Whenever my children complain about the planet to me, I say: 'Shut up! I just got here myself. Who do you think I am—Methuselah? You think I like the news of the day any better than you do? You're wrong.'

"We are all experiencing more or less the same lifetime now.

"What is it the slightly older people want from the slightly younger people? They want credit for having survived so long, and often imaginatively, under difficult conditions.

Slightly younger people are intolerably stingy about giving them credit for that.

"What is it the slightly younger people want from the slightly older people? More than anything, I think, they want acknowledgment and without further ado that they are, *without question,* women and men now. Slightly older people are intolerably stingy about making any such acknowledgment.

"Therefore, I take it upon myself to pronounce those about to graduate women and men. No one must ever treat them like children again. Neither must they ever act like children—ever again.

"This is what is known as a puberty ceremony.

"I realize that it is coming a little late, but better late than never. Every primitive society ever studied has had a puberty ceremony, at which former children became unchallengeably women and men. Some Jewish communities still honor this old practice, of course, and benefit from it, in my opinion. But, by and large, ultramodern, massively industrialized societies like ours have decided to do without puberty ceremonies—unless you want to count the issuance of driver's licenses at the age of sixteen. If you want to count that as a puberty ceremony, then it has a highly unusual feature: a judge can take your puberty away again, even if you're fifty-six, like me.

"Another event in the lives of American and European males which might be considered a puberty ceremony is war. If a male comes home from a war, especially with serious wounds, everybody agrees: Here indeed is a man. When I came home to Indianapolis from the Second World War in Germany, an uncle of mine said to me, 'By golly—you look like a man now.' I wanted to strangle him. If I had, he would have been the first German I'd killed. I was a man before I went to war, but he was damned if he would say so.

' "I suggest to you that the withholding of a puberty ceremony from young males in our society is a scheme, devised
cunningly but subconsciously, to make those males eager to
go to war, no matter how terrible or unjust a war may be.
There are just wars, too, of course. The war I was eager to
go to happened to be a just one.

"And when does a female stop being a little girl and become a woman, with all the rights and privileges appertain-
ing thereto? We all know the answer in our bones: when she
has a baby in wedlock, of course. If she has that first baby
out of wedlock, she is still a child. What could be simpler or
more natural and more obvious than that—or, in these days
and in this society, at least, more unjust, irrelevant, and just
plain stupid?

"I think we had better, for our own safety, reinstate puberty ceremonies.

"I not only declare those about to graduate women and
men. With all the powers vested in me, I pronounce them
clarks, as well. Most of you know, I'm sure, that all white
people named Clark are descended from inhabitants of the
British Isles who were remarkable for being able to read and
write. A black person named Clark, of course, would be
descended, most likely, from someone who was forced to
work without pay or rights of any kind by a white person
named Clark. An interesting family—the Clarks.

"I realize that you graduaters are all specialized in some
way. But you have spent most of the past sixteen or more
years learning to read and write. People who can read and
write expertly, as you can, are miracles and, in my opinion,
entitle us to suspect that we may be civilized after all. It is
terribly hard to learn to read and write. It takes forever.

When we scold our schoolteachers about the low reading scores of their students, we pretend that it is the easiest thing in the world: to teach a person to read and write. Try it sometime, and you will discover that it is nearly impossible.

"What good is being a clark, now that we have computers and movies and television? Clarking, a wholly human enterprise, is sacred. Machinery is not. Clarking is the most profound and effective form of meditation practiced on this planet, and far surpasses any dream experienced by a Hindu on a mountaintop. Why? Because clarks, by reading well, can think the thoughts of the wisest and most interesting human minds throughout all history. When clarks meditate, even if they themselves have only mediocre intellects, they do it with the thoughts of angels. What could be more sacred than that?

"So much for puberty and clarking. Only two major subjects remain to be covered: loneliness and boredom. No matter how old we are, we are going to be bored and lonely during what remains of our lives.

"We are so lonely because we don't have enough friends and relatives. Human beings are supposed to live in stable, like-minded, extended families of fifty people or more. In Nigeria it's common for Ibos to have a thousand relatives who know them quite well. When a baby is born, it is taken on a long trip, so it can meet all its relatives. This sort of thing is still quite common in Europe today, although the number one-thousand is far too high for there. When we or our ancestors came to America, though, we were agreeing, among other things, to do without such families. It is a painful, unhuman agreement to make. Emotionally, it is hideously expensive.

"Your class spokesperson mourned the collapse of the institution of marriage in this country. Marriage is collapsing because our families are too small. A man cannot be a whole society to a woman, and a woman cannot be a whole society to a man. We try, but it is scarcely surprising that so many of us go to pieces.

"So I recommend that everybody here join all sorts of organizations, no matter how ridiculous, simply to get more people in his or her life. It does not matter much if all the other members are morons. Quantities of relatives of any sort are what we need.

"As for boredom: Friedrich Wilhelm Nietzsche, a German philosopher who died seventy-eight years ago, had this to say: 'Against boredom even the gods contend in vain.' We are supposed to be bored. It is a part of life. Learn to put up with it, or you will not be what I have declared the members of this graduating class to be: mature women and men.

"I come to a close now by noting that the news magazines, whose business is to know and understand everything, have found this year's graduates to be apathetic. This year's graduates have tired blood. They need Geritol. Well, as a member of a zippier generation, with sparkle in its eyes and a snap in its stride, let me tell you what kept us as high as kites a lot of the time: hatred. All my life I've had people to hate— from Hitler to Nixon, not that those two are at all comparable in their villainy. It is a tragedy, perhaps, that human beings can get so much energy and enthusiasm from hate. If you want to feel ten feet tall, as though you could run a hundred miles without stopping, hate beats pure cocaine any day. Hitler resurrected Germany, a beaten, bankrupt, half-starved nation, with hatred and nothing more. Imagine that.

"So it seems quite likely to me that the class of 1978 in the United States of America is not in fact apathetic, but only looks that way to people who are used to getting their ecstasies from hatred. The members of the class of 1978 are not sleepy, are not listless, are not apathetic. They are simply performing the experiment of doing without hate. Hate is the missing vitamin in their diet, and they have sensed correctly that hate, in the long run, is about as nourishing as cyanide.

"This is a very exciting thing they are doing, and I wish them well."

❧

ONE reason I feel the need to be funnier on paper than most of my colleagues is that I have a German name, which can be counted on to remind almost any sort of American for at least a microsecond of German enemies in two world wars. I myself, a prisoner of war of the Germans, am so reminded for at least that microsecond when I hear a German name. I was on *our* side, remember?

So it is a good idea for me to tell a joke as soon as possible.

I have spoken to, and actually liked, several German veterans of the Second World War who live in America now. They, too, become screamingly funny as soon as possible.

And it may be that Mark Twain drew some of his comic energy from a similar uneasiness. He had served the Confederacy briefly, after all, in the bloodiest war in American history, and later faced paying audiences of, among others, Union veterans and their wives.

❧

AN advantage of a writer's having a joke-making capability is that he or she can be really funny in case something really is funny. Most contemporary American novelists, especially those credited with greatness because their books are so huge, cannot be funny even when it is time to be funny. So they have to pretend to be dealing at all times with matters so serious, good and evil, for example, that there could not possibly be anything funny about them. Thus are their works as consistently lugubrious as bloodhounds appear to be.

The books of jokesters are short, which is a social disadvantage in an era when literary importance is measured by the pound. The problem is that jokes deal so efficiently with ideas that there is little more to be said after the punch line has been spoken. It is time to come up with a new idea—and another good joke.

❧

I once asked my friend Joe Heller what he was up to. He said that he had an idea for a new book. I said that one idea wasn't nearly enough for a whole book. I said this because he is a funny writer.

If he had been a serious writer, I would have said one idea was more than enough for a trilogy.

❧

THE worst thing about a writer's having a joke-making capability, of course, as James Thurber of Columbus, Ohio, pointed out in an essay years ago, is this: No matter what is being discussed, the jokester is going to head for a punch line every time.

❧

SOME smart young critic will soon quote that line above against me, imagining that I am too dumb to realize that I have condemned myself, too dense to know that I have accidentally put my finger on what is awfully wrong with me.

❦

I am often asked to give advice to young writers who wish to be famous and fabulously well-to-do. This is the best I have to offer:

While looking as much like a bloodhound as possible, announce that you are working twelve hours a day on a masterpiece. Warning: All is lost if you crack a smile.

X

EMBARRASSMENT

friend of mine once spoke to me about what he called the "existential hum," the uneasiness which keeps us moving, which never allows us to feel entirely at ease. He had tried heroin once. He said he understood at once the seductiveness of that narcotic. For the first time in his life, he was not annoyed by the existential hum.

I would describe the hum that is with me all the time as *embarrassment*. I have somehow disgraced myself.

My Indianapolis relatives may actually feel that I have done so. They are not enthusiastic about my work. I have already described my Uncle John's distaste for it. As for my Uncle Alex: I dedicated *The Sirens of Titan* to him, and he said he could not read it. He supposed that beatniks would think it was wonderful. My Aunt Ella, who owned Stewart's Bookstore in Louisville, Kentucky, would not stock my books. She found them degenerate, and said so.

The only big write-up I have so far received in my home town appeared in the October 1976 issue of *Indianapolis Magazine,* a publication of the Chamber of Commerce. It began like this:

Whether they like his book or not (some don't), most of those who know Kurt Vonnegut, Jr., agree that he is a nice guy.

In Indianapolis his aunts, cousins and old friends call him Kay, and their memories of him are fond and lively. His Aunt, Irma Vonnegut Lindener, says warmly, "He's a dear, awfully nice," and her eyes light up with affection as she recounts thoughtful things he has done for the family over the years. He shared an enviable rapport with his uncle, Alex Vonnegut . . . though they were worlds apart in their convictions.

The tremendous gap between the old world gentility of Vonnegut's relatives and his own contemporary manner of living, thinking and writing has not dimmed the fondness that exists between them. Mrs. Lindener, an intellectual, articulate woman, admits that she has not read *Breakfast of Champions,* and doesn't intend to. She is also puzzled by some of his other books, but her pride in his achievement as a major novelist is not diminished by a difference in point of view . . .

More offensive to my relatives than my books, even, I think, is the fact of my being divorced. In the history of my family in America, I am only the second member to have been divorced. When I returned to Indianapolis for the funeral of Uncle Alex, at the Flanner and Buchanan funeral home, a girl cousin I had once been very close to turned her back on me—because I had not stuck with my first wife through thick and thin.

❦

THE only other Vonnegut to get divorced was my Uncle Walter—again, a first cousin of my father. He, too, had the hubris to seek his fortune in the arts in New York City—as an actor on the stage. He was a protégé of the then premiere novelist of Indianapolis, who was Booth Tarkington. I never met Mr. Tarkington, although I lived for a while only a block from his home on North Meridian Street, where he died in 1946. His use of black people for comic relief in some of his stories, no matter how kindly Mr. Tarkington's intentions, makes the stories sound somewhat dated today.

Be that as it may, Mr. Tarkington was a first-rate playwright on top of everything else, which I am not, and he saw Uncle Walter in amateur productions in Indianapolis, and urged him to come here in the late 1920s, which Uncle Walter did.

He was an instant success as a supporting actor, appearing, for example, with Humphrey Bogart in *The Petrified Forest*. His wife Marjorie also did well as a supporting actress, and Uncle Walter and Aunt Marjorie and their two children, Walter, Jr., and Irma Ruth, were all in the cast of Eugene O'Neill's only comedy, *Ah, Wilderness!*, starring George M. Cohan. Think of that: four Vonneguts all at once in a Broadway play.

When I first came to New York City as a working grown-up, as a public relations man for General Electric, based in Schenectady, older people would often ask me if I was related to Walter and Marjorie Vonnegut. They were remembered as actors and bon vivants. They drank a lot. They drank hard liquor in speakeasies, and had stories to tell about gangsters they had met.

They got divorced because Marjorie fell in love with Don Marquis, the creator of *Archie and Mehitabel.* Marquis was a bachelor then, and she married him.

Late in the 1930s Uncle Walter had trouble getting parts because of his drinking, and he came home to Indiana with a new wife, a pretty young actress named Rosalie, who was never really accepted by the family. They built a little house in an orchard in northern Indiana, which Uncle Walter's widowed mother owned. They lived there and drank a lot, and talked about starting a little repertory company there in the wilderness, as boozed-up former actors and actresses will do.

They died pretty soon.

❖

JANE Cox Vonnegut and I, childhood sweethearts in Indianapolis, separated in 1970 after a marriage which by conventional measurement was said to have lasted twenty-five years. We are still good friends, as they say. Like so many couples who are no longer couples these days, we have been through some terrible, unavoidable accident that we are ill-equipped to understand. Like our six children, we only just arrived on this planet and we were doing the best we could. We never saw what hit us. It wasn't another woman, it wasn't another man.

We woke up in ambulances headed for different hospitals, so to speak, and would never get together again. We were alive, yes, but the marriage was dead.

And it was no Lazarus.

It was a good marriage for a long time—and then it wasn't. The shock of having our children no longer need us happened somewhere in there. We were both going to have to find other sorts of seemingly important work to do and other compelling reasons for working and worrying so. But I am beginning to explain, which is a violation of a rule I lay down whenever I teach a class in writing: "All you can do is tell what happened. You will get thrown out of this course if you are arrogant enough to imagine that you can tell me why it happened. You do not know. You cannot know."

❧

So I am embarrassed about the failure of my first marriage. I am embarrassed by my older relatives' responses to my books. But I was embarrassed before I was married or had written a book. A bad dream I have dreamed for as long as I can remember may hold a clue. In that dream, I know that I have murdered an old woman a long time ago. I have led an exemplary life ever since.

But now the police have come to get me, with incontrovertible evidence of my crime. This is more or less the plot of Dostoevski's *Crime and Punishment*, of course. By coincidence, Dostoevski and I have the same birthday, too.

COULD that woman be my mother? I asked a psychiatrist that. She said that the woman might not even be a woman. She could be a man.

I went to a Hindu with occult powers, supposedly. I answered his ad in *The Village Voice,* in which he offered to tell people for a fee what they had been in previous lives. I asked him whether I had ever killed anybody in another life. He replied that I had lived only once before, and that my highest rank was as a squire to a knight in northern Europe. I had in fact killed a child accidentally. My knight and I and some others were riding through a village, and a child somehow fell under the hooves of my horse.

"It was not your fault," said the seer.

Even so.

❦

LONG after I started dreaming that dream, I did a story for *Life* magazine about a mass murderer in Provincetown, Massachusetts. He and my daughter Edith knew each other some. His name was Tony Costa.

He was adjudged guilty and insane. He was put into Bridgewater, a Massachusetts institution for the criminally insane—not all that far from Provincetown. That was where they put the Boston Strangler also. Tony Costa and the Strangler killed only women. Tony Costa killed women who were young and nubile and adventuresome, unafraid to go with presentable strangers almost anywhere. The Strangler killed any sort of woman he could catch alone.

Tony Costa and I exchanged a few letters after he was put away. He would eventually hang himself. The message of his letters to me was that a person as intent on being virtuous as he was could not possibly have harmed a fly. He believed it.

❦

I know the feeling.

❦

HAVE I ever really killed anybody, even in a war? Not that I know of. Maybe I have forgotten. I await the police.

xl

RELIGION

tOWARD the end of our marriage, it was mainly religion in a broad sense that Jane and I fought about. She came to devote herself more and more to making alliances with the supernatural in her need to increase her strength and understanding—and happiness and health. This was painful to me. She could not understand and cannot understand why that should have been painful to me, or why it should be any of my business at all.

And it is to suggest to her and to some others why it was painful that I chose for this book's epigraph a quotation from a thin book, *Instruction in Morals,* published in 1900 and

written by my Free Thinker great-grandfather Clemens Vonnegut, then seventy-six years old:

"Whoever entertains liberal views and chooses a consort
that is captured by superstition risks his liberty and his happiness."

❦

I did not know that my great-grandfather had said such a
thing, or even that he had written a book, until about ten
days ago. My brother Bernard sent the book to me then, after
picking it up on a recent trip to Indianapolis. Bernard also
sent me a copy of Clemens Vonnegut's comments on life and
death, which were read at his funeral. Clemens Vonnegut
planned his own funeral in 1874, and actually died in 1906.
His words to his mourners were these:

"Friends or Opponents: To all of you who stand here to
deliver my body to the earth:

"To you, my next of kin:

"Do not mourn! I have now arrived at the end of the
course of life, as you will eventually arrive at yours. I am at
rest and nothing will ever disturb my deep slumber.

"I am disturbed by no worries, no grief, no fears, no
wishes, no passions, no pains, no reproaches from others. All
is infinitely well with me.

"I departed from life with loving, affectionate feelings for
all mankind; and I admonish you: Be aware of this truth that
the people on this earth could be joyous, if only they would
live rationally and if they would contribute mutually to each
others' welfare.

"This world is not a vale of sorrows if you will recognize discriminatingly what is truly excellent in it; and if you will avail yourself of it for mutual happiness and well-being. Therefore, let us explain as often as possible, and particularly at the departure from life, that we base our faith on firm foundations, on Truth for putting into action our ideas which do not depend on fables and ideas which Science has long ago proven to be false.

"We also wish Knowledge, Goodness, Sympathy, Mercy, Wisdom, Justice, and Truthfulness. We also strive for and venerate all of those attributes from which the fantasy of man has created a God. We also strive for the virtues of Temperance, Industriousness, Friendship, and Peace. We believe in pure ideas based on Truth and Justice.

"Therefore, however, we do not believe, cannot believe, that a Thinking Being existed for millions and millions of years, and eventually and finally out of nothing—through a Word—created this world, or rather this earth with its Firmament, its Sun and Moon and the Stars.

"We cannot believe that this Being formed a human being from clay and breathed into it an Immortal Soul, and then allowed this human being to procreate millions, and then delivered them all into unspeakable misery, wretchedness and pain for all eternity. Nor can we believe that the descendents of one or two human beings will inevitably become sinners; nor do we believe that through the criminal executions of an Innocent One may we be redeemed."

❦

SUCH is my ancestral religion. How it was passed on to me is a mystery. By the time I got to know them, my parents were both so woozy with Weltschmerz that they weren't passing anything on—not the German language, not their love for German music, not the family history, nothing. Everything was all over with. They were *kaput.*

So I must have questioned them, finally, about what our family believed. I must have noticed that the Goldsteins and the Waleses and others proudly believed one thing or another, and I wanted a belief to be proud of, too.

How proud I became of our belief, how pigheadedly proud, even, is the most evident thing in my writing, I think. Haven't I already attributed the breakup of my first marriage in part to my wife's failure to share my family belief with me?

And did I not speak in this Free Thinking manner to the graduating class at Hobart and William Smith Colleges in Geneva, New York, on May 26, 1974:

"Kin Hubbard was an Indianapolis newspaper humorist. He wrote under the name of Abe Martin. My father, who was an Indianapolis architect, knew him some. Kin Hubbard had fault to find with commencement addresses. He thought that all the really important information should be spread out over four years, instead of being saved up for one big speech at the very end.

"That is an elegant joke, although nobody here seems to be hemorrhaging with laughter. That is just as well. I want us to be serious. I want us to ponder seriously about commencement addresses, to realize what it is that is withheld from students until the very end. In the fiction game, we call a marvelous thing withheld until the very end the 'snapper' of a tale. O. Henry probably devised more snappers than any other writer in history. So what is the snapper of a college education? What is the thing colleges hire outsiders to deliver on commencement day?

"The outsider is expected to answer the questions: what is life all about, and what are new college graduates supposed to do with it now?

"This information has to be saved up until the very end for this good reason: No responsible, truth-loving teacher can answer those questions in class, or even in the privacy of his office or home. No respecter of evidence has ever found the least clue as to what life is all about, and what people should do with it.

"Oh, there have been lots of brilliant guesses. But honest, educated people have to identify them as such—as guesses. What are guesses worth? Scientifically and legally, they are not worth doodley-squat. As the saying goes: Your guess is as good as mine.

"The guesses we like best, as with so many things we like best, were taught to us in childhood—by people who loved us and wished us well. We are reluctant to criticize those guesses. It is an ultimate act of rudeness to find fault with anything which is given to us in a spirit of love. So a modern, secular education is often painful. By its very nature, it invites us to question the wisdom of the ones we love.

"Too bad.

"I have said that one guess is as good as another, but that is only roughly so. Some guesses are crueler than others— which is to say, harder on human beings, and on other animals as well. The belief that God wants heretics burned to death is a case in point. Some guesses are more suicidal than others. The belief that a true lover of God is immune to the bites of copperheads and rattlesnakes is a case in point. Some guesses are greedier and more egocentric than others. Belief in the divine right of kings and presidents is a case in point.

"Those are all discredited guesses. But it is reasonable to suppose that other bad guesses are poisoning our lives today. A good education in skepticism can help us to discover those bad guesses, and to destroy them with mockery and contempt. Most of them were made by honest, decent people who had no way of knowing what we know, or what we can find out, if we want to. We have one hell of a lot of good information about our bodies, about our planet, and the universe—about our past. We don't have to guess as much as the old folks did.

"Bertrand Russell declared that, in case he met God, he would say to Him, 'Sir, you did not give us enough information.' I would add to that, 'All the same, Sir, I'm not persuaded that we did the best we could with the information we had. Toward the end there, anyway, we had tons of information.'

"Our most dismaying failure is in the use of our knowledge of what human beings need in the way of bodily and spiritual nourishment. And I suspect that some of the guesses made by our ancestors are partly responsible for the starved bodies and spirits we see everywhere.

"Shame on us. Less shame on our ancestors.

"I myself am an ancestor, having reproduced, having written books, being fifty-one years old. I come from simpler times. When I was a boy, all a commencement speaker had to say was, 'Go out and kill Hitler, boy. And then get married and have a lot of kids.'

"Some of you might still go looking for Hitler, in Paraguay, say. He might be there. He would be eighty-five years old now. He has probably shaved off his mustache.

"Some of you might go out and kill Communists, but that

is no longer a fashionable thing to do. And you wouldn't be killing real Communists anyway. This country has fulfilled more of the requirements of the Communist Manifesto than any avowedly Communist nation ever did. Maybe we're the Communists.

"Our politicians like to say that we have religion and the Communist countries don't. I think it is just the other way around. Those countries have a religion called Communism, and the Free World is where sustaining religions are in very short supply.

"I am about to make my own ancestral guess as to what life is all about, and what young people should do with it. I will again issue the caveat that I am as full of baloney as anybody, and that anybody who says for sure what life is all about might as well lecture on Santa Claus and the Easter Bunny, and tooth fairies, as well.

"I am, incidentally, the world's greatest authority on tooth fairies. That is how most of my life has been spent: in the study of tooth fairies. That should be carved on my tombstone. I was the one who discovered that tooth fairies are cannibals. Mostly, Tooth Fairies eat june bugs, of course. But under crowded conditions and in an atmosphere rich in carbon monoxide, tooth fairies eat each other, too.

"And who can blame them?

"Okay.

"What should young people do with their lives today? Many things, obviously. But the most daring thing is to create stable communities in which the terrible disease of loneliness can be cured. Young people should also identify and expound theories about life in which sane human beings almost everywhere can believe.

"I suggest that we need a new religion. If suggesting

that we need a new religion is sacrilege, then the emperor Constantine was guilty of sacrilege, and the emperor Nero was an admirably pious man. And I want to point out that it is impossible to discard an old religion entirely. The religion of Nero survives today, determining as it does the dates and even moods of so many of our so-called Christian holidays.

"Easter is a time for the renewal of life, and it always has been, apparently, even when people ate mastodon meat. Nothing is more human than to wish for renewal when springtime comes. And, out of respect for our ancestors, it is in the area of spiritual renewal that we are the most conservative. We must become less conservative.

"What makes me think we need a new religion? That's easy. An effective religion allows people to imagine from moment to moment what is going on and how they should behave. Christianity used to be like that. Our country is now jammed with human beings who say out loud that life is chaos to them, and that it doesn't seem to matter what anybody does next. This is worse than being seasick.

"Might not we do without religion entirely? Plenty of people have tried—not in Communist countries, as I've already said, but here. A lot of people have been forced to do without it—because the old-time religions they know of are too superstitious, too full of magic, too ignorant about biology and physics to harmonize with the present day.

"They are told to have faith. Faith in what? Faith in faith, as nearly as I can tell. That is as detailed as many contemporary preachers care to be, except when amazing audiences of cavemen. How can a preacher tell us about men and women who heard voices without raising questions about schizophrenia, a disease which we know is common in all places and all times.

"We know too much for old-time religion; and in a way, that knowledge is killing us.

"The Book of Genesis is usually taken to be a story about what happened a long time ago. The beginning of it, at least, can also be read as a prophecy of what is going on right now. It may be that Eden is this planet. If that is so, then we are still in it. It may be that we, poisoned by all our knowledge, are still crawling toward the gate.

"Can we spit out all our knowledge? I don't think that is possible. It is something I have often wanted to do. We are stuck with our knowledge, which has seeped into all of our tissues. We had better make the best of a bad situation, which is a wonderful human skill. We had better make use of what has poisoned us, which is knowledge.

"What can we use it for?

"Why don't we use it to devise realistic methods for preventing us from crawling out the gate of the Garden of Eden? We're such wonderful mechanics, maybe we can lock that gate with us inside.

"It is springtime here in Paradise. There is hope in the air!

"If I talk about the Loud family now, will all of you know who I mean? I don't mean everybody's noisy neighbors. I mean a family of prosperous human beings in California, whose last name is Loud. They were the willing subjects last year of a television documentary. Seemingly invisible cameramen and sound men were able to record for all time even the most disappointing and embarrassing moments in their lives.

"Most viewers, and the Louds themselves, claimed to be mystified by the tinhorn tragedies and unfunny comedies thus immortalized. I suggest to you that the Louds were healthy earthlings who had everything but a religion in which they could believe. There was nothing to tell them what they should want, what they should shun, what they should do next. Socrates told us that the unexamined life wasn't worth living. The Louds demonstrated that the morally unstructured life is a clunker, too.

"Christianity could not nourish the Louds. Neither could Buddhism or the profit motive or participation in the arts, or any other nostrum on America's spiritual smorgasbord. So the Louds were dying before our eyes.

"If my analysis is correct, then we have a formula for more such successful TV shows. Each show can feature an otherwise healthy family, from which a single life-sustaining element has been withheld. We might begin with the Watson family, which has everything but water. But no family could survive an entire television season without water, so we had better give the Watsons a diet absolutely devoid of Vitamin B complex, instead.

"We wouldn't tell the audience or the critics or the Watsons what was really wrong with the Watsons. We would pretend to be as puzzled as anybody about why they weren't happier with their quadraphonic sound system and their tap dancing lessons and their Pontiac Ventura and all. We would take part in symposia with ministers and sociologists, and so forth, reaching no firm conclusions—while the Watsons slowly died of beriberi.

"A microscopic quantity of vitamins could save the Watsons. But a ton of Billy Grahams couldn't save the Louds. They know too much.

"Now is as good a time as any to mention White House prayer breakfasts, I guess. I think we all know now that religion of that sort is about as nourishing to the human spirit as potassium cyanide. We have been experimenting with it. Every guinea pig died. We are up to our necks in dead guinea pigs.

"The lethal ingredient in those breakfasts wasn't prayer. And it wasn't the eggs or the orange juice or the hominy grits. It was a virulent new strain of hypocrisy which did everyone in.

"Talk about typhoid Mary!

"If I have offended anyone here by talking of the need of a new religion, I apologize. I am willing to drop the word religion, and substitute for it these three words: *heartfelt moral code*. We sure need such a thing, and it should be simple enough and reasonable enough for anyone to understand. The trouble with so many of the moral codes we have inherited is that they are subject to so many interpretations. We require specialists, historians and archaeologists and linguists and so on, to tell us where this or that idea may have come from, to suggest what this or that statement might actually mean. This is good news for hypocrites, who enjoy feeling pious, no matter what they do.

"If we were to try to grow recent strains of hypocrisy in the laboratory, what would we grow them in? I think they would grow like Jack's beanstalk in a mulch of ancient moral codes.

"It may be that moral simplicity is not possible in modern times. It may be that simplicity and clarity can come only from a new messiah, who may never come. We can talk about portents, if you like. I like a good portent as much as anyone. What might be the meaning of the comet Kahoutek, which was to make us look upward, to impress us with the paltriness of our troubles, to cleanse our souls with cosmic awe? Kahoutek was a fizzle, and what might this fizzle mean?

"I take it to mean that we can expect no spectacular miracles from the heavens, that the problems of ordinary human beings will have to be solved by ordinary human beings. The message of Kahoutek is: 'Help is not on the way. Repeat: help is not on the way.'

"What about visitors from other planets, who are supposed to be so smart? A lot of people believe that they have already been here, and that they taught us how to build pyramids. One thing that even the Egyptians can agree on, I think, is that we don't need any more pyramids.

"As an ordinary person, appalled as I am by the speed with which we are wrecking our topsoil, our drinking water, and our atmosphere, I will suggest an idea about good and evil which might fit into a modern and simple moral code. Evil disgusts us. Good fills us with joy and brings a sparkle to our eyes. That much remains the same. Might we not go farther, though, and say that anything which wounds the planet is evil, and anything which preserves it or heals it is good?

"Let me be the first to say that the idea is sappy, whatever that means. I think sappiness has something to do with being concerned about grandchildren, and the hell with them. But the worst thing about my moral code is that it invites people to have the fun of being glamorously wicked at first, which many of us feel is sexy, and then becoming almost swooningly virtuous at the end. This comes close to being the biography of Saint Augustine, and of several other famous holy men.

"On a larger scale, entire nations love to blow the hell out of other nations, and then to come like angels to pass out glass eyes and artificial limbs and Hershey bars and all that, to rebuild everything, to get everything going again.

"We would have to understand from the first the scientific fact that any wound we inflict on the life-support systems of this planet is likely to be quite permanent. So anyone who wounded the planet, and then pretended to heal it, would simply be another hypocrite. He would remain quite permanently an evil and therefore disgusting human being.

"I went to a Unitarian church for a while, and it might show. The minister said one Easter Sunday that, if we listened closely to the bell on his church, we would hear that it was singing, over and over again, 'No hell, no hell, no hell.' No matter what we did in life, he said, we wouldn't burn throughout eternity in hell. We wouldn't even fry for ten or fifteen minutes. He was just guessing, of course.

"Jimmy Breslin, on the other hand, told me one time that he sort of hankered to get back into Catholicism, because he thought there were a lot of people in the Nixon administration who deserved to roast in hell. Maybe so.

"At any rate, I don't think anybody ever dreaded hell as much as most of us dread the contempt of our fellowmen. Under our new and heartfelt moral code, we might be able to horrify would-be evildoers with just that: the contempt of their fellowmen.

"For that contempt to be effective, though, we would need cohesive communities, which are about as common as bald eagles these days. And it is curious that such communities should be so rare, since human beings are genetically such gregarious creatures. They need plenty of like-minded friends and relatives almost as much as they need B-complex vitamins and a heartfelt moral code.

"I know Sargent Shriver slightly. When he was campaigning for vice-president, he asked me if I had any ideas. You remember that there was plenty of money around, but as far as ideas went, both parties were in a state of destitution. So I told him, and I am afraid he didn't listen, that the number one American killer wasn't cardiovascular disease, but loneliness. I told him that he and McGovern could swamp the Republicans if they would promise to cure that disease. I even gave him a slogan to put on buttons and bumpers and flags and billboards: Lonesome No More!

"The rest is history.

"I was in Biafra several years ago, at the bitter end of the Nigerian civil war. The Biafrans had nothing to eat, you'll remember. They were blockaded, so no food got in. They had almost nothing to fight with, except for some Mauser rifles which were a good deal older than I was. And still they fought on. They had no recruiting program. There was no governmental scheme for the relief of refugees, and none was needed. The government did nothing to look out for the old, the sick, either. Biafra, for the short time it lasted, could be admired simultaneously by both anarchists and conservatives.

"The people could look out for each other, without any help from the central government, because every Biafran was a member of an extended family. He had hundreds of relatives he knew by name and reputation. Some Biafrans had thousands of relatives or more.

"Those families took care of their own wounded, their own lunatics, their own refugees. They shared equally whatever they had. The government didn't have to send a policeman to make sure the food was divided fairly. When the government needed new soldiers, it told each family how many recruits it was expected to send. The family decided then who was to go.

"And this admirable scheme was far from being an invention by the Biafrans. They were simply continuing to live as most human beings have lived until recently.

"I have seen the past, and it works.

"We should return to extended families as quickly as we can, and be lonesome no more, lonesome no more.

"Some of you will become leaders, although that is now thought to be a grungy destiny. Nobody wants to be Papa anymore. If you do have to lead, you may imagine that your mission is to help us find an amazing future. You should consider the possibility that you could serve the people better if you were to lead them intelligently and imaginatively back to some of the more humane and comforting institutions of the past.

"It seems certain that you will face plenty of social unrest in the future, and demands will continue to be made for economic justice. You will be very shrewd leaders indeed if you recognize that the people are in fact crying out not so much for money as for relief from loneliness.

"Let me beguile you just a little bit more about extended families. Let us talk about divorce, and the fact that one out of every three of us here has been or will be divorced. When we do it, we will very likely wrangle and wail and weep formlessly about money and sex, about treachery, about outgrowing one another, about how close love is to hate, and so on. Nobody ever gets anywhere near close to the truth, which is this: The nuclear family doesn't provide nearly enough companionship.

"I am going to write a play about the breakup of a marriage, and at the end of the play I am going to have a character say what people should say to each other in real life at the end of a marriage: 'I'm sorry. You, being human, need a hundred affectionate and like-minded companions. I'm only one person. I've tried, but I could never be a hundred people to you. You've tried, but you could never be a hundred people to me. Too bad. Good-bye.'

"Let's talk about incompatibility between parents and children, which happens often merely because of genetic rotten luck. In a nuclear family, children and parents can be locked in hellish close combat for twenty-one years and more. In an extended family, a child has scores of other homes to go to in search of love and understanding. He need not stay home and torture his parents, and he need not starve for love.

"In an extended family, anybody can bug out of his own house for months, and still be among relatives. Nobody has to go on a hopeless quest for friendly strangers, which is what most Americans have to do.

"Massage parlors come to mind—bus stations and bars.

"You graduates here are leaving an artificial extended family now. Even if you hated it here, you will find a nuclear family to be a very poor substitute for what you had here. As for those of us who have come to praise you for having graduated: we have fled here from loneliness, to be part of an artificial extended family for just a little while.

"And what we will all be seeking when we decamp, and for the rest of our lives, will be large, stable communities of like-minded people, which is to say relatives. They no longer exist. The lack of them is not only the main cause, but probably the only cause of our shapeless discontent in the midst of such prosperity.

"We thought we could do without tribes and clans. Well, we can't.

"There was a time when I was avid to invent new religions

and social orders. It has now penetrated my skull that such schemes will not work without the support of huge and gruesome police forces and prison systems, unless they are allowed to invent themselves. The emperor Constantine did not, after all, invent anything. He had many religions to choose from. He selected Christianity because it seemed to him to be the most refreshing.

"Hitler and Lenin and some others have also tried to refresh their people with ideas that had been around awhile. They chose abominably, as we know. It matters what we choose. And history and the deteriorating physical and moral environments are now telling us what we would rather not hear, what we would rather our children or grandchildren would hear: It is our turn to choose.

"At least we do not have to choose between various theories of magic, of ways to manipulate God and the devil and whatever, which is what our ancestors had to do. We no longer believe that God causes earthquakes and crop failures and plagues when He gets mad at us. We no longer imagine that He can be cooled off by sacrifices and festivals and gifts. I am so glad we don't have to think up presents for Him anymore. What's the perfect gift for someone who has everything?

"The perfect gift for somebody who has everything, of course, is nothing. Any gifts we have should be given to creatures right on the surface of the planet, it seems to me. If God gets angry about that, we can call in the Massachusetts Institute of Technology. There's a very good chance they can calm Him down.

"The new moral code we choose may already have martyrs. It is difficult to spot such things. One corpse tends to look pretty much like another one—until the historians sort them out with the benefit of hindsight.

"We shall see what we shall see.

"For two thirds of my life I have been a pessimist. I am astonished to find myself an optimist now. I feel now that I have been underestimating the intelligence and resourcefulness of man. I honestly thought that we were so stupid that we would continue to tear the planet to pieces, to sell it to each other, to burn it up. I've never expected thermonuclear war. What seemed certain to me was that we would simply gobble up the planet out of boredom and greed, not in centuries, but in ten or twenty years.

"Kilgore Trout wrote a science-fiction story called 'The Planet Gobblers' one time. It was about us, and we were the terrors of the universe. We were sort of interplanetary termites. We would arrive on a planet, gobble it up, and die. But before we died, we always sent out spaceships to start tiny colonies elsewhere. We were a disease, since it was not necessary to inhabit planets with such horrifying destructiveness. It is easy to take good care of a planet.

"Our grandchildren will surely think of us as the Planet Gobblers. Poorer nations than America think of America as a Planet Gobbler right now. But that is going to change. There is welling up within us a willingness to say 'No, thank you' to our factories. We were once maniacs for possessions, imagining that they would somehow moderate or somehow compensate us for our loneliness.

"The experiment has been tried in this most affluent nation in all of human history. Possessions help a little, but not as much as advertisers said they were supposed to, and we are now aware of how permanently the manufacture of some of those products hurts the planet.

"So there is a willingness to do without them.

"There is a willingness to do whatever we need to do in

order to have life on the planet go on for a long, long time. I didn't used to think that. And that willingness has to be a religious enthusiasm, since it celebrates life, since it calls for meaningful sacrifices.

"This is bad news for business, as we know it now. It should be thrilling news for persons who love to teach and lead. And thank God we have solid information in the place of superstition! Thank God we are beginning to dream of human communities which are designed to harmonize with what human beings really need and are.

"And now you have just heard an atheist thank God not once, but twice. And listen to this:

"God bless the class of 1974."

❦

SIX years later I would still be, outwardly at least, an unwobbled Free Thinker, for I said this at the First Parish Unitarian Church in Cambridge, Massachusetts, on January 27, 1980, approximately the 200th anniversary of the birth of William Ellery Channing:

"This will be very short. There will be almost no eye contact.

"This is only a dream. I know that this is only a dream. I have had it before. It is a dream of cosmic embarrassment. I stand before a large and nicely dressed audience. I have promised to speak on the most profound and poetic of all human concerns—the dignity of human nature.

"Only a maniac would make such a grandiose promise, but that is what I have done—in this dream.

"Now it is time for me to speak. I have nothing to say. Nothing.

"Dobedobedobedo.

"I will wake up at any moment now, and I will tell my wife about the dream. 'Where was it, honeybunch?' she will ask me. 'In a Yankee church on Harvard Square,' I will reply, and we will laugh and laugh.

"But every time I have had this dream before, I have been wearing nothing but olive drab, Army surplus undershorts. That detail is missing today—so this just might not be a dream after all. Who can say for certain?

"In this dream, if it is a dream, it is the two-hundredth anniversary of the birth of William Ellery Channing, a principal founder of Unitarianism in the United States. I wish that I had been born into a society like his—small and congenial and prosperous and self-sufficient. The people around here had ancestors in common then. They looked a lot like each other, dressed a lot like each other, enjoyed the same amusements and food. They were generally agreed as to what was good and what was evil—what God was like, who Jesus was.

"Channing grew up in what the late anthropologist Robert Redfield called a folk society, a relatively isolated community of like-thinking friends and relatives, a stable extended family of considerable size. Redfield said that we were all descended from persons who lived in such societies, and that we were likely to hanker to live in one ourselves from time to time. A folk society, in his imagination and in our imaginations, too, is an ideal scheme within which people can take really good care of one another, can share fairly, and can distribute honors to one and all.

"Maybe so. That could also be a dream, but I do not choose to think so.

"Channing's folk society, with Harvard at its center, was quite possibly the most intelligent and creative folk society the Western Hemisphere has ever known. I have to say 'possibly,' since we know so little about the Incas and the Aztecs and the Mayans—and some other tribes. I am tempted to include the Indianapolis of my grandfather's youth.

"But Channing's folk society is gone now. It has been drowned by tidal waves of strangers from simply everywhere —people like myself. Channing's folk society is now the American Atlantis, if you will.

"One of the most durable American legends has to do with the last days of the drowning of that Atlantis. It is the story of the arrest and trial and execution of Sacco and Vanzetti —of how the natives of Atlantis made war on the waves.

"That war on the waves came much too late. It happened only day before yesterday, practically. Sacco and Vanzetti were executed in Charlestown Prison in 1927. This part of New England had ceased to be a genuine folk society, had begun to admit strangers with unfamiliar ideas and customs in large numbers, one hundred years before that—when William Ellery Channing was nearly fifty years old.

"Channing did not live long enough to see the truly towering waves of immigrants come crashing in. But he did see, in my opinion, that the narrow, ethnocentric sermons suitable to a folk society should not be preached here anymore. Sermons deeply rooted in local history and sociology and politics are by and large harmless, and perhaps even charming in a relatively closed and isolated community. Why shouldn't a preacher in such a society raise the morale of his parishioners by implying that they are better servants of God than strangers are? That is a very old type of sermon—very old indeed. As old as the hills. Read the Old Testament. You can probably borrow a copy from the church next door.

"When Channing began preaching a new sort of sermon in this town, a sort of sermon we now perceive as Unitarian, he was urging his parishioners to credit with human dignity as great as their own persons not at all like their friends and relatives. The time to acknowledge the dignity of strangers, even black ones, had come.

"Couldn't strangers, even black ones, have human dignity without the acquiescence of Channing's congregation? No. Human dignity must be given by people to people. If you stand before me, and I do not credit you with dignity, then you have none. If I stand before you, and you do not credit me with dignity, then I have none. If Channing's parishioners felt that illiterate black slaves in the American South had negligible amounts of dignity, then those slaves would in fact be negligibly dignified—like chimpanzees, perhaps.

"It is easy to see dignity in relatives and friends. It is inevitable that we see it in relatives and friends. What is human dignity, then? It is the favorable opinion, respectful and uncritical, which we hold of those most familiar to us. It has been found that we can hold that same good opinion of strangers, if those who teach us and otherwise lead us tell us to.

"What could be more essential in a pluralistic society like ours than that every citizen see dignity in every other human being everywhere?

"And let us consider for a moment a society which was the exact opposite of what ours is supposed to be—which was Hitler's Germany. He trained a generation of warriors and police to be blind to human dignity, to never see it anywhere. So wherever he sent his warriors and police, there was no dignity. If he had conquered the world, there would have been no dignity anywhere. The penalty for crediting anyone with dignity in such a society? Death. And that, too, since there would be nobody to see dignity in it, would be undignified.

"Potter's field.

"Doesn't God give dignity to everybody? No—not in my opinion. Giving dignity, the sort of dignity that is of some earthly use, anyway, is something that only people do.

"Or fail to do.

"What happens if you credit a bum with human dignity —a drunken bum with his pants full of shit and snot dangling from his nose? At least you haven't made yourself poorer in a financial sense. And he can't take whatever it is that you have given him and spend it on Thunderbird wine.

"There is this drawback, though: If you give to that sort of a stranger the uncritical respect that you give to friends and relatives, you will also want to understand and help him. There is no way to avoid this.

"Be warned: If you allow yourself to see dignity in someone, you have doomed yourself to wanting to understand and help whoever it is.

"If you see dignity in anything, in fact—it doesn't have to be human—you will still want to understand it and help it. Many people are now seeing dignity in the lower animals and the plant world and waterfalls and deserts—and even in the entire planet and its atmosphere. And now they are helpless not to want to understand and to help those things.

"Poor souls!

"I am descended from fairly recent immigrants. My first

American ancestor, an atheistic merchant from Münster, arrived here about five years after William Ellery Channing died. Channing died in 1842, a reluctant Abolitionist who did not live to see all the murdering in the Civil War. I am a drop of spray from one of the waves which swamped the American Atlantis.

"The faith of my ancestors, going back at least four generations, has been the most corrosive sort of agnosticism— or worse. When I was a child, all my relatives, male and female, agreed with H. L. Mencken when he said that he thought religious people were comical. Mencken said that he had been widely misunderstood as hating religious people. He did not hate them, he said. He merely found them comical.

"What is so comical about religious people in modern times? They believe so many things which science has proved to be unknowable or absolutely wrong.

"How on earth can religious people believe in so much arbitrary, clearly invented balderdash? For one thing, I guess, the balderdash is usually beautiful—and therefore echoes excitingly in the more primitive lobes of our brains, where knowledge counts for nothing.

"More important, though: the acceptance of a creed, any creed, entitles the acceptor to membership in the sort of artificial extended family we call a congregation. It is a way to fight loneliness. Any time I see a person fleeing from reason and into religion, I think to myself, There goes a person who simply cannot stand being so goddamned lonely anymore.

"I read an essay by Harvey Cox recently, in which he quoted an early Church father as having said, 'One Christian is no Christian.' Mr. Cox said that one of the most distinctive and attractive features of Christianity for him was its insistence on forming congregations.

"We might also say that one human being is no human being.

"Many people have found a solution to loneliness by joining the paratroops. Membership in that particular family is gained and maintained by jumping out of airplanes and shouting 'Geronimo!' Not even the commanding general knows why everybody is supposed to shout 'Geronimo!' It does not matter.

"In a lonely society, the main thing is not to make sense. The main thing is to get rid of loneliness. I certainly sympathize.

"I have not mentioned love yet. I have been saving that for close to the end.

"Love was invented by a chef at the Brown Derby Restaurant in Hollywood, California, in 1939. It consists of overripe jumbo peaches with San Fernando Valley honey and chocolate jimmies on top. It is traditionally served in heated purple bowls.

"As every married person here knows, love is a rotten substitute for respect.

"I have spoken of the long tradition of religious skepticism in my family. One of my two daughters has recently turned her back on all that. Living alone and far from home, she has memorized an arbitrary Christian creed, Trinitarianism, by chance. She now has her human dignity regularly confirmed by the friendly nods of a congregation. I am glad that she is not so lonely anymore. This is more than all right with me.

"She believes that Jesus was the Son of God, or perhaps God Himself—or however that goes. I have had even more trouble with the Trinity than I had with college algebra. I refer those who are curious about it to what is known about the Council of Nicea, which took place in *anno Domini* 325. It was there that the Trinity was hammered into its present shape. Unfortunately, the minutes have been lost. It is known that the emperor Constantine was there, and probably spoke a good deal. He gave us the first Christian army. He may have given us the Holy Ghost as well.

"No matter. I do not argue with my Christian daughter about religion at all. Why should I? I have, however, begun to write a passion play for her which leaves God out entirely, but which manages to be spiritual anyway. It is still about Jesus Christ.

"I will tell you only about the last scene:

"The Roman soldiers, using ancient police methods, have done all they can to prove to Jesus that he has absolutely no dignity, so far as they can see. They have stripped him and whipped him. They have crowned him with thorns. They have made him drag his heavy cross through the streets. They have nailed his hands and feet to the cross. They have set the cross upright, so that he dangles in air.

"A group of ordinary people, who out of pity would like to take him from the cross and lay him down somewhere, and bandage his wounds and give him food and water and so on, approach the cross. The Roman soldiers stop them, tell them that they can go to the foot of the cross if they like but that they must not touch Jesus in any way, lest they give him comfort of some kind.

"That is the law.

"So the ordinary people—men, women, and children—gather beneath Jesus. They talk to him, sing to him, in the

hopes that some of it will help a little. They say how sorry
for him they are. They try to feel some of his pain—as though
whatever they could feel of it he would not have to feel.

"They go down on their knees after a while. They are
exhausted.

"Now a rich Roman tourist, a man, a successful speculator
in Mesopotamian millet futures, comes upon the scene. I
make him rich, because everybody hates rich people so
much. He is blasé about crucifixions, since he has seen so
many strangers crucified all over the Roman Empire.
Crosses then were as common as lampposts are today.

"It seems to the tourist that the people on their knees,
sighing and moaning, are worshiping this particular man on
a cross. He says to them jocularly: 'My goodness! The way
you are worshiping him, you would think he was the Son of
your God.'

"A spokesperson for the kneelers, perhaps Mary Magda-
lene, says to him, 'Oh no, sir. If he were the Son of our God,
he would not need us. It is because he is a common human
being exactly like us that we are here—doing, as common
people must, what little we can.'

"In this case this is not a dream. I thank you for your
attention."

XII

OBSCENITY

RIAH Fagan Cox was a gallant and pretty little woman from Columbia City, Indiana, which is in the northeast corner of the state, about halfway between Fort Wayne and Winona Lake. She was born into a so-called "good family," but her father was an alcoholic. He could not hold a job.

So, although little more than a child, Riah set out to rescue herself and her brother and eventually their descendents from want and obscurity. She sent herself to the University of Wisconsin, and took a master's degree in the classics. Her thesis was a high school textbook on the Latin and Greek roots of common words in English. It was adopted by many school systems all over the country, and earned enough money to enable Riah to put her brother through medical school. He set up practice in Hollywood, and became the beloved obstetrician of many famous movie stars.

She married a lawyer in Indianapolis who did not make much money. She took jobs teaching Latin and Greek and English, and became the Indianapolis representative for touring lecturers and musicians. She also sold silly, witty short stories to magazines from time to time. Thus was she able to send her son and daughter to the best private schools, even during the Great Depression. Her daughter became a Phi Beta Kappa at Swarthmore.

She died three years ago, and is buried in Crown Hill Cemetery in Indianapolis, somewhere between John Dillinger, the bank robber, and James Whitcomb Riley, the "Hoosier Poet." I liked her a lot. She was a good friend of mine. She was my first mother-in-law.

I mention her in this chapter on obscenity because she imagined that I used certain impolite words in my books in order to cause a sensation, in order to make the books more popular. She told me as a friend that the words were having the opposite effect in her circle of friends, at least. Her friends could not bear to read me anymore.

Indianapolis Magazine said much the same thing in its article about me, from which I quoted in a previous chapter. It praised the themes of my early books, *Player Piano, The Sirens of Titan,* and *Mother Night:* ". . . anger at war and killing, at the void that technology is creating in contemporary life." But it went on to say: "From then on, though the themes remained constant, his style began to change. Small obscenities crept in, and four-letter words became frequent in *Breakfast of Champions* in a riot of indecorous line drawings and misbegotten words that were suggestive of a small boy sticking out his tongue at the teacher."

This small boy, sticking out his tongue, was fifty years old at the time. It has been many decades since I have wished to shock a teacher or anyone. I did want to make the Americans in my books talk as Americans really do talk. I wanted to make jokes about our bodies. Why not? Why not, I ask again, especially since Riah Fagan Cox, God rest her soul, assured me that she herself was not wobbled by dirty words.

If I had gone to Riah's friends, they would have told me, too, that they had heard all the dirty words I used many times before, that the words did not astonish them. They would have insisted that the words should not be published anyway. It was bad manners to use such words. Bad manners should be punished.

But even when I was in grammar school, I suspected that warnings about words that nice people never used were in fact lessons in how to keep our mouths shut not just about our bodies, but about many, many things—perhaps too many things.

When I was in the fourth grade or so, I had this hunch confirmed. My father hit me for my bad manners in front of guests. It was the only time either one of my parents ever hit me. I hadn't said "shit" or "piss" or "fart" or "fuck" or anything like that in front of the guests. I had asked them a question in the field of economics. But my father was so offended by my question that I might as well have called the guests "silly shitheads." They really were silly shitheads, by the way.

The Great Depression was going on. The year would have been 1932. I had been taken out of private school a couple of years before, so that my classmates were no longer the children of the rich and the powerful. They were the children of mechanics and clerks and mailmen and so on. I thought it was wonderful that their mothers could cook. That was more than my own mother could do. Also, their fathers could fart around with motors and so on. Peer pressure, which is the most powerful force in the universe, had actually made me a scorner of my parents' class.

But I was polite enough when these two silly upper-class shitheads came over to our house one night. They were husband and wife. I remember their names well enough, but I will call them "Bud and Mary Swan." This was at a time when securities had become nearly worthless, when many banks had closed forever. Factories and stores were dead. But the Swans had arrived in a new Marmon, and Mrs. Swan had a new fur coat and a new star sapphire ring.

We all had to look out through the front door at the car, and then at the coat and the ring. So Mother and Father, with their nice manners, said they were glad that things were going so well for the Swans. The whole thing looked fishy to me. Everybody else was broke. Where would the Swans get all that money? It was as though this one couple had been allowed to defy the law of gravity.

Mother and Father told me to take another look at the sapphire, so I could see the beautiful star in there. So I did. But then, to get a better understanding of what was going on, I asked Mr. Swan how much the ring had cost him. That was when Father hit me. He hit me with an underhand blow to the seat of my pants. It lofted me in the direction of the staircase, and I just kept on going upstairs to my bedroom. I was mad.

Now then: As my parents would eventually discover, to their grief, the Swans were cat's-paws for confidence men.

They had been bankrolled by crooks to put on a show for friends of theirs who might still have a little money squirreled away somewhere. My parents would want to know where the Swans got all their easy money. My parents needed some easy money, too. If they didn't find it somewhere, they would be bounced forever from the upper class. As I say, I myself had already sunk into the lower orders.

The Swans said that they had invested what little they had left after the crash of the securities market in a wonderful company which wanted to keep itself a secret. It was quietly putting together a coal monopoly which would be as rich and powerful as Standard Oil. It was buying mines and barge lines and controlling interest in coal-hauling railroads, was getting them for a minor fraction of their true value since it was paying cash. Almost nobody else had cash. The cash was coming from individuals like the Swans and my parents, who could keep a secret, and who could scrape up a little something from the bottoms of their barrels, if they really tried.

The value of the company would increase at least a hundred times, the instant prosperity returned to the world. Meanwhile, the company was already paying dividends because it was so efficient. It was the dividends which had bought the Marmon and the coat and the star sapphire ring.

My parents of course invested. They found buyers somewhere, I suppose, for some of their oil paintings or oriental rugs, or for some of Father's fine guns. During the boom years, Father had been a collector of guns.

My parents had been taught such nice manners in childhood that it was actually impossible for them to suspect that these old friends of theirs were in league with crooks. They had no simple and practical vocabularies for the parts and functions of their excretory and reproductive systems, and no such vocabularies for treachery and hypocrisy, either. Good manners had made them defenseless against predatory members of their own class.

There we have our old friend peer pressure again, of course.

And there was no coal monopoly, of course. Whoever got my parents' money spent most of it on racehorses and chorus girls, probably, except for maybe a quarter of it, which they sent to the Swans as dividends.

❦

I had a telephone conversation recently with a young Indianapolis cousin, a married woman, during which I said that I dreaded coming out there, since I did not consider it possible that my older relatives could love me but hate my books so. She replied that I had to understand that they were all Victorians and too old to change. They could not help themselves when it came to loathing dirty books.

So I thought about Victoria, Queen of the United Kingdom of Great Britain and Ireland, and the Empress of India, who lived from 1819, long before my first ancestor arrived in this country, until 1901, when my father was a junior in Shortridge High School. And I asked myself why any mention of bodily functions should have pained this queen so.

I cannot believe that Victoria herself would have suffered a moment's genuine dismay if I had shown her the picture of my asshole which I drew for my book *Breakfast of Champions*. My asshole looks like this:

I also feature my asshole in my signature, which looks like this:

WHAT would Queen Victoria really feel in the presence of what she had declared to be obscenities? That her power to intimidate was being attacked ever so slightly, far, far from its center, was being attacked where it could not matter much as yet—was being attacked way out on the edge. She created arbitrary rules for that outermost edge to warn her of the approach of anyone so crude, so rash as to bring to her attention the suffering of the Irish, or the cruelties of the factory system, or the privileges of the nobility, or the approach of a world war, and on and on? If she would not even acknowledge that human beings sometimes farted, how could she be expected to hear without swooning of these other things?

✤

WHAT a subtle scheme Queen Victoria evolved to make people hesitant about discussing their entitlement to more control over their lives. She persuaded them that they would deserve to be self-governing only after they had stopped thinking about all the things that human beings can't help thinking about all the time.

Genteel mothers of the era could do no less than to similarly discipline their children and their servants—and their husbands, if they could get away with it, and on and on.

❦

WHAT was the dirtiest story I ever wrote? Surely "The Big Space Fuck," the first story in the history of literature to have "fuck" in its title. It was probably the last short story I will ever write. I did it for my friend Harlan Ellison, who printed it in his anthology *Again, Dangerous Visions.* It was copyrighted by him in 1972, and appears here with his kind permission. It goes like this:

THE BIG SPACE FUCK

In 1987 it became possible in the United States of America for a young person to sue his parents for the way he had been raised. He could take them to court and make them pay money and even serve jail terms for serious mistakes they made when he was just a helpless little kid. This was not only an effort to achieve justice but to discourage reproduction, since there wasn't anything much to eat any more. Abortions were free. In fact, any woman who volunteered for one got her choice of a bathroom scale or a table lamp.

In 1989, America staged the Big Space Fuck, which was a serious effort to make sure that human life would continue to exist somewhere in the Universe, since it certainly couldn't continue much longer on Earth. Everything had turned to shit and beer cans and old automobiles and Clorox bottles. An interesting thing happened in the Hawaiian Islands, where they had been throwing trash down extinct volcanoes for years: a couple of the volcanoes all of a sudden spit it all back up. And so on.

This was a period of great permissiveness in matters of language, so even the President was saying shit and fuck and so on, without anybody's feeling threatened or taking offense. It was perfectly OK. He called the Space Fuck a Space Fuck and so did everybody else. It was a rocket ship with eight hundred pounds of freeze-dried jizzum in its nose. It was going to be fired at the Andromeda Galaxy, two-million light years away. The ship was named the *Arthur C. Clarke*, in honor of a famous space pioneer.

It was to be fired at midnight on the Fourth of July. At ten o'clock that night, Dwayne Hoobler and his wife Grace were watching the countdown on television in the living room of their modest home in Elk Harbor, Ohio, on the shore of what used to be Lake Erie. Lake Erie was almost solid sewage now. There were man-eating lampreys in there thirty-eight feet long. Dwayne was a guard in the Ohio Adult Correctional Institution, which was two miles away. His hobby was making birdhouses out of Clorox bottles. He went on making them and hanging them around his yard, even though there weren't any birds any more.

Dwayne and Grace marveled at a film demonstration of how jizzum had been freeze-dried for the trip. A small beaker of the stuff, which had been contributed by the head of the Mathematics Department at the University of Chicago, was flash-frozen. Then it was placed under a bell jar, and the air was exhausted from the jar. The air evanesced, leaving a fine white powder. The powder certainly didn't look like much, and Dwayne Hoobler said so—but there were several hundred million sperm cells in there, in suspended animation.

The original contribution, an average contribution, had been two cubic centimeters. There was enough powder, Dwayne estimated out loud, to clog the eye of a needle. And eight-hundred pounds of the stuff would soon be on its way to Andromeda.

"Fuck you, Andromeda," said Dwayne, and he wasn't being coarse. He was echoing billboards and stickers all over town. Other signs said, "Andromeda, We Love You," and "Earth Has the Hots for Andromeda," and so on.

There was a knock on the door, and an old friend of the family, the County Sheriff, simultaneously let himself in. "How are you, you old motherfucker?" said Dwayne.

"Can't complain, shitface," said the sheriff, and they joshed back and forth like that for a while. Grace chuckled, enjoying their wit. She wouldn't have chuckled so richly, however, if she had been a little more observant. She might have noticed that the sheriff's jocularity was very much on the surface. Underneath, he had something troubling on his mind. She might have noticed, too, that he had legal papers in his hand.

"Sit down, you silly old fart," said Dwayne, "and watch Andromeda get the surprise of her life."

"The way I understand it," the sheriff replied, "I'd have to sit there for more than two million years. My old lady might wonder what's become of me." He was a lot smarter than Dwayne. He had jizzum on the *Arthur C. Clarke,* and Dwayne didn't. You had to have an I.Q. of over 115 to have your jizzum accepted. There were certain exceptions to this: if you were a good athlete or could play a musical instrument or paint pictures, but Dwayne didn't qualify in any of those departments, either. He had hoped that birdhouse-makers might be entitled to special consideration, but this turned out not to be the case. The Director of the New York Philharmonic, on the other hand, was entitled to contribute a whole quart, if he wanted to. He was sixty-eight years old. Dwayne was forty-two.

There was an old astronaut on the television now. He was saying that he sure wished he could go where his jizzum was going. But he would sit at home instead, with his memories and a glass of Tang. Tang used to be the official drink of the astronauts. It was a freeze-dried orangeade.

"Maybe you haven't got two million years," said Dwayne, "but you've got at least five minutes. Sit thee doon."

"What I'm here for—" said the sheriff, and he let his unhappiness show, "is something I customarily do standing up."

Dwayne and Grace were sincerely puzzled. They didn't have the least idea what was coming next. Here is what it was: the sheriff handed each one of them a subpoena, and he said, "It's my sad duty to inform you that your daughter, Wanda June, has accused you of ruining her when she was a child."

Dwayne and Grace were thunderstruck. They knew that Wanda June was twenty-one now, and entitled to sue, but they certainly hadn't expected her to do so. She was in New York City, and when they congratulated her about her birthday on the telephone, in fact, one of the things Grace said was, "Well, you can sue us now, honeybunch, if you want to." Grace was so sure she and Dwayne had been good parents that she could laugh when she went on, "If you want to, you can send your rotten old parents off to jail."

Wanda June was an only child, incidentally. She had come close to having some siblings, but Grace had aborted them.

Grace had taken three table lamps and a bathroom scale instead.

"What does she say we did wrong?" Grace asked the sheriff.

"There's a separate list of charges inside each of your subpoenas," he said. And he couldn't look his wretched old friends in the eye, so he looked at the television instead. A scientist there was explaining why Andromeda had been selected as a target. There were at least eighty-seven chrono-synclastic infundibulae, time warps, between Earth and the Andromeda Galaxy. If the *Arthur C. Clarke* passed through any one of them, the ship and its load would be multiplied a trillion times, and would appear everywhere throughout space and time.

"If there's any fecundity anywhere in the Universe," the scientist promised, "our seed will find it and bloom."

One of the most depressing things about the space program so far, of course, was that it had demonstrated that fecundity was one hell of a long way off, if anywhere. Dumb people like Dwayne and Grace, and even fairly smart people like the sheriff, had been encouraged to believe that there was hospitality out there, and that Earth was just a piece of shit to use as a launching platform.

Now Earth really was a piece of shit, and it was beginning to dawn on even dumb people that it might be the only inhabitable planet human beings would ever find.

Grace was in tears over being sued by her daughter, and the list of charges she was reading was broken into multiple images by the tears. "Oh God, oh God, oh God—" she said, "she's talking about things I forgot all about, but she never forgot a thing. She's talking about something that happened when she was only four years old."

Dwayne was reading charges against himself, so he didn't ask Grace what awful thing she was supposed to have done when Wanda June was only four, but here it was: Poor little Wanda June drew pretty pictures with a crayon all over the new living-room wallpaper to make her mother happy. Her mother blew up and spanked her instead. Since that day, Wanda June claimed, she had not been able to look at any sort of art materials without trembling like a leaf and breaking out into cold sweats. "Thus was I deprived," Wanda June's lawyer had her say, "of a brilliant and lucrative career in the arts."

Dwayne meanwhile was learning that he had ruined his daughter's opportunities for what her lawyer called an "advantageous marriage and the comfort and love therefrom." Dwayne had done this, supposedly, by being half in the bag whenever a suitor came to call. Also, he was often stripped to the waist when he answered the door, but still had on his cartridge belt and his revolver. She was even able to name a lover her father had lost for her: John L. Newcomb, who had finally married somebody else. He had a very good job now. He was in command of the security force at an arsenal out in South Dakota, where they stockpiled cholera and bubonic plague.

The sheriff had still more bad news to deliver, and he knew he would have an opportunity to deliver it soon enough. Poor Dwayne and Grace were bound to ask him, "What made her *do* this to us?" The answer to that question would be more bad news, which was that Wanda June was in jail, charged with being the head of a shoplifting ring. The only way she could avoid prison was to prove that everything she was and did was her parents' fault.

Meanwhile, Senator Flem Snopes of Mississippi, Chairman of the Senate Space Committee, had appeared on the television screen. He was very happy about the Big Space Fuck, and he said it had been what the American space program had been aiming toward all along. He was proud, he said, that the United States had seen fit to locate the biggest jizzum-freezing plant in his "l'il ol' home town," which was Mayhew.

The word "jizzum" had an interesting history, by the way. It was as old as "fuck" and "shit" and so on, but it continued to be excluded from dictionaries, long after the others were let in. This was because so many people wanted it to remain a truly magic word—the only one left.

And when the United States announced that it was going to do a truly magical thing, was going to fire sperm at the Andromeda Galaxy, the populace corrected its government. Their collective unconscious announced that it was time for the last magic word to come into the open. They insisted that *sperm* was nothing to fire at another galaxy. Only *jizzum* would do. So the Government began using that word, and it did something that had never been done before, either: it standardized the way the word was spelled.

The man who was interviewing Senator Snopes asked him to stand up so everybody could get a good look at his codpiece, which the Senator did. Codpieces were very much in fashion, and many men were wearing codpieces in the shape of rocket ships, in honor of the Big Space Fuck. These customarily had the letters "U.S.A." embroidered on the shaft. Senator Snopes' shaft, however, bore the Stars and Bars of the Confederacy.

This led the conversation into the area of heraldry in

general, and the interviewer reminded the Senator of his campaign to eliminate the bald eagle as the national bird. The Senator explained that he didn't like to have his country represented by a creature that obviously hadn't been able to cut the mustard in modern times.

Asked to name a creature that *had* been able to cut the mustard, the Senator did better than that: he named two—the lamprey and the bloodworm. And, unbeknownst to him or to anybody, lampreys were finding the Great Lakes too vile and noxious even for *them*. While all the human beings were in their houses, watching the Big Space Fuck, lampreys were squirming out of the ooze and onto land. Some of them were nearly as long and thick as the *Arthur C. Clarke*.

And Grace Hoobler tore her wet eyes from what she had been reading, and she asked the sheriff the question he had been dreading to hear: "What made her *do* this to us?"

The sheriff told her, and then he cried out against cruel Fate, too. "This is the most horrible duty I ever had to carry out—" he said brokenly, "to deliver news this heartbreaking to friends as close as you two are—on a night that's supposed to be the most joyful night in the history of mankind."

He left sobbing, and stumbled right into the mouth of a lamprey. The lamprey ate him immediately, but not before he screamed. Dwayne and Grace Hoobler rushed outside to see what the screaming was about, and the lamprey ate them, too.

It was ironical that their television set continued to report the countdown, even though they weren't around any more to see or hear or care.

"Nine!" said a voice. And then, "Eight!" And then, "Seven!" And so on.

THAT is a made-up story. Here is another true story:

When I was little, there was a female friend of my parents who was particularly admired for her vivacity and good taste and impeccable manners and so on. She married a German businessman.

When she came back to Indianapolis after the Second World War, she was as attractive as ever. She said vivaciously that Hitler had been right about most things, and that Germany should be admired for fighting so many powerful enemies all at once. "We almost won," she reminded us.

I had just come back from Germany, too. I had been a prisoner of war there. So I took my father aside, and I said to him, "Father, I can't help having mixed feelings about this old family friend."

He told me that I should pay no attention to her when she spoke of political matters, that she understood nothing about them, that she was just a charming, silly, innocent little girl.

He was right. It was impossible for her to think coherently about assholes or Auschwitz or anything else that might be upsetting to a little girl.

That's class.

XIII

CHILDREN

MY first wife and both my daughters are born-again Christians now—working white magic through rituals and prayers. That's all right. I would be a fool to say that the Free Thinker ideas of Clemens Vonnegut remain as enchanting and encouraging as ever—not after the mortal poisoning of the planet, not after two world wars, with more to come.

Can I say now, with all my heart, what he said in his little book in 1900: "We believe in virtue, in perfectibility, in progress, in stability of the laws of nature, in the necessity of improving the social conditions and relations, which should be in harmony with that benevolence which conditions the coherence of men"?

No.

"Truth," he says, "must always be recognized as the paramount requisite of human society." As I myself said in another place, I began to have my doubts about truth after it was dropped on Hiroshima.

❦

CLEMENS Vonnegut wrote of powerful and rich families founded by criminals. He despised them. He himself founded a dynasty based on hard work, prudence, and honest dealing.

At the end of his life, eight years before the First World War, his many descendents, my father and grandfather among them, must have looked like innocent, happy sailors in a flotilla of freshly painted little catboats, running before the wind in a safe harbor, always in sight of land.

The harbor was Indianapolis. The sailboats were jobs and shares in the Vonnegut Hardware Company.

Seventy-four years later, the Vonnegut Hardware Company exists no more. The "Mile Square" in the heart of Indianapolis, where it once had its bustling main store, is a desert of parking lots now. At night the Mile Square is as eerily desolate as East Berlin. The retail outlets of the Vonnegut Hardware Company were ruined by perfectly fair competition—by discount stores.

So I can bequeath no Vonnegut Hardware stock to my own descendents, nor can I offer them jobs with that firm, if life on the outside becomes too rough-and-tumble. I am the last of my grandfather's branch of the family to have worked there, to have been given a little sailboat for a while.

❧

In lieu of stock, I can only leave my descendents a story about the legendary times, now lost in the mists, when the name Vonnegut was synonymous with hardware in Indianapolis. That story will be lost forever, if I do not now take it out of my perishable head and write it down.

There was this Japanese jeweler in Indianapolis, you see, who, among other things, made class rings by hand for the graduates of Tudor Hall, the small and exclusive girls' school to which rich girls from all over Indiana were sent before going East to college. My sister, although her family was broke, went there. My first wife, although her family was broke, went there.

The name of the jeweler was Iku Matsu Moto. He had many secrets, probably because his customers asked him very little about himself. It turned out that he used to be a strong man with Ringling Brothers and Barnum & Bailey Circus.

So he appeared at the main store of Vonnegut Hardware Company on East Washington Street one day, and he wanted an anvil. His shop was on Monument Circle, three blocks away. In Indianapolis, which was laid out by Pierre Charles L'Enfant, the same Frenchman who laid out Washington, D.C., each block is one tenth of a mile on a side.

So Iku Matsu Moto found an anvil he liked, and he asked the salesman how much it cost. The salesman told him jocularly that he could have it for nothing if Iku Matsu Moto could carry it home. So Iku Matsu Moto carried it home.

❧

I scarcely know any of the few Vonneguts still living in Indianapolis, and my own children will know and care about them as much as I know or care about my German relatives. Things fall apart.

There is a Bernard Vonnegut in Albany. That's my brother, I believe. And there is a Peter Vonnegut there, who is Bernard's son, and who is a librarian, and who married a woman named Michi Minatoya, who, like Iku Matsu Moto, is of Japanese ancestry. They have two children, Carl Hiroaki Vonnegut and Emiko Alice Vonnegut, my brother's only grandchildren. They, too, are, among other things, de St. Andrés. Strange and nice.

❀

THERE is a Dr. Mark Vonnegut in Brookline, Massachusetts. That's my son, I believe.

I am proud of Mark, and I praised him and drew on his experience in this manner at a meeting of the Mental Health Association in New Jersey in Morristown on June 4, 1980:

"The title of this speech in your programs is 'Must We Do without References?' Please cross that out, in case you want to remember later on what really happened here. The new title is 'Fear and Loathing in Morristown, New Jersey,' and I want you all to know how safe I feel up here. If I go crazy, you will know all the latest things to do about it. I will be out of the nuthouse and back on the streets in no time, coked to the gills on Thorazine.

"The title in your programs is a typographical error anyway. It should have been 'Must We Do without Reference *Points?*' You might want to add that word 'Points' to the original title before you cross the whole thing out, which reminds me of a very funny story. There was a man in a restaurant, and he called the waiter over, and he said, 'Waiter —there is a needle in my soup.' And the waiter said to him, 'Oh sir, I am so sorry. That is a typographical error. It should have been a noodle.'

"When I thought I was going to talk about reference points, I had in mind the fixtures in a simpler and more stable civilization than what we have today. Examples: Shakespeare's *Hamlet,* Beethoven's Fifth Symphony, Leonardo's *Mona Lisa,* Lincoln's Gettysburg Address, Mark Twain's *Huckleberry Finn*—the Great Wall of China, the Leaning Tower of Pisa, the Sphinx. These few works of art used to be enormous monuments in the minds of public school graduates in every corner of this country. They have now been drowned in our minds, like Atlantis, if you will, by the latest sensations on television and radio, and in our motion picture palaces and *People* magazine.

"Time was when a worker in the mental health field in America would have a few reference points in common with a native-born maniac, could begin a therapeutic conversation with comments on the smile of the Mona Lisa, say. It was a beginning. But nowadays, I would think, a therapist has to be prepared to discuss in depth *Beach Blanket Bingo* or *The Texas Chainsaw Murders* or *Howdy Doody* or *Romper Room* or Walter Cronkite—and just on and on and on. Farrah Fawcett-Majors. No subject of conversation lives much longer than a lightning bug these days. I have a son who is a gag writer on the West Coast, and he wrote what he thought was a very funny skit about Howdy Doody. I had to explain to him that there were millions of Americans older and younger than he was, who did not know or care who

Howdy Doody was. He was shattered. When he was seven years old, Howdy Doody was God to him.

"But I have scrapped that particular speech, as I say. I didn't have the brains to pull it off. It was too ambitious—not only for me but for lunch at a New Jersey motel. So I have decided to talk instead about how honored I am to be here. If some of you are taking notes, you should write that down: 'Honored to be asked to speak on mental health'—something like that.

"I don't know why you invited me. Perhaps it is because my son Mark went insane. He is not the gag writer. That is another son. The one who went insane is well now. He graduated from Harvard Medical School a year ago, and is an intern in Boston now. He, too, is a magnificent speaker. He loves to ask an audience of workers in the mental health field, 'How many of you have ever taken Thorazine?' Almost no hands go up, and my son the doctor gives a little smile, and he says: 'It won't hurt you. You really ought to try it sometime, just to get an inkling, anyway, of what your patients are going through.'

"Your organizers asked me what degrees I held. Even if I were a trapeze artist, they would have to ask me that, I guess. So I ransacked the drawers of my bedside table for documents. I found a long-lost pair of cuff links, unfortunately only gold-plated. I found a snapshot of my sister Alice when she was only sixteen. She died here in New Jersey at the age of forty-one, and not in the best of mental health. I found a diploma from the University of Chicago, which is west of here. It declared that I had earned a master's degree in anthropology. I looked up the word in a dictionary. It turned out to be the study of man.

"At the University of Chicago so long ago, I had to select

a specialty from these five fields in anthropology: archaeology, cultural anthropology, ethnology, linguistics, and physical anthropology. I chose cultural anthropology, since it offered the greatest opportunity to write high-minded balderdash. Culture, of course, is every object and idea which has been shaped by men and women and children, and not by God. Cultural anthropology is a broad specialty, you might say. I never heard of a cultural anthropologist who came down with claustrophobia.

"It was that damn fool diploma which made me believe for a moment that I could speak to you as an expert on culture, about that bed of Procrustes which maladjusted persons find so uncomfortable. My own son Mark found it so uncomfortable that he tried to beat his brains out on it, and had to be put in a padded cell. Really. That is how crazy he was. He would have tried to kill himself with a Stradivarius violin, if there had been one around—or the Leaning Tower of Pisa, or Walter Cronkite's mustache.

"But I am a storyteller, not a cultural anthropologist, no matter what the diploma says. And I am not even the best storyteller in my own family when it comes to the relationship of culture to mental health. My son Mark is the best storyteller in that area. He wrote an excellent book about going crazy and recovering. It is called *The Eden Express.* Mark remembers everything. His wish is to tell people who are going insane something about the shape of the roller coaster they are on. It helps sometimes to know the shape of a roller coaster. How many of you here have taken Thorazine?

"Mark has taught me never to romanticize mental illness, never to imagine a brilliant and beguiling schizophrenic who makes more sense about life than his or her doctor or even the president of Harvard University. Mark says that schizophrenia is as ghastly and debilitating as smallpox or rabies or any other unspeakable disease you care to name. Society cannot be blamed, and neither, thank God, can the friends and relatives of the patient. Schizophrenia is an internal chemical catastrophe. It is a case of monstrously bad genetic luck, bad luck of a sort encountered in absolutely every sort of society—including the Australian aborigines and the middle class of Vienna, Austria, before the Second World War.

"Plenty of other writers at this very moment are writing a story about an admirable, perhaps even a divine schizophrenic. Why? Because the story is wildly applauded every time it is told. It blames the culture and the economy and the society and everything but the disease itself for making the patient unwell. Mark says that is wrong.

"As his father, though, I am still free to say this, I think: I believe that a culture, a combination of ideas and artifacts, can sometimes make a healthy person behave against his or her best interests, and against the best interests of the society and the planet, too.

"I have made up a story about that for this moment, and for this audience in this motel. It goes like this:

"There is this psychiatrist, you see. He is a colonel in the German SS in Poland during World War Two. His name is Vonnegut. That is a good German name. Colonel Vonnegut is supposed to look after the mental health of SS people in his area, which includes the uniformed staff at Auschwitz.

"Colonel Vonnegut has a skull and crossbones on his hat. Ordinarily, when an SS man wants to express his love for a woman, he gives her a skull and crossbones to wear. But Colonel Vonnegut is in love with an SS woman, and she already has skulls and crossbones of her own. So he sends her candy instead.

"But that is not the major crisis in the story. The most moving part is when a young, idealistic SS lieutenant comes to Vonnegut for help. His name is Dampfwalze. *Dampfwalze* means 'steamroller.' *Vonnegut* means nothing. Ask any critic on *The New York Review of Books.*

"Lieutenant Dampfwalze, who could be played by Peter O'Toole, feels that he can't cut the mustard anymore on the railroad platform at Auschwitz, where boxcars of people are unloaded day after day. He is sick and tired of it, but he has the wisdom to seek professional help. Dr. Vonnegut is an eclectic worker in the field of mental health, incidentally, a pragmatic man. He is a little bit Jungian, a little bit Freudian, a little bit Rankian—and so on. He has an open and inquiring mind.

"Actually, he cures Dampfwalze with megavitamins, the same things that cured my son. The Nazis haven't received nearly the credit they deserve for pioneering megavitamin therapy.

"So Dampfwalze is ready to return to duty. His eyes are shining again. His appetite is good. He sleeps like a baby every night. And he asks Dr. Vonnegut how serious his illness had been.

"Dr. Vonnegut tells him that, if Dampfwalze hadn't recognized nature's little danger signals early and put himself into the hands of modern medicine, he might have tried to shoot Adolf Hitler by and by. That is how sick he was.

"And the moral of that story, I think, is that a society, on occasion, can be the worst possible describer of mental health.

"I thank you for your attention."

❦

THREE of my six children are adopted nephews. They have retained their original name, the most original of all names, which is Adams. My first wife and I adopted them after, within a period of only twenty-four hours, their father drowned when his commuter train went off an open drawbridge in New Jersey and then their mother died of cancer in a hospital. Their mother was my only sister, and her death had been expected for quite a while.

There was a fourth Adams brother, an infant, who was adopted by a first cousin of his father in Birmingham, Alabama.

They were orphaned in September of 1958, nearly twenty-two years ago as I write. I came down from Cape Cod at once to run their house in Rumson, New Jersey. They held a meeting at which I was not present. They came downstairs together with a single demand: that they be kept together along with their dogs. One of the dogs, a sheep dog named Sandy, would become the closest friend I have ever had.

❦

JAMES Adams, the oldest of the orphans, as we continue to call them, was then fourteen. He is now thirty-six, the age I was when Jane and I adopted him. He attended college briefly, then became a Peace Corps volunteer in Peru, and then a goat farmer in Jamaica, and is now a cabinetmaker in Leverett, Massachusetts.

He is married to Barbara D'Arthanay, a former New England schoolteacher who lived and worked with him for several years on his goat farm on a mountaintop in Jamaica. They are as uninterested in social rank and property as was Henry David Thoreau.

They have given me a grandchild. The area in which they are raising that child consists largely of farmlands being recaptured by the wilderness. The name of the child resonates with the innocent imperialism of earlier white colonists. Her name is India Adams.

God watch over India Adams in the untamed American wilderness.

❖

A tale from Jim's bachelor days:

Jim went down the Amazon with two friends on a raft after he left the Peace Corps. One night, while the raft was tied up near Manaus, the old rubber boom town in Brazil, a speedboat came alongside. At the wheel was Yevgeny Yevtushenko, the Soviet poet. He had Brazilian friends along. He asked in English if he and his party could come aboard the raft for drinks. In exchange, he said, he would give his hosts a perfect name for their raft.

So there was some drinking on the raft, and fighting for some reason broke out between Yevtushenko and Jim.

So the party was over, and the visitors got back in their speedboat. Just before they cast off, Yevtushenko said: "I have not forgotten my promise. You should call your raft *The Huckleberry Finn.*"

Years later I myself would meet Yevtushenko, and I would ask him if the story was true.

"Ah!" he said. "Ah! That was your son? He is a very bad boy!"

Small world.

❖

STEVEN Adams was eleven when we adopted him, the same age as my natural son Mark. He was the least dependent of the lot, being a superb athlete and having joined an alternative family long before his parents died, the worldwide family of coaches and teammates and competitors everywhere. Coaches on Cape Cod, just like the coaches in New Jersey, greeted him like a long-lost son.

Steve arrived on Cape Cod wearing a jacket with this emblazoned on the back: "New Jersey Little League All-Stars." Further introductions were unnecessary.

He went to Dartmouth, where he studied English literature and played end. He is in Los Angeles now, a professional writer of comedy for television shows. He is thirty-three and has never married, and he runs a lot.

I know Steve least well of all my children, since, to his credit, he has had the least need of me. At the same time, he is the only one who has chosen to become what I am, which is a full-time writer. His work now is entirely comical. As far as I know, he will not begin a piece unless it promises to lead him at once to a joke of some kind. He is well paid for unseriousness. If he ever became serious, he would lose his job.

His job also requires him to ignore all he learned at Dartmouth of history and literature and philosophy and what have you, and to joke only about matters with which his audience is familiar, recent television commercials, celebrities of the moment, big-grossing motion pictures of the past year, extraordinarily popular records, political figures in the news incessantly, and on and on. This must become tiresome.

He is the most rootless of my children, and the one most likely to drift away. If he reproduces, his children, in California, perhaps, will never find out, probably, unless they read this book, that they are de St. Andrés and have second cousins named Carl Hiroaki Vonnegut and Emiko Alice Vonnegut and on and on.

❦

STEVE'S younger brother Kurt Adams, nine years old when we adopted him, also lives in Leverett, near his brother Jim. Kurt was the first of the brothers to settle there. He is thirty-two now, and a pilot for Air New England, and a builder on speculation of beautiful post-and-beam houses which are entirely heated by wood stoves. He lives in such a house himself. He is married to an excellent artist named Lindsay Palermo. So far, they have not had a child.

Kurt is the only canny business person of the lot. He is of modest means, but he makes satisfying gains on small investments. He has a little victory garden of dollars that he tends.

The rest do not care for money games. They cannot pay attention—any more than my father or mother or sister could, than my brother can.

This is a matter of genetics, I think. People are born caring or not caring about managing money well.

We are all experiments in enthusiasms, narrow and preordained. I write.

❧

MY brother is an enthusiast for the scientific study of thunderstorms. My late sister was born to be an enthusiast for painting and sculpture, but resisted. She said, very wisely, in my opinion, "Just because you have talent, it doesn't mean that you have to *do* something with it."

❧

THERE is a fourth Adams brother. He was an infant when his mother died. He was adopted by a first cousin of his father in Birmingham, Alabama, a judge. His mother died before she could have any influence over his character, and yet his attitudes toward life are identical with hers—and his jokes. His name is Peter Nice.

He talks of settling in Leverett—to be near his brothers, who are more like him than anyone else in the world.

❧

WHEN we adopted the Adamses, two of our natural children got artificial twins. Steve Adams was the same age as Mark Vonnegut. Kurt Adams was the same age as Edith Vonnegut. This was purely delightful for Edith, who took her new twin to "Show and Tell" at the Barnstable Elementary School. She got two more strong older brothers, as well. For Mark, the benefits of a family merger weren't so apparent at once. He was no longer the oldest child and the only male child—and so on.

❦

ALL the children remain close these days, and think of themselves as genuine brothers and sisters. They are lucky to have so many interested and responsive relatives. There are many affectionate reunions a year in the big old house on Cape Cod where they were raised together. They were such a formidable gang when they were young that one policeman became a specialist in their habits and haunts. He had a lovely name, and always left his blue flasher on when he parked in our yard. His name was Sergeant Nightingale.

Whenever Sergeant Nightingale came to interrogate this child or that one, the flasher on his cruiser splashed our house with blue as it went around and around.

Nobody ever went to prison, though.

Nobody ever dealt dope.

❦

THERE was only one really fancy auto smashup. Mark rolled and totaled a Volkswagen Microbus with about eight people in it. It scattered people out along the shoulder of the road the way a saltshaker will scatter salt. People flew out through the sun roof, out through the side doors, out through the tailgate. Mark was the last one to fly out. He landed on his feet, and found himself facing oncoming traffic like a football lineman.

Nobody was killed or seriously hurt, thank God.

Jim Adams was not the only one of my children to come close to actual combat with a major literary figure. About the time Jim and Yevtushenko were menacing each other on the

Amazon, Mark Vonnegut was considering a fight with Jack Kerouac in our kitchen on Cape Cod. These confrontations even took place in the same time zone, but in different hemispheres.

I knew Kerouac only at the end of his life, which is to say there was no way for me to know him at all, since he had become a pinwheel. He had settled briefly on Cape Cod, and a mutual friend, the writer Robert Boles, brought him over to my house one night. I doubt that Kerouac knew anything about me or my work, or even where he was. He was crazy. He called Boles, who is black, "a blue-gummed nigger." He said that Jews were the real Nazis, and that Allen Ginsberg had been told by the Communists to befriend Kerouac, in order that they might gain control of American young people, whose leader he was.

This was pathetic. There were clearly thunderstorms in the head of this once charming and just and intelligent man. He wished to play poker, so I dealt some cards. There were four hands, I think—one for Boles, one for Kerouac, one for Jane, one for me. Kerouac picked up the remainder of the deck, and he threw it across the kitchen.

It was then that Mark came in, unexpectedly home for a weekend from Swarthmore College, where he was a religion major. He was also a middleweight wrestler in very good shape. He wore a full beard and a work shirt and blue jeans, and carried a duffel bag. Everything about his costume and even his posture might have been inspired by Kerouac's books.

The moment Kerouac saw him, Kerouac stood and looked him over smolderingly from head to toe. The calm before a fight settled dankly over the room.

"You think you understand me," said Kerouac to Mark.

"You don't understand me at all. You want to fight about it?" Mark said nothing, not knowing who Kerouac was or what he was so mad about.

Kerouac praised himself as a fighter, asked Mark if he really thought he was man enough to take him on.

Mark understood this much, anyway: that he might really have to fight this person. He didn't want to, but then again, he wouldn't have minded fighting him all that much.

But then Kerouac sat back down in his chair heavily, shaking his head and saying over and over again, "Doesn't understand me at all."

Later on that night, after Kerouac and Boles left, Mark and I talked some about Kerouac, who was then completing his seventeenth and last book. He would die very soon.

It turned out that Mark had never read Kerouac.

❦

AND Mark is a physician now, married to Pat O'Shea, a schoolteacher, and they have one son, Zachary Vonnegut, the firstborn of my grandchildren, now three years old, and the only one so far to carry on my own curious last name. Mark is the first Vonnegut in America to be a healer, and only the second one to earn a doctor's degree of any sort. My brother Bernard, of course, has a doctor's degree in chemistry.

And Conrad Aiken, the poet, the one time I met him, told me that a child will compete with its father in an area where the father is weak, in an area where the father mistakenly believes himself to be quite accomplished. Aiken himself did this, by his own account. His father was a Renaissance man, a surgeon, an athlete, something of a musician, something of a poet, and on and on. Aiken said that he himself became a poet because he realized that his father's poetry really wasn't very good.

So what am I, if I believe that, to make of myself as mirrored in my own children, who cheerfully compete in every area, including writing, in which I have ever dabbled while they were watching? I played chess a little, and now all of them can beat me at chess. I painted and drew some, and now Jim Adams and Mark Vonnegut and Edith Vonnegut and Nanette Vonnegut can all paint and draw circles around me. Desperately, this old man is going to have a one-man show of his drawings this fall, but they're no damn good.

Yes, and I carpentered some, so now Jim Adams and Kurt Adams and Steve Adams and Mark Vonnegut can all do cabinet work. And on and on.

Mark has written a first-rate book. Edith has not only written but illustrated a first-rate book.

I noodled around some on the piano and the clarinet, so Steve Adams now composes his own music and performs with his guitar in cabarets, and Mark plays saxophone and a little piano in a jazz band composed entirely of physicians, and on and on.

This is terrible.

✿

I find that I want to protect the privacy of my two daughters, and so will talk about them very little. Nanette and Edith are both gifted artists. Both have found the life of an artist a lonely one. Edith has determined that loneliness is not too high a price to pay. Nanette is becoming a nurse who will make pictures for fun.

❦

AND meanwhile the man-made weather of politics and economics and technology will blow them this way and that.

❦

WHAT is my favorite among all the works of art my children have so far produced? It is perhaps a letter written by my youngest daughter Nanette. It is so *organic!* She wrote it to "Mr. X," an irascible customer at a Cape Cod restaurant where she worked as a waitress in the summer of 1978. The customer was so mad about the service he had received one evening, you see, that he had complained in writing to the management. The management posted the letter on the kitchen bulletin board.

Nanette's reply went like this:

Dear Mr. X,

As a newly trained waitress I feel that I must respond to the letter of complaint which you recently wrote to the ABC Inn. Your letter has caused more suffering to an innocent young woman this summer than the inconvenience you experienced in not receiving your soup on time and having your bread taken away prematurely and so on.

I believe that you did in fact receive poor service from this new waitress. I recall her as being very flustered and upset that evening, but she hoped that her errors, clumsy as they were, would be understood sympathetically as inexperience. I myself have made mistakes in serving. Fortunately, the customers were humorous and compassionate. I have learned so much from these mistakes, and through the support and understanding of other waitresses and customers in the span of only one week, that I feel confident now about what I am doing, and seldom make mistakes.

There is no doubt in my mind that Katharine is on her way to becoming a competent waitress. You must understand that learning how to waitress is very much the same as learning how to juggle. It is difficult to find the correct balance and timing. Once these are found, though, waitressing becomes a solid and unshakable skill.

There must be room for error even in such a finely tuned establishment as the ABC Inn. There must be allowance for waitresses being human. Maybe you did not realize that in naming this young woman you made it necessary for the management to fire her. Katharine is now without a summer job on Cape Cod, and school is ahead.

Can you imagine how difficult it is to find jobs here now? Do you know how hard it is for many young students to make ends meet these days? I feel it is my duty as a human being to ask you to think twice about what is of importance in life. I hope that in all fairness you will think about what I have said, and that in the future you will be more thoughtful and humane in your actions.

Sincerely,
Nanette Vonnegut.

xlv

JONATHAN SWIFT MISPERCEIVED

I s it possible for a man of my eminence to write so badly that he is rejected? Yes, indeed. It takes some doing, though. As my own vanity publisher, I intend to thrust one such fizzle into our culture anyway. It is an essay on Jonathan Swift, which I submitted as a preface for a new edition of *Gulliver's Travels.*

The publisher's objection was that I had sentimentalized Swift, having failed, apparently, to have read any detailed accounts of his life and character. Here is how I did it:

"Go, traveler," says his epitaph in Latin, "and imitate, if you can, one who strove with all his strength to champion liberty." Jonathan Swift (1667–1745), an Anglican priest, wrote this about his own long life. He is buried beside his wife in Dublin's St. Patrick's Cathedral, where he was dean for his final thirty-two years. It was in Dublin that he wrote *Gulliver's Travels,* a book as enduring as any cathedral. The appointment to St. Patrick's had disappointed him. He had hoped for a bishopric in England. Be that as it may, he became, according to Swift scholar Ricardo B. Quintana, "Dublin's foremost citizen and Ireland's great patriotic dean." In our own thin-skinned and solemn society, it would be impossible for such a ferocious satirist to become the head of a cathedral and a treasured public man.

He began to write *Gulliver's Travels* when he was about my age, which is fifty-four. He finished it when he was sixty. He was already recognized as one of the most bitterly funny writers of his or any time. His motives were invariably serious, however, and I now suggest that *Gulliver's Travels* can be read as a series of highly responsible sermons, delivered during a crisis in Christian attitudes, one that is far from over yet. The crisis is this, in my opinion: It simply will not do for adult Christians to think of themselves as God's little lambs anymore.

Swift died before the invention of the steam engine or the iron plow—or of the Constitution of the United States, for that matter. But he was aware of microscopes and telescopes and the calculus, and Harvey's theories about the circulation of human blood, and Newton's laws of motion, and all that. There were certainly strong hints around that the natural orders of things, so long so stubborn and mysterious, might in fact be wonderful clocks which could be tinkered with, which might even be taken apart and reassembled. Human reason was in the process of assuming powers to change life such as only armies and disasters had possessed before. So Dublin's first citizen found it urgent that we take an unsentimental look, for the good of the universe, at the great apes that were suddenly doing such puissant thinking. Lambs, indeed!

In *Gulliver's Travels,* Swift sets such high standards for unsentimentality about human beings that most of us can meet those standards only in wartime, and only briefly even then. He shrinks us, urinates on us, expands us and peers into all our nauseating apertures, encourages us to demonstrate our stupidity and mendaciousness, makes us hideously old. On paper he subjects us to every humiliating test that imaginative fiction can invent. And what is learned about us in the course of these Auschwitzian experiments? Only this, according to Swift's hero, Captain Gulliver: that we are disgusting in the extreme. We can be sure that this is not Swift's own opinion of us, thank God—for, before he allows Gulliver to declare us no better than vomit, he makes Gulliver insane. That *has* to be the deepest meaning of Gulliver's adoration of horses, since Swift himself had no more than average respect for those dazed and skittish animals. Gulliver is no longer the reliable witness he was in Chapter I.

I had a teacher in high school who assured me that a person has to be at least a little insane to harp on human disgustingness as much as Swift does. And Swift harps on it long before Gulliver has gone insane. I would tell that teacher now, if she were still alive, that his harping is so relentless that it becomes ridiculous, and is meant to be ridiculous, and that Swift is teaching us a lesson almost as important as the one about our not being lambs: that our readiness to feel disgust for ourselves and others is not, perhaps, the guardian of civilization so many of us imagine it to be. Disgust, in fact, may be the chief damager of our reason, of our common sense—may make us act against our own best interests, may make us insane.

Swift does not develop this theme, but the history of the past hundred years or so has surely done it for him. What is it that has allowed civilized human beings to build and operate death camps? Disgust. What has encouraged them to bomb undefended cities, to torture prisoners, to beat up their own spouses and children, to blow out their own brains? Disgust. Yes. In my opinion, *Gulliver's Travels* is a remarkable effort to inject us with an overdose of disgustedness, and thus to immunize us from that most dangerous disease.

This Book-of-the-Month Club edition of *Gulliver's Travels* is based on the Oxford University Press edition of 1971, which was edited by Paul Turner, Lecturer in English Literature at Oxford. That edition has what this one lacks: an introduction and hundreds of fascinating notes by him. I recommend that edition to all who want the pleasure of relating the tale to Swift's own adventures and times, and who would like help in speculating as to the plausibleness of Captain Gulliver's endless lies. Mr. Turner tells us, for example: "The scale of Lilliput is one inch to a foot of the ordinary world. Mogg mentions [F. Mogg, *Scientific American,* Vol. CLXXIX, 1948] some biological difficulties: a Lilliputian would have room for far fewer cortical cells (so far less intelligence) than a chimpanzee; his head would be too small to carry useful eyes; and he would need eight times as many calories per ounce of body-weight as a full-scale man needs —twenty-four meals a day instead of three." As for the giants of Brobdingnag, he refers to Mogg again, who "calls a sixty-foot man 'an engineering impossibility.' The skeleton would need considerable modification to support the weight (about ninety tons): shorter legs, smaller head, thicker neck, and larger trunk (to accommodate adequate internal organs to power such a huge machine)." And so on.

The justification for publishing an edition as naked of notes as this one is, of course, is that the author, like all authors, wished his book to be loved for itself alone. If the ghost of Jonathan Swift is among us, it must resent terrifically my own Yahoolike intrusion here. I apologize. Next to my being in this volume at all, my most serious offense is failing to convey how much rage and joy and irrationality must have gone into the creation of this masterpiece. In praising the sanity of *Gulliver's Travels,* I have made it sound altogether *too* sane.

XV

JEKYLL AND HYDE
UPDATED

L EE Guber, the Broadway producer, became a friend
of mine when we served on the New York State
Council for the Arts. During the summer of 1978 he asked
me to write a modern version of Robert Louis Stevenson's
Dr. Jekyll and Mr. Hyde for the musical stage. The original,
by the way, is a tiny thing, no more than sixty pages. There
is very little characterization in the original, which is surprisingly sketchy and sparsely populated. It was the first piece
of writing for which Stevenson was paid.

I never got paid for my version. I consider it excellent, if
a little slapdash and short. It is called *The Chemistry Professor,* and it goes like this:

THE TIME: THE PRESENT, SPRINGTIME. THE PLACE:
SWEETBREAD COLLEGE, A SMALL, LIBERAL-ARTS
INSTITUTION OUTSIDE PHILADELPHIA.

SCENE 1: THE COLLEGE GATE, NOON.

> [*At the rise: A chorus of male and female students is
> discovered, desperately unhappy, making extravagant
> demonstrations of grief. A particularly pretty and
> scatterbrained coed is named KIMBERLY. Her
> studious boyfriend is named SAM. Each person has a
> fresh copy of the student newspaper, which has told
> them that the college is bankrupt, and will probably
> close forever.*]

KIMBERLY: I can't stand it!
SAM: What kind of a world is this, where a thing like this can
   happen?
STUDENT 1: What a rotten, stinking society this is!

> [*And so on. The cries become more musical and the
> milling more formal, so that a song and dance about
> outrageous fortune materializes. No mention has yet
> been made, however, as to what the misery is all
> about. The number ends with the students strewn
> about in poses of dejection.*]

STUDENT 1: I feel like getting drunk.
SAM: What good would that do?
STUDENT 1: At least I could throw up.
KIMBERLY: You always do.

[*SALLY CATHCART, a Judy Garland look-alike,
enters boisterously in cheerleading garb, carrying
pom-poms high. She has not heard the news.*]

SALLY: Hey, gang—what's there to be so blue about? It's
springtime!

KIMBERLY: Where have you been, Sally?

SALLY: Cheerleading practice. [*A sample cheer*] With an S,
with a W, with an E, E, T! With a B, with an R, with an
E, A, D! Sweetbread! Sweetbread! Sweetbread!

SAM: The college is bankrupt, Sally.

SALLY: Oh, no!

SAM: [*Handing her a paper*] It's in the *Daily Pancreas.*

KIMBERLY: They wouldn't dare print it, if it weren't true.

SALLY: [*Reading*] "Bankrupt! Closing its doors forever in
two weeks' time." The most innocent college in the world.

SAM: Drop your pom-poms, Sally. Nothing to cheer for here
anymore.

SALLY: I won't drop them yet, Sam—but I'll carry them low.

CHORUS: [*Singing   as   one,   a   rich   chord*]
Lowwwwwwwwwwwwwwwwww.

[*JERRY RIVERS, a Mickey Rooney look-alike and
president of the student body, enters with his
stepfather, FRED LEGHORN, shrewd hayseed king
of the mechanized chicken industry.*]

SAM: Hey—it's Jerry Rivers, the president of the student
body.

JERRY: Gang—this is my mother's fifth and possibly final
husband, Fred Leghorn, the largest producer of chickens
in the world.

SALLY: Do you ever get tired of chickens, Mr. Leghorn?

LEGHORN: Anybody who is tired of chickens is tired of life.

SAM: You hear about the bankruptcy, Jerry?

JERRY: Yeah. I keep wondering what an ordinary bunch of kids like us can do.

> [*JERRY puts his hands behind his back, does a tap dance as he ponders the problem. He stops, speaks to the chorus.*]

JERRY: You kids got any ideas?

> [*Members of the chorus put their hands behind their backs and duplicate his steps in unison. They stop and sing the next line with a gorgeous choral effect.*]

CHORUS: [*Singing*]   What can ordinary kids like us do about anything?

LEGHORN: Maybe you could have a cake sale.

SALLY: Mr. Leghorn—couldn't you give us a few million buckaroonies or so?

LEGHORN: I came down here to see what this stepson of mine was getting for ten thousand dollars a year, and I must say I'm not overwhelmed with respect. It looks like Disneyland without the rides to me.

KIMBERLY: But we're your nation's future!

LEGHORN: That's what I mean.

JERRY: Wait a minute! I've got it! We'll put together a Broadway musical with all the talent we've got right here!

CHORUS: [*Thunderstruck, as one*]   Wow! Do you think we really could?

JERRY: Why not? We could take a piece of meretricious kid

crap up there and make enough in a season to keep this academic bucket shop running for years!

CHORUS: [*As one*]   Holy smokes!

SALLY: Jerry—just one question: Are we still in love?

JERRY: You mean in spite of the bankruptcy? It's too early to tell.

SALLY: I'll wait.

> [*ELBERT WHITEFEET, the beloved old college president and philosopher, enters wild with grief over the bankruptcy. He is comforted by DR. HENRY JEKYLL, the venerable head of the chemistry department, and by POPS, the doddering campus cop. WHITEFEET and JEKYLL wear academic caps and gowns. POPS is uniformed like a Keystone Cop. It is a wild scene. Students look on in horror and pity as WHITEFEET tears out handfuls of his own hair, rends his garments, dumps a trash container over himself, and so on.*]

WHITEFEET: I don't want to live anymore!

POPS: Please, sir—the student body is watching.

WHITEFEET: I don't care!

POPS: They shouldn't see the president of their college in this condition. They might write home.

WHITEFEET: They should hang me from the Senior Elm for what I've done.

JEKYLL: Elbert—you haven't done anything a million other nincompoops might not have done.

WHITEFEET: [*Embracing Jekyll*]   Ah—Dr. Henry Jekyll— the head of the chemistry department and my closest friend. Faithful old Henry, the only faculty member with a statewide reputation.

JERRY: President Whitefeet—Dr. Jekyll—what happened to the endowment, which was supposed to be so big and well invested—the Xerox, the Polaroid, the IBM.

WHITEFEET: [*Echoing tragically*]   The Xerox, the Polaroid, the IBM.

CHORUS: The Xerox, the Polaroid, the IBM.

[*This sets off a terrific rhythm number that builds and builds, and consists of the chanting of the names of common stocks. Everybody is caught up in a mad, slobbering war dance about wealth. It ends in panting exhaustion.*]

LEGHORN: What did happen to all those stocks?

KIMBERLY: [*Sexually aroused by wealth*]   All those woo-zum, coozum, squoozum blue chip stocks. Yum, yum! Yum, yum!

WHITEFEET: A clean-cut young investment counselor with a silver tongue came into my office two months ago. I was reading Plato at the time.

SAM: What part of Plato, sir?

WHITEFEET: [*Indignantly*]   I don't have to answer pip-squeak questions like that anymore. I was reading Plato. Period.

SAM: Yes, sir.

WHITEFEET: It's all kind of one big mixed up thing anyway. Can't tell where one thing stops and the next thing begins. This investment counselor said to me, "Lift your blood-shot eyes from the yellowed page, old philosopher. Look at the world as it has come to be! There's money to be made! In two months' time, Sweetbread College could be twice as rich as Harvard!"

SALLY: But Harvard's too big!

KIMBERLY: Harvard's too hard!

SAM: They're really serious up there.

WHITEFEET: "Put everything you've got into cocoa futures," he said.

LEGHORN: Oh Lord.

WHITEFEET: Please, for the love of God, don't anybody ever mention cocoa in my presence again.

SALLY: What are cocoa futures?

WHITEFEET: I still don't know.

KIMBERLY: I'll go to the library and look it up.

WHITEFEET: That's what you're here for—to learn how to look things up.

LEGHORN: [*To Kimberly*]   Look under "C."

KIMBERLY: [*Sincerely*]   Thanks for the tip.

   [*KIMBERLY exits.*]

WHITEFEET: If my doctor's thesis had not been about philosophical arguments against suicide, I would be a dead man now.

JERRY: Dr. Whitefeet—?

WHITEFEET: [*Indicating that he is non compos mentis with self-loathing*]   Bluh, bluh, bluh.

JERRY: Sir—I've been talking to the rest of the kids, and we thought maybe we could put on a Broadway musical.

WHITEFEET: Uck.

LEGHORN: The smartest thing you ever said.

JERRY: I haven't figured out what it should be about.

SALLY: You're a show business genius, Jerry. You can do anything.

SAM: We could do the story of Jesus Christ.

JERRY: Maybe.

SALLY: [*Singing to tune of "Ach Du Lieber Augustine"*]

> Oh, I am Mary Magdalene,
> Magdalene, Magdalene—
> I am Mary Magdalene.
> How do you do?

POPS: [*To same tune*] I have got the leprosy,

> Leprosy, leprosy.
> I have got the leprosy.
> Who will cure me?

JERRY: No, no. Kids have done Jesus Christ to death onstage. (A double take) Say, Pops, I didn't know you could sing.

POPS: I was on my way to being a star of stage, screen, and radio. But then my dog was run over, and I entered a period of deep depression from which I never recovered. Nobody starts out to be a campus cop.

JEKYLL: Cripes—you know, I ought to be able to do something to help. Come up with a chemical discovery of some kind.

WHITEFEET: You've already given the world the recipe for Betty Crocker banana cake.

JEKYLL: I'm thinking of something really dangerous, Nobel prize stuff. You can't scare the pants off people with a banana cake.

JERRY: Come on, kids! Let's get cracking! Let's go over to the Mildred Peasely Bangtree Memorial Theater, and see what we can put together. We'll stay up all night!

JEKYLL: I'll stay up all night, too! This is exciting! This is just the kind of a kick in the butt I've needed for years.

[*All students exit.*]

LEGHORN: Who was Mildred Peasely Bangtree?
WHITEFEET: Beats me.

[*KIMBERLY enters.*]

KIMBERLY: Excuse me—

[*LEGHORN, JEKYLL, WHITEFEET, and POPS
gather together as a barbershop quartet, and sing a
heart-rending ballad, "How Can We Help You, Little
Girl?"*]

KIMBERLY: You all through?
LEGHORN, JEKYLL, WHITEFEET, POPS: [*Still singing in har-
mony*] All through.
KIMBERLY: Which building is the library?

CURTAIN

❧

SCENE 2: DR. JEKYLL'S LABORATORY. TEN O'CLOCK AT
NIGHT. A PAINTED BACKDROP WITH AN OPERATING
WINDOW AND DOOR IN IT.

[*At the rise: Library clock strikes ten. Dog howls. DR.
JEKYLL is alone and going through hell, trying to
think of something really good to discover. The theater
is within hailing distance.*]

JEKYLL: Gosh darn it to heck. Let's put on the old thinking
cap, and cogitate. Jesus, this is really a doozy, trying to

think up something nobody ever thought up before. Everything I think of has been thought of.

[*JERRY appears in the window. He is dejected.*]

JERRY: Dr. Jekyll—looks like you're going to have to save the college singlehanded. We can't think up a story.

JEKYLL: Things are none too brisk in the lab, my boy. Why is it that every time you need a Nobel prize-type idea, you never can think of one?

JERRY: I'm sending over some inspiration for you. Hope it helps.

JEKYLL: Inspiration?

JERRY: You'll see.

[*JERRY exits. LEGHORN knocks on the door.*]

JEKYLL: *Entrez.*

[*LEGHORN enters with a bottle containing a green chemical.*]

LEGHORN: I wonder if you'd run an analysis on this for me. It's some kind of dope one of my competitors is feeding his chickens. I'd like to know what's in it. I'll pay you well.

JEKYLL: That's like asking Albert Einstein to balance your checkbook.

LEGHORN: He couldn't tie his own shoelaces. Everybody knows that. [*Spotting a row of bottles*] A half gallon of LSD! Amphetamines! Barbiturates! Quaaludes! Vitamin E! What are you doing with this stuff?

JEKYLL: Taken from students at different times.

LEGHORN: No wonder they think they're so talented. I'll give you five hundred bucks if you can give me an analysis of this stuff before I get out of here—tomorrow at noon. That's only in the event, of course, that your Nobel prize project falls through. Good night.

[*LEGHORN exits. JEKYLL sniffs the sample.*]

JEKYLL: Whoooeee! That'll put hair on your chest! Smells like a mixture of crème de menthe and athlete's foot to me.

[*SALLY knocks on the door, calls through it seductively.*]

SALLY: Dr. Jekyll, Dr. Jekyll.
JEKYLL: *Entrez.*

[*SALLY enters at the head of a line of coeds in diaphanous nightgowns. They have come to inspire him. KIMBERLY is among them.*]

JEKYLL: [*Petrified, retreating*]   What kind of a frame-up is this? I've never had anything to do with sex in my life!
SALLY: This isn't sex.
JEKYLL: It isn't?
SALLY: We're Muses. Jerry had us dress up like Muses, and told us to come over and inspire you.
JEKYLL: I'd hate to have to explain that to the state police.
SALLY: You just relax and enjoy it.

[*The music starts up, and the girls do a sort of here-we-go-gathering-nuts-in-May dance with and around JEKYLL, tickling him, blowing in his ears, decking him with flowers, and so on. The dance ends*]

*with JEKYLL in a sensationally compromising
position.*

*WHITEFEET enters without knocking, and is
scandalized.*]

WHITEFEET: I am revolted! I am disillusioned! I am scandalized!

JEKYLL: It isn't what it looked like.

WHITEFEET: It looked like a full professor playing here-we-go-gathering-nuts-in-May.

SALLY: It was our fault, Dr. Whitefeet.

WHITEFEET: What do you foolish virgins know? You couldn't find your own behinds with both hands.

KIMBERLY: [*Proudly, innocently*]   I just found mine.

WHITEFEET: [*Pointing to JEKYLL*]   There is the man I hold responsible. He is not only a Dr. Jekyll—he is a Dr. Jekyll and Mr. Hyde.

SALLY: [*Echoing wonderingly*]   Dr. Jekyll and Mr. Hyde. [*More firmly*] Dr. Jekyll and Mr. Hyde! That's it!

JEKYLL: Who's Mr. Hyde?

SALLY: That's the story for our musical! Dr. Jekyll and Mr. Hyde—it's never been done. Wait till I tell Jerry!

WHITEFEET: Just a minute! What about this moral outrage I saw here?

SALLY: [*On her way out, leading the other coeds*]   Buster—when you peed away the endowment on cocoa futures, you ceased to exist as a moral leader for me. You don't have the brains God gave a clay pigeon.

[*SALLY and the coeds exit.*]

WHITEFEET: I suppose I had that coming. It's probably good for me that people speak to me like that from time to time.

JEKYLL: Who's Mr. Hyde?

WHITEFEET: From the famous story, "Dr. Jekyll and Mr. Hyde," by Clare Boothe Luce.

JEKYLL: I never heard of it.

WHITEFEET: Your name is Jekyll, and you never heard of one of the most famous stories in all of our literature—a story with your own name in it?

JEKYLL: I don't make you feel like something the cat drug in because you don't know any chemistry. Don't you make me feel like something the cat drug in because I don't know any literature.

WHITEFEET: It's about a man who discovers a substance that changes his whole personality and appearance when he drinks it. He changes from nice Dr. Jekyll to terrible Mr. Hyde.

JEKYLL: He drinks it himself?

WHITEFEET: And becomes a monster.

JEKYLL: Doesn't give it to somebody else. He drinks it himself.

WHITEFEET: That's right.

JEKYLL: [*Inspired*]   Boy—that's what I call balls.

[*Cheers come from the theater as SALLY delivers the good news.*]

JERRY: [*Off, far away*]   That's it, kids! Jekyll and Hyde!

CURTAIN

❦

SCENE 3: THE BARE STAGE OF THE MILDRED PEASELY
BANGTREE MEMORIAL THEATER—A FEW MINUTES
LATER.

[*At the rise: All the students, except for JERRY,
SALLY, KIMBERLY, and SAM, are onstage. They
are excited about doing* Dr. Jekyll and Mr. Hyde.
POPS is looking on. The girls are still in nightgowns.

*Accompanied by scary music, they experiment with
turning into monsters, uttering maniacal laughs, and
generally trying to scare the hell out of each other.*

*JERRY, SALLY, KIMBERLY, and SAM enter,
loaded down with Victorian costumes and props.*]

JERRY: Okay, kids—we found all this stuff in the costume
loft. Come and get it.

[*They throw down the costumes, and people set about
clothing themselves, including SALLY, KIMBERLY,
and SAM.*]

POPS: Can I pick a costume, too?

JERRY: No. You're perfect as you are. We need a comedy cop.

POPS: [*Offended*]   There's real bullets in my gun.

JERRY: You're kidding! They shouldn't trust you with a
squirt gun loaded with lemonade!

POPS: Thanks a lot.

JERRY: Any time.

[*LEGHORN enters from the wings, impressed by a
machine he has seen back there.*]

LEGHORN: Mind if I watch you geniuses work?

JERRY: Glad to have you, Dad.

[*Everybody but JERRY and LEGHORN and POPS turns his or her back to the audience, and applies monster makeup, becoming Dracula or Frankenstein or Wolfman or whatever.*]

LEGHORN: You can stop calling me that. Your mother and I have filed for divorce.

JERRY: Well, whoever you are, take a seat somewhere.

LEGHORN: There's a hell of a machine back here. Looks like one of my old industrial chicken roasters—from the early days.

[*JERRY has a look, is thrilled.*]

JERRY: Oh, boy! A fog machine—left over from our rock and roll version of *Macbeth*.

LEGHORN: Some boat whistles, too.

JERRY: Left over from our rock and roll version of *The Old Man and the Sea*. [*He takes his place stage center.*] Okay, gang—face this way, please.

[*Everybody faces him—with horrifying effect.*]

JERRY: Oh, no—everybody can't be the monster!

SALLY: But everybody loves monsters so.

[*This starts off a production number about how everybody loves monsters, but that not everybody is lucky enough to be a monster, that some people have to be good-looking and therefore hated by everyone, and so on.*]

JERRY: Gee—I wonder how the real-life Jekyll is doing over in the lab?

LEGHORN: He can't even light a Bunsen burner, if you ask me.

CURTAIN

❦

SCENE 4: DR. JEKYLL'S LABORATORY—A FEW MINUTES
LATER.

[*At the rise: Idiotic rock music can be heard coming
from the theater through the open window. It consists
of a repetition of "Jekyll and Hyde! whoe whoe, baby,
good old Jekyll and Hyde!" JEKYLL is alone,
happily adding LSD and the unknown diet
supplement for chickens and so forth to a large
beaker, which is giving off unwholesome fumes.*

*JEKYLL closes the window, shutting out the music.
He continues about his business, singing to himself, to
the tune of "Humoresque."*]

JEKYLL: [*Singing*] We were walking through the park,
A-goosing statues in the dark.
If Sherman's horse can take it,
So can you—oo!

[*There is a knock on the door.*]

JEKYLL: [*Aside*] Hmmmm. A possible guinea pig. [*To
knocker*] Entrez, s'il vous plait.

[*Jekyll's wife, a gorgeous, tragically neglected older
woman, enters. He does not recognize her. She
immediately sings to him in a rich contralto a
show-stopping song about her total devotion to him.*]

JEKYLL: May I ask who you are?

MRS. JEKYLL: I'm your wife, Henry.

JEKYLL: Right, right, right. Got it now.

MRS. JEKYLL: When you failed to come home for supper, I called around to find out what had become of you.

JEKYLL: [*Genuinely concerned*]   Am I all right?

MRS. JEKYLL: Here you are.

JEKYLL: Thank God. I could be lying in a ditch somewhere.

MRS. JEKYLL: They said you were going all out for the Nobel prize.

JEKYLL: [*Intensely*]   It's the new me, Mildred.

MRS. JEKYLL: [*Correcting him*]   Hortense.

JEKYLL: It's the new me, Hortense. Say—you look thirsty to me.

MRS. JEKYLL: Thirsty?

JEKYLL: [*Offering the beaker*]   This'll put hair on your chest.

MRS. JEKYLL: Why would I want hair on my chest?

JEKYLL: Just a friendly expression. You have to pick me up on every last little thing? I don't know how our marriage has lasted as long as it has.

MRS. JEKYLL: That stuff smells vile!

JEKYLL: But you love me so much. That was you, wasn't it?

MRS. JEKYLL: Yes—it was I.

JEKYLL: Okay—so drink, chug-a-lug, chug-a-lug; so drink, chug-a-lug, chug-a-lug!

MRS. JEKYLL: This is the first thing I have ever refused you.

[*MRS. JEKYLL exits with dignity.*]

JEKYLL: [*Aside*]   If it's anything that burns me up, it's women's lib. [*To himself*] Okay, big boy—if you're ever going to get to Stockholm, you'd better drink this stuff yourself. Here goes nothing.

[*He holds his nose and drinks. Nothing happens for a moment, then a horrible transformation starts to take place. He claws at his throat, makes subhuman sounds, drops to the floor, rolls out of sight under a desk. When he emerges, he has become an enormous, homicidal chicken. He flings open the window, and, flapping his wings, jumps out into the night.*]

CURTAIN

❦

INTERMISSION

❦

SCENE 5: THE STAGE AT MIDNIGHT THE SAME NIGHT. THE STUDENTS HAVE BUILT A SET TO REPRESENT A NINETEENTH-CENTURY LONDON STREET. THERE ARE THREE FACADES FROM LEFT TO RIGHT: A LOW-LIFE PUB, A SINISTER STOREHOUSE WHERE JEKYLL DOES HIS EXPERIMENTS, AND JEKYLL'S RESPECTABLE HOME. ALL HAVE OPERATING DOORS. THERE ARE STREETLAMPS. THERE IS A PROMINENT SIGN ON THE SECRET LAB SAYING, "SECRET LAB."

[*Before the rise: College library clock strikes twelve.*

At the rise: Full cast, except for WHITEFEET, DR. JEKYLL, and MRS. JEKYLL, is onstage. All except LEGHORN, who is a mere observer in his regular business suit, are dressed in Victorian costumes from every level of society. POPS is a bobby, already on duty. SALLY is a whore with a heart of gold, already waiting for customers under a lamppost. JERRY, who is going to be Dr. Jekyll, wears a top hat and evening cape, and directs many students who are still working on the set, painting, driving nails. Among them is SAM, wearing a tweed suit and derby, who is to be Utterson, Jekyll's best friend, and KIMBERLY, who is dressed as a nursery maid. Her elaborate perambulator is parked on the street. LEGHORN has been interesting himself in the fog machine, which is now putting out wisps of fog.]

JERRY: Okay, kids—that's close enough. We just want to give the general idea. No point in getting it absolutely perfect tonight.

[*Students put down their tools, assemble on the street, awaiting instructions. LEGHORN goes to JERRY.*]

LEGHORN: I got your fog machine going.
JERRY: I see.
LEGHORN: It really is one of my old industrial chicken roasters. Didn't realize they were being sold now as fog machines.
JERRY: It wasn't cheap.
LEGHORN: Nothing ever is. If you ever wanted to roast a half

JEKYLL AND HYDE UPDATE ■ 591

a ton of chicken in five minutes, you still could—feathers
and all.

JERRY: That's nice to know.

SALLY: I love you, Jerry. I'd die for you, if you wanted me
to.

JERRY: That's nice to know. Places, everybody!

> [*JERRY goes into Jekyll's house. LEGHORN
> withdraws to one side of apron. SALLY stays under
> lamppost. POPS continues to patrol. Lower-class types
> go into pub. KIMBERLY, with her pram, and SAM
> exit into wings. The rest compose a London street
> scene in the late afternoon.*
>
> *A rock band in the pit strikes up appropriate music to
> be written by somebody else, and a nonstop rock ballet
> about Jekyll and Hyde begins.*
>
> *The story, to be choreographed by somebody else, goes
> roughly like this, with some information being sung:*
>
> *Everybody on the street is happy, but worried about
> nightfall and fog. There has been, only a few days
> before, the murder of a whore under the lamppost
> where SALLY stands.*
>
> *Dr. Jekyll, played by JERRY, comes out of his house,
> the image of civic decency, and is recognized and
> adored by all. He is trying to get into his secret lab
> without being observed. While biding his time, he
> performs acts of civic virtue which are noted and
> admired by one and all. He picks up a piece of trash
> dropped by somebody else, puts it in a waste barrel,
> gives money to a beggar, politely declines an invitation*

from SALLY the whore, giving her a gentle lecture, and so on. KIMBERLY enters with her perambulator, and he admires the baby, chucks it under its chin. KIMBERLY exits into wings, to return, going in the opposite direction, a few minutes later.

A fight breaks out in the pub, spills into the street. POPS rushes in to break it up. Everybody but Jekyll goes to watch. Jekyll takes the opportunity to duck into his lab. Lights go on in there.

The fight is broken up, and one of the fighters invites everyone into the pub for a drink on him.

Many accept, go into pub. Some refuse, exit into the wings instead. SALLY resumes her post by the lamppost. The street is otherwise deserted.

Utterson, the lawyer, played by SAM, enters in a state of agitation. He carries a huge briefcase on which is written, "Lawyer." He is on his way to Jekyll's house, is propositioned by SALLY. They dicker. Her price is too high and her services too limited, and he is too busy anyway. He goes and bangs on Jekyll's door. Nobody is home. He sings to the audience that his client and closest friend, Dr. Jekyll, has just written a will leaving everything to a man named Hyde, about whom Utterson has never heard before. He fears that Jekyll has gone insane or is being blackmailed. He gives up, dickers briefly with the whore again, goes into pub for a needed drink.

*JERRY, now as the monstrous Mr. Hyde, peers
furtively out the secret lab door, sees nobody around
but the whore. He whistles to her, crooks his finger at
her. She is appalled, but needs the work. She goes into
the lab with him, and the door is closed.*

*A drunk comes out of the pub, sings a song about the
beauty of love, staggers off into the wings.*

*The lab door opens. The whore reels out, her clothes
in frightful disarray. Hyde throws money after her,
heaps scorn on her as she picks it up. She exits in
disorder and shame. Hyde remains in the doorway,
looking up and down the street for other opportunities
to do evil.*

*KIMBERLY enters with her perambulator, on her
way home from the park. She seems an ideal target of
opportunity. She pauses, giving him a chance to duck
into the lab to get a black spherical bomb with a fuse
sticking out of it, which he shows to the audience. She
starts coming again, and he stops her, pretending to
be solicitous, hiding the bomb behind his back. He
tells her that she should be careful, that he thinks
someone may be following her. She looks back, and
he tucks the bomb in with the baby and lights the
fuse. She moves on, looking back over her shoulder,
exits. Hyde ducks into lab, closes door.*

*There is a terrific explosion offstage, people come
pouring out of the pub, exit in direction of explosion.*

*They return, filled with horror. Some carry pieces of
the perambulator. Utterson carries a wheel. Last of all*

*come POPS and KIMBERLY. Pops has his pad and
pencil out, trying to get Kimberly's story. Most of
Kimberly's clothing has been blown away. Her face is
black. She still holds the handle of the perambulator.*

*Utterson draws aside, muses over the clue of the
wheel. He sings that he knows his friend Jekyll has
been performing secret experiments of great
importance and behaving queerly. He wonders if he
could be making bombs.*

*Somebody suggests that everybody go into the pub to
have a drink. KIMBERLY says that she certainly
needs one. All exit into the pub, except for Utterson,
who goes to Jekyll's house and knocks again. JERRY,
now a respectable Jekyll again, comes out of the lab
unobserved, again picks up a piece of trash, puts it
into a barrel.*

*Jekyll comes up behind Utterson, scares the daylights
out of him. Utterson asks him if his research involves
bombs. Jekyll says he has discovered a means of
controlling human character with chemicals. Utterson
says this is more dangerous than bombs. Jekyll says it
is perfectly safe, with no harmful side effects. He
confesses that he turned himself into Hyde many
times, and that he isn't going to do it anymore, that
Hyde is dead. "No harmful side effects?" says
Utterson. Jekyll echoes this, but with qualifications—
blurred vision sometimes, constipation, swollen ankles,
nothing serious. Utterson asks how he feels now. Jekyll
says he never felt better, but then has an attack. He
turns into Hyde.*

He chokes Utterson to death. There are Grand Guignol effects, with Utterson spitting out catsup, sticking out an impossibly long tongue, and so on.

Still clinging to Utterson's throat, Hyde, played by JERRY, sings a tragic song about how the most idealistic experiments can sometimes go wrong.

KIMBERLY, POPS, and a few others come out of the pub, all half in the bag. KIMBERLY is still holding the handle of the perambulator. They see Hyde choking the dead Utterson. KIMBERLY identifies him as the man who probably blew up the baby, tells POPS to shoot him like a mad dog.

POPS draws his real pistol, which is loaded, and is so carried away by the drama that he actually takes a shot at JERRY, shattering a streetlamp.

Everything stops.]

JERRY: [*As JERRY, dropping Utterson*] That was a real bullet.
POPS: I told you I had real bullets in my gun. Nobody kills babies while I'm around.
JERRY: Imbecile!
LEGHORN: [*Striding onstage to disarm Pops*] I'll take that thing. [*He sticks the pistol under his belt.*]
POPS: I lost my head.
JERRY: I almost lost my life. Get out of here!
POPS: What can I say after I've said I'm sorry?
JERRY: Try "Good-bye."
POPS: This thing is never going to make it to Broadway anyway. [*He exits.*]

LEGHORN: Well—if this show has accomplished nothing else, at least it's disarmed a campus cop.

JERRY: The whole thing stunk. I really let you down this time, gang. I resign as head of the student body.

[*SALLY enters, still a mess, deeply concerned about Jerry.*]

SALLY: Jerry—

JERRY: You don't have to tell me: You don't love me anymore. I don't even love myself anymore.

SALLY: It wasn't your fault, Jerry. I mean—it was a story we found in the public domain. Everybody knows there's nothing but picked-over garbage in the public domain.

LEGHORN: A little chicken would cheer us all up about now —but I don't know where we could find a chicken this time of night.

[*POPS screams in terror outside the theater. The screams go on and on. Nobody is much concerned.*]

SALLY: What's that?

JERRY: It sounds like Pops got himself caught in his zipper again.

SAM: Happens all the time.

KIMBERLY: I don't know—that doesn't quite sound like his zipper scream.

[*POPS enters, mad with terror, breathless.*]

POPS: [*Pointing, gasping*] I just saw—I just saw—I just saw—

LEGHORN: You're not making any sense.

POPS: I just saw the biggest chicken in history.

LEGHORN: Uh huh. The biggest chicken in history weighed fifty-six pounds and four ounces, and was found on Bikini Atoll after a hydrogen bomb test there.

POPS: Bigger than that.

LEGHORN: And what was this chicken doing?

POPS: As God is my witness—it was eating a Doberman pinscher alive.

JERRY: He just wants his gun back.

LEGHORN: I don't know. Strange things happen in the chicken world. [*Aside*] Often profitable. [*To Pops*] How much would you say this chicken weighed?

POPS: With or without the Doberman inside?

LEGHORN: Without the dog.

POPS: A hundred and eighty pounds, medium build, white— yellow feet, yellow beak—believed to be dangerous. Somebody better get out an APB.

LEGHORN: A hundred-and-eighty-pound chicken would feed about two hundred people. A few birds like that would go a long way toward ending the protein shortages in India, in Africa, in Moscow—in Bangladesh. [*He considers going out to have a look.*]

POPS: Oh, sir—I hate your guts, but I beg of you, please don't go out there alone.

LEGHORN: I never met the chicken I could not dominate. Besides, gumshoe, I have a gun with five shots left in it. Remember?

[*LEGHORN draws the pistol, blows down the barrel, and exits.*]

JERRY: Well—that's all very interesting, but it doesn't have a heck of a lot to do with saving the college, does it?

POPS: You'd think it had to do with everything there ever was, if you saw a chicken that size.

SALLY: Maybe somebody should call the Humane Society.

POPS: The National Guard!

JERRY: Maybe we *should* put on a cake sale.

[*A pistol is fired outside.*]

POPS: Four shots left.

SALLY: Is it legal to shoot a chicken that size?

POPS: A chicken, no matter how big, has no rights in the state of Pennsylvania.

[*Two more pistol shots*]

POPS: Two shots left.

[*LEGHORN rushes back in, holding the smoking gun.*]

LEGHORN: Everybody out! Grab a hammer, a broom—anything! I'm gonna need help with this one. This one must have been fed pure plutonium on Mars. I think I winged it, but I can't be sure.

[*All but KIMBERLY grab makeshift weapons and rush out. SAM is the last one out.*]

SAM: You coming, Kimberly?

KIMBERLY: No. I am a follower of Albert Schweitzer. I have reverence for life. Besides, I'm very sleepy.

SAM: Okay, you take a nap.

[*SAM exits. Sounds of a chase come from outside, fading off into the distance, as KIMBERLY makes a pillow of a discarded garment and goes to sleep on Dr. Jekyll's doorstep. She snores softly, sweetly.*

There are clumsy, subhuman sounds in the wings. The great chicken which the head of the chemistry department has turned himself into enters, desperately hoping to elude its hunters. It is wounded and enraged. It does not see Kimberly at first, and KIMBERLY goes on sleeping. It tears off the door of the pub, uproots a lamppost and bends it double, and so on.

It sees Kimberly at last, approaches her sleeping form with a mixture of dim-witted awe and lust, after the fashion of King Kong. It decides to do something with her—whether to rape her or abduct her or consume her, it is not clear.

We never find out, for just in the nick of time, LEGHORN enters with his pistol cocked and aimed. He is followed by SAM, SALLY, and JERRY.]

LEGHORN: Reach for the sky.

[*The chicken raises its wings, turns around slowly.*]

LEGHORN: Don't try anything fancy. One false move, and you're fricassee.

JERRY: Some bird!

LEGHORN: I had a hunch this one would double back to the Mildred Peasely Bangtree Memorial Theater and try to hide in here. Do I know chickens, or do I know chickens?

SALLY: Who was Mildred Peasely Bangtree?

JERRY: No time to wonder that now.

LEGHORN: Quiet now. I'm going to interrogate this roaster.

SALLY: Rooster?

LEGHORN: Roaster.

> [*LEGHORN now conducts a conversation in chicken language with the chicken. It takes quite a while. It is expressive, with moments of excitement and sadness and so on.*]

JERRY: What did it say?

LEGHORN: I thought I had heard every chicken story possible, but this is a new one on me. This is the head of your chemistry department here. He drank a mixture of LSD and chicken tonic and Drano and God only knows what else, in the hopes of winning a Nobel prize. There's more of the stuff back in his laboratory.

SALLY, JERRY, AND SAM: Dr. Jekyll.

> [*LEGHORN says something rueful in chicken language, and the chicken agrees.*]

SAM: What did you just say to him?

LEGHORN: Said he couldn't go to Stockholm looking like that.

> [*Chicken says more, resignedly.*]

LEGHORN: Says he's got three bullets in him, and is dying anyway.

[*The chicken begins a tragic dying scene, which takes a minute or two.*

WHITEFEET and MRS. JEKYLL enter while it is going on. MRS. JEKYLL is carrying the beaker. Everybody is profoundly moved but WHITEFEET, who is overwhelmed with mirth.]

WHITEFEET: That's the funniest costume I ever saw!

MRS. JEKYLL: Shut up you lightweight—you intolerable sparrowfart! That is my husband there. I watched it all through the laboratory window. I have the fatal mixture here. [*She shows the beaker.*]

[*The chicken struggles upright one last time, and sings a farewell aria in chicken language, with orchestral accompaniment. It dies, its feet straight up in the air.*]

SAM: Kimberly, are you all right?

KIMBERLY: I think so. But I'll never be the same. I don't think I can be a follower of Albert Schweitzer anymore.

[*The remainder of the cast enters quietly to gawk.*]

MRS. JEKYLL: What was its last song about?

LEGHORN: I'm liable to bust out crying when I tell you. I never thought a chicken could get to me like that. There's precious little sentimentality in the modern chicken business, believe you me. It sang about the disposal of its remains. It asked to be roasted and wrapped in Reynolds Wrap and given to an orphanage.

MRS. JEKYLL: The first unselfish act of his life.

LEGHORN: Well, we're all in this together now—and the reputation of the college, not that it ever amounted to a hill of beans, depends on what we decide to do. All in favor of roasting it?

ALL: Aye.

LEGHORN: All in favor of wrapping it in Reynolds Wrap?

ALL: Aye.

LEGHORN: All in favor of giving it to an orphanage?

ALL BUT MRS. JEKYLL: No.

MRS. JEKYLL: Abstain.

LEGHORN: Abstention noted. I think you have voted wisely. Allowing even orphans to eat a chicken produced by this method is morally repugnant in a Christian society at this time. Future generations may feel differently. It is the sense of the meeting, then, that the roasted chicken be buried in an unmarked grave as soon as possible, and that nothing more be said about it, since the story, if it ever got out, would interfere with recruiting and fund raising activities of the college, and only confuse the county prosecutor.

CHORUS: [*Singing, directed by JERRY*] Aaaaaaaaaaaaa-men! Aaaaaaaaaaaa-men! Aaaaaaaaaaaaaaa-men!

[*Sobbing, MRS. JEKYLL throws herself on the remains.*]

CURTAIN

XVI

A NAZI
SYMPATHIZER
DEFENDED AT
SOME COST

I have spoken in another chapter of the thunderstorms in the head of Jack Kerouac when I knew him, or to be more truthful, when he was unknowable—near the end of his life. He was to be pitied and forgiven, of course, for all he said while the thunder and lightning was going on.

We arrive now, though, at the case of a writer who not only thought loathsomely on occasion, but who sometimes acted on those loathsome thoughts, and who, as many people have told me very pointedly, can never be forgiven. It is common for people to find his work impossible to read, not because of what he happens to be saying on a given page but because of unforgivable things he has said or written elsewhere.

He said often enough himself, one way or another and as a universally despised old man and war criminal, that he had nothing to apologize for, and that forgiveness would be yet another insult from nincompoops.

He would not like me. The evidence is that he was not strikingly fond of any human beings. He loved his cat, which he was forever carrying from here to there like a baby.

He considered himself at least the equal of any living writer. I am told that he once said of the Nobel prize: "Every Vaseline-ass in Europe has one. Where's mine?"

And yet, compulsively, with no financial gain in prospect, and understanding that many people will believe that I share many of his authentically vile opinions, I continue to say that there were good things about this man. And my name is most snugly tied to his in the Penguin paperback editions of his last three books, *Castle to Castle, North,* and *Rigadoon.* My name is on each cover: "With a new introduction," it says, "by Kurt Vonnegut, Jr."

That introduction to all three paperbacks goes like this:

He was in the worst possible taste, by which I mean that he had many educational advantages, becoming a physician, and he was widely traveled in Europe and Africa and North America—and yet he wrote not a single phrase that hinted to similarly advantaged persons that he was something of a gentleman.

He did not seem to understand that aristocratic restraints and sensibilities, whether inherited or learned, accounted for much of the splendor of literature. In my opinion, he discovered a higher and more awful order of literary truth by ignoring the crippled vocabularies of ladies and gentlemen and by using, instead, the more comprehensive language of shrewd and tormented guttersnipes.

Every writer is in his debt, and so is anyone else interested in discussing lives in their entirety. By being so impolite, he demonstrated that perhaps half of all experience, the animal half, had been concealed by good manners. No honest writer or speaker will ever want to be polite again.

Céline has been praised as a stylist. He himself mocked the endlessly repeated typographical trick that made every page he wrote easily recognizable as being his: 'Me and my three dots . . . my supposedly original style! . . . all the real writers will tell you what to think of it! . . .'

The only writers who admire that style enough to imitate it, as far as I know, are gossip columnists. They like its looks. They like the sense of urgency it imparts, willy-nilly, to any piece of information at all.

With no especial help from his eccentric typography, in my opinion, Céline gave us in his novels the finest history we have of the total collapse of Western civilization in two world wars, as witnessed by hideously vulnerable common women and men. That history should be read in the order in which it was written, for each volume speaks knowingly to the ones that came before it.

And the resonating chamber for this intricate system of echoes through time is Céline's first novel, *Journey to the End of the Night,* published in 1932, when the author was thirty-eight. It is important that a reader of any Céline book know in his heart what Céline knew so well, that his writing career began with a masterpiece.

Readers may find their experience softened and deepened, too, if they reflect that the author was a physician who chose to serve patients who were mainly poor. It was common for him not to be paid at all. His real name, by the way, was Louis-Ferdinand Auguste Destouches.

His sympathy may not have lain with the poor and power-less, but he surely gave them the bulk of his time and astonishment. And he did not insult them with the idea that death was somehow ennobling to anybody—or killing, either.

He and Ernest Hemingway died on the same day, incidentally, on July 1, 1961. Both were heroes from World War I. Both deserved Nobel prizes—Céline for his first book alone. Céline didn't get one, and Hemingway did. Hemingway killed himself, and Céline died of natural causes.

All that remains is their books.

And Céline's slowly fading infamy.

After years of unselfish and often brilliant service to mankind in literature and medicine, he revealed himself as a fierce anti-Semite and a Nazi sympathizer. This was in the late 1930s. I have heard no explanation for this, other than that he was partly insane. He never claimed to have been insane, and no physician ever declared him so.

He was sane enough, at any rate, to virtually exclude his racism and cracked politics from his novels. The anti-Semitism appears only flickeringly here and there, and usually in a context of his being absolutely gaga about all the varieties of treacherous and foolish human beings.

For what it may be worth, he wrote these words only a few days before he died: "I say that Israel is a real fatherland that welcomes its children home and my country is a shit-house . . ."

His words are contemptible to anyone who has suffered from anti-Semitism. And so, surely, were the amnesty and exoneration he received from the French government in 1951. He was punished with heavy fines and imprisonment and exile before that.

As for the words I quoted: They don't, after all, imply an apology or a wish to be forgiven. They are envious, and little more.

Since he is punished and dead, and since the Nazi nightmare is so long ago now, it may at last be possible to perceive a twisted sort of honor in his declining to speak of remorse or to offer excuses of any kind. Other collaborators with the Nazis, of whom there were tens of thousands in France and millions in all of Europe, had stories to tell of how they were forced to behave as badly as they did, and of daring acts of resistance and sabotage they committed, at the risk of their lives.

Céline found that sort of lying ludicrous in a very ugly way.

I get a splitting headache every time I try to write about Céline. I have one now. I never have headaches at any other time.

As the war was ending, he headed for the center of the holocaust—Berlin.

I know when he began to influence me. I was well into my

forties before I read him. A friend was startled that I didn't know anything about Céline, and he initiated me with *Journey to the End of the Night,* which flabbergasted me. I assigned it for a course in the novel which I was giving at the University of Iowa. When it was time for me to lecture for two hours about it, I found I had nothing to say.

The book penetrated my bones, anyway, if not my mind. And I only now understand what I took from Céline and put into the novel I was writing at the time, which was called *Slaughterhouse-Five.* In that book, I felt the need to say this every time a character died: 'So it goes.' This exasperated many critics, and it seemed fancy and tiresome to me, too. But it somehow had to be said.

It was a clumsy way of saying what Céline managed to imply so much more naturally in everything he wrote, in effect: "Death and suffering can't matter nearly as much as I think they do. Since they are so common, my taking them so seriously must mean that I am insane. I must try to be saner."

Which has brought us back to our old friend insanity again. Céline claimed from time to time to have been trepanned in the First World War, as the result of a head wound. Actually, according to his fascinating biographer Erika Ostrovsky (*Voyeur Voyant,* Random House, 1971), he was wounded in his right shoulder. And, in his final novel, *Rigadoon,* he tells of being hit in the head by a brick during an air raid in Hannover. So it might be said that he found it necessary sometimes to explain a head that so many people found unusual.

He himself must have become thoroughly sick of his head occasionally, and I will guess as to its chief defect. I think it lacked the damping apparatus which most of us have, which keeps us from being swamped by the unbelievability of life as it really is.

So perhaps Céline's style isn't as arbitrary as I've thought it was. It may have been inevitable, if his mind was so un-defended. There may have been nothing for him to do, as though he were caught in an artillery barrage, but to exclaim and exclaim and exclaim.

And his works cannot be called a triumph of the human imagination. Almost everything he exclaimed about was really going on.

He was wonderful about inventors and machines.

The inscription on his tombstone is the one with which I began this essay. Erika Ostrovsky calls it a "terse summary of a double life."

Good for her.

He expected his writings to live on and on. He described himself when he was about to die like this: ". . . by your leave, a writer, a terrific stylist, the living proof: they put me in the 'Pleiade' with La Fontaine, Clement Marot, du Bellay . . . not to mention Rabelais! and Ronsard! . . . just to show you that I'm not worried . . . in two or three centuries I'll be helping the kids through high school . . ."

At the time I write, which is the autumn of 1974, it has become apparent even to ordinary people, with their mental dampers operating perfectly, that life is in fact as dangerous and unforgiving and irrational as Céline said it was. There is some question as to whether we have two or three centuries remaining to us in which to prepare civilization for the teaching of Céline in high school.

Until that day, if it comes, I suspect that fellow writers will keep his reputation alive. We are especially shocked and enlightened by what he says. We are filled with a giddy sort of gratitude.

I have heard it suggested that Céline may live on far longer in English than in French—for technical rather than political reasons. The argument goes that Céline's gutter French was so specialized as to time and place that gobs of it are incomprehensible to Frenchmen.

Those who have translated it into English, however, have used more durable crudities, which will be clear enough still, God willing, in one hundred years.

As I say, this is not my idea. I heard it somewhere. I pass it on. If it turns out to be true, it seems that simple literary justice would eventually require that his translators be acknowledged as coauthors of Céline. Translation is that important.

There is at least one significant document by Céline that is out of print in English. And it would be punctilious of me to say that it was written not by Céline but by Dr. Destouches. It is the doctoral thesis of Destouches, "The Life and Work of Ignaz Philipp Semmelweis," for which he received a bronze medal in 1924. It was written at a time when theses in medicine could still be beautifully literary, since ignorance about diseases and the human body still required that medicine be an art.

And young Destouches, in a spirit of hero-worship, told of the futile and scientifically sound battle fought by a Hungarian physician named Semmelweis (1818–1865) to prevent the spread of childbed fever in Viennese hospital maternity wards. The victims were poor people, since persons with decent sorts of dwellings much preferred to give birth at home.

The mortality rate in some wards was sensational—25 percent or more. Semmelweis reasoned that the mothers were being killed by medical students, who often came into the wards immediately after having dissected corpses riddled with disease. He was able to prove this by having the students wash their hands in soap and water before touching a woman in labor. The mortality rate dropped.

The jealousy and ignorance of Semmelweis's colleagues, however, caused him to be fired, and the mortality rate went up again.

The lesson Destouches learned from this true story, in my opinion, if he hadn't already learned it from an impoverished childhood and a stretch in the army, is that vanity rather than wisdom determines how the world is run.

XVII

A NAZI CITY
MOURNED AT
SOME PROFIT

I have not only praised a Nazi sympathizer, I have expressed my sorrow at the death of a Nazi city as well. I am speaking of Dresden, of course. And I have to say again that I was an American soldier, a prisoner of war there, when the city was simultaneously burned up and down. I was not on the German side.

I mourned the destruction of Dresden because it was only temporarily a Nazi city, and had for centuries been an art treasure belonging to earthlings everywhere. It could have been that again. The same was true of Angkor Wat, which military scientists have demolished more recently for some imagined gain.

Being present at the destruction of Dresden has affected my character far less than the death of my mother, the adopting of my sister's children, the sudden realization that those children and my own were no longer dependent on me, the breakup of my marriage, and on and on. And I have not been encouraged to go on mourning Dresden—even by Germans. Even Germans seem to think it is not worth mentioning anymore.

So I myself thought no more about Dresden until I was asked by Franklin Library in 1976 to write a special introduction to a deluxe edition they were bringing out of my novel, *Slaughterhouse-Five*.

I said this:

This is a book about something that happened to me a long time ago (1944)—and the book itself is now something else that happened to me a long time ago (1969).

Time marches on—and the key event in this book, which is the fire-bombing of Dresden, is now a fossilized memory, sinking ever deeper into the tar pit of history. If American school children have heard of it at all, they are surely in doubt as to whether it happened in World War One or Two. Nor do I think they should care much.

I, for one, am not avid to keep the memory of the fire-bombing fresh. I would of course be charmed if people continued to read this book for years to come, but not because I think there are important lessons to be learned from the Dresden catastrophe. I myself was in the midst of it, and learned only that people can become so enraged in war that they will burn great cities to the ground, and slay the inhabitants thereof.

That was nothing new.

I write this in October of 1976, and it so happens that only two nights ago I saw a screening of Marcel Ophul's new documentary on war crimes, "The Memory of Justice," which included movies, taken from the air, of the Dresden raid—at night. The city appeared to boil, and I was down there somewhere.

I was supposed to appear onstage afterwards, with some other people who had had intimate experiences with Nazi death camps and so on, and to contribute my notions as to the meaning of it all.

Atrocities celebrate meaninglessness, surely. I was mute. I did not mount the stage. I went home.

The Dresden atrocity, tremendously expensive and meticulously planned, was so meaningless, finally, that only one person on the entire planet got any benefit from it. I am that person. I wrote this book, which earned a lot of money for me and made my reputation, such as it is.

One way or another, I got two or three dollars for every person killed. Some business I'm in.

$XV\!III$

THE
SEXUAL
REVOLUTION

So I left my first wife and Cape Cod home forever in 1971. All our children save for the youngest, Nanette, had lit out for the Territory, so to speak. I became a soldier in what many were calling a sexual revolution. My departure itself was so sexual that a French name for orgasm describes it to a tee. It was a "little death."

There were similar little deaths going on all around me, of course, and that continues to be the situation today. In the case of long marriages, such departures really are make-believe dying, a salute to a marriage in its good old days, sheepish acknowledgment that the marriage could have been perfect right up to the end, if only one partner or the other one had managed to die peacefully just a little ahead of time. Can I say this without seeming to praise death? I hope so. I am praising literature, I think—praising stories that satisfy because they end where they should, before they stop being stories.

I left the house and all its furnishings and the car and the bank accounts behind, and taking only my clothing with me, I departed for New York City, the capital of the World, on a heavier-than-air flying machine. I started all over again.

As for real death—it has always been a temptation to me, since my mother solved so many problems with it. The child of a suicide will naturally think of death, the big one, as a logical solution to any problem, even one in simple algebra. Question: If Farmer A can plant 300 potatoes an hour, and Farmer B can plant potatoes fifty percent faster, and Farmer C can plant potatoes one third as fast as Farmer B, and 10,000 potatoes are to be planted to an acre, how many nine-hour days will it take Farmers A, B, and C, working simultaneously, to plant 25 acres? Answer: I think I'll blow my brains out.

❧

IF the story of an American father's departure from his hearth is allowed to tell itself, if it is allowed to wag tongues when he isn't around, it will tell the same story it would have told a hundred years ago, of booze and wicked women.

Such a story is told in my case, I'm sure.

Closer to the truth these days, in my opinion, is a tale of a man's cold sober flight into unpopulated nothingness. The booze and the women, good and bad, are likely to come along in time, but nothingness is the first seductress—again, the little death.

To the middle-class wives and children across this land whose male head of household has recently departed, learn the truth of his present condition from yet another great contemporary poem by the Statler Brothers, "Flowers on the Wall":

> I keep hearing you're concerned
> About my happiness.
> But all the thought you've given me
> Is conscience, I guess.
> If I were walkin' in your shoes
> I wouldn't worry none.
> While you 'n' your friends are worryin'
> 'Bout me
> I'm havin' lots of fun:
> Countin' flowers on the wall,
> That don't bother me at all,
> Playin' solitaire till dawn
> With a deck of fifty-one,
> Smokin' cigarettes and watchin'
> Captain Kangaroo.
> Now don't tell me
> I've nothin' to do.
>
> Tonight I dressed in tails
> Pretending I was on the town;
> Long as I can dream it's hard to
> Slow this swinger down.
> So please don't give
> A thought to me,

I'm really doin' fine,
And you can always find me here,
I'm havin' quite a time:
Countin' flowers on the wall,
That don't bother me at all,
Playin' solitaire till dawn
with a deck of fifty-one,
Smokin' cigarettes and watchin'
Captain Kangaroo.
Now don't tell me
I've nothin' to do.

It's good to see you,
I must go,
I know I look a fright;
Anyway my eyes are not
Accustomed to this light.
And my shoes are not
Accustomed to this hard concrete,
So I must go back to my room
And make my day complete:
Countin' flowers on the wall,
That don't bother me at all,
Playin' solitaire till dawn
With a deck of fifty-one,
Smokin' cigarettes and watchin'
Captain Kangaroo.
Now don't tell me
I've nothin' to do.

❦

THIS was written by Lew DeWitt, the only one of the four
Statler Brothers to have been divorced. It is not a poem of
escape or rebirth. It is a poem about the end of a man's
usefulness.

The man understands that his wife deserves the tragic
dignity of being a widow now.

❦

OR so he feels.

And much of what any human being feels is oceanic. The
wife of a man counting the flowers on the wall may not yearn
so much to be a widow, and yet the culture in which the man
is floating may be telling him that it is right for her to yearn
for that.

He is no longer needed as a father, and no longer useful
as a soldier who could stop a bullet winging toward his loved
ones, and he has no hope for being honored for his wisdom,
for it is well understood that people only become more tiresome as they grow old.

The man is experimenting with the Christian idea of
heaven without actually dying, and more and more women, of
course, are doing it, too. In heaven, you see, or so the childish dream goes, people are liked and honored simply for having
been alive. They don't have to have any utility up there.

The man counting flowers on the wall has no appreciable
utility anymore. He probably wasn't all that good in earning
money even when he was in his prime. What is he waiting
for?

For an angel to knock on his door. Angels love anybody who has simply been alive.

❦

IT seems to me that the most universal revolutionary wish now or ever is a wish for heaven, a wish by a human being to be honored by angels for something other than beauty or usefulness.

The women's liberation movement of today in America, in its most oceanic sense, is a wish by women to be liked for something other than their reproductive abilities, especially since the planet is harrowingly overpopulated. And the rejection of the Equal Rights Amendment by male state legislators is this clear statement by men, in my opinion: "We're sorry, girls, but your reproductive abilities are about all we can really like you for."

The truth.

❦

THERE are other hard truths about the old and those without friends and those without skills or capital, and on and on.

❦

NO angel knocked on my door while I was counting flowers on the wall, but an old friend with the gambling sickness was quick to find me. He had never borrowed anything from me, but now my turn had come. He told me of a family emergency, and asked for a sum that was just about the size of the little grubstake I had built. I ran into him about five years later, and he told me that he scarcely thought of anything but the day when he could pay me back with interest.

And people reached me by mail, most often asking me to read this or that new novel and write some words of praise for the jacket.

No book had been published in the past ten years for which I had not written a blurb.

But then an old friend wrote a book so bad that even I, crossing my eyes and ransacking it from end to end, could find nothing in it which could be mistaken for even a winsome sort of imbecility. So I declined to write a blurb. This may have been a major turning point in my life.

It was a crisis in the life of another writer, too, it turned out. He had written a blurb for the book I had spurned. He called me up in the middle of the night, long distance and sounding as though he had just swallowed Drano. "My God," he said, "you just can't leave me on that book jacket all alone."

❦

AND so on. Somewhere in there my son Mark went crazy and recovered. I went out to Vancouver and saw how sick he was, and I put him in a nut house. I had to suppose that he might never get well again.

He never blamed me or his mother, as I have said before. His generous wish not to blame us was so stubborn that he became almost a crank on the subject of chemical and genetic causes of mental illness. Talk therapy made sense as poetry but not as a means to a cure, he thought.

But now, as a physician, as an open-minded scientist, he has delivered himself into the hands of a talk therapist, blabbing his head off about Jane and me and his sisters and his cousins and all that, I hope, and finding it hilariously beneficial.

Hooray.

There will be talk about how people wronged him. It's about time. It's about time.

❦

EVERYTHING is about time.

Yes, and somewhere in there I looked in on George Roy Hill while he made a motion picture based on a novel of mine, *Slaughterhouse-Five*.

There are only two American novelists who should be grateful for the movies which were made from their books. I am one of them. The other one? Margaret Mitchell, of course.

❦

THE Eastern Seaboard's intellectual ranks will probably always require one woman to be so brilliant, supposedly, that everybody else is scared to death of her. Mary McCarthy used to hold that job. Susan Sontag has it now.

Susan Sontag approached me at a party one time. I was petrified. What brilliant question would she ask me, and what would be my pip-squeak reply?

"How did you like the movie they made of *Slaughterhouse-Five*?" she said.

"I liked it a lot," I confessed.

"So did I," she said.

How sweet and easy that was, and what a great motion picture *Slaughterhouse-Five* must really be!

❦

THERE was a depression going on in the movie industry in Hollywood back then. Only two pictures were being made, both based on works of mine. The other one was *Happy Birthday, Wanda June.*

This movie, starring Rod Steiger and Susannah York, turned out so abominably that I asked that my name be taken off it. I had heard of other writers doing that. What could be more dignified?

This proved to be impossible, however. I alone had done the thing the credits said I had done. I had really written the thing.

❦

YES, and it wasn't the only bad job I ever did. I have graded my separate works from A to D. The grades I hand out to myself do not place me in literary history. I am comparing myself with myself. Thus can I give myself an A-plus for *Cat's Cradle,* while knowing that there was a writer named William Shakespeare. The report card is chronological, so you can plot my rise and fall on graph paper, if you like:

Player Piano	B
The Sirens of Titan	A
Mother Night	A
Cat's Cradle,	A-plus
God Bless You, Mr. Rosewater	A

Slaughterhouse-Five   A-plus
Welcome to the Monkey House   B-minus
Happy Birthday, Wanda June   D
Breakfast of Champions   C
Wampeters, Foma & Granfalloons   C
Slapstick   D
Jailbird   A
Palm Sunday   C

❦

WHAT has been my prettiest contribution to my culture? I would say it was a master's thesis in anthropology which was rejected by the University of Chicago a long time ago. It was rejected because it was so simple and looked like too much fun. One must not be too playful.

The thesis has vanished, but I carry an abstract in my head, which I will here set down. The fundamental idea is that stories have shapes which can be drawn on graph paper, and that the shape of a given society's stories is at least as interesting as the shape of its pots or spearheads.

In the thesis, I collected popular stories from fantastically various societies, not excluding the one which used to read *Collier's* and *The Saturday Evening Post.* I graphed each one.

Anyone can graph a simple story if he or she will crucify it, so to speak, on the intersecting axes I here depict:

"G" stands for good fortune. "I" stands for ill fortune. "B" stands for the beginning of a story. "E" stands for its end.

The late Nelson Rockefeller, for example, would be very close to the top of the G-I scale on his wedding day. A shopping-bag lady waking up on a doorstep this morning would be somewhere nearer the middle, but not at the bottom, since the day is balmy and clear.

A much beloved story in our society is about a person who is leading a bearable life, who experiences misfortune, who overcomes misfortune, and who is happier afterward for having demonstrated resourcefulness and strength. As a graph, that story looks like this:

Another story of which Americans never seem to tire is about a person who becomes happier upon finding something he or she likes a lot. The person loses whatever it is, and then gets it back forever. As a graph, it looks like this:

An American Indian creation myth, in which a god of some sort gives the people the sun and then the moon and then the bow and arrow and then the corn and so on, is essentially a staircase, a tale of accumulation:

Almost all creation myths are staircases like that. Our own creation myth, taken from the Old Testament, is unique, so far as I could discover, in looking like this:

The sudden drop in fortune, of course, is the ejection of Adam and Eve from the Garden of Eden.

Franz Kafka's "The Metamorphosis," in which an already hopelessly unhappy man turns into a cockroach, looks like this:

But could my graphs, when all was said and done, be useful as anything more than little visual comedies, cartoons of a sort? The University of Chicago asked me that, and I had to ask myself that, and I say again what I said at the beginning: that the graphs were at least as suggestive as pots or spearheads.

But then I had another look at a graph I had drawn of Western civilization's most enthusiastically received story, which is "Cinderella." At this very moment, a thousand writers must be telling that story again in one form or another. This very book is a Cinderella story of a kind.

I confessed that I was daunted by the graph of "Cinderella," and was tempted to leave it out of my thesis, since it seemed to prove that I was full of shit. It seemed too complicated and arbitrary to be a representative artifact—lacked the simple grace of a pot or a spearhead. Have a look:

The steps, you see, are all the presents the fairy godmother gave to Cinderella, the ball gown, the slippers, the carriage, and so on. The sudden drop is the stroke of midnight at the ball. Cinderella is in rags again. All the presents have been repossessed. But then the prince finds her and marries her, and she is infinitely happy ever after. She gets all the stuff back, and *then* some. A lot of people think the story is trash, and, on graph paper, it certainly looks like trash.

But then I said to myself, Wait a minute—those steps at the beginning look like the creation myth of virtually every society on earth. And then I saw that the stroke of midnight looked exactly like the unique creation myth in the Old Testament. And then I saw that the rise to bliss at the end was identical with the expectation of redemption as expressed in primitive Christianity.

The tales were identical.

I was thrilled to discover that years ago, and I am just as thrilled today. The apathy of the University of Chicago is repulsive to me.

They can take a flying fuck at the mooooooooooooooooon.

❦

AND, my goodness, haven't we come far afield from the stated subject of this chapter, which is the sexual revolution? I have spoken elsewhere of how neophyte writers, and even some old poops in the field, will veer away from subjects which alarm them. Just look how far I myself have veered away from the subject of sex. There is little that is genuinely sexual in telling a great university to take a flying fuck at the mooooooooooooooooon.

Am I too much of a sissy to discuss anal intercourse, aphrodisiacs, armpits, bidets, birth control, bisexuality, bondage, buttocks, chastity belts, circumcision, clitorises, condoms, dildoes, discipline, ejaculation, feathers, femoral intercourse, fetishes, foursomes, frigidity, genitals, hair, hair-trigger trouble, impotence, karezza, kisses, and so on? I have lifted this list from the index of *The Joy of Sex: A Gourmet Guide to Love Making* (illustrated), edited by Alex Comfort, M.B., Ph.D. (Crown, 1972). Actually, I feel quite free to discuss any and all of those matters, and even to laugh some while doing so.

What isn't congenial is an admission that I have been forced to be celibate for long periods of time. I search the index of *The Joy of Sex* in vain for "celibacy," which happens to be the most common human sexual adventure, and which could be illustrated nicely by a page as white as a snowdrift.

To take an example: I was a private in the United States Army (actually the Army of the United States, since I was a volunteer) for three years. I was one warrior ant in an enormous colony of identical ants, imprisoned in rural areas, and sent finally to an all-male battlefield in a foreign country. How many women eager to fuck me do you suppose I encountered in three long years? I could ask the same question about months and months in my civilian life, and get the same answer: to all practical purposes, none.

I was talking one time to my friend Robert Penn Warren, a lusty old gentleman and a great poet and novelist, and I asked him about another majestic literary figure, dead, who had been an acquaintance of his. Mr. Warren is seventeen years older than I am. He was born in Guthrie, Kentucky, in 1905. He drew in words an enchantingly Edwardian caricature of the man I had asked about, and he concluded it with a statement which was in no wise a joke. It was meant to have clinical significance. A person versed in psychology and medicine, he seemed to say, would be able to extrapolate an entire syndrome from this one small clue. This was the clue: "He was a masturbator, of course."

This ended the conversation. I did not protest. I was grateful, though, to remember something far more casual about masturbation which had been said to me with all possible cheerfulness by my friend Milos Forman, the motion picture director.

"You know what I like about masturbation?" he asked me.

"What is it you like about it, Milos?" I said.

"You don't have to talk afterward," he replied.

❂

I peruse what is at this moment the number one nonfiction best seller in America, written by Gay Talese, *Thy Neighbor's Wife*. It is meant to be a quite universal analysis of the current sexual revolution. According to Talese, women are becoming more hospitable and casual, less discriminating with respect to sexual contacts. I oversimplify but do not entirely misrepresent that supposed revolution if I describe it this way: Whereas an ideal woman in olden times might have given a dusty male wayfarer on the road of life a piece of pie—a modern woman may now give him a hand job or a blow job as well.

I am sorry, but that is how I read it.

I do not wish to mock the book, even having said that, for it is to me a secretly deep history of a generation of middle-class American males, my own, which was taught by parents and athletic coaches and scoutmasters and military chaplains and quack doctors and so on to be deeply ashamed of mastur-bation and wet dreams.

And the hidden plea in the book is one which first ap-peared in my eyes when I was fourteen, say, and which has not vanished entirely to this day. It is part of the mystery of me. The plea is addressed by old-fashioned males forever full of jism to any pretty human female, on the street, in a maga-zine, in a movie—anywhere. The plea is this: "Please, pretty lady, don't make me play with my private parts again."

xlx

IN THE
CAPITAL OF
THE WORLD

So here I sit on the fourth floor of a town house on the East Side of New York City, the Capital of the World, with a report card on the past thirty years of my life —signed by myself and tacked to the wall. I look at all those grades, some high, some low, and I think that I am like the compulsive gambler who borrowed so much money from me and who could not pay me back: I could not help myself.

I have spoken elsewhere of the mentor I had at the University of Chicago, who was so brilliant, who could not find anyone to publish his most audacious work, and who committed suicide. I have not proved how brilliant he was. As I set out to do so now with an example, I am hesitant, not only because I have his reputation in my hands for a moment, but because all the good things he said which I remember were so simple and clear. It has been my experience with literary critics and academics in this country that clarity looks a lot like laziness and ignorance and childishness and cheapness to them. Any idea which can be grasped immediately is for them, by definition, something they knew all the time.

So it is with literary experimentation, too. If a literary experiment works like a dream, is easy to read and enjoy, the experimenter is a hack. The only way to get full credit as a fearless experimenter is to fail and fail.

❦

A music critic once regaled a party I attended with a list of composers of serious music in the past. Nobody had heard of any of them, and the critic told us that they were all regarded in their own time as being the greatest composers alive. These were contemporaries of Beethoven and Brahms and Wagner and so on, composers for full orchestras in the Romantic mode.

We asked him why they weren't admired today. He had made it his business to hear as much of their work as he could, and he had this to say: "It was all gesture." By this he meant that musical promise after musical promise of great themes to come were made, and were not kept. The composers were honored in their own time for the gorgeousness of the promises they made but could not keep. They perhaps made promises which not even an archangel could keep.

Some of the most imposing literary reputations of my own time, it seems to me, are based on just that sort of promising.

❧

THE example of my mentor's brilliance:

Using the Socratic method, he asked his little class this: "What is it an artist does—a painter, a writer, a sculptor—?"

He already had an answer, which he had put down in the book he was writing, a book which would never be published. But he would not tell us what it was until the end of the hour, and he might discard it entirely if our answers to his question made more sense than his. This was a class composed entirely of veterans of the Second World War in the summertime. The class had been put together in order that we might continue to receive our living expenses from our government when most of the rest of the university was on vacation.

If any of us came up with good answers, I now have no idea what they might have been. His answer was this: "The artist says, 'I can do very little about the chaos around me, but at least I can reduce to perfect order this square of canvas, this piece of paper, this chunk of stone.' "

Everybody knows that.

❧

MOST of my adult life has been spent in bringing to some kind of order sheets of paper eight and a half inches wide and eleven inches long. This severely limited activity has allowed me to ignore many a storm. It has also caused many of the worst storms I ignored. My mates have often been angered by how much attention I pay to paper and how little attention I pay to them.

I can only reply that the secret to success in every human endeavor is total concentration. Ask any great athlete.

To put it another way: Sometimes I don't consider myself very good at life, so I hide in my profession.

❦

I know what Delilah really did to Samson to make him as weak as a baby. She didn't have to cut his hair off. All she had to do was break his concentration.

❦

ABOUT nine years ago I was asked to deliver an address to the American Institute and Academy of Arts and Letters here. I was not then a member, and was terrified. I had left home, and was spending most of my time counting flowers on the wall and watching Captain Kangaroo in a tiny apartment on East Fifty-fourth Street. My friend with the gambling sickness had just cleaned out my bank account and my son had gone insane in British Columbia.

I asked my wife please not to come, since I was rattled enough as it was. I asked a woman with whom I had been keeping company some not to come, either—for the same reason. So they both came, all dressed up for a fancy execution.

What saved my life? Pieces of paper eight and a half inches wide and eleven inches long.

❦

I am sorry for people who have no knack for reducing to seeming order some little thing. More and more people are doing it with film and video tape these days. My chief objection to motion pictures as art is their expensiveness. A filmmaker is like Benvenuto Cellini, who worked with raw materials which were priceless to begin with—with silver and platinum and gold.

❦

I was born into a house which was designed and built by my father in 1922, the year of my birth. It was so full of treasures that it was like a museum, and it was meant to be inherited by my brother, my sister, or me. I would not like to live there. Edwardian lives of a sort were conducted there for seven years. That isn't a long period of time, you know. To my parents, who were great lovers of music, it must have been as though a full orchestra had played the first seven bars of a symphony, and then gone home.

The house I now inhabit was built in this busy seaport by a speculator named L. S. Brooks in 1860–61, at the outbreak of the Civil War. Spiritually, it is as much my house as anyone's, since Brooks built it, along with a lot of other ones just like it in this neighborhood, with no inhabitant in particular in mind.

The first person who liked it enough to move into it, the way a hermit crab might move into an empty snail shell, was another German, Ferdinand Traud. He was president of the German Free School down at 142 East Fourth Street.

The Trauds moved out in 1875, and Julius Bruno, a broker, moved in. Julius Bruno moved out in 1887, and Peter Goetz moved in. Peter Goetz moved out in 1891, and Louisa Gerlach moved in. And on and on.

I myself bought the house eight years ago from Robert

Gottlieb, the editor in chief of Alfred A. Knopf, who moved to a house across the street—and Jill Krementz, who is now my wife, and I moved in.

Jill runs her photographic business out of the bottom floor. I run my writing business out of the top floor. We share the two floors in between.

✤

THE people in this city have been very friendly to me, although I was born far away. They have uses for strangers who do good work in the arts here, and I have done reasonably good work as a novelist from time to time.

The most satisfying kindness which has been done me here was an invitation from St. Clement's Episcopal Church, whose congregation includes many actors, to preach on Palm Sunday in 1980. It is the custom of that church, which is also a theater, to have a stranger preach just once a year.

The altar there is portable, since the front of the church is also a stage. Very few plays would work well with an altar as a fixed centerpiece. So, on the morning I preached, the altar had been trundled temporarily onto a set which was the kitchen of a Manhattan tenement of perhaps sixty years ago or more—before I was born.

I do not know what play the set was for. I have not asked. I want to imagine that it was for a play about European immigrants to New York City and their children. I was happy to speak from that set as a descendent of immigrants who settled much farther inland, immigrants about whom native New Yorkers often know nothing and imagine the worst.

I had this to say:

"I am enchanted by the Sermon on the Mount. Being merciful, it seems to me, is the only good idea we have received so far. Perhaps we will get another idea that good by and by—and then we will have two good ideas. What might that second good idea be? I don't know. How could I know? I will make a wild guess that it will come from music somehow. I have often wondered what music is and why we love it so. It may be that music is that second good idea's being born.

"I choose as my text the first eight verses of John twelve, which deal not with Palm Sunday but with the night before —with Palm Sunday Eve, with what we might call 'Spikenard Saturday.' I hope that will be close enough to Palm Sunday to leave you more or less satisfied. I asked an Episcopalian priest the other day what I should say to you about Palm Sunday itself. She told me to say that it was a brilliant satire on pomp and circumstance and high honors in this world. So I tell you that.

"The priest was Carol Anderson, who sold her physical church in order that her spiritual parish might survive. Her parish is All Angels—on West Eightieth, just off Broadway. She sold the church but hung on to the parish house. I assume that most, if not all, of the angels are still around.

"Now, as to the verses about Palm Sunday Eve: I choose them because Jesus says something in the eighth verse which many people I have known have taken as proof that Jesus himself occasionally got sick and tired of people who needed mercy all the time. I read from the Revised Standard Bible rather than the King James, because it is easier for me to understand. Also, I will argue afterward that Jesus was only joking, and it is impossible to joke in King James English. The funniest joke in the world, if told in King James English, is doomed to sound like Charlton Heston.

"I read:

" 'Six days before the Passover, Jesus came to Bethany, where Lazarus was, whom Jesus had raised from the dead. There they made him a supper; Martha served, but Lazarus was one of those at table with him.

" 'Mary took a pound of costly ointment of pure nard and anointed the feet of Jesus and wiped his feet with her hair; and the house was filled with the fragrance of the ointment.

" 'But Judas Iscariot, one of his disciples (he who was to betray him), said, "Why was this ointment not sold for three hundred denarii and given to the poor?" This he said, not that he cared for the poor but because he was a thief, and as he had the money box he used to take what was put into it. Jesus said, "Let her alone, let her keep it for the day of my burial. The poor you always have with you, but you do not always have me." '

"Thus ends the reading, and although I have promised a joke, there is not much of a chuckle in there anywhere. The reading, in fact, ends with at least two quite depressing implications: That Jesus could be a touch self-pitying, and that he was, with his mission to earth about to end, at least momentarily sick and tired of hearing about the poor.

"The King James version of the last verse, by the way, is almost identical: ' "For the poor always ye have with you; but you do not always have me." '

"Whatever it was that Jesus really said to Judas was said in Aramaic, of course—and has come to us through Hebrew and Greek and Latin and archaic English. Maybe he only said something a lot like, 'The poor you always have with you, but you do not always have me.' Perhaps a little something has been lost in translation. And let us remember, too, that in translations jokes are commonly the first things to go.

"I would like to recapture what has been lost. Why? Because I, as a Christ-worshiping agnostic, have seen so much un-Christian impatience with the poor encouraged by the quotation, 'For the poor always ye have with you.'

"I am speaking mainly of my youth in Indianapolis, Indiana. No matter where I am and how old I become, I still speak of almost nothing but my youth in Indianapolis, Indiana. Whenever anybody out that way began to worry a lot about the poor people when I was young, some eminently respectable Hoosier, possibly an uncle or an aunt, would say that Jesus himself had given up on doing much about the poor. He or she would paraphrase John twelve, Verse eight: 'The poor people are hopeless. We'll always be stuck with them.'

"The general company was then free to say that the poor were hopeless because they were so lazy or dumb, that they drank too much and had too many children and kept coal in the bathtub, and so on. Somebody was likely to quote Kin Hubbard, the Hoosier humorist, who said that he knew a man who was so poor that he owned twenty-two dogs. And so on.

"If those Hoosiers were still alive, which they are not, I would tell them now that Jesus was only joking, and that he was not even thinking much about the poor.

"I would tell them, too, what I don't have to tell this particular congregation, that jokes can be noble. Laughs are exactly as honorable as tears. Laughter and tears are both responses to frustration and exhaustion, to the futility of thinking and striving anymore. I myself prefer to laugh, since there is less cleaning up to do afterward—and since I can start thinking and striving again that much sooner.

"All right:

"It is the evening before Palm Sunday. Jesus is frustrated and exhausted. He knows that one of his closest associates will soon betray him for money—and that he is going to be mocked and tortured and killed. He is going to feel all that a mortal feels when he dies in convulsions on the cross. His visit among us is almost over—but life must still go on for just a little while.

"It is again suppertime.

"How many suppertimes does Jesus have left? Five, I believe.

"His male companions for this supper are themselves a mockery. One is Judas, who will betray him. The other is Lazarus, who has recently been dead for four days. Lazarus was so dead that he stunk, the Bible says. Lazarus is surely dazed, and not much of a conversationalist—and not necessarily grateful, either, to be alive again. It is a very mixed blessing to be brought back from the dead.

"If I had read a little farther, we would have learned that there is a crowd outside, crazy to see Lazarus, not Jesus. Lazarus is the man of the hour as far as the crowd is concerned.

"Trust a crowd to look at the wrong end of a miracle every time.

"There are two sisters of Lazarus there—Martha and Mary. They, at least, are sympathetic and imaginatively helpful. Mary begins to massage and perfume the feet of

Jesus Christ with an ointment made from the spikenard plant. Jesus has the bones of a man and is clothed in the flesh of a man—so it must feel awfully nice, what Mary is doing to his feet. Would it be heretical of us to suppose that Jesus closes his eyes?

"This is too much for that envious hypocrite Judas, who says, trying to be more Catholic than the Pope: 'Hey—this is very un-Christian. Instead of wasting that stuff on your feet, we should have sold it and given the money to the poor people.'

"To which Jesus replies in Aramaic: 'Judas, don't worry about it. There will still be plenty of poor people left long after I'm gone.'

"This is about what Mark Twain or Abraham Lincoln would have said under similar circumstances.

"If Jesus did in fact say that, it is a divine black joke, well suited to the occasion. It says everything about hypocrisy and nothing about the poor. It is a Christian joke, which allows Jesus to remain civil to Judas, but to chide him about his hypocrisy all the same.

" 'Judas, don't worry about it. There will still be plenty of poor people left long after I'm gone.'

"Shall I regarble it for you? 'The poor you always have with you, but you do not always have me.'

"My own translation does no violence to the words in the Bible. I have changed their order some, not merely to make them into the joke the situation calls for, but to harmonize them, too, with the Sermon on the Mount. The Sermon on the Mount suggests a mercifulness that can never waver or fade.

"This has no doubt been a silly sermon. I am sure you do

not mind. People don't come to church for preachments, of course, but to daydream about God.

"I thank you for your sweetly faked attention."

END